LoveDance

Awakening
the
Divine Daughter

Bedside Books
An imprint of American Book Publishing
5442 So. 900 East, #146
Salt Lake City, UT 84117-7204
www.american-book.com
Printed in the United States of America on acid-free paper.

LoveDance: Awakening the Divine Daughter

Designed by Morgan McConnell, design@american-book.com

ISBN-13: 978-1-58982-411-9
ISBN-10: 1-58982-411-3

Maragopoulos, Deborah, LoveDance: Awakening the Divine Daughter

Special Sales

These books are available at special discounts for bulk purchases. Special editions, including personalized covers, excerpts of existing books, and corporate imprints, can be created in large quantities for special needs. For more information e-mail info@american-book.com.

LoveDance

Awakening
the
Divine Daughter

By

Deborah Maragopoulos FNP

For my beloved Steve—the time is ripe for us to dance

Author's Note

I meant to write a healing book, you know the kind, a self-help manual based on my expertise… Everyone has a story: how they do what they do, how they became who they are in the world. And I have mine.

In 1984, I gave birth to a premature baby who stumped expert endocrinologists with numerous hormonal challenges. Defying medical advice, I orchestrated the care of my firstborn by learning everything I could about how hormones affect developmental behavior. My intuition proved correct—our healthy son just graduated college. In spite of my traditional training as a nurse practitioner, what I learned as a patient and a parent sparked an expertise in holistic neuro-immune-endocrinology, the interface, I believe, between the bio-physical and the psycho-spiritual being.

Through my own bio-psycho-spiritual journey, I evolved into an intuitive healer capable of honing in on the biochemical interconnections of human physiology and relating them to symbolic imbalances as lessons on a patient's soul path. Spiritual gurus, psychological geniuses, and fully grounded but very ill patients from around the world presented themselves to gain insight on the wellbeing of their physical forms. Yet, I learned the most from the children.

In 1988, my daughter was born beautifully whole and much more work than my premature son. Although developmentally advanced, speaking by six months and reading at three, he struggled in his physical form undergoing five corrective surgeries, while she delighted in her humanness. Forcing us all to stay awake, she candidly shared her inter-dimensional experiences, in constant communication with my dead grandmother, so connected to her father that at any distance she knew what he was feeling, claiming with innocent assurance that they had been father and daughter in a past life, and like I did as a child, could lay her hands on someone and "know" what ailed them. Meanwhile, my son struggled in school and at eight, asked to see a "brain doctor." The psychologist insisted that with his intense brilliance, he could not have attention deficit disorder, but my son insisted on being tested with the "video game." The psychologist was floored. How could a child know about the newly developed computer program used to differentiate learning disabilities? I just shrugged; his uncanny knowingness was part of our life. When my son agreed to submit to traditional therapeutics, "only, Mommy, if I do not lose my dreams," again, I was challenged to find a natural solution to his dilemma. Of course, the universe presented lots of opportunities for growth as pediatric patients were brought to me by their parents.

After much research, I began treating my autistic and learning disabled patients nutritionally. While gladly mixing the "brew," squeezing oil from capsules, carefully measuring powders, their parents asked me to create something easier. So by 1998, and after many exhaustive but futile attempts at finding the nutritional connection between genetics and the hypothalamic orchestration of the neuro-immune-endocrine system, I surrendered to the advice of my children and prayed. Every night for three months, I had the same dream in which my most hormonally-challenged patients came to drink from a chalice I held. We never spoke, but intuitively I knew they were better. I awoke every morning asking what the golden liquid in the cup was. The first answer came as seven letters, I thought were Hebrew, but later found were Aramaic. Amazingly they translated into the same single letter denotations used for the seven amino acids I had been studying related to the hypothalamus. Thus my nutraceutical formula, Genesis Gold®, was born. Under its influence, I began to write about my journey, but it would be another five years before I realized the significance of initially receiving the formula in Aramaic.

All through my years of healing, friends, family, colleagues, and most enthusiastically, patients encouraged me to write. They appreciated my unique take on healing, how I married eastern and western philosophies into successful therapeutics, how I seemed to know just what was out of balance to restore wellbeing, and how passionately I shared anecdotal stories from my life as a healer, wife, mother, sister, daughter. So in the summer of 2003, I began to write the book I had promised my patients. But it didn't go as planned. I had no idea how to put it together, no muse, no nothing, until September 15th...

I had a dream. I was walking down the dusty streets of Nazareth, fine linen flapping about my legs, my sandals gathering debris, as I hurried along anxious to meet my friend. Then I was there, in a humble courtyard, looking into the eyes of a boy I knew very well. In the dream, I was fourteen-year-old Mary, the soon to be bride of Yeshua.

Once the opening chapter was recorded, the muse did not leave my side day or night for eight months. I didn't know why Mary's story came to me. I wasn't religious, nor particularly interested in history, but I was compelled to record the voice of the woman history had forgotten. I lived and breathed nearly every aspect of her story while typing like mad. Here was a muse I couldn't deny. Never once did I suffer writer's block, but it wasn't easy to humanize the man deified by so many in the eyes of the woman the world believed was far from his wife. Yet how could I deny the intimate details that came in dreams and visions, some even...in Aramaic!

My poor husband, always supportive, feared for my wellbeing, but as my son put it: he could believe my experience was the product of an unstable mind or he could believe in my inter-dimensional connections, deepen our relationship, and thus gain spiritually himself. Fortunately, my husband chose the latter.

I struggled to write Mary and Yeshua's journey to Qumran for what I saw was so very different than what the scholars of the Dead Sea scrolls believed, so I called my dear rabbi friend. She advised that I forget two thousand years of what I was taught to believe was history as interpreted by modern Victorian Christendom and just "be Mary." Six months later, she called to inform me that Israeli archeologists had just discovered evidence of what I wrote. I ceased denying why this story came to me and just relaxed to birth it into the world.

Being Mary changed my life. By embodying the energy of the divine daughter, recognizing her in others, and reaping the benefits, I became my truth. I've always been a cup-half-full kind of person, sensually oriented and passionate, probably from my hot-blooded Italian family, but somehow through writing this book, life became even more joyful. I chose the first person present tense narrative because that's how it felt to me. The synchronicities between writing her story and my own have been amazing—as I wrote, it would become manifest in my life. As Mary progressed in her awakening, so did I.

I opened to admitting to my patients that, yes, in spite of my scientific training, I intuitively diagnosed and treated them. Appreciating my honesty, they began challenging me to further my healing gifts, especially encouraging me to divulge the lessons from the book. Family, friends, and even patients clamored to share in the experience, so I released chapters of the first draft for feedback. It should have been no surprise that my readers had transformational experiences, but I was in awe because that's what happened to me. I always believed in the profound potential within each of us. That's how I believe healing occurs. It's already encoded; we just have to tap in to the potential for it to become manifest.

My understanding of human consciousness is an evolution of the Mother-Father-Son-Daughter aspects of the Divine. Originally, I believe, humans worshipped the earth as the Divine Mother, her body was ours. Then we looked into the cosmos and envisioned the Divine Father as spirit. In the last two millennia, avatars teaching in parables initiated a revolution of the mind, and ever since the Divine Son has been the center of religious worship.

Now the time is ripe for the Divine Daughter to manifest in human consciousness. She is emotion weaving the mind, body, and soul into Sacred Unity with All That Is.

I believe Mary was the original embodiment of the Divine Daughter achieving Sacred Union with Yeshua, the embodiment of the Divine Son. Although lost in history due to the fear-based struggle between politics and religion, her story is fortunately being remembered. I am blessed to present my rendition of Mary's awakening to you. Writing from her perspective helped me remember who I am and why I'm here. Sharing in her journey may help you, the reader, gain a remembrance of your truth.

Thanks to all the prayers and healing energy of my beloved circle of supporters, *LoveDance* is a reality. I am eternally grateful for: my husband and hero, Steve, who rescued me whenever I questioned my purpose; my son, Jarys, who inspired me to seek my truth and whose rich knowledge of history brought to light invaluable details; my beautiful daughter, Kyra, whose delightful attitude buoyed me through three years of creation; my mother, Maria, who held the space as I evolved; and my friends: Dorothy, whose sharp pencil and wise counsel guided this work; Chris, who listened ad nauseum to Mary's tale; Hava, whose advice to surrender myself to the character was invaluable; and Carol, who supported my awakening and then released me. My deepest appreciation to American Book Publishing, who took a chance on me when others feared to and to my editor, Mary Bryan, who helped carve a long, intimately detailed story into a most lovely refinement.

As it turns out, I did write a healing book. Everything I wished to teach—the bio-psycho-spiritual healing lessons—are in this novel. In story form, the way a beloved avatar taught some two thousand years ago.

Primary Characters

Belshazzar: Akkadian; protects the king/queen. The king of Aksum who followed the unusual star to find Yeshua and watched over Mary (Mari-a) from birth.

Eleazer: Hebrew; God is helper. Tzadokim husband of Mary's sister Martha.

Eucharia: Greek; grateful. Hasmonaean wife of Syrus, mother of Martha and Mary.

Hava: Hebrew; life-giver or woman. Mentor of Mary, former high priestess of the temple of Astarte in Qumran.

Hephziva: Hebrew; my desire. High priestess of the temple of Astarte in Qumran.

Hillel: Hebrew; praised. Reigning Davidic king of the tribe of Judah aligned with the Essenes, grandfather of Yeshua living in dynastic relationship with his wife Shoshana in Qumran.

Jacob: Hebrew; heel. Third in line to the Davidic throne, English translation is James.

Joseph: Hebrew; God will increase. The direct heir of the Davidic line with alliance to the Chaverim, married to Miriam, father of Yeshua, Jacob and four other children.

Joshua: Hebrew; God saves. Son of Mary and Yeshua born in their fifth year of marriage.

Martha: Hebrew; mistress. Mary's sister, being the eldest daughter of a wealthy Hasmonaean entitled her to properties in Bethany, Magdala and Cana, married to Eleazer.

Mary: Hellenized version of Mari-a (Egyptian), the perfect one. Born in Migdol to Eucharia of the royal Hasmonaean family. Wife of Yeshua, mother of Sarah and Joshua.

Miriam: Hebrew; sea of sorrow. Wife of Joseph, mother of Yeshua, Jacob, Judah, Shimon, Rachel and Esther.

Sarah: Hebrew; princess. Daughter of Mary and Yeshua born in their second year of marriage.

Syrus: Parthian; the sun. Husband of Eucharia, Tzadokim magistrate from a family of sea merchants.

Teoma: Aramaic; twin. Son of a Roman father and Hasmonaean woman who is the sister of Joseph of Arimathaea. Yeshua's closest friend and protector of Mary and the children.

Yeshua: Aramaic; The Divine will save me, Hebrew (Y'hoshua), Greek (Jesus). Firstborn son of Joseph and Miriam, second in line for the Davidic throne. Husband of Mary and father of Sarah and Joshua.

Hebrew Year 3757

Far from his home near the headwaters of the Nile, Belshazzar steps from the periphery of drummers into the dance. The Great Sea draws back its curtain of fog from the cragged mountain crevice, leaving salt upon his tongue. Towering high above the pass, the fortress of Migdol glistens as rays of the morning sun lick the marine dew from the pale stone.

Grasping his walking stick, he beats a path to the palace gate. Servants escort him through lavish gardens into a grand hall. He is greeted by a small child.

"Hello, I'm Martha. Have you come to see my new baby too?"

Smiling, he asks gently, "And who else is paying respects to your sister?"

"A great sorceress from Alexandria." Martha takes his large dark hand in her small fair one. "Come, I will bring you to her."

Spacious enough to house two dozen children and as many caretakers, the nursery is filled not with infants, but animals. Little Martha whispers, "Mary has many friends."

Mari-a, of course, the perfect one.

Birds fly about monkeys climbing the pillars. A spotted leopard stretches lazily upon the edge of the fountain, one paw in the water. Gazelles frolic, their hooves beating charmingly upon the tile floor. In the center of the menagerie stands an imposing figure. Golden bees and an emerald-breasted hummingbird hover about the tiny bundle in her arms.

"Sahirah, what brings you out of the temple of Isis?"

Black hair capped in white, the high priestess narrows kohl-painted eyes. "I am here for the child. What brings you so far north, King of Aksum?"

"I am here by Osaze's request."

Her frown draws dark brows to meet over a sharp nose. "And what right does the Egyptian prince have…"

"You know very well."

"No! Mari-a must be raised within the protection of the temple!"

Ignoring Sahirah's sharp tone, Belshazzar looks down at his side. "Martha, please go find your parents for me." The child skips out of the nursery. "You know what must be done. Mari-a is to be raised in Galilee."

"The mother is so terrified of the child's gifts, she will never develop!" Hearing footsteps coming down the hall, Belshazzar shakes his head but the priestess' zealous plea will not be thwarted. "And her husband…! She shall be smothered in the patriarchal worship of Yahweh."

"How dare you adulterate the divine name!" A slight man of rich bearing enters the nursery, shaking with anger. Syrus.

Coiling down her arm toward the bundle, a young constrictor flicks its tongue but Syrus holds his ground. Sahirah sneers, "Once again the sacred feminine will be inhibited by man," and steps back just as a frail young woman adorned in rich silks comes through the doorway. The blanket falls away and she screams.

The babe hovers in the air.

As Belshazzar catches the swooning mother, Syrus rushes to tenderly enfold the child in his arms. Snakes and cats trailing her furious wake, Sahirah takes her leave. Settling her slender mother upon some cushions, Belshazzar asks little Martha to keep watch before approaching her father.

"I am Belshazzar, king of Aksum. I am here on Mari-a's behalf."

"I knew you would come." The babe in Syrus' arms entices a smile. "I had a vision of her birth and was guided to name her… Mary." The Hellenized form of Mari-a, Belshazzar nods his approval. "I even saw her marriage… to the king of Yisrael. Could it be the anointed one?"

Relieved that Syrus has the sight, Belshazzar explains, "Only the messah queen can bring a man to sovereignty. Mari-a's birth has been awaited in our lands, just as the birth of the prince of peace was predicted in yours." His gaze sweeps over the wild animals making themselves at home in the nursery, "When did they arrive?"

Syrus shakes his head in wonderment. "The night Eucharia began to labor. When the babe was born at the break of dawn, the animals' zest frightened the milk from my wife's breasts."

"Mari-a has special gifts. She is connected to the natural world and the creatures revere her." Belshazzar reassures him, "You have a home in Magdala, the sister city to Migdol. Bring this child up near the healing waters of the Sea of Galilee. When she is older, you can send her to Mount Karmel."

Vehemently, Syrus shakes his head. "No! She will not be exposed to such sorcery."

"You fear her gifts as well as your own. Syrus, your sight is true; the father of the Davidic prince has had your same vision. I advise that you not hinder her innate abilities."

"But you do not understand. My people are quite suspicious of anything not of Adonai."

Belshazzar laughs and the infant gurgles with delight. "She is a gift from the Divine. You shall see." He hands Syrus a small leather pouch exactly like the other he gave to the newborn prince some three years earlier. "Place this upon her body." Syrus cringes as a black crow flies through a window, cawing loudly. Belshazzar touches the man's shoulder. "Have no fear. I shall watch over her."

"Your magic is stronger than …?"

"My connection to Source is clear. You are the one to guide this child. Make haste and return to Galilee."

"But my wife has not recovered."

"I have special herbs that will strengthen her, but you must go now." Belshazzar relieves Syrus of the child so he might ready his wife and daughter. Once alone with the babe, her dark skin glistens as she speaks silently to him.

Hello, drummer! My friends are here but where is my partner? I wish to dance.

The ebony king's laughter fills the nursery, causing the monkeys to chatter excitedly over the screeching birds. Belshazzar silently reassures her. *Mari-a, I will keep the beat until you are ready to join your partner. You shall return to your home and so must all your animal companions. Please release them to be with their families.*

The newborn haze of her light eyes clears to a brilliant green as a wave of energy leads the creatures out of the palace. Against the surge of

17

gazelles, a petite but curvaceous woman enters the nursery, her dark skin setting off unusually light eyes.

"Isn't she dear?"

"Eshe, why have you come?"

"On behalf of my brother, who sent a fine wet nurse. The mother will not put her own child to her breast." She reaches for the baby, but Belshazzar holds her close. "I can love this child as one of my own."

"Time will tell why Mari-a is born into this family. Soon another child will need you. Yeshua is coming with his parents from Galilee. His father has concerns about the boy's purpose. Fortunately, the mother is well-connected to the Great Spirit. Have Osaze make arrangements for you to stay in Alexandria at the house of Arimathaea." The woman kisses the baby's forehead, whispering her love and devotion to Mari-a.

With his keen sight, Belshazzar notices that a tiny curl has been shorn from the crown of the babe's head. "Please keep watch over Sahirah. You know how to contact me."

Eyes shadowed by concern, Eshe nods her consent. Beautiful little Mari-a gurgles joyfully, the protective pouch lying at her heart. Belshazzar prays that the elestial quartz's smoky interior might absorb the darkness from her life.

Who Am I

Galilee, 3771

Do you know who you are as part of the One?
Do you know all the Me's that make up I AM?
Who shall you be once in Sacred Unity?
Be true to your self in Harmony with Love.

I am Mary

Sauntering down the road to Nazareth, I quicken my pace to pass unescorted by the women at the village well. Dust sullying my fine embroidered robe, I only stop to knock the gravel from my sandals. Great timbers from the forests of Tyre peek through worn clay walls as a cool breeze lifts faded courtyard canopies. On the western outskirts of the village, I enter the house of Joseph.

Once through the low doorway, children's laughter greets me. More alive than any of my family's grand homes, the humble cottage permeates with a wealth of love. My skin tingles—he is here.

"Yeshua, I want you to have this."

Startled brown eyes absorb me before liquefying into a warm smile. He takes the small rose quartz, fingers lingering a fraction longer than necessary. Quivering, I search for my innate strength to hold his intense gaze. His younger brothers and sisters interrupt their play to watch our exchange.

"Yeshua, mind your manners! We are not espoused."

Rude as rowdy donkeys, boys jostle into the courtyard. I am nearly knocked off the landing before Yeshua catches my arm.

"Why is she here?" the gangly son of the village potter whines.

"She possesses what we do not. We need her sacred feminine power to sanctify Mount Tabor."

"Who is she anyhow?" Yeshua's entourage grumbles amongst themselves, clearly uncomfortable with my presence. Still I hesitate to reveal myself until he gives me a nudge.

"I am...Mary." They are unimpressed so I add, "Daughter of Syrus, the magistrate." The boys quiet their protests.

Yeshua leads us through the street, ignoring the farmer who tries to sell the last of his produce to busy wives. Stomachs growl in unison but Yeshua hastens the pace, carefully avoiding sewage coursing through drainage systems. Laughing and elbowing each other, the boys make crude remarks.

"The Romans are pigs. Look at this filth in the street."

"If it were not for the Romans, we would still be pumping water from the village wells and relieving ourselves in buckets!"

Sons of the Chaverim, probably living in such conditions, look down. A scruffy one scowls at me. Teoma confides, "Mary certainly has an answer for everything!"

Yeshua nods, "That's why I like her to accompany us."

"Is that the only reason?"

I stifle a smile at Yeshua's reddened cheeks. Before passing by the well, Teoma gathers the boys into a tight-knit group, effectively shielding me from the sharp eyes of the village women. Grateful that my mother shall not discover this escapade, I thank him.

Leaving the dusty road we head southeast toward Mount Tabor, but the smell of roasting meat halts the hungry boys. Despite passionate pleas, Yeshua can get them to go no further so Teoma conspires with the goatherd to feed us in return for milking the goats. Upset by the delay, Yeshua walks in small circles. I make my way over to him and take his arm. In the coolness of the late winter afternoon, it is damp.

"Have you eaten today?"

"I'm fasting." He looks away as if I cannot possibly understand his devotion.

"Yesh, why must you suffer so?" Eyes shining like amber glass, he moves to a higher vista. Sighing, I find his cousin, a good friend to both of us.

"Teoma," I touch his shoulder as he squats down to milk a brown and black spotted doe. He looks up and grins.

"What, green eyes?"

Stroking the goat's head, I chastise myself for not curbing my passion. "I'm worried about Yeshua. He's fasting again and I think he might collapse."

"If only you were as concerned for the rest of us."

"Please, will you bring him the first cut of meat?" Hastily, I stand, but he catches the hem of my sadin, halting my step.

"What?" I cry, frustrated by the delay.

"Perhaps we might…" Teoma murmurs through a half-considered smile, "Sorry, go watch over him."

Partially obscured by weeping pepper tree branches, Yeshua rests in meditation. Carefully, I sit beside him, wishing he realized what I have always known. We are destined to be together.

"I have always loved you, Mary."

A sob catches in my throat. Singing softly in the breeze, the lime-green leaves hover about us like a bridal veil. So long I have wanted to know his feelings, but now I feel strange. His lean brown hand cups my head, pouring icy river water down my back. I shiver as sweat beads on his upper lip, glistening on the fine down that will someday be a mustache. His breath smells sickly sweet, perhaps he speaks in delirium.

Finished with the chores, the boys recline about the pepper grove hungrily enjoying their reward. Yeshua rises at Teoma's approach and takes the water skin. We silently wash our hands before sharing the meat. Yeshua's hands tremble as he gives thanks. Teoma casts a worried glance my way.

"Yesh, please eat," I beg.

Wavering on his feet, Yeshua falls into my lap, out cold.

Gray-green olive leaves rustle a warning as we return through the shadowed village. An empty courtyard greets us. Releasing Teoma's steady grip, Yeshua sinks wearily upon some cushions just as his mother rushes in.

"Ima," Yeshua implores, "please allow Mary to stay."

Tears trailing through the dust on my face, I turn toward the doorway where Teoma stands prepared to escort me home.

"Mary, come join us. It is time."

I take Miriam's hand. Unconcerned by my tattered appearance, she leads me to a simple stone kiyyor and kneels to wash my feet and hands like a servant. We rise together and through a semi-sheer veil, enter an inner sanctum. Smooth basalt walls cradle burnished copper lamps flickering upon two intersecting triangles inlaid into the marble floor.

A sweet melody courses through me, but Miriam seems unaware. In fluid motion, I abandon myself to the swirling energy. The altar beckons, yet not until the music fades away and the hayye settles into a faint buzzing do I cease dancing. I kneel at the altar, my palms and forehead pressing gently against the cool stone, envisioning a star encased in a rose upon it.

Above the frantic beat of my heart, I feel someone enter the sanctum. Turning full circle, I see that Miriam has gone and in her place is... Yeshua.

Faintly self-conscious, I rise to my feet. Never before have we been alone in a room together. This room so sensuous, how might I control my passion? For heaven knows, I am desirous of his company.

Yeshua has not moved from the doorway, nor I from the altar, yet fate tightens invisible cords that bind our hearts. Where is Miriam? As I fret, she appears behind him.

"She is intuned to the energies, my son." A sense of peace blankets me as she drapes a pale blue hooded mantle over my shoulders.

"Ima, may we have a moment alone?" Yeshua looks intently into her eyes. In spite of his charisma, Miriam shakes her head and draws me closer into her bosom.

The following morning, Yeshua and I sit before his parents in a study filled with scrolls, ancient and new. Without ceremony, his father begins. "It is tradition to announce the betrothal of a Davidic prince in Tammuz. After the winter solstice, the royal marriage will be consummated..."

Wedding! Looking at my expression, Joseph speaks much more slowly, "... so the child conceived will be born in the month of kings."

Feeling faint, I murmur, "I don't understand." Yeshua's face darkens as Joseph clears his throat.

"You were betrothed to my son when you were but three."

Twelve years and I have not known? My mother must have died a thousand deaths when my father accepted the son of a craftsman. Joseph supports his large family very well, but...All eyes study my reaction, I swallow thickly, "Yeshua is my heart's desire, but I am shocked that my Abba would give me to him."

Miriam and Joseph nod, well aware of the breach of tradition. Tzadokim never marry Chaverim!

Leaning across the table, Miriam reaches for my hand. "Dear one, your father shared my husband's vision of your marriage to our son," she

24

gives Joseph a sidelong glance, "but the elders asked Yeshua to fulfill dynastic law."

"What does that mean?" I look at my espoused.

"Nothing for you to worry about. We are to be married on the spring equinox. The Zadoks will have to be satisfied, for **this is** divine timing." Before Yeshua can speak further, Joseph raises his hand.

"Please, son, go talk this over."

Yeshua leads me down the hall to a room off the garden. Wine red, forest green, midnight blue—rich sensual colors grace the cushions and drapery. The smell of warm bread causes my stomach to quake, but Yeshua ignores the beautiful meal laid out for us on the low table.

"It is not a fast day."

Looking intently at me, he smiles. "Fasting curbs my desires."

"But don't you hunger?"

He shakes his head, tracing my mouth with the tip of his finger. "Not for food."

Deep brown eyes spiraled in gold draw me into infinity. I swallow and drop my gaze to his mouth. His lips greet mine tentatively until I open to receive him, then his kiss becomes sweetly urgent. I am melting into him to become hot liquid spilling on the cool tile floor.

"Yeshua," drawing away, I ask breathlessly, "when did you know about us?"

"Before I left for Britannia." What! That was nearly three years ago. He holds me against his chest, stroking my tangled curls. "I should have told you sooner." Trembling with unspent passion, I release a shuddering cry. "I promise that I will not cause you any more suffering."

In the portal of his eyes, the truth is revealed. "In loving you, I fear I shall experience much more suffering."

A single tear slides down his tan cheek and splashes onto mine, sealing our fate.

The odor of sandalwood permeates my nostrils from the oil massaged onto my skin. All morning I have been tended by the women, my body soaked in a jasmine bath, my hair rinsed in lavender and lemon. Silk sways tantalizingly against my smooth legs as I wander down the hall. My mother would be appalled to see me in this revealing Grecian sadin and what has been revealed to me in the chamam, she can never know.

I miss Yeshua. Three weeks ago Joseph took him into the wilderness to prepare for our coming wedding. The house feels so empty. I enter the inner sanctum through a thick black drape embroidered with the constellations and a full moon. In opposition to the sun's path, I dance with the sensuous hayye, filling thirteen oil lamps before pouring eight drops of precious oil upon lambskins arranged in the four directions. The star within a rose glows hotly beneath me as I recline on the altar. The one candle flickers, but paying no mind, I trace spirals upon my skin, noticing that my violet hue is glistening with Yeshua's silver.

Suddenly, there seems a bit less air in the room. Holding my breath, I sit up to peer into the dark. The circle of moonlight entertains a familiar shadow. Yeshua!

Ecstatic, I cover his face with kisses. "So, Mary," he whispers into my soft curls, "why are you here?" Looking into his eyes, I see the mirror of my love.

"Your Ima asked me to prepare this room for a special ceremony. The swirling hayye came so I danced and then rested here to watch the moon rise. Would you like to join me, the sky is beautiful tonight."

"I would love to join you, beloved, but first let me light the lamps."

Before he moves away, I catch his hand. "No, we mustn't waste the oil."

"I do not think it will go to waste," he whispers and moves toward the east, lighting each of the thirteen lamps in turn. I pray Miriam will not be too angry that we burn the oil before the ceremony.

Circling south of the altar, Yeshua drops to his knees. "You look so beautiful tonight with the flowers in your hair and that wonderful violet dress that matches the color of your life force. And you smell delicious. I wonder why Ima would have you prepare so elaborately only to ready this room." He does not take his eyes off me, nor does he stand. My breath catches…I am the special ceremony!

He stands and drops his robe, adorned only by the small leather pouch around his neck. Nervously, I finger my own pouch nestled between my breasts. All the elaborate ministrations over the past three days were to prepare me for this moment. Pouring off my shoulders in silky waves of violet, my gown soon lies upon the altar. Yeshua gasps.

"You are so…beautiful!"

Swallowing thickly, he kneels and slides me closer, until the tips of my toes are level with his chest. From his robe he produces a tiny bottle of oil. Holding it over us he prays in Hebrew, the sacred language of our people, and then begins anointing my feet. His touch creates waves of sensation as the pungent odor of spikenard pervades the room. When he stands to move toward my head, I feel a pillar of hayye pour from above us to enclose the entire altar. Radiance gathers to witness our union. Yeshua gently directs me to lie back and slides me north. Again he holds the tiny vial aloft, praying fervently before softly anointing the crown of my head.

The column of energy widens when he joins me on the altar. I lay completely still, mesmerized by the pulsating hayye rising in my body from the bottom of my feet to the top of my head. Tenderly, he kisses my mouth. With a cry, I pull him closer, hungrily yearning for more.

He begins stroking me softly, learning every curve. Each moment intensifies. I part my thighs and he dips into my wetness to paint spirals over my belly and breasts. I cry out as he takes a rigid nipple into his mouth. He tastes all of me and I am enchanted.

When he probes below with tender fingers, I yearn to arch up yet he holds me still. One finger, now two, now…Ouch! There is an uncomfortable tightness, something is wrong. "Yesh…?"

Rising up to face me, he whispers, "It is going to be fine, love." Of course. Miriam explained that there might be some discomfort the first time. Touching his chest, I run my hands down his hard belly …my goodness, his desire is much greater than my own!

Groaning, he lies back, but my attention is too much for he drags me up to face him. Kissing me fiercely, his lovemaking becomes more urgent. The hayye intensifies around us, crashing like waves in a stormy sea. Drumming quickens the music. I am in awe, but it is not over.

He captures my gaze, rocking gently to engage me in an entirely new dance. Seeking a deliciously furious rhythm we finally reach a point from which there is no return. The energies separate, each wave moving progressively faster until our passion becomes the purest vibration and all colors merge.

Time stops.

There is nothing but us, bathing in the now pure white light.

Yeshua collapses heavily upon me (light as a feather just a moment before) breathing raggedly. Still in awe, I watch shapes coalesce within the prism and kiss him eagerly, "Thank you. That was wonderful."

"You're welcome, my love. But what did you perceive?"

"Yesh, you were right here. Was it not the same for you?"

Kissing me tenderly, he nibbles my lower lip. "I don't think so."

Somewhat self-conscious, I whisper, "Yeshua, next time you can be the anointed one."

Just as the sky lightens, Yeshua gently shakes me awake. "Mary, did I hurt you?" Sitting up sleepily, I do not feel injured, only a bit sore. What is he talking about?

My gaze descends—blood everywhere, his groin, hips, and hands stained. Oh, no! I am unclean, and now... so is he.

"Forgive me," I explain in a strangled voice, "it is my menses."

"Barchashem!" Thanking the Divine, he reaches to embrace me, but shocked, I back away.

"Yeshua, men never touch a woman in her unclean period!" Averting my eyes, I shiver, "I should be shut away."

His fingertips lift my chin, his golden brown eyes saturated with compassion. "It's not possible for my beloved to **ever** be ritually impure." Tenderly, he lies us down on the stained lambskin and pulls me close to his chest. "In your arms, I have found what I've been seeking," he murmurs into my tangled curls, "Sacred Unity—Eloha!"

Choosing Destiny

Accompanied by the sweet musk of intimacy, Yeshua and I hurry along the corridor. Closest to the street that it might drain efficiently into the Roman sewers, the betshimush lies within a discreet tiled booth. After relieving myself in the hole for this purpose, I go to the chamam. Yeshua is there. Although ill at ease, I allow him to sponge me in a low copper basin. He even watches as I place a clean soft rag between my thighs securing the menstrual strap tightly about my hips.

"When will you be fertile?"

"In about two Shabbats."

"And we are to be married in thirteen days. Ima planned this out perfectly."

Turning away, I wind my wet hair atop my head, securing it with ivory hairpins. Miriam enters the chamam and Yeshua greets her with a kiss on the cheek, but when she tucks away my few stray hairs I slump upon her bosom.

"Mary? Ima? What is wrong?"

"Yeshua, it is all right. Please go to the gathering room."

Miriam waves him off and I give him a tear-soaked smile. With bowed head, he walks slowly away. I grasp her hands, speaking rapidly, almost incoherently.

"Oh Ima Miriam! We woke up covered in my blood and Yeshua was not offended! Then he asked about my fertile time…that is when we will be married. I…"

"You are feeling some fear. That is natural." I look up at her now, as she continues, "Yours is a challenging destiny that will be filled with love and passion, pain and sorrow. You have consented to a divine match that will pave the way for much more powerful energies to come unto the earth."

Somewhere in the depths of my soul, I know what she is saying to be true. "Will my fear prevent me from fulfilling my destiny?"

"No dear, fear, like love, is part of being human. The perfect bride for my son." Smiling, she stops for a moment to squeeze my hand, "Now I must ask you to do one more thing before adjourning to the atrium…" She pauses before saying softly, "Please say goodbye to Teoma."

Still trembling, I hesitantly enter the gathering room. Both Yeshua and Teoma stand in respect. Dressed in a fine blue robe, sashed smartly with a decorated leather belt, Teoma looks like a soldier, muscular legs encased in high sandals, arms rigid at his side. Yeshua motions for me to sit beside him and gives me a gentle hug.

Teoma's face bears great sorrow. What is wrong?

With a slight quiver of his jaw, he smiles at me. His hands slowly unclench. "Mary, I hear congratulations are in order."

From across the low round table, heat rises from his chest and faintly I smell his tantalizing sweat. My heart pounds beneath my breasts as I sigh deeply. What is happening to me? Strangely attracted to Teoma, I twist golden cords girdling my waist, my betrothed stiffening at my side.

"Please, Mary, sit with Teoma and have your breakfast. I need my son to assist me." Yeshua glances back at us as Miriam leads him away.

Left alone, Teoma's presence becomes enhanced. The sweet aching hayye surrounding us raises a lump in my throat. He motions toward the food, "Mary, eat. You look like you could use some refreshment."

He knows. Paralyzed, I cannot breathe. In surrendering to one, am I open to all men now? Or is there something between us that I overlooked in my fervor for Yeshua?

Still watching me intently, his sky blue gaze softens. Our children would have the most beautiful eyes. I am losing myself.

A sob chokes him, "I love Yeshua like a brother, but I never believed he would marry."

Pain nearly rips my heart asunder. "Perhaps then you might learn to love me like a sister." My whispered response begs an answer.

Great tears cloud his eyes. "I could never love you as a sister, sweet Mary." I take his hand and he does not pull away, but gently covers mine with his other. So warm, his hands are much larger than Yeshua's. Through the clear blue depths of his eyes, I fall into his soul. Flashes of unfamiliar images of us through the ages flow past my mind's eye. For all eternity, his love protects me, but I shudder to see such prolonged unfulfilled passion, his desire threatening to destroy him.

Saying goodbye will release him, but I cannot let him go. When I stand, Teoma does not move to stop me, so I kiss the top of his bowed head. Running from the room, my senses overloaded by emotion, his essence burns upon my lips.

Outside the doorway, my breath caught in a sob, I bring a trembling hand to my mouth. Hearing footsteps in the corridor, I turn blindly to escape and run directly into Yeshua.

"Mary!" Grasping my arms, he tries to get me to look up at him.

Not wanting to reveal my tears, I press my face into his chest, wiping them away. "Please, Teoma is waiting for you to take his leave."

"Mary, are you all right?" I only nod, for if I speak again, I will sob. He kisses the crown of my dark curls and enters the gathering room. With bowed head, I wander aimlessly.

A young boy's voice chants the sacred texts. I look up to see Yeshua's eleven-year-old brother. Jacob is a beautiful boy, a replica of his father with dark thick hair and eyes a muted shade of indigo.

"Come, I'll show you to the atrium." Jacob turns, walking so quickly that I must nearly run to keep up, but the activity lightens my mood somewhat. The enclosed courtyard's paths are lined with flowers and herbs, their fragrances mingling to produce a hazy feeling in my head like wine.

We enter a pure white tent with large open spaces between the top and the sides enticing the breeze to move freely. In the middle is a bubbling fountain that I kneel by to cool my fevered face. Jacob smiles, "Mary, there is refreshment for you at the table."

Rising, I brush off the hem of my sadin and see Jacob pointing at a feast. A large basket of fruit overflows onto the white linen tablecloth. Skins filled with yogurt sit between a small pot of honey and another basket filled with bread. My stomach rumbles. Like a gifted Tana, Jacob recites passages from the Torah verbatim. I ask him to sing me the Song of Solomon and his pure young voice sweetens my meal. Thanking him, I find a hammock suspended between the trunks of two olive trees. Jacob joins me and we swing. Soon a hummingbird hovers close looking at each of us in turn. *Be joyful,* I hear in my head. Jacob takes no notice.

"Mary, how did you know Yeshua was the one?"

"When I looked into his eyes the first time, I could see myself as love." Nothing is clearer to me than this. In Yeshua's eyes, I am beloved.

Jacob seems impressed, "That is just what the mirrors of the Essenes teach. There are seven of them." When I try to stifle a yawn, Jacob takes his leave, chanting the psalms by memory.

Not a moment later, Miriam sits on the edge of the hammock. "Mary, did you say goodbye to Teoma?"

"No, I did not realize how much he loves me…" relieved by her tender smile, I go on, "until this morning when I could feel his heart breaking."

"As your new life begins with Yeshua, you must let nothing come between you." A pillar of hayye pours down. Pure white, translucent pulsations hold the space around us, drawing my attention away from her face. The energy shifts and I hear in my head:

Beloved, you are learning that love is the vibration that connects you to other dimensions. You share a path with Teoma as well as Yeshua. One is your ever-faithful protector, while the other is your fervent lover. One will meet you at the end of your journey, while the other has met you well in the beginning.

Looking intently at me, Miriam is silent. I wonder what I saw in Teoma's eyes.

You witnessed, dear one, your shared paths through the ages to come. You will need a faithful partner to watch over you. Your destiny has been sealed by your love for Teoma. But now it is Yeshua's turn to dance with you.

Tears slip from my lashes while the hayye recedes, bringing the garden back into focus. Miriam kisses my forehead. "Please rest now, dear. You will be guided to know how to handle Yeshua."

Handle Yeshua? I close my eyes but soon the hammock rocks with the weight of another.

"Why do you cry, Mary?" Smiling, I hold open my arms. This is the way to handle Yeshua, I think, as we begin kissing softly. "Teoma took his leave in sadness; I hope he comes to the wedding." I look into his eyes for a sign of malevolence. There is none. "Do you love him?"

"Until this morning, I did not know that he loved me…," but how to say this without upsetting my betrothed? "Nor did I know that I had feelings for him."

Yeshua's hayye draws away from me, his hand cool upon my hip. I stay his touch.

"What? How can he have a piece of your heart when you gave yourself to me?" His jealousy tinges his aura with an olive hue.

Taking his hand, I hold it against my breast, "Yeshua, although I truly love you, my heart nearly broke when I saw the depth of Teoma's love for me and the bitterness of his disappointment."

He turns away, his hayye compressing into a narrow cord. I will not be with him like this, but when I try to leave, he holds me fast. Ignited by my frustration, my energy surges forth, forcing him to release me. "I can give myself to whomever I choose." His eyes widen. "And I choose you. But I will be well met!"

His brown eyes soften with unshed tears. "I love Teoma, too. I do not know how I can feel this way when one of my greatest wishes was that you would come to love one another… just not as you do." His hayye, now liquefied by his honest expression of despair, expands into its original fullness. He responds to my tentative kiss with a fervent passion that threatens to consume. Will our relationship always be so volatile or will it mellow with time?

At dusk, I slip on grass green silk in preparation to celebrate Yeshua's eighteenth birthday. Delighting in the sensuous feel of the gown, I twirl around the room and nearly collide with his mother. Raised hands clasped together, I attempt to beg her forgiveness, but she lowers my hands to the level of her breasts, looking intently into my eyes. A golden energy surges from her hands into mine and the next moment, I am transported to another time.

We are in the desert with wild flowers blooming all around. I am very young, perhaps six or seven, dressed in a pure white tunic. Walking quickly with my hands tightly cupping something fuzzy, I see her coming toward me from some large white tents. Tall and light-skinned with auburn brown hair, she holds my small hands gently as a warm golden hayye begins to seep from her palms. The tiny fuzzy body begins to move and gasping, I open my hands. The once injured queen bee explores my palms before taking flight, pausing briefly to buzz her dance of gratitude. I look up into my mother's soft brown eyes…

33

...and I am transported to the present time, looking into Miriam's eyes. "You see, Mary, why it is so natural for me to treat you as my daughter." I am overwhelmed by emotion. "Come, dear, it is time to greet the guests." Taking my hand, she leads me down the corridor. I am home.

Wandering through the crowd of strangers with sweet pomegranate wine warming my blood, I seek Yeshua but he pays me little heed attending instead to his teachers from the east. Children play around the fountain illuminated by many oil lamps. In the midst of all the foreign tongues, greetings in Aramaic catch my attention. Yeshua embraces an imposing figure on the landing. My knees begin to shake.

Broader in the chest and shoulders, Teoma takes his leave when Yeshua turns to greet another guest. He heads my way. I do not move for I wish to speak with him. "Mary, you look lovely tonight." Although his eyes are intent only on my own, I feel naked under his gaze.

"Teoma, may we speak in private?"

He raises an eyebrow. "Why certainly, but first let us share some shekar in celebration of Yeshua's birthday." After securing two cups of wine from a servant, he leads me deep into the pepper tree grove south of the outer courtyard. The delicate branches touch the ground, but close to the trunk is an open space. We are alone, hidden from the crowd.

Setting the wine aside carefully, he takes off his cloak and spreads it before me. We sit. "First, we drink to Yeshua's happiness," he raises his cup to mine and swallows down half of it. I sip mine, already feeling dizzy. "What do you want to discuss?"

Was it not just this morning that we parted, heat steaming off our chests? Taking a deep breath, I begin, "Teoma, I did not realize how you felt about me and the depth of my feelings for you."

He looks down at the cup in his hand and, lifting it to his mouth, finishes the shekar in one swallow. His voice is gruff now perhaps from the wine but I sense it is emotion, "What are you saying, Mary?"

When I gently touch his hand, his deep green hayye melts like candle wax. "I love Yeshua, truly I do, but I believe that I also love you." His breath stops for a long moment and I wait till he catches it again. "I knew that I had to release you this morning but selfishly I did not."

The masculine thickening in his throat rises like a wave. Sitting up, he clasps his hands together as if in prayer, staring at me expectantly. I take his hands in mine. Born into wealthy Tzadokim families, ours would be a more socially acceptable match. I love Yeshua, but our breach with custom will make our lives difficult indeed. "Teoma, I wish to choose my own destiny…" Halting, I breathe deeply, "if you will but…kiss me."

Teoma's jaw stiffens as he gathers his resources, "You are a temptress, but Yeshua is like a brother to me and I cannot do this."

I knew he would be honorable, but I must be sure. So moving a bit closer, I clasp his hands to my heart. His breath quickens. "Teoma, please, how can we live like this, not knowing?"

"Mary," his voice is hoarse with emotion, "no matter what you might find in our embrace, my feelings will not change. I love you. But I also love Yeshua. I am committed to honoring what is his…," swallowing, he says resolutely, "you and your future children."

Music interrupts our reverie. "Mary, finish your shekar and go dance. I must take my leave." He draws his hands from mine gently before standing and helping me to my feet.

"At least you can watch me dance before you go."

"No, my dear, it is not my turn." Teoma turns me away from him. "Go dance for your beloved." With a sob, I run from the cover of the pepper tree, his prophetic words throbbing in my ears.

East of the fountain, the men dance, the women on the other side. Looking for Yeshua, I circle the dancers in time to the music, a surge of spiraling hayye drawing me into the center of the courtyard. Dancing with the energies faster and faster, my body light, my head spinning, the crowd of onlookers becomes blurred. Finally the face I search for comes clear. I dance around my betrothed yet there is no escaping my unresolved feelings. Yeshua speaks my name, but does not move with the music. His voice seems so very far away, his face fades, the music stops.

I am being carried, my head hanging back over someone's arm. When I open my eyes, the world spins so fast, my stomach lurches in response. I groan. "She stirs." Miriam speaks but it is not she who carries me.

"Ima, please let me take her to my chambers." It is Yeshua who bears my weight.

"No, son, it is enough. She needs to rest now from the excitement and from you."

Yeshua tightens his grip, then stops so abruptly that my dizzy head might fall onto the floor. "Ima, please. I will take better care of her." I try again to open my eyes and my stomach threatens to empty itself upon us all.

"Yeshua, I have never seen you like this, not being considerate of another. Mary will be your wife, but she doesn't belong to you." Miriam's tone is severe. "She should be in the chamam with women who can tend to her needs, not entertaining you. In twelve days you will be wed, if she does not become too ill to participate in the ceremony."

Finally, he acquiesces and lays me gently on his sisters' bed. I whisper his name. Gathering me into his arms, he does not let go when Miriam returns with wet cloths. "Yeshua, it is time for you to say goodbye to our guests."

With a gentle kiss on my forehead, he leaves me wanting, still not knowing the truth in my heart.

Dod Joseph,

I pray you have found comfort for I know that it has been difficult since Doda passed away. I wish not to burden you, but I suffer. My beloved is to be wed to my best friend and brother. This is our destiny and I hope to find salvation in serving Yeshua and protecting what is his.

If only my love for Mary was not reflected in her heart, perhaps I could find a wife of my own. Yeshua's parents explained the importance of my participation in their sacred union, but I must gather all of my courage to be present with grace.

Pray for me, Dod. Please let me return with you after the wedding until the passion cools to a more bearable flame. I am in your debt.

In trust and honor, your nephew, Teoma

The women have taken over the chamam, the perfume of essential oils and fresh cut flowers saturating my senses. All morning they have bathed me, massaged my body, even using honeyed strips of linen to pull the hair from my limbs. Miriam approaches with a cup of steaming tea. In spite of her insistence that Yeshua and I be separated until our wedding day, I cannot help but return her smile.

"Now drink this, Mary. It will help you heal."

A familiar sweet fragrance is sharpened by a foreign odor. "Ima, I recognize anise, but what else is in it?"

"Ginseng from the east and chaste berry from the north. You will learn this and more from the Essene healers. It will strengthen your womb so that your first conception may not be lost." She leaves me to rest only after I finish the tea.

Although I trust her, the idea of enhancing my fertility reminds me of my vows to choose my own destiny as I drift into sleep.

A glorious light enters my dream world—the Archangel Gavriel, my secret friend since childhood. I am taught that since the beginning, women have been able to choose fertility but relinquished their power to men long ago, suffering ever since from the pain of bearing too many unwanted children.

How might I control my fertility without forsaking the pleasures of my marriage bed? The angel smiles and leads me directly into my body. Narrow at the entrance, my womb widens into a large cavern filled with rich blood for the nourishment of a child. At the end are two identical openings and through one narrow tunnel lined by feathers I am encouraged onward. The end widens into a flower, which hangs over a tiny pale pomegranate filled to popping with many, many eggs. Some are ripening and others are dormant —the essence of my future children.

Finally I am shown how, through intention and desire, I may cast a protective white light around my organs, sealing them from my husband's seed. When I desire a child, all I must do is release the protective energy and invite my child's hayye into my gan eden.

I awaken to express my gratitude for the angelic guidance, the tiny stone in the pouch at my neck heavy and warm.

Becoming As One

Over the ridge of Nazareth, spring dawns gray and misty. Although light will not penetrate the shaded courtyard window of his chambers until much later, Yeshua slips free of the warm linens to sit cross-legged upon the floor. Hands meet at his heart to give thanks, but unaccustomed to arising so early, Yeshua yawns. Whenever he closes his eyes, a sea-green gaze beckons. He resists the temptation to view through the ethers. Not until under the chupa may he look upon the face of his bride.

Excitement fills the chambers when Jacob arrives announcing, "Saada has baked massah so dress quickly before you go to the mikvah!" Fennel cake crumbs dust the corners of his young brothers' mouths.

"I cannot break my fast until the wedding feast this afternoon."

"Where in the Torah...?"

"It is tradition. But take Shimon and Judah to finish their meal, and then you may help me prepare for the ritual bath."

The children hurry noisily out, waking Teoma. Donning a robe, Yeshua enters his friend's chambers. Teoma yawns and stretches. "You're up early. Did Jacob interrupt your meditation?" He nods, smiling. "Well, I am grateful not to have to listen to your snoring anymore."

"I shall miss you."

Teoma rises and gives him a rough hug. "Before you go to the mikvah, you are wanted in the garden." Yeshua does not move until his friend pushes him away with a gruff, "Just take good care of her."

In the olive grove, Yeshua removes the pouch from around his neck and hands it to Belshazzar. The mystic nods his approval, "You have outgrown the need for my protection."

Twelve years ago, Zsao traveled from the far Himal range to teach Yeshua the ways of the Awakened One. Smiling, his almond-shaped eyes become mere slits. "Today you journey farther into manhood, but do not lose the joyful innocence of childhood as you live each day in Oneness."

Reiti sits in an impossible pose. The thin brown man from the Hindus replaced Zsao as his teacher when Yeshua was but nine. Three years later, Belshazzar arrived from far away Aksum. Now they return as promised for the most special event of his life—his marriage. At dusk, the mystics shall hold the energy during the unification ritual. A shiver of concern raises the hair on Yeshua's neck.

Reiti untangles his long limbs and rises with the grace of a crane. "Your dearest friend is deeply wounded."

Shaking his head, Zsao repeats a long forgotten lesson. "Do not allow worry to occupy space in your being. Release your fear and accept your destiny."

"I love Teoma like a brother and feel his pain as my own."

"He honors your friendship and shall give you his blessing this evening." Belshazzar's assurance does not allay all of Yeshua's concerns.

"This morning he asked me to take good care of her. Her mother bemoans that I cannot support her in the rich manner of her father. Without a betrothal ceremony last year, there has not been time, but Teoma would have built her a house with his own hands..."

"Ahh, but your parents have gifted you with a most lovely bridal chamber. At one with nature, Mary shall bask in the experience of sharing intimacies beneath the stars."

Yeshua's flushed cheeks bring laughter to their bellies. Still, he worries about Mary struggling to maintain her composure in the face of her mother's disappointment. Forbidden to see his betrothed before the wedding, he could not even wish her well on her fifteenth birthday, and has been consumed by concern after overhearing Ima complain to Hava that a whole week in their chamam would be diminished by one day in Eucharia's. The Aksum king clasps his arm.

"Your betrothed is most resilient. She shall perform the first anointing today."

He thought the women had prepared her for the sacred ritual, not a royal ceremony. How can he be anointed king, while his father and grandfather still live?

Belshazzar's laughter brightens the morning haze. "Yeshua, you are far from ready to be king; the sacred rite the messeh queen shall perform is the first of eight initiations."

His eyes widen. Mary is the messeh queen? Only royalty claim this title after being anointed by the High Priest.

"My prince, did you not anoint her upon the altar?" Yeshua nods, throat tight. In his attempt to invite spirit into their physical union, did he claim a priestly privilege? He never questioned where Ima got the sacred spikenard, did Belshazzar...?

The Aksum king nods. But if it is true, today begins his journey to enlightenment! The first of eight? From the Egyptian Therapeutae, he only learned of seven initiations.

"Two by water, two by fire, two by earth, two by air." Belshazzar nods at Yeshua's unspoken query. "The last rite is performed at death."

Swallowing thickly, he prays to be prepared for the next, "May I ask when the second rite shall be performed?"

Zsao smiles, "The awakening is a long and arduous path. You have much to learn."

"But who shall teach me? Will you return?"

"Yeshua, those closest are the best teachers. Please take advantage of your wife's wisdom." Reiti's advice is a balm to his ears for he cannot imagine leaving Mary again to travel east.

He thanks each of his dear teachers before passing by the colorfully adorned tent, praying his bride will be pleased.

Appeasing his mother, Yeshua covers his fine wedding garments with a cloak before mounting the white donkey. During the walk north, Jacob leads the entourage in song, lightening his brother's mood. Some of his cousins straggle behind, but Teoma, under Abba's orders not to be late, shepherds them along. Entering the village of Cana, a quiet synagogue and empty marketplace greets the young men, but the streets leading to the bride's home swarm with villagers.

"The magistrate invites only Tzadokim to his daughter's wedding," one of the white bearded Chaverim complains. Before Yeshua can address the elder, Teoma nudges him. Herodian guards bar the great wooden gate. Apparently, one of the tetrarchs was invited.

41

Roman soldiers push the villagers aside making way for the bridegroom. A centurion reins his bay steed close. "May your marriage bear many joyous fruits."

Yeshua thanks his old friend before entering the immense courtyard. Wealth emanates from the bubbling fountain inlaid with lapis lazuli to the polished marble pillars easily as tall as two men. Servants wash the dust from their feet and hands at an ornate silver kiyyor sitting upon a pedestal before escorting them into a richly draped gathering room. Yeshua is taken aside by his grandfather.

"Saba, why didn't Jochan come?"

Hillel shakes his head, "Since you did not honor your agreement with the Zadoks, Zechariah refused to allow his son to come." Yeshua nods, knowing his father is sorely disappointed that his cousins do not support him. "Your bride's family entertains our enemies." Hillel points to Herod Phillip speaking intimately to the Roman tribuni. Nearby the kings of Tarsus and Nabataea seek Belshazzar's attention. In embroidered robes of the finest silk, Tzadokim enjoy ripe cheeses and stuffed figs. The jewels worn by just these few men could be sold to feed half of Galilee.

Even in a simple robe, Joseph sits proudly next to the richly adorned magistrate. Syrus signals for his daughter's bridal trunk to be opened. The men express their appreciation of the display: exquisite household linens and ceremonial cloths as well as sacred ritual objects used on Shabbat, a copper pomegranate filled with precious fragrant spices, magnificent menorahs, and a pair of gilded sandals for him.

Saul acts as scribe, recording the exchange of property—a vast parcel of land west of Nazareth, a palace in Migdol, and enough gold to support his family until Yeshua is an old man.

With flushed cheeks, Joseph motions for his nephews to carry in the massive cedar table that took him a year to complete. "And the best of my vineyards will grace this table for twelve seasons."

Within the silence, Yeshua perceives the Tzadokim wryly wondering about their local magistrate who would give his precious daughter for such a pittance.

Joseph of Arimathaea stands. "Unless you have partaken of my friend's wine you cannot appreciate how rare and precious it is." Teoma's uncle is wealthier than any ten of the wedding guests and favored by Caesar as minister of the emperor's mines; only Herod's sons are more powerful.

After the ketuba is signed by witnesses, Ananias laughs, "Syrus, if I would have known you had such refined taste, I would have offered my vineyards in Damascus."

Yeshua had no idea the High Priest had designs on Mary as a bride for his son. Holding the circle of lambskin she embroidered with the emblem of their union—a star within a rose—he prays she will be pleased with his gift.

***

A beautiful cedar trunk ornately carved, obviously the work of Yeshua's father, is placed before me by two robust servants. Ima hurries them out as my aunts, cousins, and grandmother, even my aged wet nurse, gather round. Miriam sits with her sister and Hava at the back of the room, while little Esther and Ruth stuff themselves with dates.

Wed to the son of a rich textile merchant from Sepphoris just last month, my sister pushes back her richly bejeweled headdress. Although anxious for the house in Magdala to be prepared for them, Martha stayed for my prenuptials or I may have never survived our mother's sharp tongue. I reach for the protective pouch, but it lies no longer over my heart. Abba returned it to my guardian.

Martha displays Yeshua's sacred family scrolls tracing his lineage back to David for all to view before extracting Egyptian utensils from the trunk. The finely crafted copper induces nods from my father's sisters who have traveled from Tyre for my wedding.

Savta admires the Roman glass plates, "Mary, you shall serve fine meals in your new home."

"Your granddaughter will not have a home of her own." Ima bitterly tells her mother.

"What!" Doda Helena exclaims. "Eucharia, with the dowry my brother paid, my niece should have a palace!"

Afraid my aunt has embarrassed Miriam, I look over, but she seems fine. I pick a pale blue cloak from the trunk and thank her aloud for these sumptuous silks come from her own wardrobe.

Ima passes out the rest and I cringe to hear Doda Helena comment on how lightly each is dyed.

Laying the ketuba on my lap, Ima shakes her head in dismay, "This is what you are worth to them." My aunts commiserate with her as Martha reads the sacred marriage contract aloud. It ensures the transfer of property and my rights to be provided for by my husband in food, clothing, shelter, and sexual needs.

Martha whispers in my ear. "Pay them no mind. They are bitter because their rich spouses do not satisfy them in **all** ways." My cheeks flush hotly. Thankfully, Miriam stands to take curious eyes from my face.

"Martha, search the bottom of the trunk. There is a special gift my son brought from Britannia." My sister does her bidding and extracts a simple wooden box. Carefully I open it to find silvery-white branches curving into five scallops tipped with pastel opals in the form of roses. Yeshua's energy emanates from the necklace. Did he craft himself? Across the way Miriam smiles.

At my hesitancy, Martha deftly ties the necklace about my throat and my hayye shifts to encompass the rainbow of energy.

Doda Helena clucks her tongue, whispering to Savta, "Poor Mary. That will be the last piece of jewelry she will ever wear."

***

"Remove your cloak, my son." His mother's concern pierces his awareness, but she shakes her head and leads him to the ornately decorated columns signifying the gates of paradise.

Brilliant sunshine breaks through the late morning haze, directing Yeshua's attention to the steps from the rooftop. Adorned in an elegant silk gown dyed from the purple secretions of rare and precious mollusks off the coast of Tyre, his bride descends, rich dark curls cascading down her back.

Yeshua takes Mary's hand and leads her under the wedding canopy as their ketuba is read by Saul. As if protected by the chupa, Mary focuses her energy and circles him seven times, wrapping him in her violet hayye. And seven times he encircles her in silver, their intimate exchange inflaming them both.

Syrus hands Yeshua a richly beaded headdress to veil his bride. Hesitating a long moment before looking deeply into Mary's eyes, Yeshua says loud enough for all to hear, "You are my beloved partner, not my property. I will not veil your power," and casts the purple silk outside the chupa.

Horrified murmurs cut the silence as thick as clotted cream. In brilliant contrast to her dark skin, Mary's sea-green eyes express her gratitude. Relieved, Yeshua motions for the first cup of wine. His little sister Ruth sweetly holds the chalice for him to share with his bride. After they consume the ritual yayin, Belshazzar approaches with an alabaster box.

"You are the messeh queen, anoint the beloved prince."

As Mary receives the sacred spikenard with trembling hands, Yeshua takes a seat on the gilded chair. Softly singing the sweet words of love and devotion, she anoints his bowed head. Energy pours through his crown. Voice husky with passion, she kneels before him and he catches his breath as her tears bathe his feet—the first initiation by water. In a sensual peak, she wipes away the excess oil with her unbound curls. Lifting her to her feet, the groom's song floats upon the breeze before he kisses her mouth. She melts into his form, oblivious to the murmuring crowd.

Valiantly, he parts from her lips. Yeshua's youngest sister holds the second cup of yayin. Afterwards Mary sways so dizzily that he refuses a servant's offer to fill their cup with sweet shekar. When his grandparents request his presence, Yeshua asks Teoma to be sure Mary has nothing but water, but upon his return, her inebriation is heightened.

Placing her cup to his lips, he detects no wine. Kissing her mouth, he tastes none. He calls for the seudah to be served and takes his bride firmly about the waist to sit before their wedding plate overfilled with roasted lamb, sweet fennel bread, salted olives and honeyed dates. The meal does nothing to quell her.

At the conclusion of the feast, young Jacob sings a prayer of thanks and with a stomp, Yeshua breaks the plate upon which they dined. The crowds' approval does not drown Eucharia's bitterness as she ties off the linen and hands it back to him.

Although he tries to soothe Mary, he is most grateful when Martha takes her arm. In a sea of colorful headdresses, his bride's luscious curls swing free as the women dance in celebration of this first day of spring. Yeshua joins Teoma and his brothers to dance with the men.

His spirit immeasurably lightened, he is surprised when Ima takes him aside. Leading him hurriedly past two Essenes who refuse to partake a meal with the Tzadokim, she asks, "How is Mary holding up?"

"Not well. Her mother's disappointment is a bane to her. I must not leave her long."

"I'm sorry, my son, but we did not bring enough wine." Ima points to the empty urns. "The mystics taught you well. Please, the guests' cups are empty."

"Why do you ask this of me? What will Abba say?"

"He said let them drink water."

Yeshua swallows thickly, acutely aware of his father's admonitions. "My time has not come." She looks pleadingly at Yeshua and as if called by her distress, Teoma appears to place an arm around her. Yeshua sighs. "Bring me our wedding chalice and fill it with whatever wine you can find."

Teoma leaves to do his bidding and Ima turns to Saada. "Do what he asks of you."

Yeshua instructs Saada to fill six urns with water, which she has accomplished just as Teoma returns. "You must hurry. Ananias' son has alerted Eucharia. She upsets Mary as we speak," he whispers, clearly concerned. "Here, this is all I could find."

"It will do." Bowing his head, Yeshua holds the cup to his breast and prays. Energy pours through his hands and the wine soon sparkles with light. "Now, dear brother, put seven drops of this wine in each of the six urns."

Kissing his mother's cheek, Yeshua passes by the Essenes to find his bride. "Thank heavens, you returned!" Her voice unrestrained, she clings to him.

He best not leave her side again. "Beloved," he whispers, "you seem inebriated."

"How can that be? I only pretended the water was wine."

She created reality purely through desire? Watching their exchange from across the courtyard, Reiti nods and Yeshua remembers his advice. Perhaps she might teach him. Mary grasps his arm, diverting his attention.

"Look, the High Priest's cup is full and Ima said the wine had run out."

Tasting the new wine, Ananias exclaims, "What! Has the best been saved for last?"

Mary gives him a curious look. Before she can ask, Yeshua hushes her with a kiss, her passionate response so arousing that he yearns for dusk. Why not hurry things along, he thinks, as he escorts his bride across the courtyard. With a flourish, he opens the heavy gate and invites the neighbors to join the celebration. "The bridegroom is here. Drink and share my joy for I am married now to my beloved."

Amidst the growing throng of villagers, Joseph gathers the family to exit with Hava and the Seer. Mary asks concerned, "Your father is upset; why is he leaving?"

"Do not despair, precious wife. They go to prepare the inner sanctum," He reassures her but she watches Teoma's retreating back. Praying for strength, Yeshua brings a curl still shiny with spikenard to his lips, "So that you might remember this evening well, please release the effects of the imagined wine." Blushing, Mary holds tightly onto him. After a long moment her lashes flutter open to reveal a clear sea-green gaze. Giving silent thanks, he takes advantage of one of his wife's many gifts with a resounding kiss.

***

Before the sun can slip past the western ridge, we are carried back to Nazareth on a flower strewn litter. Newly married couples pepper their serenade with verses about the delights of the bridal chamber, warming me thoroughly. Yeshua takes my hand and we go to the inner sanctum. At the stone altar, Hava reads a poetic ketuba describing how our marriage unites the sacred feminine and masculine energies of Eloha. When all have taken their places around the intersecting triangles inlaid into the marble floor, we approach the altar from the east.

Her sadin dyed deep red, Hava's vibrant hayye emanates from her palms moving through our hands into our hearts. "May this union be blessed with the fertility of creation and the sacredness of the life force."

"You have embarked upon a great journey and have a unique opportunity to find yourself as Love." Adorned in a bright orange caftan, Belshazzar hands Yeshua a small stone shaped as a miniature tetrahedron. "This elestial quartz will assist in your mutual comprehension of life, death, and immortality. Place it between you and your beloved during the sacred union and the physical will align with the spiritual."

Donning saffron yellow, the Seer offers her wisdom. "May your connection be true as you follow your vision. You will not falter for you will be given strength."

So handsome in his forest green tunic, Teoma gives us his blessing, "I bring you protection from the center of All That Is. Honor the way and the path before you." Yeshua embraces his dearest friend before Teoma accepts my chaste kiss.

Regal in a dark blue robe, Joseph speaks, "My gift is the security of light which surrounds you both through this sacred union and for all eternity."

"My beloved Mary and Yeshua," a glistening tear drops onto Miriam's lavender sadin, "may you have compassion for yourselves and each other. May your hearts be filled with love and your lives be filled with joy."

When Yeshua enters the center ring, Joseph brings down the mists effectively hiding him. All eyes are on my face as Miriam gently guides me forward. Nearly at the edge of the mist, I look up to see Teoma staring at me. I halt, trembling.

I so want to be with my beloved, to experience this sacred union, but fear overwhelms me. Miriam whispers into my right ear, "Your love awaits you," and the witnesses veil their faces. Yeshua's silvery aura expands to draw me through the protective mists. Sobbing, I fall into my beloved's embrace, into the consuming fire of his love.

He holds me for a precious moment, before I lift my face to his. "Hush, my love. Release your fear. We are finally together for eternity."

Alone in the mists, I see nothing outside of the inner circle. The only sound is our breath. Cords of love and desire bind us to this destiny of ours and I do not want fear to darken its brilliance. When Yeshua slips my gown off my shoulders, its edge disappears on the other side of the mist. Smiling, he lifts me onto the circular stone.

From the altar upon which we lie, through the ceiling window and out to the heavens, a prism of hayye forms. The tetrad of angelic host bears witness as Yeshua places Belshazzar's gift in my navel. The stone's smoky interior pulsates through its transparent surface as if it is a living thing, emanating a familiar energy of comfort. From above my head, Archangel Gavriel silently introduces his companions. On my left is Archangel Uriel, on my right Archangel Michael with Archangel Rafael at my feet. Gavriel speaks from the north.

Beloved, with your union you merge heaven and earth, the lighter realities with the denser. May the divine feminine energies of sensuality, joy, and beautiful manifestation be joined with the divine masculine energies of compassion, nurturance, and seeds of creation through your sacred act.

Spreading my legs and arms wide, my body emulates the star. Hayye courses through my limbs when the angels touch my outstretched hands and feet. Over my womb heat rises on my skin in the shape of a five-petal rose. Yeshua looks up from my breast to glance down at his own groin, whispering, "There is heat in the shape of a star."

Gavriel speaks again, *Please beloved, let us not distract you with our ministrations.* The heat fades as the archangels merge into the mist. Gazing at one another before surrendering to desire, my husband stokes another fire deep within and I cry out in my need. Above us the prism is now a great tetrahedron, which houses—the eye from my dreams!

From within my mind a deep voice speaks. *Mary, have no fear. You are protected by the love of The One.*

As my passion rises to a pinnacle, I cannot seem to attend to both the One and Yeshua until the sacred dance of our lovemaking loses me in its cadence. Deepening our connection, the heat of the elestial quartz intensifies as waves of vibrant color engulf us.

Leaving our bodies, we enter the pyramid to stand before Source. The hayye of The One is love and bliss. *My beloved Yeshua and Mary, you have commenced your sacred destiny with your loving union. Yeshua, as the Essence of Divine Love, you have come into Sacred Unity with Mary who is the Presence of Divine Joy. Your love has planted the seed of hope in the heart of every incarnate soul. May you know yourself in the fullness of your truth as your willingness to enter into this union is blessed by the host of hosts.*

Cradled in my navel, the elestial quartz pulsates with the beat of my heart, its smoky depth split into two distinct hues—silver and purple, taking form as a star within a rose. Before donning our wedding garments, Yeshua kisses the emblem of our union.

We step out of the mist as one.

> 1:1 Eloha, I, Jacob bar Joseph bar Hillel descendent of Solomon bar David descendent of Judah bar Jacob bar Isaac bar Avraham, stand as keeper of the records of Yisrael, the title given by the Divine to Father Jacob for whom I am named.
> 1:2 On the first day of the year 3772, Yeshua bar Joseph of the House of David wed Mary of the Hasmonaean House. The lineage of our people has been patriarchal from the time of Avraham, but through this marriage, the bloodline shifts to matriarchal inheritance.
> 1:3 The Oneness separated itself into light and dark, masculine and feminine. In Sacred Unity, the two become as One. Ameyn.

Bringing Forth Delight

Esteemed Brother Joseph,

The tribe of Judah sends glad tidings. The forces of darkness rise from inside the Holy Temple, within the confines of the holy city and beyond the desert of Judaea growing stronger from across the Great Sea. The sons of light cast rays of hope and justice to keep the darkness at bay, yet more Hebrew blood pours down the stony mount. These are dangerous times we live in, my friend, and I agree with Judas that your mists may be penetrable by the dark shadow. Complacency shall not serve the house of David. The angels of mercy are at your disposal, just ask and you shall receive.

In faith of arms, Theudas

While packing my things into a small sack, a frown plays at the corners of my mouth. At the onset of my menses over a month ago, I had a dream that the conception was to take place in the wilderness. But Joseph insisted that we are not safe outside the mists without protection and it took over a month for Yeshua to convince him to permit us to leave the property.

With a sigh, I carry my sack to the back entrance. Miriam is there to bid us farewell. Outside the gate, Yeshua responds to a familiar voice. Teoma?

Turning to Miriam, I start to complain, but she interrupts me. "Hush, Yeshua convinced Joseph to forego a large unfamiliar guard for the devotion of his friend. Now give this to Teoma and have a wonderful time." Handing me a small leather pouch fragrant with herbs, she kisses me goodbye.

Drawing deeply of the cool morning air, Teoma has two donkeys, one packed heavily for the trip, the other for riding. His smile is endearing. "Hello, Mary. It is good to see you." How could my husband believe that this is better than an unfamiliar guard! Teoma embraces me warmly, "Did Ima Miriam give you anything for me?"

"Forgive me. I am excited about this trip."

He nods his thanks, "I would think you would be very excited about conceiving your first child."

If Mother Earth swallowed me up now, I could escape this embarrassment. I turn to glare at Yeshua but he's busy securing our things to the back of the donkey.

"Mary, do you want to ride?" Teoma's blue eyes shine brightly.

"No, thank you. I'll walk for awhile." Why is he so excited?

"I never expected to be able to accompany you. It is like old times, is it not?"

No! It is not like old times. We never camped overnight. At least I was never invited. Yeshua smiles at our exchange. Does he not realize my discomfort?

In frustration, I find myself twisting my shawl. Did Joseph send word to Teoma to return from the desert just on our behalf? I am sure that the baby is to be born in the spring, but if I conceive now she will not be due until after the summer solstice. Oh no, I will not tire myself out by walking, but rather by struggling with the twists of fate that are very much out of my hands.

Comforting me with his touch, Yeshua speaks silently, *Dearest, please relax and enjoy this adventure you so wanted to have.*

Slowly my mood brightens. Yeshua calls up to Teoma. "Mary would like to ride." Happy that my husband knows my thoughts, I kiss his cheek.

Stopping, Teoma adjusts the donkey's riding blankets, while I tie my shawl about my waist and pull the end through my legs. Now I can comfortably ride astride. Teoma sets me upon the donkey's narrow back shaking his head, "Yeshua, your wife has girded her loins in the manner of a soldier of Yisrael."

Although my lower legs are somewhat exposed, my husband shrugs. Teoma dubiously hands over the reins, and I soon find how responsive the donkey is to my silent communication. Patting her neck, I swiftly turn her toward the foothills and encourage her to gallop, intent on piercing the protective mists Joseph has cast about his lands. Something draws me toward a strange rock formation.

I sense the energy of a sacred space, but cannot see a dwelling or a cave. Not even arranged in a circle, the basalt stones lie lazily upon each other. Still, there is something here.

"Come, Mary, you have taken the wrong trail," warns Teoma, running to catch up.

"What is this place?" Ignoring me, he grasps the donkey's reins, leading us away from my discovery. My husband meets us back at the fork and encourages the donkey with a slap, thwarting any questions.

When the trail gets steeper, I slow the donkey to a walk, then halt. I am being watched. Perched on a stone ledge, a tawny wildcat basks in the sun. The donkey stands unconcerned so I greet the cat silently. She calls me Elat and explains in images that the creatures have been waiting for me. Enchanted, I bid the cat farewell and she leaps over us to disappear up the mountainside.

In moments, Teoma comes running. "Mary! Are you all right?"

Yeshua arrives, leading the pack animal. Smiling, I describe the communication. When I get to the part about the place of conception, Teoma gasps. "That is where I am taking you." A large black crow settles itself in the tree top, cawing loudly.

Yeshua laughs, "Well, now that heaven and earth agree, let us proceed."

A magical place, the sweet wild grove is blessed with the hayye of all the elements. The earth below richly comforting, the creek gurgles its praise. The leaves begin to rustle as the element of air joins the dance and I imagine that this evening when we sit by the cooking fire, all will be complete.

Having set up a fine camp, Teoma goes off to hunt. Yeshua and I could not have provided for ourselves so well, but still I am nervous about tonight with Teoma sleeping so near.

Yeshua hugs me to his side. "Mary, do not worry. In Britannia, I learned how to create kasa over another, veiling us from any eyes."

I understand how to become invisible for even as a child I would disappear when playing hide and seek with my sister and cousins, but Joseph must not truly trust the kasa for he sent us with an escort. So many secrets, I wonder…

"What was that place that Teoma led me from?"

My husband studies my face, "It is my father's. A place for him to practice what he has learned."

"What does he do?"

"He uses the ritual herbs he brought from Britannia to seek enlightenment. I believe he also has special mixes from the Egyptian healers who come from Qumran."

"Do you partake of these herbs?"

Touching my cheek, he whispers, "With my Druid master, I took a journey enhanced by sacred herbs. But it is not my way. I find a much clearer connection to Source in my prayers and meditations."

Miriam seems connected. I wonder if Joseph shares the herbs with her.

Yeshua shakes his head, "I do not believe she knows of this. Besides, Ima does not venture far from the house without Abba. She is not like you, my little nature priestess!"

I smile at his teasing. "So much has happened since our marriage. I have always been aware of things that perhaps others have not, but the angels and the animals…it is as if I am remembering something that I have forgotten."

With a tender kiss he gazes into my eyes, "I know, Beloved. Since our first night together my own awareness has increased dramatically." Our mouths linger, tasting the sweetness of one another before he continues, "At first I thought this intense enlightenment was sexual. But there is something more, for I experience openings sometimes when I but think about you."

"Yeshua, I believe that it is love which is the spark for our awakening."

"Yes, falling in love with you, I am becoming my true self."

After Teoma's delicious supper of roasted quail braised with olive oil, basilica, oregano, and crushed pepper berries, we are sated. Studying with the Essenes, I have learned much about herbs for ailments, but little about cooking.

"Teoma, that was delicious! Will you teach me how to cook? I can teach you about the healing herbs."

"Whatever you wish, Mary." He looks over at Yeshua, who laughs. What's so funny?

"Nothing, love, you look tired, Go ahead, I'll be right in."

Once in the tent, I realize how soiled I am. Before a doused fire, the men speak in hushed tones, but I cannot escape Teoma's sharp eyes. "Be careful, Mary. You may not have the same way with snakes as you do with donkeys and cats."

I hurry down to the creek to be greeted by my steed from the far bank. Praying to release the barrier that has protected me these past six months, I wash the dust from our journey before returning to the tent to sit cross-legged on a pile of blankets and close my eyes. Hmm…what next?

Conscious of my breath, I am mesmerized by the familiar purple teardrop slowly oozing throughout my being, until I am sitting in a violet egg of hayye. After unraveling the gossamer light setting my womb, the flowers, and the eggs free, I am guided to wait for Yeshua. Soon my husband stands in the doorway, his tunic sticking to his damp body.

Stripping, he joins me, "Is this part of the preparation?"

"Yeshua, let's invite the spirit of our child to come to us." When a golden hayye emerges to hover around us, my husband takes me in his arms.

Never have I felt so comfortable in Yeshua's embrace, as if destiny is being fulfilled. Beginning with tender kisses that grow more intense in longing, his insistent hands take all of me into his awareness. The elestial quartz within my navel glows intensely.

His love for me seems more than I can bear, until he meets me beyond my core. At the final release, I begin to cry. Yeshua is alarmed until he realizes the tears are of joy, not pain. Our energies merge, his silvery white aura into my deep violet hue as the golden hayye of our child nestles within my pelvis.

Winter sweeps across the plains of Esdraelon to chill Nazareth ridge. Lighting my silver menorah each night in the small window of our chambers feels strange, for Chanuka is not recognized in this house.

Perhaps if we had a home of our own, we might merge our traditions. I have not seen my family since the wedding so Yeshua invites them for the winter solstice. To my delight, Martha is due within half a moon cycle of me. While Abba congratulates our husbands, Ima draws me aside.

"You look thin, Mary. Don't they feed you?"

"Of course, Ima."

"Their Essene diet is too sparse for your royal Hasmonaean blood. I will send fresh beef and lamb." Ima clucks her tongue. "They do have a separate table to prepare meat?"

"Yes, Ima."

"Very well. Now tell me how you are feeling?"

Smiling, I reassure her. "Wonderful—especially since the new moon of Cheshvan when I first felt her move."

"So early? Are you sure it is not twins? You are too petite to carry twins." Bristling, she takes charge. "There is a fine midwife experienced with delicate pregnancies in Capernaeum, I shall have her come to attend to you."

"Thank you, Ima, but Yeshua desires to deliver our child."

"What!" Fanning herself, she takes a hasty seat. "Men know nothing of childbirth. This is unheard of..."

"But he said that his father delivered all of Miriam's children."

Drained of color, Ima motions for some wine. "I must talk to Miriam. Syrus!"

While Abba tends to Ima, I take comfort from my sister. "Mary, how do you know the baby is a girl? I have yet to feel movement."

I lay my hand over her womb, to be greeted vigorously. My sweet daughter responds with her flitting golden light to his healthy turquoise hayye. Martha places her hand over mine, "What is it, Mary? Is my child well?"

I kiss her mouth, "He is wonderfully vital. Eleazer has very strong seed."

Giggling, my sister hugs me to her, our bellies touching. The babies leap toward one another, dancing about our wombs in delighted salutations. Pressing our foreheads together, we glance down. Martha gasps, "Mary, I can feel him."

Eleazer rushes over and hugs us both. Kissing first Martha and then me, he cries, "Miracles occur in this house. Yeshua, we are truly blessed to have such wonderful wives."

Yeshua raises his cup of wine, "May we share many more moments like this as our wives and children delight in each other's company." Even Ima joins the rest of the family to seal the blessing.

***

Working with his hands, tilling the earth, tending the plants, harvesting the grain, and finally creating a meal usually brings much pleasure, but Teoma's enthusiasm is effectively tempered this morning. Saada stands with arms crossed over her ample bosom as he teaches Mary to bake. She greeted him with such fervor when he came home to the lush hills of Galilee last month that he almost wished he had stayed in the company of the rebels.

For five months, the zealot commanders used his Roman appearance to gather information from the legionaires. Rome's weakness lay in the Emperor's sickbed. Chronically ill since boyhood, Augustus took a turn for the worse after Tiberius returned from securing the territories north of the Black Sea. His tribunal powers officially reinstated, Tiberius rules the empire while his stepfather wastes away.

Hands slick with oil, Mary fashions dough into a variety of shapes— crescent moons, braided loaves, even tiny animals. Knowing how sensitive she is to her mother's strict observance of the halacha, he teases, "What is this, a pig?"

"Of course not!" With a look of consternation wrinkling her fine brow, she sprinkles the little dough creature with herbs. "Can't you see it's a lamb?"

Repressing a smile, he pushes the heavily laden baking stone into the hot oven, beads of sweat dripping into his eyes. When Saada steps out to pick more herbs, he chances to appraise his baking partner.

A smudge of flour sits like snow upon her dark skin, the color of kaffa brightened with golden honey. Mary notices his stare. "What? Do I have as much flour on my face as you?"

He chuckles softly and wipes the tip of her nose, "There, you look less like a baker now." The soft texture of her cheek reminds him of a ripe mango. He must refrain from touching her. "I do not know how it is possible, but your beauty is enhanced with the pregnancy."

To his dismay and delight, she clasps his rough hand and tucks it just under her chin. "You, my friend, have a penchant for voluptuous women."

"Honestly, Mary, can I not offer you a compliment?"

"Of course not, dear man, or I would be in danger of favoring you." He would gladly brave that danger. The expression on her face changes to one he cannot resist.

"Teoma, do you think it would be possible to go back to the wilderness for our anniversary?"

Frowning, he does not think he can tolerate escorting them to celebrate their marriage. He tries to discourage her. "In your condition, Mary, it is not wise."

Abruptly she stands placing her hands on her round belly as if for emphasis. He tries to suppress his mirth, for being due in only three months, she is still quite petite.

"My condition? I have seen many pregnant women accompanying their husbands on pilgrimages to the Holy Temple. Am I that much more fragile than they?"

"No, of course not," none could be as fervid, he quickly counters, "but it was very difficult to get Joseph to feel comfortable with you outside the mists."

Her small mouth quivers in a pout as she worries an errant sable curl, dusting its rich darkness with flour. Wringing her hands, she sighs and moves ever closer to him, looking up through long lashes black as kohl. Her green eyes capture his as she presses her delicate hands to his chest, "Please, we were perfectly safe with you."

Unable to resist, he nods a weak consent praying Yeshua has perfected kasa so that his services will not be necessary. Perhaps young Jacob is ready to master disarming techniques, for Teoma needs an outlet far removed from the heat of this kitchen.

***

Nissan, 3773

I am blessed among men. A loving family and a glorious life made complete by my marriage to my beloved. I cannot believe a whole year has passed. My beloved carries within her precious womb our daughter made manifest by our love. Growing vigorously, the child's hayye glows a golden delight nestled deeply in Mary's royal hue of purple joy.

What wonder is it to become an Abba? Never before has the world seemed so lovely, never has being human been so dear. Blessed is Eloha.

Since returning from our trip to the wilderness, I have been so tired; perhaps I should go to bed early and conserve my energy for the morrow. Martha has invited us to join them for Pesach. Our parents have made the journey to Jerusalem for only the High Priest can sacrifice the paschal lamb properly. Maybe Yeshua will take me in a cart to Magdala.

Reclining in the gathering room, I put my head on his shoulder.

"Are you ready for bed so soon, my love?" I nod, stifling a yawn. "Then let us say goodnight."

Early spring flowers lend their sweet fragrance to our chambers. As I begin to unbraid my hair, which has grown even thicker, Yeshua comes up behind me whispering, "You must never cut it and give away your power." Before I can inquire, his caresses distract me. What my pregnancy has made full and lush, our mutual desire whets further. Divesting himself of his tunic, he carefully undresses me then proceeds to take his time untangling my braids. He runs his hands through my curls, pressing himself against my back.

We both gasp, finding wonder even this far along in my pregnancy, but my heavy womb magnifies the rhythmic pulsations which begin at the top of my belly. Feeling the baby squirm as if being hugged too tightly, I have difficulty catching my breath.

Still within me, Yeshua reaches around to place his hand on my upper belly. The tightening has not relaxed, nor can I breathe very well. "Mary, what is happening?" I cannot answer. Sitting up, he holds his hands together and then separates them as if holding something round and moving. Through shallow gasps, I perceive a sphere of energy between his cupped palms.

Using the hayye, he begins circling my hard belly in spirals, then reverses the direction. The tightening lessens until I can breathe more deeply, but my womb remains sore.

Yeshua cups his hands together over his face, his shoulders shaking. Awkwardly, I sit up, "My love, all is well now. The baby and I are fine," and take him in my arms. We fall asleep with his cheek pressed to my womb.

In light of Yeshua's concern, I refrain from mentioning a visit to Magdala, but the next evening, the tightening comes back. Catching my breath, I hold my belly and try to be inconspicuous, but he notices. Leah and Saada cease serving the meal to alert Miriam. I take deeper, slower breaths while Yeshua repeatedly ministers to me with the energy. Thank goodness, it does not last as long.

"Is this the first time you have felt contractions, Mary?"

"No, Ima. Last night." I place my hand on my aching back and yet another contraction occurs on the way to our quarters. When it is over, Miriam asks if I felt the contractions after any particular activity. I nod and glance at Yeshua. Hesitantly, he explains. Sensing the heat of his shame, I feel like a child having a child. What were we thinking?

After settling me in bed, Leah teaches Yeshua how to check if my womb is opening. They determine that while my womb is softening in preparation for delivery, the baby is not in position yet. Miriam advises that I rest, and of course, not be intimate, and all will be well.

Before they take their leave, I glance at my husband, whose guilt darkens his hayye, and whisper to Miriam. "Ima, I felt fine last night. Please tell Yeshua it is not his fault."

Miriam holds out her arms and I sink into her lap. Without a backward glance, Yeshua walks into the sitting room, refusing his mother's reassurance. A calming energy blankets me. "Since Yeshua was a small child, he has heard others talk about the prophecy of a mashiach who will bring freedom from oppression to the tribes."

Held in her comforting embrace, I listen carefully, quite conscious of my breath. "Yeshua has always known he is here for a purpose. He has felt responsible for saving those he loved from harm, even from the lessons they are here to receive."

What is my lesson? Miriam strokes my hair, "When life doesn't go as he thinks, Yeshua feels he has failed in some way. He is working to accept his own humanity. You and the baby are assisting him with this journey. Yeshua must live and learn quickly to accomplish his perceived mission."

The tears that have threatened all night begin spilling down my cheeks. Miriam holds me close. "Ima, are not each of our missions to be loved and live in joy?" She nods. "Then why must he suffer so?"

A beam of white light surrounds us, "Yeshua is learning that each time he judges himself, he must acknowledge his limitations in human form and forgive himself. That is the grace of our humility, an acceptance of who we are on this earth. Until we are able to do this, over and over, we suffer our own judgment, and Yeshua is a harsh judge of his humanness."

Iyar, 3773

Perhaps the counsel of the Tzadokim, so restrictive in my eyes before, is wise after all. Desire overwhelmed wisdom for I sought the comfort of my wife's embrace and now our precious child threatens to emerge unripe. Awash with horrid images of losing them both, my days fill with fear. No amount of fasting and meditation relieves the pain, nor the lust. What is wrong with me? Even swollen with our child, it is all I can do to maintain my composure as I minister to her needs. Although Abba tries to reassure me that I am not at fault for Mary's premature labor, Ima must be of much sturdier constitution than my delicate wife.

Ironic–Mary insisted our child's birth would be in late Iyar. I pray it is so for I can tolerate our separation no longer. My beloved wife, so alive and vital, yearns to be out in nature, but the inclement weather keeps her imprisoned in our bedchambers, while the flame of my guilt keeps me in solitary confinement, unable to connect with those I love. Separated from the Divine, sacred union is only possible in communion with Mary. Until that day we meet again as one, I am lost in the void.

Pale gray morning light peeks through our bedroom window. I roll carefully out of bed, reaching down to girdle the weight of my unborn child. Pushed out by my large womb, the elestial stone protrudes with my navel. The tiles under my feet feel so refreshingly cool that standing up free from the confines of my bed becomes a treasured moment. Poor Yeshua finally sleeps after being up with me all night.

Slowly, I make my way through the courtyard that separates our chambers from the chamam, stopping occasionally to rest against the wall. Through my difficult confinement, my husband has suffered. Refusing all but my most chaste affections, he fasts and meditates constantly. Perhaps connecting to the One is something a person comes to crave like those who desperately seek kodeia, the essence of poppies.

The baby kicks me sharply in the side so I hurry to the betshimush. Afterward as I rest on a bench, Teoma walks in, rubbing his face and eyes vigorously. Perhaps he slept poorly, overwrought by the grief he has caused his own family in choosing not to take a wife. Yeshua keeps reassuring us all that his friend's decision is for the higher good, whatever that means. Nevertheless, it seems a shame for such an attractive and, I assume, virile man not to experience married life.

My cumbersome attempt to stand catches his attention.

"I am sorry; I didn't know anyone was in here…Mary?" Turning away from me, he tries to cover himself. How could he mistake the only pregnant woman in the house?

"Good morning, Teoma. I was just leaving, but it will take me a moment." I turn and begin waddling away, barely able to walk around my daughter's head.

"Wait! I'll help you back to your room." Feeling that familiar tightening, I nod and brace myself against the cool tile.

While he relieves himself another sharp contraction induces a gush of warm liquid to flow down my leg and a third nearly brings me to my knees. I cry out. Teoma rushes out of the betshimush.

"Mary, what is happening?"

"Teoma," I pant, as the last contraction slowly ends, "I think my daughter has decided to be born." Picking me up from my crouched and sodden state, he rushes so quickly that we must stop twice so that I might breathe through the contractions. Linens strewn across the floor, his loincloth twisted, Yeshua sleeps fitfully at night.

"Get up! Mary is having the baby!" Teoma yells and my poor husband leaps out of bed nearly tripping on the linens.

Another sharp contraction has me clinging to Teoma's neck, my breath ragged. Yeshua tries to get him to put me on the bed, but I resist. "I am soaked, I need to change first."

"For goodness sakes, Mary. Do not worry about the bed!"

"Please just put me down."

"No, Mary, I'll carry you until Yeshua prepares the bed."

"Please, I want to stand." Teoma carefully sets me on my feet. I hold onto his arm for a moment, "Sorry, I made a mess of you," but the next contraction forces me to crouch.

Yeshua rushes over to lift me to my feet, "Mary, do not push." The pressure so great, I must push. A gentle hayye caresses my back, as the angel guides me to kneel—chest to the floor—and I find much relief.

The men stand over me in their nightclothes, not knowing what to do. "Teoma, will you please get me a cushion for my head and get Ima Miriam? Yeshua, perhaps you could get me a fresh garment before visiting the betshimush."

Teoma secures me a cushion before giving Yeshua a rough pat on the shoulder. "Make haste, your wife is having a baby!"

When he leaves, Yeshua drops to his knees beside me, his tears melting the rigid aura that has kept his emotions in and me out. Thank The One.

"This past month has been so difficult to bear. Not only the labor and the restrictions, but…," I hesitate, wanting to be honest with him, "but it has been as if we were childhood friends, not husband and wife."

His tears pour anew as he lies next to me. "It was too difficult to be with you as a husband and also be a healer."

"The house is full of healers, but you are my only husband."

He kisses me tenderly, finally sensuously, not chastely. Lying on my side, I respond with passion, for it has been too long. We are both crying and kissing when Miriam walks in followed by Leah.

"My dears, it is wonderful to see that you have made up, but I do not think the baby should be delivered on the cold floor." Laughing, she instructs Leah to dress me. "Now, son, go to the betshimush and get ready for a long day."

When Yeshua returns, he takes me to walk in the gardens. Breakfast has been laid out for us and he eats lightly, but I find it difficult to consume much. All through the morning the contractions get stronger and closer together. By noon, I have not made much progress.

Frustrated, I ask to lie down on the hammock. Yeshua carefully helps me before climbing in, looking nearly as tired as I feel. Gathering me into his arms, he kisses me, "Do not lose faith, love. This is why it is called labor." I only manage a half-hearted smile. After a month of bed rest, I am in poor condition for this work.

In moments his breathing slows and a soft snore confirms he sleeps. At least one of us will be rested. Unfortunately, he's not the one who has to push the baby out. More attuned to him than me, the baby lies quietly. Memories of Yeshua talking and singing to her, his mouth close to my belly, from the moment I conceived, brings a smile to my lips. So even still within me, she sleeps now with her father. I caress my lower belly and she moves gently against me like a kitten. Yeshua stretches his long legs over mine. Peaceful gratitude carries me through a long afternoon evenly interrupted by contractions.

"Yeshua, wake up," I nudge him, unable to turn without toppling us over.

He yawns and stretches, "I was dreaming that I was holding our daughter, sleeping in the hammock together, she and I."

63

"You were, but now I need to get up and go to the betshimush."

My stomach has felt unsettled all day so I am not surprised that my bowels are loose, but the fresh dark blood brings a wave of concern. Immediately, the angel's presence, like a warm breeze, reassures that all will be well.

Into the night I labor, but to no avail. Finally, Yeshua requests his father's assistance. Having trained with the Essenes, Joseph carefully examines me. "This child must be born shortly; Mary is losing blood."

Yeshua looks concerned, but the faces of the women express the gravity of the situation. An incredibly wrenching contraction forces me to sit up, panting and gripping Yeshua's arms. Something tears inside and I scream. His face blanches as a gush of hot blood is released from my womb. Remembering the angel's advice, I try to breathe.

Another ripping contraction ensues, longer and more powerful than the last. Soaked in my own blood, I am lightheaded, too weak to hold onto the birthing rails. So Leah supports me with her body as Yeshua receives clean linens from his distressed mother into trembling hands.

"Can you feel the baby's head?" Yeshua nods. "Good, now begin rimming the opening with oil gently but firmly stretching around her crown." Faces go in and out of focus. Another contraction and I am asked to push. Taking a deep breath, I bear down but Yeshua shakes his head, his eyes worried. Leah whispers, "I know you're tired, but you must push much harder."

Unable to catch my breath, I nod, the room spins. Nausea overwhelms me and I begin to wretch. Leah cleans me up quickly so I can push again. Determined to get her out I push so hard my eyes might burst, but she doesn't come. How can this be? She's a month early. I reach down and feel the top of her curly head crowning. The angel assured me that the baby would be fine, but how much longer can she stay in my birth canal?

Joseph gathers the women to pray for guidance. Unfortunately, my labor does not wait and a huge contraction pushes the baby so forcefully against the opening that it begins to tear. With the next contraction, a river of blood carries my daughter into her father's arms. Ashen, Yeshua holds aloft our gray infant still attached to me by a long, bluish white cord. With each heartbeat, a fresh gush of my life force escapes. Archangel Gavriel offers silent guidance, but I am swiftly fading.

Unable to speak, I hold two images—one of Yeshua breathing for our daughter, the other of Leah kneading my womb. All is surreal, except the blood, which flows to the beat of my weakening heart. Before the darkness of incomprehension overcomes me, I hear a distant drumming herald in my daughter's cry.

To Heal Self

Swollen by winter rains, the Nile runs thick alongside the Aksum king, the rays of the sun yielding to his ebony skin. His tribe keeps the divine rhythm—drummers for the dance of humanity. A spiritual guardian, Belshazzar sacrificed his place in the peripheral circle of benevolent drummers to step into the dance.

Just before the last new moon, the messeh queen gave birth to a daughter. Belshazzar's tribe celebrated joyously. The sacred lineage will go on!

The dark Egyptian princess has come alone to meet him just south of Cairo. He embraces her warmly, "I have most joyous news, my friend. The divine dancers have birthed a daughter!"

Her unusually light eyes glow with delight as he lays the small pouch carrying the twin halves of elestial quartz in her hand.

"I shall keep these safe until the triad is complete."

He nods and bids Eshe farewell. Covering her head with a turban, she mounts the waiting camel. Watching her ride north, Belshazzar reminisces about delivering the first elestial quartz to the husband of the messeh queen nineteen years ago.

The mountain called Tabor stood as lone guard to Nazareth ridge. To leave his beloved wife and his young son when the star first appeared three months ago was a great sacrifice, but the others waited.

"Hail, Belshazzar!" Aretas traveled with heavy guard. A caravan of eight mounted men accompanied the Nabataean king.

"My friend, perhaps we should enter the village quietly."

Hor, the young king of Tarsus, laughed heartily, "Yes. We are to pay homage to the prince of peace!"

"You did not have to pay tribute to Herod before entering Samaria!"

Concerned that the aged Nabataean alerted Herod, Belshazzar inquired, "Aretas, what happened in the palace?"

"After accepting four of my finest stallions without a word of gratitude, the mad Idumaean dismissed me. My search for the child had been futile, so I took the opportunity to consult with the royal astronomers. They became quite agitated at my questioning. It took a Judaean shepherd to inform me that the child I seek resides in Nazareth."

Under what duress did the shepherd reveal such information? What did Herod know about the babe?

"Come, Aretas, one mare is all that is necessary to bear your weight!" Young Hor turned his restless steed north and rode into the village.

Listening for the rhythm of the divine dancer, Belshazzar led them to the far western edge of Nazareth. Although the streets were quiet that early evening, the villagers would talk upon seeing such richly adorned visitors enter the humble cottage. A young man of regal bearing stepped forth to greet them.

"I am Joseph bar Hillel. What honor brings such renowned guests to my home?" In deference he addressed the elder Aretas.

"We have come to pay homage to the child born into the house of David."

"My wife has borne me a son. How do you know of this? You are not Hebrew."

Hor laughed, "The child shall bring peace to the world, not only the tribes of Yisrael."

Gently, Belshazzar took the young father's arm. "Prince of Judah, our seers have foretold of the birth of your precious son. We ask that you accept our tribute."

Blue eyes darkened with suspicion until Belshazzar pierced the veil of Joseph's mind to silently console him. After depositing their weapons at the door, they were escorted through protective mists which Belshazzar recognized as the hand of a renowned Druid master. They were taken into an inner sanctum adorned by a round altar set upon the intersecting triangles of the sacred masculine and feminine.

Joseph returned with his wife. Hor's eyes appreciated the beauty of the fair-haired girl but it was the dance of light around Miriam that caught Belshazzar's attention. Within her arms lay a babe. A wave of peace flowed from the child and the three kings bowed, heads touching the ground.

"Beloved Mother, I am Belshazzar, king of Aksum. It has been foretold in our lands that a prince will be born who will bring peace. We have followed the star to pay our respects to your son. This is Aretas, King of Nabataea." The couple nodded to the gray bearded one before turning to the youngest man. "And King Hor of Tarsus. May

we present gifts to your son?"

When Miriam gave her consent, he placed a carved box on the altar. The child cooed with delight. *"Frankincense for sacred rituals in honor of your son's priestly caste."*

"Gold for the infant king," Usually a man of many words, Aretas deposited laden sacks upon the altar without further discourse.

Hor stepped forward with a linen bundle secured by golden tassels. *"Myrrh, for your son shall be a great healer."*

Joseph bowed. *"We are grateful for your recognition of Yeshua. May the Light guide you always."*

The young father offered them food as his wife excused herself. Belshazzar looked up to see Yeshua smiling over his mother's shoulder. Although Aretas and Hor took their leave after the meal, Belshazzar accepted Joseph's kind offer of lodging.

Late into the night he told the young father that seers predicted the boy would study with mystics in Egypt, Hindus, and the Himal mountains, but Joseph refused to be parted from his wife and child. "My tribe expects a legitimate heir for Yeshua was not born in the month of kings. I cannot leave my home and family, but prophesies continue to be fulfilled. Perhaps Yeshua is the mashiach who will unite the tribes against the Roman oppression."

Belshazzar smiled kindly, *"This child was sent to embody Divine Love, the one who shall bring peace to the world."* Joseph's eyes still reflected his doubt. *"When the time comes you will be guided to bring the child into Egypt. I will meet you in Alexandria and train the boy up with my own son. There are two mystics I studied with in my youth, one from the Himal range, a follower of the Buddha, his name is Zsao. The other is Reiti from Ujjain in the Hindus region. They shall come to Nazareth."*

From around his neck, he removed a small leather pouch decorated with the crown feather of a falcon. *"Place this upon the child. It contains precious elestial quartz. I shall watch over Yeshua from afar."*

Before taking his leave on the third day, he bid the dancer farewell. The small pouch with the seer's stone nestled in lion's mane lay protectively at Yeshua's waist. Holding the precious babe, Belshazzar was filled with light and love. *"Welcome, my prince, may your dance into this life bring you great joy."* And to his delight the child responded silently.

"I shall listen for your wise drumming."

He handed the child back to an auburn-haired woman with generous curves. *"I am happy to see you have come to care for the child."*

Hava smiled at him, *"You have been missed on the Mount, my friend."*

69

Down the ridge through the mists and into the valley of Jezreel, he headed for the Great Sea, keeping the sacred rhythm until it was time to welcome the divine dancer's feminine partner in Migdol.

Now to the beat of his walking stick, Belshazzar journeys home to his wife in Aksum. His eldest son has had a son of his own. He shall teach the child to beat his drum with compassion.

***

> *Welcome, precious Sarah, to the world.*
>
> *On the eve of the new moon of Sivan, like unto the dark void which births the light, you came. Your emergence from your mother's womb marked my delivery into divine humanness, my prayers answered when you received sacred breath from my mouth. Now as you suckle at her breast, I am awash with gratitude for my life. Your bronze skin kissed by the eternal glow of your hayye, like your Ima, dark and most beautiful to me. Sarah, you are perfect in body and soul. May your mind gain wisdom with your time on this precious earth. May your soul connect intimately to Eloha while your body grows strong and lovely. As your Ima kisses your dimpled cheek, my desire to merge with your spirit is profound. May your joy be complete in your human form, precious daughter of mine.*
>
> *My eternal love and devotion, Abba*

Under the dark cloak of night, my moonlight confidante is all I need to suckle my newborn back to sleep. A tiny fist opens to press my breast closer to her lips. She speaks silently, *Ima, I am happy to be with you and Abba.*

Sarah, you are my delight. Sighing with pleasure, I cannot imagine missing these precious midnight moments with her.

There has been some turmoil these past two weeks when Joseph insisted that Sarah be wet-nursed. Despite his arguments that I am weak, depleted, and need to recover, I have stubbornly refused. He went as far as to have an intimate conversation with Yeshua about how nursing will interfere with our marriage bed. Laying Sarah down safely between cushions, I snuggle in closer to my husband.

"Is she asleep?"

He responds to my affirmative kiss by pressing the hardness of his body into the softness of mine. My heart beats rapidly for it has been so long. Hearing my thoughts, he whispers into my neck, "Yes, forty-seven very long days and nights." I smile to myself. So he kept count.

Thirteen days after giving birth, my body is slow to respond. "Forgive me, Yeshua."

"Hush, beloved, I expected this," he produces a small vial of oil. "You didn't think I would only get Abba's opinion." Thank goodness he talked to Miriam.

Suddenly, it occurs to me that I had better protect myself from conceiving. I sit up carefully so not to disturb the baby. Yeshua looks dubious, "Ima said that while you are nursing you probably cannot get pregnant."

"I would feel better being sure."

In quiet repose across from me, Yeshua watches as I weave white light around my womb. My next child will be a son born when Sarah is four years old. Expressing my gratitude, I bid Archangel Gavriel goodnight.

"Is everything all right, Mary?"

"We are safe from conceiving for another three years."

"You have this all planned."

I shrug, "Just following Divine advice."

We begin making love again tentatively. Although it has been a blessing that my nipples have become insensitive to Sarah's hungry mouth, I can hardly feel my husband's caresses. Yeshua comes close to my cheek and kisses it softly. "Beloved, what is wrong?"

"It is not the same," I whisper tearfully.

"Does it not feel as wonderful to you as it does to me?" I shake my head sadly. Drawing me into his chest, he kisses me tenderly. Milk begins to leak at his touch, which offends him not. "Mmm. Sarah drinks the sweetest nectar of all."

Smiling at his playfulness, I receive his offering and a distant stirring heats my loins. When his eagerness causes me discomfort, I ask him to lie back, using the oil on both of us. His face reflects pleasure and soon I reach a long-awaited release. Pulling me into his chest to stifle my cries, he whispers, "Let us not wake her. If it's still too early we can find other ways of pleasuring each other."

I apologize, feeling slightly guilty that he is still waiting. With the oil, our mutual caresses ignite a great need so he moves between my clenched thighs and soon joins me.

Lying in his arms afterwards his fingertips trace my profile stopping at the stone receded back into my navel. He kisses the tetrahedron. "And now that Sarah contains her own light, it reflects the purity of our sacred union." The gift from Belshazzar has returned to our glorious hues of silver and purple.

In Magdala, Martha gave birth to a big healthy boy—Micah—and after forty days of the required respite, sent our mother to Nazareth. Ima arrived with an entourage of servants and gifts for her granddaughter, most distraught to discover that Yeshua shared my bedchambers.

"Mary! The Torah is quite clear. Eighty days after the birth of a girl child! Your husband will not be able to visit the sanctuary without the rites of purification!"

Knowing Yeshua would rather be with me, I changed the subject. "How are Martha and her son?"

"They are well. Her figure has nearly returned while Micah grows fat. " She held Sarah up to the light to make her appraisal. "Your daughter is beautiful, but thank Adonai, does not have skin as dark as yours." I smiled at the barbed compliment, well accustomed to my mother's tongue. "Mary, why do you not have a wet nurse? You are of royal blood. It is unseemly to put this child to your breast."

"Ima, I take much delight in nursing Sarah, and my husband is fully supportive."

"Hmm! Well, you shall see how delighted he will be when your breasts lose their beauty for the benefit of his child."

"I do not believe that nursing my baby shall harm my body!" Determined, I set my intentions to maintain my feminine wiles in all their glory. Captivated by her granddaughter's gurgles, Ima ceased her lecture and thankfully returned to Cana just before dusk.

My memory is interrupted by Sarah stirring in my lap. Sensitive to her every need, my still lovely breasts become heavy with sweet milk. A natural extension of my being, when she needs to relieve herself, I have taken to holding her over a small pot or, if outside, over the ground, so changing my soiled daughter has become a rare chore. Growing ever so quickly, already five-and-a-half months, I hope she does not walk too soon.

I want to walk, Ima! I want to see the world.

"Well, my sweet baby, until you are a bit taller, your vantage point will be no farther than my arms." Smiling a toothless grin, milk oozes around sweet lips.

The hayye of the olive grove shifts. She pulls away, milk streaming all over, and reaches for Teoma. "Wait, Sarah, you are making a mess." Kissing her milky cheeks, Teoma tosses her over his head. She laughs delighted, he is her favorite. I warn, "Dod Teo risks a dousing with curdled milk if he is not careful."

I struggle to disentangle myself from the hammock, when Teoma, with Sarah in one arm, helps me to the ground. "I believe you are lighter than you were before you became pregnant." I shrug, unconcerned. "Mary, you must make more of an effort to eat richer foods." He lifts Sarah over his head onto his shoulders. "This little pumpkin seems to be drinking away your fat. I will bring more meat and cheese to fatten you up."

"If you alert Joseph to my condition, he will want to bring in a wet nurse."

Teoma smiles down at me with Sarah clinging to his short tight curls, gurgling and biting the top of his head. "Certainly a good wet nurse would be eating richer meals." Grimacing, he tries to lift Sarah off, but she kicks and holds on tightly.

"Wait, let me help you." As he bends forward, Sarah spits up her lunch onto his head. I take his arm and lead him to the fountain, where I wet a nursing cloth.

Although I stand on the edge of the fountain to better extract my daughter and Teoma tries to lean close, Sarah pulls back in a game of keep away. "Hold still, little one." I reach over his head and grab her arms, pulling them closer. Extracting her chubby fingers from his hair wet with sour milk is difficult, but finally I hand her squirming down.

Silently, Teoma takes the baby as I attend to the mess, but his breath down my cleavage causes heat to rise in my loins. I step back, nearly falling off the narrow ledge. Teoma catches me. We are much too close. The spit up milk will have to wait.

"Abba! Abba!"

73

Sarah calls happily to a shock-still Yeshua. I cannot move. At least Teoma has enough presence of mind to lift me off the fountain and hand Sarah to her father. No one has spoken.

I retreat into Teoma's solid form away from Yeshua's anger.

Sarah corrects me, *No, Ima, it is fear.* I want to explain, but hold my tongue. Teoma nods a sad farewell.

Late in the evening, Yeshua returns to our chambers with an unwelcome announcement. I whirl around from combing my hair. "But why? What is in Judaea that Teoma must leave before the holidays?"

"It is what's **not** in Judaea."

Before passion controls my tongue, Sarah wakes up crying. I nurse her back to sleep and turn to my husband, but he lies as far on his side of the bed as he can get. Unable to sleep, I rise to walk in the garden. My baby will not wake again till after dawn.

In the olive grove Archangel Gavriel attends my meditation in full sensory form. Wings of light spanning the width of the tree, white aura luminescent with a golden edge, a face so beautiful he could be a young woman. He speaks in my mind with a bell-like voice. *Before the night is through you will be escorted by the morning star to a very dark place. Be assured, dear Mary, that this is part of the divine orchestration to assist all with a clearing of fearful energy.* In his embrace, I am at peace. He tells me to spend the rest of the night outside.

Wondering if I will be missed, but trusting the angel's guidance, I slip through the thick flap of my beloved tent and crawl onto the soft cushioned bed. So comfortable after my meditation, no more worried thoughts to interfere with my sleep, I begin to doze, only vaguely aware of being watched. Why did I not notice before?

"Mary, I was praying that I would be able to speak to you before I left." Teoma whispers from the other side of the bed.

I nod, hardly able to breathe, "I came out to the garden to meditate and was guided to lie here." This is unbelievable! The Divine plays with fire.

"The angel sent you here? What does it mean?" Perhaps he has not had many prayers answered or maybe not so quickly.

"You were praying to be able to speak to me, so now we have some private time to talk." He smiles, piercing blue eyes soft with longing. What if I can't control my passion?

"That is not all I prayed for."

I call out silently and Gavriel arrives. *Follow your heart.*

Teoma's ruggedly handsome face has a day's growth of beard. Although incredibly attracted, I love Yeshua and will do nothing to jeopardize our marriage.

"Teoma, I love and desire you," he catches his breath as I take a long deep one, "but my destiny lies with Yeshua. I love him but it pains me to see you without your heart's desire."

"I cannot imagine loving anyone else, Mary. Yeshua asked me to be your protector, but how can I if he sends me away?"

"Why do you feel you must spend your life in service to Yeshua?" His devotion is more than his desire to stay in my presence.

"Because, dear one, Yeshua is the mashiach—the one to free our people."

"I only know him as a man. We are here to experience love, thus to redeem ourselves, not to save others."

"Well, Mary, I am destined to serve him and his mission. Right now that includes serving you and Sarah."

Suddenly I realize why we are here, "Teoma, you can continue to serve us from wherever you are. Let us meditate for a moment."

"What shall I do?"

"Just follow my breath and be still." In a pillar of white light, Archangel Gavriel shows me how to unite us with silver cords of connection. Teoma gasps when the gossamer light threads its way into his heart. "Just remember the love we share then imagine each other and we will feel one another's presence."

In awe, he reaches a tentative hand to touch the hayye between us. Palm to palm, I can feel his entire essence wash over me. Teoma is duly affected. I smile at him, "Try not to hold your breath when you interact with the energies." He chuckles, then his eyes widen. Quickly he sits up.

Yeshua stands in the doorway.

Within the angel's peaceful embrace, I am protected, but grief shadows Teoma. I touch his heart energy. Yeshua's anger crashes against us like a wave. As if in a dream, I rise and embrace Teoma. This is farewell.

Passing by my husband, I am moved to say one thing, "I am sorry, Yeshua, but this will be a dark journey." The morning star shines brightly above the tent, but at my core the elestial quartz is as cold as death. Shivering, I wonder where the Divine is taking us.

Cheshvan, 3773

The fear in my heart has been made manifest—my wife is not my own. My adolescent lamentations that she would favor him over me seem ironic, our arranged marriage forced her decision—he has her heart. We do not speak, our only communication is the silence of our darkened bedchambers. What was once divine has become base, a physical release, water quenching thirst, not the sweet wine that satisfies my soul. Before we married, I dreamed of celebrating the harvest with her, making love among the golden sheaves, but my anger drove her from my arms with the excuse that the baby needed her. But I too need her.

Jealousy colors my vision, I cannot perceive her thoughts. She has shared nothing with me of what happened that night, but I sense his energy about her. In rare instances of peace, I can penetrate her mind to find her braving the ethers in search of the cords that bind their hearts.

My rage poisons our relationship, her wall of fear grows higher as she escapes under kasa. Knowing she journeys past the protective mists, I try to view her through the ethers, but all I can perceive is a black crow. As I struggle through this dark time, my wife withers away, refusing to take her meals with the family. Still the baby grows plump, but I fear we might need to bring in a wet nurse. Once I attempted to make her eat but she stubbornly refused the meal, saying food is not what she hungers for. I insisted, she gave in, her tears waking our inconsolable daughter. Frustrated, I told her that if she did not take care of herself, the baby would suffer as well. My words must have sickened her, for she purged her pain into the betshimush.

Never before have I felt so lost in the mire of fear. Perhaps I should have never married, leading our people without the burden of a wife and family. But I believed we were destined for one another. I created this painful reality to fulfill some divine purpose, but what?

Since the full moon of Tevet, the weather has become bitterly cold, and trapped inside with my sick baby, I am ever drearier. Unable to breathe through her nose, Sarah struggles to nurse, her infirmity a reflection of my own sick heart. Last Shabbat, I allowed Miriam to take her for the day, to give me time to spend with Yeshua, but he no longer seeks my company. At dusk I went to the nursery to retrieve my baby and Miriam begged me to let her stay, but Sarah is all I have now.

Tonight the pain in my heart has spread to my body. Wearily I lie beside my baby, praying she will stay asleep as Yeshua blows out the oil lamp, not even bidding me goodnight. Just as I begin to doze off, he reaches for me, his hand on my hip like ice.

"Please, Yeshua, not tonight." Never before have I refused him.

He pulls me close. "This is all we have left…" I want to be held, perhaps we can talk, but the wall of anger and fear around him seems impenetrable. "Would you refuse him?"

Teoma would never treat me like this! Unwilling to argue, I start to rise.

"Where are you going? Your lover's tent is gone."

He is right, I have nowhere to go, no one to confide in; he sent away my only friend. I am very much alone, even face to face with my husband. How must other wives feel when the passion smolders, placating their spouses and dreaming of happier times?

When I relent, his only comment is how hot my skin feels, but it is not passion. Heeding my silent tears, Sarah wails piteously.

"Go….her needs are more pressing, it seems."

Exasperated, I nurse Sarah and soon they are both fast asleep. Rising to go to the betshimush, my head spins but I never make it back to bed. Somewhere between the baths and our chambers, the sheer burden of a broken heart and a rising fever overwhelms me.

New moon of Shevat, 3774

I am losing her, not to him, but to despair. Fear and death surround me. My precious wife lies gravely ill, but I cannot find that still place from which to minister to her. When I place my hands upon her fevered brow, she becomes even weaker, her fever rising, her breathing labored. Rucha no longer resides within my being, sacred breath evaporating through my lips before I can place my mouth to hers.

Since she has been sick, the dark sky is swollen with clouds, the air bitterly cold. The birds no longer sing in her garden haven, even the trees weep in the barren groves. I am lost in my despair. If I must give her up to save her life, I will. I do! I surrender my beloved wife to the Divine. My life for hers. I leave her in Teoma's faithful hands to live happily upon this earth. May they remember me in their joy, not in their sorrow.

In a feverish delirium, I am tended by Miriam but Sarah is gone. A soft shadow hovers over my left side, never changing in spite of the rising sun. Vaguely, I am aware of snippets of conversation between Yeshua and his parents.

Joseph's voice is strained, "How can you have allowed this to happen? Look how she has wasted away. Why did you not allow me to bring in a wet nurse? Why have you not discussed this with your Ima and me?"

Yeshua says nothing, but I can feel his pain, anger muted by guilt, fear darkening his hayye. Joseph's voice rises, "Poorly prepared to take care of a wife. Keeping Teoma with you knowing how they felt about each other only aggravated the situation. But at least while he was here, she ate!" He storms out and I am awash with waves of sorrow for Yeshua. I wish I could comfort him, but I am having trouble staying awake.

Another conversation ensues, this time as Miriam sponges my fevered flesh with water drawn from an icy cold stream. I begin shivering uncontrollably. "Son, hand me some clean linens. There, Mary, rest now." She lays me back down, but I cannot focus on her face. Yeshua covers me, his hayye a bit softer now.

"Ima, I do not know how it came to this. I feel like I am living another person's life." His voice hoarse, has he been crying?

"You are living a very human life, Yeshua. Thanks to Mary and Teoma, you are going through a dark time of the soul. You will survive this, but it won't be the last." Yeshua shudders, or is it the chattering of my teeth? "What happened the night before Teoma left?" I thought she knew.

"I found her lying with him. I had already asked him to leave after coming across them in an intimate embrace by the fountain earlier." So matter of fact, almost without emotion.

"And what did Mary have to say for herself?" Miriam asks softly, somehow I feel she knows the truth, but maybe I am just being hopeful.

"After she hugged him, she said we were at the beginning of a very dark journey."

"Wise for one so young. It has been very dark indeed." I am not wise, only quoting Gavriel. "And did Teoma explain?"

"He said they talked but that he did not touch her."

"And you did not believe him?" Yeshua must have shaken his head. "Has he ever been dishonest with you?" Again, no. "Then why did you not confirm his story by hearing Mary's side?"

"She never offered an explanation." He sounds close to tears, "Ima we are not living as man and wife anymore. There is little love between us now."

"Yeshua, it is love that held her tongue." She pauses, I imagine, to reach out to him, "Now twice since you have been married, you have withdrawn yourself emotionally from her. Both times have ended in her becoming extremely ill. You have had to nearly lose her before you have surrendered to your higher Self."

"Do all dark times of the soul have to last so long," he cries, "and be so painful?"

"No, they will continue to be demanding but in a different way. You must surrender sooner and remember that you are not alone." Again a pause, "You believe your mission is to serve the world but in order to help others, you must first serve yourself."

I do not remember any more but his soft crying, probably muffled on her bosom.

Eve of first Shabbat of Shevat, 3774

Day and night, I fast and pray always at her bedside. I have not seen our daughter since her mother fell ill. Within my being, a storm brews, the fog of incomprehension beginning to lift. Somehow suffering has opened my heart to a deeper level of compassion. Thanks to Mary, I have known all the faces of fear—anger, frustration, rage, sorrow, guilt, jealousy, and unworthiness. I am truly willing now to surrender my beloved to divine orchestration. If I am blessed to see her smiling face, her pallor colored back to the beautiful bronze of her vitality, to see her stormy eyes clear to brilliant green, I shall know that I have not been forsaken. I will welcome my brother home with open arms and not allow my fear to come between us again. To remain connected to Eloha throughout this darkness is the greatest miracle of all.

The late morning sun streams through our open door to kiss my cheek. For the first time in days, I awake clear-headed but struggle to take a deep breath. My breasts have been bound. Where is Sarah? I attempt to rise but am too weak.

The Archangel Gavriel returns, as always a comfort. Why was I forsaken all through this dark time? *You were never alone but accompanied by the Archangel Uriel, the morning star.* I vaguely remember a presence like a shadow, always at my left side. Aware that most fear this dark deliverer, I thank him. Gavriel laughs, *You have earth angels here in the house.* Of course!

Silently, I call and soon Yeshua's siblings arrive. A sack over his shoulder, ten-year-old Shimon places it carefully on the bed and out crawls my baby. Sarah tries to stand but not finding proper footing rushes to me in a fast crawl. Tearful that I missed my baby's first steps, I gather her into my arms. She reaches for my breasts and finding them bound, begins to wail.

"Shimon, can you cut these knots."

He complies and Ruth helps unbind me. "Poor Mary, your breasts are squished. Will there be any milk for Sarah?"

"Let's pray there is, sweet child," sighing as Sarah happily relieves the pressure. Eight-year-old Judah watches the door, the girls gathering closer. "How did you accomplish this?"

"Well," Shimon begins, "this morning when Sarah began screaming for you, the nurse got a terrible headache, so I made tea." He smiles mischievously. "An angel showed me in a dream which of Abba's herbs to use and soon she was snoring." He motions for Judah to join us and my young guardian reluctantly leaves his post. All together, playing games like before the dark time began; I have finally awakened from a very bad dream.

Shortly, Yeshua appears. "What's this?" Sarah hears his voice and pulls away from me.

Brandishing a wooden sword, Judah bravely answers, "We are Mary's earth angels, so you better beware."

Yeshua puts up his hands, "I surrender to your demands. May I visit with my wife now?" Recognizing their brother of old, the little girls jump upon him. After a few moments, the children kiss us goodbye and dance out of the room. We are alone.

Offering silent gratitude at the sight of his silvery aura clear of fear, I open my arms. Yeshua hugs me to him, our tears merging to dampen Sarah's sweet head. The dark time finally over, all is forgiven.

After kissing my lips with loving compassion, Yeshua whispers, "Mary, can you use your connection and call Teoma back home?"

Gladly, I do his bidding.

First Shabbat of Shevat, 3774

Desperate, I paced the olive grove until a voice in the ethers interrupted my lamentations. "Why do you wail, Son?" Ambrose! Of course, I am transparent to my Druid teacher. "My, my! It appears you have lost your way, my prince. Are there not

---

three very wise men happy to help if you but ask?" I bemoaned how lost I had become, then with conscious breath, invited the hayye of my beloved mentors.

Zsao asked one question of me: what is fear? And before my eyes, fear existed as darkness where light could not penetrate. Just as darkness is the absence of light, fear is the absence of love.

Then Reiti's query prevailed: how does the healer heal the sick? Waves of energy coursed through me, as I perceived my wife's illness as a reflection of my fear. To heal her, I must heal myself. The darkness of my fear lifted and the light of love shone into my heart.

Belshazzar's deep-throated laughter preceded his question: how is this journey of love upon which I embarked with my wife serving my soul? A memory washed over me of the lessons from my youth, learned spiritually, mindfully, and, now through Mary, physically realized where I live in love.

Ambrose reminded me of our journeys together to witness the suffering and fear of most conscious beings on earth. The gift of my life with Mary, as tumultuous as it has been, and will be as Belshazzar reminded me, is that I am deepening in compassion for myself as well as for others.

I had lost my way, separated from Eloha by the veil of my fear. Thankfully, I was steered back on course by my teachers whose provocative questions acted as beacons of light. As my being expanded with love, Mary awoke from her fevered slumber. Her mind, now clear, expressed her delight at being forgiven, but it was forgiveness of my self-judgment that was necessary to heal the wound my fear had created in our relationship.

***

The journey home from Nabataea has been long, but with the speed of the white stallion, Teoma shall arrive before Pesach. The graceful strength of his mount fills him with hope. Yeshua must have forgiven them for Mary called him home, pulling on his heart just like that fateful night. When the stallion's hooves strike the rocky path, he winces, holding his right side. The Nabataean king's healers have not the skill of his friend. As the valley of Jezreel stretches before him, his mind wanders back to the desert.

After Yeshua's dismissal, Joseph sent him to Judaea under Theudas' command, a very different experience than under Judas. The zealot leader used his Roman appearance to gather intelligence from the oppression. After months of infiltrating the Herodian guard, Teoma's loyalties were nearly discovered by a sharp commander. Theudas swiftly dispatched him south of Judaea to gather resources from their Nabataean neighbors. That is where he first espied the horse.

The tribes of Nabataea had gathered for the great chariot races to be held in Herod's coliseum. The zealots amused themselves watching from the far ridge as the young men raced magnificent horses. A white stallion caught his eye. Ignoring the taunts of his companions, he brazenly approached the young sheik.

"What would you wager for that animal?"

"I would give up my wives before this stallion!" The sheik laughed and Epher tried to pull Teoma away.

Shaking off his comrade, Teoma appraised the fine horse, caressing its face and looking deeply into its dark eyes, certain that it desired to be taken to Mary. "I challenge you to a test of skills, sheik!"

Stroking his short dark beard, the Nabataean studied him. "I do love a challenge. But what do you have that I might desire?"

"I have a great inheritance!" Teoma cared not for the wealth, but his uncle would be furious if he lost his mother's inheritance on a wager. Epher shook his head.

"I am Ahad, son of King Aretas; I do not need your gold!"

Teoma knew that the Nabataean king was in great debt to Herod Antipas. "I hear your father must win this race, prince!"

Ahad's face darkened. "I will best you, Roman mongrel," taking in Teoma's shaven face and cropped hair, "and take all of your family's ill-gotten wealth!"

Feats of skill followed feats of strength. All the training Teoma had received in his youth proved insurmountable by young Ahad. By the end of the first day, he had won the sheik's wealth, including his five wives, but Ahad stubbornly refused to wager on the horse. It was nearly midnight when the king's guard interrupted their game.

Formerly unmarked, the soldiers brought Teoma bruised and bloodied before the Nabataean king.

"If my son has lost everything, why does he not look as bad as you do?"

"Prince Ahad was not the one to mar my skin, sir," his breath shallow from the great pain in his side wrought by a thick staff.

Aretas grumbled, studying Teoma a long while. "You have much courage. I have only seen one man use an atlatl as well!" The king held up the grooved piece of wood from which spears are thrown with great speed. "How do you know the Aksum king?"

"Belshazzar came to Nazareth to train me up in the ways of the young men from his land."

The white bearded king looked surprised. "You? No, there was another about your age. Who is your companion?"

Teoma hesitated. What harm could Aretas do here in Nabataea? His closed mouth incited his captor.

His eyes mere slits, Aretas warned, "Perhaps I should return you to my guard?"

Standing straight to hide his pain, Teoma vowed to protect Yeshua with his life. Let Aretas have his way, he would get nothing from him.

Aretas called for kaffa and sipped the hot dark drink slowly, draining two cups before speaking again, "I know Belshazzar well. Nearly twenty years ago, we visited a babe in Nazareth with Hor of Tarsus. You protect the prince of peace, do you not?"

Keeping his lips sealed, Teoma wondered if it was true. Was Aretas one of the three kings rumored to have paid homage to his friend? His passion took hold. "Wasn't it you who alerted Herod of his birth?"

The king nodded, his face shadowed by sorrow. "Yes, and I have paid dearly, giving my precious daughter to his crude son, Antipas. How unhappy she has been all these years because of her father's mistake. It is a wonder you survived."

His uncle had taken Teoma and his mother to Egypt during Herod's rage, while Yeshua remained safe within the mists at Nazareth. Aretas looked for his response to no avail. Defeated, he slumped back on the plush cushions.

"The stallion is yours. Take it as a gift to the young Judaean prince." The king released a great sigh. "When shall he bring us peace, do you know?" Teoma shook his head. "I remember his wedding; the miracle of the wine shall not be forgotten. But what since? Why has he not come? The Romans grow stronger while we wait for him."

Teoma was saddened by the king's words. How long would Abba Joseph keep Yeshua from the world? "His time has not come. He is not ready to make a stand."

"Well, I pledge the support of my tribes. Surely the kings of Tarsus and Aksum shall do the same! What more does he need?"

"The support of his own people."

"Ahh! What fools are they who wait for a mashiach, when the man resides amongst them!" Aretas softened his tone at the look on Teoma's face. "I mean not to offend your mother's lineage. I do not remember you at the wedding in Cana, but if I had known that Yeshua had a fondness for horses, I would have brought him a foursome as a wedding gift!"

Teoma swallowed, "The stallion is for his wife."

Aretas could hardly contain his mirth. "What use does a woman have for a horse? I shall send you back with finery fit for the wife of the prince."

"The horse will do, sir."

The great white stallion races toward the ridge of Nazareth. Excited to be so close to home, Teoma leaves his memories to attend to his mount.

They pierce through the mists and into the lands of Joseph to be greeted by Yeshua at the stables.

"My brother, you are home!" Embraced so vigorously, Teoma grunts. Yeshua releases him. "If you wish, I would be happy to heal you." Gratefully, Teoma nods. Yeshua smiles and kisses his cheeks, before turning to the horse. "What have you here?"

"A gift." He swallows thickly.

"Mary will be most pleased. I shall send her out."

Teoma busies himself grooming the horse, thinking he should have stopped and shaved. The horse nickers a greeting.

"Teoma!" Sable curls streaming behind, Mary jumps into his arms. He winces in pain. "What is it?"

"Nothing, I am so happy to be home." Holding her away, he smiles. "Baking more graven images are you?" She touches his rough cheek. "How is my Sarah? I hope she still recognizes me."

"Come into the kitchen and see for yourself. She could never forget you!" She pauses, a bit teary. "It just took so long for you to come home."

"I am sorry. I returned as soon as I could." With one finger he tips her chin up. "Do not cry, Mary, everything worked out as the angel predicted. It was as if we were players in a drama. You and I played our parts beautifully, don't you think?" She nods. "Now, I have something for you."

Tearfully, she whispers, "You did not have to bring me a gift."

"Please, you must accept it. I cannot return him." He gestures to the stallion pawing the ground.

Mary trembles with excitement. "Where did you get such a magnificent animal?" She kisses his cheek in gratitude and he gently pushes her toward the horse.

"Go on, Mary, he has been waiting for you."

Slowly she approaches, reaching out to the restless stallion. His ears flick forward, nostrils flare, stretching a graceful neck to touch her hand, then snuffles her body before settling his forehead against hers. Her dark hands lie in delicate contrast with his white coat. A light glows about the two in such intimate contact.

"Mary, it is as if you are one being."

Both turn toward him. "Teoma, but I have always known him. His name is…," she pauses as if listening to the animal, "…Sheikan."

"Thank you, Sheikan, for coming back to Galilee with me."

"He says you are welcome and to thank you…" her face reflects concern, "for fighting so elegantly for him?"

Before she can pose any further questions, Teoma rushes up the hill to retrieve Yeshua and Sarah, very grateful to be home.

Alone in Nazareth

The gilded hand mirror Miriam gave me on my seventeenth birthday reflects a face transformed. Lifting the hair from my neck, Yeshua melts me with a kiss. "Love has made your eyes ever more brilliant." He studies our reflections and then slowly turns me to face him. "I look into your beloved face and see the Divine." As he strokes my back, a wave of trepidation flows through me. "It is time for me to journey to Britannia."

What! Britannia is so very far away! Gavriel alights to envelop me. *Dear angel, will you stay when he has gone away or am I to suffer this abandonment of my beloved alone?*

"You will not be alone," They answer with one voice. "We are deeply connected, so with our hearts bound to one another, we can share intimacies over great distances and many months."

Months? My head spins. I cannot fathom being apart.

"Before we embodied in this life, we were as one. We can meet on that plane of existence whenever we like." Although I know he speaks the truth, my body aches from anticipation of unmet need, Gavriel's presence keeping me from sheer panic. "Shh, Beloved, during this separation we will come to discover an aspect of ourselves that we have forgotten."

A distant, buried memory begins to stir. A time without space, in a place without time. A sense of oneness with Yeshua who is not Yeshua, as I am not Mary, but we just are. Love so intense, so sweet, so without expectation—I have never been without him. Yet to exist within this body without the joy of physical connection…Already I miss him.

"My love, we can imagine one another when we sleep and meet in our dreams." Smiling, he adds, "Perhaps this will bring you comfort while I am gone."

From the oak trunk, he retrieves a codex, bound in soft leather, the parchment pages covered in a fine print with drawings here and there. "A record of my thoughts since I returned from my last trip to Britannia through this morning, when I wrote how difficult it will be to leave you and Sarah." Burying his head in my lap, his tears dampen my robe as mine drip upon his hair.

***

Mary…, Mary…

My husband calls early. Yawning, I arise to greet him in the ethers. *Yeshua, I was dreaming of you. We were in a forest, very dark and misty. You led me to a mossy clearing to lie upon a stone altar. Our union represented a coming together of two forces, air and water. Just as the heavens came to bear witness…you woke me.*

I can feel him groan with disappointment. *There is such a place here but I wish I had not interrupted you. Have a wonderful birthday celebration, Beloved.* The elestial stone glows from our contact.

We have met like this every morning since he left eight months ago. Using the path of light, we unite in spirit. Yet my body still yearns for his touch. With a sigh, I pick up the codex, caressing the crisp parchment as if through the ink, I can feel my beloved's hands.

Elul, 3772

Since receiving revelation about the birth of our first child, Mary has fretted over the amount of time I have needed to prepare for the conception in the wilderness. I spend my days perfecting the art of creating and maintaining a mobile kasa, for Abba believes that the world outside our home is unsafe. Through many years of study, I have learned raza—to make that which is material disappear. What appears material in this world is of a certain vibration like the deepest lowest tones of the lyre, while that of the spirit world is of a higher, lighter vibration like the silent sound only creatures perceive.

To veil oneself from the world, one must raise his energy higher, lighter, faster than that of the reality in which he exists and to the world he has disappeared, but still he sees and hears all about him. The same vibration as the healing white light which provides protection and invisibility to those within its sphere, kasa exists around our land, a technique Abba and I learned from the mystics in Britannia. Walking between the worlds of reality, Mary eloquently describes raza as dancing faster than the world, and to reappear, one must slow her dance to match that of the earth.

While Abba is in Tyre helping my uncles manage the ships, Ima comes with Martha and Micah to celebrate my birthday. Pregnant with her second son, my sister seems content, but Ima has an air of concern.

"Mary, you are too thin." A few strands of gray salt her dark hair. "You spend too much time out of doors with that horse!"

Surrounded by wooden toys, Sarah plays contently with Micah, her sable curls bouncing well past her shoulders. "Sheikan provides me with a blessed distraction in Yeshua's absence."

Martha looks up from her needlework, her slender hands never idle. "We are concerned that this separation is wearing upon you."

Sighing, I sit at her feet and Martha strokes my hair. "It has been difficult, sister, I miss him so."

Sarah runs to hug me, her plump cheeks sticky with massah crumbs. "Don't cry, Ima. Abba's here." She presses her small hand over my heart before returning to Micah.

Ima sits, her hayye laced with concern and at the core, the darkness of fear. "Men crave adventure and travel. We must understand that our husbands have greater needs than we may be able to fulfill." Foreboding laps at the edge of my aura.

Martha tries to help, "Mary, Eleazer is so happy that I am bearing his children and I am happy to be a wife and mother. But of course during the pregnancy, I cannot expect him to wait for me in our marriage bed."

How can he not wait? Perhaps she thinks that Yeshua and I were not intimate when I was pregnant. I look down, wondering if we broke some tradition which she and Ima need not know about.

"Mary, you cannot expect Yeshua to be away this long without taking other women to his bed."

I gasp as if stabbed. "You are wrong, Ima! Yeshua is faithful to me. There has never been anyone else."

She shakes her head sadly, her hand heavy on my shoulder, "Dear Mary, I just want to prepare you by revealing the truth."

That is not my truth! Sarah ceases her play so I try to appease her with a smile. "Ima," I measure my words, "are you satisfied with this arrangement?"

"Well, of course, Mary. What choice do I have?" She really believes she is powerless.

"Ima, do you not have desires as well? When Abba is gone and you believe he is taking other women to his bed, do you not feel justified in taking a lover of your own?"

Ima stands up flushed in the face. Gasping, Martha drops her needlework. They stare at me as if I have blasphemed.

"Mary," Ima gasps, "do you not realize that a woman could be stoned for adultery?" I pick up Martha's forgotten needlework. "Promise me that you will stay chaste while your husband is away."

I stand and kiss them. "I made that promise to Yeshua as he did to me." Holding Sarah up for a kiss, we take our leave.

I find Miriam in the study, but she is not alone. A familiar burgundy hayye pulsates like the heart of a hot fire. I hesitate at the threshold with Sarah in my arms.

"Please, Mary, join us." Sarah struggles to be put down and Miriam scoops her up. She listens patiently as Sarah describes our visit with my family, before asking, "Would you like to talk?" At the invitation, my emotions bubble to the surface. Turning back to Sarah, she whispers, "Guess what, precious child? There is someone here to meet you."

Sarah leans confidentially into Miriam's shoulder, "Savta, that's my Hava. Can she stay with me now?"

Miriam kisses her plump cheek and releases her. Instead of the usual hugs and kisses, Sarah greets our guest palm to palm. When they press their foreheads together, I gasp, remembering Hava greeted me in the same way. Visions of the altar force me to my knees, as waves of desire flood my body. This morning's dream continues where it was interrupted with clans from around the world witnessing our union. My passion draws Yeshua.

For heaven's sakes, Mary, what is happening?

I am here before the high priestess. Sarah knows her.

Sarah reaches from Hava's arms, "My Abba," receiving his embrace through the ethers. Tears flow over the edge of my smile.

Hello, my son. I have returned to be with your precious daughter.

With reverence, Yeshua responds, *You have my deepest gratitude, dear Hava.*

I kiss her extended hand but Hava laughs, "Please stand so I might greet you properly."

90

Still holding Sarah on her hip, she raises her left hand to my right. So intense is the energy, the rose inscribed on my body nearly three years ago pulsates with a sweet aching. Sarah breaks the spell by kissing my cheek, "Ima, stay here with Savta. I want to be with my Hava." They glide out of the room.

Miriam smiles, motioning me to sit with her on a wide cushion. "Hava has been in Qumran with the priestesses of Astarte holding the energy that was brought to earth during your union with Yeshua."

The elestial quartz glows as hotly as my cheeks. "I am sorry to act so overwhelmed."

Looking at me intently, Miriam's hayye softly probes mine. If only she can reassure me that all will be well. "Martha and my mother brought to my attention that men cannot be trusted with fidelity especially when absent from us…," my voice trails off. "I just never considered this a possibility."

"Mary, you must learn to trust." I do, but have allowed my mother to place doubt in my mind. "This separation is granting you an opportunity to learn to trust in yourself and the Divine."

But she does not reassure me that my husband will be faithful. Perhaps she had to live with this same turmoil herself when Joseph left and now it is my turn.

***

A chilly breeze blows long black hair over a drawn face. Coarse bindings secure bloodied wrists to the crossbar. Groans cascade down the stony mount. The myrrh-laced wine wore off long ago. With a muttered curse, a centurion orders the prisoner's death hastened. A quick draw of straws provokes a disgruntled groan from one of the four young soldiers who rises armed with a stout oak staff.

The sickening crack of bone precedes a piercing cry. The condemned man's head snaps back sharply against the vertical beam parting the veil of hair. Stricken eyes fix a green death glare upon him. Horrified, he backs away, stumbling down the mount.

In a cold sweat, Teoma bolts upright, nearly capsizing the hammock. After his first zealot campaign, he witnessed the crucifixion of one of his comrades. Never again! Now that cursed dream which haunted him five years ago returns. Why? Because Tiberius drowned any hopes of an uprising after Augustus' death last summer by strengthening the legions.

The more fortunate prisoners file by Nazareth on their way to the galleys, while the rebels are condemned to the cross.

He should be taking up arms beside the zealots, but instead plays father to another's child. Trapped by his loyalty to Yeshua, yet so is Mary. He wipes a damp brow. At least she experiences a measure of freedom riding far from the house on the white stallion. Not that there is another mount that can keep up nor does he wish to tempt fate by being alone with her.

Sighing, he closes his eyes but the death glare pierces his mind until a wave of sorrow disturbs the garden. Contrasting with the creamy blossoms of the apricot trees, Mary's dark beauty is soaked with despair. She sits gingerly next to him and shivering, leans into the warmth of his body.

He places the bundle he used for a pillow in her lap, "A token for your birthday."

Her careful unwrapping reveals an exquisite amethyst shawl, but she does not look up. Is it too intimate? His face flushes hotly. Perhaps she perceives his connection to the young priestess who embroidered the golden ankhs along the edge of the silk. "Do you not like it?"

She draws a shuddering breath, "I'm sorry. It's lovely. Thank you. I just…"

Wrapping the shawl about her shoulders, he lifts her silken curls free. "You're missing him more than usual." Still she stares at her clasped hands, for once struggling to express herself. "What is it?"

"Teoma, is it true that men cannot be expected to abstain?"

Her candor takes him by surprise. Embarrassed, he clears his throat. "Why would you ask such a question?"

She sighs miserably. "Because my mother informed me that while I am expected to be chaste during our separation, I cannot expect him to be."

Certain of his friend's fidelity, he asks, "And you believe that?"

"No, but I left them in the nursery and went to talk to Miriam."

He nods. "Good, so what did she say?"

"That I need to learn to trust in myself and the Divine."

"She is right, you must have faith."

She looks up, her green gaze as imploring as in his dream. He swallows thickly. "I do not know if Yeshua is strong like you."

His body stiffens, "What do you mean?"

"Why, Teoma, you are so handsome and desirable, but insist on serving Yeshua's mission and foregoing, well, you know…marriage and…intimacy."

How did he get himself into this? "I am committed to both of you, and while I do not foresee marriage," he hesitates, clearing his throat, "I am not celibate."

"Really, you have a mistress? Then why haven't I met her?" She looks about as if he is hiding some strange woman amongst the pepper trees.

He shifts uncomfortably, remembering well what he learned in the temple of Astarte. "When Yeshua asked me to leave, Joseph advised that I make some contacts in Judaea."

A flash of comprehension darkens her gaze. "He sent you to be with…women?"

He pauses to inhale deeply. "I truly believed you and I would be married, before I knew that you were betrothed, of course, and then in my fervor to serve Yeshua, I felt that I must be faithful to you both." Her lovely mouth blossoms into a smile, which eases his heart somewhat. "Joseph arranged for me to be mentored by the priestesses."

"I apologize for my naiveté. But how can you stay here with us and not be with your women friends in Judaea?"

He smiles. "Well, perhaps you are right. Once through the portal of sensuality, there is no return." Her forehead creases with concern. "But do not worry, I will not leave you."

"But if you have found it difficult, do you think Yeshua can be strong?" She presses her small hand against his chest in confirmation of his power.

"I think it might be harder for men than for women." He searches for an explanation to cover his former insensitivity, "You have Sarah to occupy your time and, of course, Sheikan."

Vehemently, she pulls away. "Do you think motherhood can satisfy that need?"

He is taken aback by the fire of her emotion.

"Women do not really understand their innate passion, so much so that they are not living the fullness of their femininity. And men perpetuate the fallacy of demurely chaste wives yet seek solace with other women!" Mary clasps his hands to her breast, "Who are these women who might express their passionate natures with men in the moment, but not for lifetime companionship?"

Teoma stares at her wondering how much to reveal, "Dear, except for the priestesses of Astarte, these women are not accepted by society openly, many are scorned and punished oftentimes in guise of the laws of Adonai."

"How terrible! The Creator made both men and women to be passionate in their love for one another."

He attempts to enlighten her. "Sex and love are not mutually inclusive."

"What?" she asks beseechingly, "You make love to women and do not feel love for them?"

How to explain without burdening her even more? "One can be intimate without being in love, but..." his voice lowers, "I imagine that sex with your heart's desire is the highest expression of love."

Her eyes overflow, comprehending his sacrifice, "I am so sorry, Teoma."

"Dearest, do not be sorry. This is my choice." He hugs her tightly, praying she receives as much comfort from the contact as he does.

***

I retire to my room exhausted. Usually adoring the words of my beloved's hand, tonight I do not open the codex. Buried beneath painful memories, his insights record more heartache than joy. Dried flowers marking the more pleasant passages bring me little solace for those are few compared to his soulful turmoil.

Pulling the silky linens over my naked flesh, soon seeped in images of our wedding union, I yearn for Yeshua. Always he perceives my nocturnal desire, but tonight he does not come.

The purple drop appears and I enter its center to follow the violet wave, raising my vibration a fraction more by deepening my breath and imagining Yeshua's hayye. Yet I cannot perceive him, no connection. I refocus my efforts, clearing my mind but to no avail. Where is he?

If something was wrong, I would feel it, but nothing. Unless...?

If I have learned to selectively use kasa to pacify Teoma, certainly Yeshua can do the same. But why seek privacy from me? Ragged breath forces me to sit up. I command myself to desist, but my fevered mind runs away with the idea that my husband may be with another woman.

I cry myself into a fitful sleep. The Archangels appear in my dreams. Uriel takes my hand as I enter another dark place. Gavriel's face is serene, but in Uriel's eyes lies my sorrow. I awaken in a cold sweat.

Rising from my lonely bed, I dress to ride. A tunic split up the middle and sewed in half lengthwise, like the horsemen of the southern deserts, works to protect my inner thighs from chaffing and I tie a sash around my chest to secure my bosom.

Prancing across the pasture, Sheikan greets me with a nicker and I mount his bare back without bridle, sensuously free. He responds to my every wish so we head to the seashore. Nearly a half-day's ride on any other mount, Sheikan covers the distance with long strides, never tiring, adjusting his pace to suit the terrain. I sit low and forward on his withers, centered with him—in unity, one with nature, borne on the wind.

The sea beckons so we plunge in to wash off the sweat and tears. Returning to the shore, Sheikan nuzzles my leg so I slip off his back to allow him to shake before rolling in the sand. I wring out my garments and lay them to dry under the late winter sky. The beloved element of water soothes my soul as the sun warms my body. Sheikan begins to graze and I sit breathing deeply in meditation. Softened by the ride, I perceive my own connection in the purple drop, but not Yeshua. With a heavy heart, I lie back and watch the sea birds.

I have lost contact with my beloved. I pray fervently that he is well, that my suspicions are not true, that I might learn trust. Within my navel the elestial quartz lies clouded by my dread. Circling a patch of long grass, Sheikan lies down beside me, allowing me to lay my heavy head upon his neck. When I awaken, the sun bows low to meet the sea. We must return or Teoma will be frantic. Hurriedly, I dress and mount Sheikan, racing east to beat the night.

The moonless sky makes it seem very late. In the stable, Sheikan looks up from his grain to nicker a greeting, and I bend to clean his hooves, ignoring Teoma's set jaw.

"You should have the grooms do that." His voice is strained. "Where were you all day? Miriam told me she sent you out to ride, but you left no word with the stable hands as to your destination." He lifts me to my feet and sniffs a lock of my hair. "You rode all the way to the shore?" I nod.

With clenched fists, Teoma barely contains himself. "How do you expect me to keep my promise to your husband if you insist on running off? What if something happened to you?"

95

Staring up at him with a heavy heart, I have no excuses, "I am sorry, Teoma. I...."

"No! You have no idea how much I worry about you. Do you know how upset Yeshua would be if I lost you?"

"He would not care."

His tight grip on my arm is nothing compared to the pain in my heart. "How can you say such a thing? After our conversation yesterday? What is wrong with you?" Teoma's frustration lies heavily in the breezeless stall.

"I cannot find Yeshua! My fears are being made manifest."

He loosens his grip, eyes softer, "Mary, you must be mistaken."

My passion rises, "Do you doubt that I can connect to him? Do you think I have not tried? We have connected every morning and night since he left in Tammuz."

Now he looks worried, "Maybe he cannot contact you. What if he is hurt or sick or...?"

"Even when ill, you can be contacted. I know that I would feel if he were...dead. It must be kasa that seals him from me. Why would he want to veil himself, unless to hide?"

Teoma shakes his head, "Perhaps he is not veiling himself, but someone else is veiling him. Let us go to Miriam, she can contact Joseph and then we will know." He tries to lead me away, but I resist. "What? Do you not want to know the truth?"

Through trembling lips, I respond, "Maybe I don't. Maybe I am supposed to just trust that all is well. Maybe I would be better off never knowing if he has been unfaithful or not."

Compassionately, he declares, "Dearest Mary, you must have faith. I will go to Miriam and be assured of Yeshua's wellbeing." He escorts me to the nursery. I kiss my daughter, who is fast asleep, exhausted from her full day with Hava.

"Mary, remember to be gentle with yourself and with him. You are both human and it is not easy in this form." Hava's golden eyes and deep auburn-colored hair reflect her fire-like aura. I manage a smile and head for the baths.

After a soothing soak, dressed in a soft linen sadin with my damp hair in long braids, I am summoned to the study, where Miriam has spent most of her time since Joseph has gone. Teoma sits grimfaced beside her. My heart skips a beat; maybe I cannot perceive Yeshua's need.

Miriam speaks, "I contacted Joseph, and apparently Yeshua is veiled from him as well." She does not appear upset, but then why would she be?

"So, Ima, you believe Yeshua is alive and well?"

"Yes, dear, I do."

Nauseated, I breathe shallowly. "Teoma," I ask, swallowing back my shame, "why are you so grim?"

Looking up slowly, Teoma makes an effort to soften his jaw, "Mary, for all of our sakes, do not forget that he is just a man."

With sheer will, I refrain from crying. "Dear friend, I thought you believed him to be something more." Teoma calls after me, but Miriam quiets him.

In the nursery, I kiss Sarah's sweet face. So connected to her father, if he was endangered she would react. But no, she sleeps peacefully. He must not be sad or afraid, or she would stir. He must be joyful or something else that I do not wish to express while standing over our child.

Unable to sleep in our bed, I head for the stables, blanket under my arm. I shall not sleep alone but will lie down in sweet straw with Sheikan. Within the comfort of his equine energy, I spend a dreamless night.

For the following week, I go into the house briefly to be with Sarah. At dawn and bedtime, I try to commune with Yeshua, but nothing. I am losing hope. Riding Sheikan far away yet I cannot escape this pain.

Miriam says very little, offering no reassurance. I can only trust myself for I am alone in this world. Now that Hava is here, Sarah does not seem to need me, but I must stay for who knows if her father will ever return. Even my angels have kept their distance and Teoma hardly looks at me, so affected by Yeshua's humanness.

The nights are long and cold under the waxing moon, the days stormy and gray like my mood. I cannot go back to my family, but do not feel at home here with Yeshua's essence pervading the house. What once made me feel attached now causes me to feel adrift.

On the eighth night after another fruitless search for my husband, I surrender to the ministration of the angels, "Marya," I succumb to prayer, using the Chaverim name for the Divine, "please lighten my heart that I may know love and abundance in my life. I cannot travel this dark path alone any longer. Please accompany me on my journey, lift my burden of pain, and help me to understand how to love myself more deeply that I might be able to love those around me with all my heart. Help me surrender my beloved to his divine destiny here on earth or in other dimensions. Please, I can do no more. Ameyn."

Both Archangels Uriel and Gavriel light up with translucent vibration and I am held in their protective embrace. Peace overwhelms my being as a tetrahedron of light appears of all colors, of none. The One speaks to me in a voice without sound and I am filled with love.

Mary, all of heaven weeps when you are in pain. Do not forget who you are, beloved. You are here to bring joy unto the world of men, your love nourishes like milk and honey. Your faith has been great, as has been your courage. My beloved Yeshua will be returned to you.

With a vast wave of love, the tetrahedron expands, encompassing me and I am awash with passion. I have never felt so adored, so cherished. Tears drench my hands clasped in fervent prayer. The angels magnify to such intensity that they are beyond my visual perception. The One is gone, but within my heart is a pure seed of compassion planted in love.

A third angel has appeared with a golden sword of light, he stands to my right. Gavriel speaks, *Mary, as you have taken Uriel's hand willingly to be escorted through this darkness, now you shall go with Archangel Michael who will escort you through the portal of your awakening.*

I extend my hayye to Michael who sweeps me through the bright portal. The world now appears bathed in light, even in this dark night. All colors and sounds enhanced by beauty awe me. Holding Michael's hand, with Uriel and Gavriel behind, I am taken to Yeshua.

He lies upon his back on an altar bathed in a soft glow, surrounded by Druids in brown hooded tunics. Dressed in white, his skin pale, his limbs thin, in a state like deep sleep, only connected to his unconscious body by a silver cord, his spirit embraces me and I am awash in love. We enter his body together and I see through his eyes all that has happened to him in the past eight days.

After our last connection with Hava, Yeshua, in the middle of a quest under the dictates of the northern clan, went into a deep trance. Unfortunately, the healers had a difficult time bringing him back. They spent days and nights ministering to him but to no avail. He was united with the One where time was not. Filled with love, he felt no attachments to this world, not even to me.

In spite of my repeated attempts to contact him, he could not be drawn away from the bliss until I finally prayed and surrendered him to the One, then he reconnected to this dimension. For the first time in a week, I feel joy.

Yeshua awakes in Britannia and I am returned to my body. The symbol of our union glows comfortingly at my core. With a heart full of gratitude, I thank my angelic escort and go to the nursery to kiss Sarah. She stirs and reaches up to hug me before whispering sleepily, "Abba's back. Be happy now, Ima." Blessed child, I should have consulted with her.

Teoma bar Flavius,

Son, in response to your request, I am sending my finest shepherds to watch over Joseph's flock. I pray that the wolves have not caused you undue concern, but understand that in moving the sheep to better grazing, care must be taken. We miss your vigor here in Judaea and look forward to the time when you may return the favor and join in shepherding our desert flocks. The temple of Astarte will be expecting an offering when you are free from your duties in Galilee. Remember that patience is greatly rewarded by the Divine. So take heed and return to the desert with pure heart and clean hands. Your loyalty shall be your redemption.

In faith, Judas

After Sarah's second birthday, the family caravans in carts drawn by donkeys to the shore of the Great Sea. With Sarah in front of me, I have a hard time keeping Sheikan in pace with Teoma's lumbering mare. Arriving ahead of the group, I take Sarah into the sea for the first time, her delight bringing a smile to Teoma's face.

Teoma sets up a tent on a lookout point just above us, the better to survey the perimeter. A small group of armed men camp at various sites surrounding the family. When I ask about the zealots, he informs me that while he trusts the mystic kasa, he is under orders by Joseph to take every precaution to keep the family safe.

The days burn one into the other until it is nearly the end of summer. Miriam asks me to take Teoma away from the encampment so they can prepare a birthday celebration. He has been working too hard and not really enjoying himself, having to keep a higher vigilance at the shore.

We head north toward the great mountain known as Karmel. The energy of the sacred space enlivens our steps, yet even some distance from our destination, sweat soaks our skin. The cool sea laps invitingly, but Teoma continues marching up the beach. Halting, I lay my sadin on the sand, dressed only in my riding sash and a short hipcloth underneath, and run into the water before Teoma notices and tries to stop me.

"For heaven's sakes, Mary what are you doing?"

Laughing, I reply from the shallows, "Let's swim for a while." Sweat glistens on his face. Perhaps he is not comfortable getting undressed.

He approaches the water's edge, "Come, we must get back."

Teasingly, I splash him, "Relax, it's your birthday. Come cool down." I swim past the breakers and look back to see him hurriedly stripping down to his loincloth. He runs and dives into the turquoise water, reaching me in short time.

A soft blue hayye, very watery and light, touches mine and my heart sings. Not alone, dolphins circle us. These creatures swam along side our ship when my family sailed the Great Sea. They come closer, looking at us with dark eyes, blowing softly out of a hole in their backs. I yearn to touch their smooth sides, to swim out farther with them.

As I move toward them, Teoma grabs my arm, "Mary, be careful." How can he feel fear near these glorious creatures? I push away and dive below the surface. Immediately, one of the dolphins swims up to me. Gliding against my side, its flesh smooth, its hayye loving, I yearn to hug it, but my breath is running out. As if sensing my need, it pushes me to the surface.

Horrified, Teoma swims swiftly over to pull me away from the creatures, easily overcoming my protests. My new aquatic friend intervenes by butting him in the side with its long nose, separating us. Catching his breath, Teoma cries out, "Mary, be still, I'm coming." Again he tries to rescue me, but the creature pushes me back with its body.

Teoma's fear magnifies so three other creatures begin to circle with calming energies. My new friend communicates in musical tones. *Greetings Elat, we have been waiting for you.*

Thank you, beautiful one. Your hayye brings me much joy. A distance from me, Teoma treads water, surrounded by dolphins.

We are your family from the seas, having been a part of your clan for a great span of eternity. Your companion is fearful to accept our hayye, ask him to relax.

I reach out to Teoma, tugging gently on his heartstrings. He looks at me and I ask him to accept their ministrations. As soon as he smiles his consent, the entire group encircles to bring us closer together. The dolphins dance about for a long time, touching us with their noses and bodies. We are bathed in light energy and filled with delight. When we tire from our long exposure in the water, they playfully escort us to the shore.

Reaching the warmth of the sand, we flop onto our backs, breathing heavily from our exertions. I bask in the dolphins' joyful hayye before turning on my side. Teoma stares at me. Pushing my wet hair off my neck, I smile. The sun warms my chilled skin but under his gaze, I am acutely aware of my clinging wet garments. A quick glance confirms that the dolphins aroused other desires in him. Laughing, I toss a handful of sand at his chest.

"That is why you have been so grumpy lately. You are stuck here with us!"

Blushing, he rolls onto his belly with his head down in the cross of his arms. I reach over and touch his muscular back, "I am sorry to tease you, but wasn't that the most wonderful experience?"

Turning his head toward me, he smiles sadly, "I am very grateful, but it is not the dolphins that arouse me."

Hmmm! What to do with this growing tension between us? My own nature is so passionate, my sensuality increasing with less restrictive garments and these experiences in nature. Only three months since Teoma has been with a woman, but nearly fifteen months since I have found relief. What is Yeshua doing right now?

What is it, my love?

Teoma raises his head. Poor man, not sure what to make of me, calling in my husband to witness our precarious situation. *We just had a wonderful experience with the dolphins. Did you meet them on your trip across the sea?*

Yes, they swam close by the ship. What amazing hayye! I suppose they spoke directly to you.

Yes, they welcomed me and ministered to Teoma, who was a bit apprehensive at first.

Yeshua laughs. *Did he try and save you from them? How is my good friend now?* He scans Teoma's hayye then quickly returns to mine. *Hmmm, it appears as if the two of you are in a bit of a situation.*

Teoma stares at me wide-eyed. "Mary, tell Yeshua to please forgive me, I will escort you safely back."

Reassure Teoma that I trust him with my life as well as my wife, but he must hurry for the family is nearly ready for you to return. And to you, my sensual wife, look forward to my visit tonight. Teoma presents a physical temptation I wish to help you forget.

Teoma seems relieved when I relay my husband's message. Taking my hand, he leads me back to the family.

***

"Ima, you be a sheep and we'll catch you," Sarah suggests, not satisfied with one human animal. Teoma smiles at me through his bridle, some ribbon she tied about his head. He has a way with wood as well as food, but the friendly Trojan horse he carved for her birthday sits alone in the nursery, for today he is her mount.

"All right, Sarah, but as soon as you catch me, it will be time to rest and have a snack."

She pouts, "But, Ima, I'm not tired."

Giving her a kiss, I pat her horse on the head. "Your steed is getting tired and needs to be put out to pasture." Teoma laughs as I assume my position.

Although I am agile, Teoma outcrawls me too quickly for Sarah's satisfaction. "No, Ima, you have to try and get away."

"I am trying, Sarah, but your horse is much faster than a sheep."

Frowning, she ponders the dilemma. "Why don't you stand up a little bit so you are faster, like this?" She hops off Teoma's back and demonstrates how to lope away on hands and feet.

I comply and soon there is a bit of a challenge. Sarah spurs her mount on, but when Teoma grasps my fleeing ankle, I trip, landing hard. "Mary, I am so sorry. Are you all right?"

Sarah lifts my sadin to expose a bloody, abraded knee. "Poor, Ima, you're hurt. Here," she beckons, "kiss it better, Dod Teo."

I try to cover my knee, "I'm fine, Sarah."

"No, Ima, Dod Teo hurt you on accident, but he must kiss it better." In her two-and-half-year-old mind only kisses will make amends so I consent, but Teoma is hesitant. "Please, Dod Teo, please, make it better." He kneels in front of me and tenderly kisses my injured knee, lingering a moment as Sarah hugs us.

A cleared throat draws our attention and we look up to see Saada holding a tray with Sarah's lunch. Teoma hurriedly stands and helps me to my feet. Sarah runs over to Saada exclaiming, "Dod Teo kissed Ima's hurt away." Saada lets out a little huff and sets down the tray before giving me a cold look.

After the evening meal, I am called into the study. Miriam greets me. "Mary, you are aware that Saada was disturbed by what she saw in the courtyard today."

"Ima, I can explain."

She shakes her head, "There is no need, but you must understand how the staff feels." I hold my tongue. "Saada and Leah have been with us since before Yeshua was born. They are very protective and see Teoma as a threat. Now I realize that you and Yeshua have come to an understanding about Teoma and while I can encourage him to make more social visits, you are still left in need." My tears well as she gets to the heart of the matter.

She kisses the top of my head. Reaching the end of my endurance, I weep in her arms. "I know, dear, how hard this is for you." She lifts my chin. "Your mother has requested your presence alone tomorrow evening. I believe she wants to speak to you about this very matter." What, are our staff related? "As I can trust no one else to escort you safely there and back, Teoma will go. He will have some business to attend to in Sepphoris while you are visiting with your family." I sigh for this does not sound like a social visit.

The next afternoon, Teoma escorts me to my parent's home in Cana. He is dressed like a Roman soldier with sandals strapped high up to his knees, a short blue tunic, and a gladius secured in his wide leather belt. Both goyim and Romans greet him as we travel north.

"Teoma, how is it that you are so comfortable with the ways of Rome?" He escorts me very formally, only offering his arm so I do not stumble over some obstacle.

"I thought you knew my father is Roman."

"Yes, and I think you look very handsome with your short hair and clean shaven face. Isn't it odd that Joseph would be comfortable with your attire?" I smile up at an impassive face.

"Mary, it is best if we save this conversation for the privacy of the house." He looks straight ahead, chin high. Why all the secrecy? If we cannot talk freely, perhaps I should have journeyed to my parent's house under kasa. As if reading my mind, he replies, "I considered using kasa as well for your protection, but it seemed unnecessary."

I remove the lovely shawl Teoma gave me as we enter the outer courtyard of my family home. "Under no circumstances are you to leave this house until I return." With that warning, he makes sure I am escorted safely inside by a servant before taking his leave. What is the matter with him?

A lovely supper is set for us with three servants attending to our every need. I chat for a bit with my parents before Ima decides to make her point.

"Mary, soon Sarah will be three." I nod, Yeshua left shortly after her first birthday. "How are you doing?"

"I am fine, Ima. I have much to keep me occupied." I really do not want to discuss this with her, especially in front of Abba.

Undaunted, she asks, "How wise is it for that young man to stay at the house while Yeshua is away?"

"Teoma has been taking care of us." Ima raises a brow. I turn to look in my father's pale eyes, "Abba, perhaps we can go riding together sometime."

Abba's balding pate belies his age, his face usually so jovial, but not tonight. "That would be nice, my dear, but I believe your Ima has more to say." I sigh and turn back to her.

"Mary, our last conversation about this over a year ago has left me with grave concerns as to your chastity."

"Ima!" Why did I have to come? But my mother is just getting started, so I must sit and listen, forever it seems, to her concerns. She believes that Teoma and I are allowed to spend too much time together without a chaperone, that my behavior is not suited to a faithful wife. They claim Teoma had designs on marrying me himself and feel that he cannot be trusted to just fulfill his duties as the family guardian. She even belabors an offer to have me live here with Sarah until Yeshua returns.

I choose not to argue with her and stay quiet. My lack of excuses further incites her, but at this point, I have broken so many rules, she will find something to scold me about. How is it that even when one has left home, is married and has a child, when with her parents, she still feels like a child herself?

"Well, I will have to talk to Miriam about the situation. She must find another guard and release Teoma or you will have to come home."

"Ima, Miriam will follow Joseph's counsel only. So you will just have to wait until Joseph and Yeshua return and talk to him about your concerns. But then Yeshua will be home so it will no longer be a problem, will it?" I stand up, shaking, as Abba reaches over and pats my arm.

"There, there, Mary, do not get upset, Ima is only trying to help." This has not helped at all. I wring my napkin, needing fresh air. "Go to the courtyard, my dear, and take some time to consider Ima's proposal." Thank goodness! I kiss his cheek and hurry out, my mother's raised voice trailing after me.

With few oil lamps lit, the courtyard is very dark, but I feel better outside. My childhood house is not home to me anymore. I do not even miss it. Saddened, I hope Teoma arrives soon.

After what seems an eternity, there is an insistent knocking on the front gate. Neither the servants nor my parents appear, so I get up, hesitantly. It must be Teoma. Where are the servants to see to the gate? The knocking becomes pounding, so I go myself but once again hesitate. I feel wary. *Don't be foolish*, I chide myself. *It's only Teoma.*

Opening the heavy gate, I peer out. There is no one at the entrance. As I take a step outwards, Teoma's warning whispers in the breeze. Fear engulfs me but before I can move back behind the gate, a strong rough hand clamps my arm and pulls me into the shadows outside the wall. Paralyzed by fear but managing to find my voice, I scream as my assailant secures me up against the wall. Breath foul with wine, he whispers crude Latin. I struggle when he tries to lift my sadin, pushing roughly against me. His dirty hand silences me. Archangel Uriel alights behind him and instructs me to call for Teoma. Concentrating my hayye, I silently scream his name.

As if my assailant can feel the angel, he moves back slightly, enough for me to twist away. I try to reach for the archangel's hand, but my assailant will not be deterred. Just as he roughly drags me back against the wall, Teoma appears!

Swiftly, silently, he pulls my attacker off and throws him to the ground. The man addresses Teoma in a rather familiar tone. Still plastered to the wall by fear, I do not move until Teoma instructs me to go back into the house. My legs shake as I back away.

Having regained his feet, the man draws his sword. Teoma does likewise, so I escape into the empty courtyard. In a short time, a man screams but before a tear can fall, Teoma steps through the gate. I rush into his arms. Gently seating us on a bench, his arm protectively around me when a servant appears. Seeing the two of us, she hurries back inside. Abba follows shortly.

"What is the meaning of this?"

Teoma does not stand because I am clinging to him, "Sir, I returned to find Mary being attacked by a soldier."

"How can this be? She was only waiting for us. Oh my daughter, I pray it is not so…" The cawing of a crow interrupts my father and he quickly returns to the house to retrieve Ima.

Buried in Teoma's chest as he strokes my hair, I cannot be comforted. With a dark flapping, the crow startles my mother, whose rage precedes her. Shielding me with his form, Teoma carries me inside and sets me down on a cushioned lounge, but I do not release him. "Please take me home, do not leave me here."

Blue eyes fill, he touches my cheek gently, "I will not return without you."

Ima tends to me as best she can, but I yearn for Miriam's healing touch. "Please, I will be fine. Sarah will miss me."

"You must wait for a few days. Your injuries will upset her."

What injuries? Shaken up and roughly handled but thank goodness, that is all. My mouth feels bruised and tender, but I just want to go home.

"Please, Teoma will take good care of me."

"If it wasn't for him, this would have never happened."

Teoma stands rigidly as I rise. "Ima, if not for him, that man would have raped me." She is shaking with emotion. "I should have paid attention to my intuition, but unfortunately I did not. I will not make that mistake again." With trembling lips, I end, "Yeshua trusts Teoma implicitly. So should you." I gingerly kiss her cheek and then Abba's.

Under the healing energy of the stars, Teoma escorts me home. Miriam is waiting for us in the study. Upon seeing my face she rushes to my side, "Mary, Teoma, what happened?" I explain in as much detail as I can remember, but my fear seems to have blurred it all. Before completing my story, I begin trembling uncontrollably.

Having sat us down side by side, Miriam kneels before us, eyes welling with tears. "I should have insisted that your parents come here." Teoma slumps forward, his head in his hands. She touches his knee, "How are you doing?"

"Not well, Ima. All I can think of is how selfish I was." He rises impassioned but pacing the room only heightens his angry despair.

"Please, Teoma." Miriam motions for him to sit. "There is an energy here that must be released. Each of you in turn reacted with guilt, blaming yourself for what happened. I did the same thing."

What am I going to tell Yeshua? He will be so upset! Teoma's sigh brings me back to the moment and I try to focus. Perceiving the darkness of guilt, images of my hesitancy to open the door before the attack go through my mind. Miriam holds the hayye as we sit before her. All the tender areas on my body inflame, burning into my core. Teoma softens as Miriam speaks.

"You are now being given the opportunity to forgive, not one another, but yourselves. Teoma, you hold within your hayye a powerful energy of devotion, but it is wrapped around a core of guilt. Time to release the guilt and forgive yourself, then you will find your devotional energies will bring you much joy." His smile is tightly laced with doubt.

Miriam turns to me. "Guilt is a magnification of your judgment of the human condition. You are learning to be more gentle with yourself and those around you. You have the opportunity to love yourself more deeply by forgiving yourself for making mistakes."

"But I am concerned about telling Yeshua. He will know!"

"Remember that this is Yeshua's lesson in forgiveness as well."

Teoma murmurs, "I pray that he forgives me."

"First, you must forgive yourself for your human errors and weaknesses." This is difficult for him. "Teoma," Miriam continues, "you deserve to have time to yourself." His cheeks redden. He was with a woman!

Miriam leaves to prepare healing herbs. Teoma and I are alone. Hesitantly he ventures, "I am so sorry. How can I make it better?"

"Sarah would suggest a kiss." When he tenderly kisses my bruised cheek, I feel safe and comforted.

Miriam stays up a long while tending me, rubbing healing creams into my bruised skin, placing poultices on the swollen areas. Gratitude fades the images of the attack. I surrender my guilt and intend to heal fully in body, mind, and soul, praying that Teoma will be relieved of his guilt and find forgiveness in his heart. Then I pray that Yeshua will be open to this lesson as well. I ask that my attacker be healed, for I wish no others to suffer from his fear. Finally, I give thanks for this experience that shall bless me with greater compassion for my humanness. When Miriam finishes, my prayer is complete.

Only Archangel Uriel appeared, and while I feel immense gratitude for his love and devotion, where were the others? *Only the light of Eloha can penetrate the veil of fear.* Gavriel explains, *That is why Uriel was given dominion over the earth as the human experience encompasses all emotions including overcoming fear. Only Uriel can bring one through her darkest time and back into the light of love where Source and it's host of angels can minister to her soul.*

I express my deepest gratitude to my savior, the morning star.

Dod Joseph,

You have yet to return from Britannia, but I must record my feelings while they are fresh. I told you about the legionnaire notorious for his crude treatment of women. While under the auspices of the zealot command, in Roman disguise, I could do nothing about his behavior. How I wish that I might have castrated him the last time I witnessed his cruelty toward an Indumean woman in Hebron.

I am unworthy of Yeshua's trust, for under my care, his wife was attacked by the brute. Barely in time did I arrive, called to the scene outside her family home by a thunderous pull. Lucias will no longer frequent the gymnasia, for I have marked him as a Hebrew, crudely albeit. While he still lives, may his lust wrought him nothing but pain.

Still Mary entrusts herself and her dear child to my protection. I vow that never again will one under my care be hurt. When I am released from my post, I pray

---

that I finally see some action with the zealots, for my sword has a great lust of its own.

Yours, Teoma

Why am I Here
Galilee, 3776

Do you know why you're here on the earth at this time?
Why you exist in the orchestration divine?
Why you chose to live this life now?
Here you shall know the Light of the One.

Welcoming Love

Mount Karmel! The highest peak on the western shore of Galilee, the last sight he saw over two years ago, now the first to welcome him home. Soon, very soon, he will be with her. Dolphins frolic alongside the ship, sleek gray flashes of delight diving through the turquoise waters of the Mediterranean.

"They seem to be escorting us, Yeshua."

Joseph of Arimathaea leans over the railing. Appointed by the late Caesar Augustus to serve as Nobilis Decurio, minister of the mines, Joseph transports tin from Britannia for the entire Empire.

"Mary sent them." Longing constricts his chest as her name passes his lips.

"Patience, son, the shore comes up to meet us."

Shouts from the stern arouse them. The sailors point toward the beach where his wife rides the white stallion into the surf completely nude! Attending closely, he realizes the others cannot see her. How clever to create a veil of kasa that only he can pierce.

Anchoring well offshore, the sailors carefully lower a rowboat onto the water, then load it with agonizing precision. Finally the boat begs to be boarded. Bidding their host farewell, Yeshua descends the rope ladder after his father. From across the water, Mary's excitement calls to him. The dolphins swim back and forth between the sluggish rowboat and the object of his desire.

Unable to wait any longer, he strips. "Abba, I will see you at home." Calling him mad to dive into the sea amidst dolphins, the sailors know not what he seeks. The promise of her violet hayye brings strength to his limbs as he glides through the water.

Riding Sheikan out to meet him, Mary dives in when he is near. He holds her precious face in his hands before catching his breath. From her usually brilliant green eyes, now gray as the North Sea, a tear escapes, slipping down the silken cheek to rest at the corner of her mouth. Tenderly, he tastes the first drops of the storm.

No words pass between them as he carries her clinging back to shore. Her rich dark flesh soaks him in like the rays of the sun, a flow of sweet nectar carrying him to her core. Through her sensuous form, earth energy merges with the prism of light, pouring like rain from the heavens. With great effort he maintains his rhythm, praying to sustain while the turquoise sea laps at them, washing away the tears, soothing their frenzy. When the final orgasmic wave crashes, the hayye expands taller and wider than ever before. They are as one once more.

"Barchashem," he whispers his gratitude to the Divine into the tender flesh of her throat, "I am finally home." Speechless, she sobs, his kiss of reassurance serving only to reignite her passion. Perhaps this need will never be filled. Searching luscious curves, he rediscovers the fingerprint birthmarks upon the tender flesh of her inner thighs and the elestial quartz glowing radiantly within her navel. He gazes into her eyes to be assured that this is no dream, disturbed by her thoughts laced with concern of a future without him.

Stroking her tangled curls, his hand lingers at the small of her back. "Beloved, there is only this moment. Be here with all of your being." Time now for his gift. With bitter sweetness, he induces wave after wave from his precious wife. The sun reaches its zenith but he does not disengage, delighted by the wonder on her face as he touches aspects never before explored. He smiles at her futile attempt to slow her response, so pleased when passion steals away her breath. An expansion of hayye fills their beings and when he finally succumbs, she nearly faints.

What has he learned while he was away? And how? He is saddened to see her entertain a brief vision of him with a faceless woman.

"There has never been anyone else but you, my love, ever."

Finally she finds her voice thickened with passion. "Forgive me for doubting you, Yeshua, but I am overwhelmed by all this newness."

He kisses away the tears that spill from her eyes. "I apologize for not lasting as long as I planned. I need practice."

"Longer?" She wonders if this is what he went away to learn.

How he missed her! "No, my sweet wife, it is but one of the many gifts from my Druid mentors." Smiling, he says no more.

For the first night in over two years, Yeshua sleeps soundly with his wife wrapped in his arms. In the morning, his second gift interrupts their repose.

Sheikan gallops by, spraying sand upon a large tawny pup with a chewed length of rope trailing behind. Mary opens her arms and the animals cease their play. The pup approaches from under the stallion's hooves to press a muzzle against her breast, brown eyes gazing into green, bonding intimately.

Placing an arm around Mary's shoulder, he strokes the dog's silken ears, "This is Tikva." He blessed her with the Hebrew name—hope of security. Mary shivers remembering the attack in Cana. The pup licks her face. "I cannot leave you unprotected."

A deep sob catches in her throat, and he silently chides himself. "Yeshua, please, I cannot bear the thought of you leaving again." He holds her tenderly while Sheikan digs up sand with a sharp hoof. The pup's confused whine deepens into a warning bark at the approach of a rider.

Teoma delivers his daughter laughing into his arms. Sarah bites his chin with a mouthful of teeth; there were only two when he left.

"I knew it. You taste the same." Choked by emotion, he cannot respond but delight renews. "My puppy has come! Thank you, Abba." Sarah throws her little arms around the dog's neck. Teoma's look of concern is relieved only by Yeshua's grateful embrace.

After a fine supper prepared by his dear friend, Yeshua has the pleasure of putting Sarah to bed. Upon his return, he draws Mary into his lap. Teoma stokes the fire.

"So Yesh, did you accomplish all that you planned?"

"There is still more to do." Feeling his wife stiffen against him, he signals to Teoma that they shall speak later. Mary rises and bids them goodnight, leaving her concern to crash against him. Trailing firelight, she looks in on Sarah before emerging from the tent with the pup. Nickering, the white stallion trots over to join their midnight stroll.

"Tikva? Thought I needed some security reinforcement?" Guilt tarnishes Teoma's humor.

115

"You are not responsible for what happened. We all learned a lesson in forgiveness, including me."

Teoma nods before looking down the beach. Mary lies upon the sand, her head cradled by the pup's tawny body with Sheikan standing watch. Teoma turns back to him. "I am sorry to burden you. I have attempted to find forgiveness, but…."

His words drift off as his mind envisions a swift revenge upon Mary's attacker. Teoma even knows the Roman by name—Lucias. What games have Theudas and Judas played with his dear friend? Standing between two worlds, Teoma's heart is divided.

"Beloved brother, do not join the brute's thorny path of self-hatred. I know your sword has a great lust for vengeance, but your heart can only be healed by love. Forgive yourself. I entrusted her to your care because your love is great. I am most grateful that you were true to your word."

"How can you say this? She was assaulted by my negligence!"

"Mary has grown from the experience, but I was speaking of your fidelity. You breached not my confidence in spite of your desire for her."

"Although I have delighted in the company of your wife and daughter, this by far has been my most difficult assignment." Teoma pauses to glance once again down the beach. "But you have more to do?" The question hovers swollen as a storm cloud.

With a sigh, Yeshua traces patterns of stars within roses upon the sand. "I do not think I can leave her again, yet I am not nearly finished with my preparations."

Nodding, Teoma asks, "So, did you contact Zsao and Reiti?"

He looks up and smiles, "I visited them in person."

"But how? Without Abba Joseph discovering?"

In his youth, Yeshua endured his father's attempts to teach him practical skills. Although approving of the art of combat taught by Reiti, Joseph wished he had shown as much interest in the sword as Teoma did. After finding out that the boys planned a trip to the Hindus region, Joseph whisked him off to Britannia, hoping that the Druid influence would make his son a man.

Returning his attention to his friend, he chuckles, "Abba and Dod Joseph were occupied in search of the secret of eternal life, while Ambrose taught me to use raza to travel in my body to distant places. The Himal range was freezing cold when I studied with Zsao."

"And Reiti? How is he?" Teoma asks, astounded.

"Our Hindus teacher is well. His people are a delight, open to many worlds of possibilities." He is encouraged by Teoma's enthusiasm. "I was even able to teach."

"Already? But Abba Joseph said that you are not ready for...."

"I am well aware of my father's opinion. I have heard only lectures from him these past two years. We do not see eye to eye on what my mission is to be. He agrees with the zealots that I am to lead the tribes against Rome."

Teoma's eyes flash, having trained with these rebels. Like the majority of their oppressed people, Abba hopes for a mashiach that will be a warrior king like unto David, not fully comprehending how his son's message of love will bring peace to this land. At this time, Yeshua is unsure himself.

Across the fire, Teoma sits patiently, well accustomed to his long silent contemplations. Yeshua finally meets the other's piercing blue gaze. "If you could travel to the Hindus and the Himal range, why didn't you visit Mary?"

"Because I could not have returned to my mentors." He leaves Teoma to put out the fire.

Mary lies dark as night upon the pale sand. The energy of the angelic tetrad surrounds her peaceful repose and he senses the message delivered to her this night. Through the passionate and sensual human form, one might connect to Eloha. How well he knows this to be true! Thankfully, his wife was shown that only fear veils her from the One. He carries her to bed, praying that she takes to heart the divine advice.

In the morning, they breakfast at the low table set under a small stand of evergreens. Precious Sarah eats well, but his wife seems to have little appetite. Teoma notices and leans over, "Mary, you can't exist on love alone," tilting her chin up to reveal tears. When Teoma gives her a hug, Yeshua's heart aches.

"Ima is going to miss Dod Teo the most."

Silently, he attends to his daughter, as his wife cries upon another's shoulder. "I won't be gone long," Teoma murmurs.

Mary's thoughts nearly tear Yeshua asunder. *I thought when he returned, I would hardly think about Teoma's absence, but I am replacing one with the other. My lover for my friend. One shares his passion but the other shares his feelings.* A long buried seed awakens to tinge his silvery-white hayye an olive hue.

"Come Sarah, let's go collect seashells." When she slips a tiny hand in his, her golden energy overcomes his despair with delight. Smiling, he begins describing the farmer's great dog far away in Britannia. Her long dark ears attending to his every word, Tikva carries a stick in her mouth. Sarah puts her free arm around the pup's neck.

"Tikva, I can't play now. Abba's telling us a story!"

***

Returning from our glorious holiday at the shore, I experience a sense of uneasiness. Unless Yeshua acquired some extraordinary equestrian skill while up north, I wonder if he is prepared for the wiggling of a three-year-old. Strange that I trusted Teoma implicitly with Sarah's safety, yet feel wary about her own father. Only a week has passed and already I miss Teoma. A streak of tan runs past Sheikan in hot pursuit of a rabbit.

"Tikva!"

Yeshua looks over his shoulder, but it is too late. The rabbit darts beneath his horse, and he struggles to control his mount as the great pup bears down on them. Sarah hits the ground with a loud crack. Leaping off Sheikan, I scramble to her side to find her left arm twisted at an unnatural angle. When I pick her up she cries out in pain. Cradling our daughter in my lap, I pray fervently that her pain be lifted and we be guided as to what to do. Yeshua's guilt-ridden aura softens into mine and Sarah's golden hue begins to merge with ours. She looks up at her father as he prays.

"Abba, my arm hurts. Please fix it."

Smiling, he cups his hands to hold concentrated hayye. I have seen Yeshua ease pain, but never a broken bone, yet Sarah seems to have complete faith as she rests in my arms. Yeshua passes his right hand over my head and I feel an immediate sense of peace. A pillar of white light encompasses us as he takes her bent arm gently in both of his and looks into my eyes. The deep dark liquid of his gaze is fathomless, I feel bathed in Divine Love. Sarah sighs and I look down at her arm. It is perfectly healed, straight and strong.

Crying with relief, I hug Yeshua's neck with Sarah struggling to sit up in my lap. The pup comes crawling up at Sarah's scolding, "You must be more careful, Tikva. We are very fortunate my Abba can fix anything."

When we arrive in Nazareth, the family greets us in the garden. Even with Yeshua's reassurance that all is well, Miriam takes Sarah to see for herself. His siblings throw questions like spears, and he settles them with promises of stories. Yeshua embraces sixteen-year-old Jacob who pulls away red-faced and comes to sit by me.

"Mary, can we talk?" The family makes its way back into the house, and I wave Yeshua inside.

"Certainly, Jacob. What is on your mind?"

Smiling sheepishly, he begins, "Remember when you said that looking into Yeshua's eyes you saw yourself as love. Well, I found my own mirror!"

"Oh Jacob, that is wonderful. You met your love."

"Yes, my mirror is in the eyes of my beloved Rebeka."

Offering my congratulations, I believe that Rebeka is his intended, at least I hope so. For like Yeshua and I, he is not privy to his arranged marriage. His parents desired that he fall in love naturally, arranging enough interactions between the two that the inevitable would happen and thankfully it did.

"Mary, how can you have any private thoughts with Yeshua?"

"Did he embarrass you?" I smile at his shy nod.

"I was noticing how happy you three are together and thought how nice it would be to be married and have children which led me to think about, well...other things."

"Jacob, it is wise for you to think about these things." His eyes beg me to understand. "Especially how wonderful it will be with Rebeka."

His cheeks flush. "But my wandering mind must offend him."

I put my arm around my young brother's waist and tell him confidentially, "I do not believe many people can do what they have not first thought about, so do not think that your thoughts are any less holy than your brother's."

He hesitates to ask, "Do all wives discuss their private affairs so openly?"

"I don't think so. Remember what you taught me about the mirrors of the Essenes?"

Nodding, he completes my lesson, "Our human relationships are the mirrors to our souls. What we see in another is what we believe ourselves to be." With the gifts of a Tana, Jacob remembers everything he has ever learned. I just wish he had more confidence in himself.

119

"You are beloved, full of fire and passion, full of love and compassion, wise beyond your years. Be gentle with yourself for it is not easy to be in human form. I know." Well aware of my suffering, he embraces me.

At the sound of a gruffly cleared throat, Jacob hastily stands up. Laughing, Yeshua slaps him on the back. "Brother, you really must approach that sweet Rebeka of yours soon. I cannot keep lending you my wife." Poor Jacob reddens as he pauses to thank me, before taking his leave.

"You just returned—must you torment him so?"

He laughs, "You should have seen what was on his mind."

"You should not abuse your gift. Give him some privacy. Don't you remember where your mind was at his age?"

Sitting, he kisses me passionately and slips a sly hand up my sadin, "I seem to remember it being right about here."

"Well, that's what I told him."

Yeshua looks at me wide-eyed, "What and ruin my reputation with my adoring brother?"

"Just bringing you down to earth so your fellow human beings, including your beloved brother, can learn to be like you."

He shakes his head, more serious now. "I am not perfect."

"I know. No one but you expects you to be."

His eyes are sad, "Since we've been married, I have made a lot of mistakes and have caused you much grief." My lips tighten, for it is true. "I wonder sometimes if it would have been better to stay single and not be in danger of hurting anyone so dear to me."

"Yeshua, most people choose to live life in relationship with others, including intimate relationships. As long as we learn from our mistakes, I cannot believe that we are not seen as worthy by the Creator."

Our embrace is only interrupted by Jacob. "Come on you two, the rest of the family is waiting to begin the meal." When we rise to join him, he looks straight at Yeshua. "Your example is comforting, brother, thank you." Winking at me, he hurries just beyond us.

Yeshua and I lie on our marriage bed tucked together, our favorite sleeping position. Since he has returned, I feel amorous all the time, especially the past two days. Kissing the back of my neck, he growls, "You smell so inviting."

Our lovemaking has an urgent quality, perhaps still reminiscent of our separation, but I sense something otherwise. As the waves of climax wash over us, he pulls me ever closer, and my womb feels full, crampy. After a languorous doze, he withdraws. "Uh, oh, time to change the linens."

After washing up and gathering the linens, I begin collecting a few personal things and place them in a pouch. "Where are you going?" Yeshua draws me upon his lap, caressing my lower belly. "I should have recognized that enticing aroma you give off right before your menses. I wonder why I am so much more attracted to you at this time."

I smile, "Perhaps because you sense that you will have to wait to have me again for a few days." Not smiling, his grip tightens.

"What do you mean?"

"Yeshua, I am going to the chamam."

"But you didn't do this when we first got married."

"I know and I am delighted that you do not find me unclean but now I look forward to joining in the rituals." He's clearly disappointed so I try to make light of it. "Strange, how most of the women are there at the same time."

He groans, "I noticed that."

"Really?"

"Yes, we men are on our own while you women congregate." Laughing, I imagine the men floundering in their attempt to take care of the household. "So what am I supposed to do?"

"We can still meet in the ethers."

"But I am here now," he pitifully pleads.

"It might be a good time to fast and pray." As I rise, he ardently tries to change my mind. Between kisses, I beg, "Please. I need to do this." Reluctantly, he lets me go.

When I bid Sarah goodbye in the nursery, Hava senses my mood. "I am pleased that you are coming into your own." I look down, feeling a bit overwhelmed. "I know it was difficult for you to be apart from Yeshua," she tilts up my chin, "but it is important that you respect your femininity in this way."

"I have enjoyed my time in the chamam and want to set an example for Sarah."

She kisses me. "This time is for you now, remember that. Live in the moment. Do not worry about the future."

How difficult it is to relax in the chamam this time. With my husband just across the courtyard, I can hardly sleep. Yeshua would never come in to retrieve me, but he does not hesitate to send Sarah in with piteous messages. "Ima, Abba misses you this much," she claims, flinging her arms so wide, the rest of the women giggle. "Why don't you come out and play with us, Ima? Abba has another gift for you."

"Tell Abba that I will join him soon, but right now I am busy taking care of myself." I send my daughter off with a stuffed date.

Late in the second evening after a luxurious soak and a sensual massage, Miriam and Hava come to sit on my bed. "Mary, this is the first time you have used the chamam with Yeshua home, isn't it?" I nod. "Is my son giving you a hard time?"

"Yes, Ima. Did you talk with him?"

"No, but we heard about Sarah's messages." There are no secrets in this house. Hava gently questions me about my family rituals regarding menstruation.

"No man could touch me or anything I touched during my unclean period. For seven days a month I was shut away."

Aware of the Tzadokim tradition, she nods and takes my hand. "The rituals can only be honored in joy. They are not meant to make you suffer." Looking up, she invites Miriam to share her thoughts.

"Yeshua is a lot like his father—his desire for you overcomes his good sense."

Not understanding their Chaverim interpretation of halacha, I frown. "So what should I do? I was torn between my strict upbringing and delight that Yeshua did not find me unclean, but when he left and I was invited to join you in the chamam, I finally learned to delight in **all** aspects of my femininity..."

Sighing, Hava advises, "Dear, you must follow your heart."

"Oh Hava, I want to be with him, but I do not want to give this up. Besides he will leave me again…"

"Mary, if you return to him tonight," Miriam caresses my cheek drawing a smile from my lips, "and express your gratitude for his patience with your absence, perhaps next time he will be a bit more gracious about your monthly respite."

So under the light of the full moon, I cross the courtyard armed with advice. When I crawl into bed, my husband pulls me close. "I want to thank you for allowing me to join the women."

"Sorry to use Sarah to bring you back. I'm not very patient." At his heartening apology, my desire descends, but he pulls me up to face him. "I can wait until you are ready. Just being next to me is comfort enough."

A giggling Sarah awakens us in the morning. "Ima, you're back!" I kiss her sweet face, still in her nightgown, hair tousled from sleep. "Good morning, Abba. Did you give Ima her gift?" She sits on his chest. "Ima?" her brow wrinkles, "are you all finished bleeding?"

"Not yet, dear."

"Then why are you not with the other women?"

I touch her nose, "Because I missed Abba." She smiles patting his cheek.

"Abba missed you, too." Leaning, she sniffs my neck, "Mmm. Doesn't Ima smell good?" He nods. "The other women rub oil all over her body. That's what I want too when I am big!"

"Next time Ima should stay as long as she needs to, don't you think, Sarah?"

"Yes, then you can spend all your time with me!" So grateful, I kiss them both.

On a brisk morning in Cheshvan, I awaken from a strange dream. In front of six people dressed in black, Yeshua and I conceive a son. I wish to tell him, but since last Shabbat when he met with his father we have not spoken. What did they discuss?

Moaning, he rolls over, "My dynastic obligation as heir to the Davidic throne—to sire a son born in the month of kings," bitter for he was born six months too early to be considered a legitimate heir.

"Yeshua, what's really the matter?"

"Royal conception must be witnessed to satisfy both political and religious factions." I do not blink an eye. He frowns, "We cannot use kasa to veil ourselves."

"Just like in my dream," I smile, but he does not.

"So you are comfortable with ALL the witnesses?"

I think so. Lightening pain flashes in the depth of his eyes and I realize that Teoma will be one. Does Yeshua believe that without the veil, my relationship with his friend might become physical? If only he would tell me his feelings.

Pulling me close, his caresses impart what his tongue refuses. "Five days before the ceremony, I cannot spill my seed."

123

"So we are to be separated?"

Lips meeting mine, he whispers into my mouth, "I think my Druid training shall prove most useful." Although my body responds to his touch, my heart desires more.

I pull away. "Please, can't we talk?"

He nuzzles my breasts murmuring, "We will, after."

I think not, I will be too besotted to think clearly and nothing will get said. "Yeshua, I am your wife, but not your friend."

"That is not true. We have been friends since childhood."

"Teoma is your friend. You tell him about your life, your concerns, your journey to Britannia. To me you say nothing, so I must pick through your half explanations and teasing to glean any truth."

Sighing he lies back. "What did you and Teoma discuss before he left?"

"We discussed this very thing. Teoma said you cannot live what you believe to be two realities at once, so you keep your mission separate from your marriage. He suggested that someday you might know them to be merged."

His smile is laced with sorrow, "Our future shall be painfully challenging." I start to question what he sees, but he places a finger across my lips. "Please, I just want to hold you or else I shall say too much." Am I so fragile in my husband's eyes that he chooses to bear the burden alone?

***

A fine bead of sweat escapes the turban to trickle down the ridge of his brow. The desert of Perea threatens to roast him. Traveling alone dressed in Roman garb has been nearly as dangerous as crossing the Jordan. In the lands ruled by the Roman procurator, native men protect what is Caesar's, but here in Antipas' eastern territory, legionnaires fraternize with Herodians and the people despise them both. After gathering information necessary to intercept supplies bound for the legions, Teoma was released by Theudas. His Roman mannerisms have served the zealot forces well.

Bright color disturbs the drab terrain—the zealot encampment. Urging his steed onward with the promise of water, he reaches his comrades in short time.

"Let me pass. I have correspondence from King Hillel."

The sallow-faced guard moves aside, bitterly mumbling, "Roman mamzer!"

Swiftly, Teoma unsheathes his long sword to render the blue sash about the Judite's torso in two. "Crudely mistaken: my father *married* my mother." Before the severed sash touches the dirt, Teoma dismounts in front of the commander's tent.

"Is it necessary to molest my guards?" Judas chides, kissing the younger man's cheek. Before Teoma can explain, a cup of shekar is thrust into his hands. Downing the cool fermented barley drink, Teoma smiles gratefully.

"Apparently your passion wasn't spent in the temple."

After delivering Joseph's correspondence to King Hillel in Qumran, Teoma paid homage to Astarte, but even the fair priestesses could not quell his yearning. Handing over the scroll, he waits while Judas reads Hillel's message.

"Ananias has been deposed. How dare Tiberius interfere! The Sanhedrin reforms to suit the oppressor. What games is our ill-begotten emperor playing?" Judas stands abruptly, crumpling the scroll in one fist, tugging at his beard with the other. Dark eyes alight on Teoma. "It is time to put your fervor to good use. Pay close heed to my eldest son; Aaron will be in charge of the campaign." Teoma harkens at this news. Perhaps now he might finally see some action. "Please take care. I do not wish to send you back to Galilee injured."

Well-respected as his father, Aaron proves to be a fine leader over the next two months. Under the cover of darkness, the zealots sneak into Herodian camps, setting fire to the Roman military supplies, then stealing weapons and valuables in the guise of common bandits. Just northeast of Babylonia, the rebels invade the last known encampment before separating into small groups to avoid being tracked. Riding far behind the others, Teoma remembers the lush valley between the great rivers—the home of Eden, wishing he could have visited the ancient city of Babylonia.

Sharp voices interrupt his thoughts. An elderly woman struggles to upright her toppled handcart, but his comrades give her wide berth. Teoma quickly rides up and dismounts to assist her with the heavily laden cart perfumed like Joseph's secret sanctuary.

125

The men chide, "Let her be, she's a sorceress," but he turns from his pious companions to receive her gratitude. The woman takes his arm; she is blind.

"Let me take you home, grandmother."

"No, my son. I have traveled this way all of my life. I know this road like my own palm." Her vacant eyes hold his and unable to tear away, he clasps her gnarled hands, yearning to understand. "Someday you shall return to discover your origins," she whispers before turning her head to take the vision with her. He swallows thickly, for he was not alone in Eden.

The woman travels east. His comrades flee west toward the river. Torn, Teoma wishes to pursue his destiny but it is mid-Cheshvan and duty calls. Once again he is expected to bear witness to a sacred event. He gathers the courage flowing through his half-Roman blood and heads home to Galilee.

Half a moon cycle later, his mare prances excitedly at the sight of the white stallion galloping over the crest of Nazareth ridge. Before their mounts fully stop, they leap off into each other's arms. He holds her a long time, not saying a word.

The aroma of lemon and sandalwood penetrates his senses. Grateful now that he stopped at that spring in Esdraelon, he brushes his newly-shaven cheek against her silken curls. She ends their embrace by pushing away to look at him. Her green gaze soaks him in as a smile graces her lovely face.

"Teoma, it is so good to have you back home."

She cannot imagine how difficult it is to be away. His voice is gruff with emotion, "I missed you and our involved discussions." She trembles, perhaps missing him as much. Trying to break the tension, he asks about the child. "How is Sarah?"

"Wonderful. She said to give you a kiss." She stands on tiptoe and he bends down with turned cheek, but she kisses his mouth. For a delicious moment he slips into Eden. This kiss is not from the child.

***

It is the kiss from my dreams. The kiss I wanted to give him before I married. A kiss I will never forget. A vision occurs, one of a dark-haired child. Our son. A surge of desire burns through the center of my being.

126

Slowly I pull away, gasping, unprepared for the depth of my reaction. I search his eyes.

Smiling down at me, he says hoarsely. "This is why I did not kiss you that night at Yeshua's party. If you would have responded, you may have made the wrong choice."

"What do you mean? I wanted to know just this. I could have married the man who would be my friend."

He holds me now at arms' length, as if any closer and this fire I started will consume us both. "Yet I am not your destiny. With Yeshua, you have much to offer the world in your willingness to bring in the sacred feminine and soon another child."

"You know about the next ceremony?" Swallowing, he nods. The sky-blue of his eyes reveal nothing more. "Yeshua is not comfortable with your presence, Teoma."

"Can you blame him?" He sighs, "You are all he has to ground him to this Earth. You hold a critical place in his mission."

"But he tells me nothing, not trusting me with his feelings. He doesn't want to share me with the world, but I must share him. I know this innately."

"Beloved, you will have to surrender him to the world if he is to complete his work."

The vision of the dark-haired child causes me to tremble, "Teoma, what about us?"

"It is not our time, dear."

We ride back in silence, our hearts heavy, burdened by an unknown future. Neither of us speaks of the kiss.

Dynastic Obligation

"In the great forests of the north live many wolves. They are very powerful hunters who live in packs but only the strongest and most beautiful male and female have babies called cubs." Sarah lies mesmerized between us in the hammock as Yeshua tells a story one autumn afternoon.

"Once there were two brother wolves who wanted the same beautiful mate. Both were good hunters, but she could choose only one, and the pair had beautiful cubs every year, which their pack helped raise. Being the cleverest hunter of all, the father wolf would lead the pack in hunting enough to feed his family.

"Unfortunately, the mother wolf could not protect herself and her babies while the father was off hunting. So father wolf asked brother wolf to stay and take care of his family. Sometimes the hunting trips were very short and sometimes the game was far away and the pack had to be gone a long time before finding enough food. Those times the brother wolf had to hunt for the mother so she could feed the cubs. She always thanked him and father wolf was grateful too." I listen intently, wondering how many of his stories contain hidden truth.

"Eventually, the food got scarce and father wolf had to take the pack very far to hunt. Mother wolf had a brand new litter of cubs, so brother wolf stayed to protect them. Unfortunately father wolf did not return. A human hunter killed him for his beautiful coat." Sarah gasps, as I stifle a cry.

"But Abba what about the cubs?"

"Brother wolf continued to take care of the cubs and the mother until they were grown. The next mating season, mother wolf chose brother wolf to be the father of her cubs."

Sarah smiles, "It was good that the father wolf left his brother to protect them or the mother and her cubs would have died too. Right, Abba?"

"Yes, dear," he hugs her to him, "Why don't you go play with Ruth and Esther?"

Wiping my cheeks with her small hand, Sarah whispers, "Don't cry, Ima, Abba will be fine."

Yeshua holds me, but I cannot imagine living without him, even with brother wolf. He kisses me tenderly, "It's just a story, dear."

"But it's based on truth and you told it to teach a lesson."

"And what did you learn?"

My voice catches in my throat, "I knew why you left Teoma behind, but I didn't think anything would happen to you. That part is just a story, isn't it?"

His eyes soften. "It is all a story invented for children. If it teaches a lesson then I am pleased. This lesson is about being prepared, that is all." I search his eyes: that is not all. "Do not mourn tomorrow, be in this moment." He carries me off to our chambers. No more talking, no more stories.

Since her father's homecoming, Sarah enters our bedchambers every morning to greet us. Yeshua adores her, wanting each moment to last as if storing memories for his next journey. In late Cheshvan, we both awaken before dawn and soon he is under the linens enacting our arousing dream.

Just as I cry out my pleasure, Sarah's little face peeks over the bed. Nearly decapitating Yeshua, I attend to our daughter. "Sweetheart, what are you doing up so early?" Yeshua groans.

"Why is Abba hiding under the covers?"

In a flourish he reappears, somehow without exposing us both, "Because I was tickling Ima and now it is your turn." Pulling her upon the bed, he tickles her until she begs him to stop. Later we breakfast with Hava, while Sarah plays in the nursery. "Although Mary and I both enjoy Sarah's company immensely, it is time that we set some boundaries."

"I was wondering when you would ask that her early morning greetings be curtailed."

Yeshua smiles back at his wise mentor, "We have been fine until this morning."

"Your thoughts create reality, as you both know. Yeshua, since you desire to spend as much time as possible with her, she is drawn to you in your waking moments, especially when you are joyful." I chuckle at his flushed face. "After consciously not desiring her presence every moment, then you must set some limits on her behavior."

"Hava, the staff must realize that we need our private time, so how is it she can slip away without anyone stopping her?"

Her laughter incites ours. "Mary, like both of you, she is quite naturally gifted at the art of using kasa." Clearly we underestimated our little girl.

Yeshua spends the next day in his father's shop fashioning a small sundial. The following afternoon, we meet in the garden. Sarah admires the small wooden instrument. "What is it?"

Taking her hand, he leads her beyond the trees into the bright sunlight and shows her how the afternoon sun casts a shadow on the sundial's face. "Why are you giving this to me, Abba?"

He motions to me over her head to come and sit by them, "Ima and I are concerned about you getting up so early in the morning. We know that you want to be with us and we want to be with you, but you need your sleep." She looks to me.

"Yes, love, if you don't get enough sleep at night, then you'll have to take even longer naps during the day."

"I don't like naps!" She says emphatically.

I want her to understand something more. "Sarah, when I was very little like you, sometimes I wanted to be somewhere else, like outside or with my sister, and I would wish that no one could see me so I could go to where I wanted to be."

"Me too, Ima! When I want to be with you and Abba in the morning, I…" she lowers her voice to a barely audible pitch, "disappear." For a long moment she holds her breath. "Even Hava cannot see me." Looking up at her father, she asks hesitantly, "Abba, are you angry?"

He hugs her close, "No, baby, but I worry that you might not be safe if you disappear from those who are taking care of you."

"All right, Abba, I will not sneak away from my Hava."

The shortening winter days bring us closer to Chanuka and the conception of our son. As Yeshua's grandfather is the king of the tribe of

Judah, a huge entourage of soldiers and staff precedes his arrival and must be accommodated. With dark drapes around her bed, Sarah sleeps in longer but since the royal couple rests in our chambers, we find ourselves with her in the crowded nursery.

The women have expressed grave concern that Yeshua shares my bed, but they know not of his Druid abilities. I yearn to be out on the land and away from their harping, but when I ask my husband to join me on a ride, he shakes his head, "I can't, my love, Abba and Saba want to discuss the proceedings for the solstice with me. Have Teoma join you." Oh, but the women will have that much more to fuss over.

Since the guests arrived, Tikva has been banished to the stable so we bring her along. Cresting the farthest hill in sight of the house, we slow our mounts to talk. Tikva has run her excitement down, only half-heartedly chasing small game.

"So, Mary, tomorrow's the big day. How are you holding up?"

I smile at Teoma's concern. "Perhaps I'm maturing. Other's expectations are not so upsetting."

"You mean your mother's?"

"Yes, and now she has Yeshua's grandmother on her side. Poor Miriam has had to rescue me from quite a few of their concerns." I pause, "If they knew I was out with you now, we would both be banished from the ceremony."

"Only me. There would be no celebration without you!"

Riding well, Teoma has the short gladius at his waist as well as a long ornately adorned sword on his mount. There seems to be no potential for violence in my gentle friend, but I will not forget how swift and furiously he came to my defense.

"You are such a sweet and gentle soul, yet you wear those weapons like they are natural appendages. Why don't you let me teach you how to use kasa to protect yourself, then you would not have to depend on your weapons."

"Don't think Joseph hasn't tried. I'm more gifted with my senses than the hayye."

"That's not true. You have an innate ability to calm others with your energy."

He smiles at me gratefully, "I suppose I can try again. We should head back or we'll be late for the lighting of the menorah."

As we pass the craggy rocks hiding the secret place, I ask, "When does Abba Joseph have time to practice his craft?"

Teoma looks sharply at me, "Did Yeshua tell you?" I nod. "It's time to return!" He reins his horse around. Sheikan rears and gallops through an overgrown trail. I lie low against his neck, but my back is scraped. Ignoring the injury, I race to catch Teoma.

"Mary, what happened? You're bleeding."

I shrug, "I must have misjudged the clearance under that tree."

Teoma brings his mount closer. "Mary, your sadin is getting soaked." We dismount and he uses his sword to expose the wound. From a leather pouch, he extracts clean cloth to stop the bleeding. He's concerned, but the wound is not painful. "Mary, the pressure isn't working. It's quite deep."

"Teoma, focus hayye from your heart into your hands. Imagine that it is a great forest green bandage staunching the blood." He is uncertain. I turn to face him, the wetness on my naked back chilling me in the winter air. Taking his hands in mine, I pray that he will find the healer within and trust his divine ability.

When I look up he's smiling. "I'll try, Mary."

I demonstrate holding concentrated hayye and soon energy faintly swirls between his hands. "Now when I turn around, imagine that my bleeding has already ceased and I will do the same. Hold your hands over my wound swirling them slowly as if you are sewing it closed." I turn my back to him.

"Oh, my goodness, it's working!" Whispering as if speaking any louder will break the spell, he winds my shawl around my chest to hold the cloth bandages in place. When we get back, Teoma asks the stable hands to assist with the animals. "Mary, you won't be able to hide this tomorrow."

"No, it will not even be visible. Find Yeshua, he will heal it."

I wait quietly in the nursery until Yeshua arrives with Teoma in his wake, "You taught Teoma how to perform a healing." He kisses me before unwinding the bandages.

"Well, Yeshua, you said it was a matter of faith."

"I'm afraid it needs more," Teoma sighs as my back is bared.

Yeshua pats his shoulder, "You did good work, but the witnesses will think I had her whipped," whispering in my ear, "not that you don't deserve it for being so reckless."

"Please, Yesh, can you just repair the damage and return me to my former unmarred self?" Teoma shakes his head. "It cannot be that bad, nothing compared to Sarah's broken arm."

Teoma relaxes only after Yeshua lays a hand on his head. Warmth radiates within the wound, first burning like fire, then immediately cooling. Teoma drops to his knees, "It's vanished!"

Yeshua helps him back up, "Here," handing him the bloodied bandages, "work your magic on that sweet laundress. She shall surely offer her assistance if you but smile at her." Teoma leaves to find Edia.

"Why won't he speak of your father's craft?"

My husband raises a brow, "You rode by the rocks today?" I nod. "Teoma takes his duties quite seriously. It is an honor to keep the family secret." I wonder if my husband visits the secret place. Yeshua shakes his head, "I have no interest in using sacred herbs to seek Eloha."

"Does he?"

He smiles. "Well, since both Jacob and I have refused our legacy, Abba thought it was best to teach Teoma the craft."

"What is the craft?"

"First I must swear you to secrecy." I give him my hand, but he kisses it, before whispering, "It is the secret of eternal life."

Wrinkling my brow, I ask, "But why don't you have any interest in this craft?"

"I believe that love is eternal. The craft of my forefathers has been handed down from father to son since the time of Solomon. But perhaps Abba should instruct you since the great king learned it from his wife."

"Is Solomon still alive?"

Yeshua's laughter fills the nursery. "I do not believe so! But the Essenes have been studying with the Egyptian Therapeutae trying to recover the knowledge."

"So if the knowledge was lost, then what is passed down?"

"Whatever each generation gathers from their travels studying with masters from other cultures is taught to the next. They protect the secret believing that it could be misused, so you must not share this with the Emperor!"

Certainly, my husband thinks the pursuit a folly. "Yeshua, didn't Solomon leave his kingdom by way of the Red Sea?"

"So it is said. Some believe he sailed away to some distant land, but I have heard that his final resting place was Aksum!"

Excitedly, I suggest, "Belshazzar is the king of Aksum, perhaps Solomon shared the knowledge with his forefathers!"

Yeshua draws me into his arms, "Perhaps not the fathers but the mothers." With a resounding kiss, he silences my further inquiry and leads me to the baths to prepare for the last gathering before the solstice.

After prayers and the lighting of the menorah, the feast is served. Although wine is served, I do not partake, but it enhances the festivities. Music begins, men and women dancing separately, yet when Joseph plays some foreign melodies, the guests become hesitant.

"Come, Mary, show them how delightful the dances of the northern clans can be." Abba rarely asks anything of me, so I oblige him with a nod, unsure of what he speaks. "Just follow the rhythm of the music, while I hold the image of the solstice celebration."

Joseph plays sensuously and soon my body, unguided by my mind, partners with his beautiful flute. To the drumming in my head, I begin gathering hayye from the earth and delivering it skywards. Then reversing the movements, I bless the earth from the heavens. Before me a vision unfolds: a great forest with large men and women dancing about me. How I wish to have the others join me, but no one does. I yearn for accompanying instruments and Saul steps forward with a lyre, Jacob with a deeper-throated flute, and Shimon on a large drum. Miriam joins Hava in a song-like chant, their voices lovely instruments. It is time now for my partner to join me.

Dancing the inner perimeter of the room, I feel Yeshua's eyes on me. Gracefully, I bow, my loose hair skimming his feet. He lifts me up and my lone dance becomes magnified, the two as one. Floating away sensuously along the length of his arms, before, with a touch of his fingertips, I return to his core. Again and again, from his chest to his back, following his spiraling movements, into the heart of the room, dancing with the energies burning through the heavens. Reaching our zenith, the music stops abruptly.

My heart beats rapidly, breath shallow, body drenched, clinging to my husband. He kisses me as if we are alone. So intoxicated with the energies, I feel no one else. The guests part like grain by a scythe as he carries me out to the atrium.

On the hammock, I cry out in my need, but he focuses only on controlling his passion. Every part of me yearns for him. This is agony, harder than being apart. Perhaps the mothers were right.

"No! They were not." Yeshua whispers hoarsely, his desire slowly softening against my belly. "By tomorrow morning, after five days of abstaining, we will not care who is watching us. We will make love with abandon, pleasing both factions surely." I might laugh, if not for the tears.

The music begins again; perhaps the guests finally dance as the northern clan. Some of the elders wander into the atrium. We lay quietly, protected by kasa. My parents walk with Yeshua's grandparents, enjoying the cool night air after the heat of the gathering room.

My mother speaks, "I must apologize for my daughter; she cannot control her passion."

Queen Shoshana answers, "The music was quite riveting and our son did invite her to demonstrate the northern dance."

Shaking her head, Ima wrings her hands. When King Hillel speaks, his voice is hoarse, "Woman, my wife and I have come to know your daughter more intimately during this visit and it is clear that Yeshua has found his match."

Yeshua stifles a chuckle. "Yesh, what is it? Your grandfather sounds upset."

"It is apparent that you have aroused his passion as well."

My cheeks feel hot, "What are you saying?"

He turns me to face him. "At this moment, every man who witnessed your dance burns with desire." Thankfully my father is silent. "I'm afraid, my love, that we will be the only ones not pleasuring ourselves tonight."

"But many of the guests came alone and…."

"Don't…now our witnesses will be quite relaxed tomorrow." Imagining who will sleep with whom, I get stuck on the Seer and Teoma. Yeshua laughs, "Well, undoubtedly not together, but then you never know."

I slap him playfully, "Yesh, she could be his grandmother."

"Do not worry, Teoma will have his choice tonight."

Smoothing our garments and unveiling, we reenter the gathering room. Thankfully, Yeshua's arm supports me. Most of the guests are, in fact, coupled off, including Teoma and Edia. I wonder if Joseph has some sort of herb to protect against unwanted pregnancies.

Yeshua whispers, "As a matter of fact, Abba did return from Britannia with some interesting ingredients for just this purpose. It is mixed in the wine for those who choose to partake." Thank goodness, we did not. He laughs, "In the north, our little ceremony is quite popular at the solstice. As the celebrations became more arousing, the women healers discovered a means to control conception." He projects an image to me of…oh my goodness…erotic intimacy with many people, enjoying each other regardless of gender.

"Yeshua, is this true?" He nods, smiling suggestively. "Wait! How would you know this?"

"Just as you do, through images. Needless to say, I surely looked forward to our communion during this time of year." And I thought he missed me more at the holidays.

We find Sarah dancing with her little aunts and scoop her up before thanking Miriam and Joseph for the wonderful day. Holding our daughter makes bidding goodnight easier. Joseph's father actually kisses my cheek and thanks me for stirring "an old man's heart." Yeshua reminds me again that it is not his heart I stirred. My mother's goodnight is curt, but my father holds me long enough to make me realize that he just now sees me as a woman and not his little girl.

Nearly running into Teoma and Edia in the atrium, I try to be gracious, and hug them, as does Sarah in her half stupor. Yeshua says something to Teoma who hurriedly leads Edia away in the direction of the wine.

The solstice dawns bright and after preparations in the sacred mikvah, we enter the inner sanctum. As we approach the altar, the elestial quartz glows hotly. Dressed in a white silk robe embroidered with five petal roses, I feel very sensuous indeed. Softly curling down my back, my hair is adorned by a crown of white flowers, my skin sweetly scented with sandalwood and lemon. Although there are only the six witnesses, the spirit of each and every one in the household blesses us with love.

The women lay their hands on my head, praying that the child I shall conceive be healthy, strong, and able to fulfill his destiny while I, as his mother, am blessed with wisdom and love. I wonder if Yeshua has been blessed as well, when he appears so handsome in his silken white robe embroidered with stars, a silver crown upon his head. Yeshua incites my yearning. The tallest man, obviously Joseph, rings a small silver bell inviting us to the altar. At the six corners of the intersecting triangles, the witnesses welcome us by singing a fertility blessing.

We enter the inner circle to pray. "Marya, blessed are we to represent the coming together of the spiritual and earthly energies. May the Divine sanctify our union. May our sacred act culminate in the bringing of new life unto this earth. May our son be one with All That Is, created in love. Ameyn."

"Mary and I would like to invite the hayye of our child to this union. Will you please join hands and complete the circle."

Our witnesses comply and the hayye swirls in a translucent pulsation. Entering from the north Yeshua drops his robe and sits upon the altar facing me, his breath slow in meditative focus. The energy, swirling sensuously around the room, in one breath is within me. Circling the inner ring, I pause to grace the witnesses with a smile. Each has a unique aura like those at our wedding, all the colors of the rainbow.

Slowly I drop my robe, my great desire blurring the watchers from my consciousness. When I raise my arms, a silver light flutters into the prism of hayye. Hovering over the amazed witnesses, our son dances about his father, before entering my heart. Yeshua smiles and rises to lift me upon the altar.

Kneeling, we cup each other's face to connect through our gaze. The liquid portal of his eyes draws me into his core where I exist as love. Carefully lifting the crown of flowers from my hair, he places it to his left. I remove his silver crown after kissing the center of his bowed head. A small cry escapes from my throat as he kisses me deeply.

He crushes my breasts against his chest, but I firmly push him back upon the altar. Five days of him joyously pleasuring me has left an indelible impression. With my dark curls, I draw stars on his skin, kissing his mouth, lightly brushing myself against him until he is gasping, realizing that he has waited so long, but not yet. Tracing a line to his groin, I seek to greet the essence of our son.

One at a time, I delicately taste the keepers of the seed. His moans invite me to the shaft of his desire, but he tolerates my ministrations only a delicious moment before drawing me up. His eyes beg for release so I comply, slowly encircling, my breath rapid and shallow. Dancing to my own rhythm, I try to pace myself, but his response overwhelms me. As I move from circles, to infinite spirals, the hayye shifts again.

The tetrahedron of nura—divine enlightenment—appears. We are lifted into the light of the One, embracing in spirit form, as our bodies continue a more frantic pace, time slowing to nothingness. The One speaks with a host of angels surrounding all.

Yeshua and Mary, my light and my joy, joined together for this life and beyond. As embodiments of the Divine Son and Divine Daughter, you are the passion that graces this humanity. Blessed is your love for one another. As you have accepted Sarah—my delight—into your life, I bless you with yet another most precious to me: Joshua holds within the seed of potential for all men. Please return with my blessings to your Earthly dimension.

As we reenter our bodies, they explode with light; the rainbow of color emanating from our witnesses encircles us, expanding greatly. With each thrusting release of seed, the rainbow moves outward, beyond the room, the house, the property, the shoreline, the world beyond my comprehension. I am connected with every light wave souls travel to embody. A gem cast upon the waters of life, the ripples moving outwards to eternity.

My climax going beyond his, crying out, tears pour down my face. The beauty of Love experienced in the presence of the One is magnified by the searing pain of separation from All That Is. Collapsed on Yeshua's chest, sobs flooding my heart, I know now what it is to be separated from Eloha for I have experienced union with the Creator. Every time I have cried in pain and joy intermingled with orgasm, at once emotional and spiritual as it is physical, I have gotten a taste of the Divine. A sweet kiss, a hug and then a quick release and I fall back into the dense realm of this world, alone but not. For in the eyes of my beloved Yeshua, I see myself as Eloha sees me. I am Love.

Yeshua seeks to comfort me, as the silent witnesses are cast in the unifying rainbow of light. Finally, finally, my tears cease, the sobbing quiets. "Beloved Mary, please, please come back." His voice grounds me and my hayye settles into my body through my heart, but I am not alone.

I look down at my belly and Yeshua follows my gaze. "Barchashem! Joshua resides in your precious womb!" Holding me tenderly, he whispers prayers of gratitude.

The witnesses stand still, their energy brightening in recognition of our son's essence. Even the king with his orange aura, between Hava and the Seer, focuses on Joshua's hayye. Teoma looks intently at me and I smile back. Miriam hands us our robes.

As Yeshua and I walk from the inner sanctum to the nursery, we are congratulated by family, staff, and guests. Placing a hand over my womb, I sigh and Yeshua pulls me closer, kissing the top of my head. "Our son. It is amazing being in love with you, living this existence so connected."

The nursery bustles with playing children. With all her grandparents gathered for the holidays, Sarah has been deluged with beautiful new toys, but she prefers Yeshua's old ark. Teoma carved a new giraffe when the original suffered a broken neck before Yeshua acquired healing skills.

She places her two small hands on my lower belly. "Hello, Joshua. It's me, Sarah." The baby's hayye dances with delight as her golden aura encompasses his silver hue.

Yeshua squats at her side, "Do you know your new brother?"

She smiles at him, without removing her hands. "Yes, Abba, Joshua and I were together before coming here."

Looking up at me then again at her, he asks, "Where were you before, Sarah?"

"Don't you remember, Abba? We were with the Light." She smiles, "Come, Ima." We are expected to lunch in the atrium so we kiss Yeshua goodbye. A cathartic premonition steals over me as I fix her hair. Sarah wiggles around and looks up, "Savta needs to be with you."

Sighing, I set my intentions to receive the blessings of the afternoon with my mother. "And you shall have a wonderful time playing with your grandparents."

"The king and queen won't be much fun with the rest there."

I smile at her concern, "Sometimes grownups think they have to act a certain way around other grownups. Perhaps you can entertain Saba for me." She loves my father.

A large fire roars in the pit with savory meat roasting for our meal. The children play happily and even Joseph's parents join in with Sarah's encouragement, seated of course, not sprawled on the blankets like Abba.

At the northeast corner of the atrium far from the bustle, Ima sits a bit forlorn. Her petite figure cloaked in apricot silk, a creamy headdress covering her fine sable hair, she is a striking woman.

"Ima, you look very nice today."

With a wave, she dismisses my compliment, but I sit and take her hand. She looks at me startled, "What is it, Mary?"

Since gratitude works with men, perhaps it might soften my mother. "I want to thank you for spending the holidays with us." Her eyes narrow with suspicion. "Really, Ima, I don't express my appreciation for you enough. I want you to know that I love you."

"Mary, you know I want the best for you." I nod, although we have different opinions about what is best. "Your relationship with Yeshua is like a very hot fire, how long can it last?" I am guided to listen. "A very different life than most young women, with your disregard for tradition, you are in danger of being burned by this fire." She looks at me but I hold my tongue. "It is going to be very difficult for you when Yeshua comes into power. He will not be accepted by the majority…I fear you will be hurt." I nod, trying to perceive the root of her fear. "Mary, as deeply as you love, you will surely suffer as deeply."

"But, Ima, I do not want to live a life without passion. Perhaps I do love Yeshua so intensely that I may suffer a broken heart someday. But I want fervor, so I'm willing to experience life fully to pave the way for my daughter and her children. I believe this is how the Creator intended women to be."

My mother's eyes well and I squeeze her hand. "When I look at you, especially with Yeshua, I realize how much I have missed."

Her hayye is so sad. "Ima?"

"No, Mary, it is my lot in life." Holding me at arm's length, she sighs, "Seeing your joy last night made me…" she hesitates, "I have not had that with your Abba."

My heart might break for her, for them, "But why not, Ima?"

"Perhaps I never really found enjoyment in my marriage bed and your father spent so much time away…."

"But, Ima, if you love Abba, how…?"

"Your Abba has been a wonderful father, but I suppose I was never in love with him. Our marriage was arranged for the benefit of both of our families, but…."

No wonder I thought myself an oddity; compared to my mother, I am. But I know in my heart, she could experience passion if she wasn't so, so…so afraid! Yes, it is her fear that keeps her from experiencing joy. "Ima, fear is the absence of light, a dark veil that keeps us from love and joy. All you must do is pray and ask that your fear be lifted."

"But Mary, I cannot ask Adonai for myself. Perhaps you can pray for me."

"I do pray for you, Ima, but if you do not ask for help to release the fear, how can it happen? Do you think Adonai will take away from you what you are clinging to so desperately?"

With a soft cry of dismay, she says, "I am afraid, but I do not know why."

I breathe deeply and ask for insight. What is this fear? "Dear, Ima, you are afraid to live fully." She still does not comprehend. I ask for assistance and Uriel comes.

The fear of death keeps humans from living fully. I repeat the insight out loud.

"Yes, Mary. Life is so difficult. There are so many rules to insure a decent afterlife. I know I am not perfect but cannot imagine existing like this for eternity."

"Yeshua tells me not to live in the future, not to worry about what will be, but to live fully in this moment." Her eyes are wide. "If you learn to live joyfully in the present, forgetting about the past, not worrying about the future, you will have a lifetime of joyful moments and then eternity will not seem so daunting." I hug her knowing this is a hard lesson, "Ima, Yeshua has to constantly remind me to stay present in this moment."

"You are so young, yet so wise already. Your husband will be a fine leader someday. And look at your daughter, the picture of joyful living." Laughing with delight, Sarah rides upon Saba's back while he rounds up the other children. Ima reaches over and places a hand on my belly, "So this is my grandson?"

All around us the hayye glistens as the shadow of remorse fades into the delight of three generations connecting through love.

The brisk predawn air chills my cheeks. Wrapped in my husband's warm body and covered with thick wool blankets is not enough to ward off the winter cold. Burrowing deeply, at least the hammock afforded us some privacy. Yeshua was pleased that I shared with him my insights from the conversation with Ima. Still, he has not told me much about his travels, but at least we talked. He stirs, "So what do you want to know about Britannia?"

"Really, Yesh? You will tell me?"

He pulls me close, kissing my cold nose. "Whatever you desire, dear." So excited, I know not where to begin. His mouth moves urgently over mine, while he strokes my body.

"Yeshua, don't distract me now. I'm thinking."

Using kasa to veil us, he moves to my breast. "I think I can talk and make love."

I laugh, "Not with your mouth full."

Proceeding down my body, he kisses the softness of my lower belly. I'll never remember what to ask now, feeling him smile at my thoughts. I laugh out loud.

"What is it, dear?" he asks between kisses.

"Oh, I was just thinking how easily I respond."

"Yes, I am rewarded over and over for my work."

I stop him, holding his head in my hands, "Yesh, if it's work for you, then...."

"Oh, no, it's a most pleasing chore. This is Divine work, a labor of love."

"That kind of statement might be considered sacrilegious by some." Looking into my eyes, he enters me and I become lost in waves of fluid color.

"Now, my love, are you not satiated with pleasure?" I nod, still catching my breath. "Are you not joyful in this moment?" Again I nod. "Then this must be the work of Eloha."

I smile and hug him closer. "I see your point, but dear, wasn't it Eloha's work that Abba said you were going to do in Britannia?"

"Yes," he sighs, "and I learned much about the energies, including new forms of healing. The northern culture reveres nature and all life, especially women and children. The ruling body is communal, made up of both men and women, respecting the feminine and masculine aspects of the Creator. They are well versed in the art of love making." My heart beats loudly. "Do you want me to continue?"

I don't know. I hesitate.... "Do I?"

He kisses me, "Did you not learn trust from your experiences?"

"Yes, but I wonder if you had sexual mentors, then perhaps I should be grateful and not worry about the details."

"I do love your sweetness, but do not worry yourself. After being with you, how could I desire anyone else?"

"For educational purposes, perhaps?"

He laughs, "I am blessed with a vivid imagination, so verbal instructions were all that was necessary." Feeling uncomfortable, I know what it is to desire another. He kisses me again, "My passions were stirred, yet I could only think of you."

A twinge of guilt burns the gratitude from my heart. I have pressured him into revealing his innocence and now my own desire for Teoma threatens me. Should I unburden myself, but then is it fair to burden him? He turns my face toward his.

"What is it?"

"You must know. I have no private thoughts from you."

He smiles, "I know that you love and desire my best friend. I know that you kissed him when he returned this last time." Barely breathing, I am crushed by the weight of my guilt. "I also know that I left you with him fully aware of how you felt about one another and that in spite of your passionate nature, you were faithful to me. You, my dear, have been sorely tested. It was much easier for me to refuse the affections of strangers than it must have been for the two of you who truly love one another."

I swallow thickly, "Yeshua, do you forgive me?"

"There is nothing to forgive. I am blessed that you chose me and not him." He kisses me again tenderly. "In spite of keeping you together, you proved yourself worthy of my trust. Faithful Teoma never breached my confidence. His love will continue to serve us for the rest of our lives."

Deliverance of Fear

Spring dawns bright and clear. I stretch through Yeshua's limbs, but he pulls me closer, tucking the curve of my bottom into the angle formed between his legs and stomach. Baby Joshua flutters in my womb. *Good morning, my precious son.*

His hayye shimmers when I place my hand over my lower belly. *Greetings, Ima.*

In my fourth month, still very slim with only a hint of my expanding womb, I feel deliciously sensual, loving my full breasts, which are not as dark as they were with Sarah. Is my body so different because my son's hayye casts a masculine glow on mine?

I wiggle ever closer to my sleeping husband, but he murmurs. "My dear, let us sleep a bit longer." To the quiet rhythm of his breath, I drift into the dream world.

Floating comfortably within a bright light, at peace, aloft among my angelic host, I cannot feel my body, but know I have just given birth. Below me—a scene of frantic chaos. Blood everywhere. Miriam crying hysterically. Hava holding brand new baby Joshua. Joseph stricken. What has happened? Where is Yeshua? Where am I? Immediately I am taken just beyond to the courtyard where Teoma is on his knees, head buried in his hands, shoulders wracked with sobs. Nearby holding a blood-soaked burden up toward the heavens, Yeshua begs the Creator. A rush of sorrow and pain flood my aura. Yeshua carries my dead body and I am with the Light.

Screaming, I awake to Yeshua clasping me to his chest. "Oh, Mary, it was awful," he whispers hoarsely, "were you having a nightmare?" I nod. His trembling vibrates through me. "You died in my dream."

Through quivering lips, I mouth…mine too. Hurriedly dressing, he leads me to Miriam. "Please, we must consult the Seer."

The blood drains from her face. "What is wrong?" He tells his mother the horrible dream we shared and clearly shaken, she escorts us to the meditation room.

Comforted by the energies, I sit upon a red cushion, Yeshua and his mother completing the triangle. Breathing softly in unison, the rainbow of light circles us with the yellow wave extending into the center, inviting us to enter. As soon as we are all on the path, the Seer appears.

What do you need, Miriam? Perceiving Yeshua and I, she asks again, *what is it?*

"We have a concern about the birth of this child."

The Seer focuses her hayye on me, but speaks to all of us. *You must surrender to this process. Know that you will be shown a way.* I feel a vague sense of peace. To my husband she says, *Yeshua, you will be given the power to do this.* Immediately, the yellow path fades.

Yeshua and I leave hand in hand to face our future but in the atrium, I tremble, perceiving my husband's fear. We lie together on the hammock. "I will find a way, dearest. I shall not lose you."

"I cannot leave my babies. Oh, Yeshua, I do not want to be parted from you."

He holds me closer, until my weeping ceases, before praying, "Eloha, we are thankful for our many blessings, especially the love we have for one another. We pray that our fear be lifted, that we might be comforted. We trust in our connection to All That Is. Ameyn."

A white light bathes us and from the center appears the nura of the One. Joshua's hayye bubbles with joy, filling my heart with peace. The One speaks.

My beloved, your love for each other and faith in creation is most pleasing. You will be blessed with the gift of everlasting life. Know that all is as it needs be. Remember, fear is the only veil the light of nura cannot pierce.

A giggle catches our attention, as precious Sarah reaches up to join us on the hammock. Yeshua lifts her up and when she extends her small hands toward the center of the light it intensifies, "Hello, Eloha. We are together again on our beautiful earth. Thank you for loving us."

The hayye compresses as if accepting her hug. *Beloved Sarah, you are my delight. Your life blesses all who know you.* Lifting gently away, the nura fades, taking the brilliance with it.

One afternoon in the study, Yeshua attempts to teach me the language of the northern clan. The son of a wealthy sea merchant, my Abba is fluent in many languages and tried to tutor me in Greek, Egyptian, and Latin, but I retained so little. The Druid runes intrigue me though with angular symbols similar to Egyptian hieroglyphics, imparting meaning through their energy.

"Ima, Ima! Look. I ruined it," Sarah cries, her new sadin stained by pomegranate. I hold out my arms and she climbs into my lap. Yeshua releases us with a kiss.

In the hall with a basketful of clean linens, Edia smiles at Sarah's predicament and leads us back into the laundry. Tall and sturdily built with straight heavy hair, large dark eyes, and a pleasant hayye, she intrigues Sarah with her skill.

"See, Ima, how nice Edia is. That's why Dod Teo likes her."

Color stains Edia's cheeks so I thank her and rise to leave, but she stops us. "Mary, can I ask you something?" I nod, sitting down at the table covered with neatly folded garments, while Sarah makes a tent with dirty linen. Wringing her hands nervously, Edia begins, "Do you think he might ever want to have a family?"

She is in love with him. How strange to be talking about this with her, but I have no right to hold him. Perhaps he can finally find some happiness. Unfortunately, Teoma has given me no indication on how he feels about her. Not that I've asked.

"I do not know." Clearly disappointed, she looks down at her hands, roughened by labor. "Perhaps you should speak with him."

"I can't. He would think me too forward."

Obviously she loves him and certainly they have been intimate. Why then can she not speak her mind? "Teoma would probably appreciate if you shared your feelings."

"I do not want to frighten him away." She takes my hand, "Please, Mary."

My stomach lurches but I agree to talk to him.

The following morning, I meet Teoma at the stables. "Good morning, Mary." He kisses my cheek, placing a hand on my belly. "How's he doing?" Joshua kicks vigorously. "Mary, he knows me!"

"Of course, you met before he implanted into my womb."

147

His grin fades as he takes our horses from the stable hand.

"Thank you, Levi."

"Anything for you, Mary." Backing away, the young man bows. Teoma smiles, "Do you realize the effect you have on men?"

Laughing, I stroke Sheikan's neck, "Of course, I have known about the power of women since I became one."

His ruggedly handsome head shakes no, "Not all women have this same effect."

"Yes they do, but just don't realize it. They're afraid of the power. Now, can you please assist me?"

Frowning, he replies, "I don't think we should ride. What about the baby?"

"Joshua loves Sheikan. I'll be fine and if anything happens, you are coming along nicely with the healing energies, I will be well cared for."

"Don't tease; I haven't progressed to people yet."

I touch his cheek, wishing he had more confidence in his healing touch. "You started with me, remember?"

We ride at a smooth pace, shadowed, of course, by Tikva, who has grown since she arrived last summer. Teoma calls his sleek two-year-old filly along to follow him like a puppy. The heavy boned mare his uncle gave him will bear Sheikan yet another foal later this year.

Time with Yeshua home and perhaps being pregnant has tempered my desire. Still I cannot deny his attractiveness, but I do want him to be happy. "Teoma, about Edia...."

He looks at me sharply, "Mary, I'd rather not."

"What is wrong? I know that you are courting her."

"I am not courting her. We are just friends."

I pursue, "She does not think of you as just a friend."

"Have you been talking to her?" I nod, in spite of his frown. "I wish you wouldn't."

Resisting me, his hayye tightens, so I soften my own and take a deep breath. "I have no wish to make you uncomfortable, but since you have not left the house in many months, perhaps you have feelings for Edia. You know, she's in love with you."

He reins in his mount, bringing it close to mine. "I would prefer to be monogamous. I enjoy my relationship with Edia and do not wish to hurt her in any way, but I am *not* in love with her." In remorse, I touch his arm.

"Forgive me, but she asked how you felt about having a family."

Looking intensely into my eyes, he says softly, "I have no desire to marry. Besides, I already have a family."

How could I have believed that my feelings have dulled when his are as strong as ever? "Teoma, I just want you to be happy."

He reaches to hug me from his mount, "I am, but please do not try to match me up with these women. You and your children are family enough for me. I am grateful to be a part of your lives."

Joshua begins moving vigorously. I place my hand on my womb, "Hush, child," but he kicks so hard I wince in pain.

"What is it, Mary? Is he upset?" I nod. Placing a hand over mine, he uses his hayye to soothe the baby, "There, there, son." Joshua quiets immediately.

"Thank you, for everything you do for us. I could never repay you, Teoma."

Not removing his hand, he smiles, "Allowing me to connect with you and the children brings me much joy."

"What about Edia?"

His lips tighten, "I will talk to her. There is no reason for her to hold out hope for me. If she wants to be married, then I shall release her." I shudder. "What?"

With trembling lips, I murmur, "That is what I should have done; then, perhaps you could have been free to live a fuller life."

Blue eyes penetrate my soul, "But I couldn't have released you from my heart." We ride back home in silence, the hayye bittersweet with longing.

In the garden, Yeshua and I lounge on a blanket after sharing a picnic lunch. Sarah wanders about the olive grove with one arm around Tikva's neck, while Teoma keeps close watch. With a cry, she runs up holding something.

"Abba, please fix it." A small brown sparrow stiff, cold, and very much dead lies in her hands. Behind her, Teoma shakes his head. "Please, Abba," Sarah begs, startling Joshua who wiggles about vigorously.

Yeshua takes the tiny creature. "Baby, this bird has been dead a long time."

"Abba, I know you can fix it!"

149

Cupping the sparrow in one hand, he places his other over it; his hayye glows, but nothing happens. Sarah cries when Yeshua reveals the still dead bird.

I draw her little body between my crossed legs, "Sarah, sometimes Eloha calls souls back to the Light. When it is time to return, the soul leaves the body, then the body becomes one with the earth."

Her tears cease, "How does the body join the earth, Ima?"

"The body is buried into the soil and months and months later, the earth absorbs it into her great body so she has materials for other bodies to be formed."

"Can we bury this poor little bird?"

"Yes, love, we will have a funeral for this bird and help her soul to become one with the Light." Taking the tiny bird from her Abba's hands, Sarah leads us to the largest olive tree. Teoma digs a small grave while Yeshua prays. Sarah pours dirt upon the body.

Looking up into the sky, she sings, "Goodbye sweet birdie, fly to the light. Someday maybe you can come back as a hawk."

Afterward, I sit on the blanket to braid Sarah's hair, wondering why she thought that her Abba could raise the dead. I shiver. How could I have forgotten? When I asked for my fear to be lifted, it was, right along with the memory of the nightmare. Yeshua stares at me as Sarah wiggles around to place her hand on my belly.

"It's all right, Joshua, Abba will bring Ima back."

Teoma looks anxiously between us. Blocking Sarah from perceiving me, I look to Yeshua and he silently answers, *Yes, I have been practicing raising the dead. Not successfully, yet, I'm afraid.* Breath catches in my throat, color drains from Teoma's face.

Obviously, we cannot discuss this now, but I am too unsettled to do nothing. "Yeshua, let's meditate."

"Right now, dear?"

"Yes, please, right now." Our breathing slows, a deep purple teardrop appearing between us. Teoma senses the hayye, but Sarah has fallen asleep in my lap. The purple teardrop dissolves with a message of compassion for ourselves.

"So how long have you been practicing?"

The men reply in unison, "About four weeks."

With narrowed eyes, I study them, "Why is Sarah involved?"

"She began bringing me injured creatures right after we spoke to the Seer." I look at my husband, incredulous.

"Yeshua thought it would be better to be prepared." Teoma tries to save him.

"But isn't healing an act of faith on the part of the healer and the healed?" Yeshua nods. "Then maybe you should practice increasing your faith, not your skills." They both look down ashamed. "Besides, there is probably a limit to when you can raise the dead after the hayye leaves."

Yeshua smiles at me, "I must have more faith in myself."

"Yes, because I am not going to be waiting around for days while you find your faith. I want to return to a still warm body." Teoma looks like he might be sick so I reach for his hand. "You, too, must have faith in this process. I am depending on you both. And Yeshua, I keep imagining a lot of damage. Could you please heal that as well?" He hugs me carefully, not to disturb our sleeping daughter, and Teoma puts an arm around him.

I pray silently that they find their faith before Joshua is born.

As is tradition in dynastic wedlock, Jacob and Rebeka have a betrothal ceremony on the summer solstice. From Qumran come the most prestigious elders of the tribe of Judah to scrupulously examine the bride's lineage before the exchange of properties. Jacob listens intently to the official proceedings with shy Rebeka at his side. After the ceremony, Jacob motions for me to meet his betrothed.

Before reaching them, I am interceded. "Mary, may I have a word with you?" The thick middle-aged woman does not wait for my consent but takes my arm and leads me to the atrium. "As Rebeka's aunt, I must ask that you limit your contact with her."

"I have no intentions of dishonoring my future sister!"

Her inflamed hayye reminds me that Rebeka's mother was quite upset about my solstice dance. Clearly, the women of her family have much anger in their hearts. Her voice is haughty, "My sister has grave concerns about your influence on her daughter. You, a married woman, shamelessly revealing herself!" With tight lips, I resist touching my uncovered hair. "The unusual betrothal agreement included Rebeka residing upon this land of Joseph's, but until then, she will not take her example from you!"

Trembling, I have never been confronted like this. Before I offer another retort, the tetrad of angels surrounds me. *Do not struggle with this*

151

being. It is her fear of the power of the sacred feminine that sharpens her tongue. Reach out to her, Mary. She is not your enemy, but a reflection of your incomplete sense of self.

"Thank you for sharing your concern." Surprised by my graciousness, I say, "I pray we might know one another as sisters."

She resists my embrace, so I return to the gathering room. Teoma puts a protective arm around me, reigniting her fury. Yeshua joins us in the atrium to kneel at my feet.

"Mary, what happened?"

Holding me closer, Teoma answers. "Rebeka's aunt dragged her out here. Who does she think she is?"

"If I knew the truth of who I am, she would not mirror for me my doubt." Yeshua takes my hands and lays his head on my lap, his mourning dampening my sadin. Teoma's fury softens to sorrow. Surrounded by their love, I am held in Divine Light.

Since Jacob's house must be built before the winter wedding, the men begin construction so we do not travel to the Great Sea until the end of Tammuz. Joseph is concerned about my riding to the shore, but Miriam reminds him that she rode upon a donkey to Bethlehem in her ninth month.

Summer at the shore slips lazily away, as I continue my training. Less and less does Yeshua have to cover my ineptness and Joseph's supply of herbs is rarely touched. While most physical ailments seem due to human choice, I always find something deeper. Perhaps I am more acutely aware of the soul's relationship to the body being the embodiment of spiritual lessons.

One day, Leah asks for some assistance with her recurrent upset stomach. Although avoiding troublesome foods, she continues to experience a burning sensation after meals. Joseph's herbal therapies bring only temporary relief.

Sitting on a blanket under the shade of a large tree, the breeze cools our skin. Not as tall as she is broad, Leah possesses a pale yellow aura rusted by worry at her core. When she is particularly concerned about something, the burning becomes unbearable.

"Perhaps your pain is related to your worry?" I suggest, softening Leah's rough edges with my energy.

"I don't know. It is as if whatever I eat cannot be absorbed." She chuckles, "Although to look at me you would never know that I was once a thin young girl. But even then, I worried."

I smile for she has named her problem. "Leah, imagine that the love of the One is the most delectable honey but your worry keeps you from absorbing this delicious essence." She places a hand on her stomach. Using my body as a mirror, I feel the most excruciating hunger pangs, as if her gut devours itself. Joshua presses himself low in my womb.

"Let's take a deep breath and exhale the pain out." She follows my example and I feel an immediate relief. "Now Leah, imagine that the next breath is the sweetness of Divine Love." We breathe again and I am filled with golden light. Her core glows too.

With a look of surprise, she smiles, "The pain is gone, Mary, but will it last?"

Joshua moves within my womb contentedly. "Leah, you have lived a long time with this fear and it is not easily released. Have faith in yourself and soon you will find that with every breath you will experience Eloha."

Hugging me tightly with her strong arms, Leah returns to help with the laundry. Healing work is wonderful, but tiring, and Joshua moves too much for me to relax. In my eighth month of pregnancy, I never imagined I could get this big. If Joshua can wait to be born in early Tishrei, yet a full moon cycle away, all will be well for the bloodline.

Yeshua appears with a basket of food. "How about a picnic, love?" Sitting, he kisses me and I lie down filled with hunger, not for food, but for him. A veil surrounds us, obliterating our presence from the rest of the world. "I love how your body fills out when you are pregnant." His hand moves to my hip, turning me to press against him. "Not that I didn't appreciate you before, but your form housing both your own beloved soul and that of our child is so sensual."

Our picnic lunch would be all but forgotten if, afterwards, Joshua did not stir with need. Laughing Yeshua places a hand on my womb, "Dear son, calm down, you will be fed." But when he proceeds to feed me, I fill up too quickly.

Waving for him to stop, I breathe, "No more, Yesh, there's not enough room." He frowns, as I try to settle into a more comfortable position. "Let us set our intentions for him to be born early in Tishrei, please…."

"I know you are concerned." It has been difficult being brave when I know what will happen at delivery. "Dearest, please try to have faith. I will find a way."

"But I do have faith in you. I lack complete faith in myself."

Sighing, he tries to comfort me, "You must pray for help. This birth is a test for all of us that I know we shall pass. I can see our future. We will raise our children together...," he pauses and I look up at him, questioning. "We will be together," he reiterates.

I sense something incomplete in his prediction, but knowing how much he insists upon staying in the moment, I dismiss it. "Yesh, please pray that I might birth Joshua earlier."

Staring off in the distance, he says softly. "We cannot change the course of our lives. I am being asked not to interfere in this way. I am sorry, love." His kiss is salted with tears.

We return from the sea in the heat of Elul to find that Jacob and Rebeka's house is complete. Rosh Hashana passes and we prepare for high holy days but still no sign of labor. Every day that Joshua thrives within me, my concern about the delivery grows.

Outside our chambers, Joseph meets with Yeshua, the courtyard carrying their voices to my ears. "Son, I am well aware of the dream and your consult with the Seer. I wonder if your prediction of such a dire outcome has not created such a reality."

Aware of my attention from the next room, Yeshua speaks softly, "Do you believe that I am purposely manifesting a difficult delivery for Mary?"

"No, but I know how you thrive on challenge. Bringing her back would be your greatest healing yet."

Yeshua's voice is louder, "I would much rather not be tested in this way, but Abba, I have to believe in myself, or I would succumb to my greatest fear. I cannot lose her, she is my life." They are silent for a moment, perhaps hugging one another, I can only hope.

Finally Joseph speaks, "The hayye of sacrifice fuels this birth, a mirror of your belief about yourself."

I gasp, but Yeshua addresses my concern. "I shall not sacrifice my wife or child to prove anything. Rest assured, I will find a way to overcome this potential obstacle. I only ask, Abba, that you have faith in me."

"Son, I have always had faith in you." Again, silence.

Yeshua returns and I touch his face, wondering how one man can feel so deeply and survive his own emotions. As if to prepare me for some excruciating pain, he uses all of his resources to bring me the utmost pleasure. We fall fast asleep wrapped in each other's arms, his seed lying deep within all night.

At the first morning light, I am awakened by a mild crampiness. Praying, I offer thanks to the Creator that my son will finally be born. I breathe quietly through the early labor, waiting for Yeshua to wake. He stretches and kisses my neck.

"Mary, is this it?" I nod.

All day, I labor until the contractions are so close together there is little rest between them. Finally, it is time to retire to our chambers for the delivery. Leah has covered the bed with thick white linens and towels surround a large basin. From the kitchen, Saada brings healing broth and strengthening teas. A small kettle bubbles gaily in the fireplace. Miriam has filled tall vases with beautiful bouquets. Before I settle down, Hava brings Sarah to me.

Many cushions comfortably support my body as my sweet daughter places a small hand on the top of my womb. A strong contraction ensues and her eyes widen. When it is finished, I take a cleansing breath and Sarah kneels near the top of my womb, cupping her hand to her mouth. My heart flutters.

"Joshua, you will soon be here. I will wait for you in the nursery." Kissing her goodbye, I hold my daughter perhaps a moment too long. Yeshua comes to take her from me, "Ima, do not worry, Abba will fix everything." Panic rises sour in my throat.

Joseph's face reveals he suspects the worse. "Abba…,"

"Hush, Mary. You should be nearly ready to deliver." Dark with concern, he palpates my belly. Time stands still. I can barely breathe when he turns to Yeshua, who looks up from his meditation. "Son, the baby is breach."

A spark of fear burns through my chest to engulf the room. The women clutch each other and Miriam trembles as her son comes to the bedside, "But I was sure she was progressing well."

Joseph shakes his head. "Perhaps you are too focused on the outcome of your dream."

"I do not remember him turning in my womb; can't I deliver him safely?" His grave look provides the answer. "Can he not be turned back around?"

"The baby's head is very large, he turned sometime in the night to present the part which would fit most easily—his hips." Joseph addresses his son, "I will try to turn him, but you must provide her with some pain relief."

Yeshua kisses me, tears in his eyes, "I'm so sorry, love."

I try to smile through yet another contraction, "Just save our son, Yesh." He nods ever so slowly and places his soothing hands on my head, as Joseph attempts to turn the baby, but after much work, it is evident that Joshua will not budge. The manipulations aggravate my womb, and there is no longer time to rest with one contraction practically on top of the other. When Joseph moves to assist Leah in the delivery position, I think how abhorred my mother would be, but am soothed by my husband who kneels at my head, prepared to guide me. Miriam, Saada, and Hava continue their preparations in eerie silence.

I can hear one thing—Teoma pacing outside the room, the click of his sandals on the tiled floor in rhythm to the beat of my heart. *Marya, please grant me strength, lift my pain and suffering. Bless all of those in attendance that they might also find the faith necessary for the deepest connection to the Divine. Ameyn.*

Miriam smiles at me, as if I have spoken my prayer out loud. My pain is less than with Sarah's birth, and active up until the end, I have more endurance. Following Yeshua's instructions, I mimic his breath, trying to stay in the moment, trying to envision the best outcome. Searching his eyes, I see only profound love.

I reach up to kiss him between contractions. "I love you, Yesh, and do have faith in us," but the next wave of contractions captures my breath.

"All right, Mary, let's try to deliver your son." Joseph instructs, flanked by Miriam and Leah offering clean linens.

With the next forceful contraction I bear down and imagine Joshua landing in his Saba's hands. "Very good, Mary, he has moved down the birth canal." Joseph's smile does not hide his fear. My son's hips may be able to emerge from my body, but what about his head?

Nearly a dozen more contractions but Joshua is stuck. Joseph stands and washes his hands again. After he whispers something to Leah, she quickly leaves the room. Still at my head, Yeshua exists between meditation and breath.

Teoma enters, obviously at Joseph's request, but I hear only snippets of their conversation. Joseph's hoarse low voice, "…yes, that one…as sharp as possible…" Teoma's face looks stricken as he makes a hasty exit. Somewhat disconnected, but the pain is not so great, my fear not so overwhelming.

Sitting with crossed legs, Yeshua quietly meditates at my head. I adjust my position, but Joshua lays very still, his hayye peaceful, as if he too is in meditation. Leah comes back to the room with a fresh supply of linens and healing herbs for poultices. Not until Teoma returns and hands Joseph an object wrapped in cloth do I begin to feel the tremendous pressure of my half-born infant trapped within me. Beginning with a dull cramp in my back, the pain squeezes my womb like a constrictor upon it's prey. My breath becomes more shallow; my heart races.

Teoma comes to my side. "Mary, everything will be fine." His handsome face creased with worry, his blues eyes shine with unshed tears. As he embraces me, I can feel the weight of the world upon him, his great love and devotion for me, his perseverance for all time. In his arms, I am grounded so much more deeply into my body that the pain of the next contraction causes me to cry out. Fearful, he releases me. The women's faces pale. Joseph turns, holding a very sharp knife. I gasp.

Looking up from his meditation, Yeshua asks, "Is there no other way?" Trembling, I breathe much too shallowly with the next contraction, while Teoma holds my hand, tears pouring down his cheeks. I look to Miriam for comfort, but she also stares at the knife. The crying women murmur until Joseph takes control.

"Listen to me. Joshua needs to be delivered. He cannot come through the birth canal. It is not my intent to sacrifice Mary to save Joshua. You must all visualize the best outcome." He looks at each individual in the room carefully. "If you haven't begun praying, now is the time." To me, he adds, "I will have to open your womb with this knife. There will be much pain, but the fear you perceive in us is because women do not survive this type of delivery. There is no other way to deliver Joshua alive."

"Do what must be done." Dry-mouthed, I turn to Teoma, "Keep pacing, dear, I can hear only your footsteps." Kissing my lips, he rushes out of the room.

Yeshua is silent. With the next contraction, I look into his calm eyes and feel a sense of relief. He places his hands on my head and the pain of the contraction lessens somewhat. The women gather around and kiss me one at a time. Miriam lingers, her tears wetting my lips. Yeshua touches his mother's shoulder, "Do not say goodbye, wish her a safe journey. She will be back."

The following contraction is the most painful yet and before anyone is in position, my hands fly to my lower belly, his life force? Where is it? "Abba," I cry, very much afraid, "Joshua's in trouble!"

Rushing to my side, he wipes my belly with a wet cloth and down comes the knife. Unprepared for the amount of pain, my faith waivers. Why is Yeshua not able to relieve me? His face, no longer calm, pales as if it is he who loses blood, not I. Joseph cuts deeper and reeling in pain, I bite my lip to keep from crying out. Blood pours from the wound, still my infant is nowhere in sight. The women cry, rushing about. The hayye swirls around us, catching on our collective panic. Only Joseph holds his one intention, to deliver my son. Yeshua's tears drip on my face. I search for something to focus on, then remember Teoma.

Straining over the commotion in the room, I hear his pacing sandals click on the tile floor, faster and faster like my heart. The pain so intense my head spins, blood stains my lip. From somewhere far away, a woman screams. The wailing cry echoes throughout the room, the footsteps slow with my heart. The scream from my dream pierces the veil of reality. So much blood, yet I cannot hear my voice, nor my heart, which stops abruptly with the scream and Teoma's footsteps.

There is no more pain. I am above myself floating about the room, no longer attached to my body—there is no silver cord. Free from pain, free from fear. There is only this moment and it is an eternity. Bathing in the cool white light, I watch from a glorious distance the chaos below. Joseph stands over my body, my stomach gaping open, blood pouring down my sides, pooling on the bed, dripping on the floor. Joshua is handed over to Hava. I hear nothing, but see him cry as she dries him vigorously, his silver aura strongly pulsating. Cheeks shiny with tears, Miriam attempts to instruct Saada, who rushes about the room. Joseph holds a bag of flesh, the afterbirth, then methodically begins cleaning the bloody mess. Teoma kneels outside the door sobbing. I float into the nursery. Sarah ceases her play to greet me with kisses.

Back at the scene of the birth, I hover over my dead body. Yeshua cries bitterly, so very far away. The Light draws me back to be greeted by the angelic host and while in their collective embrace, I watch the scene play out below. The panic dissolves as Miriam prays, naming each of the participants and asking that their fear be lifted and they be

158

guided to healing, to light, to love. Her prayer opens a portal back to where my body lies. Miriam stands at my feet, with Hava holding Joshua on my left, Joseph at my right side, still in his surgical position. On the bed at my head, Yeshua sits deep in meditation. Light beams down to encompass the circle and Yeshua glows as his life force manifests healing. The great gaping wound closes, blood fills my heart and vessels, my body made new and whole. Yet I do not return.

The Light of the One radiates upon me and I turn toward ecstasy. Knowing only bliss, merging with All That Is—I am Love. There is only joy, hope, peace, and this incredible love, greater than the most precious human emotion I have ever experienced. Recalling my earthly existence, wracking pain cuts to the core of my being and I do not want to return. I want to stay. The Divine Being holds me yet for an eternity or only a moment, I know not, as there is no time.

The One is ever powerful, "It is not yet your turn. Return to earth and live long. Complete your work in the physical realm with your dearest husband and children until the moment does come to return to the Light."

Yeshua's voice calls, "Creator of the Universe, I ask that you return my beloved. Please, Mary, come back to me, to us." His silver hayye pulls like a cord to draw me back into my body. I do not resist and as the One releases me, I glide on a violet wave into my core. My heart trembles and then with force beats once, twice and I breathe. The room comes back into focus, the loving faces about me, deep in meditation. My body is whole, healed, and I am fine.

"Where is my baby?"

Hearing my voice, Hava places my precious infant in my arms. Delightfully big, he vigorously searches for a nipple.

Saada rushes out of the room crying, "It's a miracle!"

Teoma comes quickly and with a great sigh exclaims, "It looks like you're getting better, Yesh!"

Everyone laughs, even Joseph, before the family offers thanks.

Yeshua kneels at my head. "Now I know why you took your sweet time leaving the One, Yesh. I've never known such absolute bliss." He touches the baby's head softly, before kissing my mouth. No longer do I taste blood, only the sweetness of his love.

> *Dearest Joshua,*
>
> *Welcome, my beloved son. Your Ima and I conceived you in ceremonial delight and birthed you with the drama of a Greek play, a hero with sacred rucha enlightening your beautiful form. Your precious life shall be full of emotion, well connected to the Divine, destined as you are to embody heaven on earth.*
>
> *A golden child with your Ima's dark beauty, you are the blend of all humanity. Your silvery hayye brings peace unto this world. You shall be the man that I yearn to be, loved by your Ima and sister Sarah, and adored by your Abba, accepted by this world, perfect in form, pure of heart, clear of intent, the precious essence of Eloha in your very breath.*
>
> *A gift from the One, my blue-eyed son, asleep at the breast of your beloved Ima. My heart aches with joy, my family completed by the blessing of your very existence.*
>
> *All my love, Abba*

The golden dusk glimmers softly through our open chamber door to cast a warm glow upon the face of my precious son. I thank the One for all of my blessings. He is perfect in every way and I am here to enjoy being his Ima. A beautiful chubby baby with dimples at every joint, Joshua sucks vigorously, determined to grow as tall as his Abba in a few short years.

After much hard work by Leah and Saada, our room is neat again, the flowers still fragrant, a fire glowing in the hearth. Already I have been fed a rich soup to stimulate my milk supply. And there is no sign of that terrible wound from which Joshua emerged. My husband, the accomplished healer, arrives with our daughter.

In spite of her excitement, Sarah washes with her Abba at the basin then presents her clean hands, "See, Ima, I am ready to hold my brother."

I reach out but she thwarts my embrace to study my face. "Ima, you look so pretty. You were with Eloha while Abba healed your body, weren't you?" I nod. "I saw you in the nursery, Ima. Could you see me?"

"Yes, love, I felt your kisses even."

"What a picture you are. I will always remember this moment, my three most precious beings cuddled on our bed together." Yeshua carefully sits down as not to jostle us, then leans over to kiss me.

Sarah puts her arms around our necks, "Thank you, Ima and Abba, for loving us so much to bring us here to the earth." Yeshua holds her in his lap as I adjust Joshua.

"Ima, what is Joshua doing to you?"

"He's nursing, dear, like you did when you were a baby."

Moving my hair out of the way, she watches him suckle, "He's drinking, Ima."

"Yes, love, he's drinking milk." She reaches a tentative hand to touch his cheek and he turns toward her touch, searching for another source of nourishment. She quickly pulls her hand away.

"Soon, he will be finished and then you can hold him." Yeshua raises his eyebrows. "Sarah will be very careful and we will sit right here by her."

Joshua finishes suckling. As there is little milk yet on his first day of life, he hardly needs burping so I settle him on Sarah's lap, adjusting pillows under her arms to bear his weight. Delighted with her new brother, who falls asleep in her arms, Sarah begins to sing a lullaby I have sung to her since she was an infant.

"Do you know where you're going?
Do you know where you've been?
Do you know you're a part of the great, great I AM?
So here we are on this bright shiny day
Loving each other and trusting the way."

The sun has set long ago and suddenly I am very tired. Snuggling up in the bed, Yeshua lifts a sleepy Sarah and places her on his other side, while I curl into him with Joshua near my breast. As my husband holds me close, I begin to drift off to sleep, perfectly content for us to be together like this for always.

Sometime in the night, Hava must have taken Sarah back to the nursery and Joshua into the room next to ours that she will share with him while I nurse. Four times, she wakes me to nurse my baby. I thank her between yawns as she kisses my cheek.

"Hava, it is so wonderful of you to help me like this." She graces me with a smile. Yeshua does not stir. "Isn't it strange how men do not seem to notice all our comings and goings at night?"

She chuckles, "Thank goodness, women are blessed with keen hearing after birth or babies might be sorely neglected."

"We wouldn't survive at all if men had to nourish our children." Yeshua turns over in his sleep and we hush our giggles.

The next morning, it is Yeshua who brings our son for a feeding. Hava must be sleeping, exhausted by yesterday's ordeal. Getting back into bed, he holds me while I nurse on my side. As he kisses my neck, my body responds and I press into him. He laughs. "My love, where do you get all your energy?"

I turn my head so that he might kiss my lips, "From you, dear. I feel completely whole and healed."

"Let us rest and we must come up with some kind of schedule for Hava."

"For Hava? You mean Joshua. We are all on his schedule."

Settling Joshua between two pillows, I lie upon Yeshua and breathe in his essence, "I want to thank you for bringing me back into such a whole form. I feel really wonderful, as if nothing occurred at all."

He kisses me deeply, "You are very welcome, my love. I am so grateful that I have you here with me, happy and whole."

"Really, Yesh, I feel just fine." I snuggle closer, kissing his neck, and he returns my kisses.

"Mary, we should wait. I don't want you to become fatigued and not make enough milk for the baby."

This is not my husband speaking, it sounds like his father. "Yesh, what is wrong?" He kisses me, trying to divert my attention, but I can feel something, the energy of fear, perhaps disappointment.

He sighs, "I had a long discussion with Abba." I knew it. "And he strongly, no adamantly, advised that we not have any more children."

"You are both afraid that I might really die." He nods. "Well, I considered that possibility, but I thought you would want more."

Bravely he smiles, "I do not want to take any further risks of losing you. We were very fortunate these past two times, divinely guided, but what if you delivered without me, what then?"

"Hush, all is well. So can we move past this fear of loss and into this moment of desire?"

"Yes, but I still think we should rest."

Laughing I ask, "We?"

"Well, yes, it wasn't easy bringing you back and healing all the damage." He smiles and kisses me deeply, "Not that I don't desire you, but tomorrow you can place the white light around your womb, so we do not take any chances." I look into his eyes and see how deeply affected he was by the birth, afraid to lose me.

I shall not share the vision of the dark-haired child, not now.

Discerning Disclosure

Traveling to Cana stuffed into a mule-drawn cart built for toting vegetables, I yearn for the comfort of Sheikan's back. The other women chat amiably about Rebeka's prenuptials, but I dread meeting again with her mother and aunt. Miriam's pale blue headdress flutters into my face. Conscious of my unfettered hair, I brush the fine silk away.

Before entering the house, we wash our feet and hands at the kiyyor. Casting me a barbed glance, Rebeka's aunt escorts us to a somber chamam reminiscent of my mother's. I pray for strength, wondering what lesson shall be served this day.

Rebeka greets me with a shy smile, her lime-green hayye a skittish rabbit poised to escape at the slightest threat. Looking into her clear amber eyes, I see a dark-haired boy. The same child I saw when I kissed Teoma. My heart races, unable to comprehend the meaning of my vision. I pull her close. She is my sister from another time.

Miriam approaches and hugs us both to her. Our energies merging as our breath becomes one, my worry melts away. "I welcome you, my newest daughter, to our family. I am well pleased that you have found a soul sister in our Mary."

I touch Rebeka's wet cheek. "Soon you will be with us and all will be well."

As we wash one another, the conversation centers on our relationships with men. Most of the women are married, so between us there are lifetimes of experience. Poor Rebeka cannot seem to absorb all of it, as I brush her wavy hair.

"Certainly Mary can enlighten us on how to have our choice of men." I ignore her aunt's offensive inquiry.

"Well, it appears as if without a male audience, Mary cannot perform." The juice of figs on her tongue does not sweeten Rebeka's mother's tone. Why does she dislike me?

Hava's silent advice drifts across the bath, *Unhappy with themselves, they fear your self-assured nature. Just remember who you are.*

I smile at her. "This is Rebeka's special time. It is not for our sake that we gather here, but to help her transition comfortably from a single girl to a married woman."

"It is for Rebeka's welfare that she understands the truth about men and women."

"And what do you believe to be the truth?"

Straightening up, Rebeka's mother adjusts her wrap, "Good wives might have a chance to control their husbands if not for women like you who flaunt the hair of a harlot!"

The silence in the room is deafening.

I feel a pull from Hava, *Do not engage this woman.*

Yearning for escape, my breasts suddenly feel very heavy. Rebeka turns and hugs me, the pressure of her naked body against mine causes my breasts to leak on us both. I excuse myself from our milky predicament, laughter trailing behind me.

Frustrated, I try to relieve my full breasts, but cannot. I must return to my baby! Redressing, I slip out of the house under a veil of kasa and return to Nazareth, wishing fervently that I had brought Sheikan. Already unseemly with my bare head, what more damage could riding astride do?

When I arrive in the nursery, Sarah greets me. "Josh has been crying for you, Ima!" Quickly, I relieve the wet nurse of my wailing child, who latches on as if starving. The pressure in my breasts is well relieved by the time my husband comes for me.

"Mary, why are you here?" I shake my head, unwilling to express my woes in front of the children. Yeshua takes my hand, but how can I tell him that by not veiling my power, he has left me exposed to the anger of the world?

***

166

In their bedchambers, Yeshua finds Mary kneeling over her bridal trunk. He envies the sea-foam silk embracing her every curve. How fortunate is he! After spending the past week in the company of men, preparing his brother for matrimony, he has learned much. Many of the married men placate their wives with finery in exchange for sexual favors. Last night, his beautiful wife most willingly engaged his desire with such immense pleasure to amaze him. How can that for which Adonai punished Sodom and Gomorrah so harshly bring so much delight?

Quietly he approaches, stifling a groan as she reaches further into the trunk. Long sable curls part like drapes revealing a round lush bottom. Without further hesitation, he kneels to draw her close. "I want to express my gratitude for…" She turns to him, eyes brimming with tears. "Beloved, what is it?"

She shakes her head. Is this about her hasty retreat from Cana? Before he can ask, she hands him a finely embroidered linen napkin. Violet roses flow over the edges.

"Martha helped me embroider my linens." Her voice wavers with emotion, but she picks up another napkin, not so neatly stitched. "Here's one of mine."

"It is just as beautiful, because you created it with love."

With a piercing green gaze, she begs him to understand. "I have never used any of this." Her delicate fingers brush over the contents of the trunk before diving deeper. "Yeshua…," her voice breaks into a sob.

He turns her around, the fractured wedding plate between them. Rarely has she complained about not having a home of her own, but now Jacob and Rebeka's cottage stands as a stark reminder of her loss. His preparations have called him away and soon another journey must be made, and someday back to the Himals. None of which he has told her.

"If we would have had a cottage built outside of the family home like my brother and his bride, then what would you have done when I was gone?"

Her answer is barely audible. "I would have probably been even lonelier."

He smoothes her curls as if to untangle their lives. Although serving practical purposes to remain in his parents' home, there exists a smothering air of dependency. Not yet seen as a capable man, his father still insists on accompanying him to Alexandria.

"Must you leave me again?"

Swallowing thickly, he nods. She must be told. "Not any time soon, Joshua is still so little. This next time will not be as long, for we will be going to Egypt."

"The children and I cannot come?"

"It is safer for you to stay here. The children will be much happier at home." Her eyes search his: why? "There is a teacher in Alexandria with whom I must study for a short time."

With trembling lips, she whispers, "Even a week is too long."

His eyes fill. "Mary, you know that I am preparing for my reign. I must be ready."

"I know that is what you say, but I do not understand why the teachers cannot come here."

"Because you are here and I would be distracted." His tender humor seduces a reluctant smile from her lips.

"Yesh, since we've been married I have been waiting for you to return or wondering when you will leave."

Quieting her with a kiss, he carries her to bed, hoping to quell her melancholy with caresses. But her mind is not with him.

He will leave me again and again! Why could I not perceive before marrying what my life would be like? I am led by my heart rather than my head.

He smiles down at her. "Thank goodness; if you think too much about all of this, you would want to run away."

She studies him earnestly. "But where would I go when you are my home?"

Stroking her softly, he is rewarded by a passionate kiss. Perhaps he has forgotten the wisdom of the Torah. A man shall leave his father and mother and cling unto his wife. At this moment, he clings as tightly as possible.

***

Dressing for the wedding ceremony this early Kislev morning, I pray all will be well. Yeshua struggles to sash his tunic, so I help him straighten the woven leather girdle about his deep gold garment. He's been distracted since the Zadoks arrived from Qumran for his brother's wedding. Neither Zechariah nor his son, Jochan, attended ours.

On tiptoe I kiss his lips, my wine red gown swishing enticingly around my bare legs. My husband smiles, perhaps relieved. "Are you not going to wear your necklace?"

"Yes, of course," I hurry to my trunk and retrieve the precious wedding gift from Britannia.

Placing it around my neck, he smiles. "Although you need nothing to enhance your beauty, it does look lovely on you." I am pleased with the effect of the delicate silver branches lying gracefully above the silken gown. Accepting my husband's gift, I leave my curls uncovered.

He smiles and escorts me to the cart, where the children greet us joyously.

"You look beautiful, Ima. Look, Hava put flowers in my hair too!" Sarah's delight becomes my own as I join the family on the short trip to Cana. Yeshua stays behind with Teoma and his cousins to escort Jacob. When the groom arrives at the bride's home, the celebration begins. The exchange of gifts and property satisfy both Chaverim families. How much more pleasant than my wedding. In a simple blue robe, Rebeka is lovely, and of course, discretely veiled by her husband under the chupa.

My perceptions seem greatly enhanced by the necklace. The men's sharp angled auras like sword blades, the women's soft, round, malleable bubbles distract me. Many couples appear roughly joined, filling in each other's deficiencies. Young children have soft vibrant auras of mixed geometrics with round edges, blending male and female energies.

Yeshua's hayye is the most amazing of all—a teardrop with bubble-like boundaries, yet on closer inspection, a multifaceted sacred geometry. His silvery-white is tinged violet, as our auras create the visica pisces of two conjoining spheres.

After enjoying the traditional wedding dances, we refresh ourselves with a cup of wine, but at the soulful wail of the flute, I am asked to dance. Rebeka's mother loudly voices her complaint. With bravado reminiscent of his older brother, Jacob reassures her all will be well.

The stirring music draws me to the center of the courtyard as the crowd circles around. Ancient notes in patterns of three and five flow hotly through my crown and into the earth. Faster and faster my hips move to the rhythm of the music, my arms swirling the energies. Around the perimeter, I dance in conjoined circles, changing directions at the point where the two meet over and over again. My seductive dance is not ignored by my husband, the crowd slipping from my consciousness as my passion rises to obliterate all but its object.

When the last note dies away, Yeshua draws me into the darkness outside the courtyard, but our passion play is shortly interrupted by serenading. Anxious for the privacy of our chambers, we join the other young couples to carry Jacob and Rebeka back to Nazareth. At the threshold of their new home, Jacob scoops up a giggling Rebeka as we sing to their happiness and fertility.

Under the command of the Davidic king, a grave pair of foot soldiers from Qumran guards the door. Yeshua and I continue our dance beneath the rising moon, until someone announces:

"The marriage has been consummated."

There on the door hangs the bridal linen stained red.

When Jacob and Rebeka emerge from their secluded state a month after the wedding, I instantly recognize the hayye of the dark-haired child from my visions, but keep my secret hidden.

One cool morning in Adar, I sit with Rebeka on a blanket under the barren branches of a pomegranate tree. Sarah plays sweetly with her brother who prefers teething on the small wooden blocks. Taken with their new aunt, both children recognize her unborn child.

"Ima, why is my brother inside Doda?" I hold my daughter close, knowing she perceives too much. "Doda Rebeka and Dod Jacob are going to be very sad when the baby dies." She is so matter of fact. Leaving my side, she goes to hug her aunt.

"Sorry, Doda. Remember that Eloha loves you."

Rebeka looks up from playing with Joshua who is silently telling his brother, *It is too soon.* Overwhelmed by the intensity of the moment, I can hardly breathe. I am guided to talk to my father.

At the end of second Adar, my parents arrive with my sister and her family to celebrate my twenty-first birthday. Of all the lovely presents I receive, Sarah's is the most moving. A beautiful painting depicts our family—Yeshua and I in the middle with Teoma on my other side and three children playing at our feet, a curly-haired little girl, a fair-haired boy, and a dark one. I thank her profusely as Yeshua looks over my shoulder, praising Sarah on the loveliness of her artwork.

I understand Teoma, but the third child?

170

Please, Yesh, give me some time to talk with my Abba. I promise I will discuss it with you as soon as I understand. With a kiss, he gives me his consent and arranges for my father to meet with me in the sitting area of our chambers.

Abba is delighted. "My, how marriage and motherhood become you. Your hayye is beautifully whole." He kisses my forehead. "What is it, dear?"

In a flood of tears, I reveal all that has transpired from that fateful kiss to recognizing Rebeka's baby as the same one I envision bearing Teoma. Gently taking my hands in his, Abba speaks, "You carry too much burden, my daughter. You are blessed by your connection to the energies, but being so fluent emotionally, it is difficult for you to interpret all you see."

He pauses to offer linen to dry my eyes. "Mary, I have always known that you have a powerful destiny, which you have commenced with Yeshua. Entangled in your spiritual path is Teoma, who will be with you in the end and that is when this other child shall be born. Rebeka and Jacob have their own destinies to fulfill. Neither you nor Yeshua can prevent their loss, it is their path. The spirit of this child shall serve its soul agreement before being born to you to live a joyous life."

Swallowing thickly, I broach my greater concern. "How is it that I can bear a son of Teoma's and not cause damage to my relationship with Yeshua?"

. He smiles kindly, "Do not question your destiny."

He is not telling me something, but I can only perceive his love for me, no other emotion that may influence the interpretation of his sight. "Abba, Yeshua suspects something." I hand him the artwork. "Sarah made this for me."

A doting grandfather, he beams. "A most perceptive child and quite a fine artist for her age."

"What shall I tell Yeshua?"

"Tell him the truth. Share with him how you feel. You cannot hide this from him for he is capable of looking into the heart of man and seeing all. As his wife, you know this."

I hug my father for such a long time that he has to remind me that my guests are waiting for me to enjoy the remainder of the celebration. "Abba, thank you so much, I chose well in coming to you and Ima. I have learned much and love you so."

He kisses my forehead. "Mary, you are divinely guided, but remember your choices are the gift of free will. You create your own destiny." Taking my arm, he leads me to the gathering room.

In our chambers afterwards, I lay upon my husband, my favorite position to share confidences, the solidity of his body balancing my fluid emotions, our hearts beating together. But where to start?

He kisses me. "At the beginning, love."

"You know that when Teoma returned from Judaea, I kissed him and…" I hesitate fearful to reveal myself, "and saw a vision of a dark-haired son that I would bear him."

His body stiffens slightly under mine. "How is that possible without complications for you at delivery?" He is concerned about my welfare, not that I shall bear another man's son.

"I do not know. It is what I saw. Then, the first time I hugged Rebeka at her prenuptial, I saw the same child born to her."

Yeshua's brow wrinkles, "Teoma's son as well?"

"No, it is the child she now bears in her womb, Jacob's son. Sarah and Joshua both recognize him as their brother." In my husband's intense gaze, I realize he knows that his nephew will die. A single tear catches the faint light of the full moon, before coursing down his cheek to find solace in his soft brown beard.

Silent a long time, holding one another, before he speaks, "I cannot foresee how this shall unfold, but it will serve no one for Jacob and Rebeka to mourn prematurely. Your father confirmed that there was nothing that can alter this course?"

I shake my head no. "But Yeshua, perhaps if we try to save the infant for them, then the rest of this destiny shall not be."

"The divine orchestration is already in motion. Perhaps the soul of this child is fulfilling a spiritual agreement."

"Abba did say that the great work this soul does for Rebeka and Jacob will be rewarded by a joyful life later."

He sighs, "As Teoma's and your son?"

My tears drip upon his chest. "I am sorry, Yeshua."

Kissing me softly, he whispers, "Mary, do not apologize for what has yet to become. Let us live in this moment and not mourn the future." Our bittersweet passion leaves us in tears of joy diluting the sorrow for the loss to come.

The morning before our anniversary, I finish nursing six-month-old Joshua. Unlike his sister at the same age, he has yet to indicate his need to relieve himself, so I prepare to change his soiled cloth. He enjoys the attention, and since Yeshua will not agree to another child, I relish his infancy.

"Yesh, can you hand me a fresh cloth?"

He retrieves it and picks up Joshua. "Allow me."

This should prove amusing. Smiling, I toss him a large cloth to protect the linens. He sets the baby down to reach for the supplies, but Joshua scoots away.

"Hold on, Josh," Yeshua grabs a chubby leg and drags him back. Joshua laughs, a new game, this time with a novice. I hold my tongue and watch. "He's quick. Please, Mary, dress, I'll take care of this." I keep one eye on them.

Yeshua has managed to remove the soiled cloth, but before he can get Joshua clean, off the baby scoots again. Picking up his kicking squealing son, Yeshua sighs. Joshua smiles before urinating on his Abba. "Oh, for goodness sakes, child."

"Dear, do you want help?"

Putting the baby back down, Yeshua holds him still with one hand, "It's too late now. Let me finish what I have started."

While I brush my hair, Yeshua makes progress. A fresh cloth folded under a clean bottom, Yeshua attempts to secure it and Joshua wriggles away with a wet baby laugh. For the third time, my determined husband catches our son, takes a deep breath, and quickly ties the strap.

"Thank goodness, I did it." He holds Joshua up for my approval. "What do you think?"

"I think that I am very blessed to have a husband with such perseverance." He smiles, oblivious to the fact that Joshua's genitals are quite visible through the gaping cloth.

"Will you hold him while I change my tunic?"

I try not to laugh, "Of course, dear."

We find Sarah in the atrium swinging with Teoma on the hammock. "Hello, Joshua, did you have fun with Abba?"

Yeshua rolls his eyes. *They are laughing at me.*

Teoma reaches for the baby. "Mary, this is about to fall off."

"I had a bit of trouble changing him," Yeshua explains.

Teoma looks between us, his eyes smiling, "Well, it is not easy, Yesh, since he's been scooting."

"You have some experience with changing babies?"

"Hava says I am as capable as any woman."

"Really? So did you learn this from your Roman friends?"

Slightly perturbed, Teoma responds, "No, from the women in the nursery. I used to change Sarah all the time, but Joshua is a bit more challenging since he has a tendency to urinate on you."

Yeshua is obviously upset. I kiss his cheek, "How wonderful that both of you are willing and able to help with the children," but he turns to Teoma.

"So what's your secret?"

"Hold him a moment and I'll show you."

Teoma places a blanket on the ground and takes Joshua from his father. Sitting down with his legs spread, he places the baby between his knees, talking to him continuously. Joshua is mesmerized. Quickly he unties the leather strap; Joshua takes his cue and tries to roll. Teoma puts one leg over my squealing son and refolds the cloth wrapping it tightly around the baby's hips. He ties the strap and has Joshua up so rapidly that not three breaths have passed our lips.

Yeshua shakes his head, "Cooking, childcare, and handsome as well. You are a fine catch for any woman." Teoma's cheeks flush.

Jumping off the hammock onto her father, Sarah exclaims, "Abba, Dod Teo wants to stay with us! Maybe he can teach you to cook and change babies."

"You're right, sweetheart." He turns sheepishly to Teoma, "Thank you for sharing your wisdom."

Still sitting on the ground holding Joshua, Teoma grins, "Anytime, Yesh."

"It has been too long since we practiced Reiti's art of combat."

Teoma nods, "I'll meet you at the stables after lunch."

Pulling Yeshua down to the blanket, I put my arms around both of them. "Listen; there is no need to prove anything. The children and I are grateful for all that you do for us. We love you both. If you truly want to be more like women, try asking for help and working together instead of competing with each other."

Sarah laughs, "Dod Teo and Abba can't be women. They don't have breasts!"

On the spring equinox, we return to the sacred grove to celebrate our sixth anniversary. Sheikan snorts and prances through the golden plains of Esdraelon rippling with grain. Unperturbed by Sheikan's high spirits, my husband calmly rides Teoma's lumbering mare, leading a mule burdened with supplies. Yeshua graciously dismissed Teoma's offer to escort us, not treating our friend any differently since I revealed my secret eight days ago.

Our relationship has finally merged the physical with the spiritual. Yeshua trots his horse to catch up. "So, you don't need both Teoma and me to make a perfect mate?"

"Can I not have any private thoughts?" I laugh as he shakes russet locks over his shoulders.

"Not unless you veil them. You have become like a clear body of water. I can see into the depth of your soul." Nudging close, I reach for a kiss. Our mounts stand quietly until Sheikan incites the thick muscled mare. With a coarse braying, the pack mule shakes vigorously, its large ears flopping side to side like a big gray dog.

Beautifully wild, the foothills of Moreh hide the small grove of trees surrounding the stream swollen from winter rains. Curious foxes, a lean tawny wildcat, numerous gray rabbits, and ruffled quails visit as a pair of hawks screech out their salutation from the cloud-speckled sky. Like deep-throated flutes aching in the melody of the wind, the ancient trees sing. The sun nearly sets by the time we make camp, not as efficient as Teoma, but we make do. After creating fire, Yeshua looks up.

"What is it, love?"

"I need to relieve myself," I reply heading to the stream. Milking my own breasts takes so long that when I return shivering before the fire, Yeshua is nowhere to be seen.

Sitting on my soiled sadin I warm myself by the small fire. Chirping insects punctuate the silence, lulling me into a meditative state. Soon my hayye vibrates rapidly, a more refined act of raza. The fire glows in the midst of the grove, yet I am not there but within my body, just beyond, discovering a different texture of reality. I imagine Yeshua's hayye and instantly we are together.

My love, you naturally found me in this inner dimension. I am very pleased how easily you can manifest your reality through desire.

175

Merging, our auras blend, our bodies not as solid as the earth reality, we make love weightlessly. All the same moves, but without the resistance of form, the light around us as bright as the rising sun. Our passion goes on and on, unencumbered by physical exhaustion, the loss of breath or fluids. When he was in Britannia, I would imagine him while our energies connected, but this is a full physical experience somewhere else beyond.

My dearest, this is how we can be together when we are parted.

Over any distance, Yeshua?

Yes, any distance, any time, any dimension. This is the extent of our connection. We are of the same soul seed from the beginning until the end of time. Relieved, I trust him implicitly.

Yeshua, if we are needed by those we left behind, will we be able to return?

If the children need you, you shall return to them as you desire.

But there seems to be no sense of time.

Time is but a quality we sense when we are in the earth realm.

He demonstrates how to move through this dimension, traveling to the places he has been. Foggy Britannia is most familiar to me from his stories, but when we come upon a great mountain range blanketed in white, I am surprised. *Is that snow, Yeshua?*

Yes, my love. It is the Himal mountain range where dear Zsao lives. I visited him and studied with his master.

But when?

While in Britannia, Ambrose expected that I would go alone to the Hindus region, but Abba would never agree… so I learned this means of travel to continue my training. They wish me to return once more.

I gasp, *Will you take me?*

No, love, I….

He is leaving again! My fear casts me back to earth.

Shivering, I sit naked near the fire burnt down to ashes. The sun has yet to rise. Yeshua arrives to hold me in his arms and I melt into him. "Hush, I shall not go where you cannot follow." Why did he wait until now to teach me? "My love, I have been waiting for a divine opening and our mutual expression of sorrow finally created a portal of opportunity."

Reeling from the experience of bridging time and space, I ask, "If there is no time, then can we not project into the future a happier outcome for Jacob and Rebeka?"

He smiles, "Since there is no time, there is no future. So all we have is this moment. The moments we spend with them, we will have to imagine

176

love, peace, and joy. So whatever the outcome, our experience will ultimately lead to happiness."

***

"Isn't it wonderful how much help we have, Mary?" Teoma laughs, referring to her flour-dusted son sitting in the middle of the table, little feet in the dough. All morning, Sarah has been trying to teach the baby how to roll the dough into shapes.

Mary smiles and collects the children's creations, placing them carefully on the baking stone. He lifts it into the oven then beats the dough, while she measures the ingredients for the next batch.

"Teoma, it's nice that you enjoy working in the kitchen. The children seem to love being with you." Jacob's pregnant wife has joined them. He smiles and her cheeks flush.

A pouf of sifted flour rises to cover Mary's face and she turns to sneeze, right into his chest. "Mary, you look like a spirit." The children laugh as she cleans her face.

"Did I get it all?"

Pulling her close, he wipes off the residue, "There, you're ready to face the world," then seals his observation with a kiss.

At Rebeka's disturbed look, Mary explains, "We have been friends since childhood. If not for Yeshua, I would be Teoma's plump little wife."

"Ima, you will not be plump when you are with Dod Teo."

Before Teoma can wonder what Sarah knows, Joshua crawls across the table intent on securing her finished pieces. Scooping up the sticky baby, Teoma tosses him squealing in the air.

Mary placates Rebeka. "Do not worry. My love for Teoma does not diminish my love for Yeshua." Tickling the baby, Teoma pretends not to listen.

Rebeka asks grimly. "But what did Sarah mean?"

"I do not know exactly how it will unfold, but we do have a destiny together." Teoma's chest tightens, wishing it were so.

"I am sorry I doubted you, Mary. It must be difficult knowing what the future might hold and having to wait to see the outcome." At Rebeka's words, a sob catches in Mary's throat. Teoma puts one arm around the crying women, Josh in his other.

***

Our summer passes quickly at the shore, bringing us ever closer to the birth of Rebeka's baby. Undeterred by the sand, Joshua learns to walk determined to keep up with his daring sister. Nearly tumbling in the surf, he's a challenge to watch over. Thank goodness we have help.

As I slip on a bright yellow sadin, Yeshua murmurs from our bed, "Your dark beauty needs no protection from the sun. I cherish seeing you unencumbered."

I smile at him, brushing my hair, "Let us breakfast with the children and then leave our garments behind."

Pulling me close, he kisses my mouth, stoking an insatiable fire. Long hot days melt into steamy nights, it's a wonder we dress at all. His explorations stop abruptly. "You're right; we should spend the day with the children." Aroused, but unfulfilled, I complain.

"Yesh, they can wait a bit longer."

"No, it is their holiday too." Longingly, I watch as he dresses.

After breakfast, Yeshua entices the children to build the most realistic sculpture out of sand. As they pair off, Sarah is left without a partner. "Ima, you can build with me." Yeshua works with Josh, who prefers eating the sand.

The boys, toasted brown, start building a temple of sand, while their sisters construct a house. Josh falls laughing onto the small pile of sand his father gathers. Sarah sculpts the form of a dolphin, while I embrace the sand until my hands remember and smooth the canine brow into a sleek nose. Shimon and Judah's temple becomes an Egyptian pyramid. Furnished with sticks, shells and stones, Ruth and Esther's house looks very inviting. We laugh at the impression of a baby's bottom denting Yeshua's hill.

"Very well done, Sarah. You made your dolphin look so alive."

She smiles, "I did the tail and Ima made the face."

"Quite the artist. It must be all that Greek influence." Yeshua graces me with such an appreciative smile, I need to cool down.

The children quickly divest themselves of their clothing. Before Joshua can cross the barrier of seaweed and straddle his sister's sand dolphin, Yeshua carries him laughing into the turquoise sea. After our swim, Yeshua engages his brothers with his adventures in Britannia. Saada helps me prepare a picnic lunch but it is well into the afternoon before the children are ready to rest. When daughters of some of the families who work our land stroll down the beach, the boys excuse themselves, while the girls find their mother. On Yeshua's lap, Joshua sleeps with Sarah soon to follow.

Now where were we? Yeshua teases me with provocative images until Saada looks up and whispers, "You two can run along. I'll watch the children this afternoon."

Yeshua leads me toward the tents on the deserted beach, "Come, let's see what occupies Teoma and Edia." I stop, yearning desperately to be alone with him.

"Yeshua, if you would like an audience while we make love, then by all means, find them."

My sadin slips to the sand, but he doesn't move. I run into the surf. When he fails to join me, I swim past the rolling breakers over the coral ridge and call my dolphin friends. They respond with their gentle hayye.

Greetings, Elat. Where is your mate? Gliding against my out-stretched hands they receive their answer. The largest presses her nose to my belly. *But you are in need.*

Their sensitive ministrations calm me. Smooth bodies brush past mine tantalizingly and I dive beneath the surface to meet them. Our seductive dance brings me such great pleasure that my new partners must bring me to the surface for a breath before escorting me closer to shore. Exhausted I bid the dolphins farewell.

Until we meet again, Elat.

Lying on my back in the bright sun, the water gently lapping up my legs, I close my eyes, soon asleep.

The rising tide awakens me from my slumber. I sit up, disoriented. Merging with the salt of the sea, my tears express the intensity of my need. I focus on my desire and with my next exhalation stand before him in the thick grove above the beach.

"Your swim was rewarding, I hope?" Yeshua smiles and holds out his arms. I fall into the density of his lap. How is it that I am here by desire only? "You are progressing nicely in your travels." His warm breath rekindles this morning's flame. "I would think that your aquatic lovers would have satisfied you," he murmurs stroking my damp hair, lulling me back to sleep.

I awaken after dusk, naked within the grove. Yeshua is gone again. My body aches. Taking a deep breath, I imagine soaking in a hot steaming tub and instantly I am in the baths where Yeshua awaits. I allow him to tend to me. Eyes closed as he brushes my hair, breathing deeply the steamy perfume of the waters, I focus my desire on our cozy tent, soon snuggled against him beneath soft blankets.

"Are we not going to make love?"

He laughs, "Are you not the least bit interested in how you are able to move through space in your complete human form?"

Yawning, I answer sleepily, "I do not know, other than it is exhausting. It seems as if my dolphin friends are more willing to appease me than my husband." He smiles before kissing me deeply. We make love quietly and although very nice, it is not like being with the dolphins.

"Who do you think embodied their consciousness?"

"Only you would consider such alternative practices."

In the morning I awake refreshed and full of inquiry. Thank goodness, Yeshua is still here. He returns my kiss before opening his eyes, "Now you have questions?"

"Why was I so fatigued but so easily able to locate you?"

"It takes much energy to move through space and you traveled three times in only part of a day." He tries to stroke the frown from my face.

"I could have walked that far without undue effort."

"My love, distance is of no consequence as long as you imagine clearly and desire purely. The act of manifesting physical form from one place in time to another consumes much energy."

"Yesh, how did you embody the dolphin consciousness?"

"First, with their consent, and then the same technique as traveling in the ethers. The form is left behind, so the spirit can conjoin another's physicality. Do you not remember doing this as children?" He projects an image for me.

Lying on our backs on the grassy slope, he is nine and I am six. Watching the birds, I express a desire to fly. "Then, Mary, be the hawk." Never questioning his faith in me, I need no further instruction. Soon I find myself flying overhead, soaring with the air currents caressing my wings, looking down upon two children who are watching me.

"As a child you have no limitations of belief. Closer to spirit you innately know your physical form is just one of many realities."

"Thank you for reminding me of my potential." I kiss him, and he laughs.

"As I remember my own potential I want to help awaken you to yours. Your love provides rapid enlightenment."

At the end of Elul, I awake knowing it has begun. My dark son came to me in a dream, so I rise and leave my sleeping husband. Drawn to the nursery, I find Sarah and Joshua sitting on a blanket playing with the energy of Rebeka's unborn child. Brilliantly rich as the leaves of an oak, his hayye joyously interacts with theirs.

Joshua waves as Sarah says quietly, "Ima, our brother is ready to go back to Eloha now and wait for us." She pats the blanket next to her. Silently I sit to be greeted by the flitting light of my yet-to-be-conceived son. Joshua laughs and Sarah scolds, "Hush, don't wake up the others. It's our time with him."

Joshua toddles over and sits heavily in my lap. Sarah moves closer for a cuddle so I kiss her curls tinted gold from the summer sun. Immediately, the baby's hayye moves to my face for a kiss. I comply and it enters my lips, exiting through my root.

A sense of peace, a knowing that all will be well, washes over me. I see myself holding my dark-haired son and Teoma smiling down upon us, surrounded by great trees with leaves the color of this child's hayye. Hugging my children, we say farewell to his sweet spirit, which moves beyond to merge with the light.

Shortly after breakfast, I find Rebeka wandering through the gardens, holding the small of her back. The baby's hayye has gone. "How long have you been in labor?"

She smiles through a contraction. "All night, but it is getting much stronger now."

Taking her arm, I lead her to the chamam. "Let's get you ready." I send word to Miriam and allow Leah to show me how to examine my sister. She is nearly halfway. "You are progressing very well for your first time."

"It really isn't so hard." Worry rises when Miriam looks at me. Silently, I pray to have my fear lifted and be guided to love, then I pray for Rebeka and Jacob.

Miriam smiles, *Her destiny is not yours; she will have an easy delivery.*

After preparations in the chamam, I examine Rebeka and her womb is open. "Mary, most deliveries go smoothly. Our Rebeka is perfectly built for delivering big, healthy babies." Both Jacob and Rebeka beam at Leah but my heart lurches. Miriam spends as much time patting my shoulder as fussing about the room. Alone in my knowledge, I call silently to my husband who meditates in the atrium.

Love, I will come when you need me. Do not interfere with your worry. Keep releasing it. I try, but the closer Rebeka gets to delivery, the tighter the fear clutches my heart.

Rebeka sits up from lounging on the cushions and the birth waters gush forth. The women quickly change the linens and clean her up, for she is ready to push. "Come closer, Mary. Jacob will help hold me, but I want you near."

I sit nearby silently blessing them with strength and courage. Jacob supports his wife in position to push. The baby lands in Leah's hands, not breathing. With a stricken look, Miriam signals Saada to get Joseph. I yearn for Yeshua, but fear to bring him into this.

Jacob looks up from holding his tired wife, "What's wrong?"

Worry clouds his mother's face. "Your Abba is coming."

"Why doesn't the baby cry?"

She does not answer. Rebeka clutches me hysterically. Leah cuts the cord while Miriam tries to stimulate the baby. Jacob yells for his brother, who soon appears to take the gray infant. Jacob cries silently as Yeshua prays.

Tearing open my sadin as I assist her back into position to deliver the afterbirth, Rebeka's hysteria rises to a pinnacle. Jacob goes over the edge of panic when his father enters the roomful of sobbing women.

Touching the infant, Joseph shakes his head. "I'm sorry, son. It's stillborn."

"No!" Jacob's cry rips the fabric of illusion that all will be well. Dropping to his knees in front of Yeshua, he beseeches, "If you can bring your wife back from the dead, please, please, save my son." Jacob begs, his hands beneath his lifeless child. Rebeka screams, clutching me with such grief. I try to calm her, kissing her head, but to no avail. Yeshua stares sadly at his brother.

Joseph intercedes, "Yeshua cannot save this child."

Jacob pushes his father's arm away, "No, Abba. This cannot be Marya's will," his voice coarsened by anger. Jacob takes his son, shrugging off Yeshua's comforting touch.

"Don't bother. What kind of healer are you if you cannot save my son?" Rebeka's wails become louder as Jacob approaches. They clasp one another, their dead child between them.

"I know traditionally stillborn babies are not ritually prepared for burial but it is important that you join the women and receive healing by this worldly action."

Yeshua's gaze softens and I fall into the void of his dark eyes, where there is no time, only peace and compassion for all. Touching my cheek, he brings me back to this moment. "Our eyes are portals to our souls. In yours, I perceive the watery depth of emotion that unites body, mind, and spirit. This is your gift to me and the world—your pure heartfelt emotion. Just as you have difficulty giving birth physically, the expression of your emotion can be painful."

"I am worried. When Jacob perceived that you failed him, something shifted in you.

Sighing, he draws me ever closer, "I felt it as well, but I do not know how it shall resolve. Be assured, I shall not withhold from you any longer. As it becomes clear to me, I shall share all with you, my beloved."

The profundity of my gratitude wets the front of his tunic. This is all I have ever wanted.

So with a heavy heart, lightened immeasurably by Yeshua's promise, I meet Miriam and Hava in the mikvah where we purify ourselves for the task ahead. The family tomb lies enclosed by a low stone wall. Our somber mood follows us through the gate, shadowing the quiet beauty of the garden. Miriam casts a heartening glance at a tiny lone grave.

In silence, we enter the tomb.

The air within is cold and damp. Burning oil lamps provide the only light in the windowless space. Baskets filled with white linen, sacred herbs, and precious oils surround the waist-high marble slab at the center. A small lump under the linen on the altar reminds us of why we are here. A beautiful baby with dark curls like his father, his perfectly formed hands and feet belie the fact that the life force is gone. Gazing at the child from my vision, I tremble.

Miriam carefully pours water into a basin and Hava washes the body. Burning in the hearth at the back of the tomb, the smoky incense of eucalyptus infuses the space before drifting up through a small opening in the ceiling. After we wash the body, Hava blesses the sacred burial oil and begins by anointing the baby's head and feet. The oil is then placed tenderly on the seven energy centers from the bottom up, while the rest of the body is prepared with precious pungent myrrh. Murmuring the second prayer offering, we wrap it in the pure white linen, carefully lining each layer with herbs and spice. Finally, we place the baby in the specially prepared sepulcher, a niche carved out of the cold stone. This afternoon he will be buried in the ground by the men, then next year will reenter this tomb as clean white bones within a carved ossuary. In harmonious triad, we offer up our voices to guide its soul back to the center of All That Is.

My tears begin anew as our song finishes, finding no relief in attending the corpse. Smoky eucalyptus trails us from the tomb and I sit wearily on a cold marble bench. Miriam joins me with Hava's arm around my waist. I shiver. Hava and Miriam hold the hayye as I focus on the purple drop that has become my portal into meditation. A prism of luminescent light expands to encompass us, before splitting like sunshine in a drop of water.

Through the center beam of pure white light The One emerges. I gasp. This is the same portal I entered at Joshua's birth when I died and Yeshua brought me back.

My beloved, you gather for the sacred ritual of physical death. Know that the spirit is eternal. Judge not the form rucha takes to accomplish its purpose.

Touching each of our heart centers, the hayye of The One infuses us with peace and love before merging with the light. Breathing in synchrony, our focus returns.

Gently Hava speaks, "My dear, you have had the somber energy of carrying a great burden for many months now." She hands me a linen cloth to wipe my eyes; Miriam sits motionless by my side.

With a shuddering sigh, I relate my tale. Hava wonders aloud why I did not share my knowing with Yeshua sooner. "Because it involves Teoma." My heart lightens to see no judgment in their eyes. "When he returned from Judaea two years ago, I kissed him. In that kiss, I saw a child in our future. I said nothing because I feared to believe my vision." Hava squeezes my hand.

"But, Mary, to suffer with such a burden while you were pregnant," she shakes her head. "You take on too much."

Tearfully, I whisper, "Abba said the same thing."

Miriam says softly, "Mary, your relationship with Teoma has been a source of concern to many, yet the three of you have handled it with love and compassion."

Like the trumpets of Joshua that brought Jericho down, Miriam's words crumble the walls around my heart's secret sorrow. Hava takes my hand, "My dear, we shall pass through this sad time and then perhaps you might experience the magic of Sucot with your beloved."

Walking Between the Worlds

Joshua pays little attention to nursing, distracted by the excitement around him. Hardly able to contain herself, Sarah made him a small dolphin which Yeshua helped her carve in his father's shop. Yeshua presents his son with a family of small wooden eggs. Their tiny faces painted to mimic their namesakes, their clothing the color of the aura of the person each represents, all fit in a small basket lined with lamb's wool. Delighted, Joshua tastes each one.

In spite of the chasm of silence between Jacob and Yeshua, the celebration of Joshua's birthday lightens everyone's mood. Rebeka tends to my son's every need, allowing me to stroll with Yeshua through the olive grove. "Mary, it appears part of Joshua's work is to assist my brother and his wife through the pain of their loss. Are you comfortable with that?"

"Yes, although I have borne my children unto this world, they are not mine to hold. I love them dearly, but realize that they are, like you, gifted healers."

Yeshua embraces me beneath the canopy of an ancient olive tree, heavy with fruit. "Mary, as you do your own work, your relationship with others becomes free of expectations. Your way of mothering is devoted to service of the divine path."

"Thank you, but I'm not devoted, simply in love with their essence. Your happiness is mine. If I keep any of you fast to my breast, how can I take pleasure in your growth? If this is service, it is not work." He breaks into laughter.

"Precisely my point, precious wife. We are here to live a life of service that brings us joy."

Later in the afternoon as we bid our guests goodbye, I embrace my father in heartfelt appreciation. "Abba, it has transpired as you foretold. Your advice to confide in Yeshua has opened new portals within our hearts for one another."

He hugs me tightly to his chest and I feel immense gratitude for his patient guidance all of my life. "You are most welcome, my daughter. I am happy to be of service to you." I smile at his choice of words. This life is about joyful service, harvesting the fruits of compassionate seeds sown when we serve another in love.

At the end of the grape and olive harvest, Sucot dawns very warm. An air of excitement hovers over the crowd at the edge of the last field of barley glistening golden on this bright autumn day. Every man, woman, and child in attendance is prepared to offer thanks. Three Chaverim sing beautiful songs of praise to Marya for the rich blessings of this earth, while a priestess from the temple of Astarte offers thanks to the Elat for nurturing her children.

Beneath terraced vineyards, flutes and drums entice the men to dance the gathering of sheaves of grain. When the lyre adds her voice, I join hands with the women dancing for the Elat. Finger tambourines invite Divine fertility and I laugh as Yeshua reminds me to keep the white light tightly around my womb.

Near the close of the festivities, one of the white-bearded Chaverim asks all the young couples to participate in blessing the ritual sowing of the fields. Excited laughter punctuates his drawn-out invitation as he reminisces about harvests when men were particularly virile and young women ever so ripe. Our anticipation reaches a fervor until finally, the elder straightens his bent form and releases us to the fields. Past colorful booths, ardent couples run hand in hand to find an intimate cleft. Leading me through softly waving stalks, Yeshua heads for the heart of the field. Once alone, we drop to our knees and pray.

"Marya, we are grateful for all the blessings that have been bestowed upon us. We ask that our union be blessed with light and love, that the Earth may experience our joy many fold. Bless those of our community who celebrate with us, that their hearts be filled with love. Ameyn."

Like a sunbeam through the clouds, a prism of hayye shines upon us and magically the sheaves begin to shift. Interweaving themselves to prepare a bed, individual stalks bend without breaking, clearing a space around us. We lie down in their midst.

The healing nura illuminates our passion revealing multitudes of interlocking tristans. Lying upon the woven bed of barley, beneath my lover, I am mesmerized by the hayye originating from the sun. At the moment of penetration, the beam pierces the mantle of the earth transforming the tristans into interlocking spheres. The earth has received the blessing of the heavens. We may look forward to another bountiful harvest.

Yeshua kisses my damp cheeks, "My love, you are so attuned to the hayye, it is all I can do to keep you here with me." The sun dips low, causing the westerly sheaves to cast their shadow upon us. We rise to see the interwoven sheaves have formed a perfect rose of five petals. Although the barley is unharmed, the seeds have been spilt unto the earth, in preparation for next season.

Among the last to leave the field, Yeshua and I wander back home. Teoma holds Edia's hand, catching up to tease, "So Yesh, shall the next crop be more fruitful?"

Yeshua smiles and wraps an arm around my waist. "I believe we left our mark, friend." Laughter precedes us into the courtyard, missing only Jacob's mirth.

After weeks of preparations for Yeshua's trip to Egypt, we visit my family in late Kislev. The lovely villa in Cana is decorated gaily for Chanuka. In the large window looking out to the courtyard stands the fine silver menorah filled with precious oil to glow upon us. Yeshua has agreed to stay until the eve of the winter solstice, so we can spend more time with my sister and her husband.

Nursing Joshua as we sit by the fire in the gathering room, I quietly observe my family. Across the way, Yeshua talks to Abba and Eleazer while the older children play with Ima. I put an arm around my exhausted sister and she leans into me. Joshua reaches up from my breast and strokes her arm.

"Mary, I'm late with my menses."

Using my body as a mirror, I check hers. "You are not pregnant, but your fatigue affects your cycles. You need to rest; why do you not have

189

more help?" Wearily, she sighs. Unlike Ima who designated us to wet nurses and attendants, my sister cares for all three boys with but one servant. "Martha, would you like to know a means to prevent pregnancy?" She looks up as Joshua reaches for her.

"Can you be with your husband and not risk conceiving?"

At her astonishment, I nod, "Abba Joseph has many herbal remedies for this purpose, but I remembered another way."

"What do you mean, remembered?"

I smile but Joshua needs to be changed, for still he does not indicate his need like Sarah did at this age. Martha said not to worry; when Rebeka's grieving ceases, Joshua will not remain an infant. Yeshua crosses the room.

"Why not take your sister to our chambers so you can have some privacy. I have some new stories that I think the boys will enjoy." He scoops Joshua from Martha's arms after kissing her cheek, then kisses me.

"Thank you, Yesh," I reply gratefully taking Martha's hand.

"Yeshua changes the baby?" I smile at her shocked look. "I look forward to when the boys are older, perhaps then Eleazer will be more comfortable with them."

"Martha, if you do not release your fear, they will continue to cling to you, and then you will find it more difficult to entrust their care to anyone, even their Abba."

The spacious bedchamber is in the west wing of the villa near the nursery. Sitting upon the bed facing each other, I explain the white light to my sister. After her initial surprise, she shifts as if she too remembers.

"I can show you how to place the white light of protection around your womb. You can release it whenever you are ready for more children." She gives me her consent and I proceed.

Breathing deeply with my sister I guide her through the meditation. Her aura softens as she relaxes. "Now Martha, the key to this protection is your faith. You have absolute control over your bodily functions, including your fertility. You are not at the mercy of your husband's seed." She nods, smiling at me. I take a cleansing breath. "Imagine we are going to take a trip into your gan eden."

I proceed through the imagery, truly journeying through my sister's body. Heavy with blood, the lining of her womb is ripe to flow soon with no sign of pregnancy.

"Now, Martha, visualize as I speak. See a white light like gossamer threads wrapping from the mouth of your womb around the body, over the top and splitting simultaneously to wrap around each slender tube. Over the flower-like extensions and finally, securely, around the tiny pomegranates filled with the eggs of potential offspring." We take a deep breath. "The seed cannot enter what is now protected and you can freely be with your husband without fear, choosing if and when to invite the hayye of another child."

Martha opens her eyes to look down at her womb, placing both hands over it in an inverted triangle, mimicking the form of the white light. "Mary, that was amazing. Never before had I noticed my organs except during the pain of childbirth or while having menstrual cramps. Now I feel warmth about my womb as if shielded by a veil of light. Thank you so very much."

"You are most welcome, sister. Surely you can do this on your own, perhaps teach it to your friends?" I ask hopefully.

"This remembrance could make such a tremendous difference in the lives of so many women." Taking her hand, I pray it is so.

On the full moon of Tevet, Yeshua leaves with his father to study in Alexandria. We stand on the hillside, Joshua waving long after they disappear over the crest of the valley. Sarah holds my hand, "Ima, why does Abba have to leave us so often?"

I smile at my precious daughter, "Because, my love, Abba has a great mission to serve the world and he is learning all he can to prepare for it."

Her green-gold eyes stare intently at mine. "And after he is finished with his mission, will he be able to stay with us?"

I start to answer, but something stops me—a foreboding. She searches my eyes for the truth that I do not know. Looking away from the intensity of my daughter's gaze and across the valley, I imagine Yeshua riding back to us.

Nearly a moon cycle passes before I attempt to travel in-body to Egypt. The first time I arrive, Yeshua is not alone. In the heart of a temple, he lives like an acolyte.

"Mary, you did it. I knew you could." Taking me into his arms, he kisses me passionately. His roommates do not stir as we are under a veil of kasa. Breathing in his essence, I am enchanted by our ability to be as one without limitation. Then I wonder if I can see Alexandria.

Yeshua laughs, "You are so curious. Perhaps using raza, you can see the sights without being detected. But not tonight, my love, I want you here with me."

Visiting nearly every night, I become quite adept at in-body travel. The place in which he resides is the temple of Muses. Beautiful gardens hosting wild animals provide an inviting haven for those seeking knowledge. The grand halls display Greek, Roman, and Egyptian art, as well as rare pieces from the East. Philosophers gather here to visit the great library which Yeshua says holds hundreds of thousands of scrolls. How Jacob would love this center of learning!

Unfortunately, I have seen none of this for my husband has yet to escort me outside his chambers!

Another entire moon cycle passes before I decide to share my plan with Teoma. He is not surprised that Yeshua has taught me this type of travel nor that I am visiting him. "My concern, Mary, is that you might be discovered. There are powerful mystics who live and learn in Alexandria. You should do nothing without first consulting with Yeshua."

"But he does not seem to be interested in showing me the city."

Teoma laughs, "Of course not, he wants you all to himself!"

"I will leave my purple shawl on my bed if I decide to go anytime other than when Yeshua expects me." My resolve wavers only slightly at his frown.

The next morning, I kiss Teoma on the cheek. "I'll be back." He holds my arm, shaking his head, asking silently if Yeshua knows. I smile and shake my head, no. Although concerned, he releases my arm. By visualizing my husband's hayye, I am in the temple out-of-body, floating invisible to all but him.

Yeshua sits within a great circle of mystics discussing various healing techniques. *Excellent kasa, but be careful, while you explore Alexandria.*

Floating from the temple of Muses, I am escorted by a glossy black crow. I have been to Jerusalem and many Greek cities but none as diverse as this great city at the mouth of the Nile. Magnificent temples and palaces intermingle with houses of differing styles. Busy markets with exotic goods are scattered throughout the city. Confounding as Babylon, many voices rise although Greek is most prevalent. Every shade of skin from the deepest ebony to the fairest cream adorns the inhabitants. Peeking through headdresses, somberly wrapped women walk the streets with those exposing the tops of their breasts and bellies, heavily bejeweled and tattooed with designs, faces painted to accent their features. Equally ornate, the men flaunt elaborate headdresses, tunics and robes. Exotic snakes and weasel-like creatures drape about necks and bodies with slender dogs and cats at their masters' sides. The wealthy travel on litters carried by strong men stripped to the waist.

The crow caws and the elestial quartz glows hotly in my navel. A dark familiar face in bright colored robes looks up. Oh no! Quickly I return to Nazareth.

***

To the beat of his walking stick, Belshazzar heads to the home of one of Egypt's royalty, his red and yellow caftan catching the last rays of the setting sun. The somber young man he escorts sighs but asks politely, "How is my friend Nekki?"

"He has grown strong. His wife has borne him three fine sons."

"Already? Your son only married a short time before me."

"He didn't leave his wife for two years." Belshazzar stops, "Why then was she not able to accompany you on this long journey?"

"The children…" Yeshua shakes his head. "No, it was Abba."

Belshazzar nods. He has known Joseph a long time. Always concerned about protection, keeping what he holds dear close, sometimes too close. Yeshua's father has gone ahead with Musoke, the high priest of the temple of Osiris. "Well, perhaps it is wise to keep her hidden." Yeshua glances up, barely hiding his concern.

"Belshazzar, where are we going? Abba spoke of political contacts, but I am here to study!"

"Someday when you have outgrown him, you will understand your father's purpose." The young man nods. Wondering about the second son, Belshazzar comments, "Jacob would have taken great advantage of the temple of Muses." Yeshua's infinite eyes darken. "How is he after his unfortunate loss?"

"Angry with me for not saving the child, so much entanglement between us. Mary had a foreboding, and it involves…Teoma."

"You are challenged by the gifts innate in both of you. They shall bring you great joy, sometimes wrapped in sorrow."

Learning much in his time here, Yeshua has ministered throughout the city, even raising the dead, sharing with Belshazzar his excitement at discovering a time limit of about three days before the soul is merged with the Light and unable or unwilling to return. He understands now that healing cannot be done without permission, respecting the divine plan and an individual's free will. Disturbed at how freely some use their gifts to impress others, Yeshua will soon see how many enjoy playing with the energies. Belshazzar puts his free arm around the young man's shoulders.

"Take care while you are here."

Another sumptuous gathering, the prince's vast influence evident as the most prestigious of Alexandrians share his wine, feast, and concubines. Romans and Greeks intermingle with the Egyptians. From a high balcony overlooking the vast inner courtyard, Belshazzar watches Joseph introduce his begrudging son to a few choice guests.

It is not long before his young student settles down on a cushioned lounge, arms crossed. Near the hearth, acolytes surround Sahirah. The high priestess of Isis whispers something to a lithe African beauty. She saunters over to Yeshua who looks up startled as the young woman begins a dance of seduction. Belshazzar smiles at the younger man's reaction, but soon a frown replaces his private humor.

From out of nowhere, Mari-a appears behind the seductress.

***

Pulled by my husband's desire, I find myself in the gathering room of a palace, smoky with incense. Lots of colorful people, dancing, feasting, and on closer inspection—making love. Women with their painted breasts spilling out of elegant wraps drape themselves enticingly on cushioned lounges, entertaining equally decorated men. Some couples are of the same gender and some are not couples at all but trios and more. Amazed, I become most desirous to find Yeshua.

The most graceful dancer, her slender arms encircled by bejeweled bands and tipped with brightly painted fingernails move like serpents. Her long legs descend elegantly from a well-formed bottom, a tiny waist girdled by golden chains enhances full upright breasts. Only her jewelry embellishes the ebony-skinned beauty dancing in front of my husband.

No wonder Yeshua is desirous. I feel a strange mix of surprise and passion. My husband looks about so I unveil myself behind the much taller woman. "Excuse me," I whisper and tap her silky shoulder. She nearly jumps into Yeshua's lap, who says something to her in a foreign tongue before she leaves to find another more appreciative of her talents.

In the headiness of the room, my lips entrap any explanation. Moving our garments aside, I straddle him, my breath coming in gasps. Our hayye intertwines into the pyramid of nura which has surrounded us. How surreal making love in the midst of others doing the same. The incense does not cover the musk, only heightening my passion. Our cries merge with the beat of an ancient drumming. Collapsing against his chest, tears of passion wet my cheeks.

His voice is rough, "Mary, I am sorry...."

"Don't be." Smiling at the relief on his face, I ask, "What is this place? It is so sensual."

He slips protective kasa about us. "I want to thank you for being so open. I was not with anyone else, you know."

"Well, I got here just in time."

"Really, Mary, I do not want to be...."

Hushing him with my fingertips, I murmur, "Perhaps not in your mind or heart, but your body has its own desires." My fingers glide seductively down his throat, as my mouth tastes the sweet flesh. "Besides, if you did not respond to that woman, you would have been dead." He hugs me tightly. "So why use kasa now, after making love in front of all these strangers?"

He sighs, "I should have veiled us earlier, I forgot about the energy. Many seek connection to the divine hayye, to the guides, to the One through these sensual gatherings. Our colorful climax was like a beacon drawing much attention."

Before I can look around to see who, his dark eyes search mine. "Mary, let us leave this place." So using raza, we slip through the ethers to his quarters.

Early in Nissan, I awake before dawn wondering where my angels have gone. After the children join me for our morning communion with their Abba, we go to breakfast. Kissing Teoma good morning, I spread clotted cream on his warmed massah.

"Now where are you going?" He knows me too well.

"I wish to commune with my angels in the sacred grove."

Wrinkling his brow, he asks, "The one where you conceived Sarah?" I nod. "So are you able to travel somewhere other than to Yeshua?"

I shake my head, "I haven't tried, so I'll ride Sheikan."

"You will not make it back by sunset and I do not think you should go alone. Why not commune with them in the garden?"

"Gavriel showed me the grove. I will hasten the pace as we did when we traveled to the sea, remember?"

Still shaking his head, he wraps his breakfast in a napkin, "Here, take this, you'll have to eat while you ride. Just hurry and please use kasa." With a kiss, I thank him and go to the stables.

Astride Sheikan is like riding the wind. We arrive well before noon. Sheikan rolls before drinking his fill at the stream, then trots off to graze. After refreshing myself in the cool water, I settle under a large oak tree. The angels appear, Gavriel before me, Michael on my right, Rafael behind and Uriel on my left.

Thank you, dear friends, for communing with me. It seems as if we meet only when I am in great need. I want to express my deepest gratitude for your presence in my life, your protection, your guidance.

Archangel Michael speaks with a voice like wind through chimes. *Dearest Mary, you are a most joyful charge. The emotion, which flows through you like water, fills us with delight. We bathe in your essence, experiencing the trials and challenges of the human existence as the infinite Love of the One has manifested in you.*

Archangel Uriel's brilliance shadows the grove. *Beloved, as you awaken to the truth of who you are, the depth of compassion that fills your heart is mirrored in your service to your fellow beings. Soon, you will embark on a journey with your beloved toward a deeper understanding of the human condition that shall pave the way for the mission to come.*

I shudder at the thought of another dark time with Yeshua.

Uriel's sweet laughter erases my fear. *Dearest, those lessons were duly learned. This journey involves others who exist in the darkness of their fear and whom you will bring light through your example.*

I sigh in relief, as Rafael speaks. *As your muse, I bring you inspiration to create a life of the highest manifestation of Divine Love. Your expression of love and joy is the merging of heaven and earth—malchuta.*

Silently thanking my muse, I smile. Gavriel concludes the visitation. *It is time, dearest, before you embark further on the path toward enlightenment, that you meet your divine protector.* I gasp as the angelic host disperses to be replaced by a huge creature of light.

Wings of immense proportions hugging the body of a dragon, this fiery seraph has been my constant companion since creation. I open fully

196

to her and Tamaw expands until there is no limitation to me. When I can no longer perceive where I end and the world begins, Tamaw concentrates her hayye into her long fiery tail and pierces me through the heart. Ecstasy like no other, each passionate wave flows through me, expanding my view to an infinity of stars. The intense light of the One embodied in each speck of stardust, each star seed is a soul. When I remember my own union with the One, Tamaw smiles golden flames and I am cast back into this existence. Each being on Earth is a spark of the One, originating as stardust: every human, every creature, each plant, each rock. There are no exceptions; none is greater or lesser than any other.

Yes, Mary. Gavriel intercedes, *Even highly conscious beings like Yeshua are but of the same light. As one evolves in consciousness, the divine light becomes increasingly visible to other beings. Those who live in love perceive the blessings of the awakened one. Those who live in fear cannot perceive the light and may act out of fear. The next leg of your journey will bring you in intimate contact with fear in your fellow beings.*

Shivering, I settle back into the embrace of my seraph until my inner light glows more intensely. Gavriel continues, *Tamaw will make her presence known whenever you need her protection.* Immense gratitude fills me as the angels join my seraph in musical peals of joyous laughter.

***

> Teoma bar Flavius,
>
> You have kept the flock safe, but vigilance must not be released. Three long years the Holy Temple stood unprotected by the High Priest while Ananias rested in shame. Now his daughter's husband becomes Rome's latest harlot. The governor appointed Caiaphas to head the Sanhedrin. Nothing is sacred! Tiberius holds the heart of our people in his filthy hands. Share this unholy news with the wanderers.
>
> In faith, Judas

When Yeshua finally returns, Teoma relaxes his guard. On the edge of his seat at the evening meal, Jacob inquires about the temple of Muses. An avid student, he would have made good use of the philosophers' knowledge, perhaps losing himself in the vast library. Yeshua's rich description serves only to aggravate.

"It must be nice to be the chosen one," Jacob says resentfully.

Rebeka grasps his arm, "But I needed you here with me."

"Yes, Jacob, it is difficult being left behind."

Joseph casts a long look at Mary before bringing up his son's private audience within the temple of Isis.

Yeshua either showed extreme courage or rash foolishness in refusing the request of the high priestess. Teoma cannot imagine that in Egypt those who serve in the temple of Isis have such widely differing views about men not paying tribute than those of Astarte. Yeshua must not realize the power of the women who serve the goddess.

Formerly quiet during her sons' acrid discussion, Miriam becomes agitated, "It is highly unusual, Yeshua, for Sahirah to entertain male guests."

"Ima, I was flattered to be in her presence." Yeshua's charisma defrays her worry. Jacob sits back sulkily in his seat. Rebeka puts her arm about him as Yeshua continues, "In fact, she sent along a gift for you."

The children look eagerly at their brother as their mother asks most surprised, "A gift?" She glances at her husband who shrugs.

Hardly able to contain the secret, Sarah runs off at her father's bidding. Miriam still studies Yeshua, "Perhaps, son, we could discuss your visit later?"

Nodding, he acquiesces. Sarah returns with the gift held securely to her small chest. "Here, Savta!" She hands Miriam a sleek black cat with golden eyes.

Joseph chuckles at Miriam's surprise. "A cat...how nice." Sarah's excitement makes up for her grandmother's reaction. The children take turns holding the cat until Joseph announces that it's time for them to go to bed. Hava bustles them off to the nursery. Casting a cold look at Yeshua, Jacob leads Rebeka away. Teoma tries to lighten the moment.

"So Yesh, how was your visit with the high priestess? Leave anything behind?"

Surprised, Yeshua looks at his wife. "You share everything with him?"

"I was concerned and wanted his opinion." Smiling at her candid response, Teoma thinks that there are advantages to their friendship.

Yeshua shakes his head and turns back to him. "So, what would you have done?"

Sitting forward, he places both hands on the table. "It would have been an honor to pay tribute. But then she was seeking something more from you, I am sure." Teoma waits for Yeshua's smile before continuing, "So how about those exotic gatherings? Was that part of your studies?"

His friend's smile fades, clearly disturbed at his reference. "Brother, you will just have to go to Alexandria for the experience. In the meantime, I'm sure my wife has shared enough details to fuel your imagination." Too much so, Teoma thinks, bidding them goodnight.

***

Since the tragedy, his brother stoically refuses to talk to him. While appreciating the attention Jacob dotes on his children in an attempt to comfort Rebeka, Yeshua recognizes the void in his brother's heart. While he respects Jacob's wishes, Yeshua has not been content to leave him to brood. Barely has he been able to obey the hayye of separation. Sometimes when he most wishes to approach his brother, he is stymied by Jacob's descent to invisibility, but occasionally when passing each other, their eyes gravitate into a lock. In his brother's gaze lies a deep and fluid desire, a yearning to reach out, to talk.

On the evening before the winter solstice, Yeshua happens upon Jacob in the inner atrium, translating scrolls Abba brought back from Alexandria into Aramaic. Breathing consciously, he prays that this night will be fruitful. *Please bless my dear brother with an open heart.*

Jacob follows his upward gaze as Yeshua draws the healing energy of the heavens down through his crown. For a long comforting moment, his brother's energy expands as if he too searches the stars, but before Yeshua can coax the hayye of the earth to join the heavens in his heart, Jacob withdraws into the shadow of self-consciousness. Gathering his courage, Yeshua sits down next to his brother.

Jacob's anger blossoms fresh and crimson as blood. *It has begun.*

Yeshua remains silent, ever so gently touching Jacob's aura. Perhaps his brother is impervious to his healing energy.

"How…how could you do such a thing?"

"What did I do?"

"Nothing! That's just it. You did nothing."

Yeshua's heart aches. Jacob is right; he did nothing to save the child.

"In Alexandria, you brought people back from their deathbeds; you have brought senses back to those who have thought them gone forever. You raised your wife from the dead. And you could do nothing for my son?"

"Jacob, please…."

Standing suddenly, Jacob drops the scroll to point accusingly at him. "You let him die! It is your fault I am childless!"

"Your anger clouds your mind. Your son was born dead, it was not my doing."

"But you could have done something. Admit it, this was a choice open to you. You chose to do nothing."

"I admit it."

"You demon! Is it you who decides who lives and who dies?" Jacob's voice rises to a shout. Inside the nursery, Mary soothes their frightened daughter. Before Jacob reaches hysterics, he answers the accusation.

"I have free will, just as you do, to act or not." His words command stillness.

"A god, you think yourself a god!" Jacob's voice is tremulous.

"I am your brother. I am nothing you are not."

His brother hesitates, seeming to pluck out a specific memory. "Oh, how I knelt in submission, holding my child as if offering sacrifice. I worshiped you like a god. In my mind, no man was greater. I looked up to you, tried to be like you," he pauses, but Yeshua remains still, "and this is how my love and trust is reinforced? Have I placed my dreams in the hands of a child? How is it that I did not see before, your ignorance?"

"What do you mean?"

Jacob's forefinger thumps Yeshua's chest. "You ARE responsible, and you don't even know it! Your work, your reign, your mission. When will you finally take these things seriously? You are going to be king, and you have no power over your word. How will you ever lead a people who hear whatever they want?"

Yeshua strides across the atrium, gathering his thoughts. Since returning home to Galilee, he has wondered why he is here. True, he has shared his ideology with his family, Jacob being the most apt. His dear brother constantly challenges his views, but now does Jacob's anger hide a pearl of truth?

"I know you have a point. What is my chata?"

"Your mistake is that you don't take responsibility. You just talk and talk, as if your words were as common as seeds. But your words are as valuable as gold. They have so much power to make movements of great consequence, to affect so many. You cannot be oafish with them; you have to take the greatest care. Think of aiming an arrow in a crowd of people—you are trying to hit a post, but if you don't take careful aim, somebody will die!"

"Is that not true for each of us?"

"No, no it's not! You are going to be king one day, and people think you are the mashiach."

"I cannot stop people from thinking."

"No, but you can't ignore their thinking either! People are watching you, Yesh, and if you are not careful, they will come to their own conclusions. YOU CANNOT BE OBSCURE!"

"What are you trying to say?" Yeshua wonders. "Where are you getting this?"

"There are records!" As if they might appear to bear witness, Jacob waves his hands in the direction of the study then reaching the point of hysterics, descends into the realm of the madly certain. "Prophets, statesmen, and enlightened ones say many things, but unless they tailor their words just right and pay close attention to how they are received, their mission is lost, their words escape, no longer doing as commanded. I don't want that to happen to you." Jacob calms down to draw a well-loved example from memory.

"In a temple in Greece resided an oracle who received prophesies from the god Apollo. A great general who was about to fight a deciding battle with the Parthians came to see her, asking what would be the outcome of the next day's battle. She responded by saying 'a great empire will fall.' He left arrogant and lead his men to battle certain of victory. Do you know what happened?"

Yeshua stifles a smile before hazarding, "A great empire fell?"

"Of course, Socrates, but too obscure. And that is exactly the problem. She wasn't specific enough to give him meaningful information. It was *his* empire that fell."

"So maybe she didn't know."

Jacob gives him a glare. "Or maybe she was trying to warn him, and wasn't specific enough. Greece was her empire too. When people look to you for guidance, you can't afford to not be clear. Otherwise, people will hear whatever they want."

"So you think I am like this oracle?"

"You are also like the general. You can't afford to assume victory and you can't afford to lose. You do not need to lose the faith of others the way you lost mine."

The energy of the conversation drops heavy as an anchor. Both men sit down. After a time, Yeshua breaks the silence.

"So you are leaving my side?"

"Who says I was at your side to begin with? I can't be responsible if I place all my trust in you; obviously, that isn't wise."

"How true."

"Yeshua, if you are going to act with such carelessness, I fear for our people. They should have a leader who feels as they feel, fights as they fight...."

"But...."

"I am not through! They need someone who can, through words and actions, let them know he is with them or they will lose all faith."

Yeshua pauses to infuse his brother with loving compassion. Jacob's eyes, gray with anger, brighten ever so slightly.

"I am with you, brother."

"You have made a terrible attempt at letting me know, in both word and deed." Jacob rises to leave. Before he enters the gathering room, Yeshua calls out to him.

"This oracle you speak of, she is the Oracle of Delphi. Outside her temple there are arches on which are written words of advice to those who would ask her questions. One of these reads 'Know thyself'. Please think about that."

Jacob turns away, leaving him alone beneath the stars.

After the winter solstice, preparations begin for their journey to Jerusalem. From the desert community north of Qumran, Judas arrives with an entourage of soldiers. Jacob spends an unusual amount of time with the zealot commander. Even Teoma has a vast affection for his surly mentor. The men gather nightly to discuss the situation of the Roman oppression. Much concern is expressed over camel caravans. Having little to contribute, Yeshua bides his time. The evening before Judas is to return to the desert, he gains his father's blessing to have Mary join them.

Taking her hand, he leads his wife into the study. She greets her father with an affectionate embrace, but shudders to see Judas armed as a militant within the house. Her reaction does not go unnoticed.

"Your daughter would probably be more comfortable in the company of women." Judas addresses Joseph, making Yeshua acutely aware that he is but his father's son.

"Mary will be accompanying my son so I felt it appropriate for her to take part in the last of these preparations."

"Humph!" Judas grumbles before addressing the men. "That dog, Tiberius, will soon conduct another census and will not wait for accurate tribute to be paid. Quirinus shall take advantage of the pilgrimage of our people to the Holy Temple for Pesach. Once again the leaders of the tribes must report to the city of their fathers. So you will have to go first to Bethlehem." Yeshua acknowledges with a nod. "Very well, be aware that Roman legions will accompany the prefects to protect what is Caesar's."

Judas' condescending tone incites the men into rough talk. Mary shifts uncomfortably, diminished by her ignorance of these worldly matters. Perhaps he should have better prepared her. This same cloud of frustration has cast its shadow upon him throughout the meetings. With Mary by his side, he might find a means to reach these men. At least he takes comfort in her presence.

Voices become raised and his wife leans into him as if he might shelter her from the angry onslaught expressed toward the Romans and all of their consorts. As fists are slammed upon the table and chairs are scraped across the floor, Mary drops into herself, searching. With excitement, she cries silently. *It is not anger! It is fear!*

He is pleased with her insight. *You are correct. It is the fear of separation from Source, from the One, from each other.* Perceiving her inquiry, he encourages her to speak it aloud.

Mary hesitates, looking up at him for support. *How difficult this must be for her. A woman facing these powerful men. How many times have I spoken to no avail? These rough men who believe violence is the only means to freedom, will they listen?* Her voice is very soft, and in the face of their fear, her own rises to hush her, but she prays that they each release their fear. As if spoken aloud, the men turn toward her, and there is a moment of peace in the room.

203

"Thank you all for sharing your views on the current situation, but I have a question." She looks to Judas, thinking, *His heart holds a portal, an opening, in which is buried a sweetness, like honey inside a salted bun.* Yeshua wonders why he hadn't noticed before. "How did we give our power away to our oppressors? How did we lose our divine connection?"

Mary's father smiles at her bravado. Judas' brow furrows in consternation as he shakes his head. "I do not know."

Looking into her eyes Judas visibly softens. He searches his own heart. Coming up empty, his gaze shifts to Yeshua. "Son, I have known you since you were a child. Not much of a soldier in you, but there is something else, a knowing. I believe you are the anointed one to lead us out from under our oppressors. But your wife's question begs for an answer. Can you please enlighten me?"

The room is silent. Yeshua offers a prayer of gratitude for this opening provided by his wife. Expanding his hayye to encompass the entire room, he infuses a golden light of understanding into each man's heart. Most shift as if touched intimately. Perceiving his influence, Jacob glares at him before turning away. *Dear brother, when will we be united?* Squeezing Mary's hand, he finds his voice.

"We gave away our power by allowing fear to take precedence in our hearts. Our oppressors feed off our fear, which falsely empowers them, because they too hold great fear." He pauses at the men's eyes wide in disbelief. "Our fear is the magnification of our separation from Source. Fear is what disconnects us from the Divine." Speaking his truth gives a measure of authority to his words. "Your knowledge and advice are invaluable to me. Your willingness to wield swords to protect the mission is appreciated. But the key to becoming free from our oppressors is becoming free from the fear that truly oppresses us, releasing the fear that veils us from Eloha."

All are silent for the span of many heartbeats. Jacob withdraws even further, but before he can address his brother, Teoma speaks.

"If we are to release our fear, Yeshua, what shall replace it?"

Pleased at yet another opening, he smiles. "Love shall fill the void. If all the fear that exists in human consciousness would be replaced with love, there would be no oppressors, no oppressed, no sickness, no poverty, no need in any form."

The men stare blankly, but their hearts shift ever so slightly and he infuses each with love. "This, my friends, is my mission. To help my fellow humans remember who they are as Love." Standing, he lifts Mary to her feet, and then kisses her cheek. "Did I answer the question to your satisfaction?"

She nods and looks to the men. All are nodding as if he spoke directly to them, softening as if it was their cheeks he kissed. Mary smiles, "Yes, thank you."

He leads her to thank his companions. Jacob leaves the study in haste, avoiding Yeshua. When Judas approaches, Mary gives him an impulsive hug. Judas hesitantly pats her back, trying not to touch her dark curls. He turns to Yeshua, "I see why your wife is here, but please for her safety, allow your Ima to dress her appropriately for the trip to Judaea."

Certainly, he wishes no harm to come to his wife. He nods his consent and Mary looks at him, surprised. "We will all be in costume, beloved. You shall have your power."

Her fine brows narrow, as she thinks. *What power?* How he wishes she could see herself through his eyes.

Where am I Going?

Judaea, 3780

Do you know where you're going on this journey called life?
Do you see that the path before you is wide?
Where will you go and where have you been?
Travel with faith—a way will appear.

Journey to Jerusalem

Jacob ran away to join Judas' band of zealots! While Miriam fretted inconsolably over the absence of her son, Rebeka held a brave front, clutching her husband's mikra, the parchment bearing such pain. Jacob left a broken man but returned strengthened by his experiences, perhaps knowing the truth in his heart. What a relief when he blessed his brother with forgiveness. Immensely lighter, Yeshua's delighted mood enhanced the last few days with the children. *Perhaps they will blossom while we are away.*

"Ima, Doda Rebeka and Dod Jacob will take good care of us, but Josh wants to know if you will bring us presents."

Although Joshua speaks fairly well, they still communicate silently. Yeshua laughs. *I wonder who's really interested in presents.*

"Really Abba, I told Joshua all about Jerusalem and he wants something nice."

Yeshua smiles, "And how is it you know so much about the holy city?"

Exasperated by our ignorance, our six-year-old sighs. "Abba, I have good teachers and remember all that I learn. Will you and Ima commune with us in the morning?"

He hugs her to him, "Of course, love."

Two-year-old Joshua jumps up from my lap and races about the room, collecting the egg-shaped toys Yeshua made. "Here," he hands us the tiny dolls, "'member me and Sarah."

Longingly, I watch my children run out to the garden to play. Never have I been away from them and hope to be brave and not run all the way back home. Lifting my face, Yeshua kisses me, "I thought I was home to you."

Crying, I nod, "You are, Yesh, but the children are a great part of me, of us."

He picks up the tiny dolls sitting on the bedside table. "Josh made sure we would have them with us."

"They are always in my heart, just as you are."

Riding out after dawn, the tax money hidden on Yeshua, Teoma leads the donkey that carries our things. Eager to return to the desert, Sheikan prances excitedly. Cresting over the edge of the Valley of Jezreel, the sweet breath of our sleeping children lingers on my lips.

Fertile plains, green with grain, flow into Samaria. Warning me to keep pace with him, Teoma guides us through hostile unfamiliar trails. My family always journeyed to Jerusalem on the well-maintained Roman roads, safe from robbers.

"Why don't we hasten our pace by visualizing our destination?"

"I have tried, Mary, and it hasn't worked for me."

His bay colt nickers softly to Sheikan. "We can do it together. But since you are the only one who knows exactly where we are going and what it looks like, I need you to hold the image for us."

Listening intently, Yeshua asks, "Do you understand how it works?"

"Yes," I answer with confidence. "Pretending we were already at the shore, we felt grateful, and in no time at all, we arrived."

"It was as if we took a map and folded it, bringing Nazareth and the shore together, then crossed the shorter distance."

Yeshua smiles at Teoma's vivid description and we cut our trip by two-thirds with his help, even faster than before.

Teoma's uncle lives west of the city of Ramah. An immense wall enclosing stables, fields, and luxurious gardens, as well as a family tomb, surrounds the property. The palatial house, ornately decorated by fine tapestries and rich furniture, has a strong Roman flair. Since no kasa protects all this wealth, how much tax must Joseph of Arimathaea pay?

I venture to ask Yeshua about our host. "With such a rich mind for history and culture, Jacob answered my very same question. Arimathaea can be roughly translated as prince of the sun god, an Egyptian title. His Hasmonaean mother passed down her inheritance through the matriarchal lineage much like the queens of the Nile. When in Alexandria, my family stayed in one of his mother's homes."

As I unpack the cumbersome sadins, headdresses, and numerous undergarments given to me by Miriam, Yeshua's wise counsel comes to mind, "You are afraid you won't be recognized for who you are and then again, you are afraid that you will." Nonetheless, I don my favorite sea green sadin, more appropriate in this Roman household.

Our host is strikingly handsome, very broad in the shoulders and tall, like his nephew. Dark hair with light eyes of an exotic flavor not unlike mine, Joseph of Arimathaea is a multicultural man of mixed blood. He stands as we enter the richly decorated dining hall with Teoma at his side.

"So, this is Mary." Joseph takes my hand and kisses it. A strange greeting indeed, an Egyptian custom perhaps? I smile as he seats me beside him. "You are a fortunate man, Yeshua, for I see why my nephew refuses to marry." Blushing, I glance at Teoma, who smiles back reassuringly. Now I know where he gets his teasing nature.

"Thank you, Joseph," Yeshua responds, "Judas feared we would start too many fires if we brought her along, but I couldn't be parted any longer from my beautiful wife." He squeezes my free hand and I fear I might sink into the floor.

"It is most gracious of you to welcome us into your home."

"The pleasure is all mine, my dear." Joseph brings my hand to his lips yet again. "May I offer shekar?" He begins pouring before anyone can refuse. Both Teoma and Yeshua look sternly at me when I accept a cup. Quite astute, Joseph chuckles, "Am I missing something?"

Neither of my men speak, so I answer holding my cup, "They do not believe I can handle your wine, sir."

He smiles, lowering his voice confidentially. "I do not believe in withholding anything a beautiful woman desires from her. So unless you do not care for the wine, please enjoy." I cannot help but be taken by his charm. So I lift my cup to his and after a long moment, Teoma and Yeshua do as well. The first sip goes right to my head.

The night is long and luxurious as we lounge on cushions around the low table. Dark-skinned staff serves rich foreign food. Joseph takes pleasure watching me and Teoma laughs, as tears fill my eyes after one particularly spicy dish. I nearly finish half a cup of wine trying to rid my tongue of the taste, before Yeshua stops me. "Mary, eat some bread to dull your senses." I giggle as he feeds me, leaning seductively against him. Yeshua shakes his head.

Joseph laughs, pouring more wine. "Yeshua, relax. My home is yours. You are welcome to make love in any room you desire." Too besotted to feel any shame, I smile at my husband's red face. Teoma banters with his uncle, flirting with a particularly voluptuous girl who cannot seem to stop serving him sweets. What about Edia?

Yeshua holds me. *Teoma is not married, dear, do not judge him.*

Joseph smiles at our enjoyment. How fortunate we are to have friends here in Judaea. "Mary, we have been waiting a long time for you and Yeshua to come." Gratefully, I kiss our host good night.

The next morning Joseph finds me sitting by the fountain. He wishes to talk. Perhaps with age, men speak more freely; how might my husband behave when we are old? A chill breeze blows through the garden like an ill omen.

Joseph places his cloak around my shoulders. I sigh, comfortable with him. "Do you have something on your mind?"

"I do, my dear. Do you believe that you are prepared for Yeshua's mission?" Through his clear eyes, I see fear buried deep in his soul. Fear of loss, for he has suffered a great loss in this life and has not been able to find the depth of intimacy he once had. His charm is how he keeps others at bay, enemies and friends alike. My breath becomes shallow as my hayye soaks in his essence.

"Mary, what is it?" He interrupts my vision, "You are slipping away and I feel like I am being drawn with you."

Only after a deep shuddering breath do I answer, "Your question is a reflection of your own grief. I see that you have had a tremendous intimate loss in your life and you struggle now to maintain a sense of self without bonding to another."

He nods, tears forming, "It is true. When my wife died, a part of me died as well. I have not been able to find love or comfort in many years."

I bring his hand to my cheek, my heart near breaking from holding the image of his pain. "What you are, dear man, is love. Your wife was a perfect mirror of your divine self. You can find that mirror in your life again, by allowing yourself to be love."

With bowed head, he cries and I hug him. How could Yeshua think that I would have prejudged this heartbroken man? Who cares about his connections with our oppressors or how he gets his wealth? He is human, like any other, existing in the illusion of suffering. A knowing comes. This is my work, my mission. Across the courtyard, Yeshua appears.

Joseph sits up, drying his tears. "Thank you, Mary. I haven't cried like that since I lost her. Now where do I begin?"

Warmer now under his cloak, I respond, "Pray that your fear be lifted and that you be filled with light. Be willing to risk love again, to live fully. Death is not an end but a beginning of another way of being. Your beloved will be united with you again, but until then, do not stop living." My husband makes his presence known. Joseph stands and takes his arm.

"Your wife has much loving wisdom to share with us. I feared that she could not possibly be prepared for the years to come being so young and untainted by the world, but she has an enduring strength and a depth of understanding."

Yeshua nods, not taking his eyes off me, "Yes, Mary is an integral part of my mission, for she has a unique ability to see into one's soul. We did not want to influence her with too much information, but she seems to see only the divine light in others."

Expressing his thanks, Joseph leaves us in the garden. Yeshua touches the neckline of the cloak, "Why are you chilled, dear?"

I look into his eyes, finding his soul fathomless, tending to lose myself if I delve too deeply. "I felt an ill omen wondering what you might be like at Joseph's age."

His smile is sorrowful, "You just advised Joseph to live fully now. You need to take your own advice." I nod, knowing he will not share more. "Mary, you are guided, I am sure, to do this work, but you must be careful about ministering to people."

I frown, "Why?"

"It is difficult for most men to accept help in any form. A healing from a beautiful, passionate young woman may be interpreted as an invitation for intimacy." Rigidity courses through my back. Is he concerned or jealous?

"Both," he admits. "I so want you to be with me, but it is difficult to witness you minister to another man."

"How can I refrain from touching another, especially when they are in pain? Should I not minister to men because they might misinterpret my actions?"

"No, of course not. But you must be sure Teoma or I am near."

"Yesh, I do not want to be afraid. By seeing the best in everyone, maybe I'll bring out the best."

He cups my face in his hands, his voice hoarse, "I do not want you hurt, love. You were assaulted in your own neighborhood and I have brought you into a much more dangerous place."

"Hush, love, that was my own fault. I did not listen to Teoma's advice and more importantly, I did not listen to my own intuition. Besides, at Pesach, the angel Gavriel introduced my protector to me, a seraph. Tamaw will help as well."

"Where was she that night outside your parents' home?"

Surely I did not realize he still harbored concern. "Yeshua, listen to me, what happened was a lesson for all of us, a lesson in trust and forgiveness. You must forgive yourself for being away. You cannot protect me every moment. You must trust that I will make safe decisions. How can you fully give of yourself if you are worried about me?"

"You are right, my dear. We need to pray." Holding my hands, he begins, "Marya, we are willing to travel our life path but need support and guidance. Help us to be ever present and loving to one another, forgiving each other and ourselves our human frailties. Ameyn."

A divine light—nura—bathes us in love and compassion. In the portal to Source, the archangels appear. Gavriel speaks, *Beloved, you complete each other. Your feelings for one another are the mirror to your own souls. Yeshua, it is time that you confide in Mary. Share with her your fears as you minister to her needs, thus she can help you.*

Uriel's light glimmers as he addresses us, *Dear ones, remember who you are. This life is about joy, not suffering. Do not project pain into your future through worry. Know that you are protected and guided all the days of your life. All is as it needs be. I will be ever present to bring you Eloha's light even in your darkest time. Have no fear.*

As the angels take their leave, the nura diminishes. Lightened of the burden of fear, Yeshua creates a veil of kasa so that he might know me more intimately in the garden of Joseph of Arimathaea.

Over the next few days, we prepare to travel farther south to the city of David, where Yeshua's family must be counted and pay taxes to Caesar Tiberius. Joseph stables our horses and provisions us for the trip, making us promise to return on our way back home. Once we are out of sight, Teoma laughs, "My Dod is quite taken with you, Mary. Whatever you did seems to have left an indelible impression."

"Mary ministered to Joseph, relieving some of his suffering."

Teoma looks between us, "Ministered to him? In what way? He acts like he's in love." I sigh, thinking Yeshua does not need to be aggravated.

Yeshua smiles at me, "You could say that Joseph is falling in love with himself." I pray that the healing will be complete.

Although we travel under the cover of kasa, I am surprised when Teoma leads us off the road within sight of Jerusalem. "Why must we travel this treacherous way?"

Without looking back on the steep narrow trail, Teoma answers, "It is best that we do not traverse through Jerusalem until we are expected."

"But we are under kasa. How…?"

"Please, Mary. I have my orders."

I wonder at Teoma's elusiveness. When visiting my mother's parents in Bethany, we would stay upon the well-guarded roads south into Jerusalem. Passing through the outermost northern wall, we would refresh ourselves at the Pool of Bethesda before exiting the fortress to enjoy the beautiful gardens east of the city.

Descending into the valley of Kidron by way of the shepherd's trail, the travel becomes even more rugged. The eastern walls of the city rise majestically above sheer cliffs, as we proceed past Olivet Mount and onto Jericho Road. I am most modestly dressed with a thin linen undergarment, a drab woolen sadin, and a creamy unadorned headdress. Judas made it quite clear that we are to draw no attention to ourselves.

Within sight of Bethlehem, my feet are sore and abraded. I sit on the side of the road a long while before my companions, in a heated discussion over the alignment of the tribes with the Romans, notice I am not with them. Looking back simultaneously, they hurry to my side.

"What is wrong, Mary?" Teoma asks worriedly, but I look up at my husband.

"I need you to make an exception to not doing any healings in public."

He gazes into my eyes as people continue to pass us on the dusty road. Shortly, my feet are whole again. "You can learn to do this for yourself."

"But I prefer your touch." Before I can thank him with a kiss, Teoma interrupts by clearing his throat. Yeshua takes the lead once we enter the city gates, heading straight for an inn.

"This is it!"

"This is what?" Teoma asks.

"This is where I was born."

"How can you remember the place where you were born?"

Yeshua smiles at his friend. "Because I came onto earth awakened and was raised so that I would not forget. All children are born conscious, but few are born into families who can help them stay awake. You fell asleep quickly in the family you chose."

Teoma's brow wrinkles, "What do you mean 'the family I chose'?"

Yeshua's smile broadens, "Each of us has our choice of who to live out our lives with. We choose our parents, sometimes our siblings, usually our friends. You say that you believe that your purpose is to serve me. Well, we made that soul agreement before coming here, you just do not remember now. Thankfully, you were awake enough to recognize your destiny or the mission would be incomplete."

I take Teoma's arm. "Come, let's see if there is room in the inn for us."

Not only is there room, but we are given the same one that Miriam gave birth to Yeshua in. Amazed, Teoma asks, "This is the room? The same furnishings even?"

"No, the manger I slept in is not here."

I laugh, "Your mother put you in a manger?"

"It was Abba's idea. You know how intent he is about his marriage bed." Yes, I do, for Joseph was not in agreement with my decision to bring our children into bed with us. I believe he thinks we are not making our relationship the focus of our family.

Well, he's wrong. You come first with me, dear. Smiling at my husband, I wonder where Teoma will stay since this was the last available room. "Teoma will stay here."

"No, I'll sleep in the stable if I can't find another inn."

Yeshua produces some extra bedding he secured. "I told the innkeeper my brother would share our room. We'll sleep under kasa." I laugh, gathering a fresh garment and head to the baths.

At dawn, I stretch in my husband's embrace. Teoma advised we get an early start and already stirs. When I move to slip out of bed, Yeshua pulls me back. "Wait for him to go to the baths."

"Why? We are veiled."

"I would be more comfortable after he leaves," but he responds to my advances.

By the time Teoma returns, we are dressed and fully satiated. "It appears you made good use of the time."

216

Blushing, I hurriedly repack my things. Yeshua laughs, "Don't worry, I'm sure your consorts have not forgotten you."

Teoma responds coolly, "Let's get the taxes paid as quickly as possible so we can meet *your* contacts." Before the sun rises any higher, we arrive at the Roman census.

The line of people wraps around the village square. Teoma wanders through the ranks of soldiers, planning to meet us outside the city walls, but made me promise to call him if we need assistance. While wearing the uniform of Rome, some of the soldiers do not have the appearance of Romans. Many have long hair and beards in the style of the native men. Yeshua is upset.

"Mary," he whispers, "Look at these people. They are barely surviving. How can they afford to pay taxes?" I shake my head. Large families with young children, probably from the outlying desert communities, hungry and poorly clothed, many visibly sick, all are terrified. A wave of anger passes through the crowd whenever the soldiers pass by.

In spite of our common attire, the soldiers linger near, questioning us. Although fluent in Latin, Yeshua feigns ignorance but our neighbors give us wide berth. Yeshua pulls me closer, "It is our hayye that attracts their attention."

I perceive from the soldiers' energy they are as uncomfortable as us, as angry as those they are commissioned to oppress. Most are very young men, too long away from home. Our people represent a distasteful charge, one that must be kept under control or they will be here even longer than they had planned. No one seems happy with the situation. Yeshua laments, *There must be a way to right this wrong. But how?*

As I delve deeper into the hayye of the poor people around us, fearful images of illness, abuse, and unnecessary death emerge. Too many children born into families that cannot afford to feed them. Just teaching these women about the white light of protection would be a start.

Mary, stop! You are drawing more attention to us.

A group of foot soldiers, young hungry-looking men, crowd in close, nearly pushing us out of line. One of them addresses us. "You are too fine to be with this Jew." He speaks directly to me in Aramaic as if Yeshua is not here.

His intent so obvious, I shiver and move behind my husband. *Lift your fear, Mary, and call Teoma.* Desperately, I do.

The soldier notices my attempt to cover my face. "It appears the Jews want to keep all their treasures hidden." The crowd moves as far away as possible when he confronts Yeshua with his comrades' crude encouragement.

Yeshua, I beg silently, *please create a veil,* but he's intent only on making eye contact with the indolent soldier.

The soldier raises his arm to strike Yeshua, but hesitates. Something shifts in the hayye. The fear dissipates and we're enclosed in the wings of my seraph. The soldier lowers his arm, his expression softer, his voice quiet. Yeshua says not a word, only holding his intent of peace. Uncomfortable, the rest of the soldiers look away. When Teoma appears, they seem relieved to follow his jovial command. After a brief pause, the interrogator bows his head ever so slightly toward Yeshua before joining his comrades.

Not until they are out of sight, do we move. The crowd shifts back into place, their conversation continuing as if nothing happened. Yeshua turns and holds me to his chest to stifle my tears. *It is not the time to assist these people.*

***

The hills north of the city of David provide a safe place to camp. Glancing in the direction where Yeshua and Mary lie hidden by kasa, a twinge of guilt passes through Teoma's heart. When she called to him in her terror this morning, his mind was invaded by memories of that night in Cana, once again not near enough to protect her. Somehow Yeshua quelled the situation, but Mary withdrew, unaware of the rest of the afternoon.

Yeshua's family has been counted, and thankfully the couple's modest attire did not alert the prefect to the significance of who was paying tribute. Perhaps Rome has forgotten about the Davidic line. He can only pray it is so.

Burning the remnants of the scroll, he settles into his bedroll. Although entrusting Teoma with his eldest son's security, Joseph has not faith in his memory for detail. Well aware of the delicate political situation in Jerusalem, Teoma yawns, remembering how Joseph tried to give him final instructions.

"Roman appointment of the high priesthood is an adulteration. Although Theudas recommends the sons of Ananias as potential supporters of Yeshua's mission, they are Tzadokim and cannot be trusted. Their loyalty may lie with Caiaphas." Joseph mopped his brow in consternation.

Teoma tried to cheer his mentor that final evening before leaving Nazareth. *"So, you expect me to keep Yeshua focused while gathering resources for the mission?"*

Much too somber to appreciate his humor, Joseph replied. *"Yes, you are charged with escorting, chaperoning, and inhibiting. Please restrain Yeshua from teaching, debating halacha and performing public healings."*

"Yes, sir!"

Finally Joseph smiled, *"Son, remember Mary and Yeshua will be as strangers in a new land and must attract no attention. Yeshua needs protection from the Tzadokim as well as the Romans. Do not hesitate to send word to Judas immediately if problems arise."*

Handing the scroll over, Joseph gave a last bit of advice. *"Let not the scroll, the ashes, or its memory fall into unfriendly hands."*

Teoma held it to his chest. *"I will do as you command, sir."*

"And whatever happens, do not let Mary dance."

Just after dawn, Teoma is awakened by Mary dancing about the encampment excitedly. "What arouses you this early?"

Picking up a full sack, she exclaims, "Look, Yeshua multiplied our water!"

Teoma sits up then looks about as if being watched. "Why do this now? We had enough for the short journey to Jerusalem."

Yeshua stands up stretching. "Mary just started her menses and we need to wash."

Abruptly, Teoma gets up, "What do you mean—we?"

Mary gives her husband a warning look, but he's intent. "Well, it is a bit messy."

Teoma's mouth falls open. "You didn't lay with her?"

"Of course. Why wouldn't I?"

Shaking his head, Teoma thinks that he should have attended to Joseph with a more serious attitude. Yeshua insists on commencing their trip into the holy city unclean!

Yeshua's anger rises. "There is nothing about my wife or any other woman that is unclean. That is not Divine law, it is man's!"

219

Teoma tries to calm him. "Yesh, in Jerusalem exist many who would find your foreign philosophy and behavior offensive. They would not even share a meal with you!"

"But it did commence a full week early," Mary feebly explains.

Yeshua places an arm around her waist, "I was fully aware you had begun before…." Mary raises her dark brows.

Before his imagination gallops through the possibilities, Teoma reins it in. With a deep breath, he attempts again to alleviate the situation. "Listen, I may not be offended by your behavior, but Mary will be expected to be separated from you for what will be considered her infirmity."

"I do not want to be shut away!" She looks to Yeshua who takes her hand. "I will just have to hide my **infirmity**!"

"This is not Galilee!" he mutters, packing their few things.

They walk in silence a long while. Mary finally tries to make amends, but hesitates to touch him. He turns and takes her hand with a smile, "I do not think you are unclean, but Yeshua needs to understand how very conservative our brethren are, especially in Jerusalem. I do not want to incur any difficulties before the mission even begins."

Yeshua catches up. "I apologize for becoming angry. I appreciate your efforts to protect us."

Hugging Yeshua, he teases, "I'll eat with you, Yesh, but do not expect me to kiss you."

Jerusalem—one of the greatest cities in the Roman Empire. Outside the massive walled fortress, Olivet stands higher than either Moriah or Zion. As they near the southern wall, the morning sunshine glimmers off the snow-white marble Temple which crowns Moriah with its golden pinnacles. The approach from Bethlehem must be unfamiliar to Mary; her family probably enters directly into Solomon's Porch rather than through the poorer section of the lower city.

A foul stench forces Mary to cover her face with the common headdress. Teoma chuckles, "The betshimush," and points to the southwest gate, "by that way pass the Essenes who refuse to defecate within the holy city. Especially not on Shabbat."

Yeshua confirms. "Yes, the most ascetic Essenes live strictly under the Scroll of Discipline, dictating their every behavior."

One hundred and sixty four solid rock towers surround Jerusalem; three rise ominously above the rest. "Herod built these towers. The tallest,

Phasealis, forms part of the palace, the squared off tower is Hippiclus, and the smallest—Mariamne."

Mary's gasp makes Teoma feel like a fool. Mariamne was Mary's great-great-aunt killed by King Herod who erected the tower to imprison his wife. Teoma starts to apologize but must quell Yeshua's attempt to comfort Mary with a sharp look. His charge proves more difficult with each passing moment.

Past the western gate leading to the splendid Hasmonaean palace, Teoma escorts them through the Tyropena Valley, thick with throngs of worshipers heading to the Holy Temple. Compared to the heavy Roman influence in Galilee, there is a light guard for the Roman governor housed in Herod's palace. The soldiers stare, for Mary's beauty is difficult to hide even under the shapeless cloak. Clearly unused to the modest covering, she drops her veil to return the smiles of children. Yeshua nods as if his wife has spoken aloud. "If only adults could be more like little children, there would be no need for this mission."

Abruptly Teoma halts, speaking under his breath. "Please, let us refrain from discussing the purpose of our visit outside the protection of our host."

Mary and Yeshua follow him meekly into the upper city through Genneth Gate. Teoma hastens the pace through the central square, down streets lined with lavish houses. Well beyond the house of the High Priest Caiaphas, the ancestral tomb of King David lies hidden under a Roman style villa secured behind high walls. Perhaps time will permit a visit to his mother.

Finally, they stop at a modest gate—the house of Simeon. Like their home in Galilee, the outer walls belie its inner grandeur. Graced by a lavish courtyard, the home has large central gathering rooms adorned with plants in clay pots. The high desert environment does not seem conducive to the lushness greeting them from every alcove. Servants take them to quarters in the west wing off the gardens.

When the evening meal is announced, Yeshua and Teoma head into the hall, while Mary is detained by a servant. Teoma sighs to see her hair unfettered, but Yeshua motions for her to take her place beside him.

At the head of the table, Simeon bears himself like an aristocrat. Stately and fair, his wife Shulamis whispers something in his ear. Simeon addresses Yeshua. "Perhaps your wife would be more comfortable in the chamam."

Yeshua takes Mary's arm. Teoma nudges his side as a reminder of his warning this morning, but Yeshua ignores him. "Thank you, Simeon, for your concern, but I prefer that Mary stay by my side."

"Yeshua bar Joseph, it is custom in the desert to strictly follow the halacha."

"What dictates the relationship between a man and his wife?"

"It is written in the Torah."

"An interpretation only, sir, by man, not Divine law."

All remain standing as the two staunchly debate the issue. Teoma desires greatly to interfere, fervently praying that Yeshua does not create a greater divide. Yeshua gives him a reassuring look before attending to their host.

"Why seek confrontation before we have had a chance to meet as men?"

Why indeed? Not answering immediately Yeshua instead turns to his wife, but Simeon seems to be aware of their silent communication. If only Yeshua would just be still. Teoma shakes his head in dismay when Yeshua speaks. "I disagree with this custom that divides men and women. My mission includes my wife. I will not be parted from her."

Simeon raises a brow. "The Tzadokim would find your customs of inclusion to be distasteful at best, unlawful at worst. Would you seek to create enemies of the Sanhedrin?" Teoma shifts nervously at the mention of the high court. "I was at your wedding, son, when you cast aside the bridal veil." Yeshua does not respond. "Protected by the marriage ketuba, but once veiled under the chupa, wives are the property of their husbands. You have left yours exposed to an unforgiving world by not following tradition."

"Mary is my partner, just as the masculine and feminine aspects of the One were once joined. Did not the Sacred Feminine exist in the Holy of Holies some six centuries ago? Have we not been awaiting the Elat's return to the Temple?" Yeshua barely takes a breath. "How can we, as a devout people, expect a reunification if we continue to disempower our wives by treating them as chattel?"

How rashly unwise to argue with this powerful man. Joseph will never entrust his son to Teoma's protection again if they make enemies before they begin.

Yeshua resumes his passionate speech. "Before the Temple was destroyed and the Sacred Feminine lost to Yisrael, women chose to honor their menses by cherishing the temple of their bodies. The Tzadokim shut their women away when the household chamam should be a healing sanctuary."

After a long moment, Simeon turns to Mary who pushes aside sable curls. "What do you desire?"

"To stay with my husband."

Simeon raises his arms, "So be it," inviting all to sit. After the first welcome sip, Teoma silently thanks his host for serving shekar—a potent enough drink to ease the tension.

"Yeshua, you will be facing many who are determined to find fault with you. Your lack of observance of the accepted laws will not endear you to these men. Already the legitimacy of your inheritance is in question but your liberal views will endear you to many who are not satisfied with the status quo. Just be sure that you understand all the obstacles you will encounter. You will be best received if you can maintain your passion without harboring judgment of ancient traditions."

"Thank you, sir. I mean not to offend, but this is who I am. I believe my mission is one of living a fully compassionate life and that includes the breakdown of barriers that interfere with joyful living. As you know, I have spent my youth in training, but since my marriage to this woman, whom I cherish beyond my own life, I have come to know myself as human with a divine connection." Mary looks as if she might cry when Yeshua turns and kisses her cheek. Teoma sighs so loudly that their host laughs. Rising to his feet, Teoma excuses himself to pay his respects to his mother.

***

In the mid-morning haze, we gradually ascend the streets, past the Hasmonaean palace to cross the bridge overlooking the theater and Roman forum, past the marketplace bustling with worshipers preparing for the coming Pesach. Clearly, we must introduce our way of thinking and living gracefully, but there is so much to overcome, so many beliefs that divide us. How can one man, even with powerful support behind him, change an entire nation? Feeling vulnerable, emotion bubbles up to spill unseen down my veiled cheeks.

Yeshua pulls me close. Teoma looks back over his shoulder, "Make haste, we must arrive before the publicans take their mid-day meal. And cease embracing in public."

Hope rises like smoke from a crowd gathered at the entry of the royal porch. A man dressed in a coarse camel hair tunic, his fists raised, his voice even higher, stands on the top step spouting dire opinions about the Tzadokim. When his obscenities include the Romans, more join the teeming mass and Teoma pushes us to the side. Soldiers descend like vultures and disperse the crowd. A woman screams as a burly Roman knocks the man to the ground.

"Who was that?" I ask trembling.

"A self-proclaimed mashiach." Teoma gives Yeshua a rough glance. "The prophecies are soon expected to be fulfilled and in these turbulent times, every man with a message becomes a beacon of hope. Come, we shall be safe in the Court of Goyim. The legions will not allow anything to interfere with the tax collection."

With the city full for the coming festivities, the publicans are exceptionally busy. Perhaps the lost tribes are here as well, for many colorful robes bear a variety of shields in rich contrast to the austerity of the Temple. The sight of small children clutching their mothers makes me yearn for Sarah and Josh. We communed with them earlier but I miss the touch of their little hands.

Before I can give voice to my yearning, Teoma waves me away. "Not within the Temple. There are inquisitive ears everywhere."

Why all the secrecy? Yeshua, projects images of Greek theatrics, *As actors in this play, we will have to trust that there is a master plan.*

Let us pray this is not a tragedy.

After Teoma moves to secure a better vantage point, Yeshua locates the Kohanim. His emissaries collect the tax, while the young sandy-haired priest carefully marks his ledger, engaging each citizen, thanking them for their payment. Those people in his line are exceptionally calm, almost happy compared to the others.

Yeshua tells me silently. *This man would make a fine disciple. His hayye is pure, untainted by his task as he serves his fellow man. Let's pray he recognizes us as well.* From across the courtyard, Teoma signals us to approach the young priest.

After the last person is attended, Yeshua steps forward, holding out his hands. The priest's pleasant smile turns into an expression of awe as he begins to stand. Teoma speaks quietly to him, "Stay seated, Mattathias. Do not draw the soldiers' attention."

Mattathias beams at Yeshua, "Master, you have come."

Yeshua smiles at him, "I am pleased that you remember, Mattathias. Would you and your brother, Yonatan, join me this evening at the home of Simeon?"

Brown eyes sparkle delighted, but Mattathias maintains his composure, "I will be there, Master." He turns to me, smiles, then thanks Teoma before his emissary feigns collecting payment.

After dusk, Shulamis provides a sumptuous meal. Donning a modest robe of gold and blue, I stand at my husband's side while Teoma makes the introductions, obviously intimately familiar with the men. He must have been very busy while in Jerusalem before.

Theudas is the eldest, perhaps in his late forties, his hair gray and thinning on top. A strongly-built man with some middle-age thickening, more of a scholarly appearance than the other zealot commanders, his reserved hayye warms quickly in the enthusiasm of the younger men.

Yonatan bar Ananias is Mattathias' older brother, perhaps ten years his senior. With the quiet hayye of the priestly caste, Yonatan's face registers mild concern when Yeshua answers Theudas' questions about our family.

Will their wives accompany them when we meet again? Yeshua answers me. *They will all be welcome to bring their mates, but their strict relationships may not allow them that comfort.*

With a start, I realize Simeon seems aware of our silent conversation. *Can you perceive us, sir?*

He smiles and nods. *You should use kasa to protect your conversations.* Overhearing, Yeshua flushes. *Your family is quite adept at this level of communication, son, but they are not the only ones. Take care to veil yourself in the future.* My husband nods his thanks before attending to the meal.

Overflowing with enthusiasm Mattathias engages me much more than the others. Pushing my golden veil back from shielding my view, I eagerly answer his questions about Galilee, as well as our trip to Bethlehem. He turns occasionally to Teoma, but seems more interested in my point of view. Yonatan gives him a couple of severe looks when he offers to pour my wine or pass me a dish. The servants quickly intervene, but Mattathias is much more attentive than they.

After the meal, Simeon invites us into an immense richly-furnished room. The other men speak heatedly about the zealot activity, but

Mattathias only attends when Yeshua offers a rare opinion. I find the images of violence and corruption distasteful.

"Mattathias, will you be so kind as to entertain my wife by the hearth? You seem to be already well-versed in the subject and she does not appreciate it." Yonatan looks at Yeshua as if he is insane. "Your brother is a renowned Kohanim. Besides, they'll be within sight." Simeon laughs and draws their attention with a particularly gruesome story; thankfully, Mattathias leads me away.

He offers me a cup, laughing when I wrinkle my nose at the first sip, "You've had kaffa before."

"Yes. Teoma had to put milk and honey in it to take away the bitterness."

Mattathias asks a servant to bring the condiments. "Isn't it wonderful that your husband is so near to beginning his mission?" My smile must not be very convincing. "Mary, what is wrong?"

"This talk of revolution and the wielding of swords frightens me. Yeshua believes his mission is one of peace and healing. I hope it does not come to violence."

Mattathias leans closer, whispering, "I agree, Mary; perhaps there might be a way to work this out without spilling any blood." Sincere, hopeful, and eager to please, Mattathias seems open to all that my husband has to share with him.

When I touch his arm, his hayye spikes excitedly. "Mattathias, it is so good that we have met you. We can only pray that the others will come to see the light of peace."

He looks down at my hand still on his arm, smiling warmly, "Mary, you are very passionate. It's going to take some getting used to, but I think the old ways will be quickly replaced by your fire."

I withdraw my hand. "I have trouble not touching others."

He chuckles, "You have a healing touch." He looks over at the men. "Believing my penchant for beautiful women will keep me from fulfilling my priestly duties, my brother is a bit protective."

When the men's conversation begins winding down, Yeshua joins us. He kisses my cheek, then puts an arm around my companion. "Mattathias, you are so kind to entertain my wife. She dislikes hearing the brutal details," lowering his voice, "and so do I but I must collect as much information as possible from this learned circle of advisors. May I ask you something?" Mattathias looks intently at Yeshua. "When the mission begins will you be one of my council of twelve?"

Mattathias has tears in his eyes, "I would be honored, Master."

Yeshua shakes his head, "I am not a master, Mattathias. It is you who has mastery with people that I can learn from, your hayye loving and kind as you serve the people. This is precisely the point of the mission, to serve with joy. To help them escape bondage, first from their fears. You, my good man, have the gift of lifting the fear of those you encounter and bringing them good cheer. I am most grateful for you." Their embrace attracts the others' attention.

His arm still around Mattathias, Yeshua turns toward them. "Friends, Mattathias has agreed to be one of the council of twelve. Yonatan, would you like to join your brother?"

Yonatan nods, "Yeshua, I would be happy to."

Yeshua leads us back to the group and embraces Yonatan. Turning to Theudas, he asks, "And sir, would you like to be part of the council of twelve?"

Theudas answers gruffly, "Of course, I shall join arms with you, Yeshua. You are the mashiach." I glance at Teoma. And how many others claim to be?

"Simeon, you can bring much to this mission."

Simeon bows graciously, "Yeshua, I cast my lot with you when you were but a child, but I gladly accept your invitation." Yeshua hugs the older man, who winks at me over his shoulder.

I tap Yeshua's shoulder. "Aren't you going to ask Teoma?"

"Mary, he pledged his sword to me when we were but boys." Teoma grins and Yeshua takes his arm, "But my wife is right, dear brother, will you continue to be at my side during the mission?"

Teoma nods, tears in his eyes, as they embrace. "Of course, Yesh, you do not need to ask me formally."

After another five days with the new council, Yeshua announces that we should begin our journey home. Expressing our gratitude to Simeon and Shulamis for their hospitality, we take our leave. Teoma leads us down through Genneth Gate then east through yet another gate. Bypassing the Temple, we traverse the poorer streets to exit the inner north wall by the fortress of Antonia and finally leave the city via a livestock gate. Ima would be appalled to see us making our way through the bleating flocks of sheep, but I say not a word.

When we arrive in Ramah, Joseph is delighted to have guests for Pesach. The Seder is nice but, without the children, does not have the festive air I have come to love.

That night I lay in Yeshua's arms. "When can we return home? I miss the children."

He kisses me. "I do, too. We have completed all we were meant to and more, not expecting to have commitments from the council so soon. Through Simeon, we will maintain contact with those in Jerusalem and continue to make plans with Judas as well." Caressing my naked skin, he whispers, "You did very well this trip. Only starting tiny fires that were easily extinguished."

"What do you mean 'fires'? Only that trouble in Bethlehem."

He laughs, "Do not be naïve, dear. Mattathias' fervor for you was the other fire."

"His fervor is for you and the mission."

Yeshua kisses me deeply, "No, he dreams about you as we speak." Frustrated, I try to slip away, but he holds me fast, "My dear, it is for the benefit of the mission that our disciples love and respect us. Having an adoring young priest support my wife's position as part of the mission will help the others warm to the idea. Theudas and Yonatan clearly love Mattathias, but have old-fashioned ideas about women. Mattathias' attraction to you will help soften them."

I shake my head, "Unless it creates problems for him."

"You underestimate him, my dear. With his strong influential hayye, he can easily bring them around." Before I can protest, he caresses me and I slip happily into the moment. Lovemaking soothes my deepest worries, I think. Yeshua interrupts his ministrations, "You do not need to think now, dear, just be." There is wordlessness to being, as passion and emotion blend into the hayye of joy.

Serving with Gratitude

Mary's strong desire to be with the children hastens the journey home. Once settled in Nazareth, Jacob requests Yeshua's help. So in the garden, Mary joins him to commence their healing work. Whispering through the leaves of the budding vineyard, a softly vibrant white light swirls about to form a prism. Yeshua smiles as all relax into its peaceful embrace.

Mary takes Rebeka's hands. *The baby's death magnified her feelings of unworthiness.* Unbalanced, Jacob has trouble holding her gaze. Unfortunately Mary uses her body to mirror their pain.

Relieving the discomfort in her mid-back, Yeshua reminds his wife; *Do not embody their fear,* before turning to them. "You have mirror images of fear in your hayye, centered in two places. Here," Yeshua touches his upper belly, "we hold the balance between emotion and will, while the lower energy center represents your co-creative abilities." Rising to kneel behind them, he places his hands on the crown of their heads. Fiery energy from the earth fills his lower body, while cool rays from above pour through his crown. The light merges in his heart and moves down his arms into his hands.

He invites Mary to speak. "Imagine your fear is the absence of light. See the shadow over your organs of reproduction and high in your bellies. Now imagine that you are shining a brilliant white light, illuminating these organs and dissolving the shadow." Each embraces the healing violet rays she emanates. "Good. Now extend that light upward through your belly and into your heart."

Attempting the next visualization, the two become stuck where their fear is most dense. Rebeka instinctively places her hand on her upper belly, while Jacob moves about uncomfortably. Mary looks to her husband. *One area at a time,* he advises.

Breathing deeply, she asks them to refocus their efforts on their centers of creation. They comply, visibly relaxing. "Focus this healing light before making love, praying to invite the hayye of your next child to help release this fear."

The garden dances with childish giggles. Joshua plops into Yeshua's lap as Sarah gaily proclaims, "Oh good, you taught Dod how to create a veil of kasal!" Jacob expresses his sincere gratitude before leading his blushing wife away.

"Abba, Saba wants to see you."

Mary's sea-green eyes mist when he rises. Looking back, his family's shadow stretches to the western edge of the grove.

Wood shavings dusting his tight dark curls, Teoma meets him in the hall, apparently summoned as well. Sighing, Yeshua enters the study. How many times has he been called to task at this round table? When Abba turns to place a scroll on the shelf behind him, Yeshua signals Teoma by touching two fingers between his brows. Although his own mind is veiled, his friend's thoughts will be carried by waves of concern directly to Abba's perception. Quickly, Teoma quiets his emotion.

His father takes a seat facing them. "So, how was the trip?"

"Quite successful! As I explained before, four more men joined the council."

"The humorous stories you shared with the family may have appeased your Ima, but they will not appease me."

Yeshua nods, well aware of his father's source of information. "So what did Syrus relate that concerns you so?" Teoma looks surprised, unaware that Mary's father has been watching her every move since she was a tiny child. Although Syrus rarely interferes, alerting Joseph serves his purpose.

"He's concerned about his daughter's safety, as well you should be." Yeshua does not respond, but when Teoma looks away, Joseph takes advantage of his position. "Son, I commissioned you to keep them safe…."

"And he did just that. We were fine." Yeshua catches his father's eyes. "Abba, I am not a defiant youth to be probed by interrogations, but your heart-felt concerns will be answered truthfully."

Joseph's gaze wavers. Extending a wave of peaceful energy, Yeshua prays that this day might be different. Abba resists mightily.

"Simeon expressed concern that you wished to make enemies." How clear is Syrus' distant viewing? Perhaps he must veil his bedchambers. Yeshua projects his thoughts to his father, whose face darkens. "Syrus is drawn to Mary by her fear. He only has her best interest at heart."

Too many watchers in this life! Each with his own objective, creating an entangled web about his precious wife. None seem to trust him to care for her. Least of all, his own father.

"I could not chastise her for healing Teoma's uncle, but…" Joseph speaks not his old friend's name, "I expected you to heed my warnings!"

"Mary is coming into her life's mission, as I come into mine. She created openings that shall serve us in the future."

"Your refusal to obey simple dictates of society for your own protection…."

"And whose example am I following?"

"At least I provide my family security," Joseph will not be deterred. "Can you not heed the advice of your councilors?"

Yeshua lowers his voice so his father must lean closer. "I did as you instructed and invited your old friends into the council. Sharing your fear and hatred, the zealots expect me to lead a rebellion against Rome."

"You have fulfilled the messianic prophecies. You must lead the tribes of Yisrael. It will behoove you to have a standing army when you take the crown."

"That is not my mission." Yeshua pauses and, in the silence, hears Teoma chastise himself for not stopping his argument with Simeon. "Beloved brother, you refrained yourself because in your heart, you believe in my true purpose." Teoma's eyes waver, questioning. Joseph sits back heavily in the hard wooden chair. "Abba, if only you had as much faith in me as he does."

Torn between them, Teoma clasps his hands. "Abba Joseph, Yeshua can be rash, but his passion wins their hearts. The zealots will have a difficult time understanding your son's message of peace when they have trained for so long to overthrow the Emperor," Joseph nods, as Teoma takes a breath, "but I do believe that they will come to see the light. Look how Judas softened under Yeshua's influence."

Grumbling, Joseph gestures to dismiss them.

"Abba, I wish to teach our people how to heal their lives, even the goyim…" Yeshua pauses, "and yes, the Romans."

Impassioned, Joseph stands, his chair crashing to the floor. "Yeshua, have I not prepared you for the world of men? Evil exists outside this haven. You know not what you speak. The Romans must pay for the atrocities wrought upon this land!"

Yeshua rises with Teoma at his side. "I am pleased to hear you express your true feelings, but my purpose is to bring peace."

"Peace! The mystics filled your mind with fantasy. You sound like Zsao, always lecturing about the habit of fear. Has it helped your mother? She took in his every word like golden coins, yet fear still haunts her. She is afraid for your welfare!"

Only but a peek into his father's heart, now veiled by concern for his mother. "I am well aware of Ima's fear, but it is yours that we are here to discuss."

Joseph walks out. Sighing, Teoma uprights the fallen chair. "I am sorry, Yeshua. I do understand his concern, but…."

Yeshua grasps his arm. "You were sent out into the world of men that I might be protected. I trust your judgment to be as perceptive as Abba's, but without the shadow of fear."

Teoma shakes his head. "I am not free from fear."

"No one is, but, my brother, we must strive to release our attachment to that which binds us." Questions cloud the sky of Teoma's eyes. "Let us pray that Abba will see the light before the mission begins, shall we?" By the time they complete their meditation, the shadows in the garden have diminished.

***

Before Sarah's seventh birthday, I join Yeshua in ministering to the villagers. Most are physical healings, for that is what people expect, but we also address woes of the heart. Women come from as far as Capernaeum to request my services. Apparently, my sister has been sharing her secret.

One afternoon the courtyard fills with young women and children. Yeshua smiles as I prepare a remedy in the room used to dry medicinal herbs. "They're all here for you, dear."

"How can that be? No one's sick or injured?"

Yeshua shakes his head, "No, they need your special help."

Wondering what he's up to, I ask, "All of them?"

"Not a one is ill, other than the potter's wife with a mild sunburn. I believe they want to know about the white light of protection." Smiling, he leaves me but how am I to minister to all of them? It will take much time to teach each one.

Archangel Gavriel comes to me, laughter in his voice, *Dearest, do not take on this joyful work as a burden. Teach them as a group.*

Worry never helps. I thank him and enter the courtyard to be confronted with a crowd of women, some carrying infants or accompanied by small children. The small room set aside for healings will not do, we will have to make ourselves comfortable out here. "Welcome. It is apparent that you have all come for the same type of assistance."

Soft giggling erupts. "Yes, we are multiplying rapidly." A large matron gestures toward a very young woman entering with twin babies swaddled to her bosom.

"The children are welcome to join us. Just sit comfortably and close enough to join hands." We form a large circle and the angelic host arrives with a radiant light. Only a few seem to notice.

Breathing deeply, I perceive none are pregnant at this time.

"Sisters, do you each desire to control your fertility?" Each nods her head or murmurs yes. "What I am about to teach you has always been within your power, for we never were meant to be at the mercy of man's seed." A few chuckle. "Blessed as daughters of the Elat with the powers of co-creation, we must believe in our ability to control our fertility, inviting the spirits of our children only when we desire them." I breathe out loving hayye and pass it through my heart and hands. The woman holding my left hand gasps and I smile at her.

"I shall take you on a journey into your own wombs then teach you how to protect yourself from unwanted conceptions. This may feel more like you are remembering something you have forgotten than learning something new. So take a deep cleansing breath and exhale slowly." Carefully, I begin the visualization. When the meditation ends, white light glows around each of their wombs.

"You did it! See how simple it was!"

The women touch their lower bellies, checking their work.

"So that is it, Mary? We are safe now?"

"Yes, as long as you believe in your own divine powers." They express their gratitude fervently. When the last woman leaves, I drop to my knees to pray.

"How did the conscious conception circle go?" My husband helps me to my feet.

"The what?"

His kiss draws me close. "You should offer monthly healing circles. Women would travel far for your services."

"Yeshua, I want to teach others how to do this."

"An even better idea. Before we know it, the nation of Yisrael will not have another hungry mouth to feed."

On the full moon after the spring harvest, a slight woman with three small children joins the conscious conception circle, unfortunately, already pregnant. Asking her to wait in the small room for a private consultation, I attend to the others, praying fervently to be shown how to assist her. With Martha's help, the white light of protection is received by all in short time.

Afterwards, my sister offers to take the children into the atrium while I meet with the woman. Nervously playing with her light hair, Aviva sits down. I smile and ask about her last menses.

"I am half a moon cycle late."

I take her hand. "You are pregnant." Tears spill over sparse lashes to fall upon her lap. The hayye within her womb is pure nura, lighter than even Yeshua's.

"I was praying it wasn't so. I'm only married five years and this is my fourth pregnancy. I thought nursing would prevent another."

"Aviva, do you want this child?"

"We can hardly care for the others. My husband is a shepherd...I cannot even pay you!"

"You have already brought me a gift, something I have not previously considered." She looks questioningly at me. "We have to discuss your choices."

"What choices?"

"Do you ever wonder why wealthy women seem to have fewer children? Or that the priestesses of Astarte often have none? Haven't you seen them with lovers at the festivals?" She nods. Joseph has trained me well in the art of using healing herbs. "Aviva, these women know ways of preventing pregnancy with herbs as well as flushing the womb of unwanted pregnancies."

Her eyes are wide, "That can be done?"

"Yes, but the question is if this child is meant to be born on earth at this time."

"What do you mean? How can we know the will of Adonai?"

"We can ask. If you wish, I will try to communicate with the hayye of this child."

She hesitates, wringing her hands, "I came here for help…."

"Just relax and imagine something peaceful in your life." She sits back allowing me to scan the child. *Light being, your hayye is so refined. Why are you here?*

The nura becomes more brilliant, communicating in images like the dolphins. *Elat, I am one with the Light. I bring peace and joy to you and this one in your care. Not all pregnancies are meant to bring forth life. Some are lessons on the path back to the One.*

I sigh, feeling at peace. *Light being, will you leave on your own or do we need to assist you with our earthly remedies?*

The hayye shimmers. *If you do not assist me, the physical form which houses me will continue to develop, but when delivered, will not sustain life, for I am not to be born now.* I thank the being and turn to Aviva.

"This child is not meant to be. It is here to teach us both a lesson in faith. We can assist it now to leave your body with the herbs or you can go through the entire pregnancy and deliver the child, but it will not live."

"The choice is mine?" I nod but she is not well, nursing an infant, having not recovered fully from the first two. She smiles at me through her tears, "What more do you see?"

I squeeze her hands. "You do not have enough vigor to carry this child. I am not a seer, but your body is taxed by the pregnancies so close together and nursing your youngest. It is possible that you may not survive and leave your children motherless." Although I deny being a seer, images of her demise flood my awareness.

"Then the choice is clear. I will take the herbs."

"First, let us release the hayye of this child back to the Light from which it came." I pray out loud. "Marya, we are grateful for our blessings of life, for the many expressions of joy we might experience on our soul's journey back to the Light, and especially for this light being who has come to guide us on our path. May our choices be one with the Divine plan. Please accept the hayye of this being back into Love. Ameyn."

Beaming with grace, Aviva clasps her hands as the hayye of the light being lifts away from her womb and hovers about her heart center. Divine nura shines down upon them, the same portal I entered when near death, then expands to absorb the light being before gently withdrawing. Aviva exhales her held breath.

"Thank you, Mary."

I kiss her cheek, "I am grateful for this opportunity to serve you and the Light." Archangel Rafael comes to assist as I prepare the herbs and my creation is filled with light and love. Aviva accepts the remedy, listening carefully to my instructions, and thanks me again before going out to the atrium to retrieve her children from Martha. She promises to return on the next full moon for the conscious conception circle.

Martha puts her arm around me and I turn into her bosom. As she strokes my hair, murmuring encouragement, I realize how connected I am to all of my sisters, blood related or not. How blessed I am to serve them in this way.

"Mary, you did a wonderful thing for that poor woman. Did you see how happy she was? She finally can breathe easy, knowing she made a divinely guided decision."

I look up at my dear sister, "Thank you, Martha, for helping me. If it wasn't for your sharing of this information, I would never be here serving these women."

"We need some more women to help. You cannot do it all, but you can teach us how to minister to one another." We kiss farewell. Barchashem for sisters!

Early in Tammuz, when the rest of the family heads west to the shore, we head northeast toward Magdala. Visibly armed, Teoma watches over the entourage. Only a short distance from the road leading to the Sea of Galilee, he gathers us close. "Yeshua, the road we must cross is highly traveled by soldiers heading into Capernaeum. With the women and children, I would feel better if we traveled the rest of the distance under kasa."

Yeshua nods and hands the reins over to Sarah who takes them with an air of importance. Watching his Abba bring down the mists, Joshua whispers, "Ima, we all disappear!"

We pass discreetly along the heavily traveled road with many Roman soldiers, most keeping to themselves, but some cannot seem to help but aggravate the people they pass. Finally, we arrive in Magdala. I sigh contently, awash with pleasant memories of spending sweet summers near the fresh waters of Gennesaret.

Yeshua laughs. "Come, Mary can hardly contain herself."

Beautiful vines of bougainvillea cascade vibrant waves of pink and orange over white-washed walls enclosing the extensive grounds bordering the lake. Through massive gates, Teoma leads the horses to the stables as we enter the marble tiled courtyard hosting Grecian statues. Martha has made Magdala her own.

"Welcome, brother," Eleazer hugs Yeshua, turning to me for a kiss. "Who do we have here?" Squatting, he holds out his arms.

"Dod Eleazer, you know us. Don't be silly!" Sarah scolds.

Eleazer rolls his eyes, picking up Josh, "Already a little woman," whispering to Yeshua, "although I would love to have a daughter, I do not envy you, brother. She may prove to be quite a handful like her Ima."

Yeshua shakes his head, wrapping an arm around Martha's husband. "I see your wife has shared family secrets." Eleazer nods his head in sympathy.

Taking Sarah's hand, I lead the way into the house, "Come, Sarah, let us find your Doda and leave these men in their misery." Sarah looks back, waving at her brother. Edia joins us. After the servants wash the dust from our feet and hands at the kiyyor, we enter the spacious gathering room to be nearly knocked over by my three nephews.

"Doda!" They scream in unison. Seven-year-old Micah's head is at my chin. Judah and Eli wrap their arms about my waist and hips.

"My goodness, what is your Ima feeding you? You have grown so tall."

"Boys, release your Doda!" Martha turns to her niece. "My, how lovely you look in that elegant gown." After twirling about to show her aunt the full effect, Sarah gives her a big kiss.

"Please bring your cousins to the nursery. Your lunch is waiting."

Taking Judah's hand, Sarah commands, "Show me our chambers." Micah takes a dusty Josh, who escaped his father, and runs down the hall followed by little Eli. With a flurry of laughter the children are gone, Edia close behind.

Kissing my sister, I thank her for the invitation to spend the summer. "You're most welcome. It is fortunate that Ima is not here to see such a costly gift worn as a traveling garment."

I shake my head, "My daughter is most stubborn. She insisted upon wearing the gown to show you."

With an arm about my waist, Martha laughs. "She is just like you, little sister."

In the nursery the next morning, Martha and I prepare the children for a day at the shore. "Do you remember these?" She hands me two small boats. I nod as images seep from the wood into my mind's eye.

Playing along the water's edge, Ima was quite worried that we might fall in and drown. Abba tied slender ropes to our little boats so we could pull them back, but I crept farther and farther into the water, until Ima threatened to punish me if I got my sadin wet. At two, I became distracted by a flock of waterfowl flying overhead and dropped the rope. My boat drifted away.

Six-year-old Martha cried, "Oh, no, Mary. It's gone."

I went out on the water to retrieve it. Abba knelt at the water's edge when I returned with my boat. "Mary, how did you get your boat without getting wet?"

I pulled up my dry sadin. "I walked, Abba. On the water. I not wet, see!"

He scooped me up with a kiss. "No, you are not wet, my dear. Perhaps we can take a walk on the water tomorrow."

"Well, Mary what do you think?" Martha interrupts my reminiscing, "Should we bring the boats for the children? My boys might break them."

"No, they won't. They'll be careful."

Such a bright beautiful day, so warm the water looks especially inviting. Fishing vessels float by in the distance and to the north fishermen cast nets, their wet skin glistening in the sunlight. Yeshua tries to entice Josh into the water to teach him to swim, but Josh won't release the boat. "No! My boat!"

Sarah begs, "Please, let's put it in the water."

Joshua shakes his head, "No, Sarah. No lose my boat!"

"Josh, I won't let your boat get away. Let's see if it floats like the boys'." Teoma coaxes and finally Josh relents as Sarah wades in the shallows.

Watching from the edge, Joshua's lower lip trembles. I kneel by his side and kiss his cheek. "Listen, Josh, if the boat floats away, you know how to get it." Like the creatures, children easily perceive images, so I show him my earlier memory.

238

Yeshua calls to Teoma, "Bring Sarah out of the water and leave the boat."

As the little boat starts floating away, Joshua looks at me. "Go on, baby. Go get your boat." Without hesitation, he walks across the surface of the water and gets it.

"Mary, you did that too!" Martha cries as Yeshua places an arm around my shoulders.

Finding his voice, Teoma asks, "We're still going to teach Josh how to swim, right?" Everyone laughs. Unaffected by his little miracle, Joshua clutches his boat most unwilling to share with his sister. "Help me find a nice piece of wood and I'll carve you a boat." Teoma takes Sarah's hand to search the shore.

Turning me toward him, Yeshua's expression is so serious, "You never told me you could walk on water. Can you still do it?"

"I don't know. I'm much bigger now." I laugh. "But as a child I did it because I didn't know that my desires may not be possible."

He shakes his head, "It's that simple?"

Standing on tiptoe, I kiss his nose, "You think too much. Just try it."

Much to Sarah's delight, Teoma finishes the boat in a few days. We sit on the shore watching the children float their boats and Yeshua try to walk on water. From a meditative stance to what looks like sleep walking, he splashes through the Sea of Galilee.

"Mary, he's not going to give up. This could be a very long summer."

"Come, Teoma, let's take him for a walk on the shore."

Reluctantly, Yeshua follows, his tunic damp from exertion. Just north of the docks, the trees grow close to the edge of the water. Leading them through the grove on a seldom-used trail following a vague memory, I stop to get my bearings.

"Mary, I hope you haven't gotten us lost."

I smile at Teoma, "Come, ye of little faith." In short time, we are there.

The thicket opens to a rocky point that extends into the water; the gentle lapping of the lake echoes as we approach. Peering over the edge at the overgrown trail, I can barely see the cave. I take off my sadin and Teoma turns away, but when Yeshua strips, so does he.

Carefully I descend the hot basalt, diving under the water to search for the opening. The men follow. Entering the underwater passage, we surface in a large cavern. I climb onto the far ledge.

"What is this place?" Basking in the energy of my childhood haunt, I smile at Teoma. As large as our garden gathering room, the cavern glimmers with multihued quartz. An opening in the ceiling invites the afternoon sunlight to dance upon the crystal blue water. In the alcove, a solitary mass of clear quartz stands like an altar.

"Mary, this is amazing. How did you discover it?"

"My Abba brought me to this magical place the summer after I retrieved my boat, let me play, collect quartz, swim in the pool, and show him how to walk on water."

Yeshua's hug takes my breath away. "So you'll teach me?"

"No, but the energy of the cave will. Abba felt this place would allow for safe passage through the realities so we practiced here."

"Your father walks on water too?" Teoma shakes his head.

"I don't know if he does anymore, but while you two were receiving expert instruction from the mystics, I was playing with the energies with my Abba."

Yeshua explores the cave while Teoma stands in the water and I call to my angels who come in a shimmer of light. My husband needs to learn another means to teach. I have learned quickly from him, but how is this to work with others?

Rafael laughs, *Dear Mary, your husband's muse is sensuality, as is yours. But you are correct; most humans are not comfortable enough to use these energies to fuel their creative works.* Smiling, I thank Rafael, take a deep breath, visualize my desire and walk across the pool.

Yeshua looks up as I step onto the firm rock, "Why didn't you wait for me?"

"Just testing the water, dear. Follow my breath, visualize yourself on the surface of the water and come with me." We walk hand-in-hand, breathing in unison, around the cave once, twice, three times. Yeshua lets out a great sigh. I kiss him, too passionately.

Teoma clears his throat. "Excuse me, but if you are quite finished with today's lesson, we should be getting back." He dives back under the water and exits the cave.

"So why did you insist on bringing Teoma along?"

"I thought you should learn how to teach without the sexual tension. You might want to remember this with the council."

His excitement inciting mine, he is not to be deterred. "I will definitely remember the day my wife taught me to walk on water." I pray Teoma stays outside.

So great is our passion that only afterward do I notice where he has positioned us...on the surface of the water! I nip his ear before sliding down to stand beside him, "You are audacious," and we dive back through the cavern to climb out and retrieve our clothes.

Teoma lies in the sun. "So now, Yesh, can we try and make some contacts?"

Not until the full moon of Av does Yeshua announce we will be fishing for men. Sarah is so disappointed, "But Abba, I want to catch fish! You can't eat people." Teoma can hardly contain his mirth at this suppertime discussion.

Dod Eleazer intervenes, "Sarah, while your Abba fishes for men, I will take you and the boys fishing for fish."

Although the boys are quite excited, Sarah frowns, "I want my Abba to take me fishing."

"Yeshua was never much good with the net."

Edia elbows Teoma. Yeshua acquiesces to our daughter then whispers behind his hand, "Let us hope we catch something tomorrow to satisfy the children."

Teoma smiles, "Is this your way of asking for my help?"

"Between you three men, you should be able to catch enough fish to satisfy five small children." Teoma chuckles at my assumption.

"Oh no, Yeshua cannot hurt the fish, so he warns them of our intentions and they leave the vicinity." Edia and I laugh, hardly able to swallow our drinks.

Up at dawn, exhausted since Yeshua meditated all night for an answer to his dilemma, we head to the shore. Eleazer has gathered small fishing nets while Teoma starts a bonfire to warm us and, hopefully later, cook the fish. Yeshua attempts to help Eleazer straighten the nets, but it is clear that it is not one of my husband's few worldly skills.

Before going into the water, Teoma leads the excited children in prayer. "Very good. Now you must understand that as fishermen, your hayye can either attract or repel the fish." The children listen intently. "A good fisherman understands that the fish give up their lives so he can feed his family and he expresses his gratitude to their spirits." Even Joshua is still, sitting on his Abba's lap.

Looking around at their eager faces, Teoma gives one last bit of advice, "When you call the fish to the net you must do so silently with your minds. If you make noise, they will be frightened. If you do not want to participate in catching the fish or think that you may repel the fish, then you should stay here by the fire. You can help clean and prepare the fish later, if you like." The children gravely nod. "So let's learn how to hold the net and then go into the water." Everyone jumps up and heads toward edge of the water. Everyone, but Yeshua.

Sarah notices his absence, "Abba, why aren't you joining us?"

He stands and takes her hand. "Sarah, I cannot kill the fish. My hayye will repel them and we won't be able to catch anything."

She studies his face. "But Abba, you eat fish."

"I know, dear, but I have never been able to kill any animal so I am grateful for great fishermen and hunters, like Dod Eleazer and Dod Teoma, who provide us with food."

Reaching up she kisses his cheek, "We have to thank Eloha for all of the people who take care of us." Sarah runs down to the water's edge to join her cousins and uncles. Teoma looks back and winks at Yeshua.

After a short time, the children begin silently to call to the fish while the men help hold the nets. Soon large schools begin swimming toward them. Being too short to wade as far as the others, Joshua asks to be carried. "Ima, I call the fishes, too."

No wonder fishermen do this work naked; we're drenched by the time the net is full. Martha brings a fresh change of clothing as Teoma prays, "Marya, we are grateful for this bountiful catch and thank the fish for giving up their bodies that we may be nourished. Bless the offspring of these fish that they may prosper in this wonderful lake. Ameyn."

Teoma and Eleazer patiently teach the children how to clean and skewer the fish onto long sticks to roast over the fire. Sarah presents her cooked fish to her father. "Here, Abba, you can have the first taste."

"Thank you, Sarah, and my appreciation extends to all of you great fishermen who provide me with nourishment." After tasting each of the boys' fish too, he proclaims that they are all most delicious. "Teoma, you are a wonderful teacher just like Abba."

"Yesh, I am very grateful that you were willing to share your father with me or else I might not have ever learned all that I have taught the children."

Watching both the men in my life embrace after interacting so lovingly with my children, I give thanks for all my many blessings.

Lost in Capernaeum

The next morning, we go fishing for men. Leaving Sarah and Joshua in Martha's capable hands is less difficult than receiving her blessing. Her grave look of concern follows me through the village gates, until a golden sun skipping jewels of light on the surface of the lake draws my attention. Waterfowl crowd fishermen as they cast their nets. Sturdy boats venture out into the calm waters, further now than possible this afternoon when fierce tempests will flush them back to shore.

The road snakes along the northwestern shore. Wealthy goyim dressed in the latest fashions from Rome ride on donkeys. Hebrew men in long linen cloaks walk together, while their wives follow behind, veiled most modestly. Ever alert, Teoma eyes soldiers who command strong men to carry their load a long Roman mile. None refuse, fearful to defy the Emperor's law.

We pass through the town of Gennesaret, two-thirds the way to our destination, nearly noon before reaching the crowded streets of Capernaeum. Exotic wares gaily sold by loud vendors sidle by lush displays of produce, while young animals in makeshift pens await purchase for butchering. Laughing children play in the streets, as women carry baskets on their hips. On corners, men congregate around wise Chachamim to hear them read sacred Hebrew verses of the Torah. So different than the Tzadokim is their translation proclaimed in the common language. As more men gather to debate the Chachamim's interpretation, Teoma steers us toward the center of town.

On the highest hill rises a great white marble synagogue. Constructed by a Roman centurion, some say it is greater than the synagogue in Alexandria. Milling soldiers bring us to a halt.

"There's some kind of trouble. Let us stay back until Bartholomew shows himself."

Perhaps Teoma met our next contact on his many ventures to Judaea. Suddenly a centurion gallops past. Teoma pushes us into a narrow alleyway to avoid being trampled. The Roman whirls his huge black horse around to confront us. Gasping, I hide my face in the back of Yeshua's tunic. Only at the hollow sounds of retreating hooves do I look up. My husband grasps my arms.

"Mary, what is it?"

Trembling violently, I slip into the infinite portal of his eyes to drown in a pool of memories.

***

Teoma leads them deeper into the alley, breathing heavily. Mary too remembers when they were caught in the same place some twelve years ago. Within the sea-green depths of her eyes, he loses himself to the past.

Shortly after Reiti returned to the Hindus region, Joseph surrendered the boys to the tutelage of the Aksum king. What a joy! Belshazzar gave them complete freedom. Taking great advantage of their new-found manhood, they explored Galilee, haunting the local towns, befriending Hebrew and goyim alike, even some young Roman soldiers. That is how they got out of trouble in Capernaeum. Well, sort of.

Late one night in first Adar, they stole away to Magdala. Mary met them outside the gate and with one arm, he lifted her slight form to sit behind him on the donkey. Yeshua led the way north to Capernaeum.

Yeshua's poor attempt at using kasa made it difficult to penetrate the synagogue. Disappearing and reappearing, they made their way stealthily to the inner sanctum. In great reverence, Yeshua blessed the synagogue with sacred feminine energy. Teoma prayed that it would work, for Mary was not yet a woman. Unfortunately, the candle caught the attention of a flustered young scribe who hurried to call the guards. Taking charge, Teoma led them back over the wall to race down the street where they were caught by a centurion.

"Hey, what have you there?"

"Nothing, sir. We are late and must hurry home." Teoma made a hasty excuse before Yeshua could reveal the truth, but the guard ran up exclaiming.

"These villains have desecrated the sanctuary! Arrest them!"

The centurion laughed. "It is not the Emperor's problem, nor Antipas'." He looked down and spoke in Latin. "Boy, do I know you?"

Yeshua looked up at him. "Yes. We met near Mount Karmel."

The Roman nodded, remembering it was Yeshua who healed his lame horse the past spring on the spice route. "Little one, who is your father?" The centurion asked Mary in Aramaic.

"Why she is the daughter of the magistrate! These boys have accosted her!"

The centurion turned to Teoma. "How did you travel so far from Nazareth this late at night?"

"On donkeys, sir."

"Retrieve your mounts." Teoma hurried and returned to see Mary holding tightly to Yeshua's hand. "Hand me up the girl, so she may show us the way to her home." Mary looked frightened as he did the Roman's bidding. Too soon, they arrived in Magdala.

Syrus was surprised to see his young daughter with Roman soldiers. While the flustered guard explained, the centurion took the opportunity to have his men search the villa. Hysterical at the invasion, Eucharia roughly drug Mary into the house, pursued by a large black bird.

"Be calm. It is not as if these boys planned to run off with your daughter."

Yeshua looked up. "How did you know?"

"What!" Syrus foolishly ignored the centurion. "She is only a child. Does your father know of this?" The boys shook their heads.

Remembering the terror on Mary's face, Teoma prayed that nothing would thwart their plans to go to the Himals. Soon Belshazzar would leave to return to his own tribe, but Yeshua's training was not complete. He wished to find Zsao and study with the great masters. Then they would search the Hindus for Reiti, certain there were other yogas to be learned. Yearning for more adventure than could be found in Galilee, Teoma was anxious to begin. He would watch over Mary. Besides, she loved the treks to Mount Karmel.

All color drained from Syrus' face. "You took my daughter to Karmel?"

"Yes, she wants to study with us!"

Grasping Yeshua's arm before he could say another word, Teoma faced Mary's angry father. For her sake, he spoke up, "Sir, let us return and receive Joseph's punishment." Gut twisting with concern, he prayed her father make haste and go in to his family.

Swallowing thickly, Teoma returns to the present. Mary stands before him, tears streaming from her lovely eyes. Helplessly, Yeshua looks on, unaware that Mary's mother beat her that night.

***

Teoma stokes the fire as we sit against large logs well south of the city. Stars float on the surface of the lake which laps soothingly against the pebbled shore. Still I am wary. Yeshua brushes the hair from my face, "Mary, how am I to understand how to minister to people if I do not know what they are experiencing?"

From across the fire, Teoma warns, "Some memories are better left alone."

"I have no wish to cause pain, but perhaps your perceptions are rooted in the past." I shudder as Yeshua explains, "Being punished so severely reinforced Mary's feelings of unworthiness. Even now she becomes distraught when brought before our elders, perceiving their critique as judgment. She came into this life to heal this misperception." When Teoma withdraws, Yeshua says softly, "Please come here by us."

Sighing, Teoma sits down, putting a protective arm around me, "Why does she have to relive this pain?"

"She only has to name it to release it." Yeshua moves directly in front of me. If I look into his eyes, I will know. Afraid, I turn into Teoma's shoulder, who hugs me into his chest as if to keep me from remembering. His voice is hoarse.

"Yesh, please don't."

Yeshua's hayye pulls on my heart. Patting Teoma's chest, I tell him, "Please, I need to do this," and he allows me to fully face Yeshua, his arms clasped tightly about my waist. Yeshua touches my cheek and I see in his fathomless eyes myself as a young child.

Me: very small, toddling, precocious, getting into everything. Ima: frantic, worried, upset at the slightest provocation. Martha: nearly six, quiet, good, never angering her. Climbing onto a table, I break something glass, a dish perhaps. Martha cries as Ima storms in to yank me off the table by my arm, which snaps, fragile as a chicken bone. My wailing overcomes Martha's as Ima paddles my bottom.

Pressing myself against Teoma's chest, I hold my right arm, painful at the elbow. Teoma asks, "Mary, what is it?"

248

"Ima broke my arm when I was a baby." I murmur, his heart pounding through my back. Yeshua touches the exact spot, healing hayye coursing through his hands. The pain dissolves. Gratefully looking into his eyes, I see more.

Much of my childhood Abba was away and never knew. My arm, set by a healer in Sepphoris, healed before he returned from the Tyrian port. But Joseph knew. When they returned from Egyptus at Yeshua's birthday, I was coughing so Joseph gave Ima a remedy. He asked about the bruises and Ima told him that I climbed on everything. I did, but that's not how I got hurt.

"Your father knew."

Teoma gets upset, "Why didn't he intervene?"

"There's more, Yesh." He nods, still silent. My seraph comes to encompass us all. Yeshua and Teoma perceive the shimmer of the host of angels. *Mary, if you are willing to go as deep as possible this healing will be complete.* Settling firmly into Teoma's embrace, I answer Gavriel out loud, "I am willing." Yeshua holds the energy and the hayye shifts once more.

After that summer in Magdala spent mostly with Abba, I became more willful, Ima became more upset, the punishment more severe. Catching my explorations in the bath, Ima washed me so roughly that it hurt to urinate long afterwards. Between ages four and six, I would throw tantrums at bath time.

"I don't know if I can do this, Yeshua."

Behind me Teoma tightens his grip, "That's enough...."

"Mary's mother was upset at the attention her father paid her."

Drawing my knees up to my chest, I rock, soothing the painful memories. In Yeshua's eyes, I see Ima, hurt as a child by her father and uncle. Her mother punished her too. How afraid and lonely she was. Wiping my face on my sadin, I go on. My husband's energy flowing through me as each memory surfaces, I feel lighter.

"So you see how your feelings of unworthiness were reinforced by your relationship with your mother?"

"After we were caught in the synagogue, Ima didn't touch me."

"Why not, Mary?"

In the hall, Ima grabbed Abba's walking stick and my cries woke Martha who ran to get Abba. The hayye he used to break that stick was frightening. I had never seen my Abba upset. Ima was forbidden to touch me ever again. Unfortunately, that night began the withdrawal of her affection.

I shudder, the pain of neglect far worse and repeated again by Yeshua after that incident with Teoma in the tent. "I am so sorry, my love."

Yeshua sighs, looking at Teoma. "Apparently it is worse not to be touched at all."

The weight of Teoma's sorrow presses heavily against me. "You can release this tonight, Teoma."

"Is it really over for you, Mary?"

My voice shakes, "No, because I have not remembered everything." Teoma's eyes widen as I tell him another memory, praying it is the last.

"Instead of our grand adventure together to the Himals, we were separated. You went south to Judaea, Yeshua north to Britannia, and I sailed the Mediterranean with my family. Once when I was thirteen, our ship was docked in a trading port on Crete. Anxious to see the sights, I raced ahead of my mother and sister. One particularly kind sailor escorted me, but soon we were so far from the shore that I asked him to take me back. Ima would be worried." Teoma waits but I pause too long.

"How could you have trusted him?"

"I had no reason not to, but...," I hesitate, "always before I was chaperoned. From behind a taverna, his friends offered him sikera. I asked for escort back to the boat. They laughed and started to say crude things." Again I hesitate. Yeshua reaches out, but I cannot look at him. "They, they said..." I swallow thickly, "since they had shared their wine, he must share me. He said they would get his leftovers, then he..."

Teoma's right cheek twitches with anger. With trembling fingers, I touch it, wishing... "Mary, if I would have been there, I swear, no one would have touched you."

Softly, Yeshua asks, "Mary, what happened?"

I sigh resigning myself to continue, "I tried to escape, but that made him get rougher. The others got angry or excited, I could not tell in my fear. They kept passing me around until someone held my arms so I could not defend myself." Teoma's eyes mirror my pain. "Then my father came. His menservants scattered the sailors. When we returned to the boat he asked my mother to see to me. She was very upset, blaming me for what had happened. I became hysterical, refusing to let her come near me. She assumed the worst, saying that no man would ever want me."

"Why did you not confide in anyone?"

With trembling lips I answer Teoma's question, "Because I prayed that night to forget about what had happened and I did. The next morning, I woke up wondering why I was bruised. Until tonight I had forgotten."

Yeshua's hand on my shoulder tightens, "During the incident you left your body. That's how your Abba found you and why you forgot until now. There was no indication of a prior assault because you were not conscious of it."

Teoma shakes his head, "How many things do we go through that are too painful to remain present, let alone recall?"

"Many, I'm afraid, many. Mary, you fear my judgment, choosing not to look at me while you remembered. What you perceive is your own sense of unworthiness which must be healed." His hand releases its grip on my shoulder. "Turn around, when you are ready."

Gazing at Teoma's mouth, I wonder why I don't feel judged by him. As if perceiving my thoughts, he answers, "My self-worth is lower than yours. How can I judge you?" Looking into his eyes, I speak his pain.

"Although you have loved, you do not feel beloved. Your life is a reflection of your lack of self love. Your father denied you and your mother gave you up to be raised by others. You found acceptance in Yeshua's family, but you haven't found a love of your own. And I chose Yeshua over you," tears choke me, "another rejection."

"All you say is true. But what matters is not how much others love you, but how much you love them."

Yeshua corrects him, "What matters most is how much you love yourself. Love from the world will follow and be a mirror of your love for yourself."

Teoma hugs me and I cry into his chest. I could stay right here and commiserate with him. Or I could turn around and face my destiny. Kissing Teoma, I thank him, "My dearest friend, if only we could learn to love ourselves the way we love each other." Smiling, he nods and releases me from his embrace.

Turning, I face Yeshua and in the void of his eyes, I see my true self, which is love.

"You are my beloved, Mary. It matters not to me from whence you came, only that you are here in this moment with me now." When he embraces me, my tears wash away the pain of a childhood lost, bringing in the joy of a life found. My life with him.

The three of us sleep on the shore of the Sea of Galilee, partners in this life, eternal soul mates.

First morning light finds me curled up against Teoma's back, my thumb in my mouth. Withdrawing it slowly, I leave my safe harbor. Yeshua lies a distance away. Chilled, I pray he stays asleep for I cannot look at him.

Silently walking across the sand, my only desire is to leave. Dawn beckons a soft gray. Pain invades each step, all the beatings captured within my flesh. Searching for the perfect place away from all reminders of the past, I sit facing the rising sun upon the surface of the water.

In three short breaths, I am free. Angels greet me in the ethers, but I do not heed their voices, wishing only to be one with the Light. I have no desire to return to my tortured body. As if watching a Greek play, safe in front of the stage, I observe from another place for a long time.

On the shore, Teoma stirs, reaching behind him as if I had slept against his back all night. Startled, he sits up and looks around. Yeshua sleeps soundly, while Teoma scans the lake.

"Yeshua, wake up, something's wrong with Mary."

Yeshua follows his pointing finger. "She's not in her body. I'll try and commune with her, but keep watch. You might have to swim out to her." Teoma nods as Yeshua sits in a meditative pose.

Yeshua's hayye rises from his form, reaching out to me, but I keep my distance. "Mary, please, come to me."

I cannot bear to remember more. If I open to him, I will never forget. "No, Yesh, leave me."

He reaches out again, but my fear is like a wall. Moving deeper into the space within space, there is no time, only Uriel. The others have gone.

Yeshua returns to the shore. "We must retrieve her. I do not know how much longer she can maintain out-of-body levitation, but I cannot access her. She is farther away now that I tried." Teoma secures a small boat from a fisherman and they row out to my body. Yeshua hauls me aboard.

Yanked back into my form, I scream, nearly capsizing the boat. My arms pinned, his legs securely around mine, the pain is unbearable. Engulfed in waves of panic, my heart races, my breath comes in shallow gasps. Yeshua's hayye traps me. Why won't he release me back to the light?

Finally on the shore, he carries me struggling to the sand and sits. I cannot formulate words through my screams. Teoma murmurs and I reach for him. Yeshua relents and in Teoma's embrace, the pain subsides. I look up at his tear-streaked face, feeling safer.

"Mary," he whispers, "what is wrong?"

Wracking sobs drown my voice. Yeshua sits across from us, but I dare not look at him. Like great raindrops, Teoma's tears splash upon me. The water that soothes me, the waves of the sea, the lapping of the lake. Light glistens in a tear poised to fall from his lash. There is peace in the light. I enter the light within the tear.

Free from pain, in the Light with Uriel. I watch what transpires below.

Yeshua cries, "She's gone again. I do not know what to do."

Teoma still holds my limp form. "We need to get help. We must send word to Magdala. I will go and get supplies, while you contact someone."

Wiping his face, Yeshua shakes his head. "If I touch her again, she'll panic. Leaving her body unattended, she might withdraw farther away. For now, she is close."

Teoma looks up as if to locate my essence. Yeshua stands. "I will go get what we need and send word to Magdala. She feels safe with you."

Teoma shakes his head, "But Yesh, how will you fare?"

Yeshua shrugs, leaving Teoma to sit on the shore.

I move deeper into the ethers. Uriel follows, "Mary, this is where you would go whenever you felt unsafe as a child. Those who care for you now love and honor you."

Shimmering, I move deeper past the veil. "Uriel, do not make me go back."

With angelic compassion, he bathes me with love. "I cannot force you to return, but if you do not stay embodied, you will come back again to the same scenario. Please, this life presents an opportunity for healing."

I allow Uriel to bring me close enough to see that Teoma has laid me freshly washed and dressed on a blanket under the dappled shade of a young tree. Reverently, he kneels in prayer, asking that I might complete my journey with Yeshua, willing to surrender his love for me if I am healed. A bright prism of nura surrounds him but I cannot perceive the One through the shadow of my fear. I take Uriel's hand and return.

The density of my body so suffocating, I cannot see the light. I struggle to be released, but Uriel stays me. *Mary, be patient. Fear keeps you in darkness. Focus on Teoma's light.* Only a soft glow, not the brilliance I am familiar with, my vision so muted, grief washes over me. My tears alert Teoma.

"Barchashem! Mary, you've returned." He approaches gingerly.

"I am so ashamed. I cannot bear to know more."

Teoma's tears pool with mine on the sand. "None of this was your fault."

"I must have chosen this path for a reason, but the way is so hard." He starts to reach out, but stops. I sit up and slowly hold out my hand. When our fingertips meet a wave of deep grief washes over me. Shaking with despair but not wanting to be stuck in the pain, I collapse into the security of his chest.

I awaken to a dusky sky. Teoma tends a fire. "Where is Yeshua?"

"He went to send word to your sister and get supplies, but you know he can't find his way around a marketplace." A bubble of laughter bursts before it reaches my lips. Teoma smiles, "I can't keep you in your body and find him too."

I touch his arm. "Thank you, Teoma."

"When Yeshua gets back, please let him help you."

"I'm afraid to look into his eyes and remember any more."

Teoma sighs, "At least try to stay." I murmur my consent.

Yeshua returns after dark. I get up to greet him and he drops his burden of supplies, tears in his eyes. Torn between my desire to connect and my fear to be cast back into pain, I waver. What if we can never be like we were before?

He drops to his knees. "Mary, we cannot go back, we can only go forward."

Tentatively, I reach to touch his bowed head, fingertips brushing his hair, and...*My mother saying it's my turn, forces something inside of me.* Why did I induce such anger in her? Yeshua reaches out to me, but his touch lays me open. *Leaving my tortured body, I go to Uriel.*

Yeshua holds me, sobbing. "I can't even touch her."

Teoma takes me from his arms. "Mary," he commands, "Please come back."

"I feel so incompetent. I had so much trouble finding a messenger. It took me all day to get these few things." He gestures hopelessly toward the supplies.

Teoma smiles, "We wondered how you would do."

"She spoke to you?"

Teoma nods, "She's afraid to remember more, but promised to stay."

Yeshua sighs, "That one touch brought back another horrible memory."

"What else?"

"You don't want to know."

In the ethers, Uriel speaks. "Go back, Mary. Yeshua will be shown a way to help you. You will not be hurt anymore." Shuddering, I allow him to lead me through the veil and into myself.

"Forgive me, Yesh." I whisper from the safety of Teoma's arms.

He kneels by us, but I do not look at him. "Mary, there is no reason to apologize. I only wish I could help without hurting you."

Taking a deep breath, I tell him, "Uriel said you would be shown a way. But not tonight, I am so tired."

For days, Yeshua attempts contact with me, but any touch brings a tortuous influx of memories. Especially if I look in his eyes, the pain goes beyond this life into my past. I cannot bear to know more, I just want this over. Day and night, he tries to help me in the ethers, but I flee with Uriel into the darkness. Only if Teoma holds me can I find my way back into my body.

I am losing my way.

Yeshua has made contact with the children, but I am afraid to be with them. I spend less and less time in my body, upsetting Teoma by leaving it on the water. Unable to sleep, I wander aimlessly at night trailed by the worried men. Teoma struggles to get me to eat, but nothing interests me. I can hardly remember to keep myself clean. I think I'm losing my mind, but Yeshua assures me that I am still coherent. I don't know.

The seventh day dawns. Teoma watches as I brush my hand over the sand. Birds perch upon me, small lizards and spiders finding refuge on my warm skin. When on the water, the fish school beneath me. Teoma teases that he hardly needs a net. With the animals, I can stay longer in my body. The men frighten the creatures so they keep their distance.

"We need to go back to Magdala. It will be easier to care for her with the women's help."

I stand up, startling them. "No! I will not return to my children like this!"

Teoma turns to me, "But they miss you."

My tears cause the birds to flutter, "Now that I remember, what if...?" Yeshua takes a step and the creatures and I move back nervously.

"Mary, you can break the cycle, you do not have to repeat it."

Not looking at him, I shake my head, "I can't take that chance."

Sighing, Yeshua heads to town and I sit facing the water. The energies of the light entice me to join with my angelic host.

Gavriel speaks. "Yeshua is correct, you may break this cycle of pain if you choose."

Crying in my body and in the ethers, I reply. "I do choose, Gavriel. I was willing to take this journey and now I am lost."

Gavriel's light glimmers. "You are not lost, Mary. Uriel is here to guide you. Your soul is already healing. Your mind is attempting to understand the connections to begin on the path to healing. Your body holds the memories, which serves you in this reality to ground you to earth. Not only painful memories, Mary, but joyful ones."

The angels proceed to show me many happy times.

Joyfully interacting with the children. Making love to Yeshua. Talking with him. Studying with the family. Being tended by the women in the chamam. Riding Sheikan like the wind. Swimming with the dolphins. Laughing with Teoma. Sailing the Mediterranean Sea. Spending time with the boys when we were children. Working with the energies with my Abba. Playing with my sister. Learning to embroider with my Ima. Being with the Light.

Awash in peace, I go to view my children. Playing on the shoreline at Magdala, Sarah and Joshua greet me with laughter. I love them so, I could never hurt them. I hover about their auras until drawn away by Archangel Michael back to my body.

Roman soldiers surround me. I scream and struggle, but am still restrained. "Hush, Mary." Teoma speaks to the soldiers and they take their leave.

I feel damp, but it's his body that's wet. When the soldiers are out of sight, he sits heavily upon the ground, still holding me in his arms. I look into his pained face.

"Teoma, what happened?"

He shakes his head. "We're out of food, so I was fishing and did not see the soldiers." I shudder. "Nothing happened. I was afraid you would come back into your body with them so close, and unfortunately you did when I picked you up."

Shaking I ask, "Why were they here?"

"Patrolling the area. We have been here too long. Your condition concerned them and I explained that you were sick. They are superstitious about this kind of illness."

"They thought I was insane."

Rocking me in his lap, he nods. "Please, let us go home. We are not safe here."

Before noon, Yeshua returns from Capernaeum. "I contacted Belshazzar." I nod. "He advised me how to help you."

I look up, but not at his eyes, "Really?"

He's excited, for the first time in a week. "Yes, Zsao, Reiti, Belshazzar; we are all to be in the water."

Teoma wrinkles his brow, "How is water going to help?"

Yeshua smiles and the white of his teeth stirs a faint yearning. He starts to respond but hesitates. "Mary's hayye is fluid emotion. The water will serve to connect us and you, my friend, will be the anchor so I might lay my hands on her head."

I gasp but Teoma insists, "Mary, the way has been shown. We need to do this!"

Dread settles deeply within me. At dusk, Yeshua and Teoma pray and do ritual washings of their bodies. Watching the preparations, my body quakes with pain, even my arm hurts. I disrobe to bathe in the sea and find myself covered in bruises and welts. Cold as death, the elestial stone darkens my navel. I crouch, weeping in the sand. Teoma calls out to Yeshua who kneels by my side.

"Mary, it is time."

Shaking, I whisper hoarsely. "Yeshua, what is happening?"

"My love, you are manifesting all the hurt from the past. It is coming up to be cleared. Come now into the water." He walks backwards into the Sea of Galilee. I surrender, but hesitant to look into his eyes, I gaze at the water. Behind me, Teoma gasps at the sight of my flesh.

A gentle breeze plays with my hair, my breath becomes fuller. The hayye of the blue lake soothes me to lie back and let it wash away my terror. Yeshua motions for Teoma to support me, but I float easily enough. Shivering, I close my eyes. Teoma turns and holds my feet as Yeshua prays.

"Marya, please release our fears and replace them with love and light. We are grateful for those who join us in this ministration. We ask that our attachment to this pain be released so that we may heal. We ask that we might be divinely guided and pray that we are holding the highest intent for Mary. May this healing be an opening for her and for all who suffer such pain on Earth. Ameyn."

The energy of the mystics joins us in a prism of nura. Through the water I can feel their touch, supporting me. Relaxing, my breath deepens, the pain already lessened.

Yeshua responds, "Good, my love, now focus on our hands. If you feel like you want to slip out of your body focus only on Teoma holding your feet." I wiggle my toes against the hair on Teoma's chest and feel him smile.

Yeshua touches my crown. White light, at once warm and cool, pours from his palms in waves throughout my body. The bruises and welts heal, Teoma gasping as they disappear. I perceive no more memories through Yeshua's hands and thank him.

I surrender more completely and he takes me deeper into the healing. Without leaving my body to go to the Light, the One comes to me. In a great sense of bliss, I laugh out loud and perceive all my healers smiling. I am joy!

The One speaks. *Mary, you are my joy. But as you feel tremendous joy, you have experienced tremendous pain. The polar nature of the earth realm magnifies the human experience. You have been blessed with much courage to release this belief in suffering. Healing is in seven layers from the surface to the core. You are halfway through to becoming united with the center of your being. Do not lose heart when you experience fear in your life. Your great faith keeps you on the path back to Source.*

Will I experience the joy I once had with Yeshua? The One laughs, a great bubble of mirth that none of my healers can resist joining. Like a child's laughter, it is contagious, delightful and I too laugh at myself, my humanness.

Peals of laughter form into an answer, *Your hayye humors the hosts of heaven, beloved. Without the depth of pain, your experience of joy will be multiplied.*

I take a deep shuddering breath, my belly sore from laughing. The One reminds me. *Be gentle with yourself, Mary. It is not easy being in human form. Old beliefs are stirred to the surface of your consciousness before being blown away by the winds of change. The greatest joy will follow the deepest pain.* The hayye of the One compresses and, like a kiss, settles deep within my heart center to remind me of who I am as Joy.

I look up into Yeshua's eyes. My mirror. There is no more pain. I see only Love. Barchashem. Reaching up I touch his face and he bends to kiss my forehead.

I wiggle my toes, pulling Teoma's chest hair. "Ouch, Mary."

"You can put me down now, dear Teoma. I'm back." Tenderly, they take my hands and escort me back to shore.

Layers of Healing

"You look like you've been to Hades."

Eleazer addresses Yeshua, but Teoma doesn't look much better and I care not to view myself. Taking my hand, Martha gratefully asks nothing. I mutely accompany her to the bath, just like when we were children, but as she washes my hair, the tears come. She suffered along with me, not able to intervene, living in fear. "Thank you, Martha, for all you do for me."

She turns my face toward hers and kisses me. "I am so sorry, Mary, for all you had to endure. I pray that you might forgive us."

"I could not have survived if it wasn't for you tending to me."

"But that night when you ran off, I thought Ima was going to kill you."

"Martha, I was never afraid of that. Yeshua says that I left my body so that I hardly remembered each incident. I am sorry you still have the memories, perhaps he can help you release them."

"I will ask him, but sometimes I fear I might lose my temper with the children."

I shiver, "That's why I waited so long to come home. I don't want to be like Ima."

"How could you, Mary? After what you went through."

"Martha, Ima was terribly abused and she repeated what she knew. Now that I remember what happened, I am afraid that I might do the same."

She shakes her head, kissing my cheek. "You won't, Mary, because you will ask for help. Yeshua is there and Miriam. You will be fine and if you get a fit of temper, just remove yourself from the children." Martha takes me into the nursery.

"Ima!" The children cry and I drop to my knees. Joshua climbs upon me, while Sarah squeezes my neck in her embrace. Sitting on the floor, I hold them. Joshua pets my cheek with his chubby hand. "Ima's back!" He sighs as I kiss his fair head.

Sarah studies my face. "Ima, why did you return to the past?"

I wonder how much she knows. "Because, love, I needed to release my fears and some were rooted in my past. I'm here now."

"Abba almost lost you."

"I lost myself. Abba found me, dear." She lays her head in my lap and I try to rock both of them. After the children are put in their beds, Yeshua carries me back to ours. Thankfully, he just holds me this night.

He kisses the back of my head. "I'll wait for you." I begin to cry again, unable to fathom being intimate. "Hush, love. Things will get brighter and brighter with each rising sun."

Each new dawn brings more hope and less pain. I am closer to my sister than even during childhood. Since seeking Yeshua's healing touch, her mantle of guilt has been lifted, opening her to receive me.

Teoma builds a fortress in the mud, children sitting within its walls. I kiss the top of his sandy head. "Thanks for all your help. I'm so grateful you were there."

He smiles, "It's good to have you back, Mary. Just don't ask me to go through a clearing like you did. I don't have your courage or your faith."

"You underestimate yourself but I won't ask that of you." With an exaggerated sigh, he turns back to the children. The late afternoon sun silhouettes Yeshua's lean form.

"Go to him, Mary."

"It's been so long; I fear it will be different now." I look into Teoma's clear blue eyes, supported by his love.

"It will be different, Mary. No more hidden fear, yet more honesty. And perhaps someday the same abandon, sweetened by all you have gone through together." Tears well as I hug my dearest friend. "Besides, you do not have to have great prisms of hayye every time, just relax and have fun."

He nudges me with a dirty shoulder and I go unsure. Just this morning waves of panic ensued when Yeshua pulled me close and I awakened from a nightmare about the sailors, stiffening with fear. By the time I reach his side, I am chilled thoroughly.

Yeshua puts an arm around me, "What is it, love?"

I shake my head sadly, for he knows.

Smiling, he kisses my hair, he has yet to kiss my mouth. "I shall when you are ready, dear." Sighing, I take his arm and we walk down the beach.

After the children are in bed, we lounge by a bonfire. Eleazer makes the others laugh as Yeshua strokes my hair. Looking up at the stars, I remember reclining on the altar. In absolute innocence, I trusted him then so why can I not cross the chasm that divides us now? A familiar voice stirs, the same one that guided me as a child, protecting me once with its wise counsel. *Relax and feel.*

My skin tingles as his fingers slip through my curls to graze the back of my neck, warmth travels down my spine depositing an ember in my loins. Lifting my hair to kiss the nape of my neck, a flush of heat spreads from his lips and I remember how much I feel. Leaning back, I invite his kisses, caressing his cheek as he explores my throat. With a muffled cry, I turn to face him. He kisses my lips tentatively, hands still, one sensation at a time. My lips part as do my thighs and soon the nectar begins to flow. As we lie down, there is a rustling of blankets on the far side of the fire.

The others take their leave quietly except Teoma's soft exclamation, "Barchashem!"

Sighing, I get reacquainted with my husband, but he goes so slowly. He looks into my eyes. "Are you sure, love?"

I nod. I am sure. He enters me gently, as if it is our first time.

Passion builds and I ask for more. He complies, matching my pace, until there is a great release of all the tension of loving each other through all the pain. I cry out, my tears are of joy and so, I pray, are his. He reassures me they are.

Through our window overlooking the lake, the rising sun greets us each morning. Life slowly returns to its comfortable joyfulness, but Teoma is right, as if the bitterness of the past finally fermented into sweet wine—gleuchos, I prefer to sip and savor life now rather than gulp it down. Yeshua stirs. Smiling, as he is rarely up this early, I turn to face him. "Are my thoughts so loud as to wake you?"

Touching my face with his fingertips, he replies, "Your being up rouses me. I always sleep more soundly when I hold your sleeping form against me."

"Are you disappointed that we did not find any more men for the council?" He kisses my mouth, and I praise all the hosts of heaven when my body responds.

"How can I be disappointed, love? This trip was divinely ordained for your healing. I learned more about healing the emotional aspects of being but having you fully united in body, mind, and soul is the greatest gift of all. I have no regrets; the disciples shall come in divine timing."

After spending the morning playing with the children, we travel alone to the secret cavern to swim a bit, explore the quartz-lined ledge, discover interesting outcroppings of the clear stone. Placing my hands on the glimmering crystals, the surface smoothly polished by the force of the water over millenniums, I am seeped with memories of the earth's infancy.

Yeshua speaks from the ledge, caressing the quartz altar, "The hayye of this place is incredibly healing. Let us commune with the Earth." Offering a hand, he draws my wet body into his. I sigh in the comfort of his embrace as he wrings out my wet hair, then smoothes it down my back. Leading me by the hand, he sets me upon the altar, before kneeling in front of me. The clear stone's energy warms through to my core. Yeshua prays silently, as I embrace his bowed head then move my hands out to hold the energies.

"Do you want to learn how to levitate?"

He smiles broadly, "I thought you would never ask."

I raise my vibration, not quite fast enough to disappear, but enough to be weightless, and rise off the altar to sit on a cushion of air. He strokes my legs as I float above him, "So did you ever try flying as a child?" My devious smile incites his laughter.

"Yes, but Ima got upset when I would climb the walls and float down to her."

"So why didn't you show me any of this when we were little?"

"Abba instructed me that I was not to play with the energies outside the house and never in front of guests. I did obey him, if not her." Floating away, I instruct, "Sit upon the altar, its hayye will assist you." He climbs upon it. "Now raise your vibration just a bit, not as fast as it takes

262

to disappear, and imagine yourself floating." I smile as he rises above the altar, grinning like a boy.

As he floats above the water, I playfully push him down but he maintains his position. I splash him instead, but when he catches me near the altar, our play turns into passion.

Finding all the nooks and crannies of our forms delightful, we propel through space, able to keep from bumping into any rocky surface by imagining a cushion of air. The energies of the cavern join in our dance, the colors mirrored upon the surface of the crystals causing the rainbow effect of sunlight through water.

Our passion lasts the afternoon, my newfound patience matching his Druid endurance, until we are spent from the exploration of unencumbered positions. Still hovering, he holds me, breath hot on my cheek. "You see, my love," he whispers, "how much we are a part of the energies?"

"Being with you will make it difficult for any future lovers."

Disengaging, he turns me around to face him, "What future lovers?"

"You said our forms are not eternal. I plan to come back, but cannot fathom forgetting this."

He pulls me close, kissing me deeply, "I plan to incarnate with you, dearest."

I look into his eyes, "What if we don't choose to play these same parts? Will we forever yearn for one another after this life?"

He shudders, as tears form in his eyes, "Just thinking that we may not always be as we are now causes me to mourn. Have no fear, I shall find you in whatever form you incarnate."

"But what if the Divine has other plans for us?"

He smiles, "Free will, my love, we still have free will. Besides the Divine desires us to experience joy and together we are great joy, so we are meant for one another."

Slowly, we separate and settle to earth. Diving into the pool through the tunnel, I emerge laughing, until startled by rough voices. We are not alone. Two Roman soldiers looking over the ledge call out and I panic, nearly passing Yeshua while he makes his way through the tunnel, but he catches my arm and brings me trembling to the surface.

Be calm, Mary. Breathe and veil yourself. Somehow he allows me access into his mind such that I can hear him translate the Romans' speech as well as his Latin replies. Yeshua moves to stand waist deep in the water. I am veiled directly behind him.

"Where is your lover, Jew?" the bigger man asks.

"My wife is shy and since your intentions are impure, she will not show herself."

The Roman laughs, "Come now, you cannot keep a beauty like that in the water for long. Her assets will shrivel."

The other taunts, "Come out, Jew, and bring your woman, we have been without the company of the fair sex for too long."

Yeshua casts a healing light, "My friends, you have been away from your homeland too long. Your own beautiful young women miss your attentions, I am sure."

The large man laughs crudely, "Our fair women must await fifteen years for our return while we satisfy ourselves with local harlots. Bring her now or we will come down and spill your blood first." A great black bird caws loudly, swooping down over the pool, startling the soldiers. Yeshua's eyes follow its flight.

I gasp before begging, *Join me under the kasa. Let us leave our things and bypass this way.*

Please, love, have faith. These two will see the light. Turning his attention back to the soldiers, he bathes the entire area in the lightest vibration. "Friends, you must know that the sweetest fruit is freely given ripe from the tree, not to be plucked green and bitter. Kindness may endear you to the fairer sex and make your attentions more worthwhile."

The smaller soldier laughs and elbows his companion. "There is little satisfaction taking women who do not desire us."

The bigger man shrugs, "Lazio, you are a sentimental fool. I always find satisfaction."

"Hector, you complained just last week that you tire of unresponsive partners." They both turn and look at Yeshua who attempts to soften their hayye.

"Fear causes the weak and vulnerable to withdraw and it is never much fun to make love to a cold woman." I do not believe my husband has ever had that experience. *Thankfully I have not.*

Hector comments, "You are different than most Jews. Do you not have fear?"

"I have love, which leaves no room for fear in my heart."

"I, too, would only have love in my heart if Venus was my wife."

Yeshua nods in agreement. "Love attracts love and beauty while fear attracts fear and pain. The choice is ours. I choose love. What do you choose, friends?"

They lounge on the edge of the rocky enclosure. "You and your wife, wherever she is, must be getting cold. Come out and join us."

The Roman speaks the truth, I am cold. Yeshua tells me to levitate above the water. Much better, but I cannot imagine revealing myself to these men.

"You are quite observant, friend. If you would not mind tossing down our garments, we will join you."

Laughing Hector tosses down Yeshua's tunic, but holds mine aloft. "Here you go. Cover yourself." Yeshua asks me to follow him. He dresses carefully, in no hurry.

The Romans watch, still searching for me. "Tell me, where has she gone? This is the only way out; too lovely to be a fish, she cannot still be under the water."

Yeshua laughs, "How do you know my wife is not a mermaid?" Lazio finds this very funny indeed. "I shall not expose her to rough elements, so unless you release her clothing and turn away that she might cover herself, she will not come out."

Actually, I feel perfectly content to stay veiled. *I know, my love, but we do need to get back and that is one of your favorite sadins. I would hate to have you leave it behind.* His humor lightens my mood, and must soften their hearts, for Lazio tosses my sadin to Yeshua.

"Here, just get the poor thing out of the water before she catches her death."

They both turn away and quickly I dress before unveiling. "Thank you, friends. Now we shall join you." Yeshua begins the ascent, but I hesitate. *Come, Mary, we will be fine.* I follow, fully visible.

Hector reaches down to offer Yeshua a hand. In gratitude, my husband takes it and the Roman's cloudy hayye brightens. Hector smiles and clasps my husband's shoulder, then turns and with an appreciative look, offers to assist me as well.

Go on, love, take it. I swallow my fear and take the soldier's large hand. He is very strong, lifting me up and over the ledge, as if I am but a small child. I smile my thanks and he bows his head to me.

Yeshua turns his attention to the other soldier, who hands him our sandals. As he touches the smaller man, the hayye softens around the soldier's heart center. He thanks them both before motioning for me to sit. I smile at the soldiers and Yeshua slips the sandals on my feet. Lifting me up, he kisses my forehead, before putting on his own sandals, then tells me in Aramaic to thank the kind soldiers.

I express my gratitude in Latin, mimicking his accent poorly. They laugh at my attempt and clasp Yeshua's shoulders.

"Someday, when we meet again," the large soldier says, "we would like to sit and share a meal with you and your lovely wife."

Yeshua thanks them, "Go with Eloha, friends."

"Which god is that?"

Yeshua replies reverently, "The One which is the Source of Love."

"That is one god I shall pay tribute to, if I can find as much happiness as you have, dear Jew." Hector swings an arm around his comrade and they take their leave.

"How did you do that?"

"I just loved them as I do my brethren, then I loved them more deeply and a portal of opportunity presented itself." He kisses me, "So you see, my dear, how love shall conquer all?"

***

"Sit down, Mary." Miriam beckons toward the cushions on the floor. The late summer sun dips low on the horizon casting just enough light to shimmer golden through the colored glass in the ceiling. Reminiscent of that long ago night in the synagogue of Capernaeum, spicy frankincense wafts about her meditation room. On the low round table, light dances in the crystal.

Heavy of heart, I comb nervous fingers through damp curls. Miriam rises to embrace me. Deep wracking sobs erupt.

I cry for the happier childhood I might have had. I cry for Ima's wounded heart. I cry for my children who have a damaged mother and for Yeshua who mourns my suffering. I cry for all children hurt by those they love. I cry for people who suffer in this life. I cry because I too manifested suffering. I cry until there cannot possibly be any more tears, and then I cry some more.

Miriam rocks me in her arms and I feel safe. A great eye appears in the pure white light, but there is no grand speech. Miriam speaks in that disconnected voice direct from Source. "Beloved, the healing necessary is seven layers deep. Yeshua opened a portal bringing to your consciousness that which you had forgotten. Through Miriam, a clearing of the old way in which you empathetically use your being to heal will be replaced by the lighter vibration of compassion."

The initial surge of panic at not perceiving the One bubbles into sweet laughter as the joy I embody rings clear. My incessant tears liquefy the heavy fear which begins oozing throughout my body. Silently I ask for help. Miriam smiles and invites living healers of light to pour from the heavens and enter the crystal in a rainbow of gentle waves. The healing tendrils polish the dark shadows from my aura, until my purple glows faintly, penetrating my skin to clear the surface pain before diving into the pool of my despair. Less dense with grief, my body lightens until the fear at my core is revealed. Tiny bits of dark dust disperse from my heart to be absorbed into the clear brilliant light at the center of the rainbow. I search in vain for a sad thought but none remain.

Delighted, I cry tears of joy. Miriam tightens her embrace as I wordlessly thank her. So exhausted, I go down with the sun, awakening well after dark to the press of Miriam's lips on my cheek. Yeshua takes me from his mother's arms, thanking her, while she puts out the lamp.

"You are a sweet purple again, beloved." I bury my head in his neck, too tired to reply.

Awakening the next morning in my husband's arms I feel like I have slept a lifetime. I give thanks for the divine intervention, offering my deepest gratitude to Uriel who brings light to my darkest moments. For the first time in over a moon cycle, I feel happy to be here on earth.

Yeshua stirs, "No longer veiled in fear." Rolling over I kiss his mouth. "You are curious about the seven layers of healing?" I do not even have to formulate my thoughts, he resides inside my mind. "I wish to reside in your body as well."

Without the veil of fear, my body remembers the sweet depth of joy in our union. My skin more sensitive, the heat of passion more exquisite without the desperate seeking of pleasure to cover the underlying pain. Peals of golden laughter erupt from my lips. Yeshua pauses to smile at me, looking deeply into my eyes and I see myself as Love.

"Mary, the first layer of healing begins when you love another and begin to see yourself as Love."

"But I saw this when we were first together on the altar."

267

"So you see how long ago this healing began." Yes, over eight years. "The next layer involves reaching out to those who take part in the drama of your existence. You did this four years ago when you taught your mother to live in the moment. By sharing your joyful experiences with her, you created an opening for your own healing."

"But I was unaware of what needed to be healed."

"Are you aware now?"

When we arrived home, he told me that I am healing my belief in suffering. The abuse I suffered by my mother's hand is but an aspect of my belief.

"This is one reason why you came to Earth."

I feel a bit confused, "But Yeshua, Ima is not the only player in my life's drama. What about my relationship with others, like you and the children? How is my belief in suffering being mirrored in these relationships?"

His smile is tender. "You learned the Essene mirrors well. Remember that your relationship with your mother and father represent your relationship to the Creator as a parent. Your mother represents your belief in the Creator as punishing, judgmental. Your father represents your belief in the Creator as distant, yet loving." Sighing deeply, I ingest his words. "I am the representation of co-creation in your eyes. As your husband and lover, I am the mirror image of you. The children represent how you, as a co-creator, view your creation. For some people this mirror is in their offspring, for others it is in their work, their creative efforts."

Making the connection to suffering is difficult. Oh! I know! My birthing experiences have been the embodiment of suffering.

"The next layer involves remembering why you are here. You began this when you experienced joy in our relationship. Then through the children you began to remember the joy in your own childhood. You experienced joy in the discovery of the energies and your relationship to nature and your friendship with Teoma."

"So this healing work has been going on for a long time?"

He laughs, "For most people it is over a lifetime, sometimes many lifetimes. Remember at the Sea of Galilee, the One said you were halfway done?" I nod and he continues, "Well, my work was the fourth layer, to bring to your consciousness the depth of your belief, to help you understand, the connections between your life experiences and the lessons you have come to learn."

"What is my work, Yeshua?"

"Don't you know? Through living joyfully, you model how emotions connect us to Source. Through your heart you heal those whom you touch." He seals the insight with a kiss, "Ima provided the fifth layer of healing by healing the energetic connections to the physical body. You will feel pain, but you will not allow it to take space in your being."

"Thank goodness, Yeshua, for it has been as if I have been trying to peer out through a dark veil. I have not been able to see the energies."

He strokes my cheek. "Your fear prevents you from perceiving clearly. Was the way in which you empathetically heal lifted?"

"I am not to use my being to embody others' fear."

Nodding, he reiterates, "There is no need to take on others' pain to help them heal. You can best help others by being your joyful loving self so they might see their own divinity in you."

"So what is next, Yesh?"

He laughs, "Forgiveness, love. When you find forgiveness for your own human frailties and move through this portal with grace, the world will offer no more apologies."

Then I must face my mother. Hugging me to him, he confirms, "Yes, as a player in the drama, your Ima may not fully understand the lesson, nor may she ever say she is sorry. But you will heal faster if you offer her the opportunity, even if she doesn't take it. As you approach your partners in this life who have served in bringing you closer to your Divine Self, you must forgive yourself for manifesting the belief in your separation from Oneness."

"So if I attempt to meet with Ima about what happened, will this part be over?"

Smiling sympathetically, he says, "No, love, only when you find true forgiveness for yourself will you have completed this layer of healing. That may take a long time, but you will have ample opportunity to practice forgiveness." I feel apprehensive. "We will be together through this portal of forgiveness. It is my work as well, dear." Grateful for the press of his body, I take comfort in not being alone.

"The seventh layer, the deepest of all," he continues, "is a reconnection to Source. That, my love, may take multiple incarnations, passing in and out of the veil between the realities before we find Sacred Unity. My extensive training with the mystics has prepared me for this reconnection, but in you, I have found my greatest joy, my deepest love—Eloha."

Joy clouds my vision. He kisses my closed eyes, the tip of my nose, then very softly, my lips. "I am in deep gratitude to you, my beloved Mary. Thank you for joining me on this journey back to the One." I open my eyes to look into the void of his. He will make it back to the Source of All That Is before me, this I know.

Blossoms burnt yellow by the late summer sun cast a golden glow. Arrayed in camel-tan tunics, the children hide in the long sheaves of grain heavy with seed. Blankets scattered under the shade of the olive grove protect the gossiping women from the dust.

A glowing energy calls to me and I am drawn to sit by Rebeka. Within the bowl of her pelvis resides a faint hayye of mixed hues. Rebeka looks up, "Mary, what is wrong?" I place a hand on her lower belly and she smiles nervously. "Is it true? I'm pregnant?"

"Yes, but it is very early." She begins to cry as I hug her to me.

Hava smiles. "So our Rebeka is going to have a baby?"

"Not a baby."

Hava's eyes widen and Rebeka gasps, "Mary, is something wrong?" Hava begins laughing excitedly. Whispering to Leah, the word spreads quickly, and soon all the women gather around us. "What am I having?" Rebeka demands as visions of litters float by.

I laugh, "No, Rebeka, not puppies—babies!"

"Of course, babies…." Pausing, her eyes grow wide, "Babies?"

"Yes, twins! A boy and a girl."

Hava fans her, "See how the Divine works. Your husband's seed multiplies rapidly within you." The women laugh as Rebeka's color returns.

In Joseph's study, Jacob vigorously discusses halacha with Yeshua, much more confident since his time with the zealots. Yeshua smiles as Rebeka kisses her husband.

"We did it, Jacob."

He hugs her to him, voice tremulous, "You're pregnant?" Her affirmation is muffled in his chest. Turning to us, Jacob whispers, "Thank you! Thank you!"

"Rebeka has more to tell you."

Concerned, he holds her away from him, "What is it, Beck?"

"We're having twins." Jacob nearly collapses.

"Sit down before you fall." Putting an arm around his brother, Yeshua leads them to a large cushion. "Congratulations. You are doubly blessed."

Jacob looks up with Rebeka on his lap. "Everything is going to be fine, isn't it?"

"Yes, brother, you will have two healthy babies. Apparently, one of each."

Jacob's eyes are wide, "A boy and a girl?"

"Your family is progressing twice as fast. Come, Mary, let us leave them to their celebration." After I kiss Jacob, Yeshua hugs me just outside the door, "Barchashem! I was getting worried."

I laugh, "You must have faith in your healing abilities, Yesh."

***

When the moon has fully risen and the children are safely tucked into bed, the family gathers in Joseph's study. Knowing Mary is uncomfortable exploring further the lesson of suffering, Yeshua places an arm around her waist.

"You will see that you are not alone."

Taking seats about the round table, Yeshua thanks everyone for coming together, then expands his hayye to encompass them all. "While we were away, Mary chose to explore her belief in suffering."

She cringes at his side and Teoma reaches for her hand, "I would like to know why nothing was done when Mary was still a child." His contracted hayye becomes spiky around the edges as Teoma directs his query at Joseph.

Joseph leans across the table. "I spoke to Syrus when she was..." he looks to Miriam, "I believe, six."

"But you knew about the abuse since she was three!"

Mary sinks into her chair, her consciousness drifting away from the combative men. Quickly, Yeshua cups the base of her skull and she refocuses on the new life in Rebeka's womb. Jacob lends a comforting nod. Although clearly uncomfortable, Ima joins Hava in holding the energies.

"Why did it take you so long?" Teoma's tone raises the tension in the room.

"I needed to be sure. What would you have had me do?"

271

Like a lion about to pounce, Teoma gathers his fury. "You should have brought her here, where she would have been safe."

"You would have had me take her from her parents?"

At Joseph's flashing gaze, Teoma says softly, "You took me in."

"Son, your mother and uncle sent you to us. I did not rescue you, nor could I rescue Mary." Joseph's voice breaks as he speaks her name. "After I spoke with Syrus, he stayed home more thinking it would help. Apparently it didn't. I'm sorry."

Mary cries wordlessly, deeply affected by his father's diminished energy. Yeshua explains, *Like Teoma, Abba carries the protective energies and when he was unable to help you, his guilt and sense of unworthiness magnified.* His mind is unveiled for his father's benefit. Joseph smiles wryly.

Teoma's energy withdraws as Yeshua speaks, "Her memories have caused your own to resurface." Mary rises impassioned, hugging Teoma to her breast and the combative hayye softens into a comfortable lightness. "We each play parts in this drama of life, here to learn lessons releasing beliefs that no longer serve us on our journey back to the One."

Raising his head, Teoma addresses Joseph. "Thank you for taking me in. I'm afraid I would not have turned out so well if I would have remained with my mother."

"You are like a son to me." Joseph clasps Teoma's arm.

When the men part, Hava begins, "There are many forms of suffering at the hands of others." Ima takes her hand. "Because I didn't value myself, it took many years for me to ask for a divorce. I reached the depths of despair, but after much love and support, I saw the light."

Yeshua bathes her with compassion. "Dearest Hava, what light did you find?"

"The light within myself, beloved Yeshua. I receive love from the world, because I am Love." Looking around, she extends heartfelt gratitude to all. "Discussions just like this, led by dear Zsao, helped me come to this soulful understanding. By finding the joy in each moment of my life I came into unity with the Divine."

"You are so elegant in your perceptions. I thank the Creator you were here for me and now for my children." Hava's eyes tear as she accepts his praise. He turns to Rebeka, "Dear sister, none of us would still be here if we were finished with our souls' lessons."

She shudders, unused to others knowing her thoughts. "My mother belittled me but here, I feel welcome and my feelings matter."

"I remember when Mary first came, she seemed to have a certainty about herself. How can she have been so abused yet come out of the situation conscious?"

Yeshua allows his mother to answer. "Jacob, the souls with the greatest challenges are gifted with tremendous spiritual resources. Mary has audacious confidence." After the laughter dies, Ima answers Teoma's unspoken query. "Yes, even me. An elder had to intervene when my mother hit me but that didn't soften her tongue."

Joseph sighs when Yeshua turns to him. "Like my parents, I find it hard to be demonstrative."

Teoma shakes his head, "How can we treat our own families so poorly? As a nation, we should not abuse our loved ones."

Everyone nods in agreement until Yeshua speaks, "All cultures experience internal oppression and family violence to some extent. Why are we, as Hebrews, different?"

Surprised, Teoma turns, "We have been oppressed by one group or another for the past two thousand years; we should know better. Are we to act like Romans, using violence and fear to control those more vulnerable?"

Infusing the room with peace, all attend to his words. "The Romans oppress us now and we oppress our loved ones. Is this not like the cycle of children being hurt by their parents growing up to do the same to their own children? Should they not know better? We are all human, even the Romans." With a subtle shift in the energy, Yeshua pauses. "We collectively act out the same lessons. We cannot change others, but we can learn to love ourselves so fully that we cannot help but manifest love in our lives. If each of us found the divine spark within, loving and appreciating who we are, then there would be no room for fear. Fear ignites oppression. It begins with me." Emphatically, he presses his palm to his chest.

"If I see fear, it is my own, manifested outside of me. If I experience suffering, it is my belief coming to life. If I am oppressed, it is because I feel unworthy. But if I am loved, it is because I am Love." His father has a sad, distant expression. "What is it, Abba?"

"Son, will being Love be enough to clear your soul of sacrificial energy?" Mary shivers at his side.

"I pray that I might release this belief in sacrifice, that I become my Divine Self." Every face around the table looks troubled.

273

With a sigh, he hugs each of them, spending longer with his father. Still Abba holds tremendous fear in his heart that he might do something rash.

Mary waits for him at the door. Taking his hand, she leads him back to their bedchambers. With a heavy heart, he lies upon the bed, gathering her close. Her smooth soft skin seems to soak the despair from his pores. But when her caresses venture lower, he thwarts her. "What are you doing?"

"Helping you gain insight. I believe this is how you like to do the work?" He smiles thinking how wonderfully she embodies every life lesson.

She spends so long cherishing him that he begs her to mount him. Yet she does not, instead swallowing the belief that threatens. In tears, he draws her up to his chest.

"What about you, beloved?"

Her sweet reply touches his soul. "As the Elat, I transmute your sorrow into joy, and since your joy is mine, I am well pleased."

***

I am both the dreamer and the dreamed. I am myself as a little girl being punished by my mother and I am my mother striking her child. As the child, I am in that distant place of forgetfulness accompanied by Uriel, but I am also my mother in the dark recesses of herself, also with Uriel. Witnessing with me from a space within space where there is no time, is a purer essence of Ima and that of Abba, Martha, Yeshua, Teoma, Miriam, Joseph, Sarah, Joshua, even Teoma's dark-haired son. All in audience to the earthly drama. Farther away, an even finer essence of Yeshua and me witnessing all the others. Earthly suffering is my sense of separation from the One, which is the true illusion. Moving closer to the One, I know nothing but Love.

I awaken damply sticking to my husband's body. Two long days ago, Yeshua brought me into the wilderness although I resisted. How can I help him unravel the knot of sacrificial energy when I struggle with my own? Rising, I go to bathe in the stream dancing among its rocky bed.

"When we minister to others, we are doing our own work—the healing is both for the sufferer and the healer." Yeshua explains, not joining my bath, but tracing the curve of my waist. As he touches every part of me, a prism of hayye beams down upon us. Pure tones of music entice my senses and I become lost in wave after wave of orgasmic harmony. The sound intensifies as I reach a peak, then carries me down with the softest notes to begin again.

Making love to the color and sound of the energies, Yeshua moves us into the shade, the sun high now in the sky. Trying to bring him to an end, my ministrations serve only to raise my passion and I pull away in tears, overly stimulated.

He draws me up to face him, kissing away my frustration. "Is there nothing I can do that will hasten your orgasm, Yesh?"

"No, love, I believe I have mastered my body through intention." Shaking, the heat of my passion near to consuming me as he continues, "And you, dearest, are like a fine instrument, producing sweeter music each time I choose to play you."

"Did you also hear the music?" He nods. Moving to an ancient rhythm, the vibrant sound harmonizes with us, finally, finally reaching a crescendo.

I sob into his chest, communion with Source so bittersweet. He pushes tendrils of hair away from my damp cheeks. "My love, I do not wish to cause you discomfort. I thought you enjoyed…."

"I do, but my body feels so intensely, it can no longer distinguish between pleasure and pain." When might I take the reins in our relationship?

The women from Sepphoris arrive promptly on the morning of the full moon. Beautifully attired, with colorful sadins and robes, their faces are painted to accentuate their features. A tall, full-figured woman approaches me.

"You are Mary?" I nod and she takes both my hands in hers, bejeweled and tipped by brightly painted fingernails. Her intense hayye is very passionate and self-assured. "I am Ilia and these are my ladies." A matrona! She smiles, "Do you have a purse, dear?" I shake my head, never having the need to carry coin.

Producing a large red silk bag, she turns to the others. "Put your payment here and be generous, ladies. Think how much this will save you in herbal remedies!" The women laugh and dig into their silken purses.

"Really, I do not usually accept payment for my services."

The matrona smiles, "You keep this money for yourself, dear. Don't be giving it to your husband. He certainly didn't earn it. Buy yourself something nice." Placing an arm around my shoulder, she whispers, "If this works, I have a friend in Capernaeum who would pay you handsomely to serve her ladies."

While the other women count out their coins, my new friend strokes my cheek with her very soft, perfumed hand, "You are quite exquisite." She pats my hip appreciatively. Strangely, I am at ease with her intimacy. "If you ever decide to leave your husband, you could make a fine living." I blush. She is not referring to my services as a healer.

A lovely woman with henna dyed hair hands me the very full purse. I shake my head, "Ilia, I have yet to do anything for you."

"My dear, it is our custom to collect payment before services are rendered. Now where shall we all sit?"

The energy of the group is amazingly strong. These women have the attitudes of men, not at all vulnerable, with hayye as bright and colorful as their dress. I smile as we sit in a large circle to begin the meditation. Quite attentive, following my guidance precisely, they thank me graciously afterwards.

"Mary, you are a gifted healer and we are fortunate to have found you." I smile and hug Ilia, but she pauses a moment before taking her leave. "Is there anything I can do for you?"

Sighing, I think the Divine has provided me an opening that I have no choice but to take. "Yes, I was wondering if you know of a means to hasten a man's climax."

"Why, of course, dear. It is common knowledge that to place a finger in the man's anus and press firmly toward his belly, he will immediately finish his business. You must locate the small sensitive lump about the firmness of an unripe fig." She studies my face. "An unusual question from a married woman, you must have a unique husband." I do.

Yeshua announces that my parents will arrive the night before Joshua's birthday celebration. "You might have a healing confrontation before our guests arrive."

Feeling sick, I sit up in bed. "What am I supposed to say to her? I do not know that I can truly forgive Ima or myself for orchestrating this painful lesson."

In the dark void of his gaze, I see that beneath the hayye of forgiveness is a strong root of gratitude. My purer vibration feels grateful for that of my mother, giving thanks for her willingness to play her role and she, too, is in deep gratitude to me.

Blinking, I lose focus. "Beloved, do you see how gratitude is all that is necessary for you to heal completely?" I nod, lips quivering. "Mary, it is time for you to release your attachment to the emotion of fear. It will still exist, but you shall not magnify it in your life."

Searching my heart for some remnants of gratitude for Ima, slowly, I find appreciation for what she taught me. Because of how she parented me, I learned to be a different type of parent. Relaxed in my mothering where she was restrictive, allowing my children to be children. I see beauty in the world where she does not. Perhaps it was her pessimism that endowed me with a sharp wit, for I laugh as easily as I cry. I am grateful for her polar view on life that contrasted so elegantly with my own.

Yeshua speaks softly, "But how did the abuse help you?"

I frown, having mulled over this question since I first became aware of my past. Digging deeply, I finally see the truth. If not for my mother's abuse and then neglect, I would have never left her to become part of my husband's family and be supported during our separations. If I stayed, as is tradition, in my childhood home, I very well may have repeated my mother's behaviors.

"You do not have to name all that you understand now, just be open to receive the blessing of this meeting with your mother."

Before dusk, my family arrives. Sarah and Josh greet my parents with delight, "Savta, we're so glad you came to be with Ima." Sarah hugs her as Joshua takes my hand.

"Saba needs you."

I join Abba in the inner atrium where he gathers his grandson into his lap. "Mary, I appreciate your willingness to meet with your mother tonight. Your remembrance has brought up much of her own pain. She prays for your forgiveness."

I nod and squeeze his hand, "Abba, I have come to a place of gratitude for Ima."

"Dearest daughter, I am happy for you. Your deep comprehension shall serve you well." He says no more, but clasps me tightly to him.

After Martha and I get the children settled in the nursery, Yeshua invites us all into the study. Sighing, I sit upon the floor on a crimson pillow and Yeshua sits behind me.

Ima and Abba sit opposite of us while Martha and Eleazer complete the circle to my right. The warmth and love flowing from Yeshua's touch soothes me and as he prays a prism of light intensifies between Ima and me. He gently cups my skull as if opening a portal. *Yes, my love, this is the back of the sixth energy center, the portal of insight. Releasing the veil of fear blocking the light of love will allow you to receive the most profound blessings.* I open myself to his ministrations and Abba smiles his approval.

Caressing the light with his left hand, Yeshua speaks to us. "Thank you for coming together as a family to receive the blessings of this healing circle." Martha smiles at him. "The lessons presented in living a human existence have many aspects. Mary is prepared to release her attachment to suffering." He focuses on Ima, "Eucharia, you have my deepest gratitude for the gift of your daughter. Our relationship has been blessed by this healing event." Ima's eyes widen as Yeshua sends her love.

Taking a deep breath, I am moved to begin, "Ima…." But when she holds her arms out to me, I cross the circle to kneel at her feet.

"Mary, I am so sorry."

I look into her eyes, "Ima, I want to thank you."

Her grip slackens, "Thank me? For what I did? Mary…." She begs, distraught, not comprehending.

Through quivering lips, I clarify my gratitude, "Ima, thank you for agreeing to play this part in our lives. Yours by far was the most difficult," and through her eyes, I fall into her soul.

Hovering, I nearly leave my body, my mother's pain so vast, yet with clear insight I stay to view her life with compassion. Cast into her childhood, then back through former lives where she alternated the roles of aggressor and victim over and over until we are one again with the Light. My clear purple hayye is cast about her muddy yolk of an aura then blended by a divine hand until we are a foamy white essence of our former selves. There is no differentiation between us.

Escorting the light of Eloha, Uriel appears. *This, my dearest, is the last life of suffering either as a victim or as an aggressor for you—your beloved mother's gift to you.*

Ima is crying, not tears of anger, but sorrow. Kissing her wet cheek, I hold her, but she does not feel like my mother in my arms. "Thank you, dearest Ima, for all the blessings you have given me, but most especially for who you are."

She shudders in my embrace and Yeshua advises, *she asks your forgiveness but is unable to comprehend your gratitude. In truth, it frightens her. That is why she feels so diminished.*

So I release her, "Ima, I do forgive you."

She bows her head with a fresh onslaught of tears. "Barchashem! Blessed is Adonai."

Martha cries, as Abba touches my arm. *Your healing opens a greater healing for the Earth realm. This is the beginning of the end of the cycle of victimization.*

I look at him incredulous then glance back at Yeshua. *Your father is correct, my love, but, no, not in this lifetime will human suffering end. Your personal healing is a tiny hole in the veil of fear that envelops humanity, now allowing the Light of Love to shine through. Commencing with this one tear in the fabric of the illusion, the unraveling will follow.*

Intense hayye swirls about me. Something is yet to happen. I wrap my arms about my chest to quell the deep ache in my left breast and an ancient desire rises. Yeshua smiles softly, but it is not his embrace that I yearn for. Lulled by a warm comfortable drumming, the womb-like hayye of the earth envelops me and I long to be held by my mother.

As a child Ima set me upon her knee, comforting me only with a pat. My lips never even tasted her milk. Tears still fresh on her cheeks, Ima holds out her arms and after a moment's hesitation, I ease into her embrace. With my head resting upon her bosom, I feel mothered for the first time in this life. Humming softly, she rocks me until there are no more tears.

We are left alone and I am not afraid.

Celebration of Light

The day before Chanuka dawns crisp and cold, the white cap of Mount Tabor visible from our window. Although the Essenes refuse to celebrate the Maccabees' restoration of Jerusalem, I relish the Feast of Dedication. Over a century and a half ago, my mother's ancestors rededicated the Temple and relit the lamps for the glory of the God of Yisrael. Of course the winter solstice takes precedence in this house, but I am grateful that Yeshua's family finally adopted this most glorious holiday.

Escorted by many soldiers, Judas arrived two nights ago from Qumran with his wife T'shuraw, and last night, Simeon brought Shulamis and two Essenes under his instruction. In his mid-thirties, stocky Jakob is dark from the desert sun. Taller with broad shoulders, a slender waist, and muscular legs, the younger has wavy chestnut hair and the face of Adonis.

Yeshua stirs behind me, "Jochanan is quite handsome."

"He may be beautiful, but he is not you." Yeshua returns my kiss. No one could create such a passionate reaction in me.

"I should hope not. Now let's see if I can take you to greater heights."

Laughing, I reply, "Well, if this is your way of gifting me for Chanuka, then you might want to save the best for last."

Leisurely kisses descend to create a desire so intense I beg him to fulfill me. He enhances the experience with a cushion beneath his hips, thankfully, fulfilled when the children barge in. Both hesitate, their small hands open to embrace the rainbow of hayye.

"Sarah, did the sun come up earlier than yesterday?"

A smile stifles the scolding, so she replies, "Why no, Abba, the sun comes up later and later until the solstice, then the days get longer."

"But what are you teaching Joshua?" I ask our learned daughter.

Unable to contain his secret any longer, Joshua blurts, "Today, I will use the pot!"

Yeshua and I exchange a bemused glance. He has said this nearly every day this month. Finally surrendering to the most resistant child in all of Galilee, I must trust that my son will use the betshimush sometime before he's betrothed.

"Ima, would I interrupt you if it wasn't important?"

I believe she has interrupted us for all kinds of reasons.

Although he has veiled his communication, Sarah frowns disgustedly, "Fine, Abba. You'll see!" She drags her brother from our chambers.

All day the household prepares for the first night's festivities, cinnamon and anise wafting from the kitchen. Decorations of evergreen boughs and early winter blossoms drape elegantly over the large wooden tables dressed in the finest linens. My beautiful silver menorah reigns in the largest window, prepared to be lit each night of the Celebration of Lights. Dressed in a fine wool sadin dyed dark coral, I make my way to the inner atrium.

"So this is Mary. I hear you will be visiting after the holidays." Qumran? I thought we were going to Jerusalem. Adorned in an ornately embroidered robe of sky blue, T'shuraw smiles, "Are you not prepared to travel with your husband, dear?"

"I am prepared to follow my husband wherever he must go."

The gracious woman takes my hand, "You are far too lovely to follow him about the desert like a sheep."

"Our Mary is certainly no sheep, just unaware of their destination. Joseph has yet to speak with Yeshua." Her elegant sadin a shade lighter than her hair, Miriam spares me.

Nodding, sleek T'shuraw looks into my eyes. Her hayye, like a clear morning sky, holds the promise of a glorious day. Smiling back, I await her appraisal. "Judas has told me of your importance to your husband's mission. I would like to extend myself to you." She graciously receives my thanks before sharing news from the desert clan. Hava takes my hand telling me silently, *The universe synchronizes events in your life for your development. You shall see how valuable the support of a powerful woman like T'shuraw can be.*

At dusk, the first lamp in the menorah is lit and Yeshua leads us in prayer before the feast. In the atrium the children laugh at low tables, while the adults sit around the perimeter of the gathering room. Jakob and Jochanan seem so familiar. Nearby with Saul, Teoma sits alone. Where's Edia?

Exceptionally handsome in a pale gold-embroidered tunic, Yeshua puts an arm around my waist. *But Jochanan is the shining star at this table, don't you think?* My blush does not go unnoticed, as the Essene, dressed in an emerald tunic matching his eyes, graces me with a dazzling smile. I have never seen such a beautiful man.

When my husband calls for wine, the Essenes politely refuse, but a commotion in the atrium interrupts his raised chalice. Sarah clears a path for Joshua, who carries something heavy in his little arms. "Josh, there's Abba!" As they come closer, a foul odor reveals Joshua's burden—a full pot.

"Look, Ima!" He cries in delight, "I did it!"

At the appearance of that which is unclean into the sanctified space prepared for the feast, the gay chatter abruptly ceases. Joshua's lower lip quivers. I kneel to embrace my son, the still warm pot between us. Uncertain, Sarah takes her father's hand.

The silence is shattered by Yeshua's announcement, "Please drink to Joshua as he brings great joy to his Ima and me."

All hesitate to raise their cups until Teoma cheers. Soon the rest of the family joins in, the guests slow to follow until I rise to take the pot from my stubborn son, "No, Ima. I want to show Hava and Savta."

"Josh, let's show them in the betshimush." Yeshua intervenes.

As we leave the table, Teoma tells our guests, "We've been waiting for this a very long time." Laughter escorts us out of the room.

After taking care of Joshua and washing up, we return to the celebration. Joshua runs over to hug Teoma, "Did you see, Dod Teo? I'm a big boy now."

Teoma kisses him, "I knew you could do it, Josh." Reaching for Sarah, he draws her into an embrace, "What a fine sister you are, Sarah, to help Josh like that."

"I don't change babies! Don't you think this is Ima's best Chanuka present?"

Yeshua laughs, "Yes, Sarah. It's what she's wished for most fervently." The rest of the table joins in his laughter as he turns and kisses me.

"It must be nice to take such great pleasure in life, Mary." Jochanan's charming smile makes me blush like an adolescent.

"Marriage and children have put my world in perspective."

"Will you share your secrets so that we might experience but a fraction of your joy?" Jochanan looks appraisingly at my husband who clasps his arm.

"Yes, brother. That is my wish, for each of you to live in joy."

Saul, who has been silent until now, speaks, "What a wonderful scene. I would love to sketch this moment to remember."

Teoma puts an arm around Jochanan, "Saul, go get your materials and I'll hold them captive." Jochanan looks surprised, until he realizes that Teoma jests.

Contented, Yeshua sits back; *I believe we have our next two disciples.*

I turn to Saul. "Why don't you ask Jochanan to sit for a portrait?"

Teoma studies Jochanan's face, "Yes, I'm sure you could do this fine bone structure great justice." Saul seems unusually reserved.

Jakob intervenes, "So you are an artist, Saul?"

He nods so demurely that Teoma must answer in his stead. "Saul's creations grace the known Empire."

Saul looks as if he might slip beneath the table but Jochanan's interest is sparked. "It would be an honor to see your work," Poor Saul still will not respond. "And I would love to see your rendition of Mary."

Teoma laughs, "Mary could not sit still long enough for Saul to complete a sketch let alone a painting." I frown at Teoma. Saul has asked me repeatedly since I was a young girl to sit for him, but I never have.

"It's a shame not to capture her beauty but I would be flattered to sit for you."

Jakob's face darkens with apprehension. Graven images defy the laws of Moses and most Essenes are very observant. Yeshua soothes a discomfiting silence.

"The Divine resides in beautiful art as well as that which we discard in the betshimush." He smiles, warmly clasping Jakob's arm. "Perhaps together we might find Sacred Unity in All That Is, my friend."

Finally, Saul finds his voice. "It would be a pleasure to paint your portrait, Jochanan." They smile endearingly at one another. How grateful I am that Saul has found another focus.

But I would like for Saul to paint your portrait. Yeshua complains, so I consent with a prayer that Jochanan's is first. *I'm sure it will be, dear.*

Later, as I prepare for bed, Yeshua carries a tray of sweets into our chambers. "I thought we had dessert earlier?"

Smiling, he replies, "I did not partake."

"Isn't it a bit late to eat? We are just going to bed."

Coming up behind me, he kisses my neck, "But I'm having dessert in bed, dear."

Intrigued as he arranges the sweets upon my naked flesh, the warmth of massah between my breasts is balanced by the coolness of fruit in the hollow of my throat. Smiling, he plops a dollop of sweetened cream on my belly, allowing it to drip tantalizingly down my sides.

"Do not worry," he whispers, "I'll clean that up." I am anything but worried.

Closing my eyes, I slip into this moment of delicious sensations. With a warm drizzle of honey, he awakens miniscule sensations before sweet cinnamon arouses my attention. I moan in anticipation, but he moves away from my searching hand to find every crumb and, true to his word, he cleans up every sticky drop.

I peek through long lashes as he reaches for one last delicacy. A honey-dipped stuffed date but alas, he loses it within my sacred garden. What effort he makes to retrieve it! "Please, Yesh." I beg with a kiss, surprised when he slips something between my lips. The date! Laughing, I bite it in half to share. When I cry out, the sweetest of hayye swirls about us.

"Oh, what are you waiting for?" I ask breathlessly.

He laughs, "Why this is but the first day of Chanuka."

Eight days! We have never gone longer than five.

"Have faith, love, let's see if my gift compares to Joshua's."

At breakfast, Teoma sits with Simeon, Judas, and Jacob, so I search out Edia. Her eyes well with tears when I speak his name. I take her into the outer atrium where she confesses she will be returning with Judas' family to Judaea.

"But why? Are you not happy here?"

Edia sighs heavily with remorse. "Yes, very happy, but I want a family." My heart lurches, "I'm betrothed to my Abba's second cousin. He is a good man, a farmer, much older than me but seeing that I was not pleased with this arrangement, he agreed with my Abba to allow me to come here. I was hoping to find love but…."

Tears fill my eyes. "I am so sorry, Edia."

She smiles wryly. "Here I confide in the woman who has become a friend and mentor, but who has my lover's heart." I am truly sorry, at a loss for words of comfort.

Edia hands me a piece of linen. "Maybe I shall see you when you come to Qumran this spring. I should be married by then." In her eyes, I see sons born into a strained relationship. "What is it, Mary?"

I return her smile, "Edia, you shall have beautiful sons who will love you dearly, but your husband will take longer to understand your new way of being since exposed to our different customs."

"Do you think you shall have time while in the desert to hold a conscious conception circle? My clan may not see me as a healer without your influence."

"I shall make time. You have become a dear friend." We part, feeling the pain of our entangled relationship.

As I wander into the garden, the plants' familiar green hayye offers comfort. Beneath my feet Ima Earth warms from the rising sun and the leaves of the trees show their faces to their Abba, while insects nuzzle flowers in search of nourishment. Even at the commencement of winter, our garden thrives from loving energies.

A subtle discoloration in the hayye weaves a path to the pepper grove where I find Teoma hidden beneath weeping boughs. Opening his cloak, he gestures for me to sit. My sorrow couples with his despair. He wraps an arm about my shoulder, enhancing my woe. I should be the one comforting him.

"Teoma, I am so sorry. I spoke to Edia this morning."

Nodding miserably, he confirms, "She told you?"

"Yes. So this is why you haven't been together the past week?" He nods, not saying more. Why can't he find happiness with another? He must care for her. If he would only allow himself, he might even love her.

"Please, Mary, I do not wish to discuss this further."

How is it possible to release him from my heart so that he may love someone else? I free my tongue, "You know how much I love Yeshua. I could never leave him."

Teoma gives me a startled look. "What are you saying?"

Still struggling with my heart, I plead. "You mustn't wait for me. The only way that we may be together is if something happens to Yeshua. Neither of us wants that."

"Please, if I dissolve these bonds, I would not have a life."

Tears spill at his stubborn devotion. "But you are missing an opportunity for happiness with Edia!"

Drawing away stiffly, his voice raises, "I would rather be living in your shadow, than to be with another." Lifting me to my feet, he looks into my eyes. "I can feel your love for me, Mary. I shall wait an eternity for it to be fulfilled."

Frustration and sorrow spill forth, "You deserve more. I just want you to be happy." He holds me away from him.

"Then desist in trying to make a life for me. I shall not marry another just to relieve you of your burden."

I grasp his arm, "Please Teoma, listen to me!"

He shakes me off roughly, "Leave me be, Mary," and rushes out of the garden.

A distant whistle for his mare and he rides away. Running through the olive grove, I might catch him upon Sheikan, but my arm is caught, ceasing my flight. Jochanan pulls me to him.

"Let him go."

Compassion shimmers in his brilliant eyes. I bury my face in his chest to shield my despair. A soft nicker causes Jochanan to chuckle over my head, "This great white horse responds to your distress, prepared to carry you anywhere."

"Mary must have called to Sheikan. They are connected in spirit." I look up at the sound of Saul's voice to see him busily sketching upon papyrus. A palette of paint lies near a canvas stretched upon a wooden stand. Jochanan holds me still against his chest, my hand upon it, my face wet with tears.

"Saul, I apologize for interrupting your work."

He smiles, "Hush, perhaps now I might capture your visage."

Frowning, I look up at Jochanan. "I do not wish to have him capture my sorrow."

Jochanan kisses the top of my head, "Your emotion is captivating. Relax and tell me why you chase after Teoma."

After releasing Sheikan, I follow Jochanan back under the olive tree where Saul has set his art. We sit together upon a blanket, Saul sketching all the while. "Oh, Saul, I do not want my first portrait to be such a despairing one."

He laughs good naturedly, "Dearest Mary, please. I have been trying to capture your elusive passion since you were a child."

Sighing, I wipe my tears with the edge of my sadin. Jochanan hands me a square of linen. As much as I cry, I should get in the habit of carrying some linen. I nod my thanks and Jochanan touches my hair appreciatively. "Have you ever seen such thick gorgeous locks? It is as if her passion enlivens each silken curl. You must capture the power of her hair." Nodding, Saul changes the angle of the charcoal highlighting his sketch. Stroking my hair, Jochanan implores, "It is most confusing, Mary. So deeply in love with your husband, yet you chase after handsome Teoma as if your heart is broken."

Trembling lips muffle my response, "Unfortunately, I am not pure of heart. I have caused Teoma much grief."

Jochanan looks sympathetic, "And Yeshua is comfortable with your relationship with his cousin?"

Saul intercedes, his fingers still flying over the papyrus. "Yeshua is part of the problem, encouraging them. That boy has always loved playing with fire." I look at Saul miserably, unsure how much to reveal. Although I do feel very comfortable talking to Jochanan, Yeshua has designs on asking him to join the council of twelve.

"I once was in a love triangle." Both Jochanan and I give him our full attention, but Saul looks up only to capture our essence. "I did not feel I deserved any better than my lover's second-hand affection. Although he professed his love for me, I was just one of many diversions from his unhappy marriage."

Understanding the triangle allusion, I am unsure of the lesson for us. Saul smiles at me, "It was in counsel with Miriam and Joseph, Hava and Zsao—dear Zsao, I miss him—that I found the courage to leave that painful relationship."

Jochanan listens intently, but I do not know what to do. "Saul, Teoma insists that he rather be with me as friend and confidante than have a family with another woman."

Saul stops and lays down his work to embrace me. "Dear one, Teoma cannot leave for he loves you deeply. He believes his destiny is with you and he is willing to wait until the time comes that you might be together."

I look up at him, "But, Saul, I cannot be with him unless something happens to Yeshua. Yet I love them both."

"That is the difference between your triangle and mine. You truly love him and Yeshua loves him dearly as well. You share your children with him. He is happy here with you, even if he cannot have the relationship that he most desires. Although he believed you would be his when you both came of age, in love and devotion to Yeshua, he stepped aside to serve your mutual destiny."

"Yeshua must have incredible faith in the two of you."

"He has incredible compassion for them but," smiling at Jochanan, Saul continues, "he's challenged to have compassion for himself." I shudder. We shall all be sorely tested, of this I am sure. Saul holds me close, "Hush, Mary. All will be well."

At dusk, although his horse grazes in the pasture, Teoma misses the sixth lighting of the menorah. Grief diminishes my appetite, not even the sweet pomegranate wine soothes me. Gathered by the atrium, the women, including Edia, chat amiably. Judas engages Joseph and his sons in fervent discussion near the hearth, while the children listen intently to Jochanan's animated storytelling. Saul's flute wavers over the din of conversation before Hava joins him on the lyre, her skillful fingers enticing the others into the center of the room.

I mourn Teoma's absence and with a kiss, Yeshua sends me out to find him. Hidden in the shadows, Teoma lies upon the hammock. He studies my face, his morose hayye dark with sorrow, before scooting over. I sit carefully besides him.

"Do you not want to join us? I can bring you some food."

"I am not hungry. Mary, why aren't you dancing?"

"I cannot feel the music through my sorrow." A tear escapes my eye. "Please forgive me. It grieves me to see you suffering."

Softly tracing the path of my tear, he whispers, "My pain is my own fault. You are not holding me captive."

"Yes, I am." I nod miserably, "By loving you, I prevent you from finding another because I cannot release you from my heart."

He reaches up to embrace me, "I do not want you to release me." I lie upon his chest sobbing as he smoothes my hair.

After a long while, my tears spent, he sighs as if in great relief. I raise myself up to look in his eyes and see an ancient forest with trees so large that three men might not be able to embrace one. I am with Teoma in this great forest, walking hand-in-hand. We are together at last, older, but not much. A chill passes through me; Yeshua is not there.

"Mary, what is it?" Teoma rubs my arms as to ward off the foreboding.

"We will be together later, somewhere else."

His eyes search mine, trying to understand. "When? Where?" Shaking my head, I do not know. His expression is so endearingly hopeful, desire stirs and I yearn to kiss him.

"Please, Mary, do not tempt me. Unveil us and let us return to the festivities." He holds me at arms' length until I do his bidding, then helps me off the hammock.

We return hand in hand. Yeshua greets us with hugs. "It's good to have you join us, Teoma. Thank you, Mary, for finding him." I look up at him with a heavy heart. *Hush, love. All is well. Let us enjoy this night.* Perhaps Saul is right, that Yeshua shall be challenged to find forgiveness, but by the end of the night, my husband makes me feel as if there is nothing to forgive.

All during the Chanuka celebrations Yeshua refuses to discuss preparations for the mission, but Joseph meets privately with Judas and Simeon. "Abba is up to something."

As a child, my husband's uncanny knowing forced his parents to intentionally veil their thoughts when they desired privacy, just as we do with Sarah and Josh, but he dislikes being left out. "Why don't you discuss your concerns with Simeon or Judas?"

"I do not want to undermine my Abba's authority, but I have tried to read their minds. Simeon is not easy and Judas appears to be veiled from me by Simeon's hand."

"Perhaps this particular issue does not concern you, dear."

Yeshua shakes his head, "I think it does concern me. Why doesn't Abba confide in me?"

I lead Yeshua to our favorite cushion and sit on his lap. "My love, I think it is difficult for fathers to see even their grown children as mature enough to act as confidantes."

His fathomless eyes are pained that his father will not place trust in him. "I would like to speak to Ima about this, but I am sure she is not privy to his secret and do not want to unduly concern her."

"My Abba might be able to advise us. He is a seer; perhaps he can assist us with this problem." Yeshua considers this option.

"All right, let us meditate at dawn tomorrow and consult with him." Abba and Ima are in Bethany for the holidays visiting my grandmother. Yeshua kisses me, "You have missed your Abba this Chanuka, dear."

"And Ima too, which is a nice change!" Laughing, we join our children in the garden.

Gray and cold this sixth day of Chanuka, large bonfires warm the outdoor space where the children play. Sarah runs to greet us. "Come see what Josh and I made." Taking her Abba's hand, she leads us to a blanket where Teoma sits with Joshua.

Handing us their gift, Teoma's eyes are moist with tears, Joshua's little arms wrapped around his neck. Sarah seats herself in his lap. Yeshua holds up the linen square outlined in rough embroidery that Sarah learned while under the tutelage of my sister, and painted with a scene of us all. Teoma is central to the circle with Josh and Sarah holding his hands and Yeshua and I holding theirs. Signed in the lower right corner, the square has a small handprint at the top of the beam of light.

"See, Abba, I painted Josh's hand all the colors of the rainbow and pressed it on the linen. It's the Creator's hand reaching down to our family through the light."

Admiring the gift, Yeshua comments, "It is beautiful, children, just as you see the light of Eloha."

Joshua pats Teoma's cheek. "Do you like it, Dod Teo?"

Poor Teoma can barely speak, but his pure blue eyes tell me silently, *This is my family, Mary*. With trembling lips, I nod in agreement. Yeshua pats Teoma's leg.

"This gift is a lifelong keepsake, my friend."

Teoma murmurs, "Thank you for sharing them, Yeshua"

Sarah looks between the men. "We have always been a family. Thank goodness, we remembered and found each other."

Teoma embraces the children, "Yes, Barchashem!" and they leave us with kisses to join their cousins.

Yeshua nudges me. "Sorry, apparently I am the only one in this family who has yet to see the light."

291

Teoma smiles at Yeshua, before turning to me, "As sensitive as you are, how could you deny the truth?"

Prepared for another afternoon of portrait painting, Saul passes by with Jochanan who winks at me. How nice for Saul to have such a willing subject. Yeshua chuckles. I try to grasp what is so funny, for even Teoma grins. "Are you not happy for Saul?"

"You are just glad that his focus is not on you."

"But unfortunately, when Jochanan stopped me from chasing after Teoma, he started sketching me."

Teoma laughs, the sweet sound absent these many days. Delighted, I squeeze his hand. "So Saul will finally capture your beauty, Mary?"

"No, he's intent on capturing my despair. I am sure my tears do me no justice."

"That is not true, dear. Your tears highlight your lovely sea-green eyes ever so well." Smiling, Yeshua asks, "So what was it like being held by such a handsome man as Jochanan?"

I hesitate to answer. First, because I want to be sure there is no element of jealousy in my husband's questioning and second, because I do not know. But Yeshua is only curious and Teoma seems amused rather than disturbed by this vision. Hmmm!

"Truly, I cannot say."

Yeshua raises his brows, "You are telling me that in the arms of that beautiful man, you felt nothing?"

I consider this. What did I feel? "Well, I did feel comforted."

"Comforted? That's all? Nothing else?"

I study his face, his thoughts veiled. Teoma smirks. They're on to something. "What would you expect me to feel, Yeshua?"

Smiling, he opens his arms invitingly and of course, I melt with desire. "Well, certainly I did not feel like that!"

He laughs and asks Teoma, "Please hug Mary."

Teoma reaches for me and again the melting sensation. Pushing myself away, I look at Yeshua, who smiles, "Anything?"

Blushing, I respond, "Well, yes, but..." Teoma chuckles, following Yeshua's line of questioning much better than I am.

I get up from the blanket.

"Where are you going, Mary?" Yeshua calls after me.

"I'm going to see for myself!"

Really, Yeshua can be so exasperating with his strange sense of humor. I enter the olive grove where Saul happily paints. Both men smile at my approach. "Excuse me, but I have to ask Jochanan something." Saul nods his consent and I gather my courage. "Would you mind hugging me?" He smiles and takes me in his arms. Hmmm! Nothing! I look up at his beautiful face, but alas, no. "Thank you, Jochanan." Taking my leave, I bid them farewell.

He may be handsome, but love is what melts me. Upon my return, my husband inquires, "So, what did you feel?"

"Nothing. But I think it is because I do not love Jochanan."

Looking ever so wise, Yeshua nods and turns to Teoma, "Must you love another to feel desire for them?"

Teoma shakes his head, "Not at all. I believe Mary and I had this very conversation while you were in Britannia."

Yeshua nods, "I'm sure you did." I feel the rise of irritability. Why are they making such an issue about this? Yeshua banters with Teoma as if I am not present. "I remember when my dear wife responded to my desire at that party in Alexandria." I gasp for he is right. His initial reaction was in response to that gorgeous dancer.

Trying to defend myself, I declare, "Perhaps women are different. We may need to feel love to feel great desire."

Yeshua laughs, "Come, Mary, are you denying your own reaction to that dancing girl?" Blushing, I shake my head. "Perhaps you felt nothing for Jochanan because he feels nothing for you." Well, I never considered that, perhaps not every man is attracted to every woman. Shaking his head, Yeshua responds to my thoughts, "I do not believe I have come across too many men who are not attracted to you."

I look at Teoma who confirms Yeshua's observation. "Really, you two are biased in my favor. Besides Jochanan probably has a lovely young woman waiting for him in Qumran and he can focus on nothing else!" Both of them laugh hysterically at this. I am ready to leave them to their private joke!

Before I can escape, Yeshua wraps an arm around me, "One more question, Mary. Tell me, did Saul also comfort you that day?" Slowly, I nod. "And what did you feel?"

For goodness sakes, Saul is old enough to be my Abba! Besides he prefers… men. "Are you implying that I did not feel anything but comfort in Jochanan's embrace because," I lower my voice to a whisper, "he

293

prefers men?" Yeshua barely holds back his mirth, while Teoma laughs aloud. How naïve I am! "He could have fathered such beautiful children."

"Yes, it is so sad that his beauty will die with him."

The look on my husband's face I find most annoying. "Why are you always teasing me?"

He pulls me close, "Because you are so gullible, love."

"Well, he was just too good to be true. Too handsome, a great dancer, so easy to talk to. Why we can only pray that our Saul will find him favorable."

Teoma pats my knee, "I believe a match is being made as we speak, Mary."

Yeshua is not yet finished with me, "And I thought you were so sophisticated, visiting Greece so often." Turning in frustration, I place my hands on his chest to push away from him. Instead he catches my wrists and kisses me.

"Yeshua, you are taking unfair advantage of my vulnerability," I exclaim, catching my breath.

Teoma laughs from behind me, "Come, you two, let us see if Saul has captured Jochanan's beauty or at least his heart!"

***

At dawn, Yeshua awakens his wife to commune with Syrus. As they sit in meditative poses, a beam of light flows between them. Mary's father comes in shortly, happy to be of service. *Syrus, my father will not confide in me at this time, how do you advise I handle the situation?*

Syrus sighs, *Yeshua, you no longer need him for advice. You are strongly connected to the One and have excellent advisors in the council. Your Abba has fulfilled his role as patriarch, now set to complete his own journey. His separation from you shall reinforce your sense of self-reliance. There is nothing you can do to change the tide.*

Although aware of the imminent change, he is saddened. *How am I to let my Abba go, Syrus?*

You will be asked to surrender much in this life. Your Abba's gift to you is timely preparation for the increasingly difficult separation from all that you love. Across from him, Mary catches her breath. Syrus addresses her sorrow. *Mary, remember who you are as joy. Do not mourn a loss that has yet to occur.*

I am sorry, Abba. Your advice to Yeshua ignites my fear.

In the face of all the challenges you have endured, joy has been the undercurrent of your existence.

Reaching out, Yeshua tries to comfort his wife. _I am blessed, my love, to live in the light of your joy. Your Abba is right; do not cling onto sorrow prematurely._

Mary, your grandmother is dying. Your Ima asks if you might come with the children before she passes.

Yeshua balks. _We have not planned to expose the children to the world yet, but Mary and I will certainly come to pay our respects._

Your protest is reminiscent of your father who has sheltered you far too long. It is time to be immersed in the human drama. A fortuitous channel will open allowing Martha to take possession of the house in Bethany—an ideal place to keep your children once your mission in Judaea commences.

Syrus is correct. _I may seem ungracious by not respecting tradition. This is one of many lessons of meeting the world halfway in order to demonstrate yet a more enlightened means of dealing with our humanness._

Stirring where she sits, Mary wonders if he will allow the children to visit her grandmother. Syrus joins his laughter. _Yes, precious wife, we shall go as a family to bid your grandmother farewell._

Afterwards, they find Martha in the garden with the women watching the children play. While the sisters console one another, Hava offers her condolences, "I am sorry that your grandmother is ailing, but I would like to come and help."

Ima nods her consent as he kneels by Hava. "Thank you, dear Hava. I was hoping you could help us. We will not be able to return with them to Galilee until after we visit Qumran."

Mary's worry pervades the garden. _Savta's health changes everything._ Ima puts a hand on her shoulder, "Events in our lives are not in the way of our journey, but are a part of the path. Somewhere in this drama is a gift for each of us." Mary lays her head in his mother's lap, just as he used to do as a boy. Ima smiles up at him.

As the sun sets to commence the eighth day of Chanuka, the family gathers for the last celebration before the solstice. Bellies filled with Saada's delicious cooking, the guests' mood further enhanced by shekar, all who can play an instrument make music. Yeshua becomes immersed in conversation with Simeon and Judas as the women begin to dance.

Engaging the hayye swirling about the room, Mary partners with the haunting music, sable curls dancing in her wake. Yeshua takes delight in her sensuous movements, no other woman matches her boundless energy although she engages each one in a most fluid dance. Yeshua's desire drowns his attention to the zealots. *Tonight, my love, I shall meet your passion.*

The perfume of her response wafts tantalizingly. *Do not make me wait much longer, Yesh!* In a flurry of bright silk, the women part and invite him to step into their midst.

With a hasty excuse to Judas and Simeon, Yeshua crosses the room. He catches her fingertips lingering at his throat, and cools them with his lips. The women smile as she stealthily slips away, encouraging her to tanatalize him further. Just beyond his reach, Mary uses the energies as a buffer. *He has pleasured me with his innovations all week, but tonight I shall meet him.*

"You shall not thwart my surprise," he whispers breathlessly.

With a high-pitched call, Hava harkens the women to encircle them. Mary brushes a lush bottom against him, "Perhaps, Yeshua, I shall surprise you."

He laughs, head back. "I think not, your intentions are transparent." Feigning a pout, she dances toward the courtyard of their chambers. The women tighten their circle preventing his pursuit until the music quickens. Finally they release him, but he is not quick enough to catch his wife.

Frustrated, he corners her and grasps her sadin but it tears away. Bare skinned, she eludes him. No longer to be deterred, he catches a slender arm, drawing her firmly to him, and swallows her breath. Securing her against the wall, he frees himself from his garments and devours her passion. When her pleasure rings out over the sound of the lyre, he nearly succumbs.

So much for Druid sex.

In response to her unchaste thoughts, he brings her to the edge of consciousness, but with a squeeze, he too is lost, silver merging into violet. Silky legs wrapped about him as he pants an excuse, "This is not how I planned it."

"Sometimes you just have to seize the moment, Yesh." Smoothing the hair from his face, she looks about, surprised that he failed to veil them. He scoffs and carries her to their bed.

The day after the festival of lights, Yeshua calls for a gathering in the study. The other men begrudgingly incorporate Mary into their circle and Teoma, wondering how far he will persist in breaking with tradition, becomes increasingly discomfited at Yeshua's announcement of the change in plans.

As expected, Abba expresses grave concern, "I understand that you will want to have the children near you when the mission begins, but this is premature."

"With Roman soldiers patrolling the borders, it is not safe to travel with women and children through Samaria." Knowing Teoma's preference for using zealot trails, Judas supports his father's view.

"For protection, I shall use kasa."

Simeon raises his brows. "You shall maintain a veil of protection around both your and Eleazer's family?" Unfamiliar with the reference, the Essenes look askance at one another.

Quite confident, Yeshua states, "Mary can help." Simeon looks dubiously at her, then to Joseph for confirmation. His father's friends do not trust him.

The men grumble for a bit until Yeshua reassures them that all will be well. "Abba, please stay afterwards with Teoma and we shall discuss your concerns."

"You will be going into Qumran as well?" Jakob waits for his nod before turning to Joseph. "I do not mean to offend, but Hillel is an old man and the tribe of Judah needs competent leadership." Joseph offers nothing. "When King Hillel returned from Yeshua's wedding, the people of Qumran expected his eldest son would return with him."

Mary sits forward. *Jakob and Jochanan were the Essenes at our wedding.* He sighs, she is right. They are the same two who incited Abba with reports of a miracle.

Judas' thoughts pierce his concern. *The Essene has courage to speak publicly what we old men discuss only in private. Joseph is needed in Qumran, yet he sends the boy to do his work.*

Strong-willed Jakob continues, "Yeshua, I am in support of your mission, but it would behoove you to meet with the Zadok high priest."

Simeon agrees, "Yes, son, there is much opposition growing to your leadership."

"My inheritance was sanctified by the Aviatar as soon as my Ima's pregnancy was confirmed. There should be no question of who is to become king."

Jakob explains, "The Zadoks feel Joseph has not fulfilled his responsibilities as heir to the crown. They support the strict adherence of the dynastic laws and since you did not honor your agreement with the elders, Jochan bar Zechariah hopes to lead the unification of the tribes. Some say he is the spirit of Elijah returned. And with a strong following not appreciative of your wife's Hasmonaean heritage, Jochan supports Jacob as the rightful Davidic heir."

His brother stands defiant, "And I am in support of Yeshua." He places a calming hand on Jacob's arm. Although warned by the elders, Yeshua did not truly believe the people held such prejudice.

"If you could but meet with Jochan, it might be in your favor." Simeon suggests.

Turning, he captures the attention of all. "It is not in right timing that I discuss politics with my cousin, but I shall plan on acquiescing to whatever customs we shall encounter as it serves the mission." The men nod. He turns to the Essenes. "I wish for you to become part of the council of twelve."

After he and Jakob graciously agree, Jochanan enlightens them. "Jochan lives as an ascetic, forsaking strong drink and meat, practicing celibacy, and has little tolerance for those who do not adhere strictly to the Scroll of Discipline. Feeding off the guilt of our brethren who sin in the eyes of the priests, Jochan uses the Roman oppression to confirm that Adonai is most unhappy with His chosen people."

Yeshua rises, grateful that the younger Essene has provided such an eloquent opening. "I do not plan to openly oppose my cousin, but my message is one of love and joy, not the dispiriting judgment of the reigning priesthood. There is a greater power than Adonai. It is the Light of Love from which all creation, including the gods we choose to worship, arises."

All is quiet as the men consider his words. "Not only the tribes of father Avraham shall be united, but we must include the native goyim in our mission to be freed from that which oppresses us." Looking about the table, he assures their attention, "It is not the Romans that oppress us, but our fear which holds us captive."

The men become heated when Judas stands, "You speak as if the Roman barbarians are capable of such tender feelings."

"Judas, my friend, they are human beings just as we are, capable of the full range of emotions, including love."

Even his father sits forward in support, as Judas continues. "They are a power that has conquered many peoples using violent means. Since the war of Varus, thousands of crucifixions have occurred, our brethren dying at the hands of these 'loving' Romans." His bitter tone incites the others, but Yeshua defends his point of view.

"The fear in the Roman's hearts allows them to commit such atrocities. And our fear attracts their anger and hatred. Fear suckles itself, begetting more fear." His gaze sweeps the table, before stopping at his wife. "Mary, please tell these good men what you observed in Bethlehem."

Her countenance lovely, her voice unwavering, "The soldiers were as unhappy with the situation in Bethlehem as our people. They did not want to be there and resented us. Missing their homeland and families, they felt hopeless and unwelcome."

Judas growls, "They are not welcome here." The other men add angry voices in support until Mary turns her sea-green eyes upon the zealot commander.

"Judas, they are men just as you are, full of hope for the future, desiring love and joy. They are here against their will in service to a faceless power." Judas nearly debates her position until young Jacob clasps his arm, softening the gruff older man.

"Yeshua, how do you suggest we deal with the Romans?"

Gratefully, he smiles at his brother, "We must work on lifting fear which takes space in our hearts. When fear is replaced by love, we shall see the Romans not as enemies, but as brethren." The men cannot grasp this concept, but perceiving his wife's remembrance, he counters, "Last summer, Mary and I had a wonderful experience with two Roman soldiers while swimming in a secret cove."

I cannot believe that he would subject her to such a harrowing situation.

Yeshua attends to Teoma's unspoken concern, "Mary was under a veil as soon as we realized the situation."

To the questioning men, Eleazer explains, "These three had a rough time at the lake this summer." All nod in sympathy as if they could possibly understand.

"The soldiers had impure intentions at the start of our interaction, but by the end, we were as friends." None of the men can imagine befriending any Roman, so he allows Mary to explain.

"Yeshua spoke to the soldiers as brothers, kindly and with humor and when he touched them, everything shifted. They even wanted to share a meal with us!"

Judas shakes his head in disbelief, "So your husband must touch the entire Roman legion before we shall be free?" inciting the others to join him until Mary rises impassioned.

"Judas, if you would have seen Yeshua minister to these two men who threatened to harm him for hiding me," Teoma sits forward and Yeshua tries to quiet her, but she will not cease, "you too would believe that we can live together in peace and joy!"

She pauses and the energy in the room shifts into the brilliance of a summer sky. When Mary finally resumes her passionate speech, not a single man utters a breath.

"Yeshua came to help us understand how to be divinely human. As the mashiach, his purpose is to teach us how to be Love."

Not a single one of these men understands, but thankfully his beloved wife does. He can barely control his emotion. "Mary, your great faith is all that I need to sustain me in my life's work." The azure light in the room intensifies between them as they sit mesmerized by one another.

With a clearing of his throat, Jochanan breaks the tension, "Now Saul, this is a fine portrait in the making!"

Simeon laughs, as Judas says, "My dear wife did comment only last night that if Yeshua has as much passion for his mission as he does for Mary, the nation of Yisrael shall surely be united."

Her cheeks flush even more brightly when the zealot commander embraces her, "You have softened an old man's heart."

His father and Teoma linger after the others take their leave. Yeshua asks that Mary wait for him in their chambers. After she walks slowly away, Teoma's discomfort cannot be ignored. "What is on your mind, friend?"

"Why didn't you tell me of your encounter with those soldiers before today?"

"Because it would have upset you as it does now. Teoma, I am eternally grateful for your love and devotion, but you must have faith in me."

"I do have faith in you, Yeshua. But sometimes I think you forget that the rest of us are not as far along on the path. Exposing Mary to those soldiers right after she became aware of her past assault could have been disastrous. You take too many chances with your own safety, as well as hers, and now you are planning to bring the children to Bethany."

Abba heartily agrees, *He always thinks all will be well, never considering any danger, never taking precautions.* Ignoring his father's thoughts, Yeshua places his hands on the crown of Teoma's head, infusing him with peace. "Dear brother, you are gifted with undying loyalty, but when the burden of responsibility becomes unduly heavy, take a moment to remember that this life is about joy. You shall see that this trip will turn out to be a wonderful opportunity for each of us to grow. Teoma, your joy serves me as much as your protection."

Joseph clears his throat. "Son, do you believe that your connection to the energies is enough to protect all you hold dear?"

"Abba, I realize how difficult it is for you to remain behind while I venture into hostile lands, but we agreed after returning from Alexandria that you would provide counsel only. I must approach the world as a man in my own right."

"Qumran has been waiting for a mashiach since Daniel. The scribes believe that now is the time for prophesy to come forth. Looking to the line of David for the anointed one, they wish for a leader to conquer the sons of darkness."

"Their Zoroastrian beliefs are not mine. I do not believe in the evil of which you speak, especially in reference to my wife's family." He is well versed in the coded language of the Essenes who consider themselves sons of light fighting the evil wrought by those who do not adhere piously to their strict interpretation of the halacha. Abba keeps quiet. "Our people are misled by the dark prophets of doom. That is not my message, nor will I even attempt to lead them to conquer anything through violence."

"You will be put to task by the Zadok priesthood. Your grandfather does not have much power, so do not look to him for assistance. Perhaps it is a wise choice to include these passionate young Essenes in the council, but still you must take heed of their advice. They know well the opposition you face."

"My cousin feeds off the people's fear, just as the Romans do. With the help of Jochanan and Jakob, I shall make progress in Qumran."

"Perhaps you will learn from the Egyptian Therapeutae. The royal advisors might be able to teach you what I could not."

Still his father worries about his refusal of his inheritance. "Abba, I shall take advantage of all that is offered in Qumran, but I do not believe immortality to be a privilege limited to Solomon's lineage."

Shaking his head, Abba sits heavily, defeated. "I left Qumran to escape the dictates of royalty. Now I send my son into the jaws of the serpent."

He kneels at his father's feet. "All I need is your faith that I might succeed." Yeshua receives little comfort for Joseph's fear shadows the moment.

What is My Purpose?

Judaea, 3780

What is your purpose on the earth at this time?
Will you create from fear or from love?
What are you doing, what will you choose?
Perhaps being human is all you need do.

The Birth of Death

"I can ride him by myself." Sarah boasts, leading Sheikan. In the heat of the midday sun, we walk our mounts through the heart of the Samarian desert.

Micah scoffs, "He is too fast and powerful for a little girl!"

At her cousin's rebuff, Sarah halts abruptly. Sheikan bows so she might mount him, then with a flourish, gallops off toward a far crest. My little daughter rides in perfect harmony with the stallion.

Frantic, Teoma interrupts my appraisal. "Call that horse back! They've pierced the veil."

"Do something! What if she falls?" Martha cries.

Hava calmly gathers the children into the mule drawn cart as Sheikan crests the hill. Sarah disappears. Martha screams, although Hava tries to reassure her by explaining that Sarah has veiled herself. Yeshua seems unperturbed.

Teoma turns to me, "Do something! She cannot veil the horse!"

In the midst of their fear, I go to my daughter using raza and once astride Sheikan, veil us all. On the other side of the hill, a sizeable encampment flies the colors of Rome. Leaning into my chest, Sarah cries, "I didn't want them to see me!"

Sheikan wheels around as the soldiers pursue. Running ever faster, he leaves deep tracks, but fortunately a fierce wind drives sand before it obliterating everything. Protected by kasa, I reach out to Yeshua and we are drawn safely forth.

Within Yeshua's veil of protection, all is hushed. Hava and the children hold hands, praying. Eleazer holds Martha. Teoma holds the animals. In the face of the driving sandstorm, the soldiers give up their pursuit.

Hava feeds unleavened bread and salted kippers to the children, who act as if nothing is out of the ordinary. Sarah hugs Teoma, "I disappeared just as you instructed when I saw the soldiers."

"Thank goodness; we are fortunate your Abba can command the weather."

"Yes, Abba can do most anything!" Kissing her Dod, she turns to her cousin. "See, I can ride all by myself!" Micah is more interested in how she disappeared.

"Mary, how did you go to Sarah like that?"

Smiling, I kiss my sister. "Yeshua taught me how to travel in my body." In spite of all the fuss, I am excited. Yeshua gives Martha a squeeze, smiling at a dubious Teoma.

"I was afraid that we would come upon some trouble with so many to look after."

"And you did well, Teoma, to keep us secure, but perhaps you will learn to trust your premonitions. We are blessed for now Mary knows she can be with the children whenever needed. Sarah demonstrated good sense in veiling herself. And I am most pleased to work with the element of wind."

Still upset, Eleazer exclaims, "But Sarah might have been hurt!"

"I saw this event in my morning meditation and chose not to interfere, trusting I could heal any injury she might have suffered."

"What if she would have been killed?"

Yeshua casts a comforting hayye over the children, "Even death can be overcome, Micah." Little faces question. "Over the next hill we will find a small spring where we will make camp, and tonight, we shall discuss death." He walks south and the rest of us follow.

Hidden by large boulders and surrounded by lush vegetation, the spring provides refreshing sustenance. Teoma collects some wild greens for our stew, carefully instructing the children on what is edible and what is not. After our meal, Yeshua gathers us around the campfire. Bringing in the golden light of understanding, he invites the children's questions about death.

"Doda died at Joshua's birth, did you bring her back?"

Martha gasps at Micah's unfettered question, but Yeshua smiles reassuringly. "Yes, son, I did. Mary's work was not complete, so she came back from the Light and into her body."

"The Light is where Eloha lives!"

Yeshua smiles at his youngest nephew, "Yes, Eli. Eloha is One with the Light. Just as each of us is one with the Light of Eloha."

"We all came from the Light, right, Abba?"

"Yes, Josh, we did and when we die and leave this earth, we will return to the Light."

"But can't we be with the Light when we are here, too?"

"Yes, Sarah, through prayer and meditation, people can be one with the Light."

"But aren't you one with the Light all the time, Abba?"

"Most of the time. We can all be one with the Light if we are free from fear and filled with love."

"Is the Light and Love the same thing, Dod?" Jonah asks.

"Yes, son, the Light and Love are One, the essence of Sacred Unity—Eloha."

At Yeshua's feet, the younger children absorb the harmonious discussion, but the eldest isn't satisfied, "If Savta isn't ready to die, can you save her?"

Yeshua smiles, "Micah, most humans are not ready to die even when their bodies are old and decrepit. They spend their entire lives fearing death because they do not understand that death is but a transition to another form of being. Your Savta might not be ready to die when we arrive."

Jonah shakes his head in sympathy, "Poor Savta."

Putting her arm around her younger cousin, Sarah tells him, "We will help her find her way to the Light."

Micah is full of questions, "What about young people who die? Are they ready?"

Yeshua answers carefully, "Young children remember the Light, like you do, but in growing up they begin to forget, like falling asleep and believing the dream is real. Some people wake up before they die, so they pass gracefully. But most do not remember in time, so they fear death."

"You could not save Dod Jacob's baby."

"No, Sarah, but through his death, Ima, Doda Rebeka, Dod Jacob, and I each were able to grow and be farther along on urha."

307

Jonah asks, "What is urha?"

Yeshua responds simply, "Urha is the path a soul follows to become one with the Divine. Some paths are very short, like Jacob's baby, and others are very long, like that of your great-Savta." The children seem to understand, while the adults quietly listen. *Pay attention, Mary, there is something here for you as well.*

"Our souls are eternal. Like the light, our souls have existed before the earth was even formed and will exist after it is gone. If we choose, we are born here on earth to experience this life to learn and grow. Most souls come over and over again, taking many lifetimes to learn the lessons necessary to be free from fear and return to the Light of Love." Although accepting our eternal nature, I rather like this earthly form.

Smiling at me, Yeshua continues, "Many souls come to so enjoy their physical bodies that they do not want to return as pure hayye and join with the Light. They feel as if this world is more real than the dimensions that are not so dense and physical."

Yeshua hesitates. He has been holding the hayye of understanding, casting images as he speaks. Not one of the children questions him, but Eleazer ventures to ask, "What other dimensions are there? How is that which is without form real?"

"Eleazer, do you love your wife and children?"

"Why, of course I do!"

"What form does love take, brother?" The children turn toward Eleazer and listen for his answer. He has none. Yeshua goes on, "Does love have a shape? A smell? A taste? A sound?" Nodding, I perceive love with all my senses. "Except for Mary, most of us could not describe love as a physical thing."

Laughing, the others consider his analogy of love. He goes on at my expense, "Now for Mary, everything is quite real. Even her angelic visits take form to her senses. But without such a vivid imagination, most humans would say that some things, like feelings, have no physical form. Emotion, intuition, consciousness, spirit, each exists in this dimension and others without the density of this…" He picks up a small stone. "Yet love is as real as this rock, isn't it?" Everyone nods.

He smiles, holding the rock to his chest, "In fact, I believe there is love within this rock." The children sit forward as he offers it up for their inspection. Joshua holds it to his ear.

"Abba, this rock is full of love." Each child agrees. Sarah passes the stone back to her Dod Eleazer, who dutifully examines it.

Leaning toward the children, Yeshua whispers, "Sometimes adults have trouble finding love in rocks." Eleazer hastily passes it to Martha.

Yeshua picks up a larger piece of sandstone, "Now this rock is also filled with love as is all the earth." Deftly he breaks it upon another and passes out the fragments, "Each piece is still filled with love. Do you think that one has less love in it than another?" The children shake their heads, certain that the piece of rock they hold is as full of love as any one of the rest. "Does any one piece of rock have more love than any other?" The children shake their heads again. "Not even that big piece Dod Teoma holds?"

In unison, the children respond, "No!"

Yeshua holds up his piece of rock, "Eloha is the Light of Love. As this rock is filled with love then it must be part of Eloha." Now the children nod vigorously.

Sarah announces, "Eloha is in everything."

"Yes, Eloha is Love and Love is in everything. And everything is created in Love and returns to Love after it is destroyed or broken into many, many tiny pieces like this rock. In fact, only the form dies or changes, but not the Love."

I finally hear my lesson. Love never dies.

"Yes, Mary, Love is eternal and since each of us is Love, then we are also eternal. Not this body," he pats his chest, "no, this body will die, but who I am as Love can never die. I have always been Love and so have you."

He opens his arms and the children crowd into his embrace. Hava clasps me to her side, whispering, "We are blessed to have Yeshua with us."

Yes, but it is not permanent. Hava holds me closer. Oh, why am I so attached to the comfort of a human embrace? My husband sighs. *If we were all like these little children, we would accept the truth for what it is.*

Struggling on the verge of tears, I am not afraid of death, but of separation from that which I love.

***

In the midst of the great desert of Judaea, the beauty of Bethany is striking. Flowering vines clamber onto limestone houses faded white, colorful curtains billowing through open windows. Gathered upon the low roofs, elderly men enjoy the warmth of the morning sun. Brown-armed women hang laundry in the alleyways crisscrossing the narrow streets and at the village well, wives in bright headdresses collect water and news. The eastern edge of the village hosts much grander houses with bubbling fountains. Towering palms lead them to Mary's family villa.

An open courtyard greets them, lush and alive with plants sprouting from large urns the color of sunset. Stable hands immediately see to the mounts as a well-attired goyim announces their arrival. Before entering the house, servants wash the dust from their feet and hands. Yeshua is tended before the other men, the women and children last. Joshua waits patiently as a servant pours fresh water into the kiyyor.

"Ima, maybe someone can do this for us at home."

The servant washing the boy smiles. Yeshua takes his fretting wife's arm as they are escorted to their chambers.

"Abba," Joshua runs naked from the nursery followed by a flustered young servant, "you should see how big the bath is, like a lake! They rubbed oil on my skin. Beshera is my new friend."

The young woman shyly nods, her long black hair tightly coiled upon her head. "Thank you, Beshera, for taking such good care of our son. He is excited by this fine home, but," he turns sternly to Josh, "he will pay heed to you hence forth." Meekly taking her hand, Joshua bids them goodbye.

High tiled walls separate three large Roman style baths the size of small ponds. Attended by a staff of four, Yeshua joins the men in a luxurious soak. Women's laughter echoes from next door.

"So, when Martha inherits this luxury, your family will not have to depend on your flagging skills."

Taking full advantage of Martha's wealth, Eleazer has left the selling of textiles to his younger brother. Ignoring Teoma's chide, he motions to a servant.

"Are we not to join your wife's parents for the evening meal?"

"Teoma, fear not, a bit of cheese and shekar will not hinder our appetite. Help yourself!" Quickly, the servant produces wine and a platter of fruit and cheese.

When handed a cup, Yeshua expresses his gratitude. The young servant ducks his head in embarrassment. Eleazer looks at him as if he has breached some rule. He turns to Teoma for explanation.

"Yesh," his friend lowers his voice, "they are slaves."

In the grandeur of the baths, he realizes how far removed he has lived from the rest of society. Unlike the Tzadokim, his father refuses to keep slaves. Those working the land share the wealth of their labors. The men of his family have always expressed a deep disdain for the Hasmonaean dynasty. So many divisions within the tribes of Yisrael, how might he unite them?

"Brother, drink the shekar before you spill it."

Smiling, Yeshua raises his cup to Eleazer and drinks it down.

In their chambers, he finds Mary within the arch of the balcony looking east. When he moves to join her, she presses herself deliciously against him, lifting her face for a kiss. Silken mounds tantalize the low neckline of her turquoise sadin.

"What are you gazing at?"

A smile dimples her left cheek. "Why, my beloved husband!"

Impatient, she does not wait for his kiss. They shall soon be called for the evening meal, but food will not appease this hunger. Her nipples rigidly seek his chest as the perfume of her passion mingles with the scent of her bath. Huskily, he murmurs into the softness of her neck, "I meant, what enchants you so at the window?"

She waves one slender arm in a wide expanse, pointing past lovely gardens toward large irrigated fields well beyond an immense pasture grazed peacefully by a large flock of sheep.

"All this is your grandmother's land?"

Peeking over his arm, she whispers, "Can you see all the way to the Dead Sea?" Incredulous, he shakes his head. She laughs. "No, her property extends to the foot of those far hills."

"How is it that you never mentioned all of this wealth?"

Shrugging, she replies, "I was rather unaffected by it all. Besides, my Abba limited the amount of time we spent with Savta. Before Saba died, the house was full of Herodians, Hasmonaean royalty, relations by blood or marriage, even Romans."

"Here I am, soon to proclaim my inheritance as the Davidic king to unite the people of Yisrael, and I am married into the family which conspires with our oppressors."

She studies his face with a brilliant green gaze. "It is ironic, Yeshua, that we come from such opposing lineages."

"It is not ironic. Some may call it a fine political alignment, but since both your father and mine had a vision of our union, I believe it was divinely orchestrated. What better tactic to unite our people than to tie together the tribal lines with the most radical viewpoints? Perhaps under a spiritual king, Yisrael will be united."

Mary's eyes darken, but before she can voice her concern, a servant calls them to the evening meal. Centered about a huge inner courtyard rich with flowering gardens, a large fountain and a covered atrium, the living and sleeping wings extend like spokes of a wheel with guests accommodated in the west, servants occupying the south, and the family housed in the east. In the expansive southern wing, a great room and an inner courtyard leads to the dining hall. West of the great room lies a study filled with codices and to the east, another gathering hall. At the most northern point of the house, the large kitchen accesses vegetable gardens.

When Syrus rises to greet them, Mary runs into his arms. Seated at the far end of the long table, the children chat amiably.

"Ima, we have not yet seen Savta." Martha speaks gently.

Eucharia brings fine linen to the corner of her eye. "In the morning, if it is Adonai's will." Syrus casts a warning glance as she wistfully inquires, "Yeshua, perhaps you can do something; she is in much pain …"

"Eucharia, I will try to ease your Ima's passage, but it is her time." She nods, dabbing again at her eyes and Syrus takes her hand comfortingly. The staff begins serving but Mary's mother refuses any nourishment.

Eleazer asks about recent rulings of the Sanhedrin. Mary shifts uncomfortably when her father mentions the trial of a false prophet. Syrus takes his daughter's hand, "In this time of turmoil, mashiachs abound, but only one shall unite us." Mary breathes a sigh of relief. "So Sarah told me about her encounter with the soldiers. She has your gifts with the energies." Eucharia gasps.

"A little girl should not be riding in the midst of soldiers!"

"Alas, we all love a bit of excitement, but I had it well in hand." Yeshua extends peaceful energy, calming Eucharia as Syrus looks on with gratitude.

"We dine with the true mashiach." All is quiet until Syrus laughs a deep bellow of a sound, "A sandstorm, Yeshua? What next? Shall you part the Red Sea like Moses?"

"Only if necessary, sir." Even Mary smiles as the rest of the family joins his laughter.

***

My once beautiful, robust Savta, who ruled this household with flair, is but a shadow of her former self. Lying diminished on the large cushioned bed, sallow skin framing gray lips and hollowed eyes, she appears more dead than alive. With great reservation, my sister leads me closer.

"Martha, is that Mary with you?"

Martha takes her dry bony hand, "Yes, Savta."

Reaching for me with her other claw-like hand, Savta croaks, "I have not seen your face since your wedding. Come closer, Mary." Her physical form wispy as a dry leaf, her lower energy centers barely visible. The thin sheet across the bed does not hide her swollen lower limbs in sharp contrast to her withered upper body. Her mouth sinks into her skull producing a hollow voice carried on ragged breath musty as a tomb. Involuntarily, I shudder. Savta smiles a toothless grin.

"Everyone's beauty fades in the end, dear." I sink to the floor and lay my head near her hand. Softly she pats me, "There now. Do not flaw your beauty with useless tears. Herod's granddaughters take after his comely wife Mariamne, but you possess your great aunt's most exquisite charms." As I raise my face, she cackles. "You were not here when your Saba passed away. I must be a fearsome sight."

Such humor, perhaps she has little pain. "Savta, do you suffer?"

She chuckles, a dry sound. Martha offers her a sip of water, but Savta shakes her head, pointing to a damp cloth which Martha moistens for her to wearily suck. Afterwards, she weakly replies, "It is as if I am but an infant again, suckling upon this rag. No, Mary, not as much as it must appear." She stops and takes several shallow breaths, "Before I fall asleep, I want to meet your husband, Mary."

"Savta," I reply, "you met him at my wedding."

Nodding slowly, she raises her hand, "Of course, I remember, but they say he is the mashiach, perhaps he can put in a good word for me with Adonai." Weakly she slaps my hand. "Mary, go, your sister can tend to me." Martha has my sympathy as I take my leave.

Yeshua looks up when I enter the great room. "Since I do not perceive that your Savta has died yet, why do you look like you've seen a ghost?" In tears at his teasing, I sink to a cushion and he comes to sit by my side, "Mary, you have not experienced the process of dying."

"The children should not be party to this. They never got to see my Savta when she was vital; now it is frightening."

Sighing, he places an arm around my shoulders, "My dear, you underestimate their fortitude. Our children have been exposed to the birth and death of animals at home."

"Savta kept Martha and dismissed me."

"Your sister is of hardy constitution, not as emotionally volatile as you."

I shake my head, "But her room is dark and dank like a tomb, as if she is burying herself before she dies." He finally embraces me.

"Let us bring her out here in this light room. She can die surrounded by her family instead of hidden in her den."

"Ima will not like it."

But Martha agrees and takes charge, instructing the servants to prepare the great room. Savta's second meeting with my husband is while he carries her to her new bed. "You will love this arrangement, dear Savta." Charmed by Yeshua, she does not fuss.

My sister has set up a fine space in which to die. Vases overflowing with flowers surround the bed, which looks out upon the gardens. Yeshua lays Savta upon the softly cushioned bed, settling her with many pillows behind her back so that she might breathe more easily.

"You are a kind healer, son." Smiling down upon her, he brings in a healing light, and she falls into a peaceful sleep.

Yeshua insists that we carry on all our daily activities right here in the great room, while our grandmother passes away, so Martha and I share lunch while he reads in the light of a large window. Small feet running down the hall announce the children's arrival from the gardens.

Joshua shows me what he has caught, a small toad, clasped carefully in his little hands. "I want to show Savta my new friend."

Since the drapery is not drawn about the sickbed, Savta lies in plain view. Watching for a moment, Jonah asks, "Is she dead yet?"

Sarah answers, "No, she's still breathing, see!" Holding their own breath, the children wait to see the shallow rise and fall of Savta's chest.

Jonah sighs, "Good, I haven't even kissed her hello," but their great-grandmother continues to sleep so they lose interest and join us at the low table.

"Let's draw pictures." Sarah suggests. Martha calls for sheets of papyrus and drawing implements, as well as pots of ink. Looking down at the fine tapestry carpet underneath, I ask the servants to help us roll it back.

"Looks like a party, Martha," Teoma returns with Eleazer from the blacksmith.

"Yes, we will have music later this evening to complete the festivities." In a grand mood, Martha kisses her husband. We draw with the children for the rest of the afternoon, until Savta wakes.

"Well, who are all these lovely children?" Her voice weak, but her tone is jovial. The children climb upon the bed carefully so not to jostle her. Yeshua draws a chair near as each child kisses her sunken cheeks, unperturbed by her appearance.

Joshua startles her a bit, "My friend wanted to see you, like I did," but Savta's bony finger tentatively strokes the toad's head. "Say goodbye to Savta, you will see her in the garden, soon." Joshua jumps off the bed, taking Eli.

Sarah asks, "Does it hurt to die, Savta?"

"Not really. But my energy is diminished," True, her hayye has become a tiny spark in her heart center, the color fading into white.

Sarah responds, "You are getting ready to return to the Light."

Savta looks to Yeshua for confirmation. He nods. "Your children are walking with Adonai, my son." His hayye expands with waves of peace and comfort. Sighing, I silently thank him.

My parents return, escorted by their two youngest grandchildren. "See Savta, your Ima is out here with us," Eli says.

While Abba seems most pleased with the new arrangement, Ima is shrouded by fear. Taking her hands, we bring her to Savta.

"Ima," she whispers hesitantly, "you look well this afternoon."

Savta gives her a sunken grin, "This is a good way to die."

Yeshua reaches across the bed and touches Ima's cheek, "Dear Eucharia, your smile has brightened this room." Tears wet his hand as she murmurs her thanks, before kissing her mother's forehead.

"Come Eleazer, let us pillage the wine cellar, Eucharia bought lamb." Abba laughs.

As Savta rests again before dinner, the children sprawl upon the rug around my contented husband. "Dod Yeshua, why is Savta shrinking? She used to be bigger."

Yeshua smiles at Micah, "Just as you grow from childhood into adulthood, people become smaller and more frail the longer their bodies have served them on this Earth. Your Savta's spirit, the hayye that is her individual rucha, will not die. It shall go on."

Jonah asks, "What does hayye look like?"

Sarah looks at her cousin, "Just like a person's aura only brighter. Can't you see?"

"Not everyone can see hayye, Sarah." Yeshua intervenes, "Some people can feel it more clearly than see it. Jonah, can you feel your Savta's hayye?"

"Yes, but it is very small and weak, not big and strong like yours, Dod Yeshua."

"What you feel is her life force, preparing to return to the Light. Before a person dies, the energy which usually surrounds the body becomes very concentrated, like salt in water. When the water evaporates, only the salt is left." The children seem to understand.

"Come to me, Jonah." The boy rises and stands before his Dod. Yeshua puts his hands together and produces concentrated energy.

Jonah senses something. "What is it, Dod?"

"It is hayye, son. Can you see it?"

Jonah shakes his head. "But you can feel it?" Jonah nods. "Here, move your hand through it between mine, it won't harm you. Tell me what you feel."

Tentatively Jonah passes his hand through Yeshua's. Smiling he does it again. "It's warmer in the center and near your palms and makes my skin tingle."

Yeshua beams, "Very good. Now take your hands and rub them together until they feel hot and tingling. There. Now pull them apart slowly like you are holding a ball that is as light as a feather."

Jonah's eyes widen. There is a small silvery sphere of hayye within his hands. "Dod," he whispers as if speaking any louder and the hayye will disappear, "I did it!"

Yeshua nods, patting Jonah's back, "Yes, son, you have concentrated energy. Now see if your brothers can feel it, too." Carefully, Jonah presents his sphere of hayye to his brothers who pass their hands through it, exclaiming excitedly. After the children mimic Jonah and play with hayye, Yeshua resumes the lesson. "Now, what is death?"

For a long while they consider this question until Sarah finally braves, "Is it when rucha returns to the light?"

"Yes, but even more joyful. In a spiritual sense, it is a birth."

Micah wrinkles his nose. "Death is a birth?"

Nodding Yeshua explains, "When you were but hayye, you were born into the physical form of a human body. From a baby, you transformed into a child. You can feed yourself and wash yourself and…."

"Use the betshimush instead of a cloth!"

Laughing at Joshua's interruption, Yeshua agrees, "Yes, son, and in a few years you as a child will pass on to become an adolescent. Your body will change, and your mind, and so does your soul. Then your adolescent self will die so that your young adult self can be born."

The wide-eyed children listen intently to his story of life. "From an adult you transform over many years. You may learn a trade, you may marry, you may have children. With each transformation comes a passing of the old way of being for a new you to be born. Then after many, many years, your body gets tired, but your soul has grown so much. Time to face yet another death, this time of the physical form, so that the soul may be born into the spirit world. Just as the birth of a new baby is celebrated here on earth, the birth of a soul from this physical realm to the spiritual realm is celebrated."

The children stare at Yeshua while he projects an image of a grand celebration.

Sarah suggests, "Shall we celebrate Savta's death, Abba?"

Yeshua holds up his hands to guide the hayye of understanding. "It would be wonderful to celebrate her birth into the spirit world."

Eli claps his hands. "Yes, we should have a birthday for Savta when she dies."

Joshua jumps up. "We can have massah!"

"What about presents? Can we give her presents?" Jonah asks.

Looking at me, Yeshua asks, "What do you think, Mary?"

They turn their sweet faces toward me. "I think that we could send Savta loving hayye, blessings, even music as birthday gifts."

Since Savta cannot come to the dining table, Yeshua has the table brought to her. The children are delighted to be dining in the great room. In spite of Savta's impending death, there is a celebratory hayye around her.

The aroma of roasted lamb brings tears to Savta's eyes. Yeshua offers her a piece, but she shakes her head with remorse. "Son, I have not been able to eat lamb for many years now."

Undeterred, he insists, "Come, Savta, you can still taste it. Suck on it like you do the rag." He tenderly feeds her.

After enjoying the lamb, Savta announces. "It is so nice to have everyone here. We shall have a lovely Seder with the children."

Ima looks startled, "But Pesach is months away." And the priests in the Holy Temple would be horrified to learn what our good Tazadokim family plans to do.

Savta laughs, "Then we better have it soon, for I won't make it until then." My mother's face pales. "Son, how much longer do you think I have?"

Yeshua smiles, "Less than a week, dear."

"Save the shank bone, Eucharia. And you better get started on the matza."

Ima turns to Abba, "What shall we do with all the leavened bread?"

"Give it to the poor, Eucharia."

The men head out early with the children carrying many loaves of freshly-baked bread. As we prepare for the Seder, the activity seems to soothe Ima. By the afternoon, an entity hovers near Savta's bed—my grandfather. Quietly I sit down and take her hand. She smiles, "What is it, Mary?"

"Saba is here."

"I know. I invite him to Seder every year since he passed away, but this time I can actually hear him speaking to me." On death's door, do people become more receptive to the energies? When Archangel Gavriel arrives to answer my query, Savta nearly sits up, crying, "I haven't had my Seder yet!"

Gavriel laughs like chiming bells, *She shall have her Seder.*

I relate the message to Savta, who seems surprised, "The angel spoke to you, Mary?"

"Yes, Savta, this is the Archangel Gavriel and he has been one of my most constant companions."

"I thought you only saw angels at the moment of your death."

"No, they are all around us, but most people do not attend to them."

Gavriel interrupts our conversation. *Mary, as humans get closer to physical death, the veil between the worlds appears thinner and they often perceive dead ancestors and the angelic host. Their hayye will soon merge with the Light. Your grandmother is surprised you can perceive me since you are alive and well.* Again he laughs as I explain this to Savta.

"Have you always been able to see angels, Mary?"

"Yes, but since I have been with Yeshua, my perception and communication with the energies has become expanded."

Reaching up, she touches my face, "Mary, your husband is a unique being and you are meant to be with him. Your great love for one another brings joy to those of us who do not have your clarity of vision."

I kiss her cheek before helping her settle down for an afternoon nap, but she resists drifting off, insisting on telling me why Martha shall inherit her property. "Mary, hear me. Your husband is the mashiach, but do you know who you are?" I am unsure of what she means. "My father's sister Mariamne was a dark beauty like you. The ancient blood of the Egyptian pharaohs shone through her lovely face, just as it does through yours." She pauses to catch her breath and I offer her a rag to suck upon. Finishing, she pats my hand. I move closer to hear her every word.

"Mariamne was also gifted as a seer; she studied at Karmel with priestesses of Astarte." I am shocked to hear this, for my grandmother's family has always been so pious. "Many thought she was a sorceress. Our grandfather sold her into marriage to Herod, some believed that she cast a spell upon her husband, but he was very much enchanted by her beauty. Too much so, for he proved to be a cruel and jealous man." Savta nods, looking past me as if she can see her dead aunt. "She saw her own demise and that of her sons after her, poor dear, and she made me promise as her only niece to save our family's wealth for two sisters that were to be born through my loins—one dark and gifted." Slowly she raises her bony finger to brush my forehead. "You are the child she envisioned, the one to do what she could not. I have left Martha enough to provide you refuge when the time comes—your husband's mission shall be your own." Savta speaks no more but Saba stays close.

At dusk even Savta is dressed in her finest. Yeshua begins the Seder by lighting the lamps, "While apart, these lamps mingle their flames to enlighten the path. Their light represents the light of love and understanding, illuminating our human existence."

"Praised is Marya who creates the fruit of the vine. With the consumption of this wine, may we be free from the fear which truly enslaves us." He empties his cup and we follow his example.

Quietly encouraged by Sarah, Joshua begins the questions. "Why is this night different from all others?"

"This night we eat only unleavened bread, because the Yisraelites needed to leave Egypt before their bread could rise."

Eleazer beams as Yeshua praises Micah, "In remembrance of the plight of our ancestors we eat matza. Sometimes it is necessary to accept nourishment from unconventional sources."

As we share the second cup of wine, Yeshua explains how it represents deliverance from the illusion of pain and suffering produced by fear. Savta stops sucking wine from the rag Martha offers to opine. "This is a very educational Seder."

Teoma and Abba chuckle as Yeshua raises his cup to her, before beginning the hand-washing ceremony. "Blessed is Eloha, who has sanctified us with the gift of T'hora, the ritual of purification."

Picking up the linen basket, Yeshua carefully exposes the matza. "Blessed is the Creator, who brings forth bread from the mother earth." Taking a piece he breaks it in two, "This matza is the bread our ancestors ate at the time of their affliction, but now it is the bread of remembrance of the blessings of our life." He breaks the remainder of the bread and passes it to the rest of us.

Eli asks, "Why on this night do we eat only bitter herbs?"

Sarah sits forward. "Bitter herbs represent the bitterness of enslavement."

"We can be enslaved by many things, not only by other people. Most humans are enslaved by their fear." The children's eyes widen at Yeshua's explanation.

Reaching for the small pots of morar, we each spread a tiny bit upon our matza and consume it. Joshua makes a face and I assure him that he does not have to finish it. Sarah and Micah make a show of eating a generous portion of the bitter herb.

Jonah sits up on his cushion. "Why on this night do we dip the herbs twice?"

Joshua wriggles to respond. "In our tears, we dip the herbs in tears."

"Yes, my son, the salt water represents our tears of struggle through slavery then we dip the herbs into the haroset representing the sweetness of freedom." The children dip their parsley in the salt water. "What do we desire to be free from?"

Wrinkling his brow, Micah offers, "Our oppressors?"

"Perhaps we might desire to be free from our fear, so that we are not vulnerable to oppression." Taking their time, the children consume generous portions of haroset. "Micah, what is the fourth question?"

"Why on this night do we sit in reclining positions?"

"Because free people can relax and recline, slaves must stand."

Yeshua smiles at Sarah, "Yes, this life is about experiencing joy, but if fear enslaves us, we may not fully experience all the wonders of being on earth."

As the children lie back on their cushions, Yeshua reaches behind him and starts passing plates of chicken and roasted vegetables down the table. In spite of Ima's protests, he released the servants for the evening to enjoy a meal with their families. After two cups of wine, I need to eat. Chatting happily, the children clean their plates.

"Yeshua, what about the paschal?"

Abba tries to answer Ima's concern, "Like the Essenes, perhaps Yeshua is not accustomed to referencing of the sacrificial lamb bone?"

Smiling graciously at my parents, my husband responds, "Syrus, I am not an Essene in practice, as you see I did enjoy the lamb last night."

Savta chuckles dryly, "Yes, he even fed it to me."

Yeshua smiles at her, "The paschal represents the sacrifice made by our ancestors. Believing themselves to be the chosen people of Adonai, they have seen their persecutions and afflictions as the true nature of sacrifice in order to obtain the Divine kingdom."

Ima nods in agreement, but Yeshua is not finished, "It is not necessary for us to suffer in order to be one with the Light. Our belief in suffering entices us to make sacrifices to obtain approval of a judging Creator. The judgment is our own, for the true nature of Eloha is Love."

In spite of Ima's discomfort with the breach of tradition, Savta is delighted. "You have much to teach our people, Yeshua."

Extending his loving hayye, Yeshua embraces us all. "It will be a pleasure to teach our people that the true purpose of this life is to experience joy."

A bubble of laughter bursts from Savta, "Good, then I hope you won't be reiterating the lessons from the ten plagues. I have always found them frightful."

Yeshua laughs, "No dear, and we shall not discuss the wicked child either, for I do not believe one exists on this earth." The children sit up happily.

At the conclusion of our meal, the third cup of wine is poured. Yeshua continues, "This is the cup of redemption. We drink this wine in praise of the One who gives us this bountiful earth to sustain our bodies. Only your illusions keep you in bondage from the truth of who you are." Again Savta's question echoes in my head—*Do you know who you are?* Yeshua glances at me.

"Within each of us is the Pharaoh, who mocks our escape from bondage, which is our self-doubt and feelings of unworthiness that keeps us from freedom. Thankfully, within each of us also exists Moses, the liberator, that part of ourselves that is courage to be free from the bondage of fear and faith to be who we are. Let us drink the cup of redemption." We consume our wine and the cups are refilled for the last time.

Turning toward the open door, he says, "We now invite the spirit of Elijah...."

"And Saba!" Sarah chimes in. Yeshua chuckles.

"Yes, and Saba to share a cup of wine with us."

My grandfather's rucha appears at the place set for him. Sarah claps her hands, "Sit down, Saba, and have your wine." All of us watch as she interacts with his rucha, Savta smiling a wide toothless grin. "This last cup of wine is the covenant that we have with Eloha to return to the Light. Elijah represents hope and justice and Saba is here to escort Savta back to the Light when she is ready."

Looking at Savta, Yeshua smiles, "We all left the Light willingly, agreeing to come here to learn and grow, to experience joy. We made a covenant with the Creator of the Universe that when we remember who we are, we will return to be One with the Light. We shall come back as many times as it takes to remember who we are, but only when we are fully enlightened beings do we desire to stay in the Light of the One."

The air thickens to catch in my throat. *Why doesn't this news bring you pleasure?*

Reaching deep within, I find strength. *Because Yeshua, this is your way of separating from this world. Savta's death is but a preparation for us. You shall return without me.* Sadness passes over him as our children attend to the hayye between us. Abba and Hava note the exchange as well. The silence is broken by Teoma.

"So are we to drink this last cup of wine?"

As Yeshua extends his hayye, the flames flicker then rise. "Let us drink this last cup and rejoice that we are here together to renew our covenant with Love."

Wine is drained from each cup, yet I still hold mine aloft. Yeshua touches my cup with his, "Drink, Mary."

Unable to look into his eyes, I turn toward Savta. She glows, soon to be one with the Light. I raise my cup to her and drink it down, "Have a good reunion, Savta."

Yeshua whispers, "We shall see her again in the Light." Tears spill into our embrace. "Hush, Mary, I am not leaving now." But I know in my heart that just as we are saying farewell to Savta now, that there will be a final Seder for us sooner than I can bear.

Immersed in my sorrowful premonition, I struggle with tangled curls, but Yeshua takes my comb to finish the chore, healing hayye emanating from his hands. Warmed by his light, my body soft and sensuous as he kisses the back of my neck, I am overcome by an urgency to join with him. Exploring his body, I memorize his form and waves of passion crash into the depth of our union. With a nearly full moon, I dare not look into his eyes lest I separate from this reality. Slow caresses follow the curve of my waist, brushing lightly across my flushed breasts to cup my face.

Easing my lips down, he sucks my breath away, on the edge of panic, until he kneels with me in his lap. Eye to eye, he forces me to attend to every aspect of my being. As my consciousness shifts from our forms, I search the portal of his eyes and, instead of falling, am upswept like a swirling wind. At the infinite top of the prism of light where all colors merge into none, we meet the One. The sweetness of connection in form and out is so intense that our tears of joy course together to form one salty river.

Floating upon the nectar of nothingness, our souls spill joy into eternity. Without word or thought, only pure feeling emerges—a rich abundance of love courses about and within until no boundaries exist, no us, no me. All of this intense expression in the illusion of the infinite becomes but a moment as the waves crash against the density of our forms. Consciousness differentiates into he and I, separate from the One while the orgasmic peak fades into the fluidity of our loins.

Clinging to one another, we weep in pain of separation, fully conscious now of a memory or a premonition as time has collapsed. We have been and will be united within the fiery bosom of the One. Through our very physical human act of intercourse we are able to pierce the veil of separation and experience connection to All That Is—Love. Our bodies are the vehicles to transport us to the Divine as we connect to one another, but….

Silently, Yeshua finishes my thought, *Reconnection with the One is not only possible through each other, but whenever we might surrender self we may experience the Divine in the intimate embrace of another.*

A cleft separates our bodies, the moonlight illuminating his face. "Yeshua, I do not want any other." His fingertip follows the path of a tear to the corner of my mouth, his whisper softer than the flutter of wings.

"You will when I am gone."

My chest constricts, my tears springing forth anew. Slowly, I turn away from the truth clearly revealed in his eyes. I do not wish to move, but cannot bear to stay, so I leave him kneeling upon the bed to make my way barefoot into the garden.

Between the flowering vines, a grassy knoll beckons. Lying naked upon the bosom of the Earth Ima, feeling the beat from her core match my own, hearing an owl call to its mate… who…who…, I fall asleep not knowing.

Before the gray dawn condenses into dew, hands warm my cold shoulders. "Mary, it is time." Yeshua slips a robe over my head, "The portal is open. Your Savta is ready to go."

I knock upon Martha's door and she awakens Eleazer before going to our parents' room. In the nursery, Hava rouses the children and asks me to fetch Teoma. With tousled hair and musky sensuality, he hesitates not to ask his buxom lover to assist with the children. Wordlessly, I turn back toward the center of the house.

"Mary, go now to your Savta. We'll bring the children," Teoma gently pushes me up the hall with strong hands.

A light over Savta's bed illuminates the massive space. With arms wide, Yeshua stands at her feet embracing the hayye. A brilliant whiteness of rapid vibration, the portal to the infinite fills with many souls, relatives and ancestors waiting to greet Savta. I can feel the love of the One calling to her.

The rest of the family joins us, gathering about the bed to bid her farewell. Sleepy, but enchanted by the hayye, the children hold hands. Except for Ima, there is no sense of fear and, with Yeshua's touch, even hers diminishes. No longer lucid, Savta's nafsha hovers, thinly attached to her body by a wispy silver cord. As I sit on the edge of her bed observing her drift between the realities, my consciousness joins hers.

At the mouth of the portal after a last bit of hesitancy is gently whittled away by Yeshua, she enters the light. Saba welcomes Savta before taking her nearer to the radiance of the One, but she enters the embrace of Divine Source alone. With delight she is engulfed by Love that knows no bounds. So much passionate joy, like the reunion of lovers, the intimacy so arousing that I am torn between attending and turning away in deference to their private moment. Before I can do one or the other, Savta looks back upon the world she left and I am swept up into her perspective to see the world in which her body lies is a bubble of illusion, the reality being the Light of the One.

As she bids us goodbye, the lightness intensifies, the portal collapses upon itself inhaling Savta's nafsha into the rucha of the One. With a gasp I return to my own form and see Yeshua do the same. Sarah and Joshua are back as well, attracted to the light as moths to a flame.

Yeshua draws me into his embrace, gathering the children near. *My love, there is nothing to fear in physical death.*

Nothing but the separation from that which I love.

"Did you see Eloha hug Savta? She is home now and we are here." Nodding, I caress Sarah's sweet face.

Martha covers Savta's body which must be buried before dusk.

"Shall we have the party tonight, dear?" The party? Oh yes, the celebration of her birth into the spirit world. Yeshua clasps my arms, "Mary, did you not find delight in witnessing your grandmother's reunion with the One?" I nod. "Then why is your heart so heavy?" Leaning my forehead into his chest, I close my eyes. Being with the One, Savta is blessed, while we remain here to finish our work. Mine shall take longer than Yeshua's, and I will be lost in the illusion, while he basks in the Light of the One.

After washing in the mikvah, the special tub set aside for ritual purification, Hava helps Martha and I bathe and anoint Savta with myrrh, wrapping her in herb-lined linen shroud. The children's laughter drifts in from the garden where Yeshua encourages Ima to assist them with their birthday preparations while Teoma and Eleazer dig Savta's grave.

Ready for the burial, Yeshua's laughter invites the children to come in to decorate the great room.

"Eloha, Birther of the Cosmos, we are grateful to be gathered to escort Savta's physical form back to the Earth. It has served her well. We ask that she be blessed in the spirit world as she brought blessings through her life here on Earth. Ameyn."

Sarah follows, sprinkling flowers along the way. Eleazer and Teoma carry Savta's body upon the litter as the rest of the children skip along the narrow path. Joshua picks up the petals his sister has strewn, Ima and Abba walking behind arm-in-arm. A few paces ahead of the musicians gaily playing their flutes and beating their drums, I hold hands with Martha and Hava. The staff makes up the remainder of the strange, but joyous, procession.

We gather about the freshly dug grave where Savta's body is carefully laid. The children wave goodbye as Yeshua leads us in song. Instead of the usual mourners' Kaddish, we sing a springtime melody revering birth and new life. At the conclusion, Yeshua smiles, "Today we celebrate Savta's birth into the spirit world. All of heaven is rejoicing at her return to the Light and so shall we. Does anyone want to share their thoughts?"

The children are not shy. "What will happen to Savta's body, Dod Yeshua?"

Yeshua patiently answers Jonah, "Savta's body will be returned to that of which it is made, back to the earth. In about a year, we shall dig up her clean white bones."

"What will we do with her bones, Abba?"

"We shall place them in a special box called an ossuary, then put it in the tomb by Saba's bones."

Relieved, Sarah says, "That's good, because she wants to be next to Saba."

"But she's not in her body anymore. Savta is with Eloha."

"Yes, Micah. Savta's rucha is with the Light now but some people believe that the human form can be resurrected. Like rocks, bones hold memories of their time on earth. Although some cultures burn their dead, forcing the soul to choose another form, Egyptians embalm their dead and we keep the bones of our dead so that, at the time of the resurrection, souls can recreate their forms."

Micah frowns, "But Dod Yeshua, what if your body is crippled or old and useless? Can you create a new form?"

Yeshua lowers his voice, "Son, I do not think you really need your bones to recreate the manifestation of your choice."

Behind his hand, Teoma chuckles. Abba stifles his mirth at Ima's horror, but soon everyone is laughing so the musicians begin another playful melody. Yeshua signals for Savta's body to be covered and the children toss in handfuls of soil. Teoma and Eleazer finish the work and Sarah decorates the mound with the rest of the flowers. Finally the children dance about the grave while we sing.

After celebrating late into the night, the children fall asleep where their great Savta last lay. Martha and I tuck them in. "Did you tell Savta of Eleazer's promise to support Yeshua's mission?"

Taking my hand, Martha leads me out in the hall, "No, but everything is in Divine order."

"She asked if I knew who I am."

"You are the progeny of Egyptian royalty—the keeper of the secrets." She takes my dark hand in her light one, "We must give thanks to Yeshua. I hope to only attend spiritual birthdays instead of funerals from now on."

Yeshua interrupts our further discourse by kissing Martha's cheek. "You are welcome, sister. So let us remember that when one of us dies, the others will celebrate rather than mourn."

I kiss my sister goodnight, yearning for more, but she shakes her head, whispering to let it be. As Yeshua and I enter our chambers, I turn to him. "I am so very grateful to you. This was a wonderful way for my grandmother to die. Thank you."

His eyes are soft, "Your gratitude will be completely accepted if you remember what I asked of you in the hall."

Kissing his mouth, I whisper, "I promise you, Yeshua, I shall celebrate your passing as best I can."

Holding me close, he murmurs, "That is all I ask."

Mystery of Qumran

Breath trails like smoke as our mounts race toward the pink dawn. We left the children in Martha's care with Yeshua's reassurance that we will not be in Qumran long. Still, I feel uneasy.

Immediately upon entering thirsty fields, we are surrounded by men in colorless garb, their weapons coarsely girdled by leather thongs. Although my head is covered, their attention is so uncomfortably intimate that Yeshua dismounts. Before Teoma can help me off Sheikan, Hava silently warns. *It is a breach of conduct for another man to touch your wife in broad daylight, and Mary, cover your face.* Quickly, I do as she bids while Teoma requests safe passage.

"You are King Hillel's grandson?"

Yeshua nods. My stomach flutters nervously as we follow the men, separated by a pair of foot soldiers, trailing another four pair bearing our packs. I bid Sheikan a silent farewell. The sparse grain gives way to a splattering of rough hewn houses outside the walls of the silent city. Streets lined with squat buildings crescent about a square where plainly-clad women tend to laundry. Except babes in arms, there are no children or men.

Hava, why are there only women here?
The city is segregated. Only by royal charge may soldiers pass this way.
Yeshua attends to us, *And where are the men?*
Working the fields or busy at their crafts on the other side of the city.
But when do the men and women come together?

With barely a smile Hava tightens her grip, *During the monthly festivals. They even observe Shabbat separately.* My rapidly beating heart catches my breath. *Here in Qumran, you shall learn much from the women.*

Dark eyes peek from behind chaste veils muffling excited whispers. The tension thick as clotted cream chokes Yeshua's silent reassurance, *I will come to you, love.* Hava shakes her head as we enter the palace gate. Handed over to female escorts, I beseechingly look toward my husband, being hurried away without a farewell.

Humble in comparison to my family home in Bethany, the palace of Judah bears no wealth. Stark walls flow pale as salt with nothing to attract the eye. Everything in Qumran exists for practical purposes, not simply enjoyed for its beauty. Neither are people ornamented, both men and women in pale shapeless robes sashed in blue.

My bright, fitted garments a beacon for attention, I hide within my mind musing to Hava about Yeshua's grandparents. Uncharacteristically oblivious, she does not respond. What is wrong? Can she not hear me? Reaching for Yeshua through the ethers is as impossible as moving my hand through stone.

Stopping abruptly, I grab Hava before our escorts notice. A puzzled look drifts past her golden eyes. "There is something wrong with the energies." Face close to mine, she warns me not to speak here.

In the chamam, the soil from our journey is scrubbed from our skin and then in the mikvah, we endure a ritual bath and consecration with oil. The stifling silence is broken only by chanting as priestesses exchange our garments for clean robes. Hava secures her headdress with a blue tie, but mine is rusty orange.

"Are you not of the order of Benjamin?" Hesitatingly, I nod. My mother's Kohanim lineage served the tribe of Benjamin since the time of David. So all of Qumran hales from the tribe of Judah? Before I might ask, our escort leads us to the sleeping chambers filled with excited women.

"The visitors from Galilee are here!"

A devout woman studies Hava carefully, "You were the high priestess when I was but a young acolyte." Hava nods graciously, so she is taken to the temple of Astarte.

Young women surround me. Stroking my headdress, a tall, brown-haired girl murmurs, "A daughter of the house of Hasmonaea married into the line of David."

Another girl, identical to the first, deftly unties the orange tie to reveal my hair. "The soldiers' eyes see clearly, you are most beautiful." How could these secluded women know what the soldiers think? They toss their veils upon the beds. "No need for this now. Believe me, you won't be seeing a single man anywhere near our sleeping quarters!"

"You must be Mary. I am Princess Leah and this is my twin sister, Princess Rachel. Our father, Jacob, hoped we would populate the new Yisrael." In spite of her serious expression, the rest of the girls laugh at her reference. "But alas, the crown shall not go to my father, but to Joseph and then his son, your husband. So by royal rank, you shall sit here." She forces me to take a seat on the tallest cushion.

"As your Saba is still king, I cannot sit above you," I slide down level with the rest, "and even when my husband becomes the David, I do not wish to sit above anyone."

Leah clucks her tongue disapprovingly, "And I thought the Hasmonaeans believed they were Yisrael's royalty."

I muster a gracious smile, "Not all of us, Leah. Perhaps through our marital union, the twelve tribes might become united as well."

Rachel takes my hand, "Well, until the men fight it out, we can be as sisters."

These young women old enough to marry and bear a few children make me wonder, "When do you get to be with your husbands?"

The girls look astonished. Leah answers for them. "During the festivals, if we choose, but most of us do not." How can they not want to be with their own spouses?

"I'm sorry, I do not understand."

Rachel puts an arm around my shoulder, "Mary, do you love your husband?"

"But, of course."

"I don't mean, love like you do your children, but are you attracted to him?"

"Very much so. I cannot bear to be without him."

"Sounds more like a lover than a husband." Leah laughs.

"I suppose I am fortunate in that he is my heart's desire."

"Really, it sounds very romantic, but is he a good lover?"

The twins are so forward, but I must respond, "Yes, Leah, I am more than satisfied by Yeshua in all ways."

331

Rachel squeezes me to her bosom, before planting a kiss on the top of my head, "Poor girl. It is quite apparent that she has had no other." What! My face flushes.

Sitting right in front of me, Leah speaks carefully as if teaching a child, "You must come with us tonight, then you can have a stick by which to measure your husband."

Rachel whispers in my ear, "So you won't mind if I have that handsome blue-eyed man who came with you?"

Teoma? How did they get a look at him? "He is not mine."

Kissing my cheek, she tells her sister, "Ha! I have Mary's blessing."

"We shall see about that. He belongs to whoever gets to him first." Will they accost poor Teoma? Leah laughs, "Mary, men do not have a choice in this matter. We women choose our partners, if we can decide amongst ourselves." She glares at Rachel.

A plump redhead suggests, "I am sure that he will be delighted with both of you. It's not as if you haven't had to share men before." She turns to me, "I am Princess Hester. My father is Clophas, King Hillel's third son, so I am in no way a threat to your position. Perhaps we can be friends."

I like this outspoken young woman but I'm still being clasped to Rachel's side so Hester comes over and kisses my cheek. "You can sleep next to me, Mary. If you want to go out tonight, I will take you. These two will be fighting over your male escort."

"Really, I just want to be with my husband. Is that possible?"

Hester shrugs, "I have never made such arrangements myself, other than to conceive my children." She laughs, "Oh, but Aaron can be sentimental, insisting that we spend at least one night of Pesach together."

"Are your spouses so disagreeable?"

"Our marriages were arranged to secure some political alignment. Here in Qumran everyone has a purpose and, as daughters of the house of David, our purpose is to produce enough heirs so the tribe does not die out. Perhaps your marriage is dynastic, dear? Is that why you have known no other man?"

"Yeshua and I do not live under dynastic law, although I have borne him an heir at the proper timing—our son Joshua."

"And when will you bear him another?" Hester refers to the tradition of providing at least two male heirs. I sigh.

"Childbirth is most difficult for me. My husband does not wish to chance a third."

The girls smile knowingly as Rachel asks, "So when will he take a second wife?"

What? Is this a consideration? "Yeshua loves me. He wants no other."

All sadly shake their heads. Leah speaks. "Mary, you may have only had your husband, but men, especially royalty, are bound to seek the comfort of other women."

Unlike my conversation with Ima about this very subject some seven years ago, I am not upset. "I would love to learn more about your customs in Qumran, but I am confident that Yeshua will wait until we might be together."

Rachel pulls away. "Perhaps, you do not wish to share him?"

"No, Rachel, I do not!"

Leah smiles deviously, "Listen, Mary, I would wager that if he is not under your watchful eye and one of us approaches him, your devoted husband will not refuse."

Startled, my voice catches, "If you happen upon my husband, I would ask, as your sister, that you tell him I want him and you shall see that our love for one another is true."

Heated with my frustration at these strange customs, the energy swirls threateningly. Rachel shifts about, as Hester studies me. Leah breaks the tension, "We will not take your man, even though it is selfish of you not to share, but then you are from Galilee, a barbarian culture, I am sure." It is a moment before I realize she is teasing and join the others' laughter.

Later we enjoy a sparse dinner of cooked grain and steamed vegetables. How do they maintain their plump figures on such fare? Perhaps chasing men at night is all that occupies them but I shall not tolerate being cooped up in the palace all day. Hester carefully explains that the custom of segregation has borne much creativity in Qumran. If I choose to go out at night, she laughs, I shall see a much different city.

In spite of their best efforts, I stay behind to meet my husband in the ethers, but the heavy energies prevent any contact. The girls return just before dawn smelling of men. I pretend to be asleep.

Hester touches my damp pillow. "She's been crying. Poor Mary."

"We shall make her come with us tomorrow night. It is a shame to let her wither away mourning for her husband."

"Besides, Rachel, we might need a formal introduction to her escort. He could not be found anywhere this night." Surely Teoma found pleasure in exploring the city, perhaps one of the few men who chooses his own partners.

Since the sleeping quarters face west, I awake very late and groggily try to meditate but still cannot find Yeshua. The others sleep well past noon. Hoping that my search might be more fruitful outside the palace, I join them to sneak past the guards.

Qumran is a very different city after dark. As if the rising moon calls to the inhabitants, the streets fill with both men and women, mingling, laughing, even dancing. Bonfires set in the squares attract couples, the hayye lively, sensual, full of delight. Perhaps there is some wisdom to spending time in the company of my own gender during the day, though I am not sure I could be happy with just any lover. Where, by the way, is my husband?

As suspected, the lighter energies are easier to traverse outside, but my beloved is nowhere to be found, still hidden away inside the palace. Hester leaves me to meet a friend, since the twins excused themselves as soon as we entered the square. Searching for Teoma through the ethers, I find that he is occupied, so well before dawn, I return alone to the palace.

Probing the minds of every woman in proximity, I expend much energy making some progress by late afternoon. Most muse over last night's rendezvous. How do the women of Qumran avoid pregnancy and disease? Perhaps they might appreciate attending conscious conception circles.

Outside of the heavy energy of the palace after dusk, I easily search other's thoughts. Discovering nothing about my husband, my consciousness returns to find me the focus of desire. Without concentrated effort, I cannot hear the men's actual thoughts, but their assertive attention frightens me. I escape one group only to be confronted by another. Why did I separate from the princesses?

"The most beautiful woman in all Qumran should not be alone. Come share your charms." Looking down, I move away, but more men call after me.

Before I disappear under kasa, my seraph comes. *Relax, Mary, your fear draws uncomfortable attention. Keep your head upright and breathe. I am with you always, do not be afraid.* I do as Tamaw instructs and walk past the clamoring men. *There now,* she sings softly to me, *be your sensual self. You do not have to take a lover, if you do not choose, but discover for yourself how beautifully you exist in this world.*

Walking within the wings of my seraph, I explore the city, unveiled. There is beauty in the dark, a raw sensuality in witnessing the dance of lovers on benches and against walls. The music from one square to the next implores me to dance along the streets.

In the light of day, I am only allowed to leave the palace chastely veiled. Seeking nature to contact my children, I follow the flight of a large crow to a sprawling tree and find dear Saul painting a lovely landscape. I rush into his arms, crying with delight.

"Saul, I am so happy to see you."

He looks about, "We are fortunate that my preference for men is well known here. So Mary, how do you find the ancient city?"

"I am finding pleasure in its strangeness, but being separated from Yeshua has been most difficult." Tears escape before I can wipe them away. Saul sits with me upon a blanket and I find great relief in his embrace. "I have searched the streets at night, but he has not emerged from the palace, nor does anyone seem to know about him."

Saul kisses the top of my head, "Yeshua stands against much resistance in the palace with the Zadokites and the royal advisors."

My poor husband. "What can we do to help him?"

"I have been working to garner the artisans and craftsmen's support of Yeshua. Jakob and Jochanan report much success with the Essenes. Not all agree with the rigidity of Jochan's mission."

"I am so grateful that you have helped Yeshua. Have you seen Teoma?"

"He works within the ranks of the soldiers as well as in the fields with the farmers. I have yet to speak to him, but have heard word of growing support from his efforts." Brushing my hair from my damp cheek, he says quietly, "You could help too."

"I have been stuck with princesses who sleep all day and carouse all night. I do not think they have much influence."

Saul laughs, "Use their sensuality to your advantage. Gain their favor and they shall influence with their female wiles any men who have not seen the light."

Thanking him for his wise counsel, I clasp his stained hands, "Remember trying to teach me to paint when I was a child?"

"Yes, you did show some promise, when you would sit still. Shall I send over some supplies for your amusement?"

"I would love to occupy some of these long days with art. Do you mind if I sit here to contact the children?"

Saul returns to his painting while I make myself comfortable. Within moments in the sweet air of the open land, I am in contact with my father.

Mary, what happened to you? The children expected you would visit them daily.

I am so sorry, Abba, to cause concern, but I can make no contacts from within the palace, the energies are impossibly dense. How are Sarah and Josh?

Relaxing, Abba moves into his paternal role of support. *The children are fine, having a wonderful time with their cousins. Let me see if I can help you.*

I visit with the children until Abba returns. *Mary, there is a veil of protection around the palace. Find the woman who scrambled the energies. In the meantime, stamp your hayye upon someone who can draw you to Yeshua.*

Queen Shoshana might act as a liaison between us, Abba, but I have not had an audience with her yet.

Abba laughs, *Well, perhaps you needed to meet with me first.*

Upon my return to the palace, Hava greets me. I run into her embrace. "Mary, I have not been long away, but I see that you are missing your family." Tilting up my chin, she whispers, "Especially Yeshua."

I nod tearfully, "But Hava, I have tried to find some pleasure in the holy city, going out at night with the others."

She raises a brow. "Really? You look most dissatisfied."

"Hava! I cannot find Yeshua. Did you think I would choose another?"

"I am sure the girls provided much encouragement, but no, you are too much in love with our Yeshua. Now, Mary, go and wash up. We shall dine together this evening."

Softly glowing oil lamps light the dining hall. Hava chats intimately with a tall stately woman of power—the one who scrambled the energies of the palace—the high priestess Hephziva. She looks up at my recognition, but her mind is veiled.

Smiling graciously, she invites me to sit. "Hava has told me much about you, Mary. You are the embodiment of the daughter's sacred energies. It is a lovely, sensual manifestation you have chosen, my dear."

"Thank you, Hephziva; I am honored to make your acquaintance." I bow slightly before taking my seat around the low oval table.

"You have attempted to break through the veil I have created."

"Yes, I have tried to find my husband."

She smiles at me, "And you have had some success in probing the minds around you, I see." I nod again. "But it costs you much hayye. Here, my dear, have some refreshment." She serves me a bowl of vegetable stew. "You will need this nourishment and a good night's sleep. So stay in tonight. I shall meet with you in the chamam tomorrow morning."

The chamam? I am not on my menses. Laughing, she replies, "Oh, you will be."

Sure enough the morning finds me in the chamam. It is custom in Qumran to cleanse the body thoroughly during a woman's moon cycle. Eating nothing but raw green vegetables and thin root broth purifies my insides while several ritual baths followed by deep massage draw out all tension. At the end of the first day of silence, I am brought before the high priestess.

We meditate in a triangle with Hava, a large crystal glowing between us. Deftly Hephziva leaves her body by going inside her core to emerge as a mirror image. Imitating her technique, I am out-of-body in the scrambled energies. My delight is shared by her. *I am impressed, Mary. Feel free to explore the palace, but I ask that you make no outside contacts while within this veil. The Zadoks have entrusted the security of Qumran to me.*

She teaches me much about the energies, how to access another's thoughts clearly in the density of the palace, as well as how to view distantly and move effortlessly. Excitedly I admit, "My husband has these same abilities, having trained all his life to work with the energies. I would love for you to meet him."

Touching my face gently with her long fingers, Hephziva whispers, "Your husband has no more ability than you do, dear. You are equal in the qualities of your gifts; never have I worked with a student who learns so quickly."

"I am grateful for your instruction but I believe we are all born with these gifts only most are not exposed to those who can help them stay awake and remember."

Hephziva embraces me tenderly. "So precious in your generosity, Mary. When you realize who you are, you will then truly appreciate your uniqueness."

She echoes my grandmother's words. "Yeshua tells me this as well, that when I know myself as the One knows me, then I shall be fulfilled."

"Our mashiach is very wise. And well-mated to you, my dear. I look forward to observing your progress with the people of Yisrael."

"Oh, he has plans for the goyim and the Romans as well."

For a moment she looks startled and then her countenance fades with an ancient wisdom. "His grandiose plans will be the seed of much suffering, but the fruit borne from the tree of that seed shall feed the heart of the world for many generations." I shiver from the enormity of the premonition, as Hephziva's eyes clear to their former blue-gray.

"It is best to keep your aura clear of fear, Mary, so that you do not attract that which causes you to suffer in this world."

When I offer to repay my kind mentor with the gift of conscious conception, she replies, "My dear, I am honored to work with you in this way. You do not know from whence you came, nor how it is that the remembrance of your gifts comes so easily, but someday it will be revealed to you."

After cleansing in the chamam, Hephziva asks me to share the white light with the women healers, so I hold a conscious conception circle. Anxious to practice my new skills, I accompany a sensual female entourage into the moonlight.

Searching the ethers, I find Yeshua exhausted still within the palace. After sending him love and encouragement, I return to the din of chatter, overwhelming to attend to any one mind. Those thoughts that are directed to me, about me or anyone I am familiar with come in most clearly. The rest I learn to tune out, as if I am listening not to the melody but to the music.

After I make an effort to shut out any provocative thoughts from men and, as Yeshua told me in the past, even from women, I attend to information about my friends. Men who prefer men seem delighted for Saul and Jochanan. Many are not in favor of Jochan but are open to Yeshua's message of love. Even with the Essenes, Jakob's influence seems to be effective. Teoma apparently has won the hearts of many who think highly of him and support Yeshua vicariously. Blushing to perceive that his amorous adventures have wrought an unwelcome tax, I see he's occupied with… my goodness, not one, but two lovers, and vow to find him tomorrow, praying the daylight might lessen my own need.

The following morning after a ritual washing with consecrated oils, I finally get to see Yeshua's Savta. Silver hair coiled upon her head, Queen Shoshana watches me with sharp blue eyes. "Even without ornamentation, Mary, I do not believe my grandson could have taken a lovelier wife from any of our young women."

"Thank you for your kindness, Savta." Motioning for me to sit beside her, she offers some refreshment.

"Mary, are you enjoying your time here in Qumran?"

My emotion gives me away. "I am trying to, Savta. I have been fortunate to work with the high priestess and I do enjoy the company of the princesses."

Smiling at me with regal coolness, she states, "Hephziva is quite impressed with you, Mary. That should bode well for Yeshua as her influence with the Zadoks is not to be underestimated. You realize that Yeshua faces much opposition in the elders."

"I have been told, Savta."

"You must be more careful. Fortunately, Saul is safe for a young woman." I look up at her surprised. "I am kept well informed of the comings and goings of the royal household," she says, wondering if I have been unduly influenced by the princesses.

"Savta, I have been out at night, but solely to try and contact Yeshua."

"You have not taken a lover?" I shake my head. Her look of relief is endearing. "I told Hillel that even without a dynastic relationship, and in spite of your extremely passionate nature, you would be true to our grandson."

"Savta, is it possible that I might be with Yeshua? I can travel to him now through the ethers, but I do not want to cause him any hardship."

"I can arrange a private meeting, but it must remain secret, for the Zadok believes any feminine influence to be impure. How does this type of travel work?"

"If I can but hug you, Savta, then when you hug Yeshua, I will know to come."

For a moment I think she might not agree to let me touch her, but then she nods and extends her arms to me connecting our heart centers ever so briefly. Even through her regal shell, I feel how very much she loves Yeshua. As we part, I thank her. A small nod of recognition is all that I receive before the servants escort me back to the women's chambers.

***

In stark contrast to the passionate mingling after dark, working alongside men without the distraction of women refreshes the daylight. Breathing deeply of the late morning air, Teoma feels quite accomplished. Particularly gifted with the farmers and, of course, he knows many of the zealots from time spent in the desert, he has gathered support for Yeshua while making great strides with the craft under the mentorship of the Egyptian Therapeutae. Joseph will be pleased.

"Reminiscing about last night or fanaticizing about tonight?" Epher claps him briskly on the back, interrupting his thoughts.

"Neither. I am living in the moment. At the present time, enjoying your rough companionship."

The stout man laughs deep within his belly. "Is this another concept you have learned from your mashiach?"

"Why, yes. Yeshua teaches that there is only now. Worrying about the past or the future diminishes the joy of the present moment." Not a cloud in the bright blue sky, another wonderful day in Qumran.

Nahshon interrupts their reverie from the edge of the congregating soldiers. "Brothers, pay close attention, for a vision shall pass through the square." The men turn as one.

From the palace gates saunters a petite young woman. Her elegant stride belies royal blood, but her dark hands suggest more exotic breeding than that of the fair Davidic princesses. The soldiers stand tall, each hoping to catch the eye of the elusive Galilean woman rumored to be of Egyptian heritage.

Feeling a distinct pull upon his heartstrings, Teoma brushes aside the man in front of him but can move no closer for the line of segregation is clearly marked down the center of the square. She does not come near, but with one coy glance hastens her step. His heart nearly stops.

Epher clasps his arm, "Ahh, you have been chosen, my friend."

With flushed face, Teoma steps away from the soldiers. Through several streets, he follows at an inconspicuous pace before she disappears

340

behind the outermost buildings. As soon as he turns the corner, she pushes off her headdress to enter his embrace. Pressing his cheek to her soft dark curls, his heart sings.

"Teoma, it is good to see you."

"Barchashem, you have used kasa to veil us, for I so appreciate being able to see your lovely face. Looking only at men all day is not pleasant." Her smile puts the sun to shame. Softly he caresses her cheek, the pressure of her full breasts more than he can bear. The scent of her desire overcomes him.

With seeming great effort she pushes away, breathing heavily. Green eyes feverishly bright meet his gaze. He tries to regain composure by thinking about other things, but his mind drifts to intimate freedoms gathered like wildflowers. Unlike his comrades, he enjoys the company of women, talking to them about their interests, their desires, their concerns. But he has yet to fall in love with another. *If she would have me, there would be no other.*

She looks up at him in surprise and his eyes widen. "You know my thoughts."

"Forgive me, but in attempting to locate Yeshua, I can now hear what is unspoken."

Quieting the rush of shame stirred by anger, he wonders what she perceived. Pursed pomegranate lips confirm far too much.

"Teoma, one of the reasons I came to find you, other than that I missed you, is that," she lowers her voice, "you have encountered a sexual malady."

I could have made her ill. Her cheeks flush at his chastisement.

"You need treatment and to learn to protect yourself."

"How, Mary? Can you show me?"

Sea-green eyes pool. "I'm sorry; I can as a healer," her voice quivers, "but not as a woman."

His heart brightens with hope. *She does want me after all.*

"How could you think otherwise?" She trembles passionately, "Yeshua can help you but he'll be aware of our encounter. I know no other way and frankly his knowing keeps me from seeking comfort in your embrace."

He catches his breath. "It would not feel this intense if he could have been with you these past twelve days."

"No, Teoma. It would be untrue if I said I do not desire you." Turning away from him, she runs into the field to find solace on the back of the horse.

I shall never love another woman, but as the passion between us grows, my fortitude diminishes. She looks back once before mounting the stallion and galloping away.

Overwhelmed, Teoma calms himself with a walk through the fields, but before the day grows much later, he finds that it burns to relieve himself. Cursing, he heads to the eastern edge of the city where the healers meet.

***

Day and night since arriving in Qumran, Yeshua has served the dictates of the Egyptian Therapeutae. Initially expressing disappointment that he had refused to learn the craft from Joseph, the elders soon realized that Yeshua was well accomplished in using the energies. What he learned in Britannia and Alexandria has been invaluable here in the city of his father, so he works to exhaustion alongside the Essenes healing the desert people who travel far to seek care.

When Teoma arrives, Yeshua greets him most warmly. Usually a rich forest green, Teoma's hayye sparkles with the light of many hues. "Well, if you insist on the pleasure of so many…."

"Just treat me and I will gratefully leave you to your training." Teoma gruffly interrupts, a tiny bit of violet glimmering on the surface of his hayye.

"You have been with Mary."

If you would take care of your wife, it would be easier on all of us.

Defensively he responds, "I have been struggling with more opposition than you can imagine. Jochan will not even see me. Being married, I am unclean in his eyes."

"Well, Jochan better not get anywhere near me." Yeshua cannot help but join Teoma's wry laughter. After treating the ailment, he shows Teoma how to use the white light to protect himself.

"How is she?"

"At night, she roams the streets hoping you will come out of that forsaken palace. Have you even contacted the children?" Yeshua shakes his head forlornly in the face of Teoma's lecture. "To make matters worse, in the process of trying to locate you, she has learned to read minds and I have absolutely nothing to hide from either of you!" His smile inflames Teoma. "I have always supported you, but as we get closer to the mission, I cannot support your disregard for Mary and the children." *Especially when I want nothing more than to be with them.*

Yeshua measures each word. "I know that you would love to take my place as husband and father, but it is not your time. While I am still here, I ask that you not interfere." They brace stubbornly against each other, the silence broken only by Yeshua's proclamation, "Do you think that I am unaware of my wife's desire for you? I love you as a brother but I will not share her."

I never expected you to. Backing down, Teoma leaves.

"My prince, will you please come with me?" A short, stocky Essene leads him down a familiar path.

North of Qumran, caves peer like dark eyes upon the Dead Sea. At the mouth of a large cavern, an acolyte bathes Yeshua's feet in a stone kiyyor. Adjusting slowly to the faint light of oil lamps, his eyes lock with the eye of Ra staring at the serpent intertwined about a wooden staff painted on the wall—the symbol of the Therapeutae.

"Yeshua, you are tainted by worry."

He kneels at his mentor's feet. "Kamuzu, I miss my wife."

"Hmm. In vain you seek the Zadok's blessing, purifying yourself through fasting and abstinence. Neither of which serves your purpose, Yeshua."

"But my cousin, Jochan…"

"The son of Zechariah has adopted a most stringent way of life. I understand your need as the Davidic heir to gain support of your tribesmen, for your father has left behind doubt that the eldest son can produce a worthy leader. His escape was not from Qumran but from the dictates of royalty."

"Seeing how my grandfather lives, I cannot blame my father for seeking a simpler way of life."

"You mean a less restrictive one." The renowned healer continues, "If you do not gain support of your own tribe, what hope do you have for the rest of Yisrael?"

Yeshua shakes his head. "Kamuzu, I believe my purpose is to teach all people, not just my kinsmen."

"When you assume the kingship and bind it to the healing role usually reserved for the priesthood, then all shall know your sovereignty."

"I am not ready."

"No, you are not. But soon you shall see that unbinding that which is bound shall free you to partake of the cup of immortality."

Yeshua has resisted his father's way of the seeking nura through the use of herbs, believing there is a pure connection to the Divine and thus eternal enlightenment. Under Kuzumu's tutelage, he learns that only the wise king who is willing to remix the bloodline with the Egyptian royalty retains the pure knowledge.

When he returns to his chambers, the strange veil cast upon the palace drains him further. How lush was Mary's purple stain upon Teoma's hayye. In the cast of patriarchal energies, he feels quite lost. Three more days pass before he is brought to a sparsely adorned sitting room and finally sees a woman's face. Delighted, he nearly weeps.

"My grandson, you do not look well."

"Savta, I am so much better being here with you."

"At least you have come home. Your father never returned." He nods and reaches to take her hand, but she shakes her head. "You know the Zadok beliefs."

He laughs. "My grandmother can hardly count as a contaminating influence." Rising, he embraces her. She sits stiffly for a moment before relaxing in his arms. "There. Now I feel even better." With a smile he sits back on his cushion.

Before another word passes, a delicious form fills his lap. Mary! Veiled from all but his eyes, he does not move lest he alert his grandmother. Tears on his thigh raise a passion suppressed too long. Swallowing thickly, he listens to Savta who sits undisturbed before him, apologizing for his suffering.

A delicate hand slips beneath his tunic and surely he no longer suffers! Before he can move, his grandmother hugs him briefly.

"Mary, will be here momentarily, Yeshua. You have until sunset." Although he's silenced by passion, Savta takes her leave without question. As the heavy wooden door closes, Yeshua surrenders to the moment. Mary's expression reflects the bitterness upon her tongue.

"I have not spilled my seed since last we met." And now Jochan will not see him for who knows how much longer.

She sits up abruptly, and strangely he cannot hear her thoughts. "I apologize for interrupting your visit, but you must have hugged your grandmother earlier."

How lovely is her face. "Yes, I was so happy to see her. It has been so difficult. Jakob and Simeon tried to warn me, but I did not appreciate how much resistance there is among the elders. Jochan will not bother to emerge from the desert." And may never, since he could not resist her.

She sighs and glances toward the sun low on the windowsill.

He goes on, wearily, "I have spent days healing the most gravely ill. The priests test my knowledge of scripture as if I am an acolyte. Even cleansing my body to purify myself, it was eight days before I could get an audience with Simeon the Aviatar and only yesterday, I got to see Zechariah."

"I am sorry, but I thought you would want to…."

He touches a smudge of blue that stains her silken cheek. "What's this?"

Bitterness laces her chuckle. "In spite of your struggles, the others have rallied support for you. Jakob and Jochanan with the Essenes, Saul with the artisans and craftsmen, and Teoma has the support of the entire military force, as well as most of the farmers. In exchange for learning the white light of protection, the women listen to me explain your mission of love. Convinced you are the mashiach, for only the wife of the redeemer would refuse all the handsome men in Qumran, the princesses are quickly working their way through the ranks. I have heard Jochan's disciples must be celibate but at the rate your cousins seduce men, he will not have much following here by the next festival."

He stares amazed. "You have done all of this for me?"

"Yes, we believe in you, desiring to live one with Love, like you." Her honest portrayal brings tears to his eyes.

"Since being here, I have never felt farther from the One."

She clasps him to her breast, "You are never alone, Yeshua. But when you keep us from you, how can we be of support?"

"The energies in this palace are so scrambled I cannot make any type of connection. How did you figure out how to work with it?"

"Abba told me to go to the source. The high priestess who placed kasa over the palace taught me how to pierce it." He has taken for granted her talents with the energies.

"Yes, but more importantly you have not asked for my help."

His heart nearly stops. "My mind is veiled, how can you …?"

"I know not, perhaps you cannot maintain the veil within these energies." *Oh no, she perceived my thoughts after….*"So if it's already too late, then can you tell me why you have gone against your own intuition and prepared to meet with Jochan when you told the council at home that it was too soon?"

He frowns defeated. "That is what you want, an answer?"

"No actually, I want you to be true to yourself." Her sea-green gaze becomes stormy.

Breathing deeply, he looks toward the setting sun. *How can I satisfy everyone?* Kissing him on the mouth for the first time since she arrived, Mary whispers, "Just satisfy yourself," and using raza, she disappears, leaving an ache in his heart.

***

Traveling embittered through the ethers, I find myself standing before brilliant waves of color touching souls of every hue. Whenever I paint, I am returned to that moment of ecstatic union with the One. If I never again make love, I shall relive my experiences by painting them. Not long alone with my personal woes, soon the princesses surround me.

"Mary, why are you crying?" Hester asks, putting an arm around my shoulder. Sadly, I shake my head.

Leah interrupts, "Can't you see she's too upset to talk?"

Looking at my painting, Rachel remarks, "Mary, this is pretty. What is it?"

"It is my rendition of the conception of my son."

Rachel peers closely. "Where are you? I can't make out any people."

"These are the energies I observed when my son took root in my gan eden…."

"So this is what sex is like with that husband of yours?" *When we have it,* I think bitterly, answering Leah with a nod.

"Is this because he's the mashiach or because of your talents with the energies?"

"Rachel, perhaps it's our connection through love."

Leah looks carefully at me. "So why do you look so miserable?"

I do not answer. Hester replies in my stead, "Because she hasn't been with him. How can you be so insensitive?"

"I heard from the servants that the Queen set up a secret meeting. She has just returned from being with him."

"Then what is the matter, Mary?" Hester asks kindly.

"He just wanted to talk!"

"Talk! He must be mad." Leah shouts.

"He is preparing to meet with Jochan," I explain unconvincingly.

"Jochan! Why would he want to meet with Zechariah's insane son?" Rachel asks indignantly.

"I think he is being pressured to bring their two viewpoints together. Yeshua is truly committed to the mission."

"But you said his mission is one of love. I hoped that another way of being in relationship with a man was possible." Wistful in her disappointment, Hester turns away.

"This is why sex and love should not be mixed. Look at Mary, she's mourning for a husband who believes he is our mashiach, but cannot save his own marriage."

"Leah, he's usually very committed to me. Something is wrong."

Rachel whispers, "Perhaps he's being held captive."

All is quiet for a moment, until Leah suggests, "Come, Mary, you have paint on your face." Following them into the baths, I become the object of their pity as they think how pathetic love is, glad not to deal with it.

Hester brushes my hair, *Perhaps she should just meet with Teoma tonight.* Frowning I look at her.

"Hester, how do you know Teoma?"

Her eyes widen. "How do you know what I'm thinking?"

Rachel comes rushing over. "The high priestess has been working with her. Mary, what am I thinking?"

"That you wonder if I am with Teoma tonight, will he want you at the next festival."

Rachel laughs, "Leah, see if Mary can read your mind."

Leah looks skeptical, until I tell her, "You are wondering that if you could be with Yeshua, perhaps you could climax in color." She smiles and nods as Hester speaks.

"Mary, please come out with us tonight. You'll feel better."

"Why would you think I was going to meet Teoma tonight?"

Leah's eyebrows raise, "Teoma's the one Rachel and I want?"

Hester nods, before turning to me, "Everyone knows that he followed you a few days ago."

You can get away with nothing in Qumran. "I had something to tell him. We have no plans for tonight."

"But you shall come with us, anyhow. He will help you forget about your husband."

"Leah, I cannot do that. You do not understand. Yeshua can read minds, too. Teoma is his best friend and I love my husband. Although I am upset about what happened today, it will not be made right by my being with another man, especially Teoma."

Leah nods knowingly. "I knew it. You are in love with him and I would wager he's in love with you." Shaking my head, I cannot explain this away.

Rachel produces a clean robe, pulling the stained one off me. "Here, you are coming with us, so you might as well look presentable." With that I am escorted out of the palace by eager princesses.

Although early, bonfires light the square. Heading for the center, the princesses push aside a large crowd of soldiers and other earthy men, to be followed by more young women. Excited by our presence, the men are quite vivid in their expectations for this evening. I gasp to perceive one fair-haired man's crude thoughts. Leah places an arm around my shoulders.

"Hear me, brave men of Qumran. This is the wife of our mashiach. Mary can perceive your impure thoughts, so clear your minds or her husband will not consider saving you or the fruit of your loins." I nod to confirm their immediate focus on something else, mostly their own sandals. "Good," Leah says, "now, we need your help. The new moon of first Adar is a half a week away and there is talk that Yeshua will not be allowed to participate in the festivities."

A tall, very thin man with a particularly vivid imagination joins the group forcing me to move closer to Leah. She glares at the newcomer, "Isaiah, whatever you are thinking is upsetting Mary. Don't even consider looking at her, let alone being with her in any way. This girl has great powers with the energies, so only the mashiach can handle her. You would explode in a puff of blue smoke if you but laid a hand on her." With bowed head, Isaiah steps back and the rest of the men think even purer thoughts.

I feel Teoma's energy part the crowd. Losing their nerve, the princesses step away. "Why are you out here tonight? Didn't you get to see Yeshua?" His proximity bringing mixed comfort, tears course down my cheeks. Jaw set, eyebrows furrow into a frown, "What happened?"

Hester answers for me, "He just wanted to talk." Teoma's ire rises, but he quickly quiets his rage before gently brushing the hair from my face. The crowd gasps.

"The Galilean has lived with them for so long, he is immune to the energies." Leah's explanation seems to satisfy the crowd.

Speaking over my head, Teoma addresses them, "There must be some way to get Yeshua out of the palace."

Rachel assists, "Yes, we believe he is being held captive. Mary insists that this is not his usual behavior."

"Well, I should hope not. If I had her for a wife, I would not be talking."

"Keep your voice down, Esau, you don't want to offend her."

Behind me, others stir, so I turn in Teoma's embrace to face them. "We thought Yeshua's mission was different than Jochan's."

"Yeshua does not advocate celibacy, he's only supplicating the Zadokites." Teoma raises his voice, "But it is time he met the people of Qumran."

"I met him. Nice young man, he healed my crippled foot."

"Look at that. I was wondering where your limp went." A ruddy farmer claps the once-crippled man on the back.

"Yes, he's healed many of us," Teoma whispers into my curls.

"How many of you have taken full advantage of the white light of protection?" Hester asks the murmuring crowd which cheers as soon as the women remind the men about it. "Well, you can thank Mary for that gift." With one voice, they express their gratitude.

"Let's demand that Yeshua be allowed to participate in the new moon festival." Leah insists, but the crowd wants to know why.

"Because if Yeshua attends, Mary will dance for him." Jochanan winks at me from across the fire with Saul at his side.

The grumbling settles down. "Well, if you boys could appreciate her dance, it must be something worth seeing."

"Beyond your wildest dreams." Saul entices the crowd.

Teoma squeezes my arms, "See, they all want you to be with Yeshua." *And what do you want?* He smiles, unaware of my thoughts.

"So how do we get Yeshua out of the palace and to the festival?" A very good question.

"We make our request and until it is met, nobody works."

The crowd gasps at Leah's plan, "Nothing will get done!"

"That's the point. Qumran will not survive for long without everyone helping." Murmurs run through the crowd. "And we do not meet at night, not until Mary can be with her husband."

The crowd grumbles loudly forcing Teoma to catch me as my knees give out. "The Zadoks may not appreciate you congregating, but they know it is necessary to keep the people of Qumran satisfied. You work peacefully during the day and enjoy your free time at night." The crowd murmurs its agreement. Teoma pauses for Leah to speak.

"So they will soon see we are serious in our request. We want our mashiach." The crowd cheers.

Teoma leaves them with a last thought, "Since it will be three weeks for the Davidic prince and his wife, you might all get to witness a tremendous display of hayye. At Sucot, the grain bends unbroken in intricate patterns wherever they lie." Incredulous, the people stare, mouths open.

Saul laughs, "So it is settled. We shall send word to the Zadok that the people of Qumran have spoken." With a loud cheer, the crowd starts hugging one another.

"We start tonight!" Men groan as women move away from them. Leah turns to me whispering, "See how much your sisters appreciate the white light. They will not entertain any men until Yeshua shows up."

"Thank you." I hug her.

"Please put in a good word with Teoma. Tell him my sister and I will be well worth waiting for." But he's fully aware of their intentions. The crowd begins to disperse.

Teoma walks me back to the palace, well behind the princesses, "So won't you grace me with a smile?"

I turn to smile up at him, "Thank you, Teoma."

Shrugging he replies, "Yeshua can be so stubborn sometimes, but I do love him. We had words that day after I saw you."

"I know."

Halting my steps with a hand on my arm, Teoma is surprised. "He told you?"

"No, I was still attached to you and overheard your conversation through the ethers."

"Mary, now that we have given voice to our feelings, we must try and remember that we love Yeshua, no matter how frustrated we are with him."

Nodding, I think that he has always been the strongest of us. He turns me around and pushes me toward the hidden gate behind the palace. "Sleep well, Mary."

And I do for the first time in weeks.

Portals of Passion

The morning of the festival, Queen Shoshana comes with an entourage of servants bearing gifts of sheer veils in many hues. Since Hava has such a flair for dressing, she is asked to outfit us for the evening. We thank her graciously. The queen only nods before draping across my shoulders a deep blue silk fringed with rare gold sheqels that jingle with my slightest movement.

"Thank you so very much, Savta." I cannot help but hug her.

Tears pool in her eyes, but she says stiffly, "You will be the queen someday. Wear this gift from our tribal mothers in joy." She takes her leave with a regal air.

Admiring the shawl, Hava remarks, "This is quite an honor to be presented with the royal colors before Yeshua has come into power, Mary. The Queen is showing her full support of you."

Nodding, I carefully place the shawl on the bed. "Hava, I am not a very good seamstress. How are we to make garments before this evening?"

"My dear Mary, we will use these beautiful cloths to our best advantage. This is quite a different dance than what you have experienced in Galilee."

"But Hava, how will I know what to do?"

Touching my cheek, she replies, "I will hold images for you, just do what you do best—dance with the energies."

From the various silks in contrasting colors, Hava finally decides so I stand before her and she wraps a purple cloth about my hips. A flash of memory surfaces. *I'm a little girl, perhaps seven, at the beach with Yeshua's family.*

All the children played and swam naked, but Hava wore beautiful cloths wrapped around her ample figure. Finding one lying in the sand, I tried to emulate her but she knelt before me, folding the wide linen in half then wrapping it about my tiny hips.

Looking up, she smiles, "Do you remember when I dressed you at the beach?"

I nod and touch her precious face whispering, "I think I shall need something on top this time." Hava's laughter fills the room.

By the time the sun sets, we are ready. Attired in layers of silk skirted low on their hips, sheer veils barely concealing their bellies, the princesses don colorful shawls to be placed upon the men of their choice tonight. Kohl-lined eyes peek over stained cheeks and lips. Strands of lapis lazuli and pink sapphire adorn ankles and wrists ringing cheerfully as the princesses hurry from the palace.

Hava has adorned me a bit differently. Bright purple silk tied low on my right hip, deep green on the left and my breasts covered in rich gold twisted together and tied at my neck. Over my shoulders lie sheer silks of pale gold and lavender, loosely tucked into the ties at my hips. In spite of the princesses' insistence, Hava refuses to paint more than a fine line to outline my eyes which appear more Egyptian than ever. On my head, the royal shawl jingles as I walk. Sighing, I pass my hand under the sheer cloth at my hip. I might as well be naked.

Crowded with excited people, the center of the city is alive again. Music drifts from the edge of the large square cleared for dancing but no one yet reclines on the wide carpet strewn with cushions nearest the palace. The princesses encircle to shield me from the crowd, but I do not perceive Yeshua.

Leah is upset. "He should be here waiting for you. What is taking so long?" Before sitting by the high priestess, Hava advises I veil myself with kasa. Teoma sits with Jakob, Jochanan, and Saul at the west edge of the circle. Hester whispers encouragement over her shoulder, "You'll be fine when we leave you to dance, Mary."

A loud drumming draws our attention toward an entourage of soldiers filing past to surround three sides of the carpet as the king and queen take their seats on the highest cushions. More drumming begins and a priest donning a high cap enters.

"Simeon the Aviatar!" Rachel whispers, "Well, at least one of them showed."

Last comes Yeshua. He stands humbly before his grandparents. "Hmm!" Leah purrs, "I didn't get a good look at him before. Yeshua is quite handsome."

He is. Dressed in the white robes of an Essene, girded by a deep blue sash, his hair cascades down his shoulders, his beard neatly trimmed. My appraisal stirs my desire which calls to him, for he searches the crowd. *I thought she would be here.* Giggling, the princesses wave and he graces them with a smile.

King Hillel rises. The drumming ceases and Yeshua drops to one knee.

"Children of Judah, my queen and I welcome you. In honor of Adar, the month of joy, we celebrate with the finest of the loins of David. May I present to you, Yeshua bar Joseph."

Standing, Yeshua bows to the king and queen. "Savta, Saba, I am in deep appreciation for your support and this opportunity to meet my tribe." Turning to the crowd, he bows again, "Brothers and sisters, I thank you for so warmly welcoming my wife and me."

He brings in the hayye of peace bathing all in its sunset hue, "I came here to teach, yet it is I who have learned from my dear companions that growth begins within the heart, and you are the heart of the desert." Cheering, the crowd settles into his comfortable energy. "The strength of a mountain is not at its highest point, but at its wide firm base. The people of Qumran are the foundation of this mountain of faith. I entrust to you my mission, which is of love. This life is to be lived in loving joy so let us celebrate this night together. A reunion of friends and families and, I pray, of lovers as well." The crowd yells excitedly and the king signals for the music to begin.

The women begin dancing, the princesses at the center. A sweet harmony embraces the crowd with smoky hayye. Not visible to anyone, I dance delighted in the silk swirling about my legs waiting through many songs for a sign from Hava. Choosing partners with their colorful shawls, the women slowly settle, Leah and Rachel dancing seductively in front of Teoma.

Yeshua searches, *My love, where are you?*

Hephziva chuckles as I glide close to him. *You are a temptress, my dear. Soon, very soon, it will be your turn.*

Dancing to the progressively faster music, my desire nearly pierces the kasa. Finally, all of the women have chosen and sit in a half circle in front of the men. Hava invites me into the center. My movement forms a whirlwind of energy catching Yeshua's attention. Silently, Hephziva instructs me to release the kasa.

Twirling faster and faster to the beating drum, I lower my vibration to match that of the world. Gasps and murmurs erupt from the crowd as I appear. Although moving too rapidly to see my beloved, I hear his grateful thoughts. The energies reflecting the color of my scarves, suddenly, the music stops. So do I.

Smiling, Yeshua reaches for me, but I move beyond his grasp.

Like a gliding serpent, my dance becomes long and seductive. Hava encourages me to show my face, so I drape the shawl over my outstretched arms, the tiny tambourines praising my effort. Beads of sweat pearl on oil-glistened skin, dark curls stick to my neck. The shawl burdening my shoulders drops low on my hips, its coins matching their throbbing pace. My fevered body yearns to be cooled by the night air, so without further instruction, I remove first one then the other veil from my shoulders.

Very good, Mary. Let him but glimpse your beautiful body. Hava advises. Yeshua asks silently what will cover me. *Not much.*

The colorful silks caress the night, light as butterflies' wings. Only the twisted scarf covering my breasts, gloriously bare from hip to neck. As the gossamer scarves graze the perimeter of onlookers, male desire spiky and hot is tempered by the fluidity of the females. I dance in front of Jochanan, slipping the lavender scarf coolly about his neck. He smiles up at me as my hips keep the tambourines alive.

"Is it a lover she desires or a dance partner?" With a twirl, I take my scarf, answering the question.

Upon Yeshua, I pour the lavender scarf. The crowd sings its praise as the golden scarf swirls about with a lover's caress. When I coil it too into his lap, nothing more hides me. Unencumbered I dance, leaning back into the energies, eyes closed, floating above the ground. Hephziva advises, *Let the energies hold you and drop down through your root to anchor yourself to the earth.*

Imagining a blood red cord emerging from my lowest energy center to run down my inner thighs, I ask the Great Ima to accept my connection. With a deep rumbling groan, she opens and I am rooted. Gold and lavender adorning him, Yeshua rises to his knees, calling urgently to me. Loosening the silk at my hip, I match the rhythm of the energies swirling into climax. The golden sheqels of the Queen's scarf scream out in passion. Even in silence Yeshua is hoarse with desire, *Mary, please come to me.*

So I dance as close as I dare, nectar mingling with sweat. The moisture clasps the sheer scarves to my legs when my twirling motion slows. Thinly veiled in gold, I glide to my husband. Hungrily, he grasps my legs, barely hampering my swaying hips, stripping me of the thin cloth. Freed, I dance out of his reach.

Finally unencumbered, the tiny tambourines sing out joyfully from my hips. Hava laughs heartily at my abandon. Inebriated by the blue-gold energies, I ache for my beloved splashed by the color of my passion. As the energies enclose me, the crowd disappears, Hava and Hephziva slipping away like a dream. There is no king, nor queen, no princesses behind, nor friends to the side—only me and my great unmet desire.

Raising my arms, the wet knot resists my fingers for only a moment. Yeshua rises to join me, drawing me close for a kiss. As I melt into his embrace, he releases the queen's shawl, letting it slip down to my ankles. Tearing at his robe with anxious fingers, I find his heated flesh.

Naked to the heavens, we feverishly explore one another. When he lifts me upon him, the air is pierced by my cries as wave after wave crystallizes the energies. The intense hayye lifts us from the face of the earth, the scarves floating golden and lavender. In a rainfall of energy, the color of our passion merges into pure white oozing through the mantle of the earth.

Barchashem! Yeshua thought to use kasa to shield us, for I was too besotted with desire to remember. He sets me down. "Were you to bare yourself before all of Qumran?"

"By the end of my dance, I was not aware of anything but my desire to be free of that which bound me." Looking at his precious face, I kiss him deeply, yearning for more.

He strokes my cheek, whispering, "I was a fool to let you languish alone for so long," and searches my eyes. "Mary, in but a few weeks you have learned so much about the energies. You must teach me what you know."

"Now that I can finally read your mind, I would like to exist on equal footing for a while."

He kisses me so deeply my passion re-ignites. "I shall find how you managed to overcome the density of the palace energies sooner or later." Pulling away from my hand, he continues, "So we can make a trade…"

"I will not pay for sex!" I sit up, parting us in sticky dampness.

He tries to draw me back. "I am teasing, dear."

"Was this a show for your tribe, Yeshua?" I stand abruptly, voice raised, "You have no idea how difficult it was for me to resist my desire for Teoma while you were courting Jochan with your celibacy!" Frustrated, I struggle with the scarves unable to cover my nakedness. Yeshua grabs my arm.

"Mary, please, do not leave me."

Sobbing, I drop to my knees. "If you ever do this again, I will not wait for you. Do not choose between the mission and me."

Saddened by my threats, his eyes darken. "Truly I underestimated how affected you were by my actions." *Your non-actions*, I project, grimly satisfied by his wince. He tries again, "Mary, I plan to give you up when it is time. I...."

"That is precisely the problem, Yeshua. I am living on the edge of losing you. You'll finish this mission, then leave to join with the One, giving me to Teoma like some gift. But you will be leaving behind your soul mate." Angry frustration salts the fresh wound. Suddenly, exhausted, I feel a gentle caress of hayye.

Bring him to the temple of Astarte. Come now, follow the energies.

Pulling Yeshua up with me, I obey Hephziva's command. Veiled by her hand, we walk to the far north of the city. Yeshua hesitates before yielding to the comforting feminine energy of Astarte. In the alcove of the great hall, we are welcomed by Hava, who covers us with warm robes. Once in the baths, we are left to the attentions of young acolytes.

Yeshua has not spoken since we were in the square, his thoughts a confused jumble of excuses for his behavior, none of which satisfies him enough to say aloud. I fall asleep too tired to struggle with him any more.

At dawn I am awakened by Hava sitting on the edge of the bed. Without a word, she clasps me to her ample bosom. Why do I find more comfort in Hava's embrace than my husband's? At the sound of my weeping, Yeshua rises wondering what is wrong now. *Your duties as a husband are not limited to providing for her sexual satisfaction.*

Yeshua's hayye softens at Hava's warning, "Mary, I am sorry." Yet I do not leave the comfort of her arms. Releasing his barriers, Yeshua comes to be held. The trials of the past three weeks engulf my mind, but my husband does not respond. How can he hear her silent communication, but not mine? Gently withdrawing myself, I look into his eyes and for the first time, do not fall in.

Yeshua desperately tries to grasp the situation. *What will happen to our relationship now that she will know me so intimately?*

Through quivering lips, I ask, "Why are you afraid for me to know you?" His eyes widen.

"I consciously veiled my mind, but you pierced it."

"If it will make you feel better, I will ask Hephziva how to allow you access to my mind." Hava looks at me with concern. *Will you give your power to him?*

But he is my beloved and this comes between us.

Mary, Hephziva joins our conversation through the ethers, *you will learn to control your emotion and this veil but I must agree with Hava, do not give up your newly-discovered powers—even to Yeshua.*

Yeshua recognizes her hayye. "Mary, what did she advise?"

Clasping his hands softens his stance somewhat. "Not to give away my power." His look is endearing, *but I would never hurt you.* "While here in Qumran, I learned too well that I can still be hurt unintentionally."

Great pain passes through Yeshua's eyes. Taking both my hands in his, he whispers, "I was not considering us when I made the decision to submit to the will of the Zadoks. The longer I was there, the harder it was to feel you, my love. Only when you finally came to me did I realize that you had become my closest confidante." Searching for a reaction, but stymied, he continues, "Unable to bear your unhappiness, Teoma had the courage to challenge me."

"He said we must not forget how much we love you, rather than give in to our passion for one another."

"Yes, but if I could no longer make you happy, then you would see that his love for you is greater than his love for me."

Hava puts her arms around us both. "We must give thanks to the Creator for this triangle that serves the three of you so well."

I cannot help but smile as Yeshua gives her a kiss, "Dear Hava, you are most wise. Since all the fasting and praying with the Zadoks came to naught, perhaps the priestesses of Astarte will help me see the light."

Handing us our robes, Hava chuckles, "I have never seen you act in such a coarse male fashion before last night." Yeshua's face flushes red. "I assured Hephziva that you were quite capable of creating kasa, but clearly you were lost in the moment."

Yeshua halts. "So exactly when did the high priestess veil us?"

Hava moves us along the hall, "Not until your glory was revealed." He shakes his head, seeming to shrink before us.

"The tribe of Judah did desire to meet their leader, Yeshua."

"Not like that, Mary." I do not protest, leaving him to fester.

In the sanctuary, large open windows tempt the early morning sunshine to gleam from crystal adorned altars. Like a living spring, a marble water fountain bubbles and spurts gaily. Hephziva invites us to sit at a low table. Yeshua admires the craftsmanship of the fragrant cedar.

"My Abba made this."

A subtle sensuality hides behind her smile. They were lovers once. At her nod, Yeshua asks, *What is she telling you?*

She only confirmed a feeling I had, that's all.

Hephziva thanks me in veiled silence, *Relationships between fathers and sons can be delicate, dear. In fact that is what we shall explore today.* Clearly not happy to be left out, my husband shifts and frowns. "Yeshua, do you know why you came to your father's birthplace?"

"I am here to gain support of the people of Qumran before my mission begins."

Hephziva quietly asks again, "No, son, why are you here?"

Frowning, Yeshua searches her face then turns toward Hava and me. This is about Joseph's withdrawal from him. When Hephziva nods to me, Yeshua desperately requests my help. I share my thought and his brow furrows deeply in consternation.

"So I am here to heal my relationship with my father?"

There is more. I turn and through his eyes see his soul. My husband has come to heal not only this earthly relationship, but to release his patriarchal image of Eloha.

Hephziva beams at my realization, so I allow Yeshua to access my vision. Absorbing the hayye of his soul work, tears flow and he reaches for me to hold him. In the pure silver of Yeshua's aura, a gray cord of sorrow is bound to the belief that only a great sacrifice will release it.

"Everything necessary to fulfill this mission has been afforded you. Joseph has sacrificed all that he knew in Qumran to follow the guidance, often living counter to societal norms. He has opened his home to the great mystics and has left his family to bring you to foreign teachers." Hephziva pauses, "And as we speak, he prepares for his last great sacrifice."

With wide eyes, Yeshua listens. "But he has counseled me all of my life to release my own sacrificial hayye."

"All fathers want more for their sons than they have for themselves." She waits while he absorbs this insight. "Why, in the company of men, do you lose yourself?"

"Because I see in them the reflection of my own self-judgment and then try to win their favor through sacrifice. "

"Your mother loves you unconditionally, but what she does not see is your humanness, which your father must balance for you. You are a harsh judge of your humanity, Yeshua, although like your Ima, you feel love for most others unconditionally."

My chest constricts for I know two people he loves conditionally. Turning, he cries, "It is you and me." This is also what he came to heal.

Silently, Hephziva asks Hava to join her in bringing the healing energies. The crystals glow in soft hues reflecting the white light which Yeshua's hayye expands to absorb. Tenderly taking my hand, the sacred feminine returns to our marriage.

With a great sigh, Yeshua looks up. "Thank you. I have gained more insight and healing in this short time with you than in weeks with the Zadoks."

Hephziva smiles, "Perhaps someday, son, you shall be open to allowing a patriarchal figure to envelope you in unconditional love."

He nods whispering, "I hope so."

***

Once alone in the inner sanctum, Hephziva returns her focus upon the large crystal in the center of the round table where the hayye of a visitor awaits.

My dear friend, how are you doing amongst the Essenes?

Your humor would not be appreciated here in Qumran, Belshazzar. The Essenes take their role of fighting forces of darkness quite seriously.

The Aksum king laughs heartily. *Do they not recognize the prince of peace within their midst?*

Unfortunately, young Yeshua has much to overcome with his own tribe, but last night his lovely wife created an opening with a most passionate dance.

Ahh! I have not seen Mari-a dance since she was a little girl. I took Syrus into my confidence at that time.

Although he did not interfere with her development, he provided no training.

Syrus dealt the best he could within the limitations of his beliefs. She was introduced to the teachers at Mount Karmel by the boys.

The boys?

Yes, Yeshua and Teoma would include her in their youthful adventures.

And Joseph agreed?

Unfortunately, no. He was most upset to find out that they had been covertly studying with the women. Syrus provided excellent oversight until he discovered that the boys included his daughter in their escapades. The trio was split and I was sent unceremoniously home.

The king of all Aksum dismissed by a prince of a diminishing Hebrew tribe! Hephziva smiles, shaking her head.

Belshazzar chuckles. *Joseph was sorely disappointed. He resented opening his home and sharing the fruits of his labor so that Zsao and Reiti could fill the heads of his son and wife with 'impractical mysticism'. He thought he had found an ally in me until I reminded him that he gave up the life of royalty for that of a laborer. In extreme haste, he took his son to Ambrose.*

Did our Druid friend's magic prove to be practical enough for Joseph?

He believed Ambrose would provide a more masculine balance for his young son, but Yeshua resisted, cherishing the sacred feminine that had been so carefully tended all his youth. On a second journey to Britannia, Ambrose sent Yeshua off through the ethers to study with his beloved mentors. Reiti escorted him throughout the Hindus region, yet Yeshua spent much of his time with Zsao's master in the Himal range, unbeknownst to Joseph.

How did Ambrose keep Joseph unaware of his son's activities?

The clever sorcerer kept him and his friend of the house of Arimathaea occupied with pursuits of eternal life.

The craft has always drawn Joseph's attention. As a youth, he spent much time studying with the Egyptian Therapeutae.

Ahh. Yes, but his practice lies dormant in Nazareth.

It does not appear that Ambrose had much influence for Yeshua is struggling with the patriarchal energies of Joseph and the tribal elders.

Very good! Soon he shall enter a dark time. Dear Hephziva, are you willing to support Mari-a?

Of course! She is a delight, not yet fully cognizant of her powers, but very near to sharing her gifts with the world.

Belshazzar sighs. *Let us hope that Mari-a waits for her husband to pass through the depth of his despair.*

The stars have revealed most trying times ahead for this young couple.
The two old friends bid one another farewell.

***

The desert sky swollen with clouds casts a grey light on the day I finally get to see Yeshua's Saba. With an unusual display of emotion, the king hugs me, whispering an apology for separating us. Shoshana compliments her grandson on achieving the support of Qumran.

Simeon the Aviatar joins us for lunch. The small thin man has a slight paunch, a balding crown, and a great affection for Yeshua. His very erratic hayye has multihued connections to many realities. Yeshua tells me silently that Simeon is believed to be insane.

After apologizing profusely for what he calls very poor manners on the part of Jochan for refusing to see Yeshua, Simeon announces, "When my beautiful cousin, Miriam, was brought before me, I knew I was witnessing a miracle." Looking around, he seems to lose focus, until Yeshua touches his arm.

"Thank you, son. Where was I? Oh, yes. I had the authority to sanction her pregnancy, but the priesthood was not in favor of supporting any severance of the dynastic laws. Unlike my brethren, I am not a sheep prone to following any man's law but trust my own guidance."

Again he pauses to scan our faces, stopping at me. Rising, he puts a hand on his chest, "My, aren't you lovely. Have we met?"

Yeshua intervenes again, "Simeon, this is my wife, Mary. You were telling us why you sanctioned my Ima's pregnancy."

"Well, my son, after much prayer, I received divine guidance that Miriam carried the long-awaited mashiach." With a deep breath and a grand wave of his arms, he turns to Yeshua. "So by the highest authority, I sanctioned the pregnancy and your parents were able to be wed. In spite of what some may think, you are the legitimate heir of King David, but more so, you are the embodiment of the Divine Son."

With flair, he gets up, nearly dancing across the room. Yeshua smiles. Simeon stops in mid-twirl. "That's it!" He points at me. "You are the Elat!" Rushing to my side, he drops to his knees and takes my hands in his. "I saw you dance. You rooted the Divine Light of Heavenly Father into Mother Earth."

I am touched by his deep reverence, "Thank you, Simeon. It was my pleasure to dance for you."

"You know me, Elat?" Great tears well in his eyes.

Gently, I extract my right hand to touch his bearded cheek, his tears wetting my fingertips. Within his gray eyes, a rainbow soul in touch with all but connected to nothing. Only within the pure white ray of the One does his rapidly vibrating aura settle ever so briefly upon the earth realm. He agreed to help prepare the way for Yeshua by sanctioning Miriam's pregnancy. It was his final purely lucid moment, for in the aftermath of the pressure from the Zadoks, his mind escaped into the realm of disconnected nothingness. Yeshua's presence grounds dear Simeon, for my husband's hayye is that of Love like the One's.

Leaning forward, I kiss his smooth head, "Yes, dear Simeon, I know you."

Thanking him for being so gracious to me, Yeshua helps the Aviatar to his feet, seats him upon some cushions, and places healing hands upon his head. The white light connects with the priest's fragmented aura, the multihued hayye softly blending into the pinkish orange of the setting sun. Simeon the Aviatar relaxes into a deep sleep.

Yeshua's Saba speaks from the head of the table, "Your compassion, Yeshua, for all you come in contact with will serve you well. And Mary, my dear, you are beloved by the people. Twice now I have witnessed the sacred in your union. Simeon is correct, as Yeshua is the essence, you are the presence of the Divine."

He smiles at me graciously, before turning back to Yeshua. "Let not the laws of man deter you from your purpose. Keep Mary close by your side to remind you of how beloved you are by Creation." Yeshua embraces his Saba then holds his Savta for a long time. When we finally take our leave, it is with the blessing of the David and his Queen.

Of Fathers and Sons

Shortly after dawn, we bid farewell to the temple of Astarte. Tearfully I cling to Hephziva until Yeshua draws me away. Outside Qumran, the men rub their arms briskly, the desert still under the vestiges of winter.

"Poor Teoma had to get up so early to ready our mounts, he was robbed of sleep."

Yeshua chuckles, "No, my dear, he gave it away freely!"

With flushed cheeks, I greet Sheikan who nickers and pulls away from Teoma to trot over to me. Loosening his bridle, I apologize to my dear horse. Teoma walks grumbling over to help us mount.

"Mary, that stallion is a menace. He should respect who is holding him, not break free when he sees you."

I give him a peck on the cheek. "I am sorry you are so tired." Rolling his eyes, he places me on Sheikan, then turns to Yeshua.

"Don't try to pick me up, you'll hurt yourself." Brusquely, Teoma gives him a leg up before retightening Sheikan's bridle. He is not in a good mood.

Riding north, I feel wonderfully alive as the sun kisses the earth good morning. Caves pitting the face of the hills exude a familiar hayye—the voices of our ancestors silenced for centuries. "Yeshua," I whisper, pointing, "what is hidden in those caves?"

"Scrolls, Mary, ancient scrolls, like those Abba works on," his voice lowers, "and soon it will be time for them to be hidden, but not here, somewhere else, far away."

Just beyond the caves, Yeshua wants to stop, which displeases Teoma.

"We have hardly left Qumran. We must get to Judas' encampment before dark!"

Yeshua puts a hand on Teoma's shoulder. "Please allow me to commune with my father." Saul explains that the clan of Judas is not far, but Teoma stalks off angrily.

Yeshua asks that I stay with the others. "If you don't want to share, I will try and refrain from reading your thoughts."

"I cannot ask that of you, my love, for I never willingly released access to your mind." After kissing me farewell, Yeshua climbs the mountaintop.

Teoma stakes out our mounts, then sits apart from the rest of us. His anger upsets me, but I resist piercing his mind, praying to use my new gift compassionately.

"My dear Mary, you look torn between your two loves again."

"Is my face such a transparent window into my heart, Jochanan?" He takes my hand and sits down with me.

"Mary, you are so full of passionate feeling that your every expression is like witnessing poetry coming to life. Would you like to talk?"

Sighing, I think how nice to have a man with whom to discuss my feelings. "Jochanan, I appreciate your interest and pray I do not test our friendship by revealing my heart, but perhaps you might give me an unbiased perspective."

He smiles, "While you support your husband, you are worried about Teoma?"

"Yes, and I'm trying not to read his thoughts, so his angry feelings are difficult to interpret." Looking into his soft green eyes, I await a response.

"Mary, your stare is intense, soul baring. I will try to explain what I understand." Squeezing my hand he begins, "Teoma had a most wonderful experience in Qumran, for many reasons. He enjoyed the camaraderie with the men. His contributions to the tribe were truly appreciated by young and old. But the highest compliment of all was when the men compared him to Joseph. When asked who his father was, Teoma's proud reply was that he was raised by Joseph."

Watching my expression, he continues, "The openness in Qumran allowed him to experience a measure of freedom." Touching my cheek, he asks, "Shall I go on?"

My feelings threaten to bubble over at the mention of Teoma's lovers, but I nod my consent. Jochanan smiles and continues, "Yeshua's negligence upset him for he felt he would take better care of one so dear." I wonder when this fire will ever go out.

"I doubt that he could ever love another, Mary." My lower lip trembles. He whispers, "Your seductive dance was most difficult for him to bear," placing an arm around me. "There are not enough beautiful princesses in Qumran to fill the need you have created in him."

I do not know if I can hear any more, but am guided to stay present and listen.

"It is not easy for a man to share everything he holds dear with another. His true love, his home, his family is difficult enough, but for young men, what we most desire is our father's approval."

I look up. Jochanan is speaking for himself as well as Teoma, and yes, for Yeshua too. His green eyes glimmer with unshed tears. Touching his cheek, I look deeply into the dark center of his brilliant eyes where an ancient wound abides. A strong, but not particularly affectionate man, his father resented his only son's escape into the Essene community and now his family bloodline will die with him. Jochanan harbors self-judgment and searches for approval from lovers old enough to be his father, none of whom cherished him as he deserved. The root of this wound lies in Jochanan's belief of unworthiness mirrored in his relationship with his father.

Simultaneously, we take a deep breath. "Gentle friend, your father is the representation of your relationship with the Father aspect of the Cosmos. The One unified in both masculine and feminine principles knows you only as beloved. Perhaps in your relationship with Saul, you can begin to heal your relationship with your father and with your Divine Self." As my friend's tears flow freely, I hug him to me.

"Thank you, Mary, for your insight. I had hoped to serve Yeshua, never imagining that I might be served in this way." We hug for a long while, before he whispers, "If you do this for Teoma, it might help."

"It is easier to serve strangers than those closest to us."

"Perhaps you can help him contact Joseph."

A smile struggles with the corners of my mouth, "If he is agreeable, but," I shake my head, "I must be unbiased and that might prove the greatest challenge."

"Is there anyone who can advise you on such things?"

"Yes, my Abba."

"It's all about fathers right now."

"Yes, these soul themes run long and deep, mirrored through our lives until we see the truth of who we are."

Sitting apart from Jochanan, I focus inward on my violet portal. He whispers, "Should I go?" I shake my head, close my eyes, and finding my connection to Source, visualize my father's hayye.

Within a single breath, he comes clearly to me. *Abba, I need your advice. I would like to assist Teoma in contacting Joseph.*

Mary, you have already acted as a medium for me. How is this different?

Because some of the communication may be uncomfortable.

I smile at Abba's laughter. *I am sorry, dear. Your emotion can be overwhelming. Before you begin, surrender your attachment to the outcome of the communication.*

In other words, practice non-interference like you do, Abba?

Dearest, I have learned that you can serve without being attached to another's soul path. Remember that love brings clarity to the communication while fear, including jealousy and doubt, creates obstacles to clearly connecting.

I open my eyes to see Jochanan sitting across from me in awe. "Mary, there was a shift in the hayye when you were communicating with your Abba, like a breeze coming through an open door." Smiling, I lean across and take his hand.

"Yes, entering a portal to access the mind of another, no matter how distant, is a product of desire and intention. Yeshua easily learned this as a young child and in my desire to connect with him, I remembered as well."

Jochanan asks softly, "Can you teach me?" I nod and leave him to his thoughts.

Teoma sits forlorn by our mounts. Dropping to my knees behind him, I hug his neck. He pats my arm, "What, Mary?"

"Jochanan explained why you were so happy in Qumran."

"I did have a nice time…not only at night."

"I am not reading your mind so you can free your thoughts."

With a wrinkle of his brow he asks, "Can you not do it outside of Qumran?"

"Yes, but I have learned to be more selective and I want to respect your privacy." His face softens into an endearing look.

"Really, I can think what I please?"

I take his hand, hoping his heart will also soften. "Yes, as long as you remember that thought creates reality. So try to think happy thoughts." His laughter cracks the shell about his hayye, which sweetly expands.

"Now, Teoma, I would like to offer to help you contact Joseph." The shift in his demeanor waves from surprise to hope to concern. "Of course, I will attempt to release my attachment to you so that I might be unbiased, but I will be privy to the details of your communication."

In spite of this, he looks interested, "Well, it would be nice to contact Joseph; I have so much to tell him." Pausing, he considers, "May I think about it awhile?"

I give him a kiss. "Of course, dear."

It is so much nicer to be near him when his hayye is relaxed. He holds me for a moment, before whispering, "If you weren't so exuberantly physical, Mary, it would be much easier."

Pushing away I look into his eyes, "But this is who I am."

He nods and touches my cheek, "And it's one of the many things I love."

Sheikan nickers. Following a narrow path, my husband uses the energies to float across the face of the earth, brightly glowing a translucent silvery white. With a tingling of joy that brings forth a rush of passion, I go to him.

"Mary!" He cries delighted. His hayye so light, my own feels heavy with earthiness. "Barchashem! You came! Teoma would be most displeased if I asked him to wait any longer."

Meeting my passion, he divests us of our clothing then kisses my mouth hungrily. Under the protection of the great rocks, I am transported back into his meditation. His self-disappointment dissolves as the Divine energy of the Son, which he embodies, absorbs into the wholeness of All That Is. At our mutual climax, the One's delighted laughter accompanies our prism of hayye.

We do not tarry any longer than is necessary to redress and descend to where our companions are waiting. Sheikan trots over and using a rock, we mount him and catch up to the others.

Hava smiles at us. "Did you have a nice communion with your Abba, Yeshua?"

"Very nice, thank you, dear Hava," *and a wonderful communion with the One, then yet another very fine communion with my wife.* Teoma scowls and Yeshua lowers his voice, "I believe he has gained enough worldly experience that in spite of his refusal to accept his gifts with the energies, we shall have an increasingly difficult time sneaking around his watchful eye."

Our reverie is interrupted by Jakob's wonder, *how did she disappear to return with Yeshua?* After a moment of silence, Jochanan finally asks, "Mary, how did you do that?"

"Through sheer desire. If Yeshua wants her, she just vanishes."

With an exasperated glance at Teoma, Yeshua explains, "Mary was able to travel through the dense energies of the palace, when I could not even properly veil my mind. I only pray we are not separated again, for I cannot afford for her to surpass my skills."

Scoffing, Hava asks, "And what would it cost if Mary did surpass you?"

The rest of the men await his answer. Teoma smirks while Jakob muses on how Yeshua will maintain his manhood. Astride the chestnut mare, Saul and Jochanan anxiously wonder how he might show respect for me.

Finally, my husband speaks, "What it will cost is time and effort to learn, that is, if Mary cares to teach me." All settle into the generosity of his hayye.

For a time, we ride quietly, until I perceive what happened on that cliffside. When Yeshua compared his feelings of disempowerment to what it must be like to be a paschal lamb, all of Joseph's concern about Yeshua's sacrificial nature floated to the surface of their exchange, like moss on stagnant water.

"As Abba's anger rose, my feeling of unworthiness expanded until I surrendered my fear. Then the energies turned inside out and I could see how afraid Abba was at losing me. Although I tried to remind him that as a boy I resisted his every effort to make me a man, he insisted that he should have done more."

Yeshua's voice fades with his sorrow. I whisper, "I am sorry, dear, that your father was so affected by your experience."

Wrapping his arms tightly around me, he replies, "I am not sorry, love, for this work is for us both. I have a deeper appreciation for my father and told him how much progress was made by all of you in my stead. At least one of his sons was properly prepared for the world of men." Looking ahead at Teoma, Yeshua whispers, "I think it is wonderful that you have offered to help him connect with Abba. It will be good for both of them." Teoma must be considering my offer.

Returning to Yeshua's memory, I wonder how he could possibly feel unworthy in the light of the love extended to him. The union I enjoyed with him was but a ripple upon the sea of divine communion he experienced as the beloved Son.

"We must give thanks for our blessings. The Divine connection we enjoy should be shared with our families and friends."

Kissing the back of my neck, Yeshua explains, "My love, it is only their fear which keeps them veiled from the Divine. My fear of being unworthy birthed my sacrifice in the palace and created the veil separating me from the divine energies. But you, my dear, showed me how courage and perseverance can prevail in the face of hardship." He sighs and kisses me again, "I am grateful that you came to me, for in your embrace I was able to ground this soul lesson into my human form."

"Will we always need intimacy to realize the fullness of our soul paths?"

"I suppose we have learned to embody these lessons through our passion for one another, like developing the habit of putting your right sandal on before the left." I laugh heartily, grateful not to be barefoot or alone on my path.

Shortly before sunset, we ride onto a ridge above the encampment of Judas. Pink and orange rays cast a soft glow on the brightly colored tents. Having spent my life within houses made of wood and clay, I am awed by the rich hayye weaving between the tents like living threads of light. To the far north, shepherds tend large herds of sheep and along the highest vista soldiers watch our approach. The aroma of roasting meat beckons enticingly.

"Welcome, friends. We expected you long before now," The armed guard smiles as Teoma shakes his head.

The colorfully-robed men escort us to a massive multi-roomed tent in the center of the village. Without any preparation, we are led directly into the home of Judas and T'shuraw to be warmly greeted.

"So, Yeshua, how was your visit to Qumran?"

"After a month in the birthplace of my Abba, I have become a wiser man, Judas." Our host turns to Teoma.

"I hope you made the most of the holy city."

"I did my best, sir." Saul and Jakob cannot help but laugh and soon we join them.

"You must be weary from your journey. Let us leave these men to their stories. Come with me and relax." T'shuraw takes us to the communal women's baths and provides clean garments for our use. "When you are ready, we will dine, but please, take your time."

Standing in deep copper basins, we are bathed with a generous amount of perfumed water. "Hava, we are in the middle of the desert, how can they afford this water?"

"This precious water will be used for irrigation after we're through but once again, my dear, you are being treated as the royalty you are, so relax and enjoy."

The finely woven wool robes T'shuraw provides are beautifully embroidered. Lovely in a deep mahogany with gold leaves at the hem and sleeves, Hava's auburn hair is elaborately coiled and secured with golden pins, her ample figure accentuated by shiny snakeskin. Our young assistants plait my wet curls into a crown adorned by white shell hairpins. A sleeveless turquoise sadin dips low in the back, girdled by creamy lambskin studded with turquoise.

"Hava, is there a celebration tonight that we are to attend?"

Hava smiles and touches my cheek, "You look lovely enough for any occasion, but I think not. A nice change from the white robes of Qumran, isn't it?" We thank our assistants and return to the large central tent.

"I was hoping the garments fit. Please turn around." T'shuraw smiles as we do her bidding. "Oh, yes, I am well pleased!" I thank her for adorning us so elegantly as she calls for wine. "Tell me, how did you find Qumran?"

I savor the wine, welcome after such a long respite. "At first, I was challenged by its strangeness, especially our forced segregation." Hava and T'shuraw laugh. "But I was fortunate to work with the high priestess."

T'shuraw smiles, "So how is Hephziva?" The tribe of Judah is smaller than it seems.

"She is well. I pray to meet her again."

She reaches for my hand. "You have certainly grown, my dear."

"The separation provided Mary an opportunity to focus on her own gifts, I believe, for the first time." I nod as Hava goes on, "But her dance for the new moon would have delighted even you."

"I hoped that you might stay for the spring equinox celebration." At T'shuraw's suggestion, Hava claps her hands.

"What a wonderful idea! It's Mary's wedding anniversary. Nine years, isn't it, dear?"

"Yes, but that is over a moon cycle away."

"The children will be fine, dear, and you need time. I was a bit worried when you disappeared this morning." T'shuraw raises one eyebrow, so Hava explains, "Mary is capable of using raza to travel, but Yeshua seems to call her to him whenever passion rises."

"He did not call me this morning." I fuss at my girdle hearing Hava muse how Miriam had the same trouble with Joseph.

T'shuraw chuckles at my discomfort, "My dear, I hope your visit with us will strengthen your resolve to use your sensuality to your advantage within and outside of your marriage." Her thoughts quickly shift as three lovely young women appear. "Here you are, my dears. You remember Hava, the high priestess before Hephziva." They bow politely. "And this is Mary, the wife of Yeshua, in line to be the David." The girls smile at me warmly, especially the youngest. "And my daughters; Devora, Renana, and Tamar." All three tall and dark as their elegant Ima, but Tamar is exceptionally sensual.

The girls sit very close to me. "Ima could not do justice to your beauty, Mary. Will you dance with us at the spring equinox?"

I smile at Tamar. "Thank you. If we stay, I would love to."

Hava shares a private joke with T'shuraw, but when I silently inquire, she responds with, *You shall make fine friends while you are here.*

Judas' deep voice announces the arrival of the men, all freshly washed and dressed. How handsome Yeshua looks in a dark blue robe with his long hair curling past his shoulders.

Tamar takes my hand. "Is that your husband?" I start to rise to greet him, but she holds me fast, "Stay with us, Mary. We wish to get to know you better." I relent and she kisses my cheek delighted to announce to her sisters, "She is ours for the evening."

A sumptuous supper of roasted lamb and vegetables is served, complete with wine and honey-dipped dates. After a month of vegetables, I find the food quite rich. The women's conversation drifts comfortably through children and spouses, while on the other side of the table, the men talk of Herodian politics. Although her sisters have nine children between them, Tamar seems uninterested in marriage. When the guests are shown to their sleeping quarters, Tamar starts to lead me away, but I balk.

"You will not be staying with us, Mary?"

"Tonight, I wish to be with my husband. But I hope to see you in the morning?" I kiss her cheek and she gives me a wistful smile.

Yeshua caresses my bare back, "This dress is quite revealing. No wonder Judas' daughters were reluctant to release you."

Shortly after breakfast, Teoma sends for me. We meet on a low rise west of the village and sit facing one another. Breathing deeply, I find Joseph not in the fields this early morning, but in the secret cavern. He looks about, startled by my presence.

I'm sorry Abba Joseph, but Teoma wishes to commune with you this morning. Joseph hastily emerges into the bright sunshine and I begin translating through the ethers.

Teoma relays his adventures in Qumran, emphasizing how many recognized Joseph's hand in raising him. "I want to thank you, sir. I may not have your blood in my vessels, but I consider you my father."

Clearing his throat, Joseph whispers, *I have always thought of you as one of my own sons.*

Teoma's eyes well. "I love you, Abba."

Me too, son. Gruffly, Joseph excuses himself, his emotion greater than he can bear. Even Teoma needs a moment. Perhaps if fathers and sons expressed their appreciation for one another more often, the expectations they hold would not seem so insurmountable.

Regaining his composure, Teoma gives me a hug. "Thank you, Mary. It is nice to know Joseph is but a few breaths away."

Kissing his cheek, I laugh, "Dear, you could do this yourself. I shall practice with you while we are here." He gives me a dubious nod, but I take advantage of his gratitude.

"I did not know you worked with the Therapeutae?" Teoma's face darkens, but I pursue, "Why is it such a secret?"

Teoma glances about before lowering his voice. "From the beginning, humans have attempted to learn the secret of immortality. The ancient cultures believed that only the gods could live forever, but the Egyptians have mastered the art of death and eternal life." The art of death? He smiles. "I am sworn to secrecy, yes, even from you. But perhaps someday you will learn the craft."

I wander back through the bustling village. Is this elusive craft taught only to men? Don't women wish for eternal life, or do we have secret knowledge of our own that I have yet to discover? Laughter interrupts my thoughts. Women occupied with various tasks chat joyfully, small children playing amongst them. All around is sound and color, the intense hayye of creation. I yearn to explore this sensual garden, but here is Tamar.

Taking my hands in hers, she tenderly kisses my lips, "May I show you about the village now?" She starts to lead me away.

"Tamar! Bring Mary here, I want to see something." A large round woman motions from the back of the textile tent and I am led to stand before her. Sharp brown eyes appraise my face. "Your eyes are like the sea, but turquoise is not your color, my dear." Turning to the large pile of silky linens, she selects a deep purple. "This is your color."

"Do you see the hayye around people?"

She laughs heartily and the rest of the women join her. "No, but I know the proper color of every woman I have ever dressed."

Tamar introduces us, "Mary, this is Leila. Ima asked her to make your dress." I take Leila's thick hands in mine.

"Thank you for such a lovely gown."

"You are most welcome." Draping the rich purple cloth over my shoulder, she arranges it across my bust, "Yes, this is perfect. I shall make you another gown."

I offer a weak protest. "But you must have other work to do."

She gathers the fabric and sets it aside, "My dear, please! It will bring me great pleasure to adorn you, but I will need more measurements. Adira, pull down the flap." Sandy hair plaited down her back, a small woman stands to secure the opening of the large yellow and white striped tent. "There now, Mary, take off your garment, so I might measure you properly."

Excited to receive yet another lovely gown, I remove my sadin, while Tamar searches through a pile of cloth. Gasping, she touches the small of my back, "Mary, you are so beautiful."

"Tamar, you are in my way," Leila scolds, deftly wrapping a length of linen around my buttocks and knots off the measurement. After measuring my chest and bust, she clucks her tongue. "Thank goodness you came in. This silk would not fit properly." I smile down as she secures the knot.

"But the gown you made fit."

"Wool is forgiving and T'shuraw described you as petite, so I made the dress smaller."

Turquoise cloth twisted in her hands, Tamar stares. "What is it?" I ask and she gives me a shy smile.

"Does riding astride give you such a lovely figure?"

Leila laughs, "No, Tamar, Marya gave her a beautiful face and body as a gift to her husband for being the prince of Judah!"

Joining her laughter, I comment, "Perhaps riding helps."

"I would love to ride with you, Mary." Tamar wistfully replies.

Finally, Leila has her last measurement, "I hear you have some kind of riding garment?"

"Yes, I sewed my sadin up the middle so that my legs would not get chaffed. But Tamar, if you would like to ride, you can wear it."

Shaking her head, Leila relieves me of my garment, "Let me alter it. The other is being laundered. Here, Mary, cover yourself." She hands me a blue cloth. "Tamar, hand your sadin to Adira. Thank you, dear. I thought it would be nice to get these girls on their way, so we can get back to work."

Watching Leila's thick fingers deftly manipulate the cloth, I am mesmerized, the hayye smooth and voluptuous. Song fills the air in rhythm with the sewing needles. Rich textiles call to me, texture and color delighting my senses.

Soon we redress. Tamar wraps the turquoise scrap in my hair winding it into a single braid down my back. Thanking her, I turn to Leila, "May we have two more lengths of cloth, please?" Leila smiles and hands me a length of purple and a length of blue. "Riding is very bouncy." I turn to a giggling Tamar and wrap the blue cloth around her back and over her breasts before tying it about her neck. Then I take the purple cloth and make the same support for myself. Laughing at our strange outfits, the women bid us well.

Arm-in-arm we traverse through tents colorful as wildflowers. Before calling Sheikan, I locate Teoma with the soldiers, but it is a few moments before he notices.

Mary?

Thank goodness. *Yes, Teoma. It's me.*

He moves away from the others. *I can hear your voice in my head.*

Teoma, where is the herd?

What?

I concentrate on what I desire. *Where are the horses?*

Horses? Are you looking for Sheikan? I confirm and send him loving hayye. *They are north of the village. Mary, can you hear me?*

Yes, I can hear you in my mind.

376

He's confused again. *Your what? I'm sorry, Mary. Maybe I should stand farther away from the others.*

Bidding him farewell, I don't want to overwhelm him.

To my call, Sheikan comes galloping over the northern crest, his long silvery mane blowing, tail high over his back. Standing behind me, Tamar whispers, "How shall we ride him? We have no bridle."

I caress his face and neck, letting him lip my own. Nickering softly, Sheikan bows. "Come, we don't need tack." In spite of her initial shyness, Tamar hops up behind me and Sheikan rises, adjusting to our weight.

Wrapping her slim arms tightly about my waist, Tamar whispers softly, "I've never done this before, but I trust you."

I pat her knee. "He'll take good care of both of us."

Walking west, Sheikan relaxes, so I turn my attention to Tamar, who shifts her weight about uncomfortably. "Do you dance?"

She smiles against my shoulder. "I love to dance and Ima says you dance most passionately."

"Riding is like dancing. Find the horse's rhythm and match your body to it." She soon sways with him and I give her knee a squeeze, "Good, Tamar." She hugs my waist. "Now let's go faster. The trot is bumpy but not uncomfortable if you move with him." Tamar matches his pace beautifully, bringing a thrill of excitement.

Sheikan's canter is like floating on air. "Does he go faster, Mary?" I join in her delight as Sheikan flies over the sand.

The wind swallows our laughter and threatens to steal away my turquoise wrap. Leaning back slightly into Tamar, I bring Sheikan to a halt. A large bird soaring overhead casts its shadow upon us. I look up to see a black crow far from any roosts.

Tamar exclaims breathlessly, "How exhilarating!" Her cheeks flushed from the wind, her lips soft and full against my own.

Delighted by her excitement, I ask, "Do you want to do it again?" Nodding, she leans forward and I turn to signal Sheikan. Swiftly he gallops across the open desert, as Tamar holds on tight.

Sheikan's ears flicker. Something is ahead. I try to slow his pace, but he ignores me, so rather than struggle, I lean into his neck, reaching back for Tamar. Sheikan gallops toward a lone figure with vultures circling above.

Stopping abruptly before the man, Sheikan nickers. Fortunately, Tamar maintains her balance for she could easily have unseated both of us. The man stands quietly before us, lizards at his feet and snakes slithering further behind. The birds are not vultures, but a pair of hawks crying out to him. Tall and broad, his silvery gray hair belies a much younger visage, his hayye gentle grass green to match his eyes. Somehow I know him. Slowly he approaches, hands out, extending his energy like flickering serpent tongues. Sheikan shivers in anticipation, ears pricked forward, nostrils flared. The moment the man touches Sheikan, I feel his hayye connect to mine as well.

"Ari!"

He looks up at me with kind eyes. "Mary? Is that you? I have not seen your face since you were a child. I heard that Judas was entertaining Yeshua bar Joseph, but did not expect he would bring his lovely young wife."

"Saul and Hava are here too. They will be delighted to see you."

"I am glad to hear that my old friends are so near, but please let me surprise Hava." Smiling, he asks, "And who is your friend?"

"Judas' youngest daughter, Tamar. This is her first ride!" Ari smiles at her, stroking Sheikan's sleek coat appreciatively.

"Has my Abba requested your presence because of our ill sheep, sir?"

"Yes, Tamar. If you would ride ahead and announce my arrival, perhaps I can tend to the sickest of the flock first." Bidding him farewell, we gallop back.

Sheikan easily locates a large flock southwest of the village. Amidst the sheep, spiraled around a pure white prism of hayye, Yeshua stands. Carefully we enter the flock, whose pungent odor suggests its ill state. With his right hand upon the closest ewe, Yeshua delivers healing through her and to all the other sheep following the spiral to the last lamb. When we reach the center, he looks up. My heart aches with love as my body yearns for his touch. Behind me, Tamar's body heat mimics my own.

"Dearest, are you enjoying your ride?" He smiles sweetly at Tamar who squirms slightly, her firm breasts hot against my back.

"Yeshua, Ari is coming. He wants to surprise Hava so do not tell her, but he'll tend the most ill sheep first."

Yeshua's smile brightens at the news. "Judas will welcome Ari's assistance so that we might join you for supper this evening."

Disappointment waves through me at the possibility that he may not. He reaches up and I slide into his arms, leaving Tamar alone upon Sheikan.

Although I only mean to kiss him hello, all the passionate sensations of the day emerge. I melt in his embrace, but he quells me. *Not here, love. Your friend is waiting. I will sup with you this evening and later fulfill your desires.* His silent promise whets my appetite.

One deep whiff of my neck and he lifts me back upon Sheikan. "I must smell like a hot horse, but it is far better than sick sheep."

Laughing he says, "Yes, it is. But I shall smell sweeter before we meet again."

"But what about the flock? Will you not stay to heal them?"

Yeshua puts a reassuring hand upon Tamar's knee, "I have already ministered to them. I hear you are an artist with women's dress. Could you please assist my wife?" When she consents, he bids us goodbye.

As we prepare for the evening, Tamar confides in me how distasteful men are to her senses. Now I do not particularly care for the smell of sheep, and shepherds cannot bathe often enough in the desert, but if I am attracted to a man, I find his odor enticing. Perhaps I'll introduce her to Teoma, he always smells nice.

Other than my sister Martha, I have no women friends. Tamar's affection for me is endearing, but I hope she will not fuss too much about my spending time with Yeshua.

"Why do you sigh so forlornly? Don't you like what I am doing with your hair?"

"It's lovely, Tamar. I am just thinking about Yeshua."

Sitting besides me on the cushions, Tamar puts an arm around my waist, "Why do you love him so?"

I turn and look at her. Her dark eyes sad, wistful, her hayye yearns toward me, but I hesitate to look into her soul—since arriving I have worked diligently to keep from reading minds. "Because in his eyes I see myself as love."

Tamar studies my face. "The world should know you as love, not only one man. I wish we could have known each other before you met him."

"Yeshua and I agreed before coming here to be together. But I do appreciate having you as a dear friend." I kiss her cheek, "Thank you for adorning me so beautifully."

Our sumptuous dinner cannot match Hava's delight at seeing Ari. Separating from the rest of us, they clasp hands like young lovers. Before we retire, Yeshua stands. "To love rekindled and newfound friends." When he winks at Tamar, she turns away.

Judas adds, "And may these friendships lead to lasting alliances bonded by loyalty." Although difficult to part from Tamar, my need to be with Yeshua is overwhelming.

Kissing me tenderly in the privacy of our room, my husband takes his sweet time undoing what Tamar so carefully created. "Your new friend is an artist, love. I wonder how else she might adorn you." Already flushed from his attentions, I lean into his hard body. Sweetly caressing every part of me as if mapping out a new-found land, tears well in my eyes as his tenderness crystallizes the rays illuminating our corner of the tent.

This is also why I love you so, Yeshua. I have yet to catch my breath.

Because of the intensity of our connection?

Yes, tears spill, *in your embrace, I am One with All That Is.*

"And together we are the living embodiment of Love." We fall asleep in each other's embrace, dreaming of eternity from whence we came.

For the Love of Women

Tucked into Yeshua's body, I awaken damp and sticky. Kissing my neck, he chuckles, "Even amongst the odor of the sheep, I could still detect the unique aroma of your moon cycle."

"Oh, Yeshua, now I must go to the chamam!"

Stroking the length of my body, he says softly, "Each of us is to learn with those of our own gender what we cannot teach one another." Undeterred by the mess, he moves against me, "Not that I would not love to join you. But alas I am challenged by this form and shall find myself amongst my brothers whose indelicate ways rule this world."

I giggle at his bemoaning, "Oh, but the form you chose encases such a tender heart that I cannot resist your magnetism."

Cupping my face in his hands, he presses the length of his body deliciously against mine, "You shall see that your sensuality is not limited to your attraction to me."

"Please do not bring Teoma into our intimate embrace."

My husband only smiles, as I leave to join the desert women in the circular tent dyed blood red. My body sensed the cycle of the village, for both of Tamar's older sisters are here, as well as T'shuraw, and by late afternoon Tamar joins us.

After a warm hug, she sits me down to play with my hair. I could sit forever at the knees of a devoted hairdresser, but T'shuraw clucks her tongue, "Tamar, were you not within the protection of the red tent just two Shabbats ago?" Tamar does not answer, busy with my locks.

I try to relieve the concern on her Ima's face. "I too have started early. Perhaps since we spent so much time together, she bleeds with me."

Shaking her head, T'shuraw gives her daughter a sharp look, "Perhaps, but not all desires may be met." Tamar's hands still as her hayye tightens. I smile at T'shuraw, then turn to Tamar.

"Yeshua teaches that thought creates reality, so we do manifest what we desire, if our intentions are clear."

"Do not encourage my little sister, Mary, or you shall see that she manifests her desires quite easily." Rising abruptly, Tamar casts herself upon the farthest cushions. Devora smiles at me, seemingly unconcerned. T'shuraw shakes her head.

I go to Tamar and gently stroke her back. "What is wrong?"

"My family does not want me to have my heart's desire." She sobs and I am tempted to look within her mind, but resist.

Throughout the next few days, irritable as Tamar, I hover between restlessness and fatigue. Usually the lively atmosphere of women gossiping and giggling soothes me, but now I'm near to tears. The minds of my sisters so intensely busy, I expend much energy to block the chatter. Tamar has been a comfort to me, tending to my every need.

Before going to bed one evening, she offers to give me a massage. "Mary, you will feel better and perhaps sleep more soundly. Here, undress and lie down, I'll get some oil." I agree, upset after my communication with Yeshua, who struggles to connect with the shepherds and their sons.

The rest of the women play games, chatting happily at the low table. Tamar's warm touch releases my tension into the feathery softness of the cushions. An extremely attentive masseuse, she leaves no part unattended. Of all the massages I have had in the chamam, never have I enjoyed the touch of another woman so much. "Tamar, you have wonderful hands, thank you for taking so much time with me."

Surely she must be tired after so long. "It is my pleasure to minister to you. If you will turn over, I shall work on your limbs more thoroughly." I must repay her kindness.

She takes my right hand and begins massaging my arm. How blessed I am to be treated so tenderly. Soon I close my eyes. Arriving at my belly, her massage softens. Fingertips swirling lightly upon my skin, she circles the quartz embedded within my navel.

"How lovely," she croons, her touch becoming more intimate. She kisses the stone, and I gasp, responding wetly. Opening my eyes, I see that her pleasure is even greater than my own.

"Tamar," I whisper hoarsely. She puts a slender finger to my lips and hushes me, before brushing lightly over the swell of my breast. My nipple hardens in anticipation and she smiles rewarded for her efforts. Confused, I move to sit up but she kisses my mouth pushing me gently back. Although her lips hold promise, I halt her further caresses. "Tamar, I am tired. Let us sleep."

She looks hurt, but quickly regains her composure, "I'm sorry, I thought you were enjoying the massage."

"I was," but far too much. I roll over and she lies besides me, her body pressed close to mine. Laying a hand upon the elestial stone, I expect it to feel cool, but am comforted by its glow. Perhaps the image is not of Yeshua and me, but of the union of the masculine and feminine within us.

A fitful night tossing next to Tamar and I awaken at dawn to see Hava joining us. "Oh, Hava, just as you have finally been reunited with Ari! What poor timing!"

Hava puts a warm arm around my waist, "My lover must attend to his work with the sheep, so it is perfect timing that I am here with you."

Kissing her cheek, I smile, "You love being a woman."

"Why, of course I do, Mary. This is not a separation from the world of men, but a celebration with my sisters. And it appears as if we all are joining in the festivities." She glances at our hostess and her daughters still sleeping, stopping to study Tamar.

Hava looks into my eyes, "Why do you look so peaked?" Shaking my head, I begin to cry. Tamar starts to rise, but Hava waves her away, drawing me into her embrace. "Come, we need to talk." Although open and spacious, with the women sleeping farthest from the entrance, Hava leads me to the northwest quarter of the red tent. A low oval table sits ready for breakfast. "Are you really having so much difficulty being separated from Yeshua or," she lowers her voice to a whisper, "is it something else?"

Wiping my tears on the sleeve of my robe, I sigh, "I feel so irritable. Their minds are so active, I struggle to keep mine closed."

With wide eyes, she asks, "When did you stop using your gift?"

I hesitate to reply. "After the new moon of Adar, Yeshua seemed so upset by my ability to pierce his veil, I have been concentrating on not listening to anyone's thoughts."

Hava takes my hands in hers. "How do you expect to fully develop your gifts if you refuse to use them, Mary? Did Yeshua ask you not to read his thoughts?"

"No, he said since he never willingly blocked access to my mind, he could not ask that of me. But, Hava, knowing another's intimate thoughts is invading their privacy." Pulling me close, Hava smoothes my hair until I relax in her embrace.

"Mary, let's contact Hephziva. She might better advise you."

I nod my consent and we sit opposite one another, breathing deeply. In Hava's calm burgundy glow, I feel secure. Soon the purple portal embraces my consciousness and I follow a clear blue light wave to my newest mentor. Hephziva greets me warmly, recognizing Hava's presence as well.

Mary, your hayye is so very depleted. You already learned how to attend to only that which is necessary for your soul awareness. It has cost you more to quell your gift than to maintain your conscious connection.

I sigh. *I do not understand the rules of conduct in having such free access to other's thoughts. Yeshua sees all and does not interfere, other than to tease me.* I can feel her smile.

Your young husband is very wise and those around you, gifted with the energies, respect free will in each soul, not using their knowledge for personal gain, nor interfering with another's soul path. You are a loving, joyful being, blessed with little prejudice, but all make mistakes, even those who are awakening. You will learn to forgive your humanness while you continue to grow into a sovereign being.

After I thank Hephziva, Hava hugs me with reassurance that things will be different now that she is here in the red tent. Before excusing myself, I ask to go outside to meditate.

"Dear, you are not captive. Someday you will learn to find Source in the midst of chaos." Until then I will continue to seek the quietude of the Great Mother.

"Mary, why are you leaving us?" Tamar catches me, her black eyes reflecting unfulfilled desire. Promising to return, I wonder what has been awakened in me.

Gray dawn greets the pale desert as I walk quickly to a small ridge of sandstone still chilled from the late winter night. Faint smoke drifts skyward from the rising village below. In a few short breaths the hayye of the earth envelops me and settling deeper into my body, I drift until my sense of self blurs into the rainbow of creation. Through the ethers, I look in on my children still asleep in their warm beds in Bethany, then the rest of my family. In Galilee, Joseph works diligently upon the scrolls, his *hayye* heavy with worry. In her rainbow room, Miriam clings to a dark cord of despair, but she welcomes news of the children and Yeshua, thanking me for channeling Teoma to Joseph.

I move on and Yeshua's *hayye* greets me in the ethers. *My love, what are you searching for? Are you not enjoying yourself in the red tent?*

My heart aches at his question, *I am, Yeshua, too much so, and my feelings are confusing.* He extends comforting *hayye* to me.

Take your time, dear, and do not judge your feelings. I divulge my interaction with Hephziva. *Do not stifle the memory of your divine potential, Mary. Experience the fullness of your being.*

Clearing my aura of all barriers to receive the gifts of the universe, I return to the red tent with an open mind and heart. Tamar greets me with a kiss and a wonderful idea.

"Last night during the massage, I could see an image forming on your bare skin."

I agree to be her canvas. Delighted, she hugs me then leaves to get the needed supplies. The rest of the women have breakfasted and are playing a game. Wondering what her sister asked, Renana invites me to join them at the table while I wait for Tamar to return.

"Tamar would like to paint my body and I consented." With a look of surprise, Renana glances at T'shuraw, who thinks I should not encourage Tamar, but motions for me to sit by her.

Hava asks about my meditation. "It went very well. The children are fine and I had a nice visit with Miriam."

Devora's eyebrows rise, "How do you know how your children fare, Mary?"

"I can view them through the ethers." She nods slowly, thinking that she didn't know I was a seer. "So what is this game you are playing?"

Renana describes mancala, a game of chance using polished stones on a wooden board with small hollows. Soon I find that knowing the strategy of the other players gives me an unfair advantage. Halfway through the second game, they become aware.

"Mary," Renana complains, "do not say out loud what the next throw will be."

"Even when I but think it, the stones are affected." Hava laughs at my reply.

"So is this how thought creates reality, Mary?" T'shuraw asks with a smile.

"Yes, but it's not much fun to affect the outcome of this game."

Putting down my stones, I see Tamar has returned and excuse myself. T'shuraw thinks, *if she knows our minds, why can she not see what Tamar desires?*

I turn back to the table, "T'shuraw, until this morning I have spent much hayye blocking the thoughts of others. Only now am I open to know her mind."

Tamar halts stricken, "What do you mean?"

Gently, I take her arm and lead her to the other side of the tent. "In Qumran I learned to read other's thoughts, but found it disconcerting, so I have denied myself the use of my gift. This morning Hephziva helped me understand how to use it wisely." The poor girl struggles to comprehend. "I want to be your friend and have enjoyed your attention, but I am confused."

With a great sigh, she finally responds, "Mary, I am very attracted to you and have enjoyed our time together immensely. Still I would like to paint your body."

So for the next two days, I become her blank canvas. Tamar works constantly, taking breaks only when I need to get up and stretch. Finding the touch of her fingers and the various instruments she uses to apply the paint delightfully relaxing, I finally get the sleep I've missed since being in the red tent. The other women gather around, their soft appraisals lulling me into the dream world. And Rafael's angelic presence carries Tamar late into the night, well after the rest have gone to bed.

In the flurry of activity, I learn to move in and out of meditation. Pleased with my progress, Hava announces, "Saul must look at Tamar's work. Perhaps he can even copy it on canvas so it might be cherished by her clan."

Tamar insists that never before has her art come so easily. A bright hayye surrounds my friend as through her art she transforms into a more finely-honed aspect of herself.

On the morning of the third day, Tamar completes the finishing touches. Describing her work as the depiction of the Elat, she yawns, "Please wear a loose robe over it and I'll help you bathe this afternoon in preparation for dinner."

Laying her down upon a bed of cushions, I kiss her cheek, "Sleep well, Tamar." Although anxious to leave the red tent, I look fondly at my friend. Somehow I have changed in these past few days. If not married, I might enjoy being her lover.

As if I call, Yeshua comes to me through the ethers, *Mary, are you not through yet?*

Yes, and I have a wonderful surprise for you, but ask that you refrain from reading any of the women's minds.

I will try, Mary. But perhaps we might meet before supper. I have much to tell you and desire to know how you fared with Tamar. Knowing we won't talk, I ask him to wait. Reluctantly, he bids me a sweet farewell.

By the evening, I am as anxious as Yeshua, and Tamar is fraught with sorrow. I try to soothe her, "Thank you for helping me discover that my sensuality is not limited to my relationship with my husband." Embracing her, I whisper, "I pray that you shall meet someone who will cherish you as you deserve."

With damp eyes, she finishes my hair and helps me with my turquoise gown, pleased with how beautifully it frames the tree goddess. "Will you still dance with me at the spring equinox?"

"Of course, but you will have to teach me your desert dances." Her face brightens and we go arm-in-arm to sup with the men.

Upon my shoulders drapes a delicate cream shawl that Leila embroidered with desert flowers of turquoise and purple so Tamar's art would not be revealed prematurely. Already seated when we arrive, family and guests enjoy Greek wine. Yeshua stands to greet me with a kiss and another for Tamar. Her hand on my arm becomes damp as he whispers his gratitude for taking such good care of me.

I console my confused friend, "You have shown me that my desire is not limited to men, perhaps yours is not limited to women." Red cheeked, Tamar sits by her sisters.

Again this revealing gown, how shall I concentrate on the meal? With a seductive glance, I take my seat. *What's this emanating from your back?*

He can wait until after dinner, Hava advises and Yeshua groans.

I must get Mary to sit for me, Saul muses.

I lean forward and catch his eye, "I would love to sit for you. In fact, we can start tomorrow if you are free."

"Of course, but whatever changed your mind?" I point to Tamar, who he gazes at in wonder. Jochanan tells him to be grateful I finally agreed.

She's most intimate with Judas' daughter. What happened in the red tent?

In a low voice, I address Teoma, "Hephziva advised me not to block my ability yet, so please think about something else."

His face flushes, "How are we to exist, if both of you can access my thoughts?"

"I think eventually I will be able to be more selective."

He looks to Yeshua. "When you think directly about us, your thoughts stand out among others as if you have called to us."

"Perhaps we can continue to work on your silent communication and eventually you, too, will be able to read minds." Teoma shakes his head in frustration.

Overwhelming my senses, Yeshua insists on feeding me with his fingers. Finally, T'shuraw stands, "Our family has always appreciated the artistic talents of our youngest daughter. If Mary would not mind, perhaps we can all view Tamar's art." I carefully drop the creamy shawl from my shoulders.

Praise pierces the awed silence. Gratitude for being a part of this magic pulsates within me as my husband raises his cup. "May Tamar's passion uplift all who behold her most glorious light."

Blushing across the table, she dreams of what it might be like to lie with him, but before Yeshua responds, I warn him not to overwhelm her. "You are protective of your new friend, dear."

"I understand how confusing it is to find your sensuality is without bounds."

Hmm, now that Tamar has expanded her views perhaps...

"You are too much of a man for Tamar at this point in her awakening," Yeshua warns and Teoma hastily rises to talk to Judas' son Aaron. "How long will it take for you to transcribe Tamar's art upon a canvas, Saul?"

Smiling, he calculates, "At least a week, it's quite an intricate piece. Please do not disturb it."

Before my husband can respond, Judas does, "Although you have been separated from your lovely wife, the rest of us wish to appreciate my daughter's work."

"Unless of course, you would consent to a public viewing of the complete work," Teoma suggests. "Since only a portion of the Elat is visible, perhaps..."

"It is apparent that copying an art form of this intricacy will take an inordinate amount of time and," Yeshua gives Saul an appeasing look, "I agree it would be an injustice not to have a permanent display for her clan to appreciate," his glare at Teoma causes the rest of us to laugh, "but only the master artist need view Tamar's original art."

Teoma is not to be deterred. "What a shame, and I thought that parable you told us the other night of the rich man sharing all with his neighbors was actually a reference to you sharing all you had with us." Yeshua forces a smile.

"I am pleased you were paying such close attention, but I meant sharing wisdom."

All of Judas' sons join Teoma in a collective groan.

T'shuraw halts their banter, "I am sure you will be very careful with my daughter's art, so if you and Mary would like to enjoy the rest of the evening alone, please feel free to bid us goodnight." With a grateful bow, Yeshua leads me away.

Yeshua's response to the unveiling is worth all the fuss. "Mary, it is an incredible depiction of the Earth Elat. I pray that Saul can capture it, for when you but breathe it comes to life upon your skin." Turning, I show him the rest. "Did you appreciate Tamar's attention?"

I snuggle into his neck. "Yesh, you were right about me."

"So am I to worry about you leaving me for Tamar?" I smile and for the first time, we sleep not skin to skin but separated by a gown to protect the art on my body.

Thankfully, Saul allows me to wash off the paint after only three days, yet does not release me for a week. Tamar provides her expertise on the choice of colors as well as positions me so that I am not overly exposed. The excitement between the two artists makes the long days of sitting in one position go quickly.

During my week of quietude, I explore deeper meditations, visiting the children as well as the rest of the family. Three times I am able to successfully contact Teoma, who silently teases Yeshua. *It is not unlike growing crops of grain, you spent years preparing the soil of my mind, but under Mary's tutelage I have finally come to harvest.*

I also visit Hephziva and explore deeper realms. Soon I am viewing distantly with ease. Like an invisible bird I hover above the situations I choose to witness, realizing that nothing separates me from all that I love, except my fear.

One meditation reveals the river of consciousness. In its fluidity of motion, the river of light flows in all directions—north to south, east to west, in to out, up to down. Those souls well connected to the energies float peacefully through the river. Those trapped within their illusion of reality cling to the riverbank, struggling with the currents, expending much hayye to keep from surrendering to the flow of creation.

Yeshua embraces me within the flow of the One. *As the Elat, you are the element of water soaking my airy hayye with emotion fully grounding me into the earth realm. This river is one of dreams and illusion as well as truth and manifestation. While embodied on earth, may we seek water to reconnect.*

Distant viewing has also allowed me to be with Yeshua while he works with the men who struggle with his spiritual concepts. He bemoans that it is easier to teach children. *These shepherds only understand sheep!* Believing these men understand more than sheep, I formulate a plan to help my beleaguered husband.

Before the next full moon, Edia comes to visit after T'shuraw sent word to her husband's clan. Marriage certainly becomes my friend. "Edia, I want you to be recognized for your healing skills so that you might continue to help those of your desert home."

"I have heard how successful your teachings were in Qumran. Not only have the women benefited, but of course the men reap their own rewards."

"Yes, and in light of fulfilling their desires, the men are much more open to listening to Yeshua's message."

Our hostess exuberantly agrees to a conscious conception circle, gathering all of the women of childbearing age into the center of the village. After T'shuraw introduces us to the cheerful crowd of brightly clad women, I have them sit in two concentric circles with Edia and those interested in eventually teaching in the center.

"Marya, as daughters of creation we ask to remember the divine gift of the Elat to consciously conceive our children. May we always remember our connection to Source and assist our loved ones as well. Ameyn."

Silently, I invoke angelic assistance before asking Edia to lead us in the meditation. Attending to the incredibly beautiful energies woven by each woman around her womb, I contemplate how this clear reflection of Divine Love is the hayye of protection yet also the same white light that prepares us to leave this world and merge with the One. In life and death, all is of the One. There is nothing to fear.

After I accept the gratitude of her clan, T'shuraw takes me aside. "Judas says Yeshua is having some difficulty with the men.

"Although a fine teacher of women and children, he is only now learning how to relate to men. Perhaps the women might have some influence over their spouses." T'shuraw nods thoughtfully.

"My sisters truly appreciate what you have brought to them this day and I am sure they would want to help." She considers, "A segregation until the time of the spring equinox celebration will help open the men's hearts."

Not looking forward to yet another separation but realizing how effective this tactic might be, I suggest, "Tonight, let the women demonstrate the gift of the white light, then if they agree to be separated, we shall have a grand celebration at the spring equinox. I will work with them until then." She agrees.

Within the yellow-striped walls of the textile tent, Leila dresses me in the new sadin. Purple silk wraps snuggly from breast to hip before dancing in soft folds about my legs. "Oh, Leila, how beautiful! I shall wear it tonight."

Happily, Leila gives me a great hug. "I am most pleased that my handiwork adorns you so well, Mary."

In the central clearing around a roaring bonfire, the villagers gather to celebrate the feminine energies of the full moon. Under the influence of strong fragrant shekar, Judas gregariously announces the significant events of first Adar—three betrothals, two new babies, and his daughter's art. The clan cheers enthusiastically as Saul unveils the painting as tall as a man.

Depicted with an expression of enchantment and seated upon deep purple clouds, I am adorned from buttocks to neck with Tamar's Elat. The lifelike tree shelters small creatures and birds with one slender branch encircling my outstretched arm ending in a living flower cupped within my hand. At my left thigh weave the branches within which the dove and the golden snake that Tamar had painted upon my belly come to life in a lover's embrace. Highlighted by sunshine and entwined with desert flowers, sable curls cascade over my shoulder to cover the swell of my breast.

"Tamar, I could not fully appreciate the beauty with which you adorned me, and Saul, you have made me appear incredibly lovely, thank you."

Kissing my cheek, Saul whispers, "I have hardly begun to do you justice, my dear. But if you shall sit for me again, perhaps I can create a fair image of your beauty."

I blush as Teoma comes forward. "Please allow Saul to paint another portrait that we can keep at home, for this one will remain here. Perhaps Judas' most talented daughter might want to return with us to study with Saul." Quite taken by his compliment, Tamar accepts Teoma's offer to join him in a cup of shekar.

My husband takes me aside. "What is on your mind, dear?" With a deep breath I explain the plan. "The men will not like it. I do not know how I shall stand it myself." He sighs. "Well, perhaps we can excuse ourselves now, before my birthday is over." We pass by Teoma talking intimately with Tamar. She did not participate in the white light ceremony so I silently tell him to be careful.

Thankfully, my desert sisters are exceptionally receptive. Perhaps because Yeshua is such a fine mentor, I am able to relate the spiritual messages I have come to live over the past nine years. Using my gift of perceiving the deeper soul connections, I minister to the women of Judas' clan who worry about the happiness of their mates and the wellbeing of their children.

While we do laundry, I summarize, "It is not difficult to tell you to release your fear and ask that your heart be filled with light and love. It is most difficult to do this myself, but the more I ask, the more I practice surrender, the more I look for the love and joy in life, the happier I am. And those around me react more favorably to my joy. When I react out of fear, I must remember that it isn't easy being human and be much more gentle with myself."

Watching the small children play cheerfully nearby, my heart aches for Joshua and Sarah. Tears fill my eyes as one little girl helps a toddler drink from the water urn. Touching my cheek, T'shuraw whispers, "You attend to us in support of your husband while missing your little ones. Why don't you go now, Mary, and commune with them?"

"Thank you but I already did this morning."

"Mary, would you mind holding my baby while I tend to Jaken?" Without waiting for an answer, the young woman hands me her cooing infant before turning to the little boy pulling on her robe.

Hugging the baby to my breast brings me immense relief. T'shuraw smiles, *It is good of Ava to share her child for Mary's arms have been empty too long.*

With a prayer of thanks, I rock my new charge to sleep; happily keeping her while Ava finishes her laundry.

Although I have been determined to bear this separation as well as the others, truly I detest sleeping alone and entertain the idea of sharing Tamar's bed. Needing a respite, Yeshua reports the men are becoming incorrigible. T'shuraw smiles when I communicate this to her. "The longer we make them wait, the better listeners they shall become." Hava and Devora laugh.

"T'shuraw, after less than a week, the women already discuss the concepts and offer each other words of wisdom."

My hostess agrees, "With their sisters, women are open to the teachings, but under the influence of their men, many fear to use their voices. If the men can demonstrate their full support of Yeshua, the women will welcome them with open arms."

***

Stretching his back, Teoma stifles a yawn. Long cold nights keeping watch over sheep taxes the patience of the men. Although extra vigilant in protecting ewes heavy with unborn lambs, the shepherds are unaccustomed to sharing the quietude of the desert. Even the sheep seem disturbed as if the frustrated men carry the same threat as lurking wolves.

Most nights Teoma spends listening to the soldiers' complaints. Jacob was right. They desire a mashiach who would lead them to war against Rome. The new disciples have been attempting to help, yet Yeshua's message of peace falls on deaf ears. Unfortunately, the harsh desert life seems to harden men's will as well as their hides.

Across the way, Yeshua sits alone, quietly meditating. He refused Judas' advice to demonstrate his skills in hand combat. Apparently Jacob left quite an impression on the younger zealots during his escapade last winter. Clearly Jacob is the favored Davidic son since discovering the Herodian transportation of kodeia and befriending the head of the Herodian guard who now wavers in his loyalty to Antipas. Drinking the last of his tea, Teoma wonders how he might be of assistance to his friend.

Gruff and surly, Judas stands before the men, "Marya only knows how difficult it has been to be without the comfort of our women, but my wife reports that they adamantly insist upon our full support of Yeshua."

All groan. "How long can these women hold out?"

"If it is up to my wife, for months." The grumbling continues amongst the clan.

Judas interrupts, "I believe it is up to you, men. Perhaps our prayers have been answered—our wives have received Yeshua's message and desire for us to do so as well."

The women of the desert certainly know how to use their feminine power. Rising, Teoma addresses the men, "It is evident to Yeshua and his chosen disciples that if it shall come to war, the clan of Judas is willing and able to wield their swords against Rome." The men cheer loudly, brandishing their weapons for emphasis. Teoma waits for them to settle down.

"But it appears that, like our mashiach, your women do not desire bloodshed. What can it harm to open your hearts to him?" Looking about the crowd, he continues, "Especially if your willingness to accept his message of love incites your wives to invite you back into their arms?"

Teoma smiles at their eagerness and hopes that Yeshua will come to appreciate the need of men to protect what they love.

Buoyed by his support, Yeshua speaks confidently, "Brothers, as much as I want to be with my wife, I appreciate the efforts of the women who support Mary. I do not desire war with our oppressors. I believe that our freedom can only be obtained through our connection to Eloha. Love is the means by which we may become released from fear and free from oppression."

The men are quiet as Judas asks, "So what is your decision?"

Slowly an agreement is reached—to support Yeshua. Judas praises the efforts of his men, before turning toward Yeshua.

"Inform Mary of the good news, son, perhaps my wife will relent for Shabbat."

Nodding, Yeshua smiles, but Teoma knows Mary is well aware of this morning's gathering. Motioning to his friend, they take a walk together.

"I miss being with her. I do not know how you can stand the company of men for so long." If she were his, Teoma would not favor the company of soldiers and shepherds either. Ducking his head, Yeshua responds to his thoughts. "I apologize for speaking of Mary to you."

Teoma shrugs. "I am your friend. You should be able to speak your mind, confide in me your feelings. But I was hoping to talk about your interactions with the men."

"I am not doing very well, am I?"

"Your brother was correct in his assessment that these men want a leader that they can respect, one who is strong both in word and deed."

Shaking his head, forlornly, Yeshua replies, "I am not here to lead them to war, but to teach them peace. I pray that they follow my example to manifest joy in their lives."

Poor Yeshua is not so joyful as of late. Sometimes Teoma wishes that they might take some treks together, just the two of them. Yeshua smiles, "We were quite a pair."

Placing a strong arm around his shoulders, Teoma agrees. "We still are. As boys, you used the energies to best our adversaries while I used the martial arts. Perhaps a demonstration of your particular skills would earn some respect from the men."

"But I understood from the Zadokites that many of the desert tribes are fearful of the mystics."

"Fear and respect travel arm-in-arm."

"Yes, but my message is one of love. Can a man not be respected in these times if he chooses to embrace his enemy rather than strike him down?"

"Unfortunately, no. But the world does not know you as I do. I respect you because of your compassion, the love you have always shown me, your willingness to forgive my humanity."

Halting, Yeshua turns and embraces him. "I love you, my brother. You are most willing to grow on your soul path. Besides you have known me so long."

"Well, after all these years, you have grown on me, Yesh."

The light in Yeshua's eyes dims somewhat as he murmurs, "But there is not enough time for me to grow on them."

Refreshed by a biting cold bath in preparation for Shabbat, Teoma carries a cutting of sage for Mary's twenty-fourth birthday. Although still new at manipulating the hayye, he helps shepherd the attitude of the village, astonished at the women's faith. In his experience, the desert clans are quite exclusive—prejudiced against outsiders. Apparently, these sentiments are held only by his brethren.

Outside the circle, men stand frustrated even as Yeshua exudes loving peace so Teoma joins the disciples in creating a net of support to hold back the tides of anger. Thankfully, Hava gathers women to join their efforts. Judas smiles as his men soften.

After the final prayers, Teoma looks for Mary. A large crowd of women has surrounded Yeshua, while their husbands wait impatiently to be attended. At the edge of the gathering, he hears a familiar voice and turns to see his former lover.

"You look well, Edia." Teoma smiles at her. "I pray you are happily married."

She smiles, her hair discreetly covered, but takes his hand and asks about the family in Galilee. Glad to see her happiness independent of him, he politely inquires about her new life and they part with a hug.

Separating from the growing throng of women, Tamar clasps Mary's hand fervently. A gentle night breeze blows Mary's dark curls enticingly over Tamar's face as they whisper intimately. Breathing deeply of the brisk evening air to quell his desire, his attention takes refuge within the crowd. How confident Yeshua is amongst women, in sharp contrast to his interactions with men.

Tamar finally hugs Mary who offers a bit of advice. "Dearest you, too, shall find your soul mate. Be open to love in whatever guise it presents." Her green eyes brighten at his approach.

"I wanted to wish you a happy birthday, Mary."

Graciously, she extends her hand and draws him close, thanking him with a warm hug for his humble gift. Tamar smiles at him. Perhaps Judas' youngest daughter might be receptive to his attentions this cold night and he will not have to tend sheep.

***

After I learn the dances of the desert clan, T'shuraw presents a gift for the festival. A scalloped multi-colored skirt rests low upon my hips, the deep blue girdle jingling with copper bells and a garment elaborately beaded to cover my breasts. And to dance with—a feathery-light silk dyed the deepest purple unto black.

"You are too kind, T'shuraw, it is beautiful."

Laughing as I twirl about, she replies, "My dear, it is tradition for the head matriarch to lead the women in the spring dance." She hands me a silver tambourine. "As the wife of our mashiach, I am asking you to lead us."

I can hardly express my gratitude for such an honor.

Ripe to celebrate the spring equinox, the clan of Judas gathers at dusk. Five roaring bonfires light the moonless night as the men dance in the open desert. Sweet flutes sing to the rhythm of the drums and my sisters sway with them, their heat exciting me. Tamar leans close, her breath fanning my cheek. "So who shall wear your shawl, Mary?"

"Since it is my anniversary, I shall grace my husband this night."

She gives me a faint smile, *But of course.*

The men recline in an open circle when the music changes for the women. Leading us to the edge of the circle, T'shuraw steps aside and allows me to pass.

Tambourine in hand, I lead my first dance. The significance of T'shuraw's gift to me is not lost on Judas' clan. The women have made their wishes clear, for if I am their chosen leader, then it is my choice of mate who is the clan's symbolic chieftain. If they refuse Yeshua, the tribe shall be divided.

Mary, my love, you are the Elat tonight.
And you shall be the chosen one.

Many songs later, only the young and vigorous still dance, the others sit by their men. Signaling the musicians, T'shuraw nods and we dance with our colorful veils to the seductive melodies. The heat in my body rises with my exertion, my desire stirred by the drum. Tamar engages me with an arousing dance.

From my hips, the copper bells cry out their passion to my swirling skirt. Trailing behind, the sheer purple silk undulates at my bidding. Bare skin glistening with oil, I drop to my knees just beyond Yeshua, lying back to dance serpentine.

Sensuously rising, my hair falls before my eyes, so I swing it away to see not Yeshua, but Tamar before me. Lithe arms entwine, our bodies gliding together. I dance with abandon to meet her passion. The haunting melodies of the flutes fill my ears, the drums in rhythm with my heart. A column of swirling energies surrounds us as we slide to the earth, mirroring each other. Still holding my shawl, my lover breathlessly awaiting, I lean back, arms wide inviting the hayye of the night. Tamar leans forward to embrace me. Her wet kiss so stirring I clasp her close, the shawl veiling us.

So I am her choice tonight.

Within my navel, the elestial stone burns as passionately as she, but I whisper, "Your passion is more than I can bear, but I cannot be with you this night." Slowly we part to follow where the music leads. She exits the circle and I turn to face Yeshua. Before the drums can die away, I place my shawl upon the shoulders of my husband, dropping to my knees in a bow.

Through the veil of my hair, he lifts my face. At the touch of his sweet lips, my passion surges to drip upon the desert sand.

"The Elat has chosen, Yeshua—our mashiach."

Judas' voice rings out and Yeshua rises clasping me to him. The men cheer loudly and one by one stand with their wives to celebrate their leader. The clan of Judas united once again.

Shifting Illusions

Dawn in Judaea greets us with a palette of soft hues. Lavender, pink, coral, and blue blend as the Creator takes a brush of light to paint the vast canvas of desert sky. Nocturnal creatures creep beneath the protection of great limestone rocks sprinkled throughout the bland bowl of sand. Soft as a whisper, a cool spring breeze murmurs the rising of the village. A bittersweet aching in my breast, time again to say farewell.

Laden with gifts, our mounts plod toward Bethany. Teoma needles Yeshua. "After Mary's dance, we were surprised you were her choice." Ignoring Yeshua's glare, he goes on, "Fortunately it was your anniversary or she might have chosen a goddess for a mate." Fantasies well provisioned, Teoma turns to me, "So Mary, how does Yeshua compare to Tamar?"

Still feeling her lips on my cheek from this morning's kiss, I walk tearfully ahead. Yeshua sends me comforting hayye, but only Jochanan's intervention soothes like a balm.

He puts an arm around Teoma's waist to draw him away from Yeshua. "My friend, I never told you, but before Saul, I had my eye on you. Imagine my disappointment when I discovered you had limited yourself to women!"

When Teoma turns to offer protest, Jochanan kisses him. Pulling hastily away, Teoma wipes his mouth roughly. Jochanan's look of dismay invites Yeshua's embrace.

"While the rest of us limit ourselves by judgment, only Mary is willing to explore her sensuality fully." Saul observes.

"Unfortunately, I am not free of judgment."

Yeshua shakes his head at Saul's unspoken concern, "It is not from my judgment that Mary suffers, but her own. Although open to her sensuality without the barriers of gender, what contains her is the commitment to our covenant of marriage." Saul nods.

It's what contains us all. Teoma thinks bitterly.

Yeshua puts an arm around him and for the first time, Teoma hears my husband's silent expression of gratitude. A smile steals my resolve.

Sheikan follows closely on my right, encouraging me to mount him. I hug the great horse, already overburdened with T'shuraw's gifts of embroidered garments for the children and lovely tapestries, which I shall give Martha to adorn the walls of her new home in Bethany. His soft nicker warms my heart, enticing me with images of racing across the desert to an oasis. Foreheads pressing together, our breath falls into rhythm, Sheikan speaks, *We are as one, let us run through the valley of dreams.*

Yeshua catches up to us. "My love, why don't you ride for a while? We can redistribute Sheikan's packs onto the donkeys."

Shall we unburden my heavy heart as well? "I have never loved anyone as I do you, Yeshua. But the more I discover, the more connected I feel, my love expands to encompass all. Lost in my passion, overwhelmed by my sensuality, there is less differentiation between that which I love and myself. Upon Sheikan, I am connected to All That Is, just like with you."

Caressing my face, Yeshua whispers, "You search for boundaries so that you might not expand beyond what you believe yourself to be. That is your judgment. That you are finite, mortal, limited. You are not. You are eternal, your love is boundless. Someday we shall release one another from our earthly covenant." With a tender kiss, I melt into his embrace.

After repacking the donkeys, Teoma whispers an apology and lifts me upon Sheikan's back. Unbridled and bare, Sheikan stretches low to gallop across the sandy hills. The wind whisks by as our breath matches one another until there is one spirit, rucha, residing within us—horse, rider, earth. In the austere beauty of the desert, dotted by the minute potential of life, where the golden sand touches the clear blue sky, the hayye of the Great Mother pulsates. Like a pregnant woman, the translucent golden hayye encases a rich green flicker of living potential.

Circling back to our companions, Teoma's mare nickers in welcome, yet we slip from the illusion of the desert of Judaea into the reality of living potential. The oasis Sheikan projected greets us with lush fertility. Rich green vegetation of enormous proportions surrounds a living spring whose moisture purifies the air passing through our nostrils. Birds adorned in rainbow feathers sing cheerfully, as strange furry creatures scamper underfoot. As far as the eye can see, the damp forest drips with life, chattering monkeys and vibrant snakes hanging from the fruit-laden branches. We have entered the womb of the Great Ima, for beneath the veil of sand exists this vibrant infant ripe for birth.

We explore, drinking deeply of the life-giving waters, tasting the strange but luscious fruits of the brilliant trees. So enchanted, I plunge naked into the cool clear spring. Fish of vibrant hue slip between our limbs as we enjoy the dance of life. Sheikan laughs, showing creamy teeth.

The others search for us beyond the boundaries of the illusion still within the dry austere desert from which we emerged. Teoma is frantic, while my husband reaches through the ethers.

Yeshua, I am here, right before you. The desert is but an illusion, for beneath it lays a lush jungle.

Smiling, Yeshua reassures the others and using raza, disappears before they can ask anymore. Drawn by his desire to my side, he looks about in wonder. "Mary, what have you discovered?"

"Sheikan brought me to this oasis to wash away my sorrow."

Yeshua strokes the great horse. "So beneath the illusion of the desert lies a co-existing reality. This is from whence I filled our water skins last year when we traveled to Jerusalem. I did not see this lush potential but it appears that all of creation is already here in this place without time."

His awe reflects the Great Mother's vitality. Still damp from my bath, I touch his chest longingly, "Perhaps this is Eden and if so, you are overdressed." I slip back into the water and laughing, he strips to join me.

"How long have you been here, love?" The bright fish search for passage between us, but soon there is little room for even the slimmest of water life.

Breathlessly, I kiss him, the water heightening my passion, "Before you came, we had explored this place, ate and drank, but I have no sense of time."

Pressing me into his evident desire, he whispers, "That is because there is no time here. It was only moments from when you disappeared until you contacted me."

Smiling, I reach for him. "Good, then we shall not be missed." As he enters me, the surreal nature of the environ magnifies the energies of our passion. In divine illumination, the prism of nura that accompanies our union is translucent so that the jungle surrounding us appears to exist in layers. The sandy dry desert furthest away progresses toward the center into thicker vegetation until it reaches the core of this lush Eden.

When finally we part, Yeshua tells me hoarsely, "In all of my searching for Sacred Unity, it is in your embrace that I come closest to surrender."

I kiss his precious mouth. "We are blessed to have one another, but how many times have you hinted that I might find this with another? So shall you."

His eyes are soft, fathomless, and I yearn to fall in and lose myself, but since this new awakening, I have a choice, and at this moment we are wanted by the others. Still he stares at me. *She grows beyond me, becoming more unreachable. Searching not, she surrenders to her passion and it leads her to this. I am a teacher who has much to learn.*

Yeshua, I still look to you for enlightenment. Without your fine instruction, I could have never discovered this reality, never seen the beauty beneath the surface.

His smile is endearing. *You have always seen the beauty within, for you are beauty. There is much still to do before I fulfill my purpose.*

Dressing, we mount Sheikan and return to our companions.

***

In Nazareth, a pall pervades the fields and shadows the house, but with the delivery of Rebeka's twins in mid-Iyar, the shroud lifts briefly. While the women busily tend to the new mother, Yeshua finds respite tutoring his own children.

A month goes by before he finally makes the effort to request an audience with Joseph. Pausing at the doorway, he prays to be able to control his emotion and coaxes a smile to his lips.

Lean and gray, Joseph motions for him to be seated. In the manner of his father, Yeshua commences the discourse with appreciation, "I want you to know that I am truly grateful for all that you have done for me—the training, the mystics, especially sacrificing your former way of life to bring us here to Galilee."

"You do not think me capable to be out in the world, but it is time. Time to release my attachments to all I love, so that they might in turn release me." Yeshua further probes, "Perhaps in withdrawing from the family now, you prepare for another sacrifice?"

"Yeshua, it was a conscious choice to leave Qumran. I am not sacrificing anything to make this trip!"

"Aren't you?"

Joseph's voice trembles, "Son, what does our future hold?"

Yeshua realizes—Abba doesn't know. Reiti taught him well not to interfere, so he reveals only a glimpse of his own path. "While in Britannia, I learned I am not long for this world…"

"Yeshua! Your thoughts create reality!"

"No Abba, this is my destiny. I am here to teach, perhaps not the kind of redeemer our people expect. If it serves my mission, I shall take the crown when the time is ripe." He pauses, but Joseph does not speak. "I seek to blend the role of priest and king that I might teach through example."

Swallowing thickly, Joseph's concern bubbles up to the surface of his turbid mind. *Truly he jests—the priesthood and kingship must be separate! The Tzadokim will spurn him. Even the Chaverim and Essenes will withdraw their support giving the Romans an even greater advantage. Saul is correct—my son loves to play with fire.*

"Quite a fiery barrier, I aim to cross." A spark of fear flashes in Joseph's eyes. "Speak not of this to your friends—Simeon, Judas, or Theudas. I will tell them in my own time."

"These men are your advisors. Please heed their counsel."

"Abba, I had hoped to make them disciples, but they ready their zealot troops for war against the Emperor. I will not carry a sword, but shall show them another way."

"Son, you must protect yourself, your family…"

"I have kept Teoma near as protector…"

"You depend too greatly upon him." Joseph shakes his head, "His love for your wife may prove insurmountable."

Hiding his own concern, Yeshua claims, "Your role as protector is over, Abba. I am a grown man who trusts that all will be well. My wife must make her choice and I pray that she stays by my side, but it must be for the fulfillment of her divine path, not mine."

Joseph withdraws to his thoughts. *How far my son has grown into manhood with more courage than me to tempt fate as such.*

"Not courage, Abba, but faith." Pressing his hands against the table, he captures Joseph's gaze to pierce the veil about his heart, "Be here now with all of your heart and soul while you can."

Yeshua approaches to kiss his father once on each cheek before taking his leave.

Past the stables, laughter caresses his ears. Somewhere within the barn, Mary tends to Sarah and Joshua. Sinking to his knees in the newly planted field, the rich dark mud seeps through his tunic. He covers his face with his hands, yearning for his wife.

She arrives in an instant, as fresh and real as the earth below.

"Yeshua, what is it?"

He cannot answer. Standing, she helps him to his feet, "Come, love, let us seek respite under that far grove of trees." Silently they walk arms linked until finding a comforting spot to sit.

"All of these years, I envisioned serving this mission alone." She catches her breath. "Before, I realized your importance to my work. I assumed Abba would be here to take care of the family." Shaking his head, he grieves, "But how could I accept the crown, if my father is in line before me?" With a shudder, he reaches to pull her close, "Soon Abba will leave to hide his life's work in the Himal range never to return and when Savta dies shortly after, my mission must begin."

Fervently, she brings in a prism of nura and he murmurs his thanks. Her hand gently stroking his back comforts him, but it is her sea-green eyes that fill him with hope.

"You are beloved. One with Eloha. You agreed to this work, at this time in human consciousness, because in the Light of the One, you recognized your worthiness. Here on Earth it is difficult to remember who you are though your purpose may seem clear."

"I know all of this, yet still I feel great pain. I have assisted your Savta through the portal with such ease yet grieve the loss of my Abba? How can I be a teacher if I cannot live the principles?"

Her whisper upon his cheek is soft as a breeze. "How can you be a great teacher if you don't fully experience the life that your fellow beings suffer through?"

"I expect so much of myself, yet I should know better—death is not a separation but a part of the soul's journey."

She breathes deeply as if trying to keep from falling into his despair. "You have tried to prepare me for your passing from this life. You have assured me that we will not be separated in spirit, only in form. But while in this body, form seems much more real."

They embrace each other's grief until interrupted by angelic radiance. Archangel Michael speaks in resonating silvery tones.

Dearest Yeshua, as a child, your ethereal nature allowed you to envision your mission with compassionate detachment. As a youth, unencumbered by your human relationships, you quenched your search for knowledge by absorbing truth from teachers, mentors, parents, as well as your divine connection.

With a wave of loving compassion, the angels move through them. *Now as a man in relationship to those you love, you have become fully embodied to connect to All That Is. Joyous loving desire opened the portal to your heart full of human emotion, which will serve you greatly during the time of the mission. Feeling human may seem arduous, but it is Divine, beloved Son.*

The angels surround them in winged embrace, as Michael continues his counsel. *Yeshua, no sacrifice is necessary to complete your soul path, but you agreed to embody the way back to Source, to model for your fellow beings how to be joyfully human. You are not alone, for here is Mary as well as all who agreed to support you on your journey into form. But even in the arms of your beloved, you mourn separation from Source as you predict your Abba's passing. Is not this counsel you receive as real as that which you have been given by your devoted parent? As we come to you this day, so shall your father, for in form and in rucha he is committed to you.*

With a great expansion of his hayye, Yeshua opens his heart to the radiance. "Thank you, dear friends. My heart is lightened by the wisdom of your counsel. I shall try and remember to be more gentle with myself in the density of this human form." Lying back with his wife upon the breast of the Great Ima, he takes comfort in the ministrations of the archangels. The sun sets golden when they awaken from their repose. "So much left to learn, yet I shall be thrust out into the world before I can complete my soul lessons."

Leaning upon her elbow, Mary kisses his mouth. "My love, perhaps this mission is to be the greatest part of your awakening to the truth of who you are." He smiles.

"How is it that you have grown so in wisdom?"

"Yeshua, thankfully when one of us is feeling most vulnerable, the other can provide illumination. I am grateful, you have shown me how to seek the deeper truth, for now when you are in need, I can embody the light as you have done for me so many times." Kissing her precious lips, he prays that she be blessed with patience for the path he seeks shall be arduous.

***

During the celebration of Sarah's eighth birthday, Yeshua announces our return to Magdala in spite of Joseph's protests for us to join the family at the shore. My husband spends much of the day in meditation while his father labors diligently over the scrolls. Neither man leaves much time for one another, pursuing separate soul paths.

I seek respite from the brewing storm upon Sheikan each balmy afternoon. After currying his coat with a stiff brush, I bury my face into his neck soothed by his sweet fragrance. Sheikan nickers softly when Teoma enters the stall.

"It appears we are all searching for something."

"Here, you can help me search." I hand him a comb, overcome by his enticingly earthy scent.

Teoma begins grooming Sheikan. "There is something unspoken. Cold like a death shroud." How far he has come in his sensitivities. Sheikan nips my sadin, forcing me to step back into Teoma. *This horse acts as both friend and foe. The perfume of her hair is intoxicating.*

"Teoma! Your thoughts are difficult to block."

Groaning, he leans one arm over Sheikan, "Mary, the silence is so unnerving, I wish for the gaiety of Qumran."

"Of course, you had all the company you could desire and no one to look after."

He brushes a tendril from my face. "I did enjoy the camaraderie, and I must admit that the diversions took this pressure off."

The stable feels intensely close, perhaps we should move outside. "Teoma, I want to talk to you, but do not wish to be carried away by our passion."

With a sigh, he admits, "Since our meeting in Qumran, I have been more conflicted about my feelings, Mary." I place a hand on his chest, partly to stay him, partly to connect.

"Please, you need to find a lover." He shakes his head, so I persist, "Yes, someone who will be with you…"

"And what woman would be willing to be my concubine while another has my heart?"

Desperately, I clasp the front of his tunic. "You stubbornly refuse to open your heart to another. By the time we come together, you will have deprived yourself for so long that you may have nothing to give."

By that time I will be too old to care!"

"You won't be old but maybe too closed to enjoy!"

His voice is gruff with emotion. "This is foolish talk. Joseph has worked hard to perfect his craft. Yeshua will live long, like his Abba before him."

My lower lip trembles, "Not nearly as long as his father, who will precede his own." Teoma's eyes widen.

"This is what is unspoken." He clasps my arm to draw me close, "What do you know, Mary?"

His overpowering presence cannot be refused. "I know nothing for certain. But what you feel, what we all feel, is sorrow, for Joseph is preparing to leave us. Yeshua mourns him as we speak."

Teoma's face is stricken, "This cannot be. Who shall take care of the family during Yeshua's mission, if not Abba Joseph?" In response to his pain, my own spills.

"I do not know. Please, I only told you this so you might not feel so alone. We must love one another fully so that we recognize the hayye of those who pass through the veil before us."

Great tears spill down Teoma's smooth cheeks. He responds to my embrace, holding me tightly to his chest. "I am sorry, Mary, to bother you with my passion. But I am not sorry that our encounter made clear what feels out of rhythm here. You are right. We must make the best use of our time with Abba." He kisses the top of my head before releasing me.

Later, a cool night breeze passes through our chamber window, tempering the heat of my flesh as I lie next to my sleeping husband. Whenever Yeshua chooses to contemplate his destiny with meditation, he moves so deeply within that he loses touch with his physical body. Segregation was easier than having him so near yet so far. Turning over, I can find no peace and leave our bed to meditate in the garden. Perhaps I shall exist out-of-body as well.

Under the waxing moon, I pass through our courtyard toward the garden, drawing my shawl tight to ward off the chill but I am not alone. Looking up from the edge of the fountain, Joseph whispers, "Can you not sleep, Mary?"

"No, Abba, I am ill at ease."

He pats the ground next to him so I sit to watch the night sky in silence. Finally Joseph speaks, "Tell me what is troubling you." I sigh; doesn't he feel the oppressive hayye that lies in wait like a prowling beast?

His chuckle is dry, "No longer transparent in thought, but your passion threatens to erupt."

"Is it that obvious?"

"Mary, exposing you to boundless mores has stoked an already too hot fire."

I study a face never easy to read. "You know how long Yeshua can abstain from food and…well…I do not believe our forced segregation in Qumran was as difficult for him as it was for me."

Joseph raises one eyebrow, assuming I want him to talk to his son about our marriage bed.

"No, not that! I do not know how much Teoma told you, but we were very tempted by one another in Qumran. He, at least, had other diversions so thank goodness, nothing happened." Joseph doesn't blink an eye for which I am immensely grateful, "He stubbornly refuses to take a lover. Please. He'll listen to you."

"I've had to intervene before," he sighs, "but I'll talk to him."

Kissing his cheek, I bid him goodnight. Back in bed, my restlessness awakens Yeshua. "What is it, Mary?" He tries to tuck me into his body.

As I touch his face, the tears begin to fall, "Since you can no longer read my thoughts, you do not know my turmoil."

He kisses me before speaking, "Teoma tempts you because, once again, I have left you wanting."

"I am sorry, Yesh,"

"I suppose Sheikan cannot take my place." Shaking my head, I eagerly accept his intimate embrace.

I welcome our colorful climax, but for Yeshua it releases deep layers of emotion. With a broken voice, he admits, "It appears that I have hardly scratched the surface of my despair. I do not know if I can do this."

"Perhaps if you expressed your feelings to your Abba…."

Exhausted, he shakes his head "In your arms I just feel so much more, but there is still time to speak to him."

I'm afraid when they finally come together, the tremendous release may be more than either of them can bear.

Forbidden Fruit

By the new moon of Tammuz, we head west to the Sea of Galilee. The children ride double upon the black mare. Teoma rides alone. Yeshua struggles to remain present, but casts surprised glances back at his friend's brazen thoughts.

"You realize that we can hear you." I gently remind Teoma.

"It is challenge enough to curb my behavior; must I also control my thoughts?" Yeshua tells me silently to remind him that....

"Yes, I realize that thought creates reality!" Teoma perceived us!

It appears that his desire for you is expanding his abilities.

Teoma is not amused. *Yes, desire is a great teacher. For as long as it shall be unmet, you just might find me in the ethers with you, Yeshua.*

When we arrive in Magdala, Eleazer places an arm around his shoulder. "What troubles you, my friend?" Shrugging him off, Teoma mumbles something about seeing to the animals and leaves.

Yeshua tries to explain, "It has been quite rough since we returned, Eleazer. Perhaps that pretty Greek girl who helps with the children is still in your employ?"

"When has Teoma ever had problems with women?" Shaking his head in disbelief, he continues, "Helena is married now; her husband works in the gardens and stables." Thankfully Martha does not ask me any questions as we attend to the children.

The tranquil lake provides respite as Teoma focuses his attention on teaching Joshua to swim. In a mere two days, my three-year-old son paddles to me. My gratitude induces a smile from my formerly sullen friend. Jumping from my arms to swim back to shore, Josh calls for his Abba. Teoma wades closer.

"It delights me to help your children learn and grow." Teoma watches Joshua run back to the house with great affection. Turning, his fingers graze my cheek, "When I look in your eyes, I lose myself. I do not believe I can ever love anyone as I do you." Yearning to be comforted, to comfort him, I rest between the cleft of his chest. "Ours is a strange destiny. I do not know what will become of us, but I pray to be shown a way."

Splashing vigorously, my son swims toward us as a large crow circles above. Yeshua watches from the shore wondering what more might be discovered at the Sea of Galilee. I pray nothing as painful as last summer.

Distracted one evening, I spill wine upon my creamy sadin. Offering a murmured excuse to Martha and Eleazer, I hurry to rinse out the stain. The staff has been released for the evening, so I am alone to fend for myself until Teoma enters the kitchen.

Hands on either side of the basin effectively corral me. "Please, you're blocking my light." Warm breath on the back of my neck causes a shiver. "Why do you insist on making this so difficult?"

He turns me around and without a word, takes the rag from my hands, then kneels to dab at the stain over my left thigh. "Didn't Joseph talk to you about taking a lover?"

The stained rag still in his hand, he looks up, close enough to kiss. "I have had enough meaningless encounters to last a lifetime."

"Meaningless?"

He shakes his head forlornly, "I suppose loveless would be a better word. You wouldn't know, for you have only shared intimacies within the bounds of love." Studying his earnest face, I want to reach out to him, take away this pain, fulfill this longing, but—not only for him.

"You ask me to take a lover, but I cannot love her. Even if I find a woman willing to be with me, something will be missing—something has always been missing."

My knees weaken with rising heat. Almost imperceptibly, his nostrils quiver as if scenting my desire. "Teoma, I do not know how to ease your suffering."

His eyes shine bright, expectant. *Don't you?* Gathering my resolve, I slip away from him and out of the kitchen.

"Did the stain come out?" Martha asks concerned. I nod, and sit next to her. Leaning into my sister's embrace, I shake my head at Yeshua's silent inquiry. "Do you want to talk?" I really do, but where to begin? Martha takes my hand, collects some blankets from the chest in the hall, and leads me into the starry night.

I hold nothing back, telling her everything especially how Yeshua's lack of attention frustrates me as much as Teoma's increasing advances thin my resolve.

"So what are you going to do?"

"I don't know. Yeshua's struggling with his Abba."

"Is that why he has been so distant?"

Distant is a good description for out-of-body, "Yes, not available to anyone."

Martha kisses my cheek, "How about holding some conscious conception circles? That should keep you busy. We can send word to Capernaeum; I'm sure the goyim women would like to attend." I agree with an embrace.

Later I lay tucked into my husband's body, hearing his thoughts. *I hope Martha assists her, for I do not have the strength.* I think that we all need more strength, for always in the past Teoma carried us through the burden of our desire. But now he is losing heart and I burn with unmet need while Yeshua hovers between the worlds.

Days after our talk, my tension has only increased. Yeshua meditates under the light of the full moon, while Martha and I put the children to bed. In the gathering room, Eleazer entertains Teoma with a game of mancala.

"Come join us." Eleazer pats the nearest cushion and Teoma mimics him. "We'll play partners, you two against Martha and me."

Sighing, I sit, "I've played this and have an advantage."

Eleazer raises his brow, so Teoma explains, "She can read your mind so just beware." The game begins innocently enough as I try to block their thoughts, but Teoma becomes upset when I make a poor move, "Mary, are you purposely trying to give them an advantage?"

"It takes much energy to block your thoughts! It's just a game."

He scoffs, "Well, it could be a more pleasant diversion, if you would try to be my partner," I cast him a warning look, "for the sake of the game."

"Is it my fault you have no other diversions to occupy you?"

He raises his brows. "Do you really want to discuss that now?"

"You two sound like an old married couple." Eleazer's chuckle becomes a grunt when Martha elbows him.

With a penetrating look, Teoma replies, "It has been like a nine year marriage…" adding silently for my benefit, *but without the privileges.* Gasping, I get up and disturb the game. Stones roll all over the floor.

I run out as Eleazer chastises Teoma, "For goodness sakes, man, it is just a game!"

Yeshua's body sits uninhabited upon the lakeshore, his consciousness perusing the ethers. Dropping to my knees, I bury my face in my hands. Restless, I cannot wait and call to him, irritated when he does not immediately return.

"Mary, what is it?"

Finally! I fall into his lap, but to my dismay he is slow to respond. Holding me off, he says, "Tell me what is bothering you."

Furious anger rises in me. Anger—that I must tell him everything. Anger—that I know not how to begin. Anger—that he no longer meets my passion.

I nearly leave, to go…but where? He draws me back, his fatigue thinning the silver cord that binds us. Suddenly I realize that his cord of attachment to me is nearly transparent. Searching, I see his attachment to his father is gone. My perceptions bring me no joy. "So you shall surrender me without a fight?"

His face shows concern, "Mary, why would I fight?"

"Because my heart is being stolen away. Let us see if you still desire to free yourself from all your earthly attachments after we make love." Slowly he nods. "And don't hold back this time. I want all of you."

His face is grim. "I am not ready." I start to stand up, but he holds me fast.

"Let me go, Yeshua." Reluctantly he releases my arm. "I understand that you need this time to make peace with your Abba, but I did not expect that you would surrender me, too. Unlike Joseph, I have no plans to leave you."

Unable to return to the house lest I fall into temptation, I turn toward the cavern. No one will find me there.

Yeshua calls out, "Mary, do you not have to minister to the women tomorrow?"

I halt. What am I to give them? I shudder to think how much has shifted since returning to Galilee.

The new moon of Av brings some comfort as I offer conscious conception circles to the goyim women. Word spreads quickly so the day after Shabbat, a large group of prostitutes fill the courtyard. Martha provides me with a purse that they generously fill. Afterward, I ask a burning question. "Where might one find a suitable concubine?"

"For yourself or your husband?"

I smile, "For a male friend."

The matrona studies my face, "Why go to all that expense? You should take him as a lover." Of course, I am transparent to her.

"I cannot do that, so will you help me?"

She laughs, "Of course, what do you think he'll prefer? Goyim, Hebrew? Dark-skinned, light?" I shake my head, having no idea. "A beauty like you, but that will prove difficult. Hmm. Next week there will be a fine selection from Greece at the market in Capernaeum. Send word to the grand house north of the market and I will come so the traders do not take advantage." I thank Ilia's friend.

Martha shakes her head, "Perhaps to divert Teoma's attention, but it isn't proper for you to go with them to find a concubine." Feeling the weight of the coins in my purse, I hope there is enough.

My sister doesn't think I should surprise him, so while she occupies Eleazer by the lake after supper, I take Teoma aside. He looks suspicious when I offer him shekar.

"Only if you join me, Mary." I bite my lip, hoping to soften him to the idea and pour us both a cup. We slowly sip our wine. "Where is Yeshua?"

I swallow, my husband's continuous meditation a point of contention. We rarely talk anymore and not since that night in Nazareth have we been intimate. "By the shore."

"I'm sorry, Mary." He starts to take my hand, but I withdraw it.

"Please, Teoma, don't make this more difficult."

He leans close. "I don't believe I am making this any more difficult than he is." I nod, for once again my husband travels alone on his soul path.

"Can we go to Capernaeum next week? To find more men for the council?" Venturing as he searches my face.

"What else is in Capernaeum?"

"A merchant…with some goods." I smile weakly.

"Does this have anything to do with the women you treated today?" Sitting up hopefully, perhaps he contacted one. He drowns my hope. "I do not have to pay for sex."

Wringing my hands, I pursue, "But we can go to Capernaeum and," I pull my purse out from under the cushions, "This should be enough…."

His jaw sets. He'll never budge now. "I do not need your money. No more meaningless encounters. I will wait for love."

"Please," I beg, tears spilling, "please do not wait for me."

He touches my face softly. *If Yeshua keeps this up, I will not have to wait much longer.* Be it the wine or the grief, I surrender to the comfort of his embrace.

Late into the night, Martha wakes me. I slip out of Teoma's arms and she leads me to my room. *I can only pray they were truly sleeping.*

I kiss her cheek, "Nothing more. Why didn't Yeshua come in?"

Martha shakes her head, "I sent Eleazer out to look for him. I can't tell by the way I found you, but is Teoma willing to let you buy him a concubine?" I shake my head.

Yeshua arrives to see us crying in each other's arms. Martha sits up, indignant, "Yeshua, I love you as a brother, but you better come back to earth or you are going to lose my sister."

Kneeling at our feet, he hugs us both. After a while, we dry our tears. Yeshua kisses Martha and escorts her out, "Tomorrow we shall go to Capernaeum."

Martha shakes her head, "Leave Mary here, please."

"But I need her with me."

"Then go without Teoma." No response until he sees what she knows, then he slowly shakes his head.

"We need his escort. Do not worry." He thwarts her final plea. "Your sister will be fine." Martha leaves and Yeshua turns to me.

Sighing, I tell him everything, including Teoma's last prediction. A great tear flows down one cheek. On whose behalf does he shed this tear of compassion?

Slipping under the blankets, I turn my back to him, tired of asking for his comfort, but in the morning I awaken, my thighs wet. Once again Teoma found a way to meet me in the dream world. Turning to Yeshua, I lose my resolve.

He moans, responding through the fogginess of his dreams. Wishing for more, I remember Ilia's advice. After kissing my husband to consciousness, he finally embraces me, but before that glazed look of Druid concentration steals him away, I whisper, "May I help relieve you of your burden?"

He looks intrigued, so I lick my finger and search for the fig. His eyes widen. While I am greatly rewarded, my husband looks like he might vomit. I lie quiet as he rides out his pain.

At breakfast, Teoma greets me with a smile. Shaking her head, my sister seats the children around the table. Yeshua limps in, sitting down gingerly. Teoma raises a brow, but says nothing. Eleazer is not so shy. "Sitting so long in one position in the cold night air is sure to give you cramps."

Yeshua thanks Eleazer for the advice. Silently, I ask if he wants me to do a healing. *No, love, perhaps my discomfort will remind me to pay more attention to you.*

I scold the smirk from Teoma's face. He tries to suppress his mirth. *I'm sorry, but you must admit it is just rewards. So how did you convince him to stop withholding?*

I used a technique I learned from one of the women in my healing circle.

Teoma shakes his head. *You have learned much from the prostitutes.*

Yeshua looks between us, *Where was I when you both learned about this unusual practice?*

Out of your body! With flushed cheeks, my husband finishes his breakfast.

***

The three companions travel north. Teoma prays not to face anything more challenging than inquiring Roman soldiers, as Yeshua limps along the dusty road. They'll never get to Capernaeum and back before nightfall. Teoma silently urges Mary to offer her assistance. Her bright smile at his communication warms his heart.

"Yeshua, may I relieve you of this discomfort?"

Before he can refuse, Teoma interjects, "Please, you are slowing us down." Relenting to his wife's ministrations, Yeshua soon walks at a much faster pace.

415

"Thank you. May I go on?" They nod; he's been lecturing them since leaving Magdala. "What man has assumed were the laws of Eloha concerning commitment are actually fear-based misinterpretations. The commandments are contrived by man."

Teoma raises his brow, "Careful, Yesh, the Tzadokim will have you before the Sanhedrin." Mary shudders at his side.

"Perhaps, but while in Egypt, I learned that the code of the pharaohs is identical to the laws Moses gave the Yisraelites so they might live more harmoniously in the promised land." Yeshua puts an arm around his shoulder. "So let us take for example the commandment—you shall not commit adultery."

Teoma stiffens as Mary catches her breath.

"It is a property law, listed between you shall not commit murder and you shall not steal. One soul does not own another. Your commitment to another is out of love for yourself. If you are moved to be with a person other than your espoused, that too is out of love for yourself." Mary nods, Teoma is most discomforted.

"Every human behavior has a divine purpose, birthed from the loving intention of Eloha. What truly causes grief and suffering is taking action before the time is ripe or not taking action when the time is ripe. Divine timing is about readiness. Picking a fruit before it is ripe, consuming it before it reaches peak flavor lessens the reward which is joy." Yeshua looks quite pleased with himself.

"So committing adultery is forgivable if the time is right?"

"Forgiveness does not play a part here, Teoma. The time is not right or wrong. It is tava—ripe, or bisha—unripe. Remember this is about soulful readiness. Staying in connection with Eloha allows you to recognize ripeness and reap the sweetest fruits of your human endeavors. If you pick an unripe fruit, say, have sex with another man's wife, then the experience will taste sour. But if you wait until the fruit is ripe, say, after the other man passes on, then the experience will be sweet indeed."

Teoma gets his point, but Yeshua probes deeper, "Now if you but taste the fruit ripe or unripe, without picking it off the tree, the spot where you took a bite will rot, spreading into the fruit and perhaps the tree. If the time is ripe, pick the sweet fruit and enjoy it fully. If the time is unripe, prepare to experience the bitterness of sorrow."

Abruptly, Teoma halts to stand before Yeshua. "What if the unripe fruit hangs from a sick or dying tree that cannot provide it with complete nourishment? Do you leave it there to rot or pick it and set it in a sunny window to ripen?"

Yeshua slowly nods, "I hear you, Teoma."

Swept up by the tide of people, the three enter Capernaeum. In familiar cadence, vendors sing praises of their wares, enticing villagers who cease their frantic pace only when in synchrony with the melody emerging from a stall.

Taking a deep breath, Yeshua gives his wife a quick kiss and places her hand in Teoma's. "Please take Mary to the market place. She has some money to spend."

"How are you going to locate them on your own?"

Smiling, Yeshua says brightly, "It's all about divine timing. The time is ripe for the two to come into my life so we shall find each other." Floating away into the stream of humanity, he leaves them standing dumbly in the middle of the square.

"I hope I can be as trusting as he is when you are mine."

"He is rather confident we understood his parable about fruit."

"I pray he understood mine," Teoma murmurs as Mary downcasts her gaze.

Near amber stalls of pottery, a stately matrona approaches in a flurry of bright shawls. "Mary, your friend must be most anxious for his gift! I didn't expect you until next week." With an appraising glance at him, she purrs, "So are you to introduce me to your husband?"

Swallowing thickly, Mary corrects her. "This is my friend."

The matrona draws her away, but not out of Teoma's keen hearing. "Again, I wonder why go to such expense. He would make a most satisfying lover."

"But unfortunately, I am unripe fruit."

The matona frowns, not comprehending their private humor, but returns to flourish her attention on Teoma. "My dear friend Ilia praised Mary's services. Come to the house and see for yourself." She pats his rump before taking her leave.

Distracted by her nearness, he leads a blushing Mary through the market. Passing under an ornately carved marble arch, he stops to admire it. Would time spent creating beauty relieve the burden aching in his heart?

His contemplation is interrupted by Mary squeezing his arm imploringly, "Please take me to see the concubines."

"No, I don't wish to expose you to that." He gently guides her toward the silk.

"Please, I must see for myself."

Never has he been able to refuse her. Whatever she desires, if in his power, he delivers. Reluctantly, he escorts her to the traders of flesh. In stalls built for beasts, scantily-clad girls lounge—all slaves, some stolen, most sold to feed their families.

Mary's sorrow crashes against him. She turns pleading into his chest, "Do you not see one you like? Let us purchase her freedom." Pulling out her purse she cries, "Is this enough…"

He shields her silver from greedy eyes. "Listen, we cannot set even one free. She will starve to death. Any girl we might choose will be a lifelong responsibility."

"No! No! We must help them." Hysterical, she wretches her sorrow upon the street.

He holds back her unfettered hair and when she is through carries her weeping beyond the marketplace, cursing his poor decision to expose her to such crudeness. Comforting her in a narrow alleyway, Teoma finally speaks. "There's much suffering in this world. That is why Yeshua came—to show us…."

She is snatched from his arms. Teoma quickly draws his blade.

"Teoma, sheath your sword! This is Bartholomew."

Mary peeks behind the massive bulk of the intruder whose smile bares great yellow teeth. "This man you call your brother has plucked your beautiful wife and means to taste her."

He has moments of incredible perception, Yeshua reassures them.

Moments?

Long, dirty, uncombed hair, filthy fingernails, ragged clothing; Bartholomew is not what he expected.

The giant stoops to retrieve Mary's sandal then tenderly slips it on her foot. "There, the wife of Yeshua should not be barefooted." She tries to thank him, but he abruptly paces the alley, muttering.

He's insane! Can you not heal him?

Yes, but the time is not ripe, Teoma. Yeshua places a hand upon Bartholomew's chest. He instantly calms. "Where might I find your friend Phillip?" Bartholomew turns and with enormous strides nearly loses them.

Pursuing the newest disciple through the streets, Teoma inquires, *How is this going to work, Yeshua?*

Yeshua nearly runs to keep up. "Have faith, Teoma."

Bartholomew yells over his shoulder, "Yes, we all must have faith in Yeshua."

On the lakeshore outside Capernaeum, a semicircle of goyim listens to the teachings of a middle-aged Greek man. A long white robe belted about his thin form, Phillip nods a balding pate crowned by gray curls and the four sit.

Mary struggles to comprehend the Greek's discussion of that which exists within—the Divine essence. She looks to her husband and soon smiles, delighted. Teoma chuckles, remembering that Yeshua silently translated Hebrew into Aramaic for him when they visited the Holy Temple as boys.

"Wise teacher, you have clearly demonstrated the purpose of light, but can you illuminate us on the role of darkness?" Yeshua stands as Phillip searches the crowd.

"Son, the purpose of this life is to seek the light. We move out of the darkness of this earthly existence and into the light of spiritual illumination."

Extending his hayye, Yeshua speaks, "Shem is the essence of illumination that is born out of darkness. The chaotic, swirling hayye of the dark pushes us to seek the light. Imagine a pool of water in shadow, still and clear. In the darkness of the water, we may see our true reflection. The gift of the dark is the deliverance of greater understanding and deeper connection to Eloha, which is both light and darkness."

Phillip nods slowly, awed. "You are the one sent to show us the way to Source."

"If you are quite done with these fine men, I ask that you come with me." Bidding the crowd farewell, Phillip follows Yeshua.

So by early afternoon, five travel south to Magdala. Ahead, Phillip chats amiably with Yeshua. Teoma walks behind, paying close attention to Bartholomew. When the giant takes Mary's hand, he moves to interfere but Bartholomew appears less agitated.

Entertaining Mary with stories of his adventures here and beyond this reality, Bartholomew describes entering the dark void and emerging as a star seed, recounting how he lived as a slave long ago in Egypt, building the great pyramid of Giza, when lords of other worlds intervened to move

419

the massive stones, and the great glory of being killed and entombed with his beloved master. How could he be so intimately familiar with other lives yet be so disconnected from the present reality? Perhaps this is the nature of madness.

Past lives, so vividly detailed the memory could be of yesterday, Bartholomew even describes a future life in a strange land of golden pyramids. Clearly, the man exists outside the boundaries of time. Teoma smiles at Mary's fascination. She probably finds some odd connection.

At least Yeshua has secured wise Phillip. A goyim as renowned as the Head of the Order of Shem will prove useful in the mixed cultures of Palestine. But Bartholomew? Shaking his head, Teoma shall keep a close eye on the goyim who has evidently participated vigorously with the Egyptian Therapeutae. When he returned from Qumran, Joseph made him promise to teach Joshua the craft, but he shall advise the boy carefully for the disciple's malady may stem from too great a consumption of the sacred herbs or too profound an abstinence from all that grounds most men to this earth. Who can say how a man loses touch with reality?

When they arrive in Magdala, the children rush to greet them, stopping short at the sight of Bartholomew. First to approach, Joshua comes just past his knee to pull on the soiled tunic. "Are you a giant from Britannia?"

"No, child, I am from Galilee just like you." When Joshua raises his arms, Bartholomew lifts the boy like a kitten. Mary's nephews clamber up, forcing the large man to sit in the middle of the courtyard.

Eight-year-old Sarah waits until the boys stop petting Bartholomew before standing in the circle of his massive legs. She places her hands on each side of his head. "Your mind is split in two, but it can be woven back together when you wish."

Yeshua's chin quivers and Phillip smiles. "Your shem is apparent in your seed, son." He turns to Mary. "You are a fine match for Yeshua, embodying an equal balance of light and dark."

"Thank you. Your Aramaic is wonderful." Teoma chuckles for Phillip speaks Greek.

"Mary, your husband is not assisting your comprehension." Surprised she looks at Yeshua. "Through desire, you can understand all tongues." Phillip gently takes her hand. "My, you are a rare find indeed. As the goddess, the mysteries come so easily."

Thus begins an intense time of discovery for all. Phillip and Yeshua spend mornings deep in meditation and the afternoons discussing their ethereal discoveries. Teoma joins the children—swimming, fishing, and building fortresses on the coarse shore—if they are not listening to Bartholomew's fantastical stories. Whenever disconnection threatens, Bartholomew seeks out Mary or Yeshua and often little Sarah ministers to him.

For a short while, the comparison of fruit and adultery keeps Teoma at bay, until late one summer afternoon emerging from the lake Mary's exuberant nephews push her into the water. Scolding the boys, he lifts her up, her garment clinging tantalizingly. He draws her close and sees the mirror of his desire.

"Look Josh, your Dod Teo is hungry, too. Let's bring him some sweet fruit from the garden." Turning around, the giant disciple heads back to the house with the child.

The water cools their desire. "When will the time be ripe?" His question hovers between them, the air heavy with anticipation.

Another tense week passes. Teoma stretches his muscular legs, arching his tight back, the sheet sticking uncomfortably. What havoc Queen Lilith has created with these nightly emissions.

Since Mary's dance in Qumran, their every interaction has taken on an erotic sensuality. Always most vivacious, but now…. Hadn't he tried to treat her as a beloved sister, protect her in her husband's absence—even from his own desire? Always he has lived his life honorably, yet….

Sighing, he considers an early morning swim, but the aroma of breakfast wafts from the kitchen and Martha insists they eat together. Another meal where he will be placed next to temptation.

The baths appear to be unoccupied but he soon realizes he is not alone. Coming upon Yeshua relieving his own burden, Teoma's anger threatens to engulf them both.

"Do you even realize how difficult it has been for us? How can you refuse to be with her? She is your wife!"

Yeshua responds quietly, "Do you remember last summer when my slightest touch caused Mary such agony? Well, now our intimate connection uncovers painful roots of sacrifice that I cannot bear."

"In denying her, you are sacrificing your relationship for what? Illumination?" Shaking his head, Teoma turns away. Perhaps he'll take that swim after all.

"There is no reason why you should suffer as well. Please find some diversion for yourself." Teoma does not bother to acknowledge the advice.

Late to breakfast, he apologizes to Martha, his appetite gone. Perhaps some bread might settle his...Yeshua passes the breadbasket.

"I wish you would stay out of my mind." Teoma growls as Yeshua returns his attention to his plate. He silently thanks Mary for the apologetic concern creasing her lovely forehead. How much longer will he be able to linger between loyalty and love? For the first time in his life, they are not as one in his heart.

"Dod Teo, you mustn't suffer so while you wait for Ima." Patting his arm, Sarah rises to her knees and hugs him. He kisses the children, then lingers unsure before leaving the table. Excusing them profusely to Martha, Bartholomew runs to catch him.

"Wait, friend."

They walk in silence away from the village of Magdala. Teoma's surliness begs for a fight, a stiff confrontation with a Roman to ease his discomfort. With a great heave, Bartholomew shoves him off the road. Teoma rights himself quickly, but the big man rams him again.

"What the....oof..." His wind knocked out, Teoma lies still, not foolish enough to take on this giant.

Bartholomew hauls him to his feet. "Come now. Better to take your frustration out on me than to come to any harm."

"You think," he gasps, "I cannot defend myself?"

"I know you can, but the damage you'll cause some poor soldier will get you sent to the galleys and then what shall Yeshua do?"

Brushing his tunic, Teoma mutters, "He would be better off rid of me."

Bartholomew places a heavy arm across his shoulders, "Never think that. He loves you dearly and needs you to take care of what is his."

"I cannot abide within his shadow. I'm in love with his wife," His voice breaks.

"The time will come when you shall have the sweet fruit. Have patience."

"I have waited so long!"

"And you'll wait longer. Now let us find some nice women to share our woes."

Teoma whispers, "I cannot."

"What! Are you an Essene?" Teoma shakes his head miserably. "Then you shall find pleasure in the arms of another. You need not share your love, but you will share your seed." Bartholomew roughly brushes Teoma's back. "Next time I take you to Capernaeum, you must take a bath!"

***

Restlessly, I roll over, too distressed to sleep. Teoma and Bartholomew never returned after their hasty departure this morning. My husband lies beside me most unavailable. Desiring to connect, my hand slides down his side yet his prickling skin withdraws from my touch. In dismay, I search the ethers to find Teoma in the arms of another. With a wrenching of my heart, I turn away from my husband.

"Please, Mary, do not leave me."

Melting against his hardness, his every hair a tiny fingertip, I throb with desire. Breathing in my scent, he lies still. Undeterred, I maintain a chaste distance, but imagine he fills me until climaxing in violet. With a sharp intake of breath, Yeshua cries out, drawing his knees between us. I hold him, murmuring my apology. "Mary," he gasps, "know that I love you, but even your passion is more than I can bear."

At dawn, I slip out of his embrace, greatly wishing to be in a chamam. I meet my sister in the baths and kissing her cheek, ask that she care for the children until I return.

"Please tell Teoma or he will be worried."

Martha strokes my face. "But what about Yeshua?"

"My passion causes him pain. He will appreciate the respite." Martha's look of concern dissolves into pity. "Frankly if I don't leave, Teoma will have to, for I can bear this no longer." My sister sadly escorts me to the nursery. I kiss the children goodbye and return to my room.

From the edge of the bed, I kiss Yeshua's forehead. Stirring from his slumber, he whispers, "I am sorry, Mary."

"I am going now to stay with Hephziva."

He reaches up to stroke my cheek, "I pray you find what you are looking for." I pray he does as well before traveling through time and space to the temple of Astarte.

When is the Time Ripe?

3780

When will the time be ripe to pursue
The multidimensional self that is you?
Connected to All That Is and beyond
The Self that is Love, One with Eloha.

The Dark and the Light

"Mary, it is good to have you back within the protection of the temple. What troubles you, my dear?"

Hephziva sits on plump cushions in the inner sanctum sparkling with crystals. Rejuvenated after my salt water soak, I reveal my woes as she reflects the portal of my transformation.

"So, what do you desire, Mary?"

After careful contemplation, I speak, "I want to understand what I am to learn from this path my husband has taken."

"I believe you have learned much since we parted. Tell me, have you ever traveled in your body except to be with Yeshua?"

"Yes! Once in Samaria, I was needed by my daughter and I was pulled to her."

"Ahh! But this time you were not pulled by another's need, but named your own. An entirely different experience, was it not?"

"Yes, but…" I quickly exhale my burning inquiry, "Why do I suffer so immensely without sensual contact?"

With an expression of fascination, she responds, "A rapturous soul borne out of the seductive chaos of darkness embodies into the most brightly burning light. You are the living presence of the dark and the light. Your relationship with Yeshua is a perfect mirror of your true self."

Drawing breath, I focus to better understand. "But then how is it that I desire Teoma so much? How could I be so responsive to Tamar? How, if I am with Yeshua?"

"My dear, you are capable of connecting to any other embodied soul who is willing to surrender to your passion. That is why you find others attractive. Teoma's loving desire to serve you attracts your sensuality. Tamar was your first experience with the passion of women." Seeing my look, she laughs, "Yes, first! There will be much more sensuality in your lifetime."

Sorrow merging with delight, I know it is true. "But how might I exist now, while my husband seeks illumination on sacrifice?"

"Yeshua is realizing his sacrificial nature by denying himself connection through your love. He will come to see this for himself."

"That is what Teoma told him yesterday."

"Although quite wise, your earthly love does not fully recognize his own spiritual nature, but I see he has made great strides in his pursuit of you." Dear Teoma has indeed progressed. "Others are attracted to your dark seductive hayye of potential, because you create an undeniable yearning in those who fear not to come near unto your burning flame."

"This mission is not only Yeshua's?"

Smiling, she answers softly, "No, it is yours, and all of us who wish to connect to Source. Yeshua came as gemera—a whole, completed man embodying the essence of the Divine, which is inclusive in each of us."

She pauses to study my reaction. "It is most difficult to stay in connection to the One in human form, much more so as a male. Well connected to the vast expanse of emotion, you progress most rapidly through your soul path." She must be right, for last summer, my reaction to my husband's touch lasted but a couple of weeks, while Yeshua's has gone on now for nearly three moons. "You, my dear, are also the embodiment of gemera in female form—thoroughly inclusive of Divine Creation within and without. So inclusive, that you long to share your understanding of Eloha passionately with all."

Now that our mutual desire has sparked the flame of manifestation, speaking distantly to Teoma is much easier, but one quiet afternoon, I am drawn back to the Sea of Galilee to find him standing furiously over Yeshua.

Teoma came upon the children swimming virtually unattended near their father's uninhabited body. Fishing them out of the lake, he handed Sarah and Joshua to Bartholomew who transported them, one tucked under each arm, to their waiting Doda. Then Teoma pinched Yeshua's nose shut forcing him to return gasping.

"What's wrong? You haven't done that since we were boys."

Fists clenched, Teoma barely contains his anger. "That was the most irresponsible thing you have ever done."

"What are you talking about?"

"Your children escaped from Martha, and seeing you sitting on the beach, they thought it would be fine to swim. Of course, only your body was here, while you were out perusing the ethers."

Yeshua's eyes are full of compassion. "I would never allow any harm to come to them."

"Can you be out of your body and attend to them too? What would you tell Mary if one of them drowned? 'Dear, I escorted his soul back to the One?'" In the face of Teoma's tirade, my husband sits quietly. "Do you not have an earthly commitment to three souls in your life? Or is your commitment in spirit only?"

Softly Yeshua says, "There is only one commitment and that is to Love."

Exasperated, Teoma stomps off to the house.

I am sorry, Mary. I remind my husband about split levels of consciousness. He sighs, unsure. *If Teoma learned to leave his body, his physical form would reflexively protect the children, for it is who he is.* I promise to meet him in the ethers tonight, then pass through Teoma's heart.

Abruptly he halts and clutches his chest. "Mary?"

Teoma, I realize you are upset with Yeshua, but do not go to Sarah and Josh with anger in your heart. I love you and so does he.

Conceding to my wishes, Teoma expresses his gratitude. *Whatever it is you just did to me, I feel much lighter now.*

Dearest, even so far away we can experience each other's love. Thank you for taking such good care of the children. I will be home soon.

Late in the evening I meet with Yeshua. So full of compassion, my beloved husband attempts to create peace during this challenging time. When I witness his graciousness and lack of judgment, I forget that he is human.

So, what have you learned in all of your meditations?

Mary, it has been too long since I have shared my contemplations with you. I agree, but dare not interrupt. *My embodiment as a man in connection to Source is my purpose, but those entrapped in the illusion of suffering may come to see me as a redeemer.* Doesn't he see his own suffering? He goes on, unaware of my musings. *Separation from Eloha to become individuated as a human being is my great sacrifice.*

There was a time, Yeshua, when you praised our intimate connection as a pure path to Source. How can it have changed for you?

His sorrow reflects my own. *During intercourse I am grounded so fully into my form that separation from Source feels like a fresh wound.* Quiet in the ethers, our vibrant hayye brightly bouncing against one another, wonderful, but not enough while I exist in form. *I know I am trying your patience, Mary, but I ask that you bear with me a little longer.*

With a soft cry, I reply, *Patience is not one of my best virtues, Yeshua. Although I find some comfort in stillness, my greatest connection to Eloha comes from being very human. Only this morning in the bath, I envisioned how my body is not singular but made of tiny living entities, all a part of me, all a part of the One.*

I have seen this same vision, Mary.

While in your body, Yeshua? For I believe it might be quite different living it, than just viewing it.

But I feel more comfortable doing this work ethereally.

Is your mission upon this Earth within this body of yours, that I have come to cherish, or is it spirit form? Even the archangels have told me how wonderful it is for them to witness my emotions and endeavors, for theirs is but a spiritual existence.

While I was in Britannia, we met in the ethers to connect….

We speak chastely. Do you really want to connect intimately, Yeshua? I will take anything at this point but Yeshua hesitates, wavering in his resolve. If I could whisper in the ethers, I do now. *I do not know how I can desire you so very much when you must stop and consider my proposal. If I dance naked in celebration of the next new moon, would your resolve shift then or would you care to even be there?* I do not stay for his answer, returning to my form back in the temple.

Shortly after noon the following day, Yeshua calls for me. Bitterness drowned by tears, I try to lighten my mood. *So, Yesh, what type of fruit am I?*

Laughing he replies, *A mango. You are juicy, sweet, and very rare. I have thought about your offer to dance and if you are still inclined, I would enjoy that very much.*

With a trembling lower lip, I murmur, *Yeshua, you still desire me?*

Reaching through the ethers, he embraces my aura. *I have always desired you. Last summer, you reconnected with me in spite of the agony until you entered the portal of transformation. I have contemplated our experience and am determined to try and emulate your passionate resolve and finish this piece.* I cannot stop thanking the One.

Without further ado, we begin the dance of connection in the ethers. His cool soothing hayye refreshes the fever of my midnight purple, but as if strangers, our dance is clumsy. The merging of two complete bubbles usually creates a perfect visica pisces. This time our erratic dance distorts our union for when we part—one aura swollen, the other contracted. Quaking, I pull away and in pain, Yeshua leaves me. Perhaps we may never come together again!

Back in the temple, I seek out Hephziva.

"My wise friend, in Magdala awaits my poor husband, who cannot be intimate with me in-body or out without suffering great pain. And then there is Teoma, who if I but ask, would fulfill my desires." I collapse woefully at her feet.

Hephziva settles us upon the rich cushions stroking my hair in silence until the tears begin to subside. "Tell me how you can be intimate out-of-your body, Mary?"

I look up through wet lashes. Why she has great expertise with the energies! "Like fantasizing, I suppose, but with the energy of passion, my body always responds."

She goes to a trunk and opens it, producing something wrapped in white linen. "Here, this is my gift to you." Laughing at my flushed cheeks, she explains, "Many cultures still worship the great lords of old. Unlike squash, this will not rot even after multiple uses." We cannot help but laugh together.

So I return but as soon as my husband hugs me, tears flow. "Never, did I expect that we might not always live passionately."

As if my lips might burn him, he kisses the crown of my hair. "My dear, this too shall pass." I shake my head.

"Yeshua, how can I dance for you at the new moon of Elul and not partner with you afterward?"

His lip quivers, "I cannot ask you not to dance nor do I expect you not to pick a partner." What is he saying?

Cheerfully scattered with toys existing in an imaginary world, the nursery brings me some measure of joy for my children cover me with kisses, not afraid to touch my lips.

"Ima, will you take us to the crystal cavern? Abba said when you returned we could go there," Sarah asks excitedly.

Josh jumps up and down, "Please I want to see the crystals."

431

"Perhaps tomorrow." I wonder if Yeshua will stay in-body, because I cannot do it alone.

Martha emerges hurrying the children out to join a wonderful new game with Bartholomew. We embrace a long while. "Mary, I had hoped you would have come back refreshed."

"Yeshua and I have taken many steps backwards." Martha shakes her head sadly. With resolve, I force a smile, "So, dear Hephziva gave me this."

Her face is a comical mix of shock and curiosity. "What is it?"

"Really, Martha, can't you see that it's a phallus?" Her laughter melds with mine.

"Of course, I can see that! I mean what is it for?"

Smiling, I tell her, "It is an instrument of pleasure that may be my only relief."

Examining it carefully, Martha states, "Although curious to know if it works, I don't think it can replace a man." Neither do I.

Some time after breakfast, we head out to the cavern. Yeshua invites Teoma to accompany us. Sarah's and Josh's excitement lightens my heart, so when we reach the cliff, anxious as they to swim, I quickly undress.

"Aren't you going to wear a swimming garment?" Yeshua asks, averting his eyes, so I cover myself.

At my request Teoma hands me his knife to cut two narrow strips from my favorite sadin. "Go on ahead with the children. I need time to construct this and they cannot wait."

"We will not leave you here alone, Mary."

"Please go, I'll be fine." Reluctantly, Teoma helps the children descend. Wry thoughts embitter when Yeshua leaves me behind.

By the time I join them, the children are exploring the cavern under Teoma's supervision, Yeshua already deep in meditation. Smoothing the frown from my face, I play with the children, teaching them the art of levitation, but their enthusiasm outlasts mine. Why did Yeshua come, for he is not with us now?

"It has been this way since you left. He spends less and less time here." Teoma studies my expression, "I hope you haven't lost all of your joy, dear."

I turn and watch the children scale the walls of the cavern.

"Can we greet each other properly now?" He asks, holding open his arms. I so want to, but…Yeshua and the children. "Are they unaccustomed to our mutual affection, Mary? Yeshua is not really here."

Wringing my hands, I whisper, "He is here and knows all. My mind may be veiled but yours is not."

"Mary, it's only a hug." I give in and finally feel welcomed home. My tears wet the hair on his strong chest, but Teoma is undeterred. Am I ripe yet, for I'm about to fall off the tree?

Yeshua does not return with us, nor is he home by bedtime. Slipping between the sheets alone, I decide to ease my own frustration. When I imagine my husband, he comes through the ethers, *Please, your passion is too strong. Focus on something else.*

So I clear my mind but am stymied without someone to focus on. Knowing no other's touch, I imagine Teoma. Fueled with desire, I see myself in his embrace. Soon detecting the warm musk of his skin, feeling his strong hands and tender lips, I grasp Hephziva's gift and muffle my cries into a pillow.

I sleep so soundly that not even the rising sun rouses me. Hurriedly, I dress to join the family at breakfast. My cheeks warm when Teoma enters but I bid him good morning. He ducks his head with the briefest of smiles. Looking up from her plate, my sister's face is drawn with concern.

Later as we lie upon the beach watching the children play in the water, Martha asks what happened between Teoma and me. Although I claim innocence, she frowns, "It certainly looked like you've been together."

"Yeshua asked me not to fantasize about him, and I couldn't imagine anyone else." Martha nods unconvincingly. She does not believe me!

Leaving her wondering on the shore, I swim past the cove. The clear lake water does not lend the buoyancy of the salty sea, so before the rocky point, I must turn back. Someone swiftly swims toward me. It's Teoma.

"Thank you for last night."

My heart beats rapidly. "What do you mean?"

"Did you not come to me and…?"

"No, I was…what did you…?" His smile tells the tale—he experienced exactly what I imagined. And it felt quite real to him. "Teoma, I am sorry. I thought that my ability to manifest was with Yeshua only."

433

He swims ever nearer. "I certainly do not expect an apology. We didn't actually touch one another, so I do not think it counts as tasting unripe fruit."

Not knowing what to say, I swim toward shore. When able to stand, I turn and Teoma nearly bumps into me. So enticing in the flesh, I make a hasty retreat.

I come upon Phillip standing near the fishermen and am moved to seek guidance. "May I ask how thought creates reality?"

Smiling, he motions for me to follow him into the clear water, "You naturally manifest your reality through clear intention and pure desire. Call forth fish and describe to me what you are doing."

Although I've done it since childhood, I never thought about it. "Taking a deep breath, I feel grateful to connect with the fish then call to them. I see them swimming about my legs and feel their cool, slick sides brush my skin." As I speak, the fish have arrived. "I reach down between my legs and cup my hands asking one to swim between my palms." Instantly, I am holding a silvery fish. I thank her and set her free.

Phillip smiles, "Do you have any other questions?" I follow him back to the sand.

"Yes, if I but imagine something, is it a reality?"

He studies my face with light gray eyes, his hayye clear lavender. "You have the power to create what you desire for your shem is quite pure. So whatever you have imagined has become." With a small smile, I thank him for his kindness.

Near the house, the children play hide and seek. Sarah and Josh, disappearing and reappearing, influence my nephews to follow their lead. Like a great guardian angel, Bartholomew sits in their midst. Patting the sand beside him, he gives me a wide grin.

"Sit down, perfect one." I wonder at his reference. "I do not think the children shall become lost." His large hand covers mine. So scattered, hardly held together, his aura polarizes into a muddy constricted bubble and irregular spikes of brilliant color. Attracted to the children's light, he slips out of his body. I place my hand upon his chest and he returns. Bartholomew turns to me. "I fear Yeshua is becoming lost." Me too.

After thanking the great, disconnected philosopher, I find my husband sitting upon an out-jutting rock at the point of the cove. His energy is imbalanced—an inverse teardrop, top heavy, losing contact with this dimension. A cawing crow settles into a sycamore and the elestial quartz suddenly feels very cold.

Yeshua heeds my call and returns from meditation.

I dare not touch him, but do not hesitate to speak. "Yeshua, I have created a reality through my imagination." He nods and motions for me to sit facing him. Settling on the hard rock, I wonder how he can sit so long. "Last night you asked me to focus not on you but something else."

"You seemed quite satisfied when I came to bed. I am happy for you."

"Perhaps you should wait to express your feelings. My focus was Teoma," I hesitate, looking for his response, but still he smiles at me tenderly, "and he experienced my fantasy."

Slowly his smile fades into puzzlement. "You were able to create a reality purely through thought? Teoma must be quite pleased."

"But my fantasy became real, have I not committed adultery?"

"No, the time is ripe for you to discover your power to create. With me, you assume that I am participating in the creative process, now with Teoma, you have seen how powerful you are at manifesting reality."

Why isn't he upset about this? How can he be so philosophical?

Bartholomew's warning whispers on the wind. I must find a way to bring my husband back into his form—not this mystic, ethereal being before me. "Yeshua, it is time to come home."

Shaking his head, he resists, "No, Mary, I have not completed my meditation."

I pull him to his feet, "Oh, yes, you are quite finished."

His thoughts so frantic, I ease his ruminations, "Do not worry, Yeshua. I will not touch you intimately until you are fully embodied." He relaxes somewhat, but I dare not release my grip.

As we pass by, Sarah laughs, "Look! Abba is going to join us for supper." Joshua skips ahead of the entourage with Bartholomew taking up the rear.

His laugh, a great booming sound, follows us into the baths. "Mary is bringing Yeshua back to us. Let us tell Doda Martha, perhaps we can have massah!" The children think this is a fine idea and hurry to make their request.

But within the buttery-hued room, I am not sure how to proceed and my husband is clearly uncomfortable with me.

"Mary, I bathed this morning," Yeshua offers a weak complaint.

"Not thoroughly enough, dear. Here, lie down on this table, I will oil your skin, while the staff draws the bath." Although reluctant to allow me to touch him, he sits obediently upon the table. "You will have to undress. Do you need my assistance?" He shakes his head and slowly removes his tunic.

Turning away, I find linen to cover his prone body. With a deep breath, I stand feet apart and call upon the energy from the earth. My lower body fills with red, orange, yellow heat and then raising my arms, I call to the universe to fill me with healing light. Cool rays of blue, indigo, and violet pour forth to mix with the hot energy from the earth's core in the green chalice of my heart. With compassionate detachment, I become a healer and before me lies not my husband, not even a man, but a lost soul hovering between the worlds.

Warming the oil briskly between my palms, I lightly touch him, slowly, increasing the circular pressure to chastely massage his entire form desiring that his hayye be fully realized within his beautiful male body. By the time I am finished, he is snoring softly.

***

The oil lamps glow cheerily in the hall, but Yeshua yearns for the quietude of dusk just outside. Teoma steers him by the arm as if he is a wayward craft, until reaching the safe harbor of the dining hall. Childish laughter greets them, unaccustomedly loud to his ears. Although he has no hunger, little Sarah insists on feeding him honeyed dates. From across the table, his wife watches, one hand delicately covering her mouth as if to prevent an idea from escaping. Turning to her sister, Mary draws Teoma close as well.

Tucking the children into bed brings him ever nearer to the earth realm, his form solidifying woodenly, perhaps to grow roots like a tree. In their chambers, he turns away as his wife disrobes. She climbs into bed and holds open the linens, but he protests.

"Are you more attached to the ethers than to this world?"

She has a point; perhaps he has developed a dependency upon meditation. "I appreciate what you are doing but…."

"Please stay here with me." Reluctantly, he climbs into bed, keeping a chaste distance between them. Tomorrow, he shall make another attempt to finish his work. With worry clouding his mind, fretful dreams plague his sleep.

Dawn gently rouses him. Mary lies within his arms, one soft breast resting in his hand. She stretches and her tantalizing aroma slips into his nostrils, filling his chest, winding downward to awaken a forgotten need.

With haste, she rises to leave him alone in their bed. *She treats me with the indifference of a well-trained healer.* Sighing, he considers providing his own relief but the children soon scamper into the room and pounce upon him.

"Abba's back!" Precious Joshua cries as beautiful Sarah pets his beard. How patient they have been, never complaining about his lack of attention. From beneath the clinging children, he catches his wife's green gaze. *Time to ride, Yeshua.*

On this breezeless summer morning, the lake still and flat entices Yeshua to meditate but Teoma holds the white stallion, having already lifted Mary upon its back. "Come, I'll give you a leg up." Yeshua relents with a sigh.

When he nearly loses his seat, Teoma's laughter chases them down the beach. Compared to the fluid rhythm of Mary's body behind him, his stiffness distresses the horse. Silently he tries to communicate with it, but Mary interferes.

"Yeshua, try to relax. Now bring your consciousness to your root directly in contact with Sheikan. Feel the heat of his body, the softness of his fine coat, the firmness of the ridged muscles, the hardness of the bone. There. Now feel his breath; it is much slower than yours and his heart beats at a fraction of your pace."

Adopting her visualization, his body comes into rhythm with the horse.

"Now ask him to walk by shifting your weight ever so slightly forward and contracting your legs. Place your hands gently on his neck to move with its rhythm, allowing your body to sway with his. See, it is like a dance."

"You are the dancer, my love!" She gives him a gentle squeeze around his waist.

"All human beings must learn the dance of life, Yeshua. Every creature has its own rhythm and if we wish to connect, we must allow it to lead."

They spend the entire morning riding Sheikan through the gently lapping lake. Once he is in harmony with the stallion, Mary dismounts.

Hooves pounding the earth, Sheikan races down the shore, before plunging into the water. Never before has he experienced such a fine connection with any horse. They return to Mary, the lake kissing her naked feet as she lifts heavy curls off her neck. Dismounting, he allows the horse to roll in the dry grass.

"Thank you, my beloved. That was wonderful."

Mary smiles, but her cheeks flush when Teoma retrieves the horse and winks at her. *Your magic is working.*

"You forget that I can hear you." Yeshua frowns as his friend attends only to her.

In the center of the bright dining hall, summer blossoms cheerfully adorn the linen-covered table. Crimson pomegranates, pale green figs, and purple grapes overflow the fruit bowl next to a platter of salted kippers and black olives, all to be washed down with wine. A salad of cold cucumbers drizzled with golden oil, and fresh flaky bread, round out the meal.

After he takes a seat, Mary binds his eyes. "What is this?"

"Now your tongue shall experience the Divine." Slowly, she feeds him, asking that he identify each morsel.

She has his mouth so busy, he must communicate silently. *Mary, I can think of another use for this blindfold.*

"I'm sure you can, Yeshua, but I need you to focus on the sensations in your mouth." Eleazer laughs, thinking the same.

From the other end of the table, Phillip compliments Mary, "You are quite an innovative healer," while the children blindfold Bartholomew and feed him strange combinations of food.

Teoma arrives from the stables to join them. "Now, that isn't vinegar, is it?"

Yeshua does not hesitate to accept his wife's offering. "Even if it was, it would still taste sweet coming from her loving hands."

He'll never last until the new moon. At Teoma's thought Yeshua wonders.

Later Mary takes him to the roof of the house. No talking, no thinking, just breath and beauty. Soft pink and lavender hues, streaked with clear orange and flaming yellow, dip below the crest of the distant mountains. Tentatively, he reaches through the shadowy dusk, thankful when she slips her slender hand into his.

Once in their chambers, he requests that they sleep as they have since their wedding night, skin to skin. With a smile, Mary undresses, "As long as that is all you have in mind, Yeshua."

He holds open the linens. "It is not all I have in mind, but I shall not create reality with my thoughts."

"How is it that you will not manifest what you desire? Is not your intention clear?"

He draws her into bed. "Oh, my intention is very clear, and certainly I am filled with desire, but the time is not ripe."

So there is another part of this formula?

"Yes, love, this world is not created in duality, but in triads, sacred tristans of manifestation—thought and desire manifest when in ripe time."

"How are you perceiving my thoughts?"

Smiling into her curls, he breathes in her essence, "Is your mind veiled from me?"

"I never intentionally veiled it."

Pulling her more snuggly into his body, there is no space at all between them. "Your respect for other's privacy naturally veiled your mind, but your desire to share your pure essence with me has created a window."

"I feel relieved, for it has been difficult having to speak my every musing."

"My love, I appreciate your patience with me, but more so I am grateful that you finally took the situation in hand and escorted me back home."

Her chin begins to quiver. "Yeshua, I thought you believed home is with the One."

Tenderly he kisses the tears from her cheeks. "It is, but you have shown me that Eloha is within and I can perceive connection to all through my sensory body. Mary, I am home."

The next morning, she leads him, blindfolded, carefully out of the house. The lapping of the lake on his right indicates they are heading north, the grove of trees so close they must be on a deer trail. The water sounds farther away. Has she taken him up to the cliffs which overlook the bay? The smell of curing fish from the heart of Magdala overwhelms him. Mary praises his identification of birds and creatures by their voices as well as the trees by the unique rustling of their leaves. When she leads

439

him back, the children ask him to play tag. His ability to perceive them by the pattern of their running feet and breathless giggles proves a great success. Finally, Sarah relieves him of the blindfold and begins a game with the other children.

A picnic lunch on the beach provides the perfect respite. Between bites, he stops to take in the serene setting. "I don't think I have ever tasted such good chicken, Mary."

Handing him a napkin, she smiles. "Yeshua, I don't think that you ever really stopped to taste your food." He laughs.

"Yes, after all my sensory lessons, this earthly experience will be magnified."

She packs away the remnants of the meal. "So, tell me what you have learned."

"Being fully embodied in connection with Eloha is a living meditation."

"Yes! Eloha is in everything, Yeshua—every sight, sound, touch, taste, smell!"

Her delight so irresistible, he embraces her. Tenderly kissing her forehead, he whispers, "Thank you, beloved. I know now that the pain of separation is mirrored in my eventual separation from all that I love. You have brought me back home to my body, connecting to this earthly existence. I have already experienced the pain of leaving you in these past few months. But while I am here, I shall live fully."

Afraid to lose him to the potential despair when they finally reunite, she wonders how her passion for Teoma has changed her.

Yeshua holds her tightly. "In spite of the challenge, you demonstrate incredible healing abilities returning me to my form. I am eternally grateful for both you and Teoma." Tilting her chin so that he might look into her eyes, he whispers, "But even connected to Eloha, I know myself as still very human, for I am not ready to share you."

His final lesson takes place in the baths. This time, wool plugs his ears and linen covers his eyes. Mary presents pungent, sweet, stringent, and savory aromas. He correctly identifies every herb, flower, spice, and oil. One flower does stump him.

I don't know the name of it, evidently I paid little attention to my Abba's lessons, but it smells yellow.

Does color have a scent or are you using the energies?

I am having a most difficult time blocking the hayye of the odors. But all you have presented have strong aromas, why don't you challenge me with some more subtle scents? There is a long wait as if she is unsure of what to present. He smiles and suggests. *Undress and let me but take a single whiff of each part you present.*

Hesitantly, she agrees but helps him assume a prone position, his hands lying chastely still at his sides. How simple!

The nape of your neck. Even though she attempts to confuse him, he is quite proficient. *Your left foot.*

How can you tell the difference between my feet?

He smiles. *I know your body, Mary.* A puff of air fans his beard. *Your breath passing through your right nostril.* He identifies each individual finger, as well as each breast.

In a moment, she presents the most luscious aroma of all.

Savoring what he has missed for months, the scent of her desire rises tantalizingly. He smiles around her finger, *I cannot hear you.*

Yeshua, you are not ready. Unplugging his ears before removing the blindfold with his free hand, he draws her upon his prone form. She swallows thickly, green eyes flashing distressed.

"Mary, I will wait for you, as you have me, until tomorrow night." Rolling atop, he kisses her passionately for the first time since it all began. She melts like candle wax, gasping for breath. Tenderly cupping her face, he whispers, "I am looking forward to watching you dance naked for me." He assists her to her feet and hands over her sadin, "I'll take care of this," referring to the piles of flowers and plants, spices and oils, "while you go swim."

Mary rushes so hurriedly from the baths, she runs into someone. He hears Teoma's voice. "Is the time ripe now?"

Yeshua feels his wife's pain like a rip in his chest at Teoma's thoughts: *So she shall dance for him. I don't think I can bear it.*

Her response is barely audible. "Please allow another to choose you at the new moon ceremony."

Teoma answers gruffly. "Even if I am chosen, it will not be whom I would choose." Yeshua prays she finds relief in the cool waters of the lake, as his friend enters the baths.

"I, too, would appreciate it if you would allow one of the beautiful women of Magdala to choose you, Teoma. I realize how difficult it is for you to watch Mary dance, but I am back now and there will be no more tasting of the fruit."

441

Teoma's body is rigid. "Although I admit that I have prayed for intimate contact with your wife, I did not openly invite her fantasy. In fact, I believe you gave her little choice."

"The timing was ripe for her to realize her ability to manifest. You played your part beautifully and may I say that you enjoyed every moment of it. And I am most grateful that in manifesting reality with you, Mary realized her potential and assisted me out of the void into which I cast myself. For that I thank you, Teoma." Hugging his friend, he whispers, "But once again, I remind you that she is my wife and your time has not come."

***

In spite of my anticipation, the new moon comes too soon. Martha advises me to dance only for Yeshua and ignore Teoma's response, but she cannot comprehend how difficult it is to block his thoughts.

The men have gone ahead of us. Lovely in her flowing green skirt and golden shawl, Martha allowed me to adorn her bosom with green and gold silk; even she shall bare herself tonight. I wear the embroidered garment T'shuraw gave me with the short colorful skirt and the royal shawl.

Brilliant stars warm the night as the lake laps gently at the shore. The men finish dancing and sit in a large circle while the women gather above them awaiting their music. A beautiful auburn-haired girl of about eighteen excitedly searches the crowd. Her gaze stops at Teoma who sits next to Bartholomew farthest from the water.

Murmuring a prayer of thanks, I approach the young woman. "Good evening, I am Mary."

Gracing me with a shy smile, "Hello, my name is Elana," the girl replies in Greek.

I respond in her tongue, "You are so lovely. My friend would be most pleased if you favor him."

Her eyes widen as she asks, "Which one is your friend?"

"Over there by the big man. You do think he is handsome, do you not?"

"Oh, yes, I was hoping that he wasn't already taken—is he?"

I shake my head, "He is my gift to you. Choose him quickly before another does. He's never left without a scarf and…."

Grasping my hands, she kisses my cheek, "I will heed your kind advice and be swift. Thank you, Mary." I smile at her delight, giving thanks for such divine orchestration.

When I return to my sister's side, she shakes her head, "It appears you have solved your dilemma."

Pressed sensuously against the others awaiting the sweet rewards of this night, we hear the drums beckon from the periphery of the circle. Heeding the call the women dance for their men, but I take my sister's hand to hold her back. "Let us enter after them, our husbands can wait." Laughing, Martha already sways her hips. By the time we arrive in the circle, the heat of the other women raises mine.

In the midst of the dancers, the music a bit slow, I imagine dancing with abandon. To my delight the musicians comply and hasten the beat. I partner with the rich nurturing energy of the Sea of Galilee in celebration the new moon of Elul.

Surrounded by sensuous female forms, I encourage Elana to dance before Teoma. Laughing, Bartholomew tells him, "Mary has sent you a pretty gift, my friend."

Teoma frowns. *Mary, is this true?*

I send him loving hayye. *Yes, dear, she anxiously awaits your acceptance. Please open your arms to her.* Lovely Elana makes her choice, draping her pink shawl about Teoma. *She is very young and has not had the pleasure of being with a Hebrew man.* Teoma invites her to sit beside him, freeing me to dance for my beloved.

Calling to the keeper of the rhythm, I imagine the birthing of the cosmos and the beat becomes erratic, chaotic, and dark. The other instruments fade into the background as I lead the great drum through the void, swelling in universal rhythm as more drummers join from near and far.

I am the darkness and she is me, together we dance the chaos before creation. Hidden within the shadows, I free my skirt, a fallen rainbow on cold sand. Golden sheqels chattering merrily with the drum, the embroidered top slips down to kiss the earth as I entice the shawl from its repose on my hips. Blue and gold chase me through the chaos, the veil of my hair my only adornment. Swirling, disharmonious blackness fills the center of the circle of watchers as I dance the potential within the void.

Birther of the Cosmos, the darkness brings forth light.

I imagine illumination and my beloved stands to step into the dark circle. The brilliant light of his being penetrates the darkness of mine as the lyre begins to sing. Dancing about the light, the dark succumbs to desire. Slowly, the other instruments join us until the great drum resonates with my newly-conceived rhythm, darkness in delightful harmony with the light.

Swirling attraction to the light finds form within the void. Yeshua focuses his hayye to fill my desire and we merge as one, the light within the dark. The dark within the light becomes his manifestation, pure hayye creates form, beauteous to behold. The crowd exists in silence and when the music stops abruptly, I fall to my knees. Without a moment's hesitation, Yeshua lifts me up, sealing our connection with a kiss. The crowd cheers wildly, the musicians celebrating our union with a closing melody. As the others drift away, I look into his eyes, piercing in their brilliance. Mine have become the void and thus he falls into the stormy sea of potential, drifting upon the waves of my emotion. As one, we breathe and share our essence.

Darkness covers, only faintly illuminated by distant stars. The one kiss becomes two as the light penetrates the dark once again. This time as manifest form for when the light and dark merge as one, crying out in passionate embrace, Eloha fills them. Spirit does not leave form to seek Source, but merges within our conjoined bodies, filling us with both the lightness of unique manifestation and the darkness of ever-changing potential. Yeshua and I become unified with all creation—the vibration of the cosmos revealed in the differentiation of our unique expressions of the Divine.

Sipping the sweet wine of my lips, Yeshua whispers, "Beloved, for once we brought forth Oneness with our sacred union. Experiencing Eloha within my form has filled me with great desire to manifest all of my potential."

I smile at his comprehension, pressing myself deliciously against him. "Yeshua, always in the past we left our forms to meet the One, re-experiencing the separation with every magnificent climax. Now I understand that the separation is but an illusion, for we do not have to exit the portal of our existence to be in Sacred Unity."

He breathes a final rumination, "My love, we looked within and beheld all of creation. Unity within our individual expressions of form is the truth of reality."

I receive him once again, drifting upon the sea of my own potential, delighted to manifest as One. Moving in rhythm to our breath, our auras become magnified, brilliant hues of purple and silver merging into white. Gossamer threads of connection to all creation expand our senses to taste the sweetness of our love, hear the harmony of our union, smell the passion of our connection, see the sacred Oneness of life, and feel beloved by the Cosmos.

Surrendering to Sophia

Lavender light disturbs our slumber as the rising sun crests over the Sea of Galilee. Murmuring a prayer of gratitude for the blessings in my life, a voice within my being answers: *Beloved, you are Sacred Wisdom in Unity with All That Is. Your consistent connection to the Divine shall enable you to move through your humanity with grace. As you surrender your fear, the ripe experience of joy becomes sweeter.*

Passionate desire fills my heart to know myself more fully. Turning, Yeshua speaks, "The One is within, for we have merged ourselves with Source. Our union has created space for Sacred Wisdom in the form of Chochma to evolve as a joyous expression of our human existence."

The light extending from my beloved husband's heart grows until there is no end, his silvery white hayye illuminating my deep purple hue and on through my being to meet the morning sun. Seeking my eyes, he whispers, "We have realized our enlightenment to actualize gemera as divinely merged beings. During the mission, we shall reach the sovereign state of our humanity."

This is what Hephziva spoke of in the temple of Astarte but how can we be perfect as humans? "When I suffer over my entanglement with you and Teoma, I feel far from perfect."

Touching my face tenderly, he smiles, "My love, there is not true perfection in the density of this earthly experience. You and I have the opportunity to reach the deepest potential of human existence. I am becoming like unto the adama—of the earth, as you are my other half, chava—life. Together we model the divine creation of humans."

"If we have become merged, will I not hear the angels and the One as separate any longer?"

"Like the tides of the sea that move in and out, this transformation is gradual. You will hear what you desire, but know that as a sovereign being, the merge becomes complete." As he breathes out, I breathe in and encompass his essence, feeling the truth of what he has spoken, what I have seen in his eyes.

"Still Yeshua, in relationship with all those I love, I am not yet perfected."

"Nor am I, but we are becoming completely merged with the joyous present in this life, perceiving the divinity in each human endeavor. From each entangled circumstance, shall we tease out the truth which is Love. That is all we must do to become gemera, dear, nothing more."

Stroking his cheek, I whisper, "So easily spoken, the doing is fraught with challenge."

***

Bartholomew sits heavily upon the shore next to his Greek friend. An immense egg-shaped light shimmers in front of them. He smiles to hear the voice of the Aksum king.

Greetings Phillip and is that... Bartholomew with you? An affectionate chuckle ripples the light. *Dear man, your visions are missed in the land of the pharaohs. Under the dark moon, Shasmecka and I witnessed the birth of a new creation. I am anxious to hear your assessment, philosopher.*

Phillip winks at Bartholomew. *Well, Belshazzar, Sophia has been given form.*

Bartholomew can hardly contain himself. *A dance of magic! The Joyous One brought harmony into the void of darkness by merging with the Light of Love.* As the giant man gives voice to what he witnessed, the dance is recreated in the ethers for the three to behold.

Tremulous with emotion, Belshazzar's voice penetrates the silence. *My deepest gratitude, dear friend, for sharing your vision. Here on the banks of the Nile, I felt the dancer call and lent my drumming. The chaotic rhythm thrust me into Source.*

The men on the lake shore nod their comprehension and wait until the Aksum king collects himself. *Hephziva shared her concern about Yeshua, but it appears he has passed through the despair of separation.*

Yes, Belshazzar. Like the goddess Sophia, Mary evoked his sacred senses to encourage her husband's expansion into the earth reality.

Good, very good. It appears as if he has released his attachments. Soon he will be ready.

What more can we do?

Be available to the council that has been chosen for him. Priests and leaders of his tribe, these men have a limited view. They hope for a king to free them, yet his purpose is universal.

Sitting forward to embrace the bubble of energy, Bartholomew exclaims, *He has asked us to be part of the council!*

Belshazzar's laughter expands the light. *Ahh. What good fortune. The boy has truly dissolved the patriarchal ties.*

Phillip halts the reverie. *The blessed couple approaches.*

With clarity of sight, Belshazzar perceives that Mari-a and Yeshua have begun their journey as the merge of the dark and the light. *Where one begins and the other ends is difficult to identify. Let us meditate on the completion of their transformation, my friends.*

Under a glimmering dawn of hope, the Greek philosopher, the giant Galilean, and the Aksum king merge their intentions.

***

"Mary, your sister tells me that Teoma is to leave with you tomorrow." Elana rises excitedly from her cushion. After a moment's hesitation, I look more deeply, nearly gasping out loud at my discovery—she conceived at the new moon ceremony.

"Elana, what can I do for you?"

Smiling, she clasps my hands, "I do not know if this is love, but we made a connection and I must know how he feels."

Martha gives me a concerned look, but I have already contacted Teoma and he is on his way.

When my sister departs, Elana cries, "Your dance was so erotic. When your husband embraced you, Teoma led me away. I have never known such a passionate lover." Their encounter reflected in her eyes, before a tear falls, I hear my friend's pronounced footfall.

What is wrong, Mary? Teoma greets us with a gracious smile.

Standing, I take his hand and place hers in it. "Elana would like to speak with you." I kiss her cheek and take my leave as he desperately wonders what I know. *Please, hear her then we shall talk.*

Finding Yeshua, I confide in him. "Mary, we cannot interfere. This is Teoma's path."

Sadly I shake my head, "But out of selfishness, I arranged their meeting that night to be sure he was taken care of…"

"Dearest, you played your part and she played hers. He will have to examine all he believes himself to be. This is a wonderful opportunity for growth, although he will not see it at first. You shall be sorely tested to balance your feelings with your knowing."

Teoma comes upon us while we watch the children play in the water. With a deep breath he sits. "Elana asked me to stay, and when I explained that we return to Nazareth in the morning, she asked if she could come with me."

"How do you feel about her?"

Shaking his head, Teoma is near to tears, "Honestly, Yesh, she could have been any woman." Nearly imperceptible, he whispers, "In my mind it was Mary I embraced. I am sorry."

Yeshua clasps Teoma's shoulders, but he shakes his head desperately, "Since I was young, I have never lost control. Mary, I pray she might have attended a conscious conception circle."

"No, dear, she did not." Teoma's eyes widen with suspicion so I take his hand. "Elana is pregnant with your seed."

"Oh no. No!" His face pales as he abruptly stands. "I must prepare our packs for the trip." My heart aches as I watch his retreating back.

Early the next morning, we bid my sister goodbye. Wishing us well, Phillip and Bartholomew travel north to Bethsaida while we head through the Valley of Doves. In spite of Teoma's despair, the children delight in our journey home. When the road splits, Yeshua calls for us to halt.

"Joshua would like to see the water buffalo." He points to the poorly traveled northwestern fork.

Teoma raises his concern, "That way will lead us through the swamps where we are sure to find lions as well as buffalo. It is very dangerous."

"Did you hear, son? We might even see lions." Yeshua leads us into the heart of Galilee's jungle so Joshua can see the buffalo.

450

Wildness-laden air heightens our expectations. Teoma's concern causes his mount to skitter nervously across the path. To quell their giggles, the children cover their mouths. Yeshua and I ride in peaceful joy, our mounts calm. Winding down into a verdant valley rich with waterfowl, we come upon a large herd.

Dripping lush green grass from placid lips, the buffalo watch us. A few calves separated from the cows on the north side of the path bellow piteously and race back to the herd. As Teoma's horse sidesteps nervously, the black mare carrying the children spooks. Teoma takes off and is just about to catch the runaway when his horse veers. The black mare leaps wildly over a bush, unseating the children. Sarah pulls herself back up but Joshua lands with a thump. Although unscathed, my son has fallen…into the midst of lion cubs.

Using raza, I go to my son, the mother of the cubs responding to their cries. *We must return for these babies' Ima will be here very soon.*

Hugging an exceptionally affectionate cub, Josh shakes his head, "No, I want to play with the kittens." I smile. The 'kittens' are a third his size, more like small dogs. I caress a cub valiantly trying to climb up my leg. Visualizing joy from this wild encounter, I breathe in peace and harmony. Joshua attempts to hold them all in the expanse of his short arms. "Ima, can we take one home?"

Joshua, speak without your voice. I'm sorry, but their mother would surely miss them. You wouldn't want me to leave you with her. With a shake of his head, he enjoys the remaining moments with the cubs.

Paws softly padding the earth, the lionesses growl in warning, but the kittens, happily smelling of humans, confuse them. I extend my heart energy and the largest, the mother of this litter, pauses, her golden-brown eyes softly dilating. Upon her belly, she crawls, her sisters following.

Slowly, I open my arms to them, Joshua and the cubs playing at my feet. Yeshua holds a great bubble of energy about us. Teoma leads Sarah safely astride her horse back to ours. All is well.

Distressed the lioness asks, *Elat, I mean not to offend, but my cubs?*

They are well, beautiful Ima, playing happily with my own. We mean not to disturb you and will kindly take our leave.

Purring softly, the lioness creeps closer, *Please, Elat, bless our hunt. We have been long without a kill and my milk runs dry.*

Stepping toward her, I image a successful hunt and long life for them all. She rubs against my legs in gratitude. Gently, I cup her soft tufted ear deaf since kicked by a buffalo, then cupping my own I project acuteness of perception into her damaged organ. She licks my hand with her rough pink tongue.

Thank you, Elat, for healing my deformity. My clan shall not forget your kindness. Praise the Great Spirit for bringing your cub to us.

Quietly, I lift Joshua from the bush, and in an instant, we stand before my husband.

"Josh, did you have fun playing with the lions?" He relieves me of our son.

"Oh, yes, Abba." To Sarah, he breathlessly exclaims, "When you dropped me, I landed in kittens and Ima talked with their Ima and healed her ear and then we came back here without walking!"

Sarah replies wistfully, "I'm glad you were not hurt, but I wish I could have seen the kittens."

Shaking his head, Teoma takes Joshua and puts him behind Sarah on the black mare. "Are you even vaguely concerned that he fell into the middle of a lion's den?"

Yeshua tries to reassure him. "All is well. Sometimes what appears to be frightful lions are actually playful kittens." Teoma shakes his head as Yeshua lifts me on Sheikan.

Reaching down, I kiss him. "Thank you for holding the hayye."

"My dear, you did all the work."

"You hold the space in which we can evolve. You have no idea how precious you are to us and how blessed we are to have you here." Cheeks flushed, he mounts.

When we arrive in Nazareth, Joshua and Sarah overwhelm the nursery with their adventures. During breakfast the next morning, the children's enthusiasm puts a twinkle in Joseph's eye.

"So I hear we might have a new member of the family?" Horrified, Teoma questions me silently. Joseph continues, "But Joshua told me that the mother lion would not release her cubs." Teoma sighs in relief.

"Yeshua, what is this wild story?"

"Dearest Ima, Joshua was perfectly safe in the den of lions."

Nearly faint, Miriam casts Teoma a pleading look, "And where were you, son?"

Weighted by responsibility, he replies softly, "Trying to catch the horse that ran away with Sarah. By the time I caught it, Mary was with Joshua surrounded by lions."

Before Miriam's fear ignites Teoma's guilt, Yeshua intervenes, "Joshua had a wondrous experience and Mary was given the opportunity to practice her healing skills on a wild creature which shall bode well, the lion clan is in deep gratitude to her."

Joseph places a comforting arm around his wife's shoulders. "Fear not, Miriam. How many three-year-olds can say that they played with lions?"

Sitting up as tall as possible, Joshua exclaims, "I'm nearly four!"

"Really, I thought you were only three?"

"Don't you know my birthday's coming, Saba?" Joshua pouts.

"Let's hurry and finish our meal." Joseph winks at Teoma and Joshua claps his hands in anticipation. Joseph seems to be enjoying himself!

Yeshua tells me silently. *As we loosen our bindings to this reality, the hayye of potential can shift. When we surrender those we love to the One, we free them to experience life without the limitations of our relationship.*

No wonder I feel so expansive. When he surrendered his Abba, he surrendered us all. The space he holds for me is limitless, allowing me to reach the depths of my truth. Love without ties that bind, in relation to Yeshua, we see our divine reflection.

Ignoring the family, he kisses my lips. *Mary, being within your mindfulness is a joy, for you perceive the light of love as I do.* I return his impassioned embrace.

Joseph clears his throat, "We have work to do," throwing an arm around Teoma's shoulder, they take their leave.

Squirming, Joshua whispers to Sarah, "What do you think they will make for me?" His sister shrugs and takes Esther's hand.

"I don't know, Josh. I like to be surprised, so I try not to look into their thoughts. Let's go play."

They run off with Esther, leaving Ruth behind, torn. When Miriam nods to excuse her, the girl excitedly jumps up, knocking over her bench. "Sorry, Ima." She picks it back up then runs about the table kissing us all goodbye.

"Ruth sure smells nice since she's been with the women in the chamam," Judah grunts as Shimon elbows him.

"Come, we have work to do." The two tall boys leave us alone with Miriam, Hava, and the remnants of breakfast. Saada emerges from the kitchen to clear.

Yeshua turns to Miriam, who exclaims, "Your hayye is as bright as it was when you were a child!"

"You have changed, but then," Hava peers, "so has Mary."

"I spent the summer surrendering my attachments to all of you, starting with Abba and including Mary."

"And how did you deal with Yeshua's detachment?"

Taking my husband's hand, I respond, "Not very well I must admit. Yeshua did most of his work in the ethers and...I felt so neglected, I was sorely tested by Teoma's availability." Hava frowns at Yeshua.

My husband responds with a laugh, "You are correct, dear Hava, I did neglect her while searching for Self, but Mary finally took the situation in hand."

With wide eyes, Miriam asks, "What did she do?"

Yeshua tries to reassure her. "Mary took my hand, Ima, not Teoma's, although his offer stands true to this day. Much occurred this summer at the Sea of Galilee, but most significantly, I am fully embodied. My dear wife assisted me in connecting to Eloha through my senses and since the new moon, we are in intimate union with Sacred Wisdom."

Miriam seems quite pleased, but Hava has a concern. "Teoma seems rather distressed. I cannot imagine how you handled this transformation, Mary."

"I did take time to stay with Hephziva who provided insight."

Still she is not satisfied. "Dear Hava, I am well aware of the serious intent of our wedding ketuba and my responsibility to insure my wife's satisfaction. By this light, I was amiss these past few months, which you are correct in assuming provided the tinder for their passionate flame."

Miriam's face is a mix of sorrow and compassion as she gives me a small smile, "Mary understands how you prefer to do your soul's work, son." Any mention of her son's suffering causes her pain so she is willing to believe that I am incapable of betraying my husband. Hava, on the other hand, sees Yeshua's humanness as well as mine, gently reminding him that his choices affect us both.

Yeshua takes his mother's hand. "But she has shown me another way and I pray not to challenge her patience again."

***

The sun glints off the surface of the water belying its murky interior to mirror the smile hiding the pain in his heart. From the middle of the pasture pond floats gleeful laughter, bringing some clarity to his turbid expression.

"Look, Dod Teo!" Joshua stands, nearly capsizing the tiny boat.

"Josh, sit down or you'll sink."

Quickly, he complies, as Sarah tries to balance the small craft. Teoma does not worry since both children swim, or if need be, can levitate over the water. Nearly noon and he has yet to bid them farewell. Wading into the cool water, he gently pushes a curious cow out of the way and draws upon the rope tied securely to the prow. Time spent sculpting with Joseph was like a balm, keeping his hands and mind busy. He carefully carved the dolphin at the prow, delighted by the children's appreciation.

At the edge of the pond, four-year-old Joshua sits in his lap. Patiently, he shows the boy how to tie his sandal straps, who reaches up to touch his cheek. "Where's your beard, Dod?"

"Remember, Josh, I cut it off with a sharp knife."

The child explores his own smooth cheek, "Where's my beard?"

Teoma explains, "Your beard will not grow until you are much older and then you can keep it long like your Abba."

Sarah comes to kiss his other cheek. "I like your smooth face, Dod. Maybe Josh will want to be like you when he is big."

Smiling at these precious children, Teoma wonders how he might ever love another. Perhaps love for the mother fuels devotion to the child. Will he feel the same about one of his own? Thinking of the babe in Elana's womb reminds him that it is time to say goodbye.

He bid farewell to the rest of the family this morning. Ima Miriam expressed concern but he was too ashamed to reveal his business, even to Abba Joseph. After Hava takes the children, he carries the little boat to the barn. The balmy air is heavy with grapes nearly ripe for harvest. Beyond the last barley field waiting for Sucot, Sheikan grazes in the pasture. He hastens his step. The perfume of her skin rising above the aroma of the beasts, she emerges under a veil of curls.

"Mary, do you have a moment?"

Her green eyes flash, "You've avoided me since we returned."

Taking her arm, he leads her back into the stall and seats them upon the deep straw. Confining himself to words alone will be difficult. "I am sorry. I have had much on my mind."

Like her children, she caresses his cheek. "You shall see that all will be well."

Trying to contain his emotion, he says softly, "I must do what is honorable. I cannot leave Elana stranded carrying my child. I am returning to Magdala."

She nods, and looks away for the span of many breaths. "Will you stay with her?"

His heart softens at the sadness in her voice. "No, but I hope that she will return with me so I can help her raise the child."

"Why wouldn't she return with you if you are married?"

He swallows. "I cannot take Elana as my wife but I will father the child and that will be easier if she chooses to come with me." Her expression moves him to brush a dark tendril from the downward curve of her mouth. "How can I take a wife when I love another?"

She looks down, thick lashes lying sweetly upon her cheeks. With a finger, he tilts her chin to reveal unshed tears. "I have never loved anyone but you."

Green eyes lock with blue. Once, a long time ago, she kissed him, but now it is his turn to search. Very tenderly their lips touch, hers part invitingly, his kiss becoming urgent. She runs passionate fingers through his tight curls. Lush sensuality melts in his embrace, the scent of her desire rising. Laying her back upon the straw, his mouth never leaves hers enflamed by her response.

The time is not ripe.

She places a hand between them. "I'm sorry; I cannot do this."

In his heart, regret blends with relief. "Now I know now what I must do." Passion colors her cheeks.

"What must you do?"

"I must return for you are my home." Gently, he lifts her to her feet. "Before I take my leave, I shall tell Yeshua what I have done."

Her endearing expression reveals how much she shall yearn for him. With a full heart, he whispers, "You will not miss me nearly as much as I shall miss you. But I will be back."

***

I sink to my knees in prayer. After a long while Yeshua comes, his hayye bathing me in compassion. Sitting down, he idly picks straw from my locks. "Teoma has left." I nod. "I hope you had a nice farewell, for he shall not return until late in Kislev." He gathers me in his arms, "Mary, I love you," his heart free from fear or jealousy.

Slowly, I shake my head, "You are amazing. I know he told you that we kissed. The time was not ripe, but even so, my passion nearly got the best of me."

Tilting my chin with a finger, Yeshua kisses my lips still moist from another. Not quelling my passion, I ride it back into his heart and then into my own. Tenderly, my husband caresses me, whispering, "I am blessed to have you and Hava is right, my negligence will be my undoing."

"Yeshua, I am responsible for my actions, not you."

Tracing the curve of my cheek, he responds softly, "We are all in this life together, every breath affects one another, every thought, every action, every non-action. I know my part in this drama that is our existence. Ripe action and unripe action compliment one another as day does night."

Kissing me deeply, he caresses the length of my body, opening my sadin and I shiver delighted, crying out when he fills me with passion of his own. The hayye vibrates like the strings of a lyre, our moans provide the melody.

In the aftermath, we lie naked upon our garments, limbs entwined as the tangled straw that makes our bed. Kissing my tender mouth, he sighs, "My love, our hearts must reach out to Teoma for he is going into the lion's den of his fears. He shall face that aspect of himself that is but a lamb, vulnerable and dependent upon others. In his journey back to Self, his fear shall be as vicious lions thwarting him. Let us pray that he may exist in the light of love." So I kneel in prayer with my husband to bless his friend, my lover when the time is ripe.

In my heart, I know more must be done for Teoma, for Yeshua, and for myself. Smiling at me, Yeshua responds to my thought, "Yes, it is time for you to surrender him."

***

Cleared by the Romans since the dedication of Tiberius, the caves peer accusingly at Teoma's descent through the Valley of Robbers. How he wished for a stiff confrontation, but Yeshua showed compassion. Robbed of relief, Teoma urges his horse headlong to meet his destiny arriving in Magdala well after dark.

Decorous in the Greek style, the humble courtyard hosts statues of gods. At the feet of a voluptuous Aphrodite lays floral offerings. A heavily-laden olive tree casts shadows over the entry, barely concealing a lank young man.

"What business does a Roman have here?"

Conscious of his attire, Teoma answers, "I am Teoma bar Flavius and I have come for Elana."

The other studies him a moment. "You must be the Hebrew my sister chose at the new moon. Why are you dressed as a Roman?"

Teoma smiles in an effort to put the man at ease. "My father is Roman, my mother Hebrew, but my alliance is to this land where we both make our homes."

Nodding, her brother introduces himself, "I am Nikolas. Come, my mother will want to meet you." Teoma follows him into the house to be greeted by the aroma of roasted lamb and a gregarious Greek family.

"So you are the man who has stolen my daughter's heart." Elana's mother pinches his cheek appreciatively. "How did Apollo emerge from the loins of a Hebrew?"

Coloring at her reference, Teoma holds his tongue. Elana has yet to come forth. With a raucous laugh, the eldest brother, Theologos, addresses his mother. "Meetera, cease your prattle or he may not be inclined to relinquish the full price for his bride."

Teoma swallows thickly. Their expectations might prove difficult. Theologos' young son approaches and Teoma gratefully lifts the boy onto his lap, an innocent shield from the coming interrogation.

"Are you a god, sir?" The boy traces his features before patting his broad chest.

"No, son, I am a man like your father."

The child hugs his neck. "You shall be my uncle when you marry Theea Elana."

The boy's mother elbows her husband, "See, he shall be a good father to the babe." She turns and calls over her shoulder, "Elana! Come, your bridegroom awaits!"

***

At dawn, I arise to begin the process of disentangling my cords of attachment. Yeshua follows me to the stables, "Here, love, take some sustenance." Tying a small pack about my waist, he whispers, "It will be a long day in the wilderness."

My heart constricts with knowing that I shall never view my beloved with the same eyes again. "Mary, the mirror of my love shall be that much clearer when you return." Sheikan races off. I chance a last look at Yeshua, but he is gone.

Fiercely, the wind whips through the trees, laying low the grass as Sheikan carries me toward my destiny. The sky is the brilliant blue of Teoma's eyes when lit by passion, a vast reminder of my work. Like a divine hand, the wind tears away the ribbon, unraveling my tightly woven plait with deft fingers. The winds of change escort me through another portal of transformation.

The sacred grove, my wilderness haven, beckons, a silent sanctuary. No angelic host to guide and comfort. No great voice of the One within the pyramid of nura. I am alone with myself. Yet in this place of divine connection, I am a part of All That Is. Strange, for only in the intimate embrace of my beloved, in the gasp of breath between orgasmic waves, have I felt as connected as I do now. The earth and I, the creatures and plants, all breathe in rucha, as one sacred being.

Slipping off Sheikan's back, the tangle of his silvery mane rough against my cheek, I breathe in his essence before releasing him to roll in the fallen leaves and drink deeply of the babbling stream. I lay the blanket and pack aside to sit in the crook of an ancient olive tree. In the wizened grandmother's lap, I find that my aloneness is yet another illusion.

Lightly I proceed, free from the shadow of fear, no longer a wall of solidity. Conscious breath embraces my vibrant body and the cords of attachment which bind my soul to Teoma's become visible as a tightly woven braid somewhat entangled with scattered knots. His deep earthy green separates easily from my rich vibrant purple as I use the oil of love to loosen what is bound. The knots of our sexual attraction tightening most recently between the more neatly woven braids of our chaste relationship, I gently work out the tangles. Sometimes his green cord stiffly sticks to my violet, his protection both serving and shadowing me. Twisted pieces—here I have used him to shield me from embracing my self-doubt and there I leaned on him rather than use my own fiery courage.

I breathe in his beloved soul essence and the last of the cords of attachment loosen. With the clear intention of floating free, I disentangle in loving gratitude. Far away in Magdala, Teoma clutches his chest, struggling with his breath, although free floating in this river of consciousness. While I delight in my unencumbered watery dance, he paddles toward the shore to grip the banks, struggling to stay afloat, crying, *I've been abandoned!*

My love floats to him. *Have a joyful journey back home.*

Immensely lightened, I dance with the wind whistling through the trees. Joyously, the stream beckons me to wash away the last shadowy remnants of attachment. The day yet young, I glide through the water, imaging my beloved children. Loosely braided together are we, my violet into Sarah's gold and then into Josh's silvery threads. Imagining a release of my attachment to the body, mind, and soul of each of my children, the braided cords gently fall apart, drifting as leaves upon the water.

In the garden at home, Sarah and Joshua romp through the late summer flowers, and in the river of consciousness, swim unencumbered through the waters of life. Free from my maternal encumbrance, they float in a magical world of possibility. *Beloved, Sarah, you are my delight; know joy in this human existence.*

Ima, thank you for untying us.

Joshua, you are most precious to me, a divine gift from the heart of the One.

Stripping, he jumps into the fountain and we embrace. "Hurry, Sarah, come join us!"

Laughing we connect in the life-giving water, until Hava comes upon them and pulls up her skirt to put her feet in the fountain. "Well, you are definitely your Ima's children."

"Can you feel Ima, Hava?" Josh asks in bright-eyed wonder. Cocking her head, Hava extends her hayye so I reach out and touch her heart center.

When she touches her chest, Sarah responds, "Not there, Hava, through your feet. Ima's in the water with us."

Smiling Hava tells them, "You are fortunate to be able to be with your parents anywhere."

Play comes to an end all too soon. Time to finish my work. The cool stream is comforting as I examine my attachment to my beloved

Yeshua—long cords through our hearts and beyond. Loosely woven at the root when we were young and without expectation, more intricately woven throughout the years, pulled very tight in places, changing patterns throughout our time on earth, the end of the braid not so snug where Yeshua loosened his binding. A thing of beauty, the weaving so complex that violet and silvery white blend into sparkling lavender, perhaps too lovely to disturb.

Sighing, I see myself separate from Yeshua. Holding clear intention, I spark the flame of my desire and test for ripeness. Time for the final release. Unweaving what I have woven over the past ten years, it seems impossible to refigure the pattern and not create a knotted mess. Breathing through my fear, my hayye expands with love which lubricates the bindings, loosening the braid. Here I am attached like a barnacle on the hull of a ship. Here bound like a vine, clinging to the tree roots. Dependent upon his love and approval, the tight cords must be carefully untangled; where my courage persevered, the braid slips free.

An eternity passes or only a moment, the work so stringently delicate. Nature whispers encouragement through this rough and rapid part of the river of consciousness as I move to the bank of the stream, to dry my cold skin in the sun. Caressing my naked breasts before disturbing a wet lock of hair, the wind incites my passion. My efforts renewed, I disentangle from my husband, loosening, loosening what I have created in my fear. Clearly now, I see how strongly I attached to him in fear of separation. My faith wavered and I clung, wrapping about his heart center strangling like tares about shafts of wheat. Trusting not that I could find my own way but now, I finally realize I always had the power right within my core to be as One with All That Is.

With a deep breath from my crown to my root, I arrive at the beginning of our union as man and wife. Backwards through the trials of our courtship, I unweave the braid pulled tight, arriving at the portal of my realization that Yeshua and I were destined to be together. Only eleven when the braid tightened. The loose binding of childhood slips through my fingers like fragrant oil. The cords of attachments are dissolved, leaving space for new growth.

With tears of gratitude, I give thanks and Yeshua joins me. *Beloved, you have set yourself free to become the fullness of all that you desire.*

I breathe in his essence, filling my heart now more expansive than ever before. In a second breath, I am filled by the Great Ima, and in the third by the cosmos. And still I might hold more, so I breathe in the past, the present, and the future.

Yeshua embraces my hayye. *Your hunger may not be filled all at once.*

I am anxious to experience the fullness of I for somehow the 'me's are blended into the whole.

Excitedly, Yeshua reiterates my discovery. *My love, the I that envelopes all the 'me's you believed yourself to be is but a fractional mirror of the great universal I, the I AM.*

My tiny reflection of the great I AM. Pleasure fills my being, delight floats my soul, clarity shifts my mind, passion heats my body. *Yeshua, I feel so full, so expansive.*

Smiling, he gently advises, *Consume sustenance then ride home.*

With conscious breath, I do as he advises, finding relief in the action. Although simply prepared, the meal tastes exceptionally fine. The bread enlivened by his touch, meat tenderly sliced, figs sweet in my mouth. I wipe my lips with the napkin seeped in the perfume of his skin. The wind, quieted to a gentle breeze, draws near night. Nickering softly, Sheikan offers to carry me home so off we race in intimate connection, the pure hayye of our roots mingling to flow into the earth. Connected to all, entangled with none, I am free. In releasing my family, my heart has expanded with passionate desire to be. I have surrendered all to love and love fills my being, leaving no space for fear or doubt.

When I arrive, Yeshua is there. His hayye so light it is nearly translucent, brilliant white with stars of silver rotating about a silver core. Nowhere does my purple tinge his aura, for we are unattached now. Torn between delight and despair, I dismount, falling into his open arms. Always welcome, always wanted, I am home. No boundaries exist, nor ties of any kind. Never was there a stranger marriage than ours.

Laughing at my thoughts, Yeshua brushes the tangled locks from my face to kiss me with such ardor that my own hot violet passion becomes consumed within his cool white flame.

"Yeshua?" I whisper breathlessly, his lips exploring my earlobes. Trembling as his beard tickles my neck, I try again, "Yeshua, I have not completely surrendered you, for desire overwhelms me." As he releases the linen that binds my breasts, my anticipation flows.

"Did I not tell you that the mirror of my love would be clearer?" Firmly he draws me near, but my riding skirt thwarts him. Anxiously, I assist him before the linen gives way. With a soft nicker, Sheikan announces the arrival of another, for we are in the midst of the pasture.

"Let me relieve you of this fine horse." Ari!

Yeshua picks me up with hurried thanks, before I can greet our friend. I wave as Ari leads Sheikan to the barn.

Between two rising knolls, Yeshua sets me down on a grassy bed. With fevered fingers, we undress one another, our mouths seeking sustenance between flying garments. Discovering the boundaries of my being, he meets me where I live. In the heart of desire, the violet flame transforms our souls into a single entity. Silver and purple blend into a color beyond the rainbow with the thick emptiness of a moonless midnight sky and the brightness of the midday summer sun. My great desire fulfilled again and again until the final wave crashes and we meet in our core. One breath, one color, one spirit, one being.

In unison, our breath divides to fill our individual bodies. "Mary, my precious," Yeshua hoarsely whispers, "could the mirror of our love reflect our essence any clearer than this?"

"If I knew how intensely connected we could unite with Eloha, I would have surrendered you a long time ago."

Smiling, he kisses me softly, our lips tender from passion. "Now we both exude the aroma of horse, grass, and earth. Let us go to the baths and begin again." With a deep cleansing breath, my mind focuses on the possibility that our passionate desire for one another might never be quenched in this lifetime. "Not until the end of time, then we shall create once more another eternal flame."

***

Sitting on the lakeshore, Teoma's head aches from the ouzo her brothers insisted he share last night. The anisette liquor was much stronger than any he ever consumed, so returning to Martha's was difficult indeed. The house was empty for Eleazer took his family to Jerusalem for the high holy days.

Elana seeks him out and gathers her courage. "Why did you come back?"

Gently, he takes her hand, wishing he felt more than compassion for the girl. "I want to father the child you carry."

"How do you know that I am with child?"

"Mary informed me on that day you came to her sister's house."

She pulls her hand away. "I didn't even know! How could she?"

"Mary is a healer. She…"

"Then why did you leave? If you knew I carried your seed, how could you leave?" Elana becomes distraught.

"I had a duty to escort her family back to Nazareth, with the intention to return. I am here now." He has trouble holding her gaze and she starts to rise.

"You are in love with her!"

"Please come with me. I want to support the child and you…"

In a passionate haste, Elana runs from him. Groaning, he rises to follow. His day has begun poorly.

The courtyard appears even smaller in the daylight. How so many people can exist under one roof is beyond his comprehension. Raised voices greet him.

"He came for you, girl! You will marry him!" Theologos scolds his crying sister.

"He speaks not of marriage. Only of the child! He loves another!"

Before a further word can pass, Teoma announces his presence. Theologos invites him into the house. "Here he is, drawn by the charms of our Elana. Tell us how you shall support her."

Dark eyes watch his every move. Teoma carefully responds, "I have a substantial inheritance through my mother's family. She and the child will be well cared for."

"Ahh! So you know of the blessing residing in my sister's womb." His face reflects that the pregnancy is no such thing, offending Theologos. "Most Hebrew men marry quite young. You are what? Twenty-five?"

"Twenty-eight."

"Hmm. So why have you not taken a wife?"

Straightening to his full height, Teoma takes a deep breath. "I am committed to my friend and brother, Yeshua bar Joseph. He is in line to the throne of the tribe of Judah and will unite the nation of Yisrael. I protect what is his."

Theologos studies the larger man. "My sister says you returned not for her but for the child, yet she has just informed her family of her condition. How could you know?"

Elana answers for him. "The wife of Yeshua told him!"

"A sorceress!" Elana's mother backs away. "Why I heard she cast a spell upon the women of Capernaeum so their husbands' seed would find no purchase. I forbid Elana to go to the circles."

"Mary is not a sorceress. She is a healer." Teoma's emotion cannot be quelled. "Women seek her care willingly. Perhaps if Elana might have participated in the conscious conception circles, we would not be debating her future now." His impassioned speech cannot be contained even by Theologos' growing rage.

"What are your intentions toward my sister?"

"I wish to help her raise the child. If she would return to Nazareth with me, I…"

"You will not take my sister as your harlot!" Theologos' face inflames as Nikolas rises to stand beside him

"I cannot marry your sister." He looks squarely at the two men, though he feels quite diminished.

Elana muffles her cries into her mother's breast. "That sorceress has cast a spell on you as well. She keeps you as a lover right under her husband's nose!"

With a great effort to stifle his passion, Teoma raises his hands. "You know not what you speak. I will return in the morning." The younger brother moves to stop Teoma from leaving but the elder holds him back.

"Let him go, Nikolas. If he returns with a proposal for marriage, we might consider a generous bride price. If not…."

Teoma hears no more as he enters the village proper.

That evening as he lies beneath the stars, Mary comes to him through the ethers. Her presence so palpable as if her soft form presses against his in an embrace.

Mary, it has not gone well. I do not know what I shall do and today for the first time, I feel so very far away from you.

He can feel her grief as she responds. *I released my attachment to you, dear. Although I still love you, the cords bound me to you in pain and fear, which is not what I desire.*

Teoma's panic begins anew. *You may have released me, but I can never release you from my heart, Mary.* Suddenly, she is gone.

The Chachamim teach that human suffering bears evidence of Marya's judgment and although Teoma believes the Divine to be a hallowed presence within all, at the moment he cannot perceive the sacred through his misery.

Healing Touch

Hayye trails like smoke from the sacred scrolls lying expectantly upon the shelves of Joseph's scholarly chambers. From around the carved wooden table the family warmly greets us, but I feel uncomfortable. Something is missing. No, someone is missing! Perhaps I can contact him and he might....

Gently Yeshua places his hand on my arm. "I would rather you stay here. It is precisely these attachments that we are to discuss. Teoma is not missing but doing his work from afar." Silently releasing my beloved friend once again, my heart opens to the expansiveness I experienced in the sacred grove. I breathe in the essence of all and my sight becomes acute.

Like rays of light, the cords that bind us become clearly visible. So many entanglements within this family, except Yeshua's—a silvery web of loving compassion to his parents and siblings, the children, his beloved friends. The beauty of his connection to me is breathtaking. Parallel gossamer threads woven with evenly spaced cross-ties connect my purple, nearly as black as midnight, to his silver glimmering like sunshine. Existing from the beginning of time to the end, the cords twist into a natural spiral—an intimate dance of divinity. Where we touch, the dark and the light move in harmonic vibration.

Miriam's cords are so intricately woven that it might take lifetimes to unwind. "It appears, my son, you have released us all."

Bathing us in his peaceful hayye, Yeshua smiles, "Yes, Ima. My work at the Sea of Galilee was to surrender my cords of attachment to Love. Still in spirit form of rucha, this surrender has begun. The mind can comprehend the necessity of detachment, but the body struggles with the imprint left from the tightly woven ties." My breath catches in my throat at the truth of his words. My physical form still reacts to the ancient ties that my soul so joyfully released.

"Yeshua, is this why I still feel a great pull from Teoma?"

He takes my hand, "My love, clearly setting your intention and fueling it with grateful desire to release your attachment must be done when the time is ripe."

Wrinkling my brow, I say, "But the time was ripe." His smile is for me though his attention includes all.

"It was the soul's work, but the body," he squeezes my arm as if it is fruit, "is not quite ripe. That is why your yearnings are physical." He touches the tear spilling from my lashes. Leaning into his shoulder, I sob silently.

Joseph clears his throat. "What if the one you choose to release does not choose to release you?"

With deft manipulation of the energies, Yeshua highlights the cord Joseph created to bind them. "Abba, your ties to me are no longer mirrored by mine to you." Turning toward his mother, he whispers, "And you, beloved Ima, must continually release all of us or your great compassion will be reflected within your being as great pain."

With a deep breath, he gathers in our heart energy like armfuls of spring blossoms. "There are three aspects of our human creation—the body, the mind, and the soul. These three journey together throughout eternity, the form adapting to the reality in which it finds itself."

"Pigra—the body—allows you to survive in the conditions of the world, exquisitely created to mold to the environment. Reyaya—the mind—makes sense of the reality, communicating to the body and to other forms its thoughts and intentions. Nafsha—the soul—has intimate connection with the divine plan, always ahead of the mind and the body, existing outside the confines of time, reaching ripeness like the first fruits of the season."

He pauses as we all visualize his message. The three aspects of self travel through this reality—the soul leading, the body in the rear, crossing over nook and glen, stream and mountain.

Yeshua laughs. "Mary has a wonderful view of the body, mind, and soul as traveling companions in the wilderness facing many obstacles on their journey back home." Kissing my cheek, he uses the analogy to illustrate his lesson. "Nafsha leads the three, seeing the divine vision, knowing innately that the great river of change must be crossed. So the soul flies across, encouraging the others to follow, describing the beautiful view from the far bank of the rushing waters. Reyaya, a bit more cautious, thinks about the crossing, calculating how best to ford the great rapids with the least amount of damage. Now Pigra says: 'Wait a moment. You have led me through rough waters before and I must take the brunt of your haste. So be absolutely sure that the other side is much nicer than this bank, for I wish not to suffer in the crossing.'"

Laughing, Jacob tickles a smile from his hesitant wife but the rest of us groan at the difficulty in convincing our forms of the change our souls' desire. Yeshua nods, "You each know how stubborn the human body can be. It does not seem nearly as enlightened as the soul, but it is the chosen form, the ship crafted by the mind and soul to traverse the waters of life. Perfected for this earthly journey, the body has its own knowing. Pigra will bide its time through the river of change until Reyaya can convince it that the crossing is either safe or worth the risk. We must give thanks for our incredibly gifted human forms housing our souls in this dense reality, so Nafsha might experience the joy of creation."

Joseph smiles, "I can see now how strong are my physical habits that reflect the binding attachments to those I love."

"Even when finally releasing your attachments at the soul level, well convinced in your mind of the ripeness of the act, your body will still respond in its former ways, habituated to the life it knew, slower to conform to the change. Do not reprimand the form, Pigra has served you well. Be gentle with it, compassionate to its needs and it will follow Reyaya and Nafsha like a loyal beast serves its master."

"Or as wild creatures commune with the hayye of the Elat." Ari winks at me before placing an arm around Hava.

"Yes with an open heart, one might even convince the wildest of forms to enter the circle in remembrance of Sacred Unity."

I imagine my breath is that of the One and watch all breathe in unison. Soon Yeshua leads us in Sacred Breath—rucha—intonating the vibration of YHVH with sound.

"ee-oh-oo-ah."

Over and over we sing, breathing in the essence of one another as the night air breathes with us. A fullness, an expansion like the pressure of erotic desire moves from my center outwards. Singing the nameless being's song of life, waves of ecstasy crash through my heart. My beloved's connection spirals about my aura mimicking the undulations of a serpent about her nest of eggs. Oneness without attachment fills my being like sweet breath after surfacing through deep waters. Trembling with delight, the orgasmic experience bubbles forth as laughter.

"ee-oh-oo-ah," I sing breathlessly, whispering the name of my cosmic lover after a most satisfying encounter.

Drawing me into his embrace, my earthly lover breathes in my essence, "Your fulfillment with the One Being is my heart's desire, beloved Mary."

Across the table, each couple intertwines, sharing tears and kisses. "Oh, what a joyous climax."

"Dearest, your passion has always been easily fired, but when you surrender to the One in Sacred Unity, your deepest longing is met a thousand-fold." He announces to the others, "I pray that you each might find fulfillment in the release of your bindings. Thank you for your divine presence this night."

The glow of the moon upon my face, my heart sings with a great desire to dance beneath her light. "Come, Yeshua. Let us go out into the night."

Scooping me up in his arms, he whispers, "You are insatiable, love. This is why we are well-matched, for our soul longing runs deep within us."

Peals of sweet laughter burst forth. "We are well met in many ways, Yeshua. But you will have to be most clever tonight to match the finesse of the One."

Stopping beneath the stars, he raises an eyebrow, "Really?"

I nip his lower lip lightly, whispering into his mouth, "Oh, yes, for my formless lover has outdone itself this night."

With a purring he replies, "Really? Well, we shall see. For the One has taken form in me and I shall meet your passion thrice over." A twinkling of many stars cast a shimmering light upon his beautiful face in support of his bold proclamation. I am filled with love for him, for us, for All That Is. True to his word, he fulfills my desire thrice over before the moon slips below the horizon.

A gray-blue dawn presses brisk lips to my cheek. My beloved lies upon the dewy grass, his rich brown locks bejeweled by moisture. His visage transformed by the fuller embodiment of his soul—angular jaw softened by rucha covered in downy kaffa-colored beard, an aquiline nose curved below elegant brows to the twin portals of his eyes. I resist the temptation to move up and kiss his full lips.

Stroking the length of my body, his fingers settle within the tangled curls at the small of my back. "What are you looking for?"

I lay my cheek against his chest, comforted by the thudding of his heart. "You are so beautiful. It is a wonder no other woman ravished you the many times we have been apart."

Placing one arm behind his head, he tilts up to look at me. "Away from you, I only missed your charms more. No other could have met me as you have, Mary."

I cup my chin in the curve of my crossed arms. "Yeshua, how can you encourage me to explore my sensuality, yet I am the only one for you?"

"Before we wed, Abba took me to Britannia, but I was reluctant to share my essence with another who could not meet me. I observed many rituals, not unlike our new moon celebrations, and perceived that after intimacy, peoples' hayye shifted." He pauses to create a visual of distorted auras following sexual liaisons.

"Their unions were incomplete—in body, perhaps in mind, rarely in spirit. Only when a great devoted love existed between the couple and they had remembered their connection to Eloha did their hayye seem magnified equally." Carefully, he searches my face, "As a child, I felt whole until puberty shifted everything. My body changed so rapidly, my emotions began influencing my mind, and my aura became formless without clear boundaries."

Caressing my cheek, he whispers, "I have grown in loving connection to All That Is as a fully embodied man through our relationship for you, my beloved, are whole in body, mind, and soul, absolutely integrated."

Perhaps he is overly concerned about his vulnerability. "Yeshua, with all your searching to seek Eloha are you not curious to know if you might be able to connect in union with another?"

With both hands, he cups my face. "You are the curious one and I know you can find connection with another being. Take the experience last night with Sacred Breath, you exhibited the deepest connection by far."

"I did not notice how deeply the others were connecting." His mouth breaches a smile beneath mine.

"So deeply connected there was nothing but you and the One. Mary, for me sexual expression is sacred. Just as I choose not to intoxicate myself with strong drink, I choose not to share my essence with just anyone."

"Besides," he mouths into the softness of my cheek, "you have fulfilled my every desire with joyful eagerness. You meet my imagination over and over with your creative sensuality. Time has only made you more desirable as you continually open to fuller expressions of yourself."

Nibbling my chin, he continues, "Why would I ever leave this paradise since in you my dreams have become manifest."

Breathing in your essence, I am fulfilled
The sweet wine of your lips intoxicates me
Silky dark curls, your only adornment
I yearn to taste the fruit of your lush garden
Parting desire, I plunge into the river of dreams
In the sea green depth of your eyes, I find
The perfect reflection of my Self as Love
Twin flames borne from a single spark
United at last to create a most joyous existence
Sacred Wisdom delights in our sensual song
Alone I wandered between the worlds
My single manifestation quite separate from reality
Until into your embrace I at last succumbed
Lying upon your breast I connect to the earth
Finally well met in form and vibration, I am home
Before time began Source was passionate desire to be
From the dark womb of potential the light emerged
Sacred Unity diversified into joyous love, you and I
Souls part as stardust, born unto Earth
Reconnect as One in breath and being—Eloha.

***

Arising early, Teoma dons long robes and heads to Caperneuam praying to be shown a way. Within the bustling marketplace, he hesitates at a stall to admire a robust bullock.

"My friend, you have returned." A heavy arm is placed upon Teoma's already overburdened shoulders. Bartholomew!

Teoma embraces the large man. "It is good to look upon a friendly face."

Bartholomew pats the calf appreciatively. "Is your offense so great to consider the life of this animal?"

His friend's knowing is uncanny. Teoma looks up. "I know not the proper price for my mistake."

"Well, this fine young bullock is enough to consecrate the High Priest on Yom Kippur. Perhaps there is a sage in the synagogue who might provide counsel."

Just outside the sanctuary courtyard, Bartholomew secures a learned one. The white-bearded sage questions Teoma. "What is your chata, son?"

"I have lain with a Greek woman who now carries my seed."

"Are you married?" Teoma shakes his head. "Is she?" Again, no. "But your heart is greatly burdened."

"What should I do?"

After studying his face, the sage suggests, "Go to the Holy Temple. Your people are Tzadokim. Only a blood sacrifice will appease your guilt."

Teoma nods, knowing what must be done. He thanks the sage. His conflict lies between duty and freedom. Why can't they be one and the same? When his best friend married his true love, Teoma chose to wander unencumbered, to experience life beyond Nazareth. Now this freedom has led to yet an unwanted responsibility to father a child he so thoughtlessly planted in the womb of a woman he barely knows. Without love, duty seems an unbearable burden.

Bartholomew escorts him back to Magdala. "It is a long way to Jerusalem. Perhaps if you offer tribute to the gods of your father, your burden might be lifted?"

Intent on making amends, Teoma ignores such sacrilege and seeks out Elana. Near the placid lake they sit quietly, Teoma wishing he felt more for the girl.

"So when you return, we will be married?"

Forlorn, he shakes his head, "I will care for you and the child, but I cannot take you as my wife."

"Why are you willing to live in the shadow of her love rather than the reality of mine?" Looking at her fair face, he wonders this as well. His silence further aggravates the girl who leaves in a passionate haste.

Rising wearily, Teoma goes after her. As he winds through the narrow streets, trepidation creeps into his heart. He hastens his step and nearly passes by her crumpled form. Muffled sobs draw his attention.

"Elana?"

Gently, he picks her up, praying that she be well. She must have slipped and fallen for by the time he reaches the courtyard, both their garments are stained with blood. Her mother greets him, shouting for her young grandson to make haste and find his father.

Not once has he been within the vine-covered walls of this courtyard in peace. Now the air heavily-perfumed by ripe grapes is punctuated by the cries of the women. Elana is losing the baby and her mother assumes that he is to blame. Perhaps he is. He prayed for a way to be revealed and that path lies bloody before him.

"What has happened? What did you do to my sister?" Nikolas is prepared to pummel him for causing her such grief.

Older and a bit more sensible, Theologos tries to extract the truth from the women.

"He means to placate his god with an offering in the great temple. Aphrodite is powerless!" Elana's mother cries, "His seed pours from her womb."

Her eldest son is not so sure that the Hebrew god could best the Greek goddess. This is the work of a mortal man, one who refuses to take responsibility for his actions, one who will pay for hurting his sister.

Nikolas needs no encouragement to attack. Weighted by his guilt, Teoma refuses to defend himself, taking cruel comfort. Theologos becomes disgusted by the one-sided fight and drags the battered man into the alley.

"Perhaps your god will save you or does he only smite your weak victims?" Tonight, Theologos will offer sacrifice to Aries, god of war, for the pleasure of this vengeance.

Before the moon has risen, Bartholomew discovers his gravely-injured friend lying in the dark streets of Magdala. With great tenderness, he carries Teoma back to Martha's house. The disciple tends to the younger man, who slips in and out of consciousness. Bartholomew prays that Yeshua come and heal his friend, but not until Teoma asks on Yom Kippur does his master arrive.

***

Sitting down upon a blanket, I pick up Jonathon and watch Rebeka nurse Jonina, sparkling with devotion. Before little Jonina can clasp a chubby hand around her mother's hair, I deftly twist it down her back and out of the baby's reach. Nearly bouncing his curly head into my chin, I kiss Jonathon's dimpled cheek and he turns to suck on mine hungrily.

"I should feed him first, but he leaves so little for her." Rebeka sighs, drained from nursing them. She refuses a wet nurse, unwilling to release her cords of attachment to the twins.

With a flurry of giggles, Sarah drops upon the blanket. "Do you want to see what Abba has been teaching us?" Joshua settles himself next to her. "Watch, Ima!"

With great concentration, Sarah focuses her hayye on a stone lying a short distance away and holds her hands out as if to catch it. Slowly, the stone rises from the grass hovering in the air, level with her outstretched hands. Miriam walks into the garden and pauses at the sight of her granddaughter, remembering Yeshua perform levitation as a child. All of us in silent awe, until the stone swerves viciously into Joshua's face.

Rebeka screams and the twins begin howling. Miriam panics. Handing over Jonathon to his terrified Ima, I bring in the white light. Immediately bathed in calm reverence, the still place within allows me to assess the situation. Lying unconscious with a rapidly swelling knot on his forehead, Joshua's face is covered in blood. Sarah cries, one hand on his chest.

Shifting slightly, I take Joshua's head into my lap, then reassure my daughter. "You are not to blame. Please sit across from me and hold your brother's feet."

Sarah settles herself into the comforting circle of light. "All right, Ima. How else can I help?" I smile at my sweet daughter.

"Please anchor your brother's hayye through your root and into the earth." Accessing the image I hold, Sarah performs her task with ease.

Joshua slipped out of his body the moment the stone smashed into his forehead. I invite the energy of the earth and that of the heavens to help. Calling him back, I begin healing the damage, seeing his face unmarred. Like drops of rain coalescing on the surface of a leaf, the drops of blood find their way back into the laceration. The swelling diminishes until his forehead is smooth and lovely without a sign of the injury. Still Joshua hovers above, a silvery cord attaching him to his form then into the earth at Sarah's root. I leave my own form to escort him back.

Ima, isn't it nice here?

Embracing my son's nafsha, I tell him, *It is wonderful, but now it is time to return to your body, Josh. Look, it is whole again.*

Josh relaxes and slides back into himself. Bending forward, I kiss his precious face and he rewards me by opening his eyes.

"Sorry, Sarah, for taking your stone."

Partially hidden by curls, she whispers tearfully, "It's all right, Josh. I'm sorry you got hurt."

He wiggles his feet against her belly, "Thanks for holding onto me," laughing as she tickles his legs.

Outside the circle of healing, hysteria reigns. From my heart center to Rebeka, then to the crying babies, I extend peaceful hayye until they calm. Miriam, collapsed on the grass at the sight of Joshua's blood, still entertains horrifying images of her children's various injuries. What catches my breath is one of Yeshua in the future, hurt and surrounded in fearful trepidation. She shares my knowing!

Within the healing circle, Sarah and Josh attend to my concern. I calm myself and they settle into each other's embrace. "Joshua, when you try to levitate something to you, see what you desire in your hands, not in line with your sight."

"I love you this much, Ima." He spreads his arms wide.

"I love you too. But it looks like Savta can use some of our love right now." Sarah stands and pulls her brother to his feet leaving the healing circle. Miriam reaches up to them and they cover her with kisses.

Over Joshua's head she gives me a grateful smile. *Thank you, dear, for healing him. He is most precious to me, like his Abba.* I return her smile, planning to help refine my son's skill at levitation. In the meantime, the children will not be allowed to levitate anything heavier than a cushion.

***

When Yeshua arrives in Magdala, Bartholomew greets him vigorously but the disciple's face is creased by the strain of long nocturnal vigils. A once renowned healer within the Egyptian Therapeutae, Bartholomew submits to his ministrations. "Your loving compassion for my brother is like a balm to your mind, Bartholomew."

Teoma lies battered upon the bed. Although Bartholomew has tended his wounds and washed his body, the damage is great. Eyes swollen shut, nose fractured crookedly, and lips scabbed, his face unrecognizable.

Even working day and night, Yeshua's healing skills are blocked by his friend's great self-judgment. Choosing a most bitter path, Teoma sacrificed his own blood to redeem himself, but his healing will continue in layers over a long period of time.

Gently Bartholomew touches his shoulder. "Teoma is burdened by his sense of duty, but let not his yoke be yours."

Yeshua is brought to tears by the wisdom of the goyim, "What once brought him joy in service to those he loves, now brings him pain. When we choose to live in sorrow we cast the mold for manifestations of fear. Our perceived separation from Eloha keeps us from realizing our full potential as conscious creators of our existence."

Nodding, Bartholomew returns to sponging Teoma's body.

On the morning of the fourth day Teoma finally revives. "Do no more, Yeshua. Let me be."

Bartholomew tenderly bathes his brow. "Please, friend, allow Yeshua to heal you completely. For even now your appearance is not your own."

Teoma's voice is muffled through swollen lips, "Yeshua, I am grateful you have come but this is my burden to bear."

Cupping his friend's face, Yeshua kisses his forehead. "I wish for you to come home but Mary will be most upset to see you like this. Please, for her...."

Perhaps my deformity will harden her heart and I will be forgotten.

"Your soul paths are as one. She will love you no matter what form you take."

With a great sigh, Teoma relents, "Then I will stand in your way no longer. But leave one scar upon my face to remind me of my duty."

Giving thanks, Yeshua completes the healing of his beloved brother. Shortly, Teoma is made whole, save one small scar near the corner of his right eye.

"Thank you, Yeshua." Taking his hand, Teoma promises, "Never shall I commit this same chata," and lies back wearily. "I need time to heal my heart but I will return with the council."

Exhausted and ill at heart, Yeshua gratefully returns the next evening to Mary's arms. "If I find my own brother's pain so difficult to bear, how am I to help others?"

477

She feeds him his own advice, not to take on others' pain while healing, her kisses a reminder of his joyous existence. *Although I pray that Teoma finds such happiness, I know that until we release one another from our earthly commitments the fullness of joy will be veiled.*

Late the next evening, Ima calls them to her meditation room, asking fretfully about Teoma. Taking her hand, he tries to soothe her worry. "Physically, he is well. Emotionally, he has much more healing to do. He will be leaving Magdala to stay with his Dod until the winter holidays."

She nods, her eyes moist with tears, "Joseph will take care of him." As she speaks Dod's name, her hayye softens with longing.

"All is well, Ima. Your sons are fine." Ima thinks that in his perspective everything is always fine. What is this horrifying image at the hub of her wheel of fear? Mary hides a smile behind a delicate hand, easily veiling her mind from him.

"Ima, we are blessed to have so many healers in the house for with such boisterous children, accidents are bound to occur." *Strongly attached, most especially to me, her attachment duplicated to Joshua, she perceives that you and Sarah do not need her but she is entangled with us.* Mary nods.

Miriam looks up, "I cannot bear to see any of you hurt."

Kissing her forehead, he whispers, "Our human forms are vulnerable in this dimension. Our eternal souls use these physical lessons to connect to Source. Joshua is blessed by his accident to learn more about the energies, and so is his sister who begins her healing work. As for Mary, her ability to minister peacefully in the midst of chaos will serve us all well in the future."

His mention of a tumultuous future ignites Ima's fear. "Yeshua, my premonitions about you are becoming stronger."

Raising her chin up, he whispers, "Release your fear, Ima. All of the events of our lives serve us in the divine orchestration of malchuta. You shall see that in connection to the One, even what appears to be a horrible tragedy is a gift of love." With wide eyes, she nods, but her hayye has not fully encompassed the comfort he extends, his words becoming icons of pain in her mind.

As Mary calls forth the white light of healing, he is eternally grateful for her. His appreciation expands into a sense of awe as the violet hayye emanating from her heart mesmerizes him. With a single breath that fills his being, he becomes fully connected to All That Is. From this space his awe transforms into adoration. Flowing like a waterfall into the everlasting pool of love, adoration reflects unto infinity. Joining with the prism of light, Yeshua holds Ima in both arms, his heart center against her back, his hands cupping hers in front of her chest. The peaceful hayye of loving compassion for Self flows through him and into her heart center. With a gasping breath, Ima completely lets go and receives the fullness of his essence.

The profound nature of the healing energies lulls Ima into a deep sleep. Carefully, Yeshua lays her down upon the cushions then covers her sweet form with a blanket. Leaving a single oil lamp lit near the door to the chambers, he extinguishes the rest.

Down the hall, lamps still burn in the study. Yeshua leads Mary to the door. "Abba, we left Ima asleep in her meditation room."

"I pray you helped her. She fears for you, son."

Yeshua reaches to embrace his father. "Leave this and go to her. Neither of you should be alone this night."

Joseph extracts himself gruffly, "I'm nearly finished."

Sadly, Yeshua motions for them to leave. "To release his cords of attachment Abba feels he must be separate in form as well from those he has bonded himself to."

"It is not easy letting go and your Abba recognizes how physical his habits are. His isolation is how he surrenders."

"But it causes pain to those who are still attached. I must work more diligently on releasing them both since I am still affected by their sorrow."

Mary halts in the courtyard leading to their chambers. "Yeshua, how can you not be? They are your parents and it is very easy to surrender those you love when you are separated by distance but most difficult to be in physical contact as they struggle to reestablish their bonds to you."

"Thank you, for your wisdom." Tenderly he kisses her mouth, knowing that they shall both be challenged when Teoma returns.

***

Soon after Miriam's healing, Jacob approaches with concerns about his wife. Sitting in the olive grove, we are sure of our privacy since Rebeka rarely leaves their cottage since Joshua's accident. "Mary, I do not know how to help her. I am afraid she will become ill from caring for the twins without respite."

"Jacob, perhaps she must become ill before she can ask for help."

He takes my hand in despair. "I could not bear to see her suffer. While the babies grow fat, she wastes away."

I see in his eyes their relationship, strained by his worry and her deterioration. An attentive father and husband, Jacob tries to relieve her of some of the burden of caring for the twins but Rebeka refuses to release her hold on them. "Mary," he whispers with tears in his eyes, "she doesn't seem to want to be with me anymore. I never anticipated children would come between us."

Patting his hand, I extend loving hayye, "Dearest brother, you must understand that she will only release this suffering when she is ready. She still grieves your first baby's death and clings to the twins, always fearing the worst. She believes she's the only one who can love and protect them."

"More and more lately, she will not allow me to be alone with them for very long—nor Hava. I am their Abba! I would never allow harm to come to them."

"In her heart, she knows that but her fear overwhelms her since she expends much hayye to maintain a mantle of protection against the illusion of pain and suffering."

"The **illusion** of suffering? Mary, the pain of losing our first son was very real."

"Yes, but beneath the pain was a great blessing waiting to be discovered which you received by asking for help. Rebeka must find it in her heart to ask for help, Jacob. Healing is received in soulful readiness. It cannot be forced upon another."

Wiping away an errant tear, he sighs, "What shall I do?"

I rub his back, "Release your fear, Jacob. Ask to be filled with light and love. Untangle yourself from Rebeka and the twins, trusting that all will be well. Love yourself as deeply as possible and they will bask in your light and know themselves as love." He sobs quietly but allows the white light to heal his broken heart. "Rebeka loves you, dear. She doesn't love herself as she deserves so her expression of love is laced with fear. Our work is on our own souls first before we realize the effect of our divinity on others."

Sitting up, Jacob tries to make sense of my message, "How can I concentrate any effort on myself while my wife is suffering so?"

Touching his cheek that he might look my way, I answer, "Because that is all you can do, Jacob. You can only heal yourself. There is no other soul that you can save but your own."

"But what about Yeshua? Is he not the mashiach?"

Smiling, I reply, "Our people wish for salvation but your brother came to model how to live as a human being in connection with the Divine. Believe me, it is constant work to release the fear and expectations related to unworthiness. Yeshua is a work in progress as we all are. He is just a bit ahead of the rest of us."

Jacob smiles, his lashes wet with tears, "I don't believe he is ahead of you...."

"Hush, you know how hard your brother works on these issues of the soul!"

At my jest, his smile broadens, "Yeshua is well matched and he knows it, dear sister." Laughing, he continues, "It must be aggravating for him when you move through your issues with ease."

"Jacob, what appears to be ease is really much emotional turmoil. I am a very hot flame that cooks the meat of my soul rapidly. Yeshua slow-roasts his much more thoroughly."

***

Joseph of Arimathaea welcomes him in the outer courtyard of the villa in Ramah. "What a wonderful surprise. Always most welcome, but if you had sent word, I would have engaged some dancing girls for your pleasure."

Teoma stiffens in his uncle's embrace, his face darkening with sorrow. "Your kind gesture, sir, would be wasted upon me."

Kissing his forehead, Joseph replies, "Then perhaps you might take comfort in your cousin."

Teoma nods, "Is Abner here with his family?"

"He's with his wife and sons visiting her mother in Caesarea, but here is yet another cousin of yours." Wondering who could possibly offer him comfort, Teoma follows his uncle through the lavish gardens and into the grand villa. "May I present Gidon."

Extravagantly dressed as royalty yet harsh as a legionnaire with hair, eyes and skin of the same rich brown color, his cousin has a decidedly Roman style. Joseph elaborates, "Known as Prince Phillip to the Romans,

481

not the Herod Phillip of the northeastern tetrarch, your cousin prefers the Hebrew name given to him by his mother, Mariamne."

Gidon clarifies his position, "I am no longer crown prince having lost my inheritance when my mother and her two brothers attempted to take over my father's rule. I was but a youth when we were banished." Noting the confusion on Teoma's face, he continues, "My mother is not the Mariamne you might believe. My father had many wives. After he put the first Mariamne to death, he needed another Hebrew wife to calm his kingdom and placated her father by appointing him to be high priest."

"Cousin, you have the appearance of a soldier."

"Ahh! That is the price of losing one's crown. I made my home in Rome but served my brothers here by commanding the Herodian guard which, I believe, is where I recognize your face."

Teoma draws quick breath. He does know this man! In his work with the zealots he had much contact with Antipas' guard in Samaria. Not face to face but from afar, Teoma witnessed the leadership of the prince among the Herodian military. What was his uncle thinking to invite the enemy into his home? Now Gidon will surely remember his face, making him of no use to the zealots.

Joseph chuckles and places an arm about his nephew. "Let us have some wine and discuss why the two of you are here."

Most disenchanted with Rome, Gidon speaks vehemently against his own kin. An honorable man who wishes to be part of something greater, he is very interested in Yeshua. "So, tell me, does he have a chance to overthrow the foreign rule?"

Studying his deeply wounded cousin, Teoma sees his pain mirrored in the other's eyes. Throughout the evening, confidences are wooed by a great amount of Greek wine. While in Rome, Gidon's brother Antipas stole his wife Herodias. Disillusioned, Gidon sought refuge with Dod Joseph. How tangled is Teoma's blood with his enemies!

Impassioned, Teoma rises to his feet. "I have known Yeshua since we were but boys. The most compassionate man alive, he believes not in war. He shall unite the tribes of Yisrael and the peoples of this land through love."

His testimony warms Gidon. "Your love for him is great indeed, cousin. You and I shall spend much time together finding peace within this fine home. Our mutual desire to free ourselves from the oppression that afflicts our hearts shall unite us."

Joseph nods as his nephews embrace. Although with many years between them and vastly different upbringings, the cousins have honor and duty flowing through their veins. They shall form a strong alliance by healing one another's spirit, and later might even welcome some dancing girls. Their camaraderie reminds him of his old friendship with Yeshua's father. Years ago he gave Joseph bar Hillel the land and house in Nazareth with the hopes that it become an esteemed place of learning. Perhaps the dream shall finally be realized when the council meets this winter.

Gathering of the Council

Chill winter wind blows guests through the protective mists. From the Judaean desert arrives Judas with Jakob, Jochanan, and Saul. Judas kisses me like one of his daughters, "Mary, our clan has changed since you graced us with your visit."

Always forthright, T'shuraw replies, "Yes, shepherds spend much more time with the herds on holiday from the passion of their wives." She whispers, "I am looking forward to observing your interactions with the disciples."

"It is wonderful to see you again, son."

Receiving Judas' kiss, Yeshua smiles, "I am delighted that you have brought your family to spend the holidays with us."

With a flurry of scarves, gorgeous Tamar kisses me most passionately. "Mary, I missed you." I hug her tightly, not unaware of Joseph and Miriam's response.

Before I allay their concerns, Yeshua saves me the fuss. "It is wonderful to have you here with us, Tamar." His kiss flusters her.

"I am looking forward to the solstice celebration my Abba has told me about."

"We are all looking forward to my wife's dancing, Tamar." Blushing, she follows her Ima into the house.

Always fashionably attired, Saul smiles with handsome Jochanan in his wake. "You both look well." Studying us, he visualizes a portrait.

"Oh, Saul!" How might I have the patience to sit through another?

Laughing, Yeshua teases, "I imagine that I will have enough trouble legitimizing myself with our more conservative brethren, let alone pose for an idolatrous painting."

Saul's face flushes red, but Jochanan laughs, "Saul, let us relax and enjoy our visit."

We greet Jakob with hugs. "Yeshua, since you left Qumran, there is much change and I believe most is for the better. It looks like Jochan will welcome you now."

Smiling at our friend, Yeshua replies, "Certainly, I will meet with him, but let us not discuss these matters before the rest have arrived. Why don't you all come in for some refreshment?"

In the morning, the women meet in the inner atrium. With Miriam's insistence, Rebeka joins us, of course, carrying Jonina and Jonathon, one on each hip. Hava gathers us in a circle to sip our tea. Miriam raises a brow as Tamar takes a seat very close to me.

"Rebeka," T'shuraw addresses her in an unabashed way, "have you taken advantage of Mary's services?"

"What do you mean?"

With a shake of her head, T'shuraw catches Jonathon crawling quickly across the circle. "How old are the twins?"

"Eight months." Rebeka responds demurely.

"Too young to become an older brother." With that she kisses his cheek and releases him to crawl over to his Savta.

"Well, that will not happen anytime soon, T'shuraw."

"Ah, and it is no wonder, dear." T'shuraw chides, "You are quite exhausted from mothering these babies and have no time to spend with your husband." Hava hides a smile as Rebeka shrinks back into her cushion. Jonina makes her escape and joins her brother. Hava scoots over to assist Ima with the rambunctious twins.

"Your family has beautiful children, Mary." Her mother's glance hushes Tamar.

"Let's hold a white light ceremony right now for dear Rebeka. Tamar did not participate when you were with us and this will give her an opportunity as well."

"I certainly see no need for the white light." Tamar fusses, her palm clammy against mine. T'shuraw's clever expression would stop a legionnaire in his tracks.

486

"You never know, dear, what the future might hold." Dropping my hand in her frustration, Tamar pouts.

Rebeka rises to leave, but Miriam gently suggests, "It would be best to protect yourself against pregnancy while you are still nursing."

"Are you not getting any assistance from a wet nurse?" Seeing her suspicions confirmed, T'shuraw clucks her tongue. "Well, no wonder you appear so frail. The babies are sucking the life out of you. It is a shame that you have not partaken of Mary's gift. For the sake of your marriage, I must insist that you join us."

With a hesitant nod, Rebeka agrees. Smiling, I try to reassure her, "Dear, you will be able to relax and enjoy your relationship with Jacob, free from the fear of pregnancy. When you are ready to have another, you can release the protection."

An expansion of the energies, the white light infuses Rebeka's heart center. At first she holds her breath and nearly panics. Looking for a way out, she reaches for her infants, but they have fallen fast asleep. "Rebeka, your resistance to the healing is causing you discomfort. Ask now that your fear be lifted and you be filled with love."

Gasping, Rebeka weeps, her tears cleansing her aura as blood cleanses the womb. Softly I ask, "May I begin the conscious conception circle?" She gives her consent and I take them on a journey. T'shuraw's womb is lush and healthy, her marriage bed enlivened with the freedom of the white light. Tamar welcomes my ethereal touch as something sensual, not ready to release me from her heart strings, her sexuality is yet to be fully explored. An inner voice gently whispers—*neither is mine.*

Lush with femininity, Hava's womb lays dormant. *As you see, I have my own form of the white light, dear.*

A combination of herbal remedies over the years reinforced by sheer will has controlled Miriam's fertility since Esther's birth. *I have found means to prevent pregnancy which I promised to show you before you revealed to me your secret.*

Would you like further protection from disease? She nods.

With great reverence, I minister to this very special gathering of women. When it is finished, a chiming of bells sounds in the ethers, now free to express our sexuality with whomever we desire. What doorways might open for the women in this particular circle?

"The energies have brought in a new harmony to us, one that shall enhance our sensual experiences."

T'shuraw sits up and stretches, "I just love these ceremonies, more relaxing than soaking in the Dead Sea." Turning toward Rebeka, she states, "Well, go on, dear. Find that handsome husband of yours and share your good news." Rebeka rarely leaves the babies. T'shuraw clucks her tongue, "Go now, they shall not need another feeding for a long while. We'll take good care of your precious babies while you take good care of your precious husband." Rebeka hesitates, but Hava waves her away.

Miriam lets out a great sigh, "Thank you, T'shuraw. Hava and I have not been able to get through to Rebeka all these months."

T'shuraw looks at me, "Did you not offer this to her before?"

I shake my head. "Her resistance has been great and I was guided to wait until the time was ripe."

Hava laughs, "Well, ripe or not, the fruit has been picked."

Silently I call to Jacob, *Your wife participated in our conscious conception circle with much encouragement from T'shuraw. Please make yourself available this moment for the twins are sleeping contently in their Savta's lap.* Jacob sends me waves of gratitude and I share his message with the others.

T'shuraw gracefully bows her head while Miriam's eyes fill with tears. Smiling, Hava tells me: *The men should be the ones to make payment for your services, dear.*

Later that evening lying in Yeshua's embrace, he attunes to my thoughts. "Dearest, Tamar's presence is a reminder that you are far from complete in the exploration of your sensuality."

"But Yeshua, I am feeling most satisfied in my relationship with you. Why would this possibility intrigue me so?" I turn to kiss his mouth, seeking comfort as well as illumination.

Returning my kiss tenderly, he strokes my cheek, "Because passionate joy is who you are. Our relationship is but one aspect of your potential." Chuckling he continues, "When dear Teoma returns, I shall be doubly challenged."

Sighing, I wonder when this triangle shall ever be released. Yeshua whispers, "It is a fallacy to believe in duality, for the world is made of sacred triads of possibility. The triangle is the cornerstone of creation. If one but looks, she will find that there is always another choice in this free will universe. There is never just one answer, but from the perception of any individual, at least two others."

He begins tracing tristans on my skin with the feathery ends of my hair. "From the point where it appears one is offered only polar choices—right or left, dark or light, this or that—there are in actuality three choices. To move one way, or the other, or to stay still. To be you with me, or to be you with another, or to be you—whole within your Self. You have at least three choices, three points on the triangle of potential. Even time appears to have three points of reference, the past, the present, and the future. All are now, for time does not exist unless the One takes form as in your lovely visage, then there is the Mary that was, the Mary that is, and the Mary that will be. Time exists in triangular relationship to creation as a means to identify Self."

Drops of perception splash down upon me. Yeshua's crystalline hayye consists of many connecting triangles softened into a great spherical teardrop. A memory surfaces of making love in the barley fields and witnessing multitudes of sacred tristans illuminating the surface of all reality.

"You are correct; creation is multiple trinities of possibility."

Pleased at my comprehension, Yeshua beams, "You are my finest student, love. Perceiving through the depth of your being, through the triad of the soul, mind, and body, you become the teachings." I cannot help but smile.

"Yeshua, I have an unfair advantage being your first and only disciple at this time. I am both your best and your worst."

Shaking his head, he breathes softly through my lips, "You shall see that because of your tremendous faith and courage, as well as your uncanny ability to embody your knowing, of all the disciples, you are the finest." As he kisses me, I think that if the other students could experience his essence as I do then each would become as fine gems embodying the truth of who they are.

Gathering me into his lean form, he whispers, "You see the divine in all creation but, Mary, until they recognize their own spark of divinity, the other disciples will not fully embody Eloha as you do. It is not my essence that brings you Sacred Wisdom; it is your own. For you see mirrored in me your own divine light. The clarity you experience in our relationship is not because of who I am, but because of who you are."

With Sacred Breath, I inhale our mutual essence to see that he exists with me as his other half. The children are one point of reference, and the family, including Teoma, the other. I am no longer a choice for him, but an aspect of him. Smiling at my insight, he rolls atop of me. "We have merged. I seek not to experience life as you do for as we are one, whatever your choices wrought becomes mine own. Your joy is mine, beloved. I bask in your sensual relationships with creation for we are one in spirit, now in mind, and in only a moment in body." With that, he punctuates his point of view.

Caught up in the wave of passion, the triads become fluid emotion washing through our beings. Sacred triangles form the physical essence of life—our precious body fluids, the sweat, blood, and tears, all created from tiny triangular cornerstones of watery potential. No wonder my element is water, awash by passionate insight as the depth of my love liquefies to transform our separate beings into one. From his perspective of Self, of which I am part, the rest of our lives are points on multiple triangles. It is not me or another for him. It is us and choices between all the other souls who share this existence. We are as One with All That Is.

In the coolness of the next afternoon, we are called away from our guests to greet the disciples from Jerusalem. Pleased, Yeshua greets Simeon and Shulamis with a hug. "Our family becomes more complete each passing day."

After I kiss his wife, Simeon whispers in my ear, "Be gentle with them, Mary." Gruff Theudas greets us both formally, not softening until Yeshua insists upon an embrace.

"Come now, we are as family. Hold me as a son." With the briefest of smiles, Theudas hugs my husband, giving me a curt nod.

In palpable delight, Mattathias greets us. "Mary, I am so happy that we can join you and Yeshua for Chanuka. Come and bid my brother well."

Beneath Mattathias' joy is a kernel of worry about his travel-worn brother. With the briefest of smiles, Yonatan greets me, "How are you, Mary?"

"I am well, Yonatan, but you have left a part of yourself behind. How is your wife?" Sighing, he shakes his head, not wanting to speak of these things with me, nor with anyone. Mattathias thinks that if I but touch his brother, Yonatan would be relieved of some of his distress.

Not wishing to offend the Kohanim, I wait for Mattathias to intervene. "Yonatan, take Mary's hand and greet her properly." Reluctantly, he barely touches my hand but I sense his pain. After spending the last couple of weeks in the matrimonial chambers, Yonatan had to leave his wife, unable to live outside the dynastic law of the high priesthood for she did not conceive during the prescribed time each of the past three years. Searching, I move my consciousness into his center of creation and am transported to her root hayye where a tiny spark of life glows within her womb.

Yeshua's hand on my shoulder draws me back to the moment. "Won't you share your insight with Yonatan, my love?"

I hesitantly consent, "You are to be an Abba in ten moons."

Yonatan cannot believe it, but Mattathias cries, "What is it, Mary? A boy or a girl?"

"Your wife is carrying a fine son." Yonatan's lower lip quivers a moment, before he regains his composure. Mattathias hugs him, nearly dancing with joy.

"You see, brother. I told you she would know. Now you must release this worry, for you shall have an heir."

Turning to Yeshua, Yonatan says thickly, "I would like to offer thanks to Adonai for the blessing of my son. Where might I find a holy place to pay homage?"

My husband smiles at Yonatan, "Someday you will find that the holiest of Holies is within your own being and the grandest of temples is just beneath your feet." Yonatan looks down at the rich earth upon which he stands. "But I shall have my brother Jacob escort you to the mikvah, and then into the inner sanctum of our home, where you shall find sanctity beneath the light of the cosmos." Jacob steps forward and, after brief introductions, leads Yonatan into the house.

Shortly after breakfast, the following morning, Phillip and Bartholomew arrive from Bethsaida. Amazed at the illusion of the house within the mists of kasa, Phillip commends Joseph repeatedly. Sarah and Josh delight in being reunited with Bartholomew who is quite at home in the nursery much to Hava and Miriam's initial concern. The giant man's hayye is not frenetic but oddly subdued.

"Yeshua, perhaps if Bartholomew could spend the mornings outside in the daylight, he might be more himself by the evenings when you wish to meet with the disciples."

Bartholomew's split moods seem to be affected by the cycles of light and dark. So for a couple of bright mornings, Sarah watches over the great disciple until the council is ready to meet.

This time there is no grumbling about my presence, for Judas keeps the others at bay. Yeshua quietly listens to the news from their homelands, carefully gathering their perceptions about the Roman oppression, the latest rulings of the Sanhedrin, the division between the Tzadokim and Chaverim and where the goyim stand. Attending to the others' unspoken thoughts, Simeon draws out their opinions for the rest to consider. Phillip holds the energies reminding me of Hephziva's support. Smiling, Yeshua tells me silently, *Phillip is a wonderful blend of the masculine and feminine, like Jochanan, dear.*

With our minds veiled, we are not penetrable to the probing of the mystics. Judas and Theudas hotly debate the use of force in creating change while the Essenes and the Kohanim question the appropriateness of political and religious reform to unite the factions. The only goyim, Phillip and Bartholomew, wish for an inclusive philosophy to unite all against Roman oppression. Always the philosopher, young Jacob suggests that our reality is based upon our collective perceptions. Although Mattathias and Jochanan attend, his ethereal viewpoint floats away from the more grounded men.

Yeshua uses his brother's lead to introduce the concept of thought creating reality. "What one believes becomes. Each of us manifests his own aspect of reality and as a people we hold common beliefs that become the reality of our world." The men look at him thoughtfully as he softens the fear that keeps them from perceiving the truth. "Most humans create unconsciously. Unaware that their thoughts are being fueled by their emotion, they believe that their existence is a destiny beyond their control. Creation is a simple formula—Clear Intention coupled with Pure Desire in Ripe Timing—becomes manifestation. I ask that each of you consider yourselves as conscious creators."

With a deep breath, he perceives their individual realities then exhales into the room a more harmonious potential. "Now breathe in my rucha that you might share my vision." In unison the disciples inhale and the hayye of the room shifts as their dreams become realized in the ethers.

Every man desires peace and harmony in their lives, each dreaming about a time of joyfulness, a time of love. From my root I color their collective dream until it sings with harmonious vibration. Adding shadows from the darkness of the void within my being brings depth of dimension. Yeshua basks in the light of the swirling reality, praising my efforts for the benefit of those who cannot see. "Thank you, Mary for highlighting their dreams. Is it not a lovely vision, Bartholomew?"

Our giant friend laughs in delight. "Oh yes! Mary, make them dance as one."

Yeshua smiles at him, "Dear man, it is up to each of you to find the love within your beings. Then you might see the same love reflected back to you in the eyes of one another. Until then each dream will dance alone in the ethers." Standing, he leads me from the room leaving the men to consider his counsel.

"Teoma's missing these lessons."

Drawing me close, Yeshua whispers, "Since he has asked that we not view him from afar, I do not know when he shall return but worry not, he knows these lessons well."

The lightness of Joseph's study is shadowed by the men's heated debate. Some are not sure that they are truly responsible for all that has occurred in their lives. Yeshua spends quite some time naming their individual experiences and how their beliefs and emotions birthed their realities. Not a one can fool my wise husband as he sees clearly into their hearts. He reminds me silently that his disentanglement from all and the loving acceptance of the men allow him a most pristine view into their consciousness. As the hayye swirls, I perceive that they all love him but some are still unsure about me.

The factions become most clear when I feel a strong pull. "Yeshua," I announce excitedly, "Teoma will be here shortly. Please excuse me, so I might ride out to meet him."

The men's collective thoughts rise like smoke. With a cleansing breath, Yeshua takes my hand. "Dearest, ride swiftly and bring my brother home." I kiss his cheek and am about to skip out of the room when Yonatan clears his throat.

"Yeshua, is it wise to allow your wife to go unescorted to meet another man?"

Turning toward Yonatan, Yeshua casts forth the hayye of comfort, "Do you think that I can hold her to me, Yonatan?"

Joseph and Saul stifle snickers, well aware of my impetuousness. Jochanan rises, "I would be happy to ride out with Mary…" *to ward off the others' concern.*

Yeshua smiles at his friend, "Only if you desire."

493

"Jochanan, thank you, but I know you would like to stay. I…."

Shaking his head, Jochanan takes my arm, "No, I would rather be with you. Just do not out ride me on that stallion of yours."

Kissing his cheek gratefully, I whisper, "You can ride Teoma's mare while I transmit the discussion for you."

"I was hoping that you could do that," is his quiet reply.

Yonatan seems satisfied, although Yeshua tells me silently; *I pray that you not give them any more to fuss over.*

I shall not allow my passion to take over, I reassure him but his faint smile tells me that he still prays.

We fly across the southern fields on horseback. Although Sheikan is excited, Jochanan's black mare keeps pace. I extend my gratitude to my dear steed before projecting the image of meeting Teoma, thus further hastening him.

North of Esdraelon, Teoma and I leave our companions behind. With tears of gratitude, I fall into his embrace. As he holds me, I close my eyes, experiencing the solidity of his form, his beating heart in comforting rhythm with the earth. Jochanan and the other rider pull up beside our mounts, not saying a word.

After a long while, Teoma pushes me gently away, "Eloha only knows how much I missed you," he whispers, tears falling from sky blue eyes. The pain of his journey sculpted his face like sandstorms do desert stones, a tiny crescent scar near the outer corner of his right eye marring his once perfect complexion. Tenderly I touch it and he holds my hand to his cheek kissing the palm. I shiver with delight but he clasps my hand to his heart. "Hush, we'll talk later."

Arm around my waist, he greets Jochanan and the stranger smiles at us, "Who is this beautiful woman who rides so fast to welcome you?"

"This is Mary, Yeshua's wife."

Dismounting, the man bows, "I was told of your passion, but I must wonder at this mashiach who does not keep such a precious thing close." Jochanan dismounts as well. The lively man clasps Teoma's other arm, "Shall I introduce myself?"

"I am sorry for my cousin's rudeness, Mary. This is Gidon. Born into the family of King Herod, he has been ousted for being a troublemaker."

Jochanan laughs at Teoma's sarcasm, causing Gidon to stomp away. "What kind of introduction is that, cousin? This lovely woman shall never find favor in me if you feed her all the gossip before she gets to know my finer qualities."

Clasping me protectively, Teoma responds, "She does not have the time nor the patience to search for your fair side. Come, let us ride home. I promised Yeshua a surprise and we shall have to pray that my brother's compassionate heart shall overlook Gidon's uncouth behavior."

Before Teoma lifts me upon Sheikan, I take Gidon's hand, "Surely I shall see your light."

He makes a show of bowing until his forehead touches the back of my hand, "My dear, you are most gracious. I look forward to meeting your fine husband and family."

Teoma places me firmly upon Sheikan. "Gidon, this is Jochanan, one of the finest Essenes you shall ever meet."

With an unabashed air sitting tall atop his steed, dark brown hair cut short in the Roman style, his royal lineage clearly evident by his carriage and elegant riding cloak, armed like Teoma, with more scars to show, Gidon has an undeniable presence.

A bit overwhelmed by Gidon's bravado, gentle Jochanan catches up to Sheikan, *I'm not the best chaperone for the likes of these two.*

I laugh, *Jochanan, I am never in danger except from my own emotion. But I thank you for your perseverance.* He graces me with a smile from his handsome mouth.

It was well worth being able to communicate silently. By the way, what is happening?

***

The light trailed Mary out, leaving shadows of judgment upon the faces of the council. Even Abba casts a worried look his way. Yeshua sighs, struggling with his own concern. The scraping of Yonatan's chair across the tiled floor finally breaks the silence.

"What man do we follow that allows his wife to lead?"

Phillip clears his throat. "The anointed one is wise to bow his head in reverence to his queen." Yeshua silently thanks him.

The younger men turn toward Yonatan but the priest holds his peace. Simeon speaks, "Do you remember my advice not to create enemies before fortifying your council?" His father sits back heavily, wondering if his son shall ever heed his elders.

495

A clutching of his heart at Mary's delight in reuniting with Teoma forces him to gather his resources. "Do I not have the promise of each of you to act on my council?"

The men nod in unison. After casting a long look at Yonatan, Theudas addresses Yeshua. "There is much about you that is clearly different than what we have been taught."

Does his father's friend question the wisdom of lending his support?

"I have invited you to my home that you might witness how I live in relationship with my family. Some of my decisions and actions may seem quite strange but as we are a diverse group, whose customs shall I follow?" No one responds. "I follow the dictates of my own conscience. I work to stay in connection to the Divine while in human form. I accept that all is as it needs to be and..." He gazes poignantly into each man's eyes, before stating resolutely, "I have great faith in Mary as my life partner."

Rising, he leaves the men to their thoughts.

The gray-green cast of olive trees highlights his concern as he awaits her return. Four riders gallop through the fields, stopping abruptly at the foot of the terraced grove. Broad-shouldered Teoma turns to petite Mary who nods before dismounting. She runs up the hill, tinged with a longing that he prays is for him. Her lips seek his with lush promise.

Smiling, Jochanan approaches. "It is quite a surprise Teoma has brought you."

Yeshua clasps his arm, "Thank you, dear friend, for escorting my wife." With long strides, Teoma crests the hill to embrace him. "Welcome home, my dearest brother."

Teoma whispers into his neck, "Thank you for all your help."

"You know I would do anything for you," he swallows thickly at Teoma's brazen thought, "except that."

The men part to greet the newcomer. Yeshua holds out his hand, "Welcome, prince."

"He lost his crown, Yesh."

With a sweep of his cloak, Gidon kneels before Yeshua. "You are the prince of Yisrael, soon to be anointed King. I pledge my sword to you, my mashiach." Elegantly, he unsheathes his long sword and lays it at Yeshua's feet.

Placing both hands on Gidon's bowed head, Yeshua blesses him. "May your courage serve the Divine within, your faith be as a great ship to carry you along your soul path. May you know yourself as love and your light shine forth upon all whom you shall encounter." Silvery white light emanates from his heart center through his hands, filling Gidon's deep turquoise hayye until it is translucent.

Gidon rises to kiss him first on one cheek then the other. "I shall be your most devoted servant for the rest of my days."

Yeshua gazes into his light brown eyes. This prince of a foreign king knows much about the Roman Empire, but his heart, freshly tilled with grief, is keen for learning a new way of life. "I ask that you be one of my council."

"I would be honored, master."

Yeshua kisses his bowed head. "So be it."

A tiny smile reveals Teoma's pleasure. Yeshua thanks him silently. His friend's love shall continue to serve him well and his brother has demonstrated his unconditional support. The council is finally complete.

Dancing Unity

Solstice morn breaks brisk and clear, enticing family and guests to recline comfortably in the gathering room. Boughs of green rest upon the oiled mantle, scarlet and cream blossoms stand in elegant vases, golden yellow squashes sit within painted bowls. Ima and Hava outdid themselves this year. Settled upon cushions in the center, Yeshua attends to the various conversations.

Near the hearth, Mattathias discusses theology with Jacob, "You are quite well versed in the Torah, Jacob."

"I have studied with the Chachamim but nothing as challenging as my heated debates with my brother."

Mattathias glances over. "I cannot imagine Yeshua in argument."

"Oh, my brother can be quite passionate about his viewpoint."

Near the atrium, Simeon thinks that stubborn is a better word. Phillip winks at Mary who attends to that which is unspoken.

"Our Jacob remembers everything he has ever learned verbatim, a true tana." Mattathias nods as Teoma continues, "Unlike some," he gestures towards his cousin, "who do not hear the sages."

Gidon ignores his cousin. "So why aren't you married yet, Mattathias? You look like you could use the comfort of a wife and home."

The young priest colors brightly. "I am betrothed." He diverts attention by turning to Mary, "You have changed since last we met," but Teoma's grunted response captures the room.

"Much has happened since we were in Jerusalem."

Simeon attempts to probe Mary's veiled mind. *Yeshua's lovely wife has progressed with the energies. I wonder who she has studied with.*

"The high priestess in Qumran, Hephziva."

"How did you pierce my veil, young woman?"

"Since they returned from the desert of my forefathers, we are all open to Mary and Yeshua, although she takes more care than my son at not invading our privacy."

Phillip puts a hand on Simeon's shoulder, "Fear not. Mary shall not abuse her connections to the hayye. I had the pleasure of meeting them this summer and it is evident to me that this man you refer to as the mashiach is much more than that." All eyes turn to the Greek philosopher. "He is the embodiment of the divine masculine as Mary is the embodiment of the divine feminine. At the Sea of Galilee, I was honored to witness the union of the dark and the light. They birthed Sacred Wisdom into this reality through their dance."

"I, too, am well familiar with the power of women," Judas smiles at his wife who sits in quiet conversation with Miriam and Hava. "On my first visit here some three winters ago, it was clear that Mary is key to Yeshua's mission. Since their visit to Judaea, we have been infused with their hayye, T'shuraw says, but whatever it is, a great change has been made." The older women smile at Judas' proclamation, his wife particularly pleased.

"I do not understand these energies of which you speak."

Most of the guests nod in agreement with Theudas before turning to Yeshua for clarity. Now is the time to open the men to his wife's wisdom. "Mary, could you please illustrate the concept of hayye for them?"

She consents with a hesitant smile. Holding the space but not interfering, Yeshua watches as she visualizes the energy within the room, until the auras of all are illuminated. On his right, Bartholomew immediately notes the shift as do Simeon and Phillip. Yeshua smiles gratefully as his mother and Hava move apart to create a triad with Mary. With a melodious voice, his precious wife commences teaching the council of twelve.

"Have you ever entered a home, a room, or even the marketplace, and perceived the emotion of the inhabitants before you could see what was going on, before you could hear their words? You sensed their fear or excitement, joy or anger." She looks about expectantly, her passion bringing to life her very words. Each man nods mesmerized. "That is an aspect of hayye, a feeling, a sense, a knowing. Hayye can also be visualized as color and shape. It can be heard or felt as music or vibration. It can be sensed as a flavor, an aroma, a tactile sensation."

"Have you not entered a suspicious place and felt," she runs delicate fingers over one dark forearm, capturing their attention, "the quiver of your skin in response to the hayye of fear, of danger?" When Mattathias gasps affirmatively, Gidon nudges him.

"Around and within each of our beings is an aura with a distinctive color, shape, feel, sometimes smell, taste, touch. Another's hayye can incite an emotional response, like that of a precious infant, a beloved parent, a feared authoritarian, a desirable lover." The men shift, some uncomfortable with her visualizations, some running away with their fantasies.

"Are the energies part of the attraction one feels when meeting another?" Mary flushes until Teoma tames his cousin's uncouth mind with a brusque warning.

"Yes, Gidon, but it can be repulsion as well. We can all sense energy, some of us have more finely tuned instruments, but most rarely use their abilities."

"Mary, what does my hayye look like?" Bartholomew entices a smile from her lips.

"When I first met you, it was quite a sight. Imagine," raising her arms, she demonstrates, "many bolts of lightening from within and without, multicolored and splayed irregularly all around your being." She brings her hands together close to her belly, "But within the core was a dark shadow like a separate entity."

The once renowned teacher now childlike in his inquiry, "But it is different now, isn't it?"

"Yes, dear, when you first arrived, the darkness had risen like a cloud over the rainbow but since your work with the children, it is more blended and less shadowed." The affection Mary has for Bartholomew spills forth upon them all.

"I do feel much better."

"And you look much more like your beautiful self." Impassioned, she rises to embrace Bartholomew, but Mattathias grasps her arm. Yonatan's disapproving look forces his younger brother to release her, but Mattathias' question will be heard.

"How can we learn to see hayye?"

She touches the young priest's cheek. "Try sitting cross-legged like Yeshua and place your hands in the prayer position, fingers touching lightly." Glowing from the contact, Mattathias ignores his brother and holds his hands clasped fervently in front of his chest.

Touching his stiff shoulders, she whispers, "Now relax and drop the triangle formed by your hands to your root. There," she points, "between your legs."

Undeterred by her intimate instruction, Mattathias inverts the masculine blade into the feminine chalice. The other men sit mesmerized by her throaty whisper.

"Breathe deeply and open to receive Divine Abundance."

Smiling, Mattathias takes a deep breath and the energy about him settles into his core through the chalice of his hands.

"Now close your eyes and turn your sight inward. What do you see? What do you feel? Can you sense anything?"

The rest of the men scramble to imitate the young priest. Yeshua smiles as those closest to Mary open to the energies. Across the room, Theudas and Yonatan resist inverting the triangle of their hands from the accustomed prayer position but Judas tries valiantly, assuming the receptive posture. Jakob peers through the darkness of his mind, praying fervently to see something. Jochanan's and Saul's natural eye for beauty enhances their perception. Not visualizing the hayye as Mary explains, still Abba has a deep knowing. Open to the earth at his root, Ari senses the energies tactilely. Simeon compares his perceptions with Phillip. Grateful that the men are taking instruction from a woman, Yeshua offers a silent prayer.

Mary's sensual voice interrupts his reverie. "We all perceive the energies differently, there is no correct way. For those of you having some difficulty, take a deep cleansing breath and relax as if you are floating upon water. Now what do you perceive?"

Sensing the zealot commander's struggle, she gives him special assistance, "Judas, breathe deeply in through your nose and out through your mouth. Imagine lying on the sand on a warm spring day, the sun trying to rouse you through your closed lids. There are colors and tiny shapes."

Laughing he cries, "I can see something."

"Thank goodness, man, there is some imagination in you yet!" T'shuraw's exclamation causes the women to chuckle.

Silently, Yeshua praises his wife. *My love, you are a natural teacher. The most stringent of these men are softening to your divine feminine ministrations. I love the inversion of the blade into the chalice, very clever. Tonight, you shall give them a multi-sensory display of the energies.*

But I do not wish to upset this fine balance with too sensual…

I shall pay close heed so not to lose you to your fiery passions. I desire the disciples to know us well. Now rouse them, dear, before Gidon gets carried away by his fantasy.

Softly, she speaks, "Very gently bring your consciousness back with your breath, focusing on your inhalations, exhaling into the room, and return when you are ready."

One by one, they respond.

"Once again, a lovely healing circle," T'shuraw sighs. Arriving with a baby in each arm, Rebeka sits down by Jacob who relieves her of Jonina. Teoma reaches for Jonathon and after only a moment's hesitation Rebeka gives the baby up and settles more comfortably on her cushion.

Bubbling laughter, Joshua comes running into the room and lands on Bartholomew's lap, splashing his joyous energy into the great man's chalice. Sarah follows with Tamar, Esther, and Ruth in tow. While the older girls settle down by their mothers, Sarah asks, "What game are you playing now, Abba? Can we play too?"

Yeshua gathers her into his lap and kisses her cheek. "Ima has been teaching the men how to perceive the energies and tonight she will give them a special gift."

Clapping her hands, Sarah says excitedly, "Oh good! Ima will dance in celebration of the birth of the sun." Joshua cheers, hugging Bartholomew tightly about the neck.

Anticipating a challenging evening, Teoma's worry ignites concern in the other men.

Yeshua puts out the fire. "I look forward to a wonderful solstice celebration with my family and ask that each of you come with open hearts to partake of the feast of fine food, wine, company, and, of course, the energies." Setting Sarah down, he walks over to lift his wife to her feet. "Come, my love, let us rest before sunset."

***

Dressing for the celebration, my husband's amused attitude fills the room. He runs a seductive hand beneath my skirt, lifting the silken fabric away from my thighs as he encircles my form, the six deep-colored panels blending into one another to create twelve in motion. Stopping behind me, he takes the ties from the beaded top and secures them around my neck. His hot breath stirs my passion, but he makes no further move to seduce me. Finally, he secures a golden chain about my waist, where it lies perfectly upon the soft swell of my lower belly. As the skirt sits low upon my hips, the emblems dance merrily with my every breath.

"Teoma has your form well memorized, my beloved."

In the privacy of the atrium on the second day of Chanuka, Teoma gifted me with this exquisite chain adorned by thirteen emblems of the tribes of Yisrael, the tribe of Yosef having both the palm tree and the grape.

"You and Yeshua have come together to unite our nation. I hope to add more charms as we gather other nations."

I thanked him with a kiss on his smooth cheek, the warm musk of his skin arousing my passion. Before igniting a fire, I prayed for strength. "Teoma, it is a very long necklace."

Softly chuckling, he stretched the length of the chain and placed it against my belly, "You wear it here, Mary."

"But no one shall see its beauty." That little boy smile nearly enticed me to kiss his mouth.

My memory dissolves as my husband places his hands above the chain and lifts me into the air, exactly how Teoma has always lifted me upon Sheikan. "You see, my dear, how sensitive his hands are. What his mind might forget his body is acutely aware of. Now let us join the others." Draping a silk scarf of brilliant gold upon my shoulders, he waits as I secure the royal shawl about my hips.

Bright as desert flowers, Ruth and Esther are adorned in pinks and yellows, while Sarah twirls gold and green about the guests. My anticipation for the music quells my appetite for the feast set before us.

"You must eat, Mary, Joseph says the dancing shall go on all night."

Sitting by Gidon, Teoma chuckles, "Do not worry, Mattathias, Mary always has enough energy to dance. You shall see, she shall be the first and the last on the floor. Just pray the musicians can keep up with her."

Phillip smiles and tells Teoma, "If not, she shall produce her own music as she did at the Sea of Galilee." Yeshua nods at the philosopher, pleased with his perceptiveness.

Watching from afar, Tamar finally makes her way over to sit by me. "Dear Teoma, were you saving this space for me?"

504

Placing an arm around her, Teoma whispers, "But of course, Tamar. We were just discussing Mary's dance. Gidon, this lovely lady may be able to keep pace with her." Blushing, Tamar tries to attend to me, but the elegant older man draws her focus away.

"We have just met, yet I am quite taken by you, Tamar, and wonder why your husband has not accompanied you to Galilee."

Teoma thwarts him, "No man has found favor with Judas' most lovely daughter, cousin. She saves herself for a more genteel mate and clearly it is not you."

Our side of the table rolls with laughter at the bantering of the cousins. Kissing Tamar's cheek, I whisper, "Stay close to Teoma. He shall keep you from harm's way."

"I would prefer to stay close to you."

"Tamar, you shall have a most wondrous experience this night." She can hardly contain her excitement at Yeshua's prediction.

Teoma's interest peaks, "What is so stimulating, Tamar?"

She laughs, "You shall see." Teoma looks quizzically at us.

Blowing him a kiss, I say, "Relax and you too shall be pleasantly surprised."

I can only pray it is so, returning his attention to his cup of wine.

From the other end of the table, Miriam watches my encounter with Tamar, disturbed by our mutual attraction. *Ima has not experienced life as you have. Let us pray that she finds joy in whatever guise it presents.* I kiss Yeshua's mouth, in remembrance of all the joy I have experienced with him.

Too long and passionate, our kiss incites Tamar and Teoma. With a great guffaw, Judas says, "It appears Yeshua wishes that the music commence. Joseph, gather your sons and let us begin."

Saul and Jochanan smile, always pleased with our affection for one another, but Yonatan is clearly uncomfortable. Yeshua attends to him. "As Kohamim, you must demonstrate great passion for the Word. I am the living Word and I am passion for life. Your existence upon earth is a divine gift. Feast upon the bounty that the Creator has provided. To experience joy you must live and love passionately."

He stands pulling me up for another deep kiss. Breathless, but he is not, "Mary is my life, my joy, my passion. I pray you each find your own. Tonight, you have feasted at the table of my Abba, consuming the best of our wine, our crops, our herds. I invite you now to enjoy the multi-sensory feast of my beloved wife's dance."

505

Cushions strewn around the perimeter of the gathering room clear a space for dancing. Anticipating the music, the energies play with my heartstrings like a lyre. Ari joins Joseph on his flute, while Shimon and Judah drum, and Saul plays Hava's lyre so she might dance with the women. As the men take their seats, the women gather about Miriam, for she will lead us in the traditional dances in celebration of the solstice. The disciples have formed a harmonious orchestration of their own.

Laughing with delight, Sarah dances by each man, placing her small hand on the center of his chest, before returning to the circle of women. In his Abba's lap, Joshua reaches for a kiss when she passes by. As the evening grows late, the women choose partners of the disciples, carefully returning them to their places in the circle. Tamar is not shy about dancing with the men, but neither are Ruth and Esther who share her exuberance. When Yeshua signals the music to change, the women form an outer ring to anchor the energies. Miriam sits opposite of Yeshua, with Hava in the east and T'shuraw in the west. The rest intersperse themselves between the triad, Sarah at Miriam's side while Joshua has the comfort of Savta's lap.

Before the middle of the longest night of the year, I begin my dance for the twelve. Calling to the drums to match my rhythm, I take pleasure in the synchronicity of the energies represented by the men, enticing their heart centers opened by my daughter until the hayye begins to sing. Twirling about the circle, my hips rapidly vibrating, the tiny tambourines beg to be set free. Matching the colors of my skirt, the auric colors of the disciples pour through their heart centers to swirl about me.

From Judas comes forth blood red, the root of creation, blending into the fiery sunset of Bartholomew, who is most settled this night. The orange of Theudas is like unto the fruit, sweet and juicy, dripping into Yonatan's mango colored hayye. Simeon's yellow, hot as midsummer, cools slightly as it blends into Jakob's hayye fresh as tender new grass. Verdant forest green is my Teoma, melding into his cousin Gidon's turquoise, which pours like water into the rich blue of Mattathias. Brother Jacob's indigo dye seeps into the pale lavender of Phillip. Finally, gentle Jochanan's purple-pink hue rises like the sun into Yeshua's crystal clear aura.

All the colors of the rainbow represented by the twelve reflect through the diamond of Yeshua's being. My body heated by the dance desires freedom from the shawl so it pools liquid gold in the center of them all.

Twirling, my multi-hued skirt catches the light of the disciples, the tribes of our people chained over my womb singing to their ancestors. I dance with abandon, my feet pounding the floor, the flutes sing in harmony with my breath. Calling once more to the drums to deliver my own hayye forth, they respond with the passion of a lover.

Shimon is surprised, *Mary, my drum plays itself, my hands dance to its beat, for it no longer dances to mine.*

Laughing, Yeshua responds in my stead, *Dear little brother, follow its lead as it follows Mary's.* Young Judah offers no complaint, lost to the music as me.

Song stirs deep within my loins, the low growl of a lioness emerging from my root, the base tone of the earth, the depth of the void. My color bursts forth as the blackest of midnight skies, deep purple shining from light. Creation births from my womb-like essence to split into the twelve colors of the rainbow of light through time and through space until merging as one with the light of my beloved. From across the center of creation, Yeshua reflects back to me the beauteous glory of the earthly array.

As the sound of the void of creation escapes my lips, the tones of the disciples join in. From lowest to highest, from Judas to Jochanan, twelve notes arise in harmony. Accompanying the earthly instruments like a heavenly host, the men's tones swirl about to glorify creation. My own sound vibrates through my very being, my beloved's tone beyond hearing. His crystal clear energies entice my spirit to rise from my form. There, I know his tone. It is the song of Love.

Beloved, we are as one in harmony with All That Is
Sacred Sound from the core of your being has birthed life
Behold the beauteous colors of the rainbow
From the darkness of the void of your potential
Passionate womb bears creation sparked by Desire
Made manifest in the light of my Love
All color, all sound returns as vibration
To that which I AM, to Love
Joyful one, your delight is mine own
May this earthly existence beget
A new way of being in synchronistic dance
With the music of living nature

Sacred Breath fills me as I breathe you in
Rainbow of light blessed with knowing
All is as it needs be in the eyes of the One Being
Mary, you are my life and my home
Dance into existence our collective dream.

Passion plays with my heart, nectar drips from my sacred vessel. I give thanks to my beloved who has seeded my creation, breathed life into my being. In each man, a passionate fire is sparked. I dance with their collective desire surging forth into the center of the circle held intimately in the lap of the women about them. Holding the rainbow in the core of my being, I present the council of light to my beloved. In his embrace, they are thus absorbed, returned to Love again and again.

Yeshua, I sing, *my beloved husband, hear my call. Delight bursts through my heart. As my body dances for them, my soul yearns for you. Meet me for passion's play beyond this dimension and then we shall return renewed.* With heaving breasts, I encircle the lightness of being that we have birthed into this room. All respond with hot fires of their own, priest and goyim meld like metal in a blacksmith's oven. There are no men nor women, only lust for life, dreams of desire, portals of passion.

All in all, there is only I AM.

As I think it, raza takes me to the lap of the Great Ima Earth. Seeped in passion, I call to my lover. *Come, do not tarry. Let them cast their own dreams into a wondrous reality. Join me now before my desire overwhelms my being, Yeshua....* In one eternal moment, he is before me. Whole within his being, his great desire a staff upon which I fall, absorbing his essence furthers my passion. He cries out my name.

Seeking my lips to taste his own salt, he removes all encumbrances, crushing my softness against his lean form. I cannot wait any longer, but wait I must as he savors every swell, every curve. Aching for release, only the golden chain adorns me. The elestial stone glows as nectar pours onto the ground.

Surely new life will spring forth from this very spot.

"You are the energies and the music is you. The hayye of the rainbow of light blesses our union once again."

As I ride my passion back into his heart, we explode into light. Tiny tristans encircle us to sing with the vibration of the Divine. "Yeshua, Yeshua, I am completed."

Laughing into my mouth, he sings, "Beloved, not yet. For this is but a taste my love for you." At the moment, I can take no more.

Triads of Creation

The warm rays of the sun lick our cheeks like a cat her kitten. With a feline stretch, Yeshua bids me good morning and we make our lazy way to the house. I am accosted by Tamar at the baths. "Mary, please, I must talk with you." With a knowing smile, Yeshua takes his leave.

I lead her to a steaming basin of water, "Can we bathe while we talk?" With flushed cheeks, she undresses, her hayye uncharacteristically hesitant, embarrassed as I sponge her yet she returns the favor. "Did you not have a wonderful time last night?"

Her lips quiver, "Yes, but…" and she clasps my hands, "I have been with Teoma and…" Holding my hand to her breast, she begs, "Please, just look into my memory." With a deep breath, I do, seeing more than I should know. Their passionate embrace began in the gathering room, but seeking privacy, Teoma led her to his chambers…swept into her perception of the experience, I am in their embrace.

"Mary, I didn't know men enjoy all that I have enjoyed with women, but he did, everything, and more." Yes, I can see much, much more than her previous liaisons. She touches my cheek, "I don't mean to upset you."

Slowly, I shake my head, breasts flushed, loins aching. "I am not upset." Moving closer, she cups my head and kisses my mouth. My response nearly overwhelms us both, my deep purple crashing into her golden orange hayye.

With a gasp, Tamar backs away, "Now I am even more confused. Your passion is so strong. I…." My chest constricts my breath, the hot scented bath, our delicious nudity, her throaty whisper. "For it was you I wanted last night and I believe he desired you too. That is what brought us together, but what shall we do now?"

I shake my head to clear the fogginess, yet cannot think clearly. "Maybe you should discuss this with Teoma."

Dressing afterwards, I perceive Teoma's call just as T'shuraw enters. "My dear Mary, it appears you have opened many new doorways, especially for my daughter." She thankfully relieves me of Tamar.

I find Teoma pacing through the olive grove. "Barchashem! You finally arrived."

Slightly wary for intimate musk exudes from him, I allow him to lead me under a low-branched tree. We sit upon the grass and he sighs loudly. "Judas accosted me this morning. 'Son,' he said, 'I told the men that you would be accountable to me if your conduct was less than proper when Mary rode out to meet you. Then you nearly ravish my daughter in front of them.' I couldn't tell if he was upset or pleased. You know how gruff he can be even when happy. I don't know what came over me."

Another triangle has formed between him, Tamar, and me. A sacred tristan or one that shall bring us sorrow. "Teoma, what are you asking of me?"

He takes my hand and like Tamar holds it against his chest. "I desired you, but then so did she and what an amazing experience." His mind spills into mine to overwhelm me with feelings for him, for her, for them.

Flushed, I try to speak, "We did tell you that you would be pleasantly surprised."

An endearing smile passes over his lips, blue eyes twinkling merrily. "You saw us together?"

I must restrain myself, I think feverishly. "Not before, only a knowing that you would be pleased."

Teoma comes closer. "You are not upset with our coming together?" Slowly, I shake my head gasping as he traces my jaw. "Rather, you are aroused." Even closer, his breath hot upon my face, I cannot tear my eyes from his. "I think your affection for both of us feeds this passionate fire that threatens to consume."

A triad of temptation. Swallowing thickly, I search for something…a clearing of this heated tension…once long ago I cooled our mutual passion by calling to… my husband.

Yeshua appears.

"Come now. We all had an exhausting night, so let us spend this sixth day of Chanuka in quiet repose."

Teoma looks up as if in a dream, "Yeshua, why are you here?"

Smiling, my husband offers him a hand, "Come, brother, make haste. You and I are in sore need of a bath which is now clear for our use. My love, Hava and Ima wish to breakfast with you." With a kiss on the cheek, he escorts me to the atrium.

"Ima, you requested my presence?" Still dazed, I clasp my trembling hands. Miriam looks up from the low table, where she and Hava lounge.

"The children have been fed and are playing with Bartholomew in the garden. He really is a lovely man, very sensitive to the energies and Sarah and Joshua adore him." She motions that I sit between them.

Putting an arm around my waist, Hava kisses my cheek, "Once again, you outdid yourself, my dear. I have never known a dancer who could arouse so many, young and old, male and female. Some even putting aside their preferences for the nearest warm body."

So everyone knows about Teoma and Tamar? What must the Kohanim be thinking?

Miriam serves me a plate of fruit. "You must maintain your vigor." I cannot even think about food. I need to take a long walk, perhaps a fast ride, alone.

They chat merrily. "The separation and reunion of the light was most magnificent." Miriam hands me a warm piece of bread.

"So what do you imagine the men thought when you disappeared?"

What? My raza is also of concern? "Hava, I do not know. I could not stay and make love to Yeshua in front of them!"

Laughing, Hava says, "Well, some are quite conservative, I suppose you could not." Miriam shakes her head.

"Hava, really! The children were in attendance."

"I get too carried away with the energies, Ima. And now I am enthralled by this triangle I have created with Teoma and Tamar."

Miriam tries to contain her surprise, but Hava does not stifle her mirth. "My dear, you opened many eyes last night, apparently including your own."

I clasp my head between damp palms. Miriam touches my shoulder, "Mary, when you dance with such abandon, it is quite apparent that you are connected to the One, bringing great healing into this dimension. Yeshua encourages your use of the energies for the benefit of us all. Last night, the disciples opened to their soul paths as you showed them their connection to one another, to you and to Yeshua."

Looking up at her, I whisper, "Yeshua has taught me about sacred triangles of connection. I see now how you and he and I are one triad." Turning to Hava, I whisper, "And you and Miriam and I are another. Connections everywhere I turn, interlocking tristans. Triads of creation."

Both women stare intently at me, witnessing the vision I present. Nodding, Miriam whispers, "I can see the triangles. The connections are infinite in every aspect of our lives."

Clasping her hand, I whisper, "Ima, if I but think of these triangular relationships, I am overwhelmed by passionate desire."

Hava rubs my back. "Your passion is for the Divine which you see in all. These triads magnify sacred perception bringing you closer to the realization of your divinity."

"We have much to learn from one another, my daughter. I pray that our participation in your dance with the energies shall connect us more intimately. Hava and I are always here for you. I know you believe that I may not always understand, but I appreciate my own humanity and shall never look at you with judgment."

Tears spill from my eyes, "I thought you might not understand how I can be attracted to Tamar, but I see that it matters not, only that you love me." She kisses my forehead and holds me close.

Chuckling on my other side, Hava states, "You have much more to discover about who you are, Mary. I pray you keep us informed of your adventures since we no longer can access your thoughts. We just might be of some assistance along the way." So tired, I begin to doze and soon my husband appears to carry me to our chambers.

After undressing, he settles us on the bed, his back against cushions. Holding me between his legs, he wraps his arms around my torso with my hands in his.

"Yeshua," I whisper, "I feel overwhelmed by my passion. I have created a triangle that tempts me sorely between Teoma and Tamar. Thank you for coming to me."

Kissing the back of my head, he whispers, "My love, you are somewhat disconnected. Your dance ministered to us all then our night of passion taxed your resources. Your root and crown are immensely out of balance with your heart center."

The blood-red of my root expands beyond my pelvis spilling down my inner legs. At my crown, a wide portal funnels in the cosmos. My heart center, so constricted, limits my very breath.

"Allow me, dear, to help you balance your hayye." Warmth like the summer sun pours through my back to fill my chest. Deepening my breath consciously, I receive his essence and feel my heart center expand to its normal capacity.

Gently, Yeshua places his hands on my crown and reduces the portal. As this center returns to its original size, my disorientation fades. Next he pulls my bottom flush with his groin, gently spreading my thighs. With his left hand between my breasts, he presses the middle finger of his right hand firmly against the tight flesh at my root. Immediately the inflamed and swollen energies quiet and shrink to a healthy glow. My original comfortable balance is fully restored.

"Thank you, Yeshua. Will you lie with me now?"

Resettling into our favorite position, he whispers, "Yes, love, for your energetic display last night was quite taxing for me to hold...." If he spoke more, I do not know.

I awaken refreshed and playfully turn in my husband's embrace, but he cools my passion with a whisper, "Let us not enflame the embers that smolder within."

"I do not wish that my fiery desire for you ever be extinguished, Yeshua."

"There is not a chance in all eternity that you shall ever be without your passionate flame. It is who you are. But for now, it is best that you become more grounded."

Sighing, I pout, "Yeshua, is not sexual union a most grounding experience?"

Taking my face in the cup of his palms, he continues, "Yes, but for you, it has become a portal of connection to the Divine. It is time to reconnect to this lovely form. We must eat before we gather with the others."

"Really, I am not hungry for food."

"In your passionate fervor, you forget to nourish yourself. If you would have eaten more last night, it might have been less traumatic an imbalance of your energies. That is why I insisted you breakfast with Ima and Hava, but I see that you partook only of their wisdom."

I snuggle closer, "A massage would help ground my hayye."

"Do not tempt me. I have yet to chastely minister to you as you did me in Magdala." Exactly what I'm counting on, but he shakes his head, drawing me from our bed, "Come, let us dress and eat."

After the midday meal, I feel ready to face the gathering of men. Holding open the wooden door of the study, Yeshua presents me to the council. The first to greet me with a great hug, Judas whispers gruffly into my hair, "Once again, you have changed my life. I am grateful to serve both you and Yeshua." The love he has for me, for Yeshua pools in the depth of his dark brown eyes. Through his chest, I feel the triad between his wife, himself, and us as one being.

Crossing the circle, I approach Yonatan and Theudas. Their softened visage invites me to touch them as I did Judas. Yonatan places a hand over mine, "Mary, I do not know what to say, but something has changed." His heart is beginning to open as I exist in triangulation with him and his brother, with him and Theudas.

The elder speaks, so I give him my attention, "You are not what I expected, but then neither is your husband. I have much to learn from you both."

"Thank you, Theudas," and to my delight he returns my smile.

Another triad grasps my attention as I turn to Jakob. "I had some concern when you disappeared, but as you appear quite whole, I am relieved." Pulling me close, he whispers, "Yeshua will address this, won't he?" I nod before noting the other leg of this Qumran triangle.

Enraptured, Jochanan clasps me, tearfully. "A most amazing experience. I feel as one with you and Yeshua, and now with this fine group of men, thank you."

After kissing his cheek, I turn to Saul who takes me in his arms. "Your seduction of the energies must be captured on canvas."

Kissing him, I laugh, "Dearest Saul, can you not paint my dance from memory?"

He releases me gently. "I will try."

A pull from behind draws me to Abba Joseph. "So when did you learn to play the instruments, my dear?" I smile as he passes me on.

Kissing both my cheeks, Simeon states, "You have accomplished much more than any high priestess, Mary." I study his amber eyes.

"Simeon, it is in remembrance of my being that I might display such intimate connection to the energies." He nods and I turn to the other angle of this triad—Phillip.

With dancing gray eyes, the philosopher hugs me, "Sophia, esse eene agappe."

Translating his native tongue into my own, "Chochma, sacred wisdom, you are love," I kiss the wise Greek's cheek. "And so are you, dear man."

Bartholomew picks me up, "Do you see my hayye today?"

"It is most lovely." He sets me down as lightly as a leaf.

When Gidon gives me a hug, a triangle forms between us and Teoma. "Mary, never in all of my travels have I witnessed such a passionate display. I wonder if you might grace us with dance at every such gathering of the disciples."

"If the time is ripe, I shall."

Next to him, Teoma. My heart beats frantically, but Yeshua soothes me. Being hugged into the firmness of Teoma's body should be no different than the others—but it is. "Thank you for the lovely chain. It enhanced my dance."

His voice so very low, I must look up at him. "It is your beauty that illuminates the jewelry. Your passion that ignites us all." Again my heart beats so hard, he must feel it through my breast.

Jacob saves the moment by extracting me from Teoma's embrace. "It is my turn to thank my sister." With one arm, he holds me to his side, taking my other hand and placing it against his chest. Another triangle appears between Rebeka, him, and me. "Beloved sister, how can I thank you for what you have done for my wife and me." They shared a most passionate night. "She did not even leave my embrace this morning. In fact Hava had to come with the twins, and…," his voice almost breaks, "she even made mention of using a wet nurse from time to time."

I kiss his cheek, "I am so happy for you both."

Mattathias trembles with delight. Taking both my hands, he pulls me close and whispers excitedly, "Mary, you gathered our energies like ribbons of the rainbow and presented us to Yeshua who absorbed our color into his white light." I am delighted he perceived so much.

Jacob laughs, "Mattathias, did you hear the music as well?" The priest wrinkles his forehead. "Each of us has a unique tone. Mary played our music quite beautifully, don't you think?" With a gentle extraction, Ari leads me from the two young men's comparison of their perception of the energies.

Tenderly he whispers, "Even the human creature is not immune to your call, is he?" I smile at my friend as he turns me over to my husband.

Yeshua tenderly touches my face, "Sit, my love. All this gratitude in one day can be wearisome." Settling me upon deep cushions, he sits close before motioning for the others to form a circle. With his left hand at the base of my spine, he grounds me into my form. With the other, he invites questions.

"Brothers, we share this life that we might experience great joy. Mary's dance was her gift to you and I am pleased to see that you have all opened your hearts to receive her love. I know that you have many questions at this time, for most of you the energy seems newly discovered. Jakob, what would you like to know?"

The elder Essene responds carefully, "How does one traverse through time and space as Mary appeared to last night?"

"Raza is accomplished simply through desire. Fueling her vision of an intimate cleft within our eastern pasture with her heartfelt desire, she manifested a reality in which she arrived quite whole in her form within the cleavage of Mother Earth."

"Then you disappeared as well, master."

"Oh, my desire was great to be one with my wife at that very moment. So holding the image of her in my arms, I felt immense gratitude and accessing raza, my material form disappeared then reappeared safely into her embrace."

Mattathias blushes at the image, causing his brother Yonatan to ask, "Yeshua, why is it through your wife's dance of seduction, we experienced openings?"

"Emotion is the connection that unites the triad of the body, mind, and soul. Passion sparks the transformation of the illusion of separation from the Divine. Love for Self brings the three aspects of the human being into Oneness with Eloha."

"But are we not slaves to our carnal desires which further separate us from Adonai?"

Smiling, Yeshua expands his heart energy to encompass the room, now bathed by his crystalline tristans. With every breath of his essence, my own transformation becomes complete as I am filled with the lightness of being in the presence of his love. "Yonatan, Marya created this very body which houses your soul as the ultimate vehicle of transformation to Source. In the sensual nature of the human form, we experience the gift of creation. Through touch, sight, smell, taste, sound we witness the Divine."

Theudas agrees with Yonatan, "Yeshua, we have been taught that through prayer we might find communion with Adonai."

"I believe the Therapeutae teaches a meditative silence whereupon your consciousness leaves the confines of your body to seek connection. That is one way, but my dear wife has taught me another." Winking at Phillip, he goes on, "Through our senses, Sacred Wisdom is born. You heard Phillip refer to Mary as Sophia. She embodies Chochma by using her sensuality to connect with the Divine. She feasts upon creation and invites you to join her, in dance and in song. This summer in Magdala, my dear wife relieved me of my misperception that the only means to reconnection with the One Being was to escape my physical form."

Nodding at Teoma, he continues, "My brother presents a constant reminder that I am here to serve as a living example of Divine Connection in my human body. While in relationship to those I love and cherish—my wife, children, parents, siblings, friends, and now you, my expanded family—I find the most glorious connection to Eloha." He turns back to Yonatan. "We will come to Jerusalem to celebrate your second marriage, dear friend. Perhaps your wife might benefit from time spent with mine."

Poor Yonatan is clearly not comfortable with this idea, but Mattathias pipes in, "Oh, yes, brother, Mary could provide wise counsel to your bride and then perhaps she can visit mine."

I smile at him, *I would be delighted to meet your betrothed, dear Mattathias.* His jaw drops open in wonder.

"Mary, I can hear you speak to me in my mind!"

Jochanan laughs, "Well, that didn't take long for you!"

Yeshua smiles at the young priest, after hearing Teoma wonder why it took him so long. *Because, my dearest brother, you do not believe in yourself.*

"Yeshua, I studied with the finest mystics in Samaria to master the craft, but at such tender ages you and your wife surpass me."

Looking intently at Simeon, Yeshua says softly, "Did not Mary suggest that the craft you refer to is but a remembrance of who you are?" The elder nods. "We are all but a seed of potential, connected to All That Is. Mary continually blossoms into the fullness of herself. You have the same potential, Simeon."

Between Bartholomew and Teoma, Gidon sits amazed. "I am just a man, albeit of royal heritage, but uneducated and inexperienced with all that you have spoken of this day. Yet I feel something within my breast that stirs my passion to know more. I desire to understand as you do, my mashiach, to live passionately as does your beautiful wife. I am here in service of the Light, as Mattathias so eloquently described our mutual purpose, but somehow I believe we each shall undergo a transformative experience while under your tutelage. In knowing you, we might never be the same."

All stare at the newest disciple. Teoma puts an arm around his cousin, as Bartholomew gently touches the crown of Gidon's head with his massive hand.

"My mission is to serve you by being the embodiment of Divine Love. My wish for you is that you might know yourself as Love that you might live passionately in immense joy. May you know your intimate connection to Sacred Unity through your breath and your senses. Sacred Wisdom is our gift to you, beloved."

***

By mid-Tevet, the last of the council takes its leave. T'shuraw allowed her daughter to remain behind, so Teoma could not be in a finer mood when Gidon requests a tour of the property. Since Tamar has never been to the sea, Teoma makes plans to traverse through the Valley of Jezreel to the shore.

At the last moment Yeshua declines the invitation with an excuse that he must spend this time with his father, but encourages his wife to entertain Tamar. Mary seems out of sorts as her husband bids them farewell.

Through the rich dark fields, Tikva runs to join them. Teoma tries to send the enormous dog home, but she will not leave Sheikan's side. Tail in the air, she bows down and woofs at him.

Gidon laughs, "Waste not your time, cousin, we must accept her company."

Teoma attempts to lose Tikva, but Mary asks Sheikan several times to stop for the dog. When they finally race down to the beach, the horses are hot. Tikva quenches her thirst at the spring before lying under the eucalyptus grove.

Mary laughs, taking Tamar's hand, and introduces her to the Great Sea. Splashing playfully, Mary dives beneath the surface. Thoroughly aroused by their antics, Teoma calls to a reluctant Gidon.

"Come, let us join them."

Excited by the laughter of his mistress, Sheikan comes crashing through the surf. Tamar screams and seeks Teoma's protection as Mary swims out past the breakers with her steed. Soon the dolphins appear and surround her.

After much hesitancy, Tamar follows the men to swim with the dolphins. Enchanted by their antics she exclaims, "How I wish to paint their likeness upon canvas. Or perhaps your body! I can mix some dyes from winter berries we passed upon the trail."

"I do not wish to be without my husband long enough for you to adorn me."

"What are you girls laughing about?" In four strong strokes Teoma comes quite near, grateful as Tamar widens the portal to his greatest desire. A large dolphin dives right in front of him. Soon others follow, separating Teoma from the women. Gidon laughs.

"It appears Yeshua has enchanted these creatures, cousin, to keep his precious wife safe from your amorous advances."

Teoma swims away, exasperated, "It is Mary who communicates with them!"

Tamar looks at Mary with wide eyes. "Did you tell the dolphins to keep him away?" In denial Mary claims that the dolphins are acting on their own accord.

She swims away but he hears her silent voice. *They said I was a wild thing and advised that I be true to myself, for I belong to no human.* When Teoma agrees with the creatures, she hastily heads to shore.

Tamar is most ready to seek dry land, so they swim back. While Gidon makes a fire, she rests under a pile of blankets watching Mary approach with appreciation matching his own.

"Aren't you cold?" Tamar's teeth chatter.

"No, the hayye of the dolphins is invigorating. I didn't even notice the chill." She turns to Gidon. "Do you need help?"

Laughing, he looks up. "Can you cook, Mary?" With a shake of her dark head, she provides a true answer. "My cousin informed me that the mashiach and his wife require our worldly assistance."

With a glance at Teoma, Mary blushes. Tamar reaches to caress her slender ankle, "I surprise myself in my attraction to him, but you must admit he is very appealing even for a man. I do not know how you have resisted his charms for so long, Mary."

Teoma hides a smile, feeling exceptionally invigorated by the crisp air. His passion warms him well enough. Securing the thin wrap about his waist, he appraises the two lovely women.

Gidon clears his throat, "I hear in Egyptus that eunuchs make the best guardians for royal wives."

Growling, Teoma turns, "What is that supposed to mean?"

His cousin shrugs, "I was just thinking that Yeshua might consider a eunuch to watch over his beautiful wife. Of course, if you insist upon the position, I am sure we can find someone to perform the necessary procedure."

Teoma considers teaching Gidon some manners, but his cousin fends him off with a long spoon.

"Gidon, what is a eunuch?"

"Well, Tamar, it is a man who is no longer a man."

With a wrinkled brow she looks to Teoma for clarification. He grumbles, "It is a man who has been castrated."

Gasping, she cries, "How terrible! Why would anyone do that?"

Gidon shakes his head, feigning sorrow. "Sometimes it is necessary to make a great sacrifice to keep what is most precious secure. It appears that my cousin is not really willing to protect his charge."

Flustered, Mary turns and heads swiftly up the beach.

Knowing she will consider traversing back home, Teoma races to catch her about the waist. "Mary, what is it?"

"I cannot even imagine such a thing! Yet it's true—no longer are you the best escort for me."

"But I've always tried to keep you safe."

"Yes, from others, but what about from my desire, what about from yours?" In tears she runs away.

Just past the rocky outcropping, well out of sight of the others, he deftly pulls her into his form. "Since returning to Galilee, I can no longer quell my passion for you!"

Catching her breath, she looks up with feverish gaze. As the heat of her body reflects off his naked torso, he groans, conscious that his own desire has become quite evident beneath the thin covering at his hips.

Veiling her green eyes beneath thick lashes, she tries to look away. Her look of vulnerability entices him to draw her ever nearer.

And he is knocked roughly down. Casting Mary aside so he might not fall upon her, he lands on his back, a pink tongue vigorously licking his face. Groaning, he wrestles Tikva, nearly disrobing himself.

"Get off me, you great beast!"

From her seat in the sand, Mary laughs. Tikva crouches behind as if her petite form could protect the great dog from her suitor's wrath. He reaches to help Mary up and she does not resist brushing the sand from his skin.

"Teoma, you must admit, she has uncanny timing."

The dog wags her tail apologetically. "Yeshua sent her, didn't he?" She nods. "Mary, what do you expect of me? I have done my best to protect you, Yeshua, and the children for as long as I can remember. I never meant to fall in love with you. Why would I want to live with my heart's desire just beyond my reach? It is most torturous."

Trapping her hand so firmly to his chest, she seems to hold his heart. "Since the blessing of your fantasy in Magdala, it is hopeless to keep the image of us from my mind. With Tamar's mutual desire for you, it is as if I am nearly within your embrace. Mary, please….," he drops to his knees imploringly, "how much longer must I wait? After thirteen years of loving you, is it not time?"

Tears spill to splash upon his face. "Teoma, if we give into our passion before the time is ripe, we will reap most bitter fruits."

His eyes brim and her lower lip quivers invitingly. One kiss to relieve this painful yearning. He gently pulls her closer. With great resolve, she whispers, "Dearest, we will not only hurt the one who you have committed your life to, but more importantly we will cause ourselves great pain. If you breach your own confidence, what hope will you have left? Please, let us tempt one another no longer. Let us resolve to wait until the time is truly ripe to fully experience our love for one another."

Bowing his head, his shoulders shake, "It is not yet ripe?"

Hugging his head, she murmurs, "No, but I do believe when it is ripe, our actions will reap sweet blessings upon each of us."

Whining, Tikva nuzzles them, as if to say, *Cheer up, all is as it needs be. Besides, I adore you both.* Turning, Teoma gives the great dog a hug, then gets to his feet. Kissing the top of Mary's head, he leads her back to the others.

By a roaring fire, his cousin has set a fine meal. After sharing the stew and a flask of wine they discuss their lives. Speaking from their four very different perspectives, the friends become quite close at the seashore. Teoma takes Tamar to his bed and Mary sleeps alone, Tikva guarding her.

Late the next morning they arrive in Nazareth to find Yeshua waiting at the stables. Smiling, Gidon dismounts and clasps his arm. "Yeshua, you have much faith in your loved ones."

"My faith is rooted in their profound ability to follow their soul path."

Teoma sighs as he helps Tamar down. "Once again I find myself facing great obstacles in my relationship with you."

"And as always you handle the challenges with grace, beloved brother."

When Yeshua kisses his cheek, Teoma responds by drawing him into a great hug. "My love for you makes loving your wife that much more exasperating."

"I have always loved you, Teoma. You are the first and the last in my relationship to my fellow men. My prayer is that you find joy in this existence."

Wondering how their mutual destinies shall unfold without uprooting them all, Teoma squeezes Yeshua tightly before releasing him. Touching his chest, Yeshua responds, "Change is a wondrous part of our soul paths. Our perception of it can be either through the filter of fear or loving gratitude. It is your choice."

Reaching up, Yeshua lifts Mary from Sheikan's back. "Beloved, your commitment to our relationship in light of your love for Teoma prepares the way for the commencement of our mission. Thank you."

Their challenges have only progressed to deeper levels. Shivering, her response is barely perceptible. "Beloved husband, I shall know myself as love before I share my essence with another."

Teoma swallows thickly as Yeshua touches her cheek. "As well it must be."

***

"Mary, come to bed, I wish to talk to you." Yeshua holds open the blankets that I might slip besides him. Lying upon our sides facing one another, we touch not, lest our voices remain unheard. His fathomless eyes reflect my desire, but he places his hand chastely between us. "My love, on the spring equinox I would like to celebrate our commitment to…"

Before he can finish, a sob catches in my throat. In spite of my best efforts, I still am torn between my two loves.

With compassion, my husband smiles. "Ah, but on the contrary, your actions prove otherwise." Flashes of temptation in my relationship to Teoma cloud my vision. "Love, your search to connect while I was trapped by my fear in the palace at Qumran and then partnering with me last spring reinforced your commitment. And in Magdala, you ministered to me with great compassion, inviting sacred wisdom into our relationship. Your dance for the disciples wove their hayye into my light preparing the way for the mission."

Still I feel a precarious balance between these acts and my unfaithful heart. Hot tears threaten to spill over the brim of my eyelashes as I whisper, "Yeshua, you speak of a celebration of our commitment but perhaps we might recommit ourselves to each other, at least me to you."

A flash of white teeth creates a quake within my breast. "Beloved, the commitment I speak of is not to our marriage, but to our soul paths. Your tumultuous feelings for my brother have fueled your journey as you reach deeper into self for guidance. Your connection to Eloha is in part because of your strong emotions, which are revealed in your relationships to those you love, including me and Teoma."

Yes, it is true that this past year has been one of great spiritual growth for all of us.

"Mary, you are the embodiment of the Divine Daughter for you fully embrace your humanity using the human form, fired by emotion, to connect to rucha. Your life is a most exquisite example of Sacred Wisdom." He takes a deep breath, thinking *I must quell my desire to touch her or I shall not complete my objective. With this woman, I lose myself again and again to rediscover who I AM in the most divine of perspectives.* His visage is so achingly beautiful that a wave of passion splashes from my core into his.

Hoarsely, he whispers, "Please, Mary, let me finish." Another deep breath and he continues, "When I was in Britannia, Ambrose told me that before eight years were completed from the time I reconnected to the One, another reconnection would take place. It is time for you and I to anchor in the energies that shall open the portal for our mission to be realized."

I smile, my hands clasped tightly against my belly, lest I reach for him.

"All around the Earth will be gathered others to hold the hayye just as they did when we were married. The divine orchestration of malchuta is in place that our message of love might be received in this dimension."

Finally, he touches me, his fingertips lightly brushing the skin of my arm. "This is why I have not been able to complete a full massage of your body. Even with the slightest contact, your very skin responds like miniscule lips drinking in my essence. Your heat is consuming, while the scent of your desire perfumes the air so heavily that I taste your nectar upon my tongue. Your passionate response to the most chaste touch is what thwarts my every effort." His very words raise the fire within, blurring my vision with smoky desire.

With a deep kiss, he draws me to his form, chuckling. "Teoma is right. I shall not be satisfied if only after absolute depletion, I finally manage to conquer this challenge. Alas, perhaps I must let this one go."

My sight now quite clear, I study his face. "Really, you acquiesce?"

His caresses move seductively down my sides. "I do acquiesce in using you as a subject. Perhaps another woman might not be so responsive to thwart my effort."

I cannot help but smile, "I don't know, Yesh, your charms can be overwhelming."

"To you, dear."

Sighing, I lie back to fully enjoy this moment. Loving seduction with the promise of joyous connection is how he has drawn the council of twelve into his realm.

My husband shall see that in ripe time the people of Yisrael shall not resist, nor the goyim, nor the world.

***

The bright sun barely warms the winter morning as Teoma and Gidon spar with the boys. From the hillside, Mary and the children watch until suddenly, the fierce scream of a stallion punctuates the crisp air. Having gotten between the older northern stallion and his lead mare, Sheikan limps over to the stables, like Teoma, his strong desires unmet.

While Mary leads the injured horse into a stall, Teoma brings water and rags. Gidon entertains the children outside as the couple works silently. Placing his forehead against Sheikan's, Teoma bemoans, "It appears you must bide your time as well, my friend."

526

The horse nickers softly, as if to say that Yeshua keeps her from them both. Abruptly Mary stands, "Sheikan!"

When she attempts to move away, Teoma catches her arm and she melds into his chest, but resolutely he speaks his mind, "Mary, you realize that his intent with the spring equinox ceremony is to cast a protective barrier about you. No longer will you look at me with the same eyes."

"Teoma, how are we to proceed with the mission if I am torn between you both? I must give you up until the time is ripe and that will be after Yeshua is gone." Tears spill from her eyes as she speaks, her palms pressed passionately against his chest.

Teoma cups her face as he had Sheikan's. "I have seen us together and he is still with us."

Her lips quiver as if she did not truly consider an act of infidelity. With a great sigh, he loosens his hold, placing one hand on the wall while the other strokes her silken curls. "Mary," he emotes hoarsely, "Yeshua asked me to protect you and the children, but my feelings for you overwhelm my senses. I cannot protect you from my desire."

Waiting for but the subtlest of invitation so this tide might wash them away, he leans closer. In the proximity of the stall, her breath tantalizing his cheek, he ceases playing with her hair and decidedly pulls her close. Once more she fits against him like a sheath upon a sword. Incited, the stallion races out of the barn and back into the fray. Before Mary can call to him, Teoma covers her lips with his own.

With great effort she breathes her words into his mouth, "Teoma, when the time is ripe, we will come together naturally, without a thought. Now our hearts are heavy for we shall regret any act that might seem to fulfill our desires."

Gidon comes running into the stable, his thoughts as loud as his racing heart. *I have been lax in my duties, for my cousin has nearly ravished the wife of the mashiach.* "Come, cousin, we must leave for Sepphoris soon. I am sure the most desirable of women would prefer we were bathed and properly attired."

Teoma stares at Mary's beloved face. *No other diversion shall fill this need.*

Pressing her hand to his heart, she tells him silently, *I must release you again and recommit myself to my own soul path of which you are a part, but not in the way you desire, not yet.*

Am I the only one with desires?

Tears spill down her cheeks as she shakes her head—no.

Gidon places a hand on his shoulder, "Come now. Let us prepare for this evening."

"Please try to surrender me, please!" Mary whispers desperately, but Teoma does not know how.

***

Yeshua approaches the stable, his heart thundering, and takes Teoma's arm. Leaving Gidon behind to walk through the pastures, he finally speaks. "Yes, I did wish to place a barrier about my wife that could not be pierced by your passion." Teoma nods. "I was hoping that by including our family in the ceremony, our marriage might be sanctified in all of our eyes, but especially..." pausing, he looks at Teoma, "in yours."

Silence ensues as Teoma restrains his emotion. Searching the horizon as they walk, Yeshua says hoarsely, "And I too see you with her before I go."

Teoma halts. "Forgive me, Yeshua, for coveting your wife. I do not know why, after ten years of suppressing my feelings for her, they come raging forth."

"Perhaps it is because the mission is about to begin which shall bring much change into all of our lives. For you—the freedom to love without the burden of duty. For me—to surrender all in order to be One with Love. Although I have surrendered in spirit, still I suffer in form."

"Is this part of your sacrifice, Yeshua?"

A humorless chuckle accompanies his dry answer. "I was told by the archangels that no sacrifice is necessary in the fulfillment of my purpose, but at this point in my soul's journey giving up my wife feels like a sacrifice."

Clearing his throat, Teoma clasps his arms. "Let us pray that we might have compassion for ourselves when this part of the drama plays out. Mary has said that she shall not act until the time is ripe. I pray that I will recognize the moment of harvest and that it might be sweet for you as well."

Near to tears, Yeshua kisses Teoma on the forehead. "Always I have strived to live in the moment, but as I look into our future, I see much pain. I am committed to go before you, but pray that you and Mary, my children, and my family each might find the way after I have gone."

Swallowing thickly, Teoma promises, "I will hold the gate until the last beloved lamb passes through and only then will I join you."

Yeshua embraces the man who is his brother in spirit if not in blood. "I know you will. That is how I might lead the way knowing you so faithfully bring up the rear."

The shadows grow long before he leaves Teoma under the protection of a sycamore grove to prepare for a ceremony of his own. From the ethers, Yeshua watches as Teoma releases his cords of attachment to Mary who praises his efforts. And this time there is no struggle for any of them, only great relief.

Epilogue

The Second Anointing

Spring equinox 3782

Born from the great rock where Moses met the Divine, stones skitter underfoot. White smoke curls into clouds devoid of rain from a decapitated pyramid resting on the summit of Horeb. Creosote bushes stand as occasional sentries offending the senses with the odor of burnt oil. Rainfall so rare, the priests descend every morning to the muddy hole at the base of the mount to fill their water skins. How I yearn for a bath.

A horned lizard meditates in the late morning sun, inviting me to bask on the warm red granite. When we arrived, Belshazzar arranged for me to meet with the head of the Therapeutae. Under Eshe's watchful eye, the priestesses of the half-finished temple massaged my body with fragrant oils before dressing me in a pure white robe of the finest Egyptian cotton. Only then was I allowed to see Kamuzu.

"Mari-a," Kamuzu referred to me by my Egyptian name. "You were brought here to anchor new energies into this dimension. Yeshua rides across the desert to join you. As the messeh queen, you will anoint him again." His hair still shiny black, his face unlined, but his eyes wise with many years lived, or perhaps, many lives remembered. "Belshazzar tells me you visit the portals which shall be held open for the sacred event."

In my dreams, I travel to places, some familiar, most not. The first night here, I dreamt of Belshazzar's son gathering a circle of drummers far to the south in Aksum. I traversed the next across the great waters where golden pyramids glinted under a midday sun and a priest adorned in colorful feathers bowed to me. The third night, I was swept away to cliff dwellings to be greeted by musicians playing melodious clay flutes and on the fourth I visited a land blanketed in snow. Beneath a vividly colored sky, people covered in animal skins chanted around raging bonfires. I told Kamuzu of my visions.

"You are hek mat—the breath of wisdom…"

A frown shadowed me for I felt not wise, but very, very lost.

"This second anointing will prepare your husband for the path of realization, then you shall part to finish your own initiations. Only when water gives way to fire will you perform the third anointing." Providing no further enlightenment, Kamuzu left me to my thoughts.

That night, I dreamt of a familiar forest in Britannia where Ambrose confirmed Kamuzu's predictions. The next night on the snowcapped Himals, I discovered gentle Zsao surrounded by chanting monks in yellow robes. On the seventh, my dreams took me to the Hindus region. Reiti sat twisted in a strange pose while people paraded through the streets burning torches. My eighth dream brought me to the crux of two great rivers, where a priestess of Ishtar, her slender arms encircled in silver, rang brass bells, gathering the masses to the temple.

From cliffs high above the Dead Sea, Hephziva assured me on the ninth night that her acolytes would hold the energy we were to bring in. The following evening I found myself in Alexandria before a priestess who sat on a throne in the temple of Isis, hair capped in white, black eyes glowing with recognition. In my eleventh dream, I was swept high upon Mount Karmel; women healers rose to embrace me, and dear Hava was with them. Last night, I dreamt of Miriam's rainbow room back in Nazareth where all the family gathered, including our precious children.

Were these the same twelve portals that witnessed our sacred marriage union ten years ago? The elestial stone in my navel glows to highlight the star within the rose. I shiver and the lizard stirs at my side. Time to prepare.

With conscious breath, I connect to the earth drawing precious water forth from the red granite, then soak in the fountain spraying rainbows in the sunshine, at home in my element. Droplets glisten down dark curves, sable curls blossoming. My right hand tingles aching for another.

Yeshua stands before me.

Discarding his tunic and kicking off his sandals, he steps into the blessed water and, finally, takes my hand. Our lips meet to bring a divine perspective. The clouds hovering over Horeb drift apart revealing—a rosebud of light.

As the first triad of petals open, my three lower energy centers hotly glow. When the second triad blooms my fourth, fifth and sixth alight. A third triad beginning at my crown, then the boundary of my aura, then the aura of the Earth, opens softly. The final triad blossoms to connect me to the sun, then the stars, then the universe beyond.

In the midst of the four tristans lay a single white petal—the essence of masculine in the womb of the feminine. Entering the center of the thirteen-petal rose, I am cast back into my being through a point above my breasts. Dark as midnight yet with an amethyst glow, this portal leads to timeless places. Flashes of other realities in the past, present, and future—strange and surreal in their very nature—lay strewn before my consciousness.

Yeshua's passion nearly overwhelms my senses. "Mary, as the Divine Daughter, you are this strange new rose, the tristans—our relationships, the center—the portal to the Source of All."

My vision reflects in his fathomless gaze. "When Teoma comes upon this fountain, surely he'll complete our triad."

Hand in hand, we step out of our aqua haven. And while our dearest friend partakes of the life-giving water, I anoint my husband upon the altar in the sanctuary. Twelve portals around the world open to receive the energy Yeshua and I bring through our sacred union, on this eve of our mission of Love.

Herein Ends the Words of Book One

LoveDance Continues in Book Two:
Realization of the Magdalen

Jerusalem, 3782

Veiled in shadows, dark and lean, the man hovers over me, sharp brows drawn into an angle over the avian nose, eyes gleaming like glass. Panicked, I clasp my right hand, searching, frantically searching. Gone!

"Hush, beloved, it's on the other," murmurs Yeshua, his touch warm over the icy ring, "all is well, go back to sleep." He draws me nearer undeterred by the beads of sweat pearling upon my oiled flesh.

Tucked into the comforting curve of his body, I twirl the carved band until my heart ceases its panicked pace. Crafted by Ambrose to reflect the soul path of the wearer, our rings, initially pink as the dawn of awakening, became golden with realization. Yeshua yearns for the white hue of sovereignty to claim his kingdom, but I pray to be released from these nightmares plaguing me since receiving this ring.

A faint knocking disturbs my slumber, but my husband does not stir. Lavender light slips through the window and I slip out of his warm embrace, pausing a moment to gaze at his precious face before donning a robe.

Shulamis is at the door. "I am sorry, Mary, but your mother is here. She insists on speaking to you."

Ima? Bare feet padding softly on the cool mosaic tiles, I follow my hostess to private chambers off the garden. Shulamis draws the drapes behind her, leaving us alone.

Pinched with worry, Ima wrings her slender hands. "I had to come before you left Jerusalem. Can you imagine how I felt when I heard what happened between you and Teoma in Magdala? My fears have become realized!"

Silencing me with a wave of her hand, she continues, "Can you believe that I am but a guest in the Hasmonaean palace? Antipas had much nerve bringing his brother's wife to Yonatan's belated wedding!"

True, the bride's threatening miscarriage postponed the second ceremony until nearly Shavuot, but that gave us one last Seder with Yeshua's father before he ventured east to hide the sacred scrolls.

"And my own daughter disgraces me by attending the wedding of the High Priest's eldest son unveiled!" Ima rants, pacing the room. Will she ever let this go?

Ten years ago, my husband decried tradition by refusing to veil me under the chupa. While appreciating his magnanimous gesture to preserve my power, without the matrimonial headdress, I have suffered much judgment. My mother cracks the shell of my reverie.

"Some wear their sin like a crown. Others must hide their shame..." Words trail off as she peers beyond me. I glance over my shoulder. In the open window perches a crow, its black feathers glistening with fine morning dew. Neither of us moves.

Ima swallows, her slender throat rising in a lump, the center of her eyes darken within a wide rim of white. "Mary," she pleads hoarsely, "please make it go away."

Turning toward the bird, I expand my energy. It greets me not in images but speaks in my mind, like the dolphins. *I will not leave until she reveals the truth.*

Never has my mother communicated with the creatures, always before her fear was too great, but somehow she understands it. "Please, I am!" Defeated, she sinks into a cushioned lounge. I stand between them, not knowing what to do. "My daughter, you shall fall into temptation, just as I did..."

With one shiny black eye, the crow urges Ima to continue. "I prayed to forget my sin, but you would not let me! Nothing I did would make you cease..."

536

Cease what? The bird unfurls its wings and Ima shrinks back. "I was afraid of what you might become. Your wicked magical ways… I was being punished." Her voice barely perceptible.

The crow caws shrilly. "The darkness of your skin is a constant reminder of my sin."

How many times has she said that the Egyptian blood in our Hasmonaean lineage came forth in me like the curse of the pharaohs? Yes, I am darker than my sister, but…

"Ima, what are you saying?"

With pained effort, mustard eyes focus on mine. "I was seduced! I knew not that he was a sorcerer. To my shame I gave birth to his seed." Her trembling finger points accusingly.

"What! What about Abba?"

Shaking her head, she glances at the window where the crow poises for flight. "Syrus returned because he had a vision. Vowed to protect and raise you." Her voice drops again. "But he is not… your father."

With halting steps, I approach, but she refuses to look at me. Her hair streaked with gray, her face so much older. Has guilt aged her this much?

"Ima, who is my father?"

Flapping wings graze past my head, terrifying her. Before I can go to Ima, the crow flies out the window without a sound.

In a daze, I brush my hand against her pale cheek, as Shulamis abruptly enters to tend to Ima's still form. "Mary, do not worry, she has only fainted. Go now to your husband."

My head spins, but somehow I find Yeshua in the courtyard among the lush vegetation bidding Simeon farewell. When he takes my right hand, I hardly feel him. Looking at our intertwined fingers, I cannot tell which are mine. My body feels hollow.

"Come, Mary," Yeshua's voice seems so distant. "Our escort waits." He takes a step and using raza, slips away.

***

Disoriented, Yeshua walks right into Teoma. He looks down at his left hand— empty… A scream pierces the haze about his mind; the white stallion rears up. Cursing, Teoma lunges for the reins, but Sheikan gallops away. With the reflexes of a centurion, Gidon mounts and takes off after the runaway.

"Where is Mary?"

Yeshua does not know. Taking a deep breath, he looks past Teoma and into the ethers. Within the prism of creation, his hayye merges with the light. She is not there. Not within the tetrahedron separated into many colors, nor within the void. Where can she be?

A violent shaking interrupts his search. "Did you leave her at Simeon's? Shall I go back for her? Tell me what to do…"

"Be calm." With effort, Yeshua penetrates his friend's veil of fear. "See for yourself."

Bowing his head, Teoma places his hands together as if in prayer. A long moment passes. "I cannot feel her."

"Neither can I." Yeshua tries to recreate this morning's events. Did she greet him? No! What was she wearing? Cast back to the moment he first took her cold hand to step through time and space… "She slipped."

"She what?" Teoma cries, "Has this ever happened before?"

Yeshua shakes his head. "She wasn't prepared to go. You must have clear intent and pure desire to travel using raza, and she was distracted, not even dressed."

"She left without…" Narrowing his eyes, Teoma accuses, "you never pay attention! Who packed?" Yeshua hands over the sack with their belongings. Teoma's search quickly reveals Mary's riding garments and her sandals. He looks up exasperated. "She was barefoot as well? Something must have happened!"

Blowing heavily, Gidon's lathered mount gallops up the hill. "I could not catch the stallion." A growing crowd gathers to watch the Herodian confront them outside the city walls. "Come; let us find a quiet place."

Northeast of Jerusalem, the Holy Temple's golden pinnacles sparkle high above the fortress walls. The ride is short to the peaceful gardens of Olivet Mount.

"So did something happen at the temple?"

Teoma will not rest, so Yeshua patiently describes what Mary told him about the conflict with the priestesses.

"And at the wedding?"

Gidon shifts nervously. Yeshua places a hand on his knee. "I am sorry, but she was there." Herodias favors the wealth and power of Gidon's gluttonous brother.

"I am most saddened for Antipas' wife. Sent off to her father like a broken thing." Teoma pats the abandoned man's arm.

"I once met the Nabataean king. Aretas confided that his daughter was quite unhappy with your brother."

"Yes, but she did not deserve to be treated like this."

"Neither did you." Teoma embraces his cousin. "Perhaps my brother might teach you to release your cords of attachment to Herodias." Yeshua smiles to see Gidon nod.

Beneath a wizened olive tree, Yeshua begins a meditation. From a distance, he views Simeon's home, but his wife is not there. Neither is she with Joseph of Arimathaea, nor with Hephziva in Qumran. At home in Nazareth, Sarah and Joshua greet him delighted, which he takes as a good sign. So attached, his children would perceive their mother's distress if she was endangered. But where could she be?

Still in the Hasmonaean palace, where the wedding was held, Martha and Eleazer prepare to return to Bethany, while Syrus, attending to his wife, hastily halts Yeshua's further explorations. *What are you doing?*

I am looking for Mary.

Why? Isn't she with you?

This morning while using raza to meet Teoma, Mary slipped.

What! Syrus' fear severs their connection.

Abruptly Yeshua's consciousness returns. To clear his own trepidation, he breathes deeply and focuses on the slate sky between the branches.

"Well, where is she?" Teoma asks anxiously.

"I do not know, but her father became upset when I told him."

"Of course, he did! He's concerned about her welfare."

Yeshua shakes his head. "Syrus is usually quite unattached, never interfering with Mary. But he was perturbed at my intrusion."

"Perhaps we should track down the horse."

At Gidon's suggestion, Teoma looks up hopefully. While appreciating his friend's devotion, Yeshua prays that Teoma continues to release his cords of attachment to Mary. Both men look to him for leadership. Already it begins.

Asking them to prepare the horses and secure provisions, he finds that still place within and expands his consciousness to be immediately greeted by a friendly voice.

What assistance can I provide, my prince?

Dear Ambrose, I am looking for Mary. We became separated while traveling through the ethers and now I cannot locate her.

How fortunate. His Druid teacher advises, *it is time to prepare alone. You must find the masters to further your enlightenment and teach those amenable to your beliefs. Only then will you be ready to fulfill your purpose.*

But Mary?

She must continue her path to complete your initiations. We discussed this eight years ago when you came to Britannia, now is the time to strive for sovereignty.

The ring on his right hand glows golden. He is not yet sovereign. Ambrose continues the silent discourse. *Unravel the last of your earthly bindings…*

But he did last month at the Sea of Galilee. The winds of change always haled transitions in their lives, yet the water lay still as glass that night, without a hint of the afternoon's fierce gales. Where thirteen milk white petals marked the site of their sacred union, he and Mary set the stage.

A log settled heavily sending sparks into the darkness as he carefully unrolled their ketuba onto his linen tunic. Drawn in kohl, the ornate letters stood out on the pale parchment in reverse of the stars in the sky above. Mary's breath caught in her throat when he laid it across her lap.

"Disentangle the last of our bindings."

Through another's eyes, one might perceive the soul's journey, its dark chaotic potential, the light of its most beautiful manifestation. In her's, she saw himself as love—infinite and eternal. She smiled and without hesitation cast their wedding ketuba into the flames. The parchment curled before quickly being consumed.

Tenderly cupping her face—the arched brows framing eyes startling light in the richness of her honey-tempered dark skin, the delicate bridge of her nose above the most luscious of lips, ripe cheeks soft as silk curving into the fine-boned jaw—he drew her attention from the smoke that carried their connubial promises into the night.

"We shall journey upon our soul paths, unbound now, free to learn, to live, to love…" Her ring paled to white—her sovereignty assured.

Perhaps Ambrose is right. He must seek the eastern masters before claiming his kingdom. Piercing Yeshua's internal reverie, his mentor starkly advises. *You will be united again in the spring of your thirtieth year.*

What and not see her beloved face for two years! *Ambrose, we have come so far together. Is it necessary to separate once more?*

You know it is and Teoma must go too. If you attempt to contact her, she may not fulfill her purpose.

What about the children?

Time to begin their training at Mount Karmel. And with the breeze rattling through the gray-green leaves, the voice of his mentor floats back to Britannia.

He looks up from the crux of the olive tree. Teoma and Gidon stand expectantly before him. Holding his hand to the warmth of the sun, Yeshua prays that his beloved wife will take it once again.

***

Sweating profusely in the oppressive heat, Teoma dismounts and motions for his companion to do the same. Removing his sandals, Yeshua stands feet apart in the river, palms facing skyward, perhaps communicating with Mary. Before Yeshua's mount can step on its reins, Teoma catches the long leather straps. Micah shakes his head.

Inexperienced at traveling the trade routes, Teoma welcomed the zealot's company for Yeshua's silence mimicked the desolate desert. With Mary's disappearance, Teoma refused to leave Nazareth until Gidon promised to escort the children safely to Mount Karmel. After crossing the Jordan and trading donkeys for camels, the Egyptian cavaneer begrudgingly carried extra grain for the Herodian prince's fine Nabataean mares.

The caravan traversed the desolate Ituraean desert to a rising plateau where a ridge of barren hills entrapped the southern plain. Far to the west, snowcapped Mount Hermon rises pristine. Drinking deeply, the horses pull impatient to feast on the green fields spread placid as a lake on each side of the swift Abana. Rushing through canals crisscrossed by bridges, the river delivers them into Damascus unmolested. Taxes were collected in Hazor.

"Fare well, my friends." Micah embraces them. While the caravaneers busily trade Egyptian perfumes for lapis lazuli, the zealot will stealthily gather information in the greatest trade center of the Roman Empire.

Sweet anise from Mesopotamia softens the bite of Hindus pepper. Teoma ignores the display of beautifully designed Parthian carpets draped over bundles of angora wool, drawn instead to a bolt of silk dyed purple from the secretions of rare mollusks. The color of Mary's hayye, he presses the silk to his cheek.

"It would be a fine gift for her."

Teoma's face flushes hotly. How foolish he is to allow his mind to wander. Tongue enlivened by the Abana, Yeshua goes on, "I have never thought of her as my property."

Perhaps not, but jealousy has threatened their friendship more than once. And now she is free while Teoma ventures off to lands unknown. What is he doing here?

"Following your destiny." Wrapping an arm around his shoulder, Yeshua continues, "I need you both to realize your truth before we meet again. Only then can our message of love be received."

"Ours? I have known since we were children that you are the one to unite the tribes of Yisrael. I am only a protector, a shepherd to watch over your flock. I am no teacher, no leader."

Yeshua kisses his cheek. "My brother, you do not yet realize your own mission in this life. It runs deep and long, parallel to mine, merging like the Euphrates and the Tigris into the sea. By the time we return to Galilee, we will all know why we left."

Glossary

Abba: Aramaic; Father.

Aviatar: Hebrew; title of priest second in line to the Zadok, given the Essene title of Gavriel.

Adama: Hebrew; earth.

Adonai: Hebrew; the Lord.

Aksum: a country in east Africa (Ethiopia).

Archangels: Greek (angelos); messengers. Spiritual or energetic messengers of the One Being: Michael (who is like God), Gavriel (strength of God), Rafael (God's healer), Uriel (God's light).

Astarte: a Canaanite goddess known as Isis in Egypt, Ishtar in Babylonia.

Bar: Aramaic; son of, as in "Yeshua bar Joseph."

Barchashem: Aramaic; Thank God.

Betshimush: Hebrew; latrine.

Bisha: Aramaic; bad (unripe, out of rhythm) translated as evil.

Brit: Hebrew; circumcision denoting a covenant with YHVH.

Calendar: Hebrews began each month at the new moon. Every three years approximately eleven days were added as an abbreviated thirteenth month or second Adar. In accordance with the Torah, New Year begins on the Spring Equinox:
Nissan (March/April) Pesach
Iyar (April/May)

Sivan (May/June) Shavuot
Tammuz (June/July) Summer Solstice
Av (July/August)
Elul (Aug/Sept) Rosh Hoshana
Tishrei (Sept/Oct) Yom Kippur, Sucot, the month of kings
Cheshvan (October/November)
Kislev (November/December) Chanuka
Tevet (December/January) Winter Solstice
Shevat (January/February)
Adar (February/March)

Chamam: Aramaic; baths, the place for women to use during menstruation.

Chata: Aramaic; a missed thread, Chet: Hebrew; missing the mark is less of an offense than Aveyra; violating a boundary.

Chaverim: Hebrew; associates, friends. The group of Hebrews that accepted oral interpretation of the Tanach, known as mishna, relying on sages (Chachamim) for guidance conflicted with the more conservative Tzadokim who crudely referred to the them as Perisha (Pharisees) or separatists.

Chokhma: Hebrew; sacred wisdom, a feminine principle of utilizing the sacred Senses, Greek; Sophia.

Chupa: Hebrew; wedding canopy.

Council: In the manner of ancient kings whose advisors represented the tribes of Yisrael, Yeshua chose a council of twelve:
   Judas, Simeon, and Theudas—zealot commanders
   Yonatan and Mattathias—Kohanim sons of high priest Ananias
   Jakob and Jochanan—Essenes under the tutelage of Simeon
   Phillip—a Greek, Head of the Order of Shem
   Bartholomew—a Galilean in the Egyptian Therapeutae
   Jacob and Teoma—Yeshua's brother and cousin

Gidon—the disinherited son of Herod

David: Hebrew; beloved. The king of the Yisraelites.

Dod: Hebrew; uncle.

Doda: Hebrew; aunt.

Dynastic Wedlock: ritualistic marriage arrangement to insure birth of royal heirs at the proper timing, practiced since the time of the Yisraelite captivity in Babylonia.

Egyptian Therapeutae: a community which practiced curative healing and preserved sacred mysteries.

Elat: Aramaic; goddess, the feminine aspect of Eloha.

Elestial Quartz: a translucent gemstone with a smoky interior, found in Africa, known as the gift of the angels.

Eloha: Aramaic; The Divine One

Essene: healers who broke away from Jerusalem in opposition to the Hasmonaean family takeover of the high priesthood. Strictly opposed to both the Tzadokim and Chaverim, the Essenes referred to the Hasmonaeans as forces of Darkness and to themselves as the Sons of Light.

Gan eden: Hebrew; garden paradise (the female womb).

Gemera: Aramaic; finished, concluded. Translated as perfect.

Goyim: Hebrew; the nations that are not Yisraelites.

Halacha: Hebrew; path, way, direction, the Laws of Moses.

Hasmonaean: Kohanim distinguished in Hebrew history for rededicating the Holy Temple and restoring Yisrael from the Assyrians, but were rejected by some Hebrews for taking over royal duties.

Hayye: Aramaic; life force, energy.

Herodians: those who support Roman rule by the sons of Herod.

Ima: Hebrew/Aramaic; Mother.

Ketuba: Hebrew marriage document ensuring the transfer of properties and the rights of the wife to be provided for by her husband in food, clothing, shelter, and sexual satisfaction.

Kasa: Aramaic; veil. (A protective energetic field making those within it undetectable.)

Kiyyor: Hebrew; hammered out, a round basin used to wash the hands and feet.

Kohanim: the Hebrew priesthood, descendents of Aaron.

Malchuta: Aramaic; where the metaphysical (heaven) meets the physical (earth). Translated as Kingdom.

Marya: Aramaic; My Lord.

Mashiach: Aramaic; the anointed one, Greek (Christos). Prophesized in the Nevi'im to be the redeemer born of the House of David to reunite physical sovereignty (political freedom) to Yisrael on earth with allegiance to God

Mikvah: Hebrew; a pool of living water used for ritual purification.

Mikra: Hebrew; the writings, Greek (graphe), Latin (scriptum).

Nafsha: Aramaic; the individual spirit that resides in the body to be returned to the Divine.

Nura: Aramaic; light. Illumination or Divine Intelligence.

Ossuary: Greek; a decorated box encasing the bones of the dead.

Pesach: celebration in the spring of the freedom of the Hebrews from Egypt.

Pigra: Aramaic; corpse. the physical body without the breath of life.

Raza: Aramaic; secret. (The disappearance of something material. In-body travel.)

Reyaya: Aramaic; understanding. Mind, grasping intelligence.

Rucha: Aramaic; soul, sacred breath or spirit.

Saba: Hebrew; old man, Grandfather.

Sanhedrin: supreme Hebrew court of seventy run by Tzadokim.

Savta: Hebrew; feminine, Grandmother.

Shabbat: Hebrew; to stop. Day of rest beginning at dusk on the sixth day and ending an hour after sunset on the seventh.

Shekar: Hebrew; intoxicant, a fermented drink distilled from grain, fruit, or honey.

Shem: Hebrew; the name of the Divine.

Sheqel: Hebrew coin stamped with a chalice on one side and a triple lily on the other replaced by the Roman dinari.

Star: in the 17th century German astronomer and mathematician, Johannes Kepler found that Saturn and Jupiter moved so close together that they appeared to be a single star in the year 7 BCE.

Sucot: harvest holiday in Tishrei marked by dwelling in booths.

Tava: Aramaic; good. Ripe, harmonious.

Tanach: the entire collection of Hebrew scripture, the name is an acronym of the titles of the three collective works the **Torah** (5 books of Moses), the **Nevi'im** (the prophets) and the **Ketuvim** (the writings).

Tikva: Hebrew; hope.

Tzadokim: Hebrew; righteous. Greek: (Sadducees) Inherited aristocrats including priestly families, who accepted only the written Tanach as sacred.

Yayin: Hebrew; effervescing. medicinal wine.

YHVH: Hebrew; (Yud-Hay-Vav-Hay) to be. Unique to Yisrael for the Creator.

Yisrael: Hebrew; one who wrestles with God. The people of Yisrael are descendants of Patriarch Jacob bar Isaac bar Avraham whose twelve sons fathered the tribes of Yisrael.

Zadok: Hebrew name of an established priesthood who served the lineage of David.

Zealot: the Hebrew resistance bitterly opposed to Roman oppression.

About the Author

Deborah Maragopoulos is a gifted healer with a passion for writing. After receiving her Master's degree from UCLA as a nurse practitioner, she studied neuro-immune-endocrinology, genetics, functional quantum physics, psycho-spirituality, nutritional biochemistry, and bio-energetics to establish a holistic health care practice. Realizing patients responded best to her story-telling, Deborah began her journey as a novelist in which the heroine is a wife, mother, healer, and spiritual seeker just like herself. Deborah lives with her beloved husband, children, and their menagerie of animals in Ojai, California.

Visit **www.lovedance.com** for more information.